American Empire: Blood and Iron

HARRY TURTLEDOVE

AMERICAN EMPIRE:
BLOOD&IRON

THE BALLANTINE PUBLISHING GROUP
NEW YORK

American Empire:
Blood and Iron

Introduction

The Great War is over. After three years of brutal conflict, the United States have defeated the Confederate States and Canada—as, in Europe, the German Empire and Austria-Hungary have defeated France, Britain, and Russia. Now, all across North America, people are trying to pick up their shattered lives.

In Boston, Sylvia Enos mourns the loss of her husband, George, who was killed when his destroyer, the USS *Ericsson*, was sunk by a torpedo during the last moments of the war. As the Confederate States had already asked for an armistice, she believes a British submersible sank the *Ericsson*. She has more urgent things to worry about, though: keeping her job when so many men are returning from the war, and bringing up her young son and daughter.

In fact, though, Commander Roger Kimball of the CSS *Bonefish* sank the *Ericsson*, a last blow against the United States even though he knew the Confederacy had asked for quarter. His executive officer, Tom Brearley, tried to talk him out of this, but he ignored Brearley and went ahead. As the USA prohibited the CSA from keeping submarines after the armistice, Kimball is on the beach in Charleston, South Carolina, looking for whatever he can find.

Roger Kimball is Anne Colleton's sometime lover. Her plantation, Marshlands, a ruin because of the Red Negro uprising of 1915–16, Anne is now living in St. Matthews, South Carolina, not far from Columbia, the state capital. After the war ended, she and her brother Tom and a militia they recruited have finally succeeded in clearing out the last remnants of the black rebels who called themselves the Congaree Socialist Republic from the swamps along the banks of the Congaree River.

Colonel Irving Morrell is one of the U.S. heroes of the moment. The young officer spearheaded the column of armored traveling forts known as barrels that broke the Confederate defenses around Nashville, Tennessee, and allowed the United States to capture the important city. Pushing south from Nashville, he was one of the first officers to receive a Confederate request for a cease-fire.

Lieutenant Colonel Abner Dowling is adjutant to Colonel Morrell's commanding officer in the Nashville campaign, George Armstrong Custer. As the war ended, he was summoned to Philadelphia, the *de facto* capital of the United States, along with Custer, whom Democratic President Theodore Roosevelt has just promoted to full general as a reward for his long, faithful, and—in the end—successful service. Custer's headlong aggressiveness found a perfect match with the use of barrels *en masse.*

In Philadelphia, young Socialist Congresswoman Flora Hamburger has earned the nickname "the conscience of the Congress" for her principled stands on important issues. Her younger brother, David, is also in Philadelphia, at the Pennsylvania Hospital—he lost a leg fighting in Virginia not long before the end of the war. To her dismay, David has become a Democrat and supports a hard line against the CSA. Flora has become friendly with Hosea Blackford, the veteran Socialist congressman from the state of Dakota, who lives in the same block of flats as she does.

Nellie Semphroch, a widow, lives in Washington, D.C., with her grown daughter, Edna. They have run a coffeehouse throughout the Great War in the *de jure* capital of the United States, which was occupied for two and a half years by Confederate soldiers. Nellie has also gathered information from Confederates in the coffeehouse and passed it on to the cobbler across the street, Hal Jacobs, an important member of a U.S. spy ring. Nellie and Edna were both decorated by President Roosevelt for their services, and Nellie has just accepted a proposal of marriage from Jacobs.

Anne Colleton's former butler, Scipio, has found a job waiting tables in Augusta, Georgia. The cultured, educated Negro is glad to have escaped from the ruin of the Congaree Socialist Republic, and perhaps even gladder to have escaped from his former mistress' vengeance: the Red uprising, of which Scipio had been an unwilling part, had begun at Marshlands with the murder of her brother, Jacob, a fact that helps drive her push for revenge against the Negroes involved. Scipio hopes for nothing more than to live out the rest of his life in obscurity.

In Lexington, Kentucky, another Negro, Cincinnatus Driver, is adjusting to life in the United States. The adjustments aren't easy; Kentucky was forcibly rejoined to the USA after its conquest in the Great War. Confederate diehards remain active in the state. So do Red factions consisting mostly of Negroes. Cincinnatus has been uncomfortably and unwillingly involved with both groups, and both view him with suspicion—as does Luther Bliss, the head of the Kentucky State (secret) Police. He has been driving a truck for the U.S. Army, but with the end of the war finds himself out of work and looking for a way to support his wife and young son.

On a Canadian farm not far from Rosenfeld, Manitoba, Arthur McGregor has avenged himself on the U.S. occupiers who executed his teenage son, Alexander, for rebellion against their authority. His bomb killed Major Hannebrink, the officer who ordered Alexander up before a firing squad, during a celebration of the end of the war. Arthur McGregor has no intention of confining his vengeance to Major Hannebrink alone. This worries his wife, Maude. His surviving daughters, Julia and Mary—especially Mary, the younger—don't precisely know what he is doing, but hope he will do more of it.

Lucien Galtier is also a farmer working land formerly belonging to the Dominion of Canada. These days, though, his farm near Rivière-du-Loup is part of the Republic of Quebec, a U.S. creation during the Great War. Galtier at first opposed the U.S. occupation of Quebec, especially after U.S. authorities took part of his farm—part of his patrimony—and built a hospital on the land. Lately, though, his reservations about the United States have faded, not least because his daughter, Nicole, who was working at the hospital, married an American doctor, Leonard O'Doull.

Just returned to the United States from the province of Ontario is Jonathan Moss, who served as a pilot all through the Great War. Moss, who lives in the Chicago area, plans to resume his study of the law. While in Canada, he fell in love with a Canadian woman, Laura Secord. Even though she emphatically does not love him in return— she is descended from a famous Canadian patriot of the same name—he cannot get her out of his mind.

Steelworker Jefferson Pinkard has just returned to Birmingham, Alabama, after fighting in the Confederate Army in West Texas. He looks forward to returning to his job at the Sloss Works. He is not so sure he looks forward to returning to family life. During the war, his wife, Emily, was unfaithful with his best friend, Bedford Cunningham, who had come home for good after losing an arm in Tennessee.

Steelworker Chester Martin will be returning to Toledo, Ohio. He fought in the Great War from first shot to last, and was lucky enough to be wounded only once. As a sergeant, he had commanded a company in the closing days of the fighting in Virginia (he was, in fact, David Hamburger's company commander). He is eager to return to the United States to see his parents and his sister, Sue.

Petty Officer Sam Carsten remains in the U.S. Navy. He has seen the effects of aviation on naval warfare off the South American coast, when the USS *Dakota* was bombed by land-based aeroplanes. His superior officer, Commander Grady, has hinted that the U.S. Navy has something new in mind when it comes to naval aviation. Carsten is eager to learn what it is.

Reggie Bartlett, a pharmacist's assistant, has returned home to Richmond, Virginia, capital of the CSA. He has had a hard war. He was captured once in Virginia, but escaped from a U.S. prisoner-of-war camp. Returning to action, he was badly wounded in Sequoyah and captured again. This time, he remained in a U.S. hospital in St. Louis till the fighting ended. His long talks with Rehoboam, a colored Confederate soldier also at the hospital after losing a foot, have made him thoughtful about parts of life in the Confederate States he had always taken for granted before the war.

Sergeant Jake Featherston, former battery commander in the First Richmond Howitzers, has also come home to Richmond. He too fought from first shot to last in the Great War, and never rose above sergeant, not least because the War Department was angry at him for exposing the shortcomings of his former CO, Captain Jeb Stuart III. Furious and bitter at the War Department in particular and the world in general, Featherston wonders what to do now that he has no place in the Army any more.

I

When the Great War ended, Jake Featherston had thought the silence falling over the battlefield as strange and unnatural as machine-gun fire in Richmond on a Sunday afternoon. Now, sitting at the bar of a saloon in the Confederate capital a few weeks later, he listened to the distant rattle of a machine gun, nodded to himself, and took another pull at his beer.

"Wonder who they're shooting at this time," the barkeep remarked before turning away to pour a fresh whiskey for another customer.

"Hope it's the niggers." Jake set a hand on the grip of the artilleryman's pistol he wore on his belt. "Wouldn't mind shooting a few myself, by Jesus."

"They shoot back these days," the bartender said.

Featherston shrugged. People had called him a lot of different things during the war, but nobody had ever called him yellow. The battery of the First Richmond Howitzers he'd commanded had held longer and retreated less than any other guns in the Army of Northern Virginia. "Much good it did me," he muttered. "Much good it did anything." He'd still been fighting the damnyankees from a good position back of Fredericksburg, Virginia, when the Confederate States finally threw in the sponge.

He went over to the free-lunch counter and slapped ham and cheese and pickles on a slice of none-too-fresh bread. The bartender gave him a pained look; it wasn't the first time he'd raided the counter, nor the second, either. He normally didn't give two whoops in hell what other people thought, but this place was right around the corner from the miserable little room he'd found. He wanted to be able to keep coming here.

Reluctantly, he said, "Give me another beer, too." He pulled a couple of brown dollar banknotes out of his pocket and slid them across the bar. Beer had only been a dollar a glass when he got into town (or a quarter in specie). Before the war, even through most of the war, it had only been five cents.

As long as he was having another glass, he snagged a couple of hard-boiled eggs from the free-lunch spread to go with his sandwich. He'd eaten a lot of saloon free lunches since coming home to Richmond. They weren't free, but they were the cheapest way he knew to keep himself fed.

A couple of rifle shots rang out, closer than the machine gun had been. "Any luck at all, that's the War Department," Jake said, sipping at the new beer. "Lot of damn fools down there nobody'd miss."

"Amen," said the fellow down the bar who was drinking whiskey. Like Featherston, he wore butternut uniform trousers with a shirt that had seen better days (though his, unlike Jake's, did boast a collar). "Plenty of bastards in there who don't deserve anything better than a blindfold and a cigarette, letting us lose the war like that."

"Waste of cigarettes, you ask me, but what the hell." Jake took another pull at his beer. It left him feeling generous. In tones of great concession, he said, "All right, give 'em a smoke. *Then* shoot 'em."

"Plenty of bastards in Congress, too," the bartender put in. He was plump and bald and had a white mustache, so he probably hadn't been in the trenches or just behind them. Even so, he went on in tones of real regret: "If they hadn't fired on the marchers in Capitol Square last week, reckon we might have seen some proper housecleaning."

Featherston shook his head. "Wouldn't matter for beans, I say."

"What do you mean, it wouldn't matter?" the whiskey-drinking veteran demanded. "Stringing a couple dozen Congressmen to lampposts wouldn't matter? Go a long way toward making things better, *I* think."

"Wouldn't," Jake said stubbornly. "Could hang 'em all, and it wouldn't matter. They'd go and pick new Congressmen after you did, and who would they be? More rich sons of bitches who never worked a day in their lives or got their hands dirty. Men of good family." He loaded that with scorn. "Same kind of jackasses they got in the War Department, if you want to hear God's truth."

He was not anyone's notion of a classical orator, with graceful, carefully balanced sentences and smooth, elegant gestures: he was skinny and rawboned and awkward, with a sharp nose, a sharper chin, and a harsh voice. But when he got rolling, he spoke with an intensity that made anyone who heard him pay attention.

"What do you reckon ought to happen, then?" the barkeep asked.

"Tear it all down," Jake said in tones that brooked no argument. "Tear it down and start over. Can't see what in God's name else to do, not when the *men of good family*"—he sneered harder than ever—"let the niggers rise up and then let 'em into the Army to run away from the damnyankees and then gave 'em the vote to say thank-you. Christ!" He tossed down the last of the beer and stalked out.

He'd fired canister at retreating Negro troops—and, as the rot spread through the Army of Northern Virginia, at retreating white troops, too. It hadn't helped. Nothing had helped. *We should have licked the damnyankees fast,* he thought. *A long war let them pound on us till we broke.* He glared in the direction of the War Department. *Your fault. Not the soldiers' fault. Yours.*

He tripped on a brick and almost fell. Cursing, he kicked it toward the pile of rubble from which it had come. Richmond was full of rubble, rubble and ruins. U.S. bombing aeroplanes had paid repeated nighttime visits over the last year of the war. Even windows with glass in them were exceptions, not the rule.

Negro laborers with shovels cleared bricks and timbers out of the street, where one faction or another that had sprung up since the war effort collapsed had built a barricade. A soldier with a bayoneted Tredegar kept them working. Theoretically, Richmond was under martial law. In practice, it was under very little law of any sort. Discharged veterans far outnumbered men still under government command, and paid them no more heed than they had to.

Three other Negroes strode up the street toward Jake. They were not laborers. Like him, they wore a motley mix of uniforms and civilian clothing. Also like him, they were armed. Two carried Tredegars they hadn't turned in at the armistice; the third wore a holstered pistol. They did not look like men who had run from the Yankees. They did not look like men who would run from anything.

Their eyes swept over Jake. He was not a man who ran from anything, either. He walked through them instead of going around. "Crazy white man," one of them said as they walked on. He didn't keep his voice down, but he didn't say anything directly to Jake, either. With his own business on his mind, Jake kept walking.

He passed by Capitol Square. He'd slept under the huge statue of Albert Sidney Johnston the night he got into Richmond. He couldn't do that now: troops in sandbagged machine-gun nests protected the Confederate Capitol from the Confederate people. Neatly printed NO LOITERING signs had sprouted like mushrooms after a rain. Several bore handwritten addenda: THIS MEANS YOU. Bloodstains on the sidewalk underscored the point.

Posters covered every wall. The most common showed the Stars and Bars and the phrase, PEACE, ORDER, PROSPERITY. That one, Featherston knew, came from the government's printing presses. President Semmes and his flunkies remained convinced that, if they said everything was all right, it would be all right.

Black severed chains on red was another often-repeated theme. The Negroes' Red uprisings of late 1915 had been crushed, but Reds remained. JOIN US! some of the posters shouted—an appeal from black to white.

"Not likely," Jake said, and spat at one of those posters. No more than a handful of Confederate whites had joined the revolutionaries during the uprisings. No more than a handful would ever join them. Of so much Featherston was morally certain.

Yet another poster showed George Washington and the slogan, WE NEED A NEW REVOLUTION. Jake spotted only a couple of copies of that one, which was put out by the Freedom Party. Till that moment, Jake had never heard of the Freedom Party. He wondered if it had existed before the war ended.

He studied the poster. Slowly, he nodded. "Sure as hell do need a new revolution," he said. He had no great use for Washington, though. Washington had been president of the United States. That made him suspect in Jake's eyes.

But in spite of the crude illustration, in spite of the cheap printing, the message struck home, and struck hard. The Freedom Party sounded honest, at any rate. The ruling Whigs were trying to heal an amputation with a sticking plaster. The Radical Liberals, as far as he was concerned, played the same song in a different key. As for the Socialists—he spat at another red poster. Niggers and nigger-lovers, every one of them. The bomb-throwing maniacs wanted a revolution, too, but not the kind the country needed.

He peered more closely at the Freedom Party poster. It didn't say where the party headquarters were or how to go about joining. His lip curled. "Goddamn amateurs," he said. One thing spending his whole adult life in the Army had taught him: the virtue of organization.

With a shrug, he headed back toward his mean little room. If the Freedom Party didn't know how to attract any members, odds were it wasn't worth joining. No matter how good its ideas, they didn't matter if nobody could find out about them. Even the damned Socialists knew that much.

"Too bad," he muttered. "Too stinking bad." Congressional elections were coming this fall. A shame the voters couldn't send the cheaters and thieves in the Capitol the right kind of message.

Back in the room—he'd had plenty of more comfortable bivouacs on campaign—he wrote for a while in a Gray Eagle scratchpad. He'd picked up the habit toward the end of the war. *Over Open Sights,* he called the work in progress. It let him set down some of his anger on paper. Once the words were out, they didn't fester quite so much in his mind. He might have killed somebody if he hadn't had a release like this.

When day came, he went out looking for work. Colored laborers weren't the only ones clearing rubble in Richmond, not by a long chalk. He hauled bricks and dirt and chunks of broken stone from not long after sunrise to just before sunset. The strawboss, of course, paid off in paper money, though his own pockets jingled.

Knowing the banknotes would be worth less tomorrow than they were today, Jake made a beeline for the local saloon and the free-lunch counter. He'd drawn better rations in the Army, too, but he was too hungry to care. As before, the barkeep gave him a reproachful look for making a pig of himself. As before, he bought a second beer to keep the fellow happy, or not too unhappy.

He was stuffing a pickled tomato into his mouth when the fellow with whom he'd talked politics the day before came in and ordered himself a shot. Then he made a run at the free lunch, too. They got to talking again; Featherston learned his name was Hubert Slattery. After a while, Jake mentioned the Freedom Party posters he'd seen.

To his surprise, Slattery burst out laughing. "Oh, them!" he said. "My brother took a look at those fellows, but he didn't want any part of 'em. By what Horace told me, there's only four or five of 'em, and they run the whole party out of a shoebox."

"But they've got posters and everything," Jake protested, startled to find how disappointed he was. "Not *good* posters, mind you, but posters."

"Only reason they do is that one of 'em's a printer," the other veteran told him. "They meet in this little dive on Seventh near Canal, most of the way toward the Tredegar Steel Works. You want to waste your time, pal, go see 'em for yourself."

"Maybe I will," Featherston said. Hubert Slattery laughed again, but that just made him more determined. "By God, maybe I will."

Congresswoman Flora Hamburger clapped her hands together in delight. Dr. Hanrahan's smile was broader than a lot of those seen at the Pennsylvania Hospital. And David Hamburger, intense concentration on his face, brought his cane forward and then took another step on his artificial leg.

"How does it feel?" Flora asked her younger brother.

"Stump's not too sore," he answered, panting a little. "But it's harder work than I thought it would be."

"You haven't been upright since you lost your leg," Dr. Hanrahan reminded him. "Come on. Give me another step. You can do it." David did, and nearly fell. Hanrahan steadied him before Flora could. "You've got to swing the prosthesis out, so the knee joint locks and takes your weight when you straighten up on it," the doctor said. "You don't learn that, the leg won't work. That's why everybody with an amputation above the knee walks like a sailor who hasn't touched land in a couple of years."

"But you *are* walking, David," Flora said. She dropped from English into Yiddish: "*Danken Gott dafahr. Omayn.*"

Seeing her brother on his feet—or on one foot of his and one of wood and metal and leather—did a little to ease the guilt that had gnawed at her ever since he was wounded. Nothing would ever do more than a little. After her New York City district sent her to Congress, she'd had the chance to slide David from the trenches to a quiet post behind the lines. He wouldn't have wanted her to do that, but she could have. She'd put Socialist egalitarianism above family ties . . . and this was the result.

Her brother shrugged awkwardly. "I only need one foot to operate a sewing-machine treadle. I won't starve when I go home—and I won't have to sponge off your Congresswoman's salary, either." He gave her a wry grin.

As a U.S. Representative, Flora made $7,500 a year, far more than the rest of her family put together. She didn't begrudge sharing the money with her parents and brothers and sisters, and she knew David knew she didn't. He took a brotherly privilege in teasing her.

He also took a brotherly privilege in picking her brains: "What's the latest on the peace with the Rebs?"

She grimaced for a couple of reasons. For one, he hadn't called the Confederates by that scornful nickname before he went into the Army. For another . . . "President Roosevelt is still being very hard and very stubborn. I can understand keeping some of the territory we won from the CSA, but all he's willing to restore is the stretch of Tennessee south of the Cumberland we took as fighting wound down, and he won't *give* that back: he wants to trade it for the little piece of Kentucky the Confederates still hold."

"Bully for him!" David exclaimed. He had been a good Socialist before he went off to war. Now, a lot of the time, he sounded like a hidebound Democrat of the Roosevelt stripe. That distressed Flora, too.

She went on, "And he's not going to let them keep any battleships or submersibles or military aeroplanes or barrels, and he's demanded that they limit their Army to a hundred machine guns."

"Bully!" This time, her brother and Dr. Hanrahan said it together.

Flora looked from one of them to the other in exasperation. "*And* he won't come a dime below two billion dollars in reparations, all of it to be paid in specie or in steel or oil at 1914 prices. That's a crushing burden to lay on the proletariat of the Confederate States."

"I hope it crushes them," David said savagely. "Knock on wood, they'll never be able to lift a finger against us again." Instead of knocking on the door or on a window sill, he used his own artificial leg, which drove home the point.

Flora had given up trying to argue with him. He had his full share of the Hamburger family's stubbornness. Instead, she turned to Dr. Hanrahan and asked, "How much longer will he have to stay here now that he's started to get back on his feet?"

"He should be able to leave in about a month, provided he makes good progress and provided the infection in the stump doesn't decide to flare up again," Hanrahan said. Flora nodded; she'd seen he gave her straight answers. He finished with a brisk nod: "We'll shoot for November first, then."

After giving her brother a careful hug and an enthusiastic kiss, Flora left the Pennsylvania Hospital. Fall was in the air, sure enough; some of the leaves in the trees on the hospital grounds were beginning to turn. She flagged a cab. "The Congressional office building," she told the driver.

"Yes, ma'am." He touched the shiny leather brim of his cap, put the Oldsmobile in gear, and went out to do battle with Philadelphia traffic. The traffic won, as it often did. Philadelphia had been the *de facto* capital of the USA since the Confederates bombarded Washington during the Second Mexican War, more than thirty-five years before. Starting even before then, a great warren of Federal buildings had gone up in the center of town. Getting to them was not always for the faint of heart.

"I have a message for you," said Flora's secretary, a plump, middle-aged woman named Bertha. She waved a piece of paper. "Congressman Blackford wants you to call him back."

"Does he?" Flora said, as neutrally as she could. "All right, I'll do that. Thank you." She went into her inner office and closed the door after her. She didn't turn around to see whether Bertha was smiling behind her back. She hoped not, but she didn't really want to know.

Dakota, a solidly Socialist state, had been returning Hosea Blackford to the House since Flora was a girl. He was about twice her age now, a senior figure in the Party, even if on the soft side ideologically as far as she was concerned. And he was a widower whose Philadelphia apartment lay right across the hall from hers. He had left no doubt he was interested in her, though he'd never done anything to tempt her into defending herself with a hatpin. To her own surprise, she found herself interested in return, even if he was both a moderate and a gentile.

"Now," she muttered as she picked up the telephone and waited for the operator to come on the line, "is he calling about Party business or . . . something else?"

"Hello, Flora," Blackford said when the call went through. "I just wanted to know if you had seen the newspaper stories about strikes in Ohio and Indiana and Illinois."

Party business, then. "I'm afraid I haven't," Flora said. "I just got back from visiting David."

"How is he?" Blackford asked.

"They've fitted the artificial leg, and he was up on it." Flora shook her head, though Blackford couldn't see that. "Even with one leg gone, he talks like a Democrat." She inked a pen and slid a piece of paper in front of her so she could take notes. "Now tell me about these strikes."

"From what I've read, factory owners are trying to hold down wages by pitting workers against each other," he said. "With soldiers starting to come home from the war, they have more people wanting jobs than there are jobs to give, so they're seeing who will work for the lowest pay."

"That sounds like capitalists," Flora said with a frown. A moment later, she brightened. "It also sounds like a political opportunity for us. If the factory owners keep doing things like that—and they probably will—they'll radicalize the workers, and they'll do a better job of it than we ever could."

"I happen to know we've urged the strikers to stay as peaceful as they can, unless the bosses turn goons loose on them or their state governments or the U.S. government move troops against them," Blackford said.

"Good." Flora nodded. Blackford couldn't see that, either, but she didn't care. Something he'd said touched off another thought. "Has Roosevelt made any statement about this yet?"

"One of the wire reports quotes him as calling the factory owners a pack of greedy fools," the Congressman from Dakota said, "but it doesn't say he'll do anything to make them stop playing games with people's lives."

"That sounds like him," Flora said. "He talks about a square deal for the workers, but he doesn't deliver. He delivered a war."

"He delivered a victory," Hosea Blackford corrected. "The country was starved for one. The country's been starved for one for more than fifty years. You may not like that, but you can't stick your head in the sand and pretend it isn't so."

"I don't intend to do any such thing," Flora said sharply. "The people *were* starved for a victory. I've seen as much, even with my own brother. But after a while they'll discover they have the victory and they're still starved and still maimed and still orphaned. And they'll remember Teddy Roosevelt delivered that, too."

Blackford's silence was thoughtful. After a few seconds, he said, "You may very well be right." He did his best to hold down the excitement in his voice, but she heard it. "If you are right, that would give us a fighting chance in the elections of 1918, and maybe even in 1920. A lot of people now are afraid we'll be so badly swamped, the Democrats will have everything their own way everywhere."

"A lot of things can happen between now and the Congressional elections," she said. "Even more things can happen between now and 1920."

"That's true, too," Blackford said. "But you've seen how many Socialists are wearing long faces these days. Even Senator Debs is looking gloomy. Maybe they should cheer up."

"Maybe. The real trouble"—Flora took a deep breath—"is that

we've never won a presidential election. We've never had a majority in either house of Congress. Too many people, I think, don't really believe we ever can."

"I've had doubts myself," Blackford admitted. "Being permanently in the minority is hard to stomach sometimes, if you know what I mean."

"Oh, yes," Flora said quietly. "I'm Jewish, if you'll remember." On the Lower East Side in New York City, Jews were a majority. Everywhere else in the country, everywhere else in the world . . . *permanently in the minority* was as polite a way to put it as she'd ever heard.

She wondered if reminding Blackford she was Jewish would make him decide he wasn't interested in her after all. She wondered if she wanted him to decide that. In many ways, her life would be simpler if he did. With a large family, though, she'd rarely known a simple life. Would she want it or know what to do with it if she had it?

The only thing Blackford said was, "Of course I remember. It means I have to eat crab cakes and pork chops by myself." His voice held nothing but a smile. "Would you care to have dinner with me tonight? If you like, I won't eat anything that offends you."

"I'm not offended if you eat things I can't," Flora said, "any more than an Irishman or an Italian would be offended if I ate corned beef on Friday. I'd be offended if you tried to get *me* to eat pork, but you'd never do anything like that."

"I should hope not!" Blackford exclaimed. "You still haven't said whether you'll have dinner with me, though."

"I'd like to," Flora said. "Can we wait till after six, though? I've got a shirtwaist manufacturer coming in to see me at five, and I aim to give him a piece of my mind."

"Six-thirty, say, would be fine. Shall I come to your office?"

"All right." Flora smiled. "I'm looking forward to it." She hung up the telephone and went to work feeling better about the world than she had in some time.

Reginald Bartlett was discovering that he did not fit into the Richmond of late 1917 nearly so well as he had in 1914. Fighting on the Roanoke Valley front and in Sequoyah, getting captured twice and shot once (shot twice, too, actually: in the leg and the shoulder from the same machine-gun burst) by the Yankees, had left him a different man from the jaunty young fellow who'd gaily gone off to war.

Richmond was different, too. Then it had been bursting with

July exuberance and confidence; now the chilly winds of October sliding into November fit the city's mood only too well. Defeat and autumn went together.

"Going to rain tomorrow, I reckon," Reggie said to Bill Foster as the two druggist's assistants walked along Seventh Street together. He reached up with his right hand to touch his left shoulder. "Says so right here."

Foster nodded, which set his jowls wobbling. He was short and round and dark, where Bartlett was above average height, on the skinny side (and skinnier after his wound), and blond. He said, "I heard enough people say that in the trenches, and they were right a lot of the time." He'd spent his war in Kentucky and Tennessee, and come home without a scratch.

After touching his shoulder again, Reggie said, "This isn't so much of a much." He'd had a different opinion while the wound stayed hot and full of pus, but he'd been a long way from objective. "Fellow I worked for before the war, man name of Milo Axelrod, he stopped a bullet with his face up in Maryland. He wasn't a bad boss—better than this McNally I'm working for now, anyhow."

"From what you've said about McNally, that wouldn't be hard." Foster might have gone on, but a small crowd had gathered at the corner of Seventh and Cary. He pointed. "I wonder what's going on there."

"Shall we find out?" Without waiting for an answer from his friend, Reggie hurried over toward the crowd. Shrugging, Foster followed. "Oh, I see," Bartlett said a moment later. "It's a political rally. That figures, with the Congressional election next Tuesday. But what the devil is the Freedom Party? I've never heard of 'em before."

"I've seen a couple of their posters," Bill Foster said. "Don't rightly know what they stand for, though."

"Let's get an earful. Maybe it'll be something good." Reggie scowled as his wounded leg gave a twinge, which it hadn't done in a while. "Couldn't be worse than the pap the Radical Liberals and the Whigs are handing out."

"That's about right." Foster nodded. "Everybody who's in is making noise about how he never much cared for the war, and everybody who's out is saying that if he'd been in he never would've voted one thin dime for it."

"And it's all a pack of lies, too," Bartlett said with deep contempt. "Why don't they admit they were all screaming their heads off for the war when it started? Do they think we've forgotten? And when Arango ran against Semmes for president two years ago, he said he'd do a better job of fighting the Yankees than the Whigs were. He didn't say anything about getting out of the war, not one word."

The Freedom Party spokesman didn't have a fancy platform or a fancy suit, which proved he belonged to neither of the CSA's major parties. He stood in his shirtsleeves on a box or a barrel of some kind and harangued the couple of dozen people who were listening to him: "—traitors to their country," he was shouting as Reggie and Bill Foster came up. "Traitors and fools, that's what they are!"

"A crackpot," Bartlett whispered. He folded his arms across his chest and got ready to listen. "Let's hang around for a while. He may be funny."

Somebody in the crowd already thought he was funny, calling, "By what you're saying there, the whole government is nothing but traitors and fools. You've got to be a fool yourself, to believe that."

"I do not!" the speaker said. He was an overweight, balding fellow of about fifty-five, whose fringe of gray hair blew wildly in the fall breeze. His name was Anthony Dresser—so said a little sign Reggie needed a while to notice. "I do not. I tell you the plain, unvarnished truth, and nothing else but!" His eyes, enormous behind thick spectacles, stared out at his small audience. "And you, my friends, you hug the viper to your bosom and think it is your friend. Congress is full of traitors, the War Department is full of traitors, the administration—"

Reggie stopped paying much attention to him about then. "And the moon is full of green cheese!" the heckler shouted, drawing a roar of laughter from the crowd.

Dresser sputtered and fumed, the thread of his speech, had it ever had one, now thoroughly lost. Reggie and Foster grinned at each other, enjoying his discomfiture. The speech surely would have been boring. This was anything but. "Not as easy to get up on the stump as the old boy thought, is it?" Foster said with a chuckle.

"You are all traitors to your country, for not listening to the plain and simple truth!" Dresser shouted furiously.

"And you're a maniac, and they ought to lock you up in the asylum and lose the key!" It wasn't the first heckler, but another man.

Dresser looked to be on the point of having a fit. Somebody reached up and tugged at his trousers. He leaned over, cupping a hand behind his ear. Then, with a fine scornful snort, he jumped down from his perch. "All right," he said. "All right! You show them then, if you think you know so much. I can tell you what you will show them—you will show them you do not have any notion of what to say or how to say it."

Up onto the platform scrambled a lean man somewhere in his thirties, in a day laborer's collarless cotton shirt and a pair of uniform pants. He looked around for a moment, then said, "Tony's right. A blind man should be able to see it, too. The government *is* full of traitors and fools."

Dresser had been argumentative, querulous. The newcomer spoke with absolute conviction, so much so that before he caught himself Reginald Bartlett looked north toward Capitol Square, as if to spy the traitors in the act.

"Yeah? You can't prove it, either, any more than the other jerk could," a heckler yelled.

"You want proof? I'll give you proof, by Jesus," the lean man said. He didn't talk as if he had any great education, but he didn't seem to feel the lack, as did so many self-made men. "Look what happened when the Red niggers rose up, back at the end of '15. They damn near overran the whole country. Now, why is that, do you reckon? It's on account of nobody in the whole stinking government had the least notion they were plotting behind our backs. If that doesn't make everybody from the president on down a damn fool, you tell me what in the hell it does do."

"He's got something, by God," Foster said, staring at the new speaker.

"He's got a lot of nerve, anyhow," Reggie said.

"That's why you ought to vote for Tony Dresser for Congress," the lean man continued: "on account of he can see the plain truth and you can't. Now the next thing you're going to say is, well, they're a pack of fools up there, all right, with their fancy motorcars and their whores, but they can't be traitors because they fought as long as they could and the Yankees are pretty damn tough.

"Well, this here is what I've got to say about that." The lean man let loose with a rich, ripe raspberry. "I know for a fact that people tried to warn the government the niggers were going to rise, on account of I was one of those people. Did anybody listen? Hell, no!" Contempt dripped from his voice like water from a leaky roof. "Some of those niggers were servants to rich men's sons, important men's sons. And the rich men in the Capitol and the important men in the War Department shoveled everything under the rug. If that doesn't make 'em traitors, what the devil does?"

"He *has* got something," Bill Foster said in an awed voice.

"He's got a big mouth," Bartlett said. "You throw charges like that around, you'd better be able to name names."

Instead of naming names, the newcomer on the stump charged ahead: "And after that—after that, mind you, after the niggers rose up—what did the government go and do? Come on. You remember. You're white men. You're smart men. What did they go and do?" The lean man's voice sank to a dramatic whisper: "*They went and put rifles in those same niggers' hands, that's what they did.*" He whispered no more, but shouted furiously: "If *that* doesn't make 'em traitors, what the devil does?"

Reggie remembered Rehoboam, the Negro prisoner of war who'd shared his U.S. hospital ward after losing a foot in Arkansas—and after being a Red rebel in Mississippi. Things weren't so straightforward as this new Freedom Party speaker made them out to be. The older Reggie got, the more complicated the world looked. The lean man was older than he, but still saw things in harsh shades of black and white.

And he contrived to make his audience see them the same way. "You want to put Tony Dresser into Congress to give the real people of the Confederate States a voice," he shouted, "the working men, the men who get their hands dirty, the men who went out and fought the war the fools and the traitors and the nigger-lovers got us into. Oh, you can throw your vote away for somebody with a diamond on his pinky"—with alarming effectiveness, he mimed a capitalist— "but who's the fool if you do?"

"Why the hell ain't *you* runnin' for Congress instead of that long-winded son of a bitch?" somebody shouted.

"Tony's the chairman of the Freedom Party," the lean man answered easily. "You promote the commander of the unit, not a new recruit." He took out his billfold and displayed something Bartlett could not make out. "Here's my membership card—number seven, from back in September."

"Where do we sign up?" Two men asked the question at the same time. One of them added, "You ain't gonna stay a new recruit long, pal, not the way you talk. Who the hell are you, anyway?"

"My name's Featherston—Jake Featherston," the lean man answered. "Sergeant, Confederate States Artillery, retired." He scowled. "The fools in the War Department retired damn near the whole Army." With what looked like a deliberate effort of will, he made himself smile. "Party office is a couple blocks down Seventh, toward the Tredegar works. Come on by. Hope you do, anyways."

"Damned if I'm not tempted to," Bill Foster said as the little rally began to break up. "Damned if I'm not. That fellow Featherston, he's got a good way of looking at things."

"He's got a good line, that's for certain," Reggie Bartlett said. "If he were selling can openers door to door, there wouldn't be a closed can in Richmond this time tomorrow. But just because something sounds good doesn't make it so. Come on, Bill. Do you think a stage magician really pulls a Stonewall out of your nose?"

"Wish somebody'd pull one out of somewhere," Foster answered.

Reggie's laugh was rueful, five-dollar goldpieces being in notably short supply in his pockets, too. He said, "The world's not as simple as he makes it out to be."

"Well, what if it isn't?" his friend returned. "I wish it was that simple. Don't reckon I'm the only one who does, either."

"Reckon you're not," Bartlett agreed. "But most folks are the same as you and me: they know the difference between what they wish and what's really out there."

"Yeah?" Foster raised an eyebrow. "How come we just fought this damn war, then?" Reggie thought about that for a while, but found no good answer.

Guided by a pilot intimately familiar with the local minefields, the USS *Dakota* made a slow, cautious entrance into New York harbor. Sailors on tugs and freighters waved their caps at the battleship. Steam whistles bellowed and hooted. Fireboats shot streams of water high into the air.

Sam Carsten stood by the port rail, enjoying the show. The late-November day was bleak and gloomy and cold, but that didn't bother the petty officer at all. Anything more clement than clouds and gloom bothered him: he was so blond and pink, he sunburned in less time than he needed to blink. After Brazil entered the war on the side of the USA and Germany and their allies, the *Dakota* had gone up into the tropical Atlantic after convoys bound for Britain from Argentina. He was only now recovering from what the cruel sun had done to him.

Off to the west, on Bedloe Island, stood the great statue of Remembrance, the sword of vengeance gleaming in her hand. Carsten turned to his bunkmate and said, "Seeing her gives you a whole different feeling now that we've gone and won the war."

"Sure as hell does." Vic Crosetti nodded vigorously. He was as small and swarthy as Carsten was tall and fair. "Every time I seen that statue before, it was like she was saying, 'What the hell you gapin' at me for? Get out there and kick the damn Rebs in the belly.' Now we gone and done it. Can't you see the smile on that bronze broad's kisser?"

Remembrance looked as cold and stern and forbidding as she had since she'd gone up not long after the Second Mexican War. Even so, Carsten said, "Yeah." He and Crosetti grinned at each other. Victory tasted sweet.

"Carsten!" somebody said behind him.

He turned and stiffened to attention. "Sir!"

"As you were," Commander Grady said, and Sam eased out of his brace. The commander of the *Dakota*'s starboard secondary armament was a pretty good fellow; Sam cranked shells into the forwardmost five-inch gun under his charge. Grady said, "Do you recall that matter we were discussing the day the limeys gave up the fight?"

For a moment, Carsten didn't. Then he nodded. "About aeroplanes, you mean, sir?"

"That's right." Grady nodded, too. "Were you serious about what you meant about getting in on the ground floor there?"

"Yes, sir. I sure was, sir," Sam answered. Aeroplanes were the coming thing. Anyone with an eye in his head could see that. Anyone with an eye in his head could also see the Navy wouldn't stay as big as it had been during the war. Since Sam wanted to make sure he didn't end up on the beach, getting involved with aeroplanes looked like a good insurance policy.

Commander Grady said, "All right, then. I have some orders cut for you. If you'd said no, you'd have stayed here. There wouldn't have been any trouble about that. As things are, though, we both catch the train for Boston tomorrow morning. You'll see why when we get there." His smile made him look years younger.

"You're leaving the *Dakota*?" Vic Crosetti demanded. When Sam nodded, Crosetti clapped a hand to his forehead. "Jesus Christ, who'm I gonna rag on now?"

"I figure you'll find somebody," Carsten said, his voice dry. Crosetti gave him a dirty look that melted into a chuckle, then slapped him on the back. Sam had a gift for getting in digs without making people angry at him.

"Only problem with this is the train ride," Commander Grady said. "This Spanish influenza that's going around is supposed to be pretty nasty. We might be better staying aboard the *Dakota*."

"Sir, if the limeys couldn't sink us and the Japs couldn't sink us and whoever was flying that damn bombing aeroplane out from Argentina couldn't sink us, I don't figure we need to be afraid of any germs," Sam said.

Grady laughed. "That's the spirit! All right, Carsten. Pick up your new orders, get your paperwork taken care of, and we'll go ashore tomorrow morning—if you can stand an officer for company, that is."

"I'm a tough guy, sir," Carsten answered. "I expect I'll put up with it." Grady laughed and mimed throwing a punch at him, then went on his way.

"What's this about aeroplanes?" Crosetti asked.

"Don't even know, exactly," Sam said. "I joined the Navy five years before the war started, and here I am, buying a pig in a poke. Maybe I need my head examined, but maybe I'm smart, too. Smart, I mean, besides getting away from you. I hope I am, anyway."

"Good luck. I think you're crazy, but good luck." Crosetti shook Sam's hand, then walked off shaking his own head.

Getting orders was the easy part of getting off the *Dakota*. Carsten filled out endless separation forms. Only after the last of them was signed would the paymaster grudgingly give him greenbacks. With money in his billfold and a duffel bag on his shoulder, he walked down the gangplank from the *Dakota* to the pier with Commander Grady.

Even at the edge of the harbor, New York boiled with life. When Grady flagged a cab for the ride to the New York Central Railroad Depot, three different automobiles almost ran him and Sam down in the zeal for a fare. The drivers hopped out and screamed abuse at one another in both English and a language that seemed entirely compounded of gutturals.

Grady knew his way through the crowded old depot, which was fortunate, because Sam didn't. He had to step smartly to keep from being separated from the officer; the only place where he'd felt more crowded was the triple-decked bunkroom of the *Dakota*. Everyone here was moving, intent on his own business. About every third man, woman, and child was sneezing or sniffling or coughing. Some of them were likely to have influenza. Carsten tried not to inhale. That didn't work very well.

He and Grady got a couple of seats in a second-class car; the Navy saved money on train fares that way. They were the only Navy men there, though soldiers in green-gray occupied a fair number of seats. The civilians ranged from drummers in cheap, flashy suits to little old ladies who might still have been in Russia.

Once Grady and Carsten pulled into Boston, the officer paid for another cab ride, this one over the Charlestown Bridge to the Navy Yard on the north side of the Charles River. Seeing the battleships and cruisers and submersibles and tenders tied up there made Sam's heart swell with pride. A few ships from the Western Squadron of Germany's High Seas Fleet stood out from their American allies because of their less familiar lines and light gray paint jobs.

Sam followed Commander Grady, each of them with duffel bag bouncing on his back. Then, all at once, Sam stopped in his tracks and stared and stared. Grady walked on for a couple of steps before he noticed he didn't have company any more. He turned and looked back, a grin on his rabbity features. "What's the matter, Carsten?" he asked, sounding like a man trying hard not to laugh out loud.

"Sir," Sam said plaintively, "I've seen every type of ship in the U.S. Navy, and I reckon damn near every type of ship in the High Seas Fleet, too." He pointed ahead. "In all my born days, though, I've never seen anything that looked like *that*, and I hope to God I never do again. What the hell is it supposed to be?"

Now Grady did laugh out loud. "That's the *Remembrance*, Carsten. That's what you signed up for."

"Jesus," Sam said. "I must have been out of my goddamn mind."

The *Remembrance* looked as if somebody had decided to build a battleship and then, about a third of the way through the job, got sick of it and decided to flatten out most of the deck to hurry things along. An aeroplane sat on the deck aft of the bridge: not a seaplane that would land in the water and be picked up by the ship's crane but a Wright two-decker fighting scout—a U.S. copy of a German Albatros—with utterly ordinary landing gear and not a trace of a float anywhere. Sam shook his head in disbelief.

Laughing still, Commander Grady clapped him on the back. "Cheer up. It won't be so bad. You'll still mess forward and bunk aft. And a five-inch gun is a five-inch gun." He pointed to the sponson under that unbelievably long, unbelievably level deck. "You'll do your job, and the flyboys will do theirs, and everybody will be happy except the poor enemy bastards who bump into us."

"Yes, sir," Sam said dubiously. "What the devil did she start out to be, anyway? And why didn't she turn out to be whatever that was?"

"They started to build her as a fast, light-armored battle cruiser, to slide in close to the Confederate coast, blast hell out of it, and then scoot before the Rebs could do anything about it—a monitor with legs, you might say," Grady answered. "But that idea never went anywhere. Some bright boy got to thinking how handy it would be to take aeroplanes along wherever you needed them, and . . . there's the *Remembrance*."

"I thought of that myself, after the *Dakota* got bombed off Argentina," Carsten said, "but I never imagined—this." He wondered if he'd get into fights because sailors on ordinary, respectable vessels would call the *Remembrance* the ugliest ship in the Navy. Dammit, she *was* the ugliest ship in the Navy.

"Come on, let's go aboard," Grady said. "She won't look anywhere near so strange from the inside."

Even that didn't turn out to be true. The hangars that held nearly three dozen fighting scouts and the supply and maintenance areas that went with them took up an ungodly amount of space, leaving the bunkrooms cramped and feeling like afterthoughts. As a petty officer, Carsten did get a bottom bunk, but the middle one in the three-tier metal structure was only a few inches above him. He could stand it, but he didn't love it.

The only place in which he did feel at home was the sponson. The five-inch gun was the same model he'd served on the *Dakota*, and the sponson itself might have been transferred bodily from the battleship. The chief gunner's mate in charge of the crew, a burly veteran named Willie Moore, wore a splendid gray Kaiser Bill mustache. He wasn't half brother to his counterpart from the *Dakota*, Hiram Kidde, but Sam couldn't have proved it by the way he acted.

He turned out to know Kidde, which surprised Sam not at all. "If you served with the 'Cap'n,' reckon you'll do for me," he rumbled when Carsten mentioned the name of his former gun commander a couple of days after coming aboard.

"Thanks, Chief. Hope so," Sam said, and punctuated that with a sneeze. "Damn. I'm coming down with a cold."

He was off his feed at supper that evening, which surprised him: the *Remembrance*, however ugly she was, boasted a first-class galley. Everything was fresh, too—an advantage of sitting in port. But Sam didn't realize how sick he was till the next morning, when he almost fell out of his bunk. He stood, swaying, in front of it.

"You all right?" asked George Moerlein, who slept just above him. Sam didn't answer; he had trouble figuring out what the words meant. Moerlein peered at him, touched his forehead, and then jerked back his hand as if he'd tried picking up a live coal. "We better get this guy to sick bay," he said. "I think he's got the influenza." Sam didn't argue, either. He couldn't. He let them lead him away.

* * *

Arthur McGregor took a certain somber satisfaction in listening to the wind howl around his farmhouse. That was just as well; the wind in Manitoba was going to howl through the winter whether he took any satisfaction in it or not.

"One thing," he said to his wife. "In weather like this, the Yanks stay indoors."

"I wish to heaven they'd stayed in their own country," Maude answered. She was short and redheaded, a contrast to his rangy inches and dark hair that was beginning to show frost as he edged into his forties.

Her eyes went to the photograph of their son, Alexander, that hung on the wall of the front room. The photograph was all they had of him; the U.S. troops who occupied Manitoba had executed him for plotting sabotage a year and a half before.

McGregor's eyes went there, too. He was still paying the Americans back for what they'd done to Alexander. He would never be done paying them back, as long as he lived. If they ever found out he made bombs, he wouldn't live long. He couldn't drive the Yanks out of Canada singlehanded. If they were going to try to rule his country, though, he could make their lives miserable.

Julia came in from the kitchen. She also looked toward Alexander; these days, the family almost made a ritual of it. McGregor looked at his daughter in what was as close to wonderment as his solid, stolid nature could produce. Some time while he wasn't looking, Julia had turned into a woman. She'd been eleven when the Americans invaded, and hardly even coltish. She was fourteen now, and not coltish any more. She looked like her mother, but taller and leaner, as McGregor himself was.

"What are you going to do about that school order, Pa?" she asked.

The wind gusted louder. McGregor could have pretended not to hear her. His own sigh was gusty, too. "I'm going to pretend I don't know the first thing about it for as long as I can," he answered.

He'd pulled Julia and her younger sister, Mary, out of school a couple of years before. The Americans were using it to teach Canadian children their lies about the way the world worked. Since then, McGregor and Maude had taught reading and ciphering at home.

Now, though, the occupying authorities had sent out an edict requiring all children between the ages of six and sixteen to attend school at least six months out of the year. They didn't intend to miss any chances to tell their stories to people they wanted to grow up to be Americans, not Canadians.

"It'll be all right, Pa," Julia said. "I really think it will. You can send Mary and me, and we won't end up Yanks, truly we won't." She looked toward Alexander's photograph again.

"I know you won't, chick," he said. "But I don't know that Mary would be able to keep from telling the teacher what she really thinks."

At nine, Mary wore her heart on her sleeve, even more than Alexander had. She also hated Americans with a pure, clear hatred that made even her father's pale beside it. Letting the Yanks know how she felt struck McGregor as most unwise.

Julia had washed the supper dishes; Mary was drying them. After the last one clattered into the cupboard, she came out to join the rest of the family. She was sprouting up, too, like wheat after planting. She would, McGregor judged, make a tall woman. But she still kept some of the feline grace she'd had since she was very small, and also some of a cat's self-containment. McGregor hadn't needed to teach her much about conspiracy. She understood it as if by instinct.

Now he said, "Mary, if you have to, do you suppose you can put up with listening to the Yanks' lies in school without telling them off?"

"Why would I have to do that, Pa?" she answered. "Maybe they can make me go to school, but—" She caught herself. Her gray eyes, so like those of her father and her dead brother, widened. "Oh. You mean put up with them so I wouldn't get in trouble—so *we* wouldn't get in trouble."

"That's right." Arthur McGregor nodded. No, no one needed to teach Mary about conspiracy.

She thought it over. "If I have to, I suppose I could," she said at last. "But telling lies is a sin on their heads, isn't it?"

"So it is." McGregor smiled to hear that, but not too much: he'd passed his own stern Presbyterian ethic down to the new generation. "The Yanks have so many other sins on the book against them, though, that lying doesn't look like so much to them."

"Well, it should," Mary said. "It should all count against them, every bit of it. And it will. God counts *everything*." She spoke with great assurance.

McGregor wished he felt so sure himself. He believed, yes, but he'd lost that simple certainty. If he'd had any left, Alexander's death would have burned it out of him, leaving ashes behind. He said,

"You will go to school, then, and be a good little parrot, so we can show the Americans we're obeying their law?"

His younger daughter sighed. "If I have to," she said again.

"Good," McGregor said. "The more we look like we're doing what they want us to, the more we can do what we want to when they aren't looking."

Julia said, "That's good, Pa. That's very good. That's just what we'll do."

"That's what we'll have to do," Maude said. "That's what everyone will have to do, for however long it takes till we're free again."

"Or till we turn into Americans," Arthur McGregor said bleakly. He held up a work-roughened hand. "No, I don't mean us. Some of our neighbors will turn into Americans, but not us."

"Some of our neighbors have already turned into Americans," Julia said. "They don't care about what they were, so they don't care what they are. We know better. We're Canadians. We'll always be Canadians. Always."

McGregor wondered if, with the strongest will in the world, his grandchildren and great-grandchildren would remember they were Canadians. And then, perhaps wondering the same thing, Maude spoke as if to reassure herself: "Germany took Alsace and Lorraine away from France almost fifty years ago, but the people there still remember they're Frenchmen."

Canadians had heard a great deal about their ally's grievances against the Kaiser and his henchmen (till the Americans overran them, after which they'd had to endure lies about Germany's grievances against France). Now France had more reasons to grieve, for the Germans were biting off more of her land. And McGregor, still in his bleak mood, said, "The Germans settled a lot of their own people in Alsace and Lorraine to help hold them down. If the Americans did that . . ."

His wife and daughters stared at him in horror. Mary spoke first: "I wouldn't live next to Americans, Pa! I wouldn't. If they came here, I'd . . . I don't know what I'd do, but it'd be pretty bad."

"We won't have to worry about that till next spring at the earliest," McGregor said. "Won't be any Yanks settling down to farm in the middle of winter, not here in Manitoba there won't." His chuckle was grim. "And the ones who come in the spring, if any do, they're liable to turn up their toes when they find out what winters are like. We've seen that the Americans don't fancy our weather."

"Too bad for them," Julia said.

After the children had gone to sleep, McGregor lay awake beside his wife in the bed the two of them shared. "What am I going to do, Maude?" he whispered, his voice barely audible through the whistling wind. "By myself, I can hurt the Americans, but that's all I can do. They won't leave on account of me."

"You've made them pay," Maude said. He'd never admitted making bombs, not in so many words. She'd never asked, not in so many words. She knew. He knew she knew. But they formally kept the secret, even from each other.

"Not enough," he said now. "Nothing could ever be enough except driving them out of Canada. But no one man can do that."

"No one man can," Maude said in a musing tone of voice.

He understood where she was going, and shook his head. "One man can keep a secret. Maybe two can. And maybe three can, but only if two of them are dead." That came from the pen of Benjamin Franklin, an American, but McGregor had forgotten where he'd first run across it.

"I suppose you're right," Maude said. "It seems a pity, though."

"If Alexander hadn't hung around with a pack of damnfool kids who didn't have anything better to do than run their mouths and make foolish plots, he'd still be alive today," McGregor said harshly.

Maude caught her breath. "I see what you're saying," she answered after a long pause.

"And the strange thing is, if he was still alive, we wouldn't hate the Yanks the way we do," McGregor said. "They caused themselves more harm shooting him than he ever would have given them if they'd let him go."

"They're fools," Maude said. That McGregor agreed with wholeheartedly. But the American fools ruled Canada today. God must have loved them, for He'd made so very many.

The notion of God loving Americans was so unlikely, McGregor snorted and fell asleep bemused by it. When he woke up, it was still dark; December nights fifty miles south of Winnipeg were long. He groped for a match, scraped it alight, and lit the kerosene lamp on the nightstand.

He didn't want to get out from under the thick wool blankets: he could see his own breath inside the bedroom. He threw a shirt and overalls over his long johns and was still shivering. Maude got out of bed, too. She carried the lamp downstairs as soon as she was dressed. He followed her.

She built up the fire in the stove and started a pot of coffee. It wasn't good coffee; if the Americans had any good coffee, they kept it for themselves. But it was hot. He stood by the stove, too, soaking in the warmth radiating from the black iron. Maude melted butter in a frying pan and put in three eggs. McGregor ate them along with bread and butter. Then he shrugged on a long, heavy coat and donned mittens. Reluctantly, he opened the door and went outside.

It had been cold in the bedroom. As he slogged his way to the barn, he wondered if he would turn into an icicle before he got there. A wry chuckle made a fogbank swirl around his face for a moment, till the fierce wind blew it away. People said there wasn't so much work on a farm in winter. In a way, they were right, for he didn't have to go out to the fields.

In spring and summer, though, he didn't have to work in weather like this. The body heat of the livestock kept the barn warmer than the weather outside, but warmer wasn't warm. He fed the horse and cow and pigs and chickens and cleaned up their filth. By the time he was done with that, he was warmer, too.

His eye fell on an old wagon wheel, the sort of junk any barn accumulated. Under it, hidden in a hole beneath a board beneath dirt, lay dynamite and fuses and blasting caps and crimpers and other tools of the bomb-maker's art. McGregor nodded to them. They would come out again.

Rain, some of it freezing, poured down out of a bleak gray sky. A barrel rumbled across the muddy Kansas prairie toward Colonel Irving Morrell. The cannon projecting from its slightly projecting prow was aimed straight at him. Two machine guns projected from each side of the riveted steel hull; two more covered the rear. A pair of White truck engines powered the traveling fortress. Stinking, steaming exhaust belched from the twin pipes.

The charge would have been more impressive had it been at something brisker than a walking pace. It would have been much more impressive had the barrel not bogged down in a mud puddle that aspired to be a pond when it grew up. The machine's tracks were not very wide, and it weighed almost thirty-three tons. It could have bogged on ground better than that it was traveling.

Morrell snapped his fingers in annoyance at himself for not having brought out a slate and a grease pencil with which he could have taken notes here in the field. He was a lean man, nearing thirty, with a long face, weathered features that bespoke a lot of time out in the sun and wind, and close-cropped sandy hair at the moment hidden under a wool cap and the hood of a rain slicker.

His boots made squelching noises as he slogged through the ooze toward the barrel. The commander of the machine stuck his head out of the central cupola that gave him and his driver a place to perch and a better view than the machine gunners and artillerymen enjoyed (the engineers who tended the two motors had no view, being stuck in the bowels of the barrel).

"Sorry, sir," he said. "Couldn't spot that one till too late."

"One of the hazards of the game, Jenkins," Morrell answered. "You can't go forward; that's as plain as the nose on my face. See if you can back out."

"Yes, sir." Lieutenant Jenkins ducked down into the cupola, clanging the hatch shut after himself. The engines changed note as the driver put the barrel into reverse. The barrel moved back a few inches, then bogged down again. Jenkins had spunk. Having shifted position, he tried to charge forward once more and escape the grip of the mud. All he succeeded in doing was getting deeper into it.

Morrell waved for him to stop and called, "You keep going that way, you'll need a periscope to see out, just like a submersible."

He doubted Jenkins heard him; with the engines hammering away, nobody inside a barrel could hear the man next to him screaming in his ear. Even so, the engines fell silent a few seconds later. The traveling fortress' commander could see for himself that he wasn't going anywhere.

When the young lieutenant popped out through the hatch again, he was grinning. "Well, sir, you said you wanted to test the machine under extreme conditions. I'd say you've got your wish."

"I'd say you're right," Morrell answered. "I'd also say these critters need wider tracks, to carry their weight better."

Lieutenant Jenkins nodded emphatically. "Yes, sir! They could use stronger engines, too, to help us get out of this kind of trouble if we do get into it."

"That's a point." Morrell also nodded. "We used what we had when we designed them: it would have taken forever to make a new engine and work all the teething pains out of it, and we had a war to fight. With the new model, though, we've got the chance to do things right, not just fast."

That was his job: to figure out what *right* would be. He would have a lot to say about what the next generation of barrels looked like. It was a great opportunity. It was also a great responsibility. More than anything else, barrels had broken two years of stalemated struggle in the trenches and made possible the U.S. victory over the CSA. Having the best machines and knowing what to do with them would be vital if—*no, when,* he thought—the United States and Confederate States squared off again.

For the moment, his concerns were more immediate. "You and your men may as well come out," he told Jenkins. "We've got a couple of miles of muck to go before we get back to Fort Leavenworth."

"Leave the barrel here for now, sir?" the young officer asked.

"It's not going anywhere by itself, that's for sure," Morrell answered, with which Jenkins could hardly disagree. "Rebs aren't about to steal it, either. We'll need a recovery vehicle to pull it loose, but we can't bring one out now because it would bog too." Recovery vehicles mounted no machine guns or cannon, but were equipped with stout towing chains, and sometimes with bulldozer blades.

More hatches opened up as the engineers and machine gunners and artillerymen emerged from their steel shell. Even in a Kansas December, it was warm in there. It had been hotter than hell in summertime Tennessee, as Morrell vividly remembered. It had been hot outside there, too. It wasn't hot here. All eighteen men in the barrel crew, Jenkins included, started shivering and complaining. They hadn't brought rain gear—what point, in the belly of the machine?

Morrell sympathized, but he couldn't do anything about it. "Come on," he said. "You won't melt."

"Listen to him," one of the machine gunners said to his pal. "He's got a raincoat, so what the devil has he got to worry about?"

"Here," Morrell said sharply. The machine gunner looked alarmed; he hadn't intended to be overheard. Morrell stripped off the slicker and threw it at him. "Now you've got the raincoat. Feel better?"

"No, sir." The machine gunner let the coat fall in the mud. "Not fair for me to have it either, sir. Now nobody does." That was a better answer than Morrell had expected from him.

Lieutenant Jenkins said, "Let's get moving, so we stay as warm as we can. We're all asking for the Spanish influenza."

"That's true," Morrell said. "First thing we do when we get in is soak in hot water, to get the mud off and to warm us up inside. And if thinking about that isn't enough to start you moving, I'll give two dollars to any man who gets back to the fort ahead of me."

That set the crew of the barrel into motion, sure enough. Morrell was the oldest man among them by three or four years. They were all veterans. They were all convinced they were in top shape. Every one of them hustled east, in the direction of the fort. They all thought they would have a little extra money jingling in their pockets before the day was through.

Morrell wondered how much his big mouth was going to cost him. As he picked up his own pace, his right leg started to ache. It lacked the chunk of flesh a Confederate bullet had blown from it in the opening weeks of the war. Morrell had almost lost the leg when the wound festered. He still limped a little, but never let the limp slow him down.

And he got to Fort Leavenworth ahead of any of the barrel men. As soon as he reached the perimeter of the fort, he realized how worn he was: *ridden hard and put away wet* was the phrase that came to mind. He'd ridden himself hard, all right, and he was sure as hell wet, but he hadn't been put away yet. He wanted to fall into the mud to save himself the trouble.

Soaking in a steaming tub afterwards did help. So, even more, did the admiring looks he got from his competitors as they came onto the grounds of the fort in his wake. He savored those. Command was more than a matter of superior rank. If the men saw he deserved that rank, they would obey eagerly, not just out of duty.

That evening, he pored over German accounts of meetings with British and French barrels. The Germans had used only a few of the traveling fortresses, fewer than their foes. They'd won anyhow, with England distracted from the Continent because of the fighting in Canada, and with mutinies spreading through the French Army after Russia collapsed. Morrell was familiar with British barrels; the CSA had copied them. He knew less about the machines the French had built.

When he looked at photographs of some of the French barrels—their equivalent of the rhomboids England and the CSA used—he snickered. Their tracks were very short compared to the length of their chassis, which meant they easily got stuck trying to traverse trenches.

Another French machine, though, made him thoughtful. The Germans had only one example of that model: the text said it was a prototype hastily armed and thrown into the fight in a desperate effort to stem the decay of the French Army. It was a little barrel (*hardly more than a keg,* Morrell thought with a grin) with only a two-man crew, and mounted a single machine gun in a rotating turret like the ones armored cars used.

"Not enough firepower there to do you as much good as you'd like," Morrell said into the quiet of his barracks room. Still, the design was interesting. It had room for improvement.

He grabbed a piece of paper and a pencil and started sketching. Whoever designed the first U.S. barrels had thought of nothing past stuffing as many guns as possible inside a steel box and making sure at least one of them could shoot every which way. The price of success was jamming a couple of squads' worth of soldiers into that hellish steel box along with the guns.

If you put the two-inch cannon into that turret instead of a machine gun, you got a gun firing every which way all by itself. You'd still want a machine gun in front. If the cannon were in the turret, the driver would have to go down into the lower front of the machine. Could he handle a machine gun and drive, too?

"Not likely," Morrell muttered. All right: that meant another gunner or two down there with him.

You wouldn't always want to use the turret cannon, though. Sometimes that would be like swatting a fly with an anvil. Morrell sketched another machine gun alongside the cannon. It would rotate, too, of course, and the gunners who tended the large gun could also serve it.

That cut the crew from eighteen men down to five or six—you'd likely need an engineer, too, but the machine had better have only one engine, and one strong enough to move at a decent clip. Morrell shook his head. "No, six or seven," he said. "Somebody's got to tell everybody else what to do." A boat without a commander would be like a boat—no, a ship; Navy men would laugh at him—without a captain.

He was forgetting something. He stared at the paper, then at the plain whitewashed plaster of the wall. Forcing it wouldn't work; he had to try to think around it. That was as hard as *not* thinking about a steak dinner. He'd had practice, though. Soon it would come to him. Soon . . .

"Wireless telegraph!" he exclaimed, and added an aerial to his sketch. Maybe that would require another crewman, or maybe the engineer could handle it. If it did, it did. He'd wanted one of those gadgets in his barrel during the war just finished. Controlling the mechanical behemoths was too hard without them.

He studied the sketch. He liked it better than the machines in which he'd thundered to victory against the CSA. He wondered what the War Department would think. It was different, and a lot of senior officers prided themselves on not having had a new thought in years. He shrugged. He'd send it in and find out.

"Miss Colleton"—the broker in Columbia sounded agitated, even over the telephone wire—"I can do only so much. If you ask the impossible of me, you must not be surprised when I do not hand it to you on a silver platter."

Anne Colleton glared at the telephone. She could not exert all her considerable force of personality through it. But she could not leave St. Matthews, South Carolina, to visit the state capital, either. And so she would have to forgo the impact her blond good looks had on people of the male persuasion. She'd manage with hard-headed common sense—or, if she didn't, she'd find a new broker. She'd done that before, too.

"Mr. Whitson," she said, "are the Confederate dollar, the British pound, and the French franc worth more in terms of gold today, January 16, 1918, than they were yesterday, or are they worth less?"

"Less, of course," Whitson admitted, "but even so—"

"Do you expect that these currencies will be worth more in gold tomorrow, or less again?" Anne broke in.

"Less again," Whitson said, "but even so, you are gutting your holdings by—"

She interrupted: "If I convert my holdings in those currencies to gold and U.S. dollars and German marks while the C.S. dollar and the pound and the franc are still worth *something*, Mr. Whitson, I will have *something* left when the Confederate States get back on their feet. If I wait any longer, I will have nothing. I've waited too long already. Now, sir: will you do as I instruct you, or would you sooner converse with my attorneys?"

"I am trying to save you from yourself, Miss Colleton," Whitson said peevishly.

"You are my broker, not my pastor," Anne said. "Answer the question I just gave you, if you would be so kind."

Whitson sighed. "Very well. On your head be it." He hung up.

So did Anne, angrily. Her brother, Tom, came into the room. "You look happy with the world," he remarked. His words held less in the way of lighthearted humor and more sardonicism than they would have before the war. He'd gone off, as if to a lark, a captain, and come back a lieutenant-colonel who'd been through all the horrors the Roanoke front had to offer.

"Delighted," Anne returned. She was still sorting out what to make of her brother. In a way, she was pleased he didn't let her do all his thinking for him, as he had before. In another way, that worried her. Having him under her control had been convenient. She went on, "My idiot broker is convinced I'm the maniac. Everything will be rosy day after tomorrow, if you listen to him."

"You're right—he's an idiot," Tom agreed. "You know what I paid for a pair of shoes yesterday? Twenty-three dollars—in paper, of course. I keep my gold and silver in my pocket. *I'm* not an idiot."

"It will get worse," Anne said. "If it goes on for another year, people's life savings won't be worth anything. That's when we really have to start worrying."

"I'll say it is." Her brother nodded. "If the Red niggers had waited to rise up till that happened, half the white folks in the country would have grabbed their squirrel guns and joined in."

"If they hadn't risen up when they did, we might not be in this mess now," Anne said grimly. "And they did bad enough when they rose."

Tom nodded. The Marxist Negroes had killed Jacob, his brother and Anne's, who was at the Marshlands plantation because Yankee poison gas left him an invalid. They'd burned the mansion, too; only in the past few months had their remnants been cleared from the swamps by the Congaree River.

"Hmm," Tom said. "We need an idiot to take Marshlands off our hands for us. Maybe we ought to sell it to your broker."

"As a matter of fact, I think we need an imbecile to take Marshlands off our hands," Anne said. "God only knows when anyone will be able to raise a crop of cotton on that land: one fieldhand in three is liable to be a Red, and how could you tell till too late? And the taxes—I haven't seen anyone talking about taking the war taxes off the books, have you?"

"Not likely." Tom snorted. "Government needs every dime it can squeeze. Only good thing about that is, the government has to take paper. If they don't take the paper they print, nobody else will, either."

"Small favors," Anne said, and her brother nodded again. She went on, "I'd take just about any kind of offer for Marshlands, and I'd take paper. I'd turn it into gold, but I'd take paper. If that doesn't prove I'm desperate, I don't know what would."

"A hundred years," Tom said. "More than a hundred years— gone." He snapped his fingers. "Like that. Gone." He snapped them again. "Better than fifty years of good times for the whole country. That's gone, too."

"We have to put the pieces back together," Anne said. "We have to make the country strong again, or else the damnyankees will run over us again whenever they decide they're ready. Even if they don't decide to run over us, they can make us their little brown cousins, the way we've done with the Empire of Mexico."

"I'm damned if I'll be anybody's little brown cousin," Tom Colleton ground out. He swore with studied deliberation. He'd never cursed in front of her before he went off to the trenches. He still didn't do it in the absentminded style he'd no doubt used there. But when he felt the need, the words came out.

"I feel the same way," Anne answered. "Anyone with an ounce of sense feels the same way. But the Congressional elections prove nobody knows how to take us from where we are to where we ought to be."

"What?" Her brother raised an eyebrow. "Split as near down the middle between Whigs and Radical Liberals as makes no difference? And a couple of Socialists elected from Chihuahua, and one from Cuba, and even one from New Orleans, for Christ's sake? Sounds to me like they'll have everything all straightened out by day after tomorrow, or week after next at the latest."

Anne smiled at Tom's pungent sarcasm, but the smile had sharp corners. "Even that mess shouldn't get things too far wrong. We have to do enough of what the Yankees tell us to keep the USA from attacking us while we're flat. Whatever dribs and drabs we happen to have left after that can go to putting us back on our feet. Lean times, yes, but I think we can come through them if we're smart."

"Outside of a couple of panics, we haven't had lean times before," Tom said. "We do need better politicians than the gang we've got. We could use somebody who'd really lead us out of the wilderness instead of stumbling through it for forty years."

"Of the current crop, I'm not going to hold my breath," Anne said. "I—" The telephone interrupted. She picked it up. "Hello?" Her mouth fell open, just a little, in surprise. "Commander Kimball! How good to hear from you. I was hoping you'd come through the war all right. Where are you now?"

"I'm in Charleston," Roger Kimball answered. "And what the hell is this 'Commander Kimball' nonsense? You know me better than that, baby." Unlike her brother, Kimball swore whenever he felt like it and didn't care who was listening. He not only had rough edges, he gloried in them. And he was right—she did know him intimately enough, in every sense of the word, to call him by his Christian name.

That she could, though, didn't mean she had to. She enjoyed keeping men off balance. "In Charleston? How nice," she said. "I hope you can get up to St. Matthews before long. You do know my brother, Lieutenant-Colonel Colleton, is staying with me here in town?" *You do know that, even if you get up to St. Matthews, you're not going to make love with me right now?*

Kimball was brash. He wasn't stupid. Anne couldn't abide stupidity. He understood what she meant without her having to spell it out. Laughing a sour laugh, he answered, "And he'll whale the living turpentine out of me if I put my hands where they don't belong, will he? Sweetheart, I hate to tell you this, but I haven't got the jack for pleasure trips without much pleasure. I'm on the beach, same as every other submarine skipper in the whole goddamn Navy." Where he could banter about passing on a chance to pay a social call that was only a social call, his voice showed raw pain when he told her the Navy had cut him loose.

"I'm very sorry to hear that," she said, and trusted him to understand she understood what grieved him most. "What are you going to do now?"

"Don't know yet," Kimball said. "I may try and make a go of it here, or I may head down to South America. Plenty of navies there that could use somebody who really knows what he's doing when he looks through a periscope."

That was likely to be true. The South American republics had chosen sides in the Great War as the rest of the world had done. Losers would be looking for revenge. Winners would be looking to make sure they didn't get it.

Anne said, "Whatever you decide to do, I wish you the very best."

"But not enough for you to send your brother out to hunt possums or something, eh?" Kimball laughed again. "Never mind. We'll get another chance one of these days, I reckon. Good luck to the lieutenant-colonel, too, the son of a bitch." Before she could answer, he hung up.

So did she, and she laughed, too. She admired the submariner; he was, she judged, almost as thoroughly self-centered as herself. Tom raised an eyebrow. "Who's this Commander—Kimball, is it?"

"That's right. He captained a submarine," Anne answered. "I got to know him on the train to New Orleans not long after the war started." He'd seduced her in his Pullman berth, too, but she didn't mention that.

"How well do you know him?" Tom asked.

"We're friends," she said. *I was in bed with him down in Charleston when the Red Negro uprising broke out.* She didn't mention that, either.

She didn't have to. "Are you more than ... friends?" her brother demanded.

Before the war, he wouldn't have dared question her that way. "I've never asked what you did while you weren't fighting," she said. "What I did, or didn't do, is none of your business."

Tom set his jaw and looked stubborn. He wouldn't have done that before the war, either. No, she couldn't control him any more, not with certainty. He said, "If you're going to marry the guy, it is. If he's just after your money, I'll send him packing. What you're doing affects me, you know."

Nor would he have had that thought in 1914. "If he were just after my money, don't you think *I* would have sent him packing?" she asked in return. "I can take care of myself, you know, with a rifle or any other way."

"All right," Tom said. "People who fall in love are liable to go all soft in the head, though. I wanted to make sure it hadn't happened to you."

"When it does, you can shovel dirt on me, because I'll be dead." Anne spoke with great conviction. Tom came over and kissed her on the cheek. They both laughed, liking each other very much at that moment.

In the trenches down in Virginia, Chester Martin had heard New Englanders talk about a lazy wind, a wind that didn't bother blowing around a man but went straight through him. The wind coming off Lake Erie this morning while he picketed the Toledo steel mill where he would sooner have been working was just that kind. In spite of coat and long underwear, in spite of hat and ear muffs, he shivered and his teeth chattered as he trudged back and forth in front of the plant.

His sign was stark in its simplicity. It bore but one word, that in letters a foot high: THIEVES! "They want to cut our wages," he said to the fellow in front of him, a stocky man named Albert Bauer. "We went out and got shot at—hell, I got shot—and they stayed home and got rich. No, they got richer; they were already rich. And they want to cut our wages."

Bauer was a solid Socialist. He said, "This is what we get for reelecting that bastard Roosevelt."

"He's not so bad," Martin said. A Democrat himself, he walked the picket line with his more radical coworkers. "He visited my stretch of the front once; hell, I jumped on him when the Rebs started shelling us. Later, when I got wounded, he found out about it and sent me a note."

"Bully!" Bauer said. "Can you eat the note? Can you take it to the bank and turn it into money? Roosevelt will oblige. Feudal nobles do. But does he care about whether you starve? Not likely!"

"Hush!" Chester Martin said suddenly. He pointed. "Here come the scabs." The factory owners always had people willing to work for them, no matter how little they paid. They also had the police on their side.

Jeers and curses and all manner of abuse rained down on the heads of the workers taking the places of the men who'd gone on strike. So did a few rocks and bottles, in spite of Socialist calls for calm and in spite of the strong force of blue-uniformed policemen escorting them into the steel mill. "Well, now they've gone and done it," Albert Bauer said in disgusted tones. "Now they've given the goddamn cops the goddamn excuse they need to go on and suppress us."

He proved a good prophet. As soon as the police had hustled the scabs into the plant, they turned around and yanked the nightsticks off their belts. A whistle blew, as if an officer during the war were ordering his men out of the trenches and over the top. Shouting fiercely, the police charged the strikers.

Chester Martin had not been an officer. But, thanks to casualties in the ranks above him, he'd briefly commanded a company in Virginia not long before the CSA asked for an armistice. Almost all the men on the picket line had seen combat, too. "Come on!" he shouted. "We can take these fat sons of bitches! Let's give 'em some bayonet drill."

He tore the cardboard sheet off his picket sign. The stick he was left holding wasn't as good a weapon as a billy club, but it wasn't to be despised, either. All around him, his companions imitated his action.

Here came the cops, a solid phalanx of them. Even so, they were outnumbered. They relied on discipline and on being able to create fear to get their way. After gas and machine guns and artillery and Confederate barrels, Martin found absurd the idea that he should be afraid of conscription-dodgers with clubs. He heard laughter from the men to either side of him, too.

In the instant before the red-faced policemen slammed into the picketers, Martin saw surprise and doubt on the features of a couple of blue-uniformed goons. Then he was at close quarters with them, and had no chance to study their expressions in any detail.

One of them swung a nightstick at his head. As if the cop were a Rebel with a clubbed rifle, Martin ducked. Things seemed to move very slowly, as they had in combat in the trenches. As he would have with a bayoneted rifle, Martin jabbed the end of his stick into the policeman's beefy side. A bayonet would have deflated the fellow for good. As things were, the cop grunted in pain and tried to twist away. Martin kicked him in the belly. He folded up like a concertina, the nightstick flying out of his hand.

Martin wished he could have grabbed the solid club, but it landed on the sidewalk, well out of his reach. He caught another policeman in the throat with the end of what had been the handle for his picket sign. Anyone who'd been in the trenches would have had no trouble blocking that lunge or knocking it aside. The cop let out a gargling shout and went over on his back.

"See?" Martin shouted. "They aren't so goddamn tough—the Rebs'd eat 'em for breakfast. And we can whip 'em, too."

"Rally!" one of the policemen shouted. The cops were taking longer than the strikers to figure out what was going on. Not until something close to half their number had fallen or had their night-sticks taken away did another cry ring out: "Drop back and regroup!"

Yelling in triumph, the men from the picket line surged after them. "Down with the scabs!" they roared. "Down with the cops!" They trampled underfoot the policemen who couldn't fall back and regroup.

Maybe one of those police officers was first to yank out his pistol and start shooting at the men who were stomping him. But after one or two sharp cracks rang out, it suddenly seemed as if every cop in Toledo were drawing his revolver and blazing away at the striking steelworkers.

Against gunfire, the strikers had no defense. Some fell screaming in pain. Some fell silently, and would not rise again. A few kept trying to advance on the police in spite of everything. Most, though, Chester Martin among them, knew how hopeless that was. He was not ashamed to run.

Bullets zipped past his head. Now that the police had opened fire, they seemed intent on emptying their revolvers and slaying as many strikers as they could. In their shoes, Martin probably would have done the same. After the men from the picket line had come so close to overwhelming the cops altogether, they wanted their own back. If strikers got to thinking they could defeat the police, no man in blue would be safe.

"Next time," somebody not far away panted, "next time we bring our own guns to the dance, by Jesus!"

"That's right," somebody else said. "They want a war, we'll give 'em a fucking war, see if we don't."

All Martin wanted was to be able to work and to bring home a halfway decent wage. He didn't think that was too much to ask. The men who ran the steel mill—the trust bosses with their top hats and diamond pinky rings, so beloved of editorial cartoonists—evidently thought otherwise. A bullet slapped into the flesh of a man close by. Martin had heard that sound too many times on too many fields to mistake it for anything else. The steelworker crumpled with a groan.

Martin dashed around a corner. After that, he didn't need to worry about getting shot. The people on the street weren't striking; they were going about their ordinary business. If the cops suddenly started spraying lead through their ranks, they—or their survivors—could complain to city hall with some hope of being heard.

It looked to be open season on picketers, though. Martin realized he was still holding the stick he'd used against the police to such good effect. As casually as he could, he let it fall to the pavement. Pulling his cap down over his eyes (and wondering how it had managed to stay on his head through the melee), he trudged down the street toward the nearest trolley stop.

Several policemen, pistols drawn, ran past him while he stood waiting. His eyes widened; maybe he'd been wrong about how much mayhem the cops were willing to dish out to the general public.

Since he didn't do anything but stand there, they left him alone. If he'd tried to flee . . . He didn't care to think what might have happened then.

When the trolley came clanging up to the stop, he threw a nickel in the fare box and took a seat even though it was heading away from his parents' flat, where he was staying. He rode for more than a mile, till he'd put the steel mill well behind him. When he did get off, he was only a block or so away from the county courthouse.

Across the street from the building stood a statue of Remembrance, a smaller replica of the great one in New York harbor. Remembrance had finally brought the United States victory over the CSA. What sort of statue would have to go up before anyone recognized that the working man deserved his due? How long would it take before he did?

Those were questions that made Martin look at Remembrance in a new way. His left arm bore a large, ugly scar, a reminder of what he'd suffered for his country's sake. What was his country willing to do for him?

"Shoot me again, that's what," he muttered. "Is that what I fought for?"

Teddy Roosevelt made noises about caring over what happened to the ordinary working man. Martin's brief meeting with the president in the trenches had made him think Roosevelt was sincere. He wondered what Roosevelt would say about what had happened in Toledo. That would tell whether he meant what he said.

Martin wondered if writing him a letter would do any good. He doubted it. He knew what happened when a private wrote a general a letter: either nothing, or somebody landed on the private like a ton of bricks. Roosevelt would do what he would do, and Chester Martin's view of the matter wouldn't count for beans.

"That's not right," he said. "That's not fair." But it was, he knew too well, the way the world worked.

After a while, he took a streetcar back to his parents' apartment building in Ottawa Hills. His younger sister, Sue, was at work; she'd landed a typist's job after he recovered from his wound and went back to the front. His father was at work, too. That graveled him some; Stephen Douglas Martin had been a steelworker longer than Chester had been alive. He labored down the street from the plant his son was striking. *He* had a good job and a good day's pay; Chester wondered if he himself would have to wait till he was gray and wrinkled to say the same. He wondered if he'd ever be able to say the same.

His mother, Louisa, who looked like an older version of Sue, exclaimed in surprise when he came through the door. "I thought you'd be out there all day," she said. She didn't approve of his striking, but he was her son, and she stayed polite about it.

At the moment, he knew a certain amount of relief he'd made it here ahead of the news of trouble. "It got a little lively when the scabs came in," he said, which was technically true but would do for an understatement till a better one came along.

"Were the cops busting heads?" his mother asked. He nodded. She shook her own head, in maternal concern. "That's why I don't want you out there picketing, Chester. You could get hurt."

He started to laugh. He couldn't help it. It wasn't that she was wrong. It was much more that she had no idea how right she was. "If I came through the war, I'm not going to let Toledo goons worry me," he answered.

"You need to worry. You could step in front of a streetcar tomorrow," his mother said. He nodded. She said that a lot. If he was going to worry, trolley cars wouldn't go high on the list. Two other questions topped it. One was, had anyone recognized him while he nerved the strikers to resist the police? The second followed hard upon the first: would any of those people let the police know who he was?

Jefferson Pinkard kept a wary eye on the crucible as it swung into position to pour its molten contents onto the Sloss Works foundry floor. The kid handling the crucible had some notion of what he was doing, but only some. Herb Wallace, the best crucible man Jeff had ever known, had gone off to fight the damnyankees—conscription nabbed him early—but he hadn't come home to Birmingham. His bones lay somewhere up in Kentucky.

This time, the pouring went smoothly. Only a tiny, fingerlike rivulet of molten steel broke through the earth and sand walling the mold, and Pinkard and his partner had no trouble stemming it with more earth. Leaning on his rake afterwards, Jeff said, "Wish they were all that easy."

His partner nodded. "Yes, suh, Mistuh Pinkard," Vespasian agreed. The big, bulky Negro—as big and bulky as Pinkard himself—took off his cloth cap and wiped sweat from his forehead. Winter might rule outside, but it was always summertime in hell on the foundry floor. Vespasian pointed toward the crucible operator.

"Hope to Jesus Billy up there figure out his job before he kill somebody. Ain't happened yet, but he come too damn close a couple times."

"Yeah—one of 'em was me last month." Pinkard jumped sideways to show how he'd escaped the misplaced stream of metal.

"You was right lively, that's a fact," Vespasian said.

"Damn well had to be." Pinkard shored up the edge of the mold at another place where it looked as if it might give way. "The floor did run smoother before the war, and that's a fact, too."

Vespasian didn't answer. He hadn't been on the foundry floor before the war. Back then, Negroes had fed the furnaces and done other jobs that took strong backs and no brains, but the better positions had been in white hands. Jeff's partner then had been his next-door neighbor and best friend, Bedford Cunningham.

But the war had sucked white men into the Confederate Army. The CSA had still needed steel—more steel than ever—to fight the damnyankees. Negroes started filling night-shift jobs once solely the property of white men, then evening-shift, and then, at last, day-shift, too.

Back then, before he got conscripted himself, Jeff hadn't wanted to work alongside a black man. He'd done it, though, for the sake of his country. Bedford Cunningham had come back to Birmingham without an arm. A lot of other steel men had come back as invalids. A lot more, like Herb Wallace, hadn't come back at all.

And so even now, with the war over for half a year, Negroes remained in some of the places they had taken during the war: they'd gained experience. Pinkard couldn't argue against experience, not when he'd just been griping about Billy. And Vespasian, who was in his forties, didn't get uppity the way a lot of younger blacks did. As far as the work went, he made a good enough partner. Jeff still felt uncomfortable working beside him.

He didn't quit. He'd have felt a lot more uncomfortable unemployed. Steel was all he knew. If he got a job at another foundry, he had no guarantee he wouldn't be working with another Negro, and one harder to get along with than Vespasian. He didn't care to move out of Sloss company housing, either (though he wished he didn't live next door to Bedford any more). He endured.

He never once wondered what Vespasian thought of working next to him.

At shift-changing time, the steam whistle blew a blast that cut through the rest of the din on the floor like a hot knife through pork fat. "See you in the mornin', Mistuh Pinkard," Vespasian said.

"Yeah," Jeff answered. "See you."

They clocked out separately, and left the enormous foundry building separately, too. It wasn't the way it had been, when Pinkard and Bedford had sometimes gone home to their side-by-side yellow cottages with their arms draped over each other's shoulders. Vespasian didn't have a yellow cottage. His cabin was painted primer red, which was cheaper.

Some of the white men going home waved to Pinkard, as did a couple coming onto the evening shift. He waved back. He was always glad to see familiar faces. He didn't see that many. Shift changes reminded him how little remained the same as it had been in 1914. Being reminded hurt.

His breath smoked as he hurried home. They'd had snow the week before, which wasn't common in Birmingham. On top of everything else, it had been a hard winter. The grass was yellow-brown and dead. Somebody sneezed not far from Jeff. He hoped it was from a cold, or from a tickling mustache hair. The Spanish influenza was killing men who'd lived through all the bullets the damnyankees aimed at them—and killing their wives and mothers and children, too.

In spite of the cold, Fanny Cunningham was standing in front of her house, gossiping with the woman who lived on the other side of her from the Pinkards. She waved to Jeff as he walked by. He waved back, calling, "How's Bedford doing?"

"Right good," she answered. "He's been cheerful the whole day through."

"Glad to hear it," Pinkard said. He was especially glad to hear Fanny had had her husband under her eye the whole day through.

She said, "You don't come over like you used to, Jeff. Bedford'd be powerful pleased to see more of you."

Jefferson Pinkard didn't answer that. He waved again, almost—but not quite—as if to say he'd think about it, then headed up the walk to his own cottage. He hesitated before opening the door. He had to do it, though, if he intended to go inside. When at last he did, the savory smell of stewing pork made his mouth water.

"That you, darlin'?" Emily called from the kitchen.

"It's me, all right," Jeff said.

Emily came out, a smile on her face. She had a barmaid's good looks and a barmaid's good buxom figure and hair of a bright shade somewhere between red and gold. Now that she wasn't working in a munitions plant any longer, she was letting it grow out. Now that she was out of the plant, too, the jaundice working with cordite had given her was gone, leaving her rosy and altogether desirable.

Jeff took her in his arms. She pulled his face down to hers. Her lips were greedy against his. She'd always been greedy for loving. When Jeff hadn't been there to give it to her . . . That was when he'd become a less than happy man.

"What did you do today?" he asked her after they broke apart.

"Usual kinds of things," she answered. "Did my cleaning. Did my cooking. Went out and bought me some cloth to make a dress with." She nodded toward the sewing machine in a corner of the front room. Then she stuck out a hip, tilted her head a little, and looked at him sidelong. "Thought about you. Thought about you a lot, Jeff."

"Did you?" he said.

Emily nodded, batting her eyelashes. She played the role of seductress to the hilt. That didn't mean Jeff failed to respond to it. The collarless neck of his shirt suddenly felt like a choker. Some evenings, supper turned out to be later than he expected when he walked through the door.

"Did—?" That was the question Jeff knew he shouldn't ask. *Did you see Bedford Cunningham today?* If he wanted to let the poison seep out of their marriage instead of putting more in, he couldn't keep harping on that. He changed course in midstream: "Did we have any more beer in the icebox?"

Alabama had gone dry not long before the war. What that meant, Pinkard had found, was that you had to know somebody before you could buy beer or whiskey, and that the quality of the stuff you could buy, especially the whiskey, had gone down. He'd evidently managed to ask the question without perceptible pause, for Emily nodded again. "Sure do," she said. "Couple bottles. Shall we have 'em with the stew? It ought to be just about ready."

"That sounds pretty good," Jeff said. Supper, for the moment, was more on his mind than going back to the bedroom. He found another question that wasn't dangerous, or wasn't dangerous that way: "What did you pay for the cloth?"

Now Emily's blue eyes flashed with fury, not any more tender emotion. "Dollar and a half a yard. Can you believe it?" she said. "I wasn't buying fancy silk taffeta, Jeff. I know we ain't rich. It wasn't anything but printed cotton dress percale, like I used to get before the war for eleven cents a yard. Wasn't as nice as what I could get then, neither."

He sighed; he'd feared the answer would be something like that. "They haven't bumped my pay in a bit," he said. "Don't know when they'll do it again." His laugh held fury, too. "Here I am, making more money than I ever reckoned I would in all my born days, and I can't even keep my head above water. That ain't right, Em. That purely ain't right. And hellfire, the little bit we'd stashed away in the bank before the war—what'll it buy us now? Not what we hoped it would, that's certain sure."

His wife didn't argue. Instead, she went into the kitchen, pulled the cork from a bottle of beer, and brought it out to him. "Here," she said. "Won't make things better, but it'll make 'em *look* better for a spell." While Jeff took a long pull, she got the other bottle for herself.

Things did look a little better after some beer. Getting some pork stew under his belt made Pinkard more charitably inclined toward the world, too. It even made him more charitably inclined toward Emily. He hadn't married her for any other reason than getting her drawers down, but she'd shown him some others in the years since they tied the knot.

While she washed the supper dishes, he read yesterday's newspaper by the light of a kerosene lamp. Kerosene was heading through the roof, too, especially since the Yankees weren't going to let go of Sequoyah, from which the Confederate States had drawn a great part of their oil.

A story caught his eye. "Look here," he said to Emily when she came out of the kitchen, drying her hands on a towel. "They had themselves a riot in Richmond: folks saying we're selling ourselves down the river to the USA. We're sure as hell selling ourselves down the river to somebody. Dollar and a half a yard for cotton! That kind of thing means we need to get ourselves set to rights, but I'm hanged if I know how."

"I don't want you hanged, Jeff, sweetheart, but I like the way you're hung," Emily said. She cared nothing for politics. Sweeping the newspaper aside, she sat down on her husband's lap.

His arms went around her. One hand closed on her breast. She sighed in his ear, her breath warm and moist. He knew she wanted him. He'd never stopped wanting her, even when. . . . That hand squeezed tight. Emily whimpered a little, but only a little.

Later, in the bedroom, she whimpered in a different way, and gasped and moaned and thrashed and clawed. Sated, sinking toward sleep, Jeff slowly nodded. She wanted him, all right—no doubt of that. But whom would she want when his back was turned? He drifted off, wondering, wondering.

Nellie Semphroch woke with a start to find a man in her bed: a gray-haired fellow with a bushy mustache. The reason she woke, and woke with a start, was not hard to find, for he was snoring like a sawmill.

As her racing heart slowed toward its normal rhythm, she relaxed and let out a small sigh. Here she'd been married since before the turn of the year, and she still wasn't used to sleeping with her husband. She wasn't used to thinking of herself by her new name, either. She'd worn the one Edna's father had given her for a good many years—most of them without him, as he'd died when his daughter was little, and Edna wasn't little any more.

"One of the few decent things he ever did," Nellie muttered. Then, softly, she repeated her new name to herself, over and over: "Nellie Jacobs. Nellie Jacobs. Nellie *Jacobs*." She hadn't had so much trouble the first time she was married. That lay a quarter of a century in the past, though. She was more set in her ways now. "Nellie Jacobs."

Hal Jacobs grunted and rolled over toward her. His eyes opened. Did he look a little confused, too, as if wondering where he was? He'd been a widower for a long time, as she'd been a widow, and had grown used to fending for himself. The room in which he'd lived, above the cobbler's shop across the street from her coffeehouse in Washington, D.C., was aridly neat.

Then, seeing her, he smiled. "Good morning, my dear Nellie," he said, leaning over to kiss her on the cheek. He did that every morning they woke up together.

"Good morning, Hal," Nellie said. Her husband, though far from young, remained very much the enchanted new bridegroom. Nellie wasn't so young as she wished she were, either. For her part, she remained bemused she'd ever agreed to marry him.

His hand slid along under the covers and came to rest on the curve of her hip. "You have made me the happiest man in the world," he declared.

He *was* sweet. Because he was sweet, Nellie had never told him how much she disliked having a man reach out and touch her like that. He wasn't young. He didn't seek his marital rights all that often. When he did, she had no trouble getting through it. She'd got through far worse back in her own younger days.

He wanted to please her. She let him think he did. Once or twice, he really had come close, which surprised her. She'd thought that part of her dead forever, not that it had ever had much life.

She threw off the wool blankets. She wore a thick flannel nightgown and long underwear beneath it, but she was still cold. She'd been cold for months. "When will this winter end?" she asked, though that was not a question her husband could answer.

Hal Jacobs got out of bed, too. He also had on long johns under a nightshirt, and he also looked cold. "It has been a hard one," he agreed. "March and no sign of letup. And it has to be making the influenza epidemic worse."

They both dressed rapidly. Nellie said, "I hate the influenza. It makes people afraid to go out in crowds, and that's bad for business."

"With so much snow on the street, they have trouble getting about anyhow," Hal said. "This will not keep me from enjoying a cup of your wonderful coffee, though, or I hope not, Mrs. Jacobs."

"I think we can probably take care of something like that, Mr. Jacobs," Nellie said. She'd always liked his old-fashioned, almost Old World, sense of courtesy. Now that they were married, she found herself imitating it.

They went downstairs together. Edna, whose room was across the hall, joined them a few minutes later. They all stuck close to the stove, which heated the kitchen area as well as water for coffee.

Sipping at his steaming cup, Hal Jacobs let out a grateful sigh. He looked from Nellie to Edna and back again. "My beautiful wife and her beautiful daughter," he said, beaming. "Yes, I am a lucky man."

Edna glanced over to her mother. "You better keep him happy, Ma. He sure does talk pretty."

"Foosh," Nellie said. She and Edna did look alike, with long faces, brown hair, and very fair skin. She didn't think she was particularly beautiful. Edna made a pretty young woman. She smiled more than Nellie did, which made her look more pleasant—but then, she was looking for a man. Nellie's opinion was that the joys of having even a good one were overrated, but Edna paid as little attention to Nellie's opinions as she could get away with.

A customer came in and ordered a fried-egg sandwich to go with his coffee. He was young and moderately handsome, with a brown

Kaiser Bill mustache whose upthrust points were waxed to formidable perfection. Edna took care of him before Nellie could. That might have been funny, were it happening for the first time. Having seen it throughout the war, Nellie was sick and tired of it.

She made eggs for herself and her husband, too—after so many years as a widow, she found the idea of having a husband very strange. When Hal had eaten, he said, "I'm going to go across the street and get some things done." He chuckled. "Can't have folks say my wife does all the work in the family, now can I?"

"Not when it isn't true," Nellie said. "Go upstairs and get your overcoat, though, before you set foot outdoors." Jacobs nodded and headed for the stairs.

Edna laughed. "There you go, Ma! You're telling him what to do like you've been married twenty years." Nellie made a face at her, and not a happy one. Jacobs laughed again going upstairs. That was luck, nothing else. He could as easily have grown angry at the idea of being ordered about.

Well bundled, he walked across the snowy street and opened the cobbler's shop. He wouldn't get much business today. He had to know it, too. The shop was part of his routine, though, as running the coffeehouse was part of Nellie's. She was glad he kept his independence and let her keep hers.

A barrel with a bulldozer blade welded to the prow rumbled down the street, pushing snow aside—and up onto the sidewalk, making the drifts higher and making it even harder for people to come into the coffeehouse or the cobbler's shop. The barrel driver cared nothing about that. Having been occupied by the Confederates for more than two and a half years and then devastated in the U.S. reconquest, Washington remained under martial law with the war months over.

Trucks roared by in the barrel's wake: it was for them that the bigger, heavier machine had cleared a path. Rubble filled their beds. Had rubble been gold, Washington would have spawned a rush to make the stampede to California seem as nothing beside it. But it wasn't gold. It was only rubble. It had to be disposed of, not sought out.

When Nellie opened the front door to take a cup of coffee to Hal, she found she couldn't, not without shoveling her way to the street. By the time she and Edna did the shoveling, the coffee was cold. She poured it out, got a fresh one, and took it across the street. Then she discovered she had to shovel her way into her husband's shop. That meant another trip back for coffee that was hot.

Some of the things she said about the U.S. government were less than complimentary.

Her husband was fixing a soldier's boot when she finally came in. The only difference between 1918 and 1916 was that it was a U.S., not a Confederate, boot. "Coffee? How nice. How thoughtful," he said. His eyes twinkled. "And what do you hear in the coffeehouse that might interest an old shoemaker, eh?"

Nellie laughed. He hadn't just been a shoemaker during the war. He'd been part of a spy ring keeping tabs on what the Confederates did in and around Washington. He'd helped Nellie get coffee and food when they were scarce and hard to come by. Since she had them, her place had been popular among Confederate officers and homegrown collaborators. In turn, she'd passed on what she overheard to him.

She had an Order of Remembrance, First Class, straight from the hands of Theodore Roosevelt because of that. Edna had an Order of Remembrance, Second Class, which was richly undeserved: she'd been on the point of marrying a Confederate officer when he died in a U.S. artillery barrage. So far as Nellie knew, Hal had no decorations of his own. That struck her as dreadfully unfair, but he'd never once said a word about it where she could hear.

Nor did he now. He drank the coffee quickly, savoring the warmth she'd had to work so hard to get him. Then he remarked, "If you look over there, you'll see they are building the Washington Monument a little higher now."

She looked out the window. Before the war, she would have been able to see only the tip of the monument over the buildings between it and the shop. Rebel bombardment and U.S. counterattacks had truncated the white stone obelisk. She could still see more of it now than she'd seen before the war, because the fighting had also leveled most of the buildings formerly in the way.

Hal said, "I hear they're starting to rebuild the White House and the Capitol, too."

"They'll be pretty," Nellie said. "Past that, I don't know why anybody would bother. They'll just get blown up again when the next war comes, and I can't see the president and Congress coming down from Philadelphia, can you?"

"To spend all their time here, the way they used to do?" Hal Jacobs shook his head. "No. Not when we are still so close to Virginia, even though the USA will hold the land down to the Rappahannock. But maybe to come down for ceremonial sessions: that, yes. That I could see."

"I suppose you may be right," Nellie said after a little thought. "Teddy Roosevelt *is* the sort to enjoy ruffles and flourishes, no doubt about that. He'd love to make the Rebs grind their teeth, too. They were going on about how Washington would be theirs forever. Reckon they didn't know everything there is to know."

"They were wrong," her husband agreed. "They will pay the price for being wrong. But we have paid a great price because they were wrong, too. I hope that will never happen again."

"Oh, I hope so, too," Nellie said. "I hope so with all my heart. But when I said people wouldn't come back to the White House and the Capitol on account of they'd get blown up in the next war, I didn't hear you telling me I was wrong."

"We have fought three wars against the Confederate States," Hal said. "I hope we do not fight a fourth one. I pray we do not fight a fourth one. A man should plan by what he has seen, though, not by what he hopes and prays. The older I get, the more certain I am this is true."

Nellie studied him. No, he wasn't handsome. No, he didn't make her heart flutter. And yet, as she had seen during the war and as she saw even more strongly now, he had a core of solid good sense that was altogether admirable. She did admire it, and him.

She hadn't been looking for anyone to make her heart flutter. That was for people Edna's age. Good sense, though—good sense lasted. The older Nellie got herself, the plainer that became.

She smiled at her new husband. It was the most wifely smile she'd ever given him. It was also the smile of someone beginning to realize she'd made a good bargain after all.

John Oglethorpe came up to Scipio as the Negro was clearing dishes off a table a customer had just left. The restaurant owner coughed. Scipio knew what that sort of cough meant: Oglethorpe was about to say something he only half wanted to say. Scipio could make a good guess about what it was, too.

His guess wasn't just good. It turned out to be right. After clearing his throat a couple more times, Oglethorpe said, "You've done a right good job for me here, Xerxes. I want you to know I mean that."

"I thanks you very much, suh," Scipio answered. Xerxes was the name he'd used since escaping the collapsing Congaree Socialist Republic and making his way across South Carolina to Augusta, Georgia. In his proper persona, he had a hefty price on his head, though Georgia worried more about its own black Reds on the loose than about those from other states.

"You've been just about as good a waiter as Aurelius, matter of fact," Oglethorpe went on. The other Negro had conveniently put himself out of sight and earshot. Oglethorpe coughed yet again. "But him and me, we go back years, and I ain't got enough business to keep two waiters busy any more, not with so much of the war work closed down, I ain't."

"You's lettin' me go," Scipio said. The dialect of the Congaree was slow and thick as molasses. Scipio could speak far better formal English than his boss—years of training to be the perfect butler at Marshlands had forced him to learn—but that wouldn't help now. It was likely to make things worse, in fact.

Oglethorpe nodded. "Hate to do it, like I say, but I've got to keep my own head above water first. You on the trail of another job waitin' tables, you tell whoever's thinking about hiring you to talk to me. You're a brick, and I'll say so."

"That right kind o' you, Mistuh Oglethorpe," Scipio said. "You been a good boss." He was, on the whole, sincere. Oglethorpe expected his help to work like mules, but he worked like a mule himself. Scipio had no complaints about that. Fair was fair.

Digging in his wallet, Oglethorpe peeled off brown banknotes. "It's Wednesday today, but I'm payin' you till the end of the week. Couple extra days of money never did anybody any harm."

That was more than fair. "Thank you kindly, suh," Scipio said. He counted the money, frowned, and counted it again. He took out a banknote and thrust it at the man who ran the restaurant. "Even if you is payin' till the end o' the week, you done give me twenty dollars too much."

"Keep it." Oglethorpe looked annoyed that he'd noticed. "Ain't like it was twenty dollars before the war. Money was worth somethin' in those days. Now—hell, look at you. You got all that money in your hand there, and you ain't rich. What kind of world is it when you can be standin' there with all that cash, and you got to worry about—" He checked himself. "No, you don't have to worry about where your next meal is comin' from. You get on back here with me."

Scipio got. His boss hacked off a couple of slices of egg bread, yellow as the sun, then put them around a slab of ham that would have choked a boa constrictor. He added pickles and mustard, gave Scipio the monster sandwich, and stood there with hands on hips till he'd eaten it.

"I gets me a new job, I comes back here to eat," Scipio declared. "Want another one?" Oglethorpe asked, reaching for the bread again. Scipio shook his head and, belly bulging, managed to make his escape. Only when he was out on the streets of Augusta did he wish he'd taken the restaurant owner up on his generosity. A sandwich like that kept a man's belly from complaining for most of a day.

Augusta had a shabby, run-down look to it these days. From things he'd heard, Scipio suspected the whole Confederacy had a shabby, run-down look to it these days. A lot of men, white and black, were walking along not quite aimlessly, looking for anything that might be work. As Oglethorpe had said, the factories that had boomed during the war—cotton mills, brickworks, fertilizer plants, canneries—were booming no more.

More than a few men remained in their uniforms, though the war had been over since the summer before and spring wasn't far away. Most of the whites who still wore draggled butternut looked to be wearing it because they had nothing better to put on. The Negroes in uniform, though, might have been in business suits. They were advertising that they had served their country, as plainly as if they carried sandwich boards, and were hoping that would help them land work. What sort of place the Confederate States were going to give their black veterans remained to be seen.

Scipio headed east along Telfair toward the Terry, the colored district in Augusta. Somebody was holding a rally in May Park, a couple of blocks south of Telfair; he saw waving flags from the corner of Telfair and Elbert. He didn't really need to go back to his room: he was, at the moment, a gentleman of leisure. He wandered down toward the park to find out what was going on.

The flags were Confederate flags. They flew at the edge of the street to draw people toward the rally—as they'd succeeded in drawing Scipio—and fluttered in a mild breeze on and beside the platform on which the speaker stood. Behind the fellow was a sign that did not look to have been painted by a professional. It read, FREEDOM PARTY.

What was the Freedom Party? Whatever it was, Scipio had never heard of it before. No one at Anne Colleton's elegant dinner parties had ever mentioned it, so far as he recalled. Of course, he hadn't paid that much attention to politics, at least till he'd been dragooned into the leadership of the Congaree Socialist Republic. Why should he have? He couldn't vote; the Confederate States didn't recognize him as a citizen. Maybe this new outfit would help make things better.

And maybe it wouldn't, too. The skinny fellow up there on the platform was long on complaints: "Aren't our generals pretty in their fancy uniforms? Wouldn't you have liked it better if they'd had any notion how to fight the goddamn war? Wouldn't you have liked 'em better if they weren't in the damnyankees' pockets?"

Scipio blinked at that. Generals had occasionally visited Marshlands. He knew good and well they'd done everything they knew how to do to beat the United States. They hadn't known enough, but they'd tried.

Most of the men in the crowd looked to be either white veterans or men who'd had wartime factory jobs and had no jobs now. They'd never seen any generals, except perhaps whizzing by in fancy motorcars. When this loudmouthed madman ranted about traitors in high places in Richmond, they ate it up and shouted for more.

And he gave them more, saying, "And if the goddamn generals weren't traitors and fools, how come they sat there with their thumbs up their asses while the niggers plotted up the biggest goddamn rebellion in the history of the world? Were they blind, or did they shut their eyes on purpose? Either which way, throw 'em on the rubbish heap, every stinking one of 'em."

"That's right!" voices in the crowd said. "Tell it!" As far as they were concerned, the speaker might have been one of the colored preachers who went around the plantations testifying to the power of the Lord. These battered white men responded the way colored fieldhands, as oppressed a group as was ever born, did when the preacher started going strong.

"And we'd have whipped the damnyankees—*whipped* 'em, I tell you—if the niggers hadn't risen up," the man from the Freedom Party shouted. He believed every word he was saying; Scipio could hear conviction jangling in his voice. "They stabbed us—they stabbed our country—in the back. Get rid of the traitor niggers and the traitor generals and I'll tell you, we'd have been past Philadelphia and heading for New York City!" He pumped his fist in the air.

His audience pumped their fists in the air, too. Scipio stood only on the outermost fringes of the audience. By the glares coming his way, he suddenly realized even that was much too close to the platform. He made himself scarce before anybody decided pounding him into the ground would be a good way to settle lunch.

Behind him, the crowd erupted in more cheers. He didn't turn around to find out why. He suspected he'd be happier not knowing. Once he got back inside the Terry—local colored dialect for *Terri-*

tory—he felt better. Being surrounded by black faces eased the alarm he'd felt at the Freedom Party rally.

Not all white men were like that shouting would-be politician. Scipio patted his hip pocket, where the money John Oglethorpe had given him rested. Oglethorpe was as good as they came, black or white. Even Anne Colleton didn't scare Scipio the way he'd been scared in May Park. Miss Anne wanted to go on running things, and she wanted revenge on the people who'd killed her brother and gutted Marshlands and almost killed her. That made sense to Scipio, even if it had put him in hot water. The fellow on the platform . . .

"Ain't gwine think about he no more," Scipio muttered. That was easy to say. It wasn't so easy to do.

He stuck his head into every little hole-in-the-wall café and cookshop he passed, to see if anybody was looking for help. Even if a waiter didn't get paid a whole lot, he didn't go hungry, not if his boss had so much as a particle of heart. Waiting tables was easier than factory work, too, not that any factory work was out there these days.

He didn't find any restaurant jobs in the Terry, either. He would have been surprised if he had. Half of these joints didn't have any waiters at all: the fellow at the stove did everything else, too. At a lot of the other places, the waiter looked to be the cook's son or brother or cousin. Still, you never could tell. If you didn't bet, how were you going to win?

The Terry had even more places to get a drink than it did places to get food. Scipio was tempted to stick his head into one of them, too, not to look for work but to find somewhere he could kill an afternoon over a mug of beer or two. In the end, he stayed out. Unless a man had silver to spend, beer cost three or four dollars a mug even in the dingiest dive. Without a job at the moment, Scipio didn't care to throw his banknotes around like that.

He ended up back at his roominghouse. The landlady gave him a fishy stare. A working man who unexpectedly showed up long before quitting time couldn't figure on anything else. The landlady didn't say anything. She didn't need to. If Scipio was late with his rent, he'd end up on the sidewalk, and everything he owned—not that that amounted to much—out there with him. He was paid up till the end of the week, and he had plenty for the next week's rent.

He hoped he wouldn't have to worry past then. He'd never before had trouble finding a job. That cheered him, till he remembered he hadn't looked for one since the war ended. Everybody was scrambling for work now.

He went upstairs. The furniture in his room was no better than could be expected in a Terry roominghouse, but he kept the place spotlessly clean. The books on the battered bookshelf were his. He pulled out a beat-up abridgement of Gibbon's *Decline and Fall* and read with a smile on his face of the Moorish conquest of the blond Visigoths of Spain.

General George Armstrong Custer was not a happy man. "God damn it to hell and gone, Lieutenant Colonel," he shouted, "I don't want to go back to Philadelphia. I'm perfectly content to stay here in Nashville."

"I'm sorry, sir," Lieutenant Colonel Abner Dowling said. Custer's adjutant was in fact a good deal less than devastated, but knew better than to show it. "The telegram just now came in. I'm afraid it leaves you little room for discretion."

"I don't want to go back to Philadelphia," Custer repeated. He *had* scant discretion. Once set on a course, he kept on it, and derailing him commonly took the rhetorical equivalent of dynamite. He'd been stubborn and hard-charging for more than seventy-eight years; no wire from the War Department would make him change his ways. Abner Dowling was convinced nothing would make him change his ways.

"Sir," Dowling said, "I suspect they want to honor you. You are, after all, the senior soldier in the United States Army."

"Don't pour the soft soap on me, even if you're shaped like a barrel of it," Custer growled. His description of Dowling's physique was, unfortunately, accurate, although he was hardly the dashing young cavalryman himself these days. He tapped at the four stars on the shoulder of his fancy—as fancy as regulations permitted, and then some—uniform. "Took me long enough to make full general, by God. When I think of the fools and whippersnappers promoted ahead of me . . . I could weep, Lieutenant Colonel, I could just weep."

Custer's slow promotion had also meant Dowling's slow promotion. Custer never thought of such things, nor that calling a fat man fat to his face might wound his feelings. Custer thought of Custer, first, last, and always.

Dowling scratched at his mustache, in lieu of reaching out and punching the distinguished general commanding the U.S. First Army right in the nose. He took a deep breath and said, "Sir, they may have taken a while to recognize your heroism, but they've gone and done it."

In an odd sort of way, he was even telling the truth. As with the rest of his life, Custer knew only one style of fighting: straight-ahead slugging. First Army had paid a gruesome toll for that aggressiveness as it slogged its way south through western Kentucky and northern Tennessee.

When Custer saw his first barrel, he'd wanted to mass the traveling forts and beat his Confederate opponents over the head with them, too. War Department doctrine dictated otherwise. Custer had ignored War Department doctrine (lying about it along the way, and making Dowling lie, too), assembled his barrels exactly as he wanted to, hurled them at the Rebs—and broken through. Other U.S. armies using the same tactics had broken through, too. If that didn't make him a hero, what did?

If he'd failed . . . if he'd failed, he would have been retired. And Dowling? Dowling would probably be a first lieutenant in charge of all the battleship refueling depots in Montana and Wyoming. He knew what a narrow escape they'd had. Custer didn't even suspect it. He could be very naive.

He could also be very canny. "I know why they're calling me to Philadelphia," he said, leaning toward his adjutant so he could speak in a conspiratorial whisper. "They're going to put me out to pasture, that's what they're going to do."

"Oh, I hope not, sir," Dowling lied loyally. He'd fought the good fight for a lot of years, keeping Custer as close to military reality as he could. If he didn't have to do that any more, the War Department would give him something else to do. Anything this side of latrine duty looked more pleasant.

"I won't let them," Custer said. "I'll go to the newspapers, that's what *I'll* do." Dowling was sure he would, too. Publicity was meat and drink to him. He might even win his fight. He'd won many of them in his time.

All that was for the moment beside the point, though. "Sir, you are ordered to report in Philadelphia no later than Sunday, twenty-first April. That's day after tomorrow, sir. They've laid on a special Pullman car for you and Mrs. Custer, with a berth in the next car for me. You don't have to take that particular train, but it would be a comfortable way to get there." Dowling was, and needed to be, skilled at the art of cajolery.

Custer sputtered and fumed through his peroxided mustache.

He did know how to take orders—most of the time. "Libbie would like going that way," he said, as if to give himself an excuse for yielding. Dowling nodded, partly from policy, partly from agreement. Custer's wife *would* like going that way, and would also approve of his acquiescence. But then, Elizabeth Bacon Custer, in Dowling's view, had more brains in her fingernail than her illustrious husband did in his head.

The train proved splendid. Dowling wondered if the Pullmans and dining car had been borrowed from a wealthy capitalist to transport Custer in splendor—and he himself got only a reflection of the splendor Custer had to be enjoying to the fullest. As he ate another bite of beefsteak in port-wine sauce, he reflected that life could have been worse.

A brass band waited on the platform as the locomotive pulled into the Broad Street station—and not just any brass band, but one led by John Philip Sousa. Next to the band stood Theodore Roosevelt. Dowling watched Custer's face when he saw the president. The two men had been rivals since they'd combined to drive the British out of Montana Territory at the end of the Second Mexican War. Each thought the other had got more credit than he deserved—they'd quarreled about it in Nashville, as the Great War was ending.

Now, though, Roosevelt bared his large and seemingly very numerous teeth in a grin of greeting. "Welcome to Philadelphia, General!" he boomed, and advanced to take Custer's hand as the band blared out "The Stars and Stripes Forever" and photographic flashes went off like artillery rounds. "I trust you will do me the honor of riding with me at the head of the Remembrance Day parade tomorrow."

Dowling could not remember the last time he had seen George Custer speechless, but Custer was speechless now, speechless for half a minute. Then, at last, he took Roosevelt's hand in his and huskily whispered, "Thank you, Mr. President." Beside him, Libbie (who thought even less of Roosevelt than he did) dropped the president a curtsy.

And Abner Dowling felt something that might almost have been a tear in his eye. Roosevelt had done Custer honor, not the other way round. President Blaine had instituted Remembrance Day at the close of the Second Mexican War as a memorial to the humiliation of the United States by their foes. It had always been a day of mourning and lamentation and looking ahead to fights unwon.

And now the fight was over, and it had been won. Instead of lying prostrate in defeat, the United States stood triumphant. With

Remembrance Day come round again, the country could see that all the sacrifices its citizens had made for so many years were not in vain. Flags wouldn't fly upside down in distress any more.

Custer asked, "Mr. President, where will you seat my wife? That I have come to this moment is in no small measure due to her."

"Thank you, Autie," Libbie said. Dowling thought Custer dead right in his assessment. He hadn't thought Custer perceptive enough to realize the truth in what he said. Every once in a while, the old boy could be surprising. Trouble was, so many of the surprises proved alarming.

"I had in mind placing her in the motorcar directly behind ours," Roosevelt answered, "and putting your adjutant with her, if that be satisfactory to you all. Lieutenant Colonel Dowling has given his country no small service."

Dowling came to stiff attention and saluted. "Thank you very much, sir!" His heart felt about to burst with pride.

"The people will want to look at the general and the president, so I am perfectly content to ride behind," Libbie said. In public, she always put Custer and his career ahead of her own desires. In private, as Dowling had seen, she kept a wary eye on Custer because his own eye, even at his advanced age, had a tendency to wander.

"Good. That's settled." Roosevelt liked having things settled, especially his way. "We'll put you folks up for the night, and then tomorrow morning . . . tomorrow morning, General—"

Custer presumed to interrupt his commander-in-chief: "Tomorrow morning, Mr. President, we celebrate our revenge on the world!" It was a typically grandiose Custerian phrase, the one difference being that Custer, this time, was inarguably right. Theodore Roosevelt laughed and nodded and clapped his hands with glee. The victory the United States had won looked to be big enough to help heal even this longtime estrangement.

Up until the war, the Hindenburg Hotel had been called the Lafayette. Whatever you called it, it was luxury beyond any Dowling had ever known, surpassing the train on which he'd come to Philadelphia to the same degree the train surpassed a typical wartime billet. He feasted on lobster, drank champagne, bathed in a tub with golden faucets, plucked a fine Habana from a humidor on the dresser, and slept on smooth linen and soft down. There were, he reflected as he drifted toward that splendid sleep, people who lived this life all the time. It was enough to make a man wish he were one of the elect—either that, or to make him a Socialist.

The next morning, he was whisked along with the Custers on a whirlwind inspection of the units that would take part in the parade. He endured rather than enjoying most of the inspection: he'd seen his share of soldiers. But some of the barrels and their crews were from the First Army brigade Colonel Morrell had assembled and commanded. They greeted Custer and Dowling with lusty cheers.

Dowling thought those cheers lusty, at any rate, till the parade began and he heard the Philadelphians. Their roar was like nothing he had ever imagined. It was as if they were exorcising more than half a century of shame and disgrace and defeat—Lee had occupied Philadelphia at the end of the War of Secession—in this grandest of all grand moments.

Some women in the crowd looked fierce as they waved their flags—thirty-five stars, now that Kentucky was back in the USA, and the new state of Houston would make it thirty-six on the Fourth of July. God only knew what would happen with Sequoyah and with the land conquered from Canada. Abner Dowling didn't, and didn't worry about it.

Other women, he saw, seemed on the point of ecstasy at what their country had finally achieved. Tears streamed down the faces of old men who remembered all the defeats and embarrassments, of boys who hadn't been old enough to go and fight, and of men of fighting age who had given of themselves to make this parade what it was. Even a young man wearing a hook in place of his left hand wept unashamed at this Remembrance Day to be remembered forever.

In the motorcar ahead, Custer and Roosevelt took turns rising to accept the plaudits of the crowd. And the crowd did cheer each time one of them rose. But the crowd would have cheered anyhow. More than anything else, it was cheering itself.

Libbie Custer leaned close to Dowling and said, "Lieutenant Colonel, I thank God that He spared me to see this day and rejoice at what we have done."

"Yes, ma'am," he said, and then, half to himself, "And what do we do next?"

Having been beached, Roger Kimball, like so many of his comrades, was making the painful discovery that very little he'd learned at the Confederate Naval Academy in Mobile suited him to making a living in the civilian world. He was a first-rate submarine skipper, but there were no civilian submarines. The C.S. Navy was no longer allowed to keep submersibles, either; otherwise, he would have stayed in command of the *Bonefish*.

He had a fine understanding of the workings of large Diesel engines. That also did him very little good. Outside the Navy, there were next to no large Diesel engines, nor small ones, either. He understood gasoline and steam engines, too, but so did plenty of other people. None of them seemed willing to sacrifice his own position for Kimball's sake.

"Miserable bastards, every last one of 'em," he muttered as he trudged through the streets of Charleston, South Carolina. Then he laughed at himself. Had he had a steady job, he wouldn't have let go of it, either. Maybe he should have headed down to South America, as he'd told Anne Colleton he might.

A lot of former Navy men were trudging the streets of Charleston these days, most of them overqualified for the jobs that turned up—when any jobs turned up, which wasn't often. Kimball kept money in his pocket partly because he wasn't too proud for any kind of work that came along—having grown up on a hardscrabble farm in Arkansas, he was no pampered Confederate aristocrat—and partly because he was a damn fine poker player.

He walked into a saloon called the Ironclad. "Let me have a beer," he told the barkeep, and laid a ten-dollar banknote on the bar.

He got back a beer and three dollars. Sighing, he laid some briny sardellen on a slice of cornbread from the free-lunch counter and gobbled them down. Pickled in brine, the little minnows were so salty, they couldn't help raising a thirst. He sipped the beer, and had to fight the urge to gulp it down and immediately order another. Provoking just that response was the free lunch's *raison d'être*.

A couple of men farther down the bar were talking, one of them also nursing a beer, the other with a whiskey in front of him. Kimball paid them only scant attention for a bit, but then began to listen more closely. He emptied his schooner and walked over to the fellow who was drinking whiskey. "You wouldn't by any chance be from the United States, would you?" he asked. His harsh Arkansas drawl made it very plain he was not.

He was looking for a *yes* and a fight. As the man on the bar stool turned to size him up, he realized the fight might not be so easy. He was a little heavier and a little younger than the other man, but the fellow owned a pair of the steeliest gray eyes he'd ever seen. If he got in a brawl, those eyes warned he wouldn't quit till he'd either won or got knocked cold.

And then his friend laughed and said, "Jesus, Clarence, swear to God I'm gonna have to stop taking you out in public if you don't quit talking that way."

"It's the way I talk," the man with the hard eyes—Clarence—said. He turned back to Kimball. "No, whoever the hell you are, I am not a damnyankee. I sound the way I sound because I went to college up at Yale. Clarence Potter, ex-major, Army of Northern Virginia, at your service—and if you don't like it, I'll spit in your eye."

Kimball felt foolish. He'd felt foolish before; he expected he'd feel foolish again. He gave his own name, adding, "Ex-commander, C.S. Navy, submersibles," and stuck out his hand.

Potter took it. "That explains why you wanted to wipe the floor with a Yankee, anyhow. Sorry I can't oblige you." He threw a lazy punch in the direction of his friend. "And this creature here is Jack Delamotte. You have to forgive him; he's retarded—only an ex–first lieutenant, Army of Northern Virginia."

"I won't hold it against him," Kimball said. "Pleased to meet the both of you. I'd be happy to buy you fresh drinks." He wouldn't be happy to do it, but it would make amends for mistaking Potter for someone from north of the Mason-Dixon Line.

"I'm pleased to meet damn near anybody who'll buy me a drink," Delamotte said. He was a big, fair-haired fellow who sounded as if he was from Alabama or Mississippi. He kicked the bar stool next to him. "Why don't you set yourself down again, and maybe we'll get around to buying you one, too."

Being closer to Clarence Potter, Kimball sat beside him. The bartender served up two more beers and another whiskey. Kimball raised his schooner on high. "To hell with the United goddamn States of America!"

Potter and Delamotte both drank: no Confederate officer cut loose from his country's service in the aftermath of defeat could refuse that toast. The ex-major who talked like a Yankee and looked like a tough professor offered a toast of his own: "To getting the Confederate goddamn States of America back on their feet!"

That too was unexceptional. After drinking to it, Kimball found himself with an empty schooner. He wasn't drunk, not on two beers, but he was intensely and urgently thoughtful. He didn't much care for the tenor of his thoughts, either. "How the hell are we supposed to do that?" he demanded. "The United States are going to be sitting on our neck for the next hundred years."

"No, they won't." Potter shook his head. "We *will* get the chance."

He sounded positive. Roger Kimball was positive, too: positive his new acquaintance was out of his mind. "They made you butternut boys say uncle," he said, which might have come close to starting another fight. Confederate Navy men, who'd battled their U.S. counterparts to something close to a draw, resented the Army for having to yield. But now, not intending pugnacity, he went on, "Why do you reckon they'll be fools enough to ever let us do anything again?"

"Same question I've been asking him," Delamotte said.

"And I'll give Commander Kimball the same answer I've given you." Potter seemed to think like a professor, too; he lined up all his ducks in a row. In rhetorical tones, he asked, "Toward what have the United States been aiming ever since the War of Secession, and especially since the Second Mexican War?"

"Kicking us right square in the nuts," Kimball answered. "And now they've finally gone and done it, the bastards." He'd done some nut-kicking of his own, even after the cease-fire. That last, though, was a secret he intended to take to the grave with him.

"Just so," Clarence Potter agreed, emphasizing the point with a forefinger. "Now they've finally gone and done what they've been pointing toward since 1862. Up till now, they *had* a goal, and they worked toward it. Christ, were they serious about working toward it; you have no notion how serious they were if you've never seen a Remembrance Day parade. Scared me to death when I was up in

Connecticut, believe you me it did. But now they don't *have* a goal any more; they've *achieved* their goal. Do you see the difference, Commander?"

Before Kimball could answer, Jack Delamotte said, "What I see is, I'm thirsty, and I bet I'm not the only one, either." He ordered another round of drinks, then ate some sardellen and lit a cigar almost as pungent as the fish.

After a pull or two at his beer, Kimball said, "Major, I don't follow you. Suppose their next goal is wiping us out altogether? How in blazes are we supposed to stop 'em?"

"Goals don't work like that, not usually they don't," Potter said. "Once you got to where you always thought you were going, you like to ease back and relax and smoke a cigar—a good cigar, mind you, not a stinking weed like the one Jack's stuffed into his face—and maybe marry a chorus girl, if that's what you reckoned you would do after you made it big."

"So that's what you figure is going to happen, eh?" Kimball chuckled. "You figure the United States scrimped and saved for so long, and now they'll buy a fancy motorcar and put a beautiful dame in it? Well, I hope you're right, but I'll tell you this much: it won't happen as long as that goddamn Roosevelt is president of the USA. He hates us too much to care about chorus girls."

"I never said it would happen tomorrow," Potter replied. "I said it would happen. Countries live longer than people do." He knocked back his whiskey with a sharp flick of the wrist and ordered another round.

While the bored man behind the bar was drawing the beers, Jack Delamotte leaned toward Kimball and said, "Now you're going to hear Clarence go on about how we need to find a goal of our own and stick to it like the damnyankees did."

"It's the truth." Potter looked stubborn—and slightly pie-eyed. "If we don't, we'll be second-raters forever."

"Won't see it with the regular politicians," Kimball said with conviction. "They got us into the swamp, but I'm damned if I reckon they've got even a clue about how to get us out." Neither Potter nor Delamotte argued with him; he would have been astonished if they had. He went on, "I heard this skinny fellow on the stump a week or two ago. The Freedom Party, that was the name of his outfit. He wasn't too bad—sounded like he knew what he wanted and how to get there. His name was Feathers, or something like that."

To his surprise, Clarence Potter, who'd struck him as a sourpuss, threw back his head and guffawed. "Featherston," the ex-major said. "Jake Featherston. He's about as likely a politician as a catfish is on roller skates."

"You sound like you know him," Kimball said.

"He commanded a battery in the First Richmond Howitzers through most of the war," Potter answered. "Good fighting man—should have been an officer. But that battery had belonged to Jeb Stuart III, and Jeb, Jr., blamed Featherston when his son got killed. Since Jeb, Jr.'s, a general, Featherston wouldn't have got past sergeant if he'd stayed in the Army till he died of old age."

Slowly, Kimball nodded. "No wonder he was ranting and raving about the fools in the War Department, then."

"No wonder at all," Potter agreed. "Not that he's wrong about there being fools in the War Department: there are plenty. I was in intelligence; I worked with some and reported to others. But you need to take what Featherston says with a grain of salt about the size of Texas."

"He's got some good ideas about the niggers, though," Kimball said. "If they hadn't risen up, we'd still be fighting, by God." He didn't want a grain of salt, not one the size of Texas nor a tiny one, either. He wanted to believe. He wanted his country strong again, the sooner the better. He didn't care how.

Clarence Potter shook his head. "I doubt it," he said. "A good big man will lick a good little man—not all the time, but that's the way to bet. Once we didn't knock the USA out of the fight in a hurry—once it turned into a grapple—we were going to be in trouble. As I said, I was in intelligence. I know how much they outweighed us." Even with a good deal of whiskey in him, he was dispassionately analytical like a scholar.

Kimball cared for dispassionate analysis only when calculating a torpedo's track. Even then, it was a means to an end, not an end in itself. The end was action—blowing up a ship. Featherston wanted action, too. "You know how I can find out more about this Freedom Party?" he asked.

"They've started up an office here in town, I think," Potter answered, distaste on his face. "Jake Featherston calls Richmond home, though, and I think the Party does, too."

"Thanks," Kimball said. "Do me a little poking around, I think." He signaled to the bartender. "Set 'em up again, pal."

Cincinnatus Driver—the Negro was getting more and more used to the surname he'd taken the year before—had hoped the war's end would bring peace to Kentucky, and especially to Covington, where he lived. Now here it was the middle of spring, and Covington still knew no peace.

Every day when he left his house to start up the ramshackle truck he'd bought, his wife would say, "Be careful. Watch yourself."

"I will, Elizabeth," he would promise, not in any perfunctory way but with a deep and abiding sense that he was saying something important. He would crank the truck to noisy, shuddering life, climb into the cabin, put the machine in gear, and drive off to hustle as much in the way of hauling business as he could.

He wished he were inside one of the big, snarling White trucks the Army used to carry its supplies. He'd driven a White during the war, hauling goods that got shipped across the Ohio from Cincinnati through Covington and down to the fighting front. The Whites were powerful, they were sturdy, they were, in fact, everything his antiquated Duryea was not. That included expensive, which was why he drove the Duryea and wished for a White.

As he turned right onto Scott from out of the Negro district and drove up toward the wharves this morning, he kept a wary eye open. A good many U.S. soldiers in green-gray uniforms were on the streets. They also looked wary, and carried bayoneted Springfields, as if ready to start shooting or stabbing at any moment.

They needed to be wary, too. After more than fifty years in the Confederacy, Kentucky was one of the United States again. It was, however, like none of the other United States, in that a large part of the population remained unreconciled to the switch from Stars and Bars to Stars and Stripes.

The city hall had U.S. machine-gun nests around it. Somebody—odds were, a Confederate diehard—had taken a shot at the mayor a couple of weeks before. Cincinnatus wouldn't have been brokenhearted had the malcontent hit him. The mayor cooperated with U.S. authorities, and tried to placate the locals with rabblerousing speeches against blacks.

Blue St. Andrew's crosses, some of them new, marked buildings and suggested the Confederate battle flag. Two horizontal red stripes with a white one between similarly suggested the Confederate national flag. Some of those were new, too. The diehards hadn't given up, not by a long chalk. I AIN'T NO YANKEE, someone had written beside one of those not-quite-flags.

New posters marred walls, too, some of them slapped over the proConfederate graffiti. The posters were solid red, with broken chains in black stretched across them. The Red uprising had not got so far among the Negroes of Kentucky as among their brethren still in Confederate-owned territory at its outbreak. But it had not been brutally suppressed here, either. Being a Red wasn't illegal in the USA, even if it was hazardous to a black man's health.

Red posters and blue crosses were both thick around the waterfront. Cincinnatus wondered if the diehards and the Reds had bumped into each other on their clandestine rounds of pasting and painting. Down in the CSA, they would have been deadly foes. Here in Kentucky, they sometimes reckoned the U.S. government a common enemy. Cincinnatus whistled softly. They sometimes didn't, too.

Both soldiers and police patrolled the wharves. Confederate policemen had commonly worn gray, like soldiers from the War of Secession. Now that Kentucky belonged to the USA, policemen— sometimes the same policemen—wore dark blue, as their grandfathers might have done had they fought for the Stars and Stripes.

And some policemen wore no uniforms at all. Some of the idlers, some of the roustabouts who strode up and down the piers and along the waterfront, were sure to belong to Luther Bliss' Kentucky State Police, an outfit that made Kentucky the only U.S. state with its own secret police force. Cincinnatus knew Luther Bliss better than he wanted to. Knowing Bliss at all was knowing him better than Cincinnatus wanted to; the chief of the State Police made a formidable foe.

Roustabouts were hauling crates and barrels off a barge. Cincinnatus braked to a halt: cautiously, as the Duryea didn't like to stop any more than it liked to start. He hopped out of the cab and hurried over to a discontented-looking fellow holding a clipboard. "Mornin', Mr. Simmons," he said. "What you got, where's it got to get to, and how fast does it got to be there?"

"Hello, Cincinnatus," the steamboat clerk answered, pointing to some of the barrels. "Got oatmeal here: five for Twitchell's general store, and another five for Dalyrimple's, and three for Conroy's. You fit all of them in there?" He pointed to Cincinnatus' truck. "Damn tight squeeze, if you do."

"Mr. Simmons, they'll go in there if I got to make one of 'em drive," Cincinnatus said, at which the white man laughed. Cincinnatus went on, "Half a dollar a barrel for haulage, like usual?"

Simmons looked more discontented than ever. At last, he said, "Wouldn't pay it to any other nigger driving a raggedy old truck, that's for damn sure. But yeah, fifty cents a barrel. Bring me your receipts and I'll pay you off."

"Got yourself a deal, suh." Cincinnatus beamed. That was good money, and he might have the chance to pick up another load, or maybe even two, before the day ended. Then he hesitated, really hearing the third name Simmons had given him. "That Joe Conroy?" he asked. "Fat man, used to have hisself a store before it burned down?"

"Let me check." Simmons flipped papers. "Joseph Conroy, that's what it says. I don't know about the other part. How come?"

"Didn't know he was back in business, is all," Cincinnatus replied. It wasn't all, not even close, but he kept that to himself. "Where's his new store at?"

Simmons checked his papers again. "Corner of Emma and Bakewell, it says here. You know where that is? This ain't my town, you know."

"I know where it's at, yeah," Cincinnatus said. "Over on the west side, gettin' out towards the park. Twitchell's over here on Third, and Dalyrimple's on Washington, so I reckon I'll deliver theirs first and then head over to Conroy's." He held out his hand. "Give me the papers I got to get signed."

"Here you go." The steamboat clerk handed them to him. "That's the other reason I pay you like I would a white man, or almost: you read and write good, so things get done proper."

"Thank you," Cincinnatus said, pretending not to hear that *or almost.* He couldn't do anything about it. Stowing the papers in his shirt pocket, he started crowding barrels of oatmeal into the back of the truck. He did end up with one of them on the seat beside him; Simmons was a keen judge of how much space merchandise took up.

The truck rode heavy, the weight in back smoothing out its motion and making it laugh at bumps that would have jolted Cincinnatus had it been empty. He appreciated that. The ponderous cornering and the greater likelihood of a blowout were something else again. He drove carefully, avoiding the potholes that pocked the street. A puncture would cost him precious time.

His first two stops went smoothly, as he'd thought they would. He'd delivered to both Hank Twitchell and Calvin Dalyrimple before. Twitchell, a big, brawny fellow, even helped him lug barrels of oatmeal into his general store. Calvin Dalyrimple didn't; a strong breeze would have blown him away. They both signed their receipts and sent Cincinnatus on his way in jig time.

He drove out to the west side of town with much more trepidation. That didn't shrink when he discovered Conroy's new general store sat between a saloon and a pawnshop. None of the looks he got from passersby as he stopped the truck in front of the store was friendly, or anything close. Most of them translated to, *What the hell you doing here, nigger?* He hoped the truck would still be there when he got done with his business with Conroy.

He also hoped the storekeeper wouldn't recognize him. When he brought the first barrel into the store, all he said was, "Here's your oatmeal, suh, straight off the docks. Got two more barrels in the truck; fetch 'em right in for you. All you got to do is sign the receipt shows you got 'em, and I be on my way."

Joe Conroy grunted. He was a round, middle-aged white man with narrow, suspicious eyes. He was also a Confederate diehard, and a friend of Cincinnatus' former boss, Tom Kennedy. Kennedy had involved Cincinnatus with the diehards, too, having him plant firebombs on cargoes heading down to U.S. forces. Eventually, Cincinnatus had planted one in Conroy's old store, but the white man had never figured that out.

Cincinnatus had never decided how smart Conroy was. Smarter than he let on, was the Negro's guess. He proved smart enough to recognize Cincinnatus, whom he hadn't seen in a year, and who would have been glad never to see him again. "Well, well," he said slowly, the unlit cigar in his mouth jerking up and down. "Look what the cat drug in."

"Mornin', Mistuh Conroy." Cincinnatus hurried out to the truck to haul in the second barrel of oatmeal. As long as he was working, he didn't have to talk. He wished a customer would come into the cramped, dark general store. Conroy couldn't afford to talk, not where anyone could hear him.

But nobody came in except Cincinnatus. Conroy gave him an appraising stare. "Hear tell it was that damnyankee you was workin' for who shot Tom Kennedy," he said.

"Yes, suh, that's a fact. Hear him say so my ownself," Cincinnatus agreed. He got in a dig of his own: "Wasn't the Reds, like you told me in the park last year."

"No, it wasn't the Reds," the storekeeper said. "But it was a friend of yours, just the same. We don't forget things like that, no indeed, we don't."

"I saved Tom Kennedy's bacon from the Yankees back when the war was new," Cincinnatus said angrily. "I hadn't done that, I never would've met you—and believe you me, that would've suited me fine."

"We know where you're at." Conroy put menace in his voice.

"And I know where you're at, too," Cincinnatus said. "I get into trouble from you and your pals, Luther Bliss'll know where you're at and what you've been doin'. Don't want no trouble, Conroy." He used the white man's unadorned surname with relish, to shock. "But I get trouble, I give it right back."

"Damn uppity nigger," Conroy growled.

"Yes, *sir*." Cincinnatus went outside and manhandled the last barrel of oatmeal into the store. He thrust the receipt at Joe Conroy. "You want to sign right here, so I can go on about my business."

"Why do I give a damn about that?" Conroy said.

"On account of if you don't sign, I take this here oatmeal back to the docks and you don't get no more shipments." Cincinnatus wondered how much Conroy cared. If the store was nothing but a front for the diehards, he might not care at all. That would make Cincinnatus' life more difficult.

But Conroy grabbed a pencil, scrawled his signature, and all but hurled the paper back at Cincinnatus. "Here, God damn you."

"Much obliged, Mistuh Conroy." Cincinnatus headed for the door. "Got me a lot of work left to do."

"Come on," Sylvia Enos said to her children. "Get moving. I've got to take you over to Mrs. Dooley's so I can go to work."

"I like it better when you're not working, Ma," Mary Jane said. She would be five soon, which Sylvia found hard to believe. "I like it when you stay home with us."

"When she stays home with us, though, it's because she's out of work again, silly." George, Jr., spoke with the world-weary wisdom of his seven years—and wasn't shy about scoring points off his sister, either. "We have to have money."

He had a hard streak of pragmatism in him. His father had been the same way. George, Jr., looked very much like his father, though he was missing the brown Kaiser Bill mustache Sylvia's husband had worn. Seeing her son, Sylvia again cursed the fate that had put a submersible in the way of the USS *Ericsson* the night after the Confederate States yielded to the USA.

With the CSA out of the war, she thought, *it had to be a British boat.* George hadn't worried about the Royal Navy. A Confederate submarine had almost sunk his destroyer earlier in the war. He'd fought Rebel boats all the way up to the end. To have his ship sunk by the limeys after that . . . even now, it was hard to take. George hadn't deserved that much bad luck.

"Come on," Sylvia said again. "I can't be late on account of you. I can't be late at all."

That was nothing less than the gospel truth. With men home from the war in droves, jobs for women were harder and harder to come by. She didn't know how long the work at the galoshes factory would last, and she couldn't afford to anger the people over her in any way. She was the sole support for her family as much as any man was for his, but nobody looked at things that way. Men came first. Women had been fine during the war. Now . . .

Now she couldn't even vote for anyone who might better her plight. Massachusetts had no women's suffrage. Had she been able to cast a ballot, she would have voted Socialist in a heartbeat. The Democrats had been fine when it came to winning the war. What were they good for in peacetime? Only counting their profits, as far as she could see.

She hurried the children out of the apartment and down to the clamorous streets of Boston. With a sigh of regret, she walked past a newsboy hawking the *Globe*. She couldn't justify laying out a couple of cents on it, not when she didn't know if she'd have work next week.

"England signs treaty!" the newsboys shouted, trying to persuade others to part with pennies. "Limeys give up all claim to Sandwich Islands and Canada! England signs treaty! Recognizes Ireland and Quebec!"

It was, she supposed, good news. The best news, though, as far as she was concerned, would have been for the ocean to swallow England and all her works. And while the ocean was at it, it could swallow the CSA, too.

Mrs. Dooley was an aging widow with wavy hair defiantly hennaed, and with bright spots of rouge on her cheeks. To Sylvia, it looked more like clown makeup than anything alluring, but she would never have said so. The woman took good care of her children and did not charge too much.

After kissing George, Jr., and Mary Jane good-bye, Sylvia went back to the trolley stop, tossed another nickel in the fare box (and soon she would have to start paying Mary Jane's fare, too: one more expense), and headed to the galoshes factory. To her relief, she got there on time.

The place stank of rubber from which the rubber overshoes were made. Sylvia's post came just after the galoshes emerged from the mold. She painted a red ring around the top of each one. Had the firm been able to train a dog to do the job, it would have. That failing, it grudgingly paid her.

When she'd worked in a mackerel-canning plant, she'd been

able to operate the machine that glued gaudy labels to cans almost without thinking about it; sometimes, when she was lucky, she would hardly notice the time going by between getting to the factory and dinner or between dinner and going home. She hadn't had that luxury at the shoe factory where she'd been working when George was killed. If she didn't pay attention to what she was doing there, the powerful needle on the electric sewing machine would tear up her hand. She'd seen it happen to operators who'd been at the place longer than she'd been alive. A moment's lapse was all it took.

All that could happen with a moment's lapse here was her ending up with red paint on her hand, not red blood. Still, she couldn't let her mind wander, as she'd been able to do in the canning plant. What she did here wasn't simple repetitive motion, the way that had been. She had to pay attention to painting the rings precisely. If she didn't, the foreman started barking at her.

Frank Best wasn't a hardened old Tartar like Gustav Krafft, the foreman at the shoe factory where she'd worked, who gave a walking demonstration of why the limeys and frogs thought of Germans as Huns. Best's style was more the sly dig: "Thought you were going to slip that one by me, did you?" was a favorite remark.

The other difference between the two men was that Krafft had been too old to serve in the Army. Frank Best wore a Soldiers' Circle pin with the year 1904 on it. That being his conscription class, he was only a handful of years older than Sylvia. He was also single, and convinced he was the greatest gift to women God had ever set on the planet.

A lot of women who worked in the galoshes factory were widows, some still wearing mourning, others not. Most of them, like Sylvia, heartily despised the foreman. "Like to put a certain part of him in the mold—the size-two mold," Sarah Wyckoff, one of those widows, said at dinner on a day when Best was being particularly obnoxious. "Wouldn't need nothin' bigger."

That produced a good set of giggles. Sylvia said, "No, for goodness' sake, you don't want him vulcanized *there*. He'd never keep quiet about it then." More giggles rose.

"If so many of us hate him," said May Cavendish, another widow, "why does *he* think he's so bully?"

"He's a man," Sarah Wyckoff said, as if she expected that to cover everything. By the way the other women nodded, it probably did.

May Cavendish tossed her head; her blond curls bounced on her shoulders. "What frosts me is that some of the girls *do* like him."

"I can't imagine that anybody would really *like* him," Sylvia said with a shudder. Her companions nodded. She went on, "But if he says, 'Be nice to me or go look for another job,' some of the girls are going to be nice to him. Times are hard. Believe me, I know."

"We all know, sweetheart," Sarah said. "If he said anything like that to me, though, I'd break him in half." She was built like a long-shoreman; Sylvia didn't think she meant it any way but literally.

"There ought to be a law," Sylvia said. She'd had that thought before, when she lost her job at the canning plant because she'd had to stay home and tend to her children after they came down with the chicken pox.

"There ought to be a lot of things that there ain't," Sarah Wyck-off said with authority. "If I was Teddy Roosevelt—"

"You'd look silly with a mustache, Sarah, and you haven't got enough teeth to be TR," May Cavendish said. She pulled a pack of cigarettes from her handbag, scraped a match on the sole of her shoe, got the cigarette lighted, and blew out a creditable smoke ring. Then she coughed. "Sorry. I'm still getting the hang of this."

"Doesn't it make people think you're fast?" Sylvia asked.

May shook her head. "Not the way it would have before the war," she said, and drew on the cigarette again. The coal glowed red. She let the smoke go without showing off this time. "It's not like it's a big, smelly cigar or anything. It's not like it was hooch, either. You don't get drunk or anything—you feel better about things for a little while, that's all." She extended the pack toward Sylvia. "Want to try one?"

"Sure. Why not?" Sylvia said. "It's not like they can hurt you or anything." She took a cigarette. May Cavendish struck another match. Sylvia didn't drag deeply on the cigarette, the way May had done. She drew in a cautious mouthful of smoke—or so she thought. When she tried to suck it down into her lungs, she hacked and wheezed and started to choke.

"Very same thing happened to me the first time I tried," May assured her. "It gets easier, believe me it does. You get used to it."

Sylvia's mouth tasted as if someone had just doused a campfire in there. She stared at the cigarette in dismay. "Why would you want to get used to it?" she asked, and coughed again. But she felt tingly all the way out to her fingers and toes, tingly and light-headed in a strange and pleasant sort of way. Ever so cautiously, she took another puff.

It still tasted bad. It made her chest burn. But the tingles and that good feeling in the middle of her brain got stronger.

"Don't do too much the first time," May Cavendish advised her. "You can get sick if you do. Think about whether you like it or not. It's not like cigarettes are expensive, or anything like that."

"That's true," Sylvia said. "They've come down since the war ended, too. I've noticed that, even if I don't usually buy them."

May nodded. "And the tobacco's better now. It's the one good thing you can say about the Rebs—they grow better tobacco than we do. Some of the stuff they were selling while the war was still on . . . Honey, I swear to Jesus they were sweeping the horseballs off the street and wrapping paper around 'em."

"People kept smoking, though," Sarah Wyckoff said.

"Why not?" Sylvia said. "It's not a bad thing, and May's right—it does make you feel nice for a little bit." Despite saying that, she had no great urge to smoke the rest of the cigarette May Cavendish had given her. She let it fall to the ground and crushed it with her foot. Maybe she'd acquire the habit and maybe she wouldn't. If she did, she'd do it slowly. If she tried to do it in a hurry, she had the feeling she would get sick instead.

"Time to get back to work," Sarah said, "or Frank'll start sweet-talking us again." She rolled her eyes to show how much she looked forward to that.

When Sylvia went back into the plant, it didn't stink so badly of rubber, or so it seemed. After a while, she realized the cigarette had numbed her sense of smell. That seemed a good reason to start smoking all by itself.

The line began to move. Sylvia painted red rings on a pair of galoshes. The machinery sent them down the line to the next worker, who would trim off extra rubber. Sylvia dipped her brush in the paint can and painted more rings.

Lucien Galtier was the sort to enjoy summer while it lasted. Up here, close to the St. Lawrence, a few miles outside the town of Rivière-du-Loup, it did not last long. The farmer did not hold that against summer. It was what it was. He accepted along with enjoying.

He accepted weeds, too, but he did not enjoy them. At the moment, he was hoeing the potato patch. When he saw a bit of green of the wrong shade and in the wrong place, the hoe lashed out without his conscious direction. The decapitated weed toppled.

"Strike them all dead, *cher papa*," Lucien's son, Georges, said from a couple of rows over, seeing the hoe come down. At eighteen, Georges overtopped his father by several inches, and was wider through the shoulders, too—Lucien's strength was of the wiry, enduring sort. Georges' humor was also wider than his father's; he enjoyed playing the buffoon, while Lucien met the world with irony.

"Strike them all dead, eh?" Lucien said as he got rid of another weed. "One fine day, my son, you will make your country a fine general."

"If the Republic of Quebec needs *me* as a general, it will be in a great deal of trouble," Georges said with conviction. He looked down at the ground. "Come on, you weeds—get out of the potato trenches and charge the machine guns! Die, and save me the trouble of grubbing you out." Beaming at Lucien, he went on, "Perhaps you have reason. I can talk like a general, *n'est-ce pas?*"

His father snorted. "As always, you are a nonpareil." He bent his back to the weeding, not wanting Georges to see any surprise on his face. He'd forgotten, as he sometimes could in the daily routine of farm life, that this was, and had been for the past year and more, the Republic of Quebec, dancing attendance on the United States, and not the province of Quebec, a French-speaking appendage to the British Empire.

He laughed—at himself, as he often did. He'd forgotten the American-fostered Republic of Quebec, and that with an American son-in-law. There was absentmindedness worthy of a professor or a priest.

When he straightened again, he glanced over in the direction of the hospital the Americans had built on his land to care for their wounded from the fighting north of the St. Lawrence. The hospital remained, but no longer flew the Stars and Stripes. Instead, the Republic's flag (which had also been the provincial flag) floated above it: a field of blue quartered by a white cross, and in each quadrant a white fleur-de-lys. These days, the hospital drew its patients from the people of Quebec.

As the sun went down, he and Georges shouldered their hoes like rifles and trudged back toward the farmhouse. A Ford was parked by the house: not one in a coat of green-gray U.S. official paint, nor the Republic's equivalent blue-gray, but somber civilian black. Georges grinned when he saw it. "Ah, good," he said. "My sister is here for me to harass."

"Yes, and her husband is here to give you what you deserve for harassing her, too," Lucien replied, to which his son responded with a magnificent Gallic shrug.

Charles, Georges' older brother, came out of the barn just as Lucien and Georges headed toward it to hang the hoes on the rack

Lucien's grandfather had built long years before. Charles looked like Lucien, but was more sobersided—he had to take after his mother there.

Marie greeted her husband and sons on the front porch, as much to make sure they wiped their feet as for any other reason. She was a small, dark, sensible woman, ideally suited to be a farm wife. Her younger daughters, Susanne, Denise, and Jeanne, who ranged in age from sixteen down to eleven, also came out. Susanne sixteen! Galtier shook his head. She had been a child when the war started. Seeing her ripening figure forcibly reminded him she was a child no longer.

Lucien waded through his younger daughters to give Nicole a hug. She looked very much the way Marie had as a young wife. She also looked happy, which made her father happy in turn. When she turned Lucien loose, he shook his son-in-law's hand. "And how does it march with you, the distinguished Dr. O'Doull?" he asked.

Dr. Leonard O'Doull looked back over his shoulder, as if to see whether Galtier were speaking to someone behind him. With a chuckle, he answered, "It marches well enough with me, *mon beau-père*. And with you?"

"Oh, with me?" Galtier said lightly as he got out a jug of the applejack one of his neighbors—most unofficially—cooked up. "It is good of you to ask. It is good of you to deign to visit my home here, instead of returning to the palace in which you dwell in Rivière-du-Loup."

"Father!" Nicole said indignantly.

"Be calm, my sweet," Leonard O'Doull said, laughter in his green eyes. "He was trying to make you squeak, and he did it." He'd spoken French—Parisian French—before he came up to Quebec. He still spoke Parisian French, but now with a heavy Quebecois overlay. In another few years, he would probably sound like someone who'd grown up here.

Nicole sniffed. "I expected such behavior from my brother, not from my own dear papa." She laid the treacle on with a trowel. Her eyes glowed.

"Why?" Georges asked innocently. "What did you expect Charles to do?" That set Nicole to spluttering, Charles to glaring, and the young ladies of the family to chaffing both their brothers impartially.

In the midst of that racket, Lucien spoke more seriously to Dr. O'Doull: "It is always good to see you." He handed his son-in-law a glass of the apple brandy. "To your health."

"And to yours," O'Doull said. They drank. Galtier gasped a little as the applejack clawed its way down to his belly: this was a rougher batch than most his neighbor made. If it fazed Leonard O'Doull, he didn't let on. Irishmen were supposed to have well-tempered gullets, and he lived up to that. After another sip, he went on, "Nicole and I finished our work at about the same time, and we thought we would pay you a visit."

"You should have such thoughts more often," Galtier said, but then qualified that by adding, "Are you certain it has been good for Nicole to continue to work instead of keeping house full time?"

"She has become a good nurse," O'Doull answered, "and the hospital would be the poorer if it lost her. And she desires to work, and I, believe me, I am perfectly happy with the way she keeps house."

"So long as a man is happy, everything will march well," Lucien said gravely, and his son-in-law nodded. The farmer raised an eyebrow. "Is it for this reason—to boast of your happiness—that you do us the honor of this visit?"

"By no means." O'Doull could match Georges absurdity for absurdity and Lucien dry for dry. "It is because a little bird whispered in my ear that Nicole's mother was fixing a great stew of *lapins aux pruneaux*."

"Ah, is that the reason?" Lucien slowly nodded. "Very well. Very well indeed, in fact. The rabbits think I set the cabbages there for them to enjoy. I, on the other hand, think God put the rabbits there for me to enjoy. After you taste of the stew"—whose hot, meaty odor filled the farmhouse—"you will decide."

"Any rabbit who presumes to taste of your cabbages surely deserves to end up *aux pruneaux*," his son-in-law agreed with a face so perfectly straight that Galtier, well pleased, elbowed him in the ribs as if he were a son of his own flesh and poured him another glass of the homemade Calvados.

The meal was a great success. Afterwards, Nicole helped her mother and sisters with the dishes—with so many hands, the work could not help being light. O'Doull handed fragrant Habanas to Lucien and his sons and lit one for himself. Galtier savored the aroma before drawing the first sweet smoke from his own panatela. He whistled. "*Tabernac*," he said reverently. "By the tobacco they grow there, Habana must be very close to Paradise."

"Closest part of the Confederate States, anyhow, not that that's saying much," Dr. O'Doull replied.

Charles said nothing, which was not surprising. Georges said nothing, which was an astonishment. Both young men puffed happy clouds. So did Lucien. He could not recall the last time he'd been more content, at least outside the marriage bed.

And then another astonishment took place: Nicole came out of the kitchen, followed by Marie and Susanne and Denise and Jeanne. Galtier did not find that an astonishment of the pleasant sort; custom was that the women let their menfolk linger over liquor and tobacco. He reckoned that a good custom, one in no need of breaking. "What's this?" he asked. "A parade?"

"No, *cher papa,* only something I have to tell you—something I have to tell everyone," Nicole said. "Everyone except Leonard, that is, for he knows." Even by the ruddy light of kerosene lamps, Lucien could see her blush. He knew then what was coming, knew it before she spoke: "*Cher papa, cher maman,* you will be grandparents next year."

"A grandfather?" Lucien exclaimed. Even knowing what was coming, he found himself surprised. *But I am too young to be a grandfather!* he wanted to cry. Foolishness, of course: if he had a married daughter, he was not too young to be a grandfather. Still, he felt as if he were.

He looked down at his hands, gnarled and scarred and callused by years of farm work, tanned by the sun when there was sun, roughened by the wind and the snow. They were not the hands of a man too young to be a grandfather.

From them, he looked to Marie. She, without any possible doubt, was too young to be a grandmother. But her beaming face said she didn't think so. It also said she looked forward to the role.

"What of me?" Georges said with fine mock anger. "I will be an uncle next year, but do you say one word about that? No! You leave it to me to figure out for myself. Is that fair? Is that just?"

Nicole said, "What you will be next year is what you are this year and what you have always been: a nuisance."

"Thank you." Georges nodded, as at a great compliment.

"We'll be aunts," Susanne and Denise and Jeanne chorused. Jeanne, who was the youngest of them, added, "I can't wait!"

"You'll have to," Nicole said. "I am not ready to have the baby just yet."

Lucien got up from his chair and embraced his daughter. "Congratulations," he said. "May all be well. May all be well with you always." He let her go and shook his son-in-law's hand. "Who would have thought I would have a grandchild named O'Doull?"

The young doctor's eyes twinkled. "See what you get for letting your daughter go to work in the American hospital?"

"At the time," Galtier said gravely, "I did not think that a good idea. Perhaps I was right." Leonard O'Doull just grinned at him. He had to wait for Nicole to let out an irate squawk before he could go on, "Perhaps, too, I was wrong. But only perhaps, mind you." Someone—he did not see who—had filled his glass with applejack again. If it was full, it needed emptying. Before the war, he'd never imagined a half-American grandchild. Now, though, he discovered he liked the idea.

Jonathan Moss sat in a coffeehouse not far outside the Northwestern University campus. A breeze from Lake Michigan ruffled his light brown hair. An internal breeze ruffled his thoughts.

"What's the matter, Johnny my boy?" asked his companion at the table, a curly-haired fellow named Fred Sandburg. "You look like you've got bullets whizzing past your head again."

Sandburg had served on the Roanoke front in Virginia, helping to take the riverside town of Big Lick and the nearby iron mines away from the Confederate States. That had been some of the worst fighting of the whole war. He knew all about bullets flying past his head. He had a Purple Heart with an oak-leaf cluster to show how much he knew.

He knew more about it than did Jonathan Moss, and Moss would have been the first to admit as much. He'd been a flier up in Ontario through the fighting, and never had been shot. When the war was new, he'd thought of himself as a cavalier, meeting other cavaliers in single combat. Three years of flying had convinced him he was as much a gear in a killing machine as an infantryman in the mud. Only the pay and the view and the hours were better.

Moss sipped at his coffee. Conversation buzzed in the background. It was the sort of coffeehouse where vast issues were hashed out and settled every day: the nature of the universe, the effect of the war on the history of the world, whether the waitress would go home with the college kid who'd propositioned her. Vast issues whirled through Moss' head, too.

"I'm trying to sort out whether I really give a damn about studying the law," he said.

"Ah," said Sandburg, who was also in law school. "You finished your first year before the war started, same as I did, right?"

"You know I did," Moss answered. "Then, it seemed important.

Now . . . I have a tough time caring now. I guess the war made me look at the scale of things differently, if you know what I mean. I mean, in the big picture, what difference does it make whether or not I hang out my shingle and start drafting wills for wheat traders with more money than sense?"

"Maybe it doesn't make any difference in the big picture," his friend said. "It sure as hell does make a difference in the way your life goes. Don't you care about that? Me, I want to be in a spot where nobody can make me pick up a Springfield for the rest of my days."

"Something to that, no doubt about it," Moss admitted. He finished his coffee and waved to the waitress for another cup. Had she said she would go home with the student or she wouldn't? Try as he would, Moss couldn't tell. "But I have trouble giving a damn. I have trouble giving a damn about almost everything."

"Aha!" Fred Sandburg stabbed out a forefinger. He would make a formidable attorney: he listened. "Almost everything, eh? All right, Johnny my boy, what do you give a damn about?"

Suddenly, Moss wished the coffee the waitress brought were whiskey. In the officers' clubs during the war, he'd had plenty of high-proof lubrication against the slings and arrows of outrageous fortune. He'd needed it, too. He needed it now, needed it and didn't have it. At last, slowly, he said, "Up in Ontario, in Canada, there was this girl, this woman . . ." He ran out of steam.

"Oho!" Sandburg laid that forefinger by the side of his nose. "Was she pretty? Was she built?" His hands described an hourglass in the air.

"Yeah, I guess so," Moss answered, a puzzled tone in his voice: he wasn't really quite sure. "She was . . . interesting." He nodded. That was the right word. He repeated it: "Interesting."

"Hell with whether she was interesting," said Sandburg, a relentlessly practical man. "Was she interested?"

"In me?" Moss laughed. "Only to spit in my eye. Her name's Laura Secord. She's somehow related to the original who had the same name a hundred years ago, and played Paul Revere against the USA in the War of 1812. She hates Americans. She told me where to head in I don't know how many times. Besides," he added morosely, "she's got a husband."

"Oh, bully." Fred Sandburg made silent, sardonic clapping motions. "You sure know how to pick 'em, don't you?"

"Sure do," Moss said. "Last time I saw her was just after the

Canucks surrendered. I drove over from Orangeville, where our last aerodrome was, back to this little town called Arthur, where it had been. She was keeping a farm going there. She didn't know whether her husband was alive or dead. She hadn't heard from him in a long time—he was in the Canadian Army. But everything would be ready for him if he came down the road."

"So if she was keeping the home fires burning for him, what did she say to *you*?" Sandburg asked.

Moss' face heated at the memory. "She told me she never wanted to set eyes on me again. She told me she wished the Canucks had shot me down. She told me she wished her husband had fired the bullet that shot me down. She told me she hoped the train I took back to the USA went off the rails and smashed to bits. After that, she got angry."

Fred Sandburg stared, then started to guffaw. "And you call this broad interesting? Jesus Christ, Johnny my boy, you can go down to New Mexico and marry a rattlesnake and do it cheaper. You'll live happier, too."

"Maybe," Moss said. "Probably, even." His grin lifted up only one corner of his mouth, making it more grimace than smile. "But I can't get her out of my mind."

Sandburg was just warming to his theme: "Or you could take to drinking absinthe to forget, or smoking cigarettes doped with opium or hashish. Then if she ever saw you again, she'd take pity on you because you were so pale and wasted and decadent-looking, and clutch you to her bosom." He leaned forward and made as if to clutch Moss to his bosom.

"Funny," Moss said, evading him. "Funny like a crutch." With so many veterans on one crutch or two these days, the cliché had taken on fresh life.

"All right, all right," Sandburg said. "But what are you going to do, moon about this woman the rest of your life? When you have grandchildren, you can talk about her the way fishermen go on: the one that got away. You're probably better off, you know. You're almost sure to be better off."

"Yeah, I know," Moss said. "I've been telling myself the same thing ever since I got back to the States. Trouble is, I can't make myself believe it."

"What are you going to do, then? Head back up to wherever it was in Canada you said she lived?" Sandburg shook his head. "That sounds like an awful lot of trouble to go through to have some girl tell you to go to hell twice." He glanced over toward the waitress, a pert brunette. "She'll probably tell you to go to hell right here. And if she doesn't, what does this Canuck gal have that she's missing? They're all the same when the lamp goes out."

"I never thought so," Moss said. He'd never thought of going back to Arthur, Ontario, again, either, not seriously. In musing tones, he went on, "Maybe I should. I'd get her out of my system, anyhow."

"That's the spirit." Sandburg raised his coffee mug in salute. "The hell with courses. The hell with examinations. If you can only see this woman who hates your guts one more time, you'll die happy. I expect they'll make a moving picture about it, and every organ player in the country can milk the minor chords for all they're worth."

"Oh, shut up," Moss said. But the more his friend ridiculed the idea, the more it appealed to him. If he felt like going up to Ontario, he could do that, provided the occupation authorities didn't give him any trouble. Had he not come from a family with money, he wouldn't have been studying law at Northwestern in the first place. Leaving for a semester wouldn't be hard.

He wondered what his parents would say. Variations on the theme of *You're out of your mind* occurred to him. Maybe he'd be wiser just to tell them he was going up to visit someone he'd met during the war, without going into too many details. They might think he meant an Army buddy. He'd have a lot less to explain afterwards if he came home unsuccessful.

He was not a fool. *I'm not a fool except about this,* he thought. No matter how foolish he was when he thought about Laura Secord, he understood the odds weren't in his favor. The odds weren't always in his favor when he played poker, either. Of course, he generally lost money when he played poker, which meant he didn't play it very often.

"Come on," Sandburg said after a look at his pocket watch. "We've got Bricker's lecture on courtroom defense and cross-examination tactics to go to, and he's worth listening to. Besides, he hasn't lost a case in years, and if that doesn't prove he knows what he's talking about, I don't know what would."

Moss laid a quarter on the table to cover his two cups of coffee. The waitress brought back fifteen cents' change; he left her a nickel tip. As he was heading out the door, he said, "I'm glad we're not down at Clemson or one of those other Confederate universities. If we were, we'd be paying five bucks for coffee, not five cents."

"Yeah, but we'd be somewhere close to millionaires—in Confederate dollars, anyhow," Fred Sandburg said. He shook his head. "Before the war, their dollar was at par with ours. God only knows when it will be again."

"They're giving us their specie and letting the printing presses run for themselves," Moss said. "You let that go on for a while and pretty soon you take five pounds of bills to the grocery store and trade 'em for five pounds of beans."

"Either that or the bills start getting crowded on account of all the extra zeros they have to put on each one," Sandburg agreed. He checked his watch again. "Come on. Shake a leg. We're going to be late."

By shaking a leg, they got to Swift Hall on time. Moss liked the campus, with its buildings scattered among emerald-green lawns and the deeper tone of trees. Lake Michigan beyond could almost have been the sea.

As Fred Sandburg had said, Professor Bricker was an impressive lecturer. Not only was he a strikingly handsome man, with broad shoulders and a thick head of black hair, he also had a deep and musical voice and a presence an actor might have envied. Moss could see how juries would believe anything he said; no wonder he'd been a burr under the saddle of local district attorneys for years.

And yet, however fine a lecturer Bricker was, Jonathan Moss had trouble paying attention to him today. His thoughts kept wandering up to Canada, wondering what Laura Secord was doing, wondering what she would say when she saw him again.

He would find out. No doubt that was stupid. He recognized as much. But he was sure—almost sure—he'd do it anyway.

Anne Colleton's broker looked like the very unhappy man he was. "It was good of you to come up to Columbia when I asked," he said. "I do appreciate it, believe me. I wanted to tell you in person that, as of August first, I shall no longer be able to represent you."

"I'm sorry to hear that, Mr. Whitson," Anne said, not altogether truthfully. "Are you retiring altogether from your profession?" Whitson was not a young man, but not so old as that, either.

"Yes, and not voluntarily," he answered, his voice bitter. "As of that date, I shall be declaring bankruptcy to protect myself from my creditors. I doubt very much whether you or anyone else would have any use for a bankrupt broker."

"I'm sorry to hear of your misfortune." But Anne could not

resist getting in a shot of her own: "You might have done better if you'd invested along the lines I chose—the lines about which you had some unkind things to say when I presented them to you."

"Go ahead—rub it in," Whitson muttered. Anne did not dislike him enough to do any more gloating, so she pretended not to hear. He went on, "I must admit, your ideas proved sounder than mine. I am, as I say, bankrupt, with holdings in worthless stocks. Your financial position is not as it was before the war—"

"Whose is, in the Confederate States?" Anne asked harshly.

"Not many folks', I'll tell you that," the broker said. "But you are merely poorer than you were. In the CSA, and especially here in South Carolina, that's an impressive accomplishment. Most plantation owners have long since gone belly up. You're still in the fight."

"Who else is?" Anne asked, interested in the competition.

"Importers," Whitson answered. "Steel men. Petroleum men in Texas and Louisiana—they're thriving, because Sequoyah's gone. Some of the Sonoran copper kings: the ones whose mines the Yankees didn't reach. But anybody who grew anything with Negro labor—cotton, tobacco, rice, sugarcane, indigo—has troubles the way a stray dog has fleas."

"Can't trust 'em, not any more," Anne said. "That's never going to be the same again. That's why I've still got Marshlands like a mill-stone around my neck. Who would want the place now? What would anyone do with it if he bought it?"

"I haven't the faintest idea," Whitson said, "but I don't know what that proves, either." His mouth tightened to a thin, pale line. "The ideas I have had haven't been good ones."

"The whole country is having a rough time," Anne said with more sympathy than she'd thought she would show. "It's hard for anyone to prosper. We need to put some heart back into ourselves, but I don't know how."

"This inflation is eating us out of house and home," the broker said. "Before long, everybody will be a millionaire and everybody will be broke."

I told you so trembled on the edge of being spoken, but Anne held her tongue. She *had* told Whitson so, and he hadn't listened, and now he was paying the price. Because she'd converted her holdings into currencies that still meant something in terms of gold, she'd come through pretty well. When the upturn finally arrived, she would be rich again—if she could wait long enough.

Whitson said, "If you like, Miss Colleton, I can recommend a new broker for you. I know several very able men who—"

Anne got to her feet. "No, thank you. I hope you will forgive me for saying so, but your recommendation does not strike me as the ideal warrant for a man's quality."

Whitson bit his lip. "I deserve that."

"Maybe you'll have better luck in times to come. I hope you do," Anne said, telling more of the truth than not—she had nothing personal against the luckless broker. "I see you have all my papers here. Please give them to me now."

"Very well." Whitson sighed as he handed them to her. "I should have been listening to your investment advice, not the other way round. The world has turned upside down since the end of the war."

"Since the beginning of the war," Anne said. "But you're right. The Confederate States were on top, and now we're on the bottom. Some people are going to be content to stay on the bottom, too. Some are going to try to see how to get back on top again. What will you do, Mr. Whitson?"

She didn't wait for an answer, but swept the papers into her valise and left the broker's office. As she turned around to close the door, she saw him staring after her. She let out a tiny sigh. Whitson was going to be one of the ones who stayed on the bottom for a long time.

His office stood only a few blocks away from the Capitol. Anne thought about going over to see the governor, but sighed again. She didn't have the influence she'd enjoyed before the war, either. Not only had her fortunes suffered, she'd called in too many favors fighting the black Reds who lurked in the swamps by the Congaree long after their revolt was stamped out elsewhere. She'd almost had to seduce the governor to pry a machine gun loose for the militia.

"God damn you, Cassius," she muttered. The former chief hunter at Marshlands had proved a far more stubborn and resourceful foe than she'd imagined any Negro could. She'd underestimated the blacks at Marshlands time and again, underestimated them and let them fool her.

"It won't happen again," she muttered as she hurled the valise into the back seat of her beat-up Ford. Before the Negro uprising, she'd driven a powerful Vauxhall. When the revolt broke out, she'd driven it up from Charleston toward Marshlands. South of the front—the Negroes of what they called the Congaree Socialist Republic had been able to hold a regular front for a while—a militia officer had confiscated the Vauxhall for use against the black rebels. She'd never seen it again. She wondered how many bullet holes scarred the fine coachwork these days.

After cranking the Ford's engine to rough, noisy life, she climbed in and drove south down the Robert E. Lee Highway, from which she would eventually turn left to get to St. Matthews. She was about thirty miles away from home: a little more than an hour, if she didn't have a puncture or a breakdown. If she did, the time might double, or it might go up by some much larger factor.

What struck her as she rattled along in the decrepit motorcar was how still and empty the countryside felt. Cotton and tobacco should have been ripening in the fields, and Negro laborers should have been tending both crops. Here and there, they were. But so many fields were a rank tangle of weeds and vines and shrubs, with no one even trying to bring in a crop on them.

It wasn't the way it had been. It would never again be the way it had been. Tears stung her eyes, so that she had to slow down till they cleared—not that the Ford could go very fast anyhow. The cotton fields at Marshlands looked like this these days.

Colletons had thrived on the plantation since the end of the eighteenth century. Even so, she was ever more tempted to cut her losses on it, quit paying the exorbitant taxes, and let the state of South Carolina take it off her hands. As far as she was concerned, the state of South Carolina was welcome to it.

The Lee Highway crossed the Congaree on a steel suspension bridge. The Red rebels had damaged the bridge, but hadn't managed to destroy it. Well before she came to the river and the swamps to either side of it, Anne took a revolver from the valise and laid it on the seat, where she could grab it in a hurry. As a force for rebellion against the government of South Carolina and that of the CSA, the Congaree Socialist Republic was dead. Not quite all the Negroes had been hunted out of the swamps yet, though. Some still made a living of sorts as bandits.

If bandits were lurking there, they gave no sign. She spotted a couple of pickaninnies fishing and passed an old black man leading a skinny, swaybacked mule laboring along under some enormous burden tied to its back. She thought about stopping and making the old man show her what the mule carried. How many rifles and pistols had traveled through the CSA in bundles like that before the uprising of 1915? Too many, surely.

In the end, she drove on. She felt bad about it afterwards, but one person could do only so much. If the old man was moving guns or explosives, what was she supposed to do with him? Arrest him? Driving with one hand on the wheel and one on the pistol didn't appeal to her. Shoot him on the spot? That did appeal to her, powerfully, but it wasn't so simple as it would have been before the war, either. She would certainly have to go to court about it, which wouldn't have been certain at all before 1914. The number of Negro veterans enrolled on the South Carolina voting lists remained tiny. The uprising during the war, though, showed how dangerous ignoring Negro opinion could be.

When she got into St. Matthews, she smiled. Several women on the street were wearing trousers. She'd started that fashion herself, getting Aaron Rosenblum the tailor to make her several pairs so she could go into the swamps to fight the Reds in clothing more convenient than an ankle-length skirt. These women didn't wear pants because they intended to hunt Reds. They wore them because one of the most prominent women in Calhoun County did.

Tom Colleton chuckled when she remarked on that. "I had noticed it myself, as a matter of fact," he said. "Gives a whole new kick to watching a pretty girl."

"Does it?" Anne wasn't sure whether to be angry or amused. She ended up a little of both. "That's not why I got them, you know."

"I never said it was," her brother answered. "That doesn't make what I did say any less true, though." While Anne digested that and finally nodded, Tom went on, "Have we got any money left?"

"All things considered, we're doing well—as well as we can be, anyhow." With a certain amount of malicious pleasure, she added, "We're doing a lot better than clever Mr. Whitson," and explained how he'd gone bankrupt.

"So the broker's broke, is he?" Tom said.

Anne made a face at him. Then she started to laugh. "That's the sort of thing you would have said back before the war. You're usually more serious these days."

"I can laugh when somebody else falls on his face in the mud," Tom told her. "Laughing when I'm down there myself is harder. Laughing when the whole country's down there is hardest of all. I still don't know how we're going to get back on our feet, Sis."

"Neither do I, not with the damnyankees standing over us with a club," Anne said. "Sooner or later, though, they'll ease up. They have troubles of their own, what with all their strikes and trying to hold the Canadians down and Socialists yelling their heads off. When they get too busy at home, that's when we'll find somebody who can help us get moving again." She sighed. "I wish it would happen faster, though."

IV

Even months after getting over the Spanish influenza, Sam Carsten knew he wasn't quite the man he had been. The disease had done its best to steamroller him into the grave. Something like a dozen sailors aboard the USS *Remembrance* had died. Many more, like him, remained weaker and slower than they were before they got sick.

He could still do his job, though, and do the hundreds of jobs any sailor had to do when he wasn't at his battle station. And, as the *Remembrance* worked with the aeroplanes she carried, learning what they could and couldn't do, he occasionally found time to marvel.

This was one of those times. He stood by the superstructure as the *Remembrance* steamed in the North Atlantic, watching while a Wright two-decker approached the stern. A sailor with semaphore paddles directed the aeroplane toward the deck. The pilot had to pay more attention to the director than to his own instincts and urges; if he didn't, he'd end up in the drink.

"Come on," Sam muttered. He'd been watching landings for a while now. Just the same, they made him sweat. If he couldn't take them for granted, what were they like for the fliers? Pilots were the most nonchalant men on the face of the earth, but anyone who was nonchalant through one of these landings would end up dead. "Come on."

On came the aeroplane. Smoke spurted as its wheels slammed the deck of the *Remembrance*. The hook on the bottom of the Wright machine's fuselage missed the first steel cable stretched across the deck to arrest its progress, but caught on the second one. The two-decker jerked to a halt.

"Jesus." Carsten turned to George Moerlein, who'd watched the landing a few feet away from him. "Every time they do that, I think the aeroplane is going to miss the deck—either that or it'll tear in half when the hook grabs it."

His bunkmate nodded. "I know what you mean. It looks impossible, even though we've been watching 'em for months."

As the Wright's prop slowed from a blur to a stop, the pilot climbed out of the aeroplane. Sailors with mops and buckets dashed over and started swabbing down the deck. With oil and gasoline spilling all the time, swabbing was a more serious business than on most ships.

Sam said, "The thing I really fear is one of 'em coming in low and smashing right into the stern. Hasn't happened yet, thank God."

"Yeah, that wouldn't do anybody any good," Moerlein agreed. "Could happen, too, especially if somebody's coming in with his aeroplane shot to hell and gone—or if he just makes a mistake."

"What I hope is, we never come into range of a battleship's big guns," Carsten said. "Taking a hit is bad enough any which way— I've done that—but taking a hit here, with all the gasoline we're carrying . . . We'd go straight to the moon, or maybe five miles past it."

"It'd be over in a hurry, anyhow," his bunkmate answered. Before Sam could say he didn't find that reassuring, George Moerlein went on, "But that's one of the reasons we're carrying all these aeroplanes: to keep battlewagons from getting into gunnery range in the first place."

Carsten stamped the flight deck, which was timber lain over steel. "We can't be the only Navy working on aeroplane carriers."

"I've heard tell the Japs are," Moerlein said. "Don't know it for a fact, but I've heard it. It wouldn't surprise me."

"Wouldn't surprise me, either, not even a little bit," Sam said. "I was in the Battle of the Three Navies, out west of the Sandwich Islands. Those little yellow bastards are tougher than anybody ever gave 'em credit for."

Moerlein looked sour. "And they just walked away from the war free and clear, too. The Rebs are paying, England and France are paying, Russia's gone to hell in a handbasket, but Japan said, 'Well, all right, if nobody else on our side's left standing, we're done, too,' and we couldn't do anything but say, 'All right, Charlie—see you again some day.' "

"We will, too," Carsten said. "I was just a kid when they took the Philippines away from Spain right after the turn of the century. And now we've taken the Sandwich Islands away from England—I was there for that, aboard the *Dakota*. So they're looking our way, and we're looking their way, and nobody's sitting between us any more."

"That'd be a fight, all right. All that ocean, aeroplanes whizzing around, us bombing them and trying to keep them from bombing us." Moerlein got a faraway look in his eye.

So did Sam. "Hell, if both sides have aeroplane carriers, you could fight a battle without ever seeing the other fellow's ships."

"That would be pretty strange," Moerlein said, "but I guess it could happen."

"Sure it could," Sam said. "And you'd want to sink the other bastard's aeroplane carriers just as fast as you could, because if he didn't have any aeroplanes left, he couldn't stop your battleships from doing whatever they wanted to do." He stamped on the flight deck again. "And if the aeroplane carrier is the ship you have to sink first, that makes the *Remembrance* the most important ship in the whole Navy right now."

For a moment, he felt almost like a prophet in the middle of a vision of the future. He also felt pleased with himself for having had the sense to figure out that aeroplanes were the coming thing, and grateful to Commander Grady for having brought him to the *Remembrance*, no matter how ugly she was.

Then something else occurred to him. He hurried away. "Where's the fire at?" George Moerlein called after him. He didn't answer, but hurried down a hatch to go below.

He guessed Grady would be checking one sponson or another and, sure enough, found him in the third one into which he poked his head. The officer was testing the elevation screw on the gun there, and talking about it in a low voice with the gunner's mate who commanded the crew for that sponson. Sam stood at attention and waited to be noticed.

Eventually, Commander Grady said, "You'll want to make sure of the threads there, Reynolds. Good thing we're not likely to be sailing into combat any time soon." He turned to Sam. "What can I do for you, Carsten?"

"I've been thinking, sir," Sam began.

A smile spread across Grady's rabbity features. "Far be it from me to discourage such a habit. And what have you been thinking?"

"We've taken the Confederates' battleships away from them, sir, and we've taken away their submersibles," Carsten said. "What do the agreements we've made with them say about aeroplane carriers?"

"So far as I know, they don't say anything," Commander Grady said.

"Shouldn't they, sir?" Sam asked in some alarm. "What if the Rebs built a whole raft of these ships and—"

Grady held up a hand. "I understand what you're saying. If the *Remembrance* turns out to be as important as we think she is, then you'll be right. If she doesn't, though—" He shrugged. "There are a lot of people in Philadelphia who think we're pouring money down a rathole."

"They're crazy," Sam blurted.

"I think so, too, but how do you go about proving it?" Grady asked. "We need to have something to do to prove what we're worth. In any case, I believe the answer to your question is no, as I said: if the Confederate States want to build aeroplane carriers, they are not forbidden to do so. When the agreements were framed, no one took this class of ship seriously."

"That's too bad," Carsten said.

"I think so, too," Grady repeated. "Nothing I can do about it, though. Nothing you can do about it, either."

Carsten looked southwest, in the direction of the Confederacy. "Wonder how long it'll be before the Rebels have one of these babies." Then he looked east. "Wonder how long it'll be before England and France do, too."

"It'll take the Rebs a while, and the frogs, too, I expect," Commander Grady said. "We're sitting on the CSA, and Kaiser Bill is sitting on France. England ... I don't know about England. They didn't have the war brought home to them, not the way the Confederates and the French did. Yeah, they got hungry, and the Royal Navy finally ended up fighting out of its weight, but they weren't *whipped*—you know what I mean?"

"Yes, sir," Sam said.

Grady went on as if he hadn't spoken: "And from Australia through India and Africa, they're still cocks o' the walk. If they decide they want to get even and they find some friends ..." His laugh was anything but mirthful. "Sounds like the way we won this last war, doesn't it, Carsten? We decided we were going to get even, and we cozied up to the German Empire. I hope to God it doesn't work for them ten years down the line, or twenty, or thirty."

"Yes, sir," Sam said again. "I guess we just have to do our best to keep ahead of them, that's all." He sighed. "I wonder where all this ends, or if it ever ends."

"Only way I can see it ending is if we ever figure out how to blow a whole country clean off the map," Grady said. He slapped Sam on the back. "I don't figure that'll happen any time soon, if it ever does. We'll have work to do for as long as we want it, the two of us."

"That'd be good, sir," Carsten said equably. "That's the big reason I wanted to transfer to the *Remembrance*. As soon as they bombed us off Argentina, I knew aeroplanes were going to stay important for a long, long time."

"You're a sharp bird, Carsten," Grady said. "I was glad to see you get that promotion at the end of '16. You're too sharp to have stayed an able seaman for as long as you did. If you were as pushy as you're sharp, you'd be an officer by now."

"An officer? Me?" Carsten started to laugh, but Commander Grady wasn't the first person who'd told him he thought like one. He shrugged. "I like things the way they are pretty well. I've got enough trouble telling myself what to do, let alone giving other people orders."

Grady chuckled. "There's more to being an officer than giving orders, though I don't suppose it looks that way to the ratings on the receiving end. I think you've got what it takes, if you want to apply yourself."

"Really, sir?" Sam asked, and Commander Grady nodded. Sam had never aspired to anything more than chief petty officer, not even in his wildest dreams. Now he did. He'd known a few mustangs, officers who'd come up through the ranks. Doing that wasn't impossible, but it wasn't easy, either. How much did he want it? Did he want it at all? "Have to think about that."

Jake Featherston rubbed brilliantine into his hair, then combed a part that might have been scribed with a ruler. He looked at himself in the tiny mirror above the sink in his room. He wasn't handsome, but he didn't figure he would ever be handsome. He'd do.

He put on a clean shirt and a pair of pants that had been pressed in the not too impossibly distant past. Again, he didn't look as if he were about to speak before the Confederate Congress, but he didn't want to speak before the Confederate Congress, except to tell all the fat cats in there where to go. He grinned. He was going to tell some fat cats where to go today, too, but they weren't so fat as they wanted to be, nor so fat they thought they were.

He donned a cloth workingman's cap, put his pistol on his belt, and left the room. Fewer people bothered wearing weapons on the streets in Richmond than had been true in the first desperate weeks after the Great War ended, but he was a long way from the only man sporting a pistol or carrying a Tredegar. Nobody could be sure what would happen next, and a good many people didn't care to find out the hard way.

Featherston hurried down Seventh toward the James River. The back room in the saloon where the Freedom Party had met wasn't big enough these days, but a rented hall a couple of doors down still sufficed for their needs. After meetings, the Party veterans would repair to the saloon and drink and talk about the good old days when everyone had always stood shoulder to shoulder with everyone else.

Sometimes Jake was part of those gatherings, sometimes he wasn't. After tonight, either he would be or he wouldn't have anything to do with the Party any more. He saw no middle way—but then, he'd never been a man who looked for the middle way in anything he did.

A small crowd had gathered on the sidewalk in front of the meeting hall: men in caps and straw hats crowding around the doorway, jostling to get in. They parted like the Red Sea to let Jake by. "Tell the truth tonight, Featherston!" somebody called. "Tell everybody the whole truth."

"Don't you worry about that," Jake answered. "I don't know how to do anything else. You wait and see."

Several people clapped their hands. But somebody said, "You don't want to be Party chairman. You want to be king, is what you want."

Whirling to turn on the man, Jake snapped, "That's a goddamn lie, Bill Turley, and you know it goddamn well. What I want is for the Freedom Party to go somewhere. If it wants to go my way, fine. If it doesn't, it'll go however it goes and I'll go somewhere else. No hard feelings."

No matter what he'd said a moment before, that was a thumping lie. Hard feelings were what made Jake Featherston what he was. If the Freedom Party rejected him tonight, he would never forget and never forgive. He never forgot and never forgave any slight. And this rejection, if it came, would be far worse than a mere slight.

Inside, people buzzed and pointed as he walked up the aisle toward the long table on the raised stage at the front of the hall.

Anthony Dresser already sat up there, along with several other Party officials: Ernie London, the treasurer, who was almost wide enough to need two chairs; Ferdinand Koenig, the secretary, a headbreaker despite his fancy first name; and Bert McWilliams, the vice chairman, a man who could be inconspicuous in almost any company.

Dresser, London, and McWilliams all wore business suits of varying ages and degrees of shininess. Koenig, like Jake, was in his shirtsleeves. As Jake sat down at the table, he looked out over the audience. It was a shirtsleeves crowd; he saw only a handful of jackets and cravats and vests. He smiled, but only to himself. Dresser and his chums no doubt thought they looked impressive. The crowd out there, though, would think they were stuffed shirts.

"And they are," Jake muttered to himself. "God damn me to hell and gone, but they are."

Anthony Dresser rapped a gavel on the tabletop. "This meeting of the Freedom Party will now come to order," he said, and turned to Ferdinand Koenig. "The secretary will read the minutes of last week's meeting and bring us up to date on correspondence."

"Thank you, Mr. Chairman," Koenig said in a rumbling baritone. Jake Featherston listened with half an ear as he droned through the minutes, which were approved without amendments. "As for correspondence, we've had a good many letters from North and South Carolina and from Georgia concerning joining the Party and forming local chapters, this as a result of Mr. Featherston's speaking tour. We've also had inquiries from Mississippi and Alabama and even one from Texas, these based on newspaper stories about the speaking tour." He displayed a fat sheaf of envelopes.

Dresser gave him a sour look. "Kindly keep yourself to the facts, Mr. Koenig. Save the editorials for the papers." He nodded to Ernie London. "Before we proceed to new business, the treasurer will report on the finances of the Party."

"Thank you, Mr. Chairman." London's voice was surprisingly high and thin to be emerging from such a massive man. "As far as money goes, we are not in the worst situation. Our present balance is $8,541.27, which is an increase of $791.22 over last week. I would like that better if it were in dollars from before 1914: then we would have ourselves a very nice little piece of change. But even now, it is better than a poke in the eye with a sharp stick."

"Question!" Jake Featherston said sharply. "Where did all that new money come from?"

Dresser brought the gavel down sharply. "That doesn't matter now. Only thing that matters is how much money we've got." He banged the gavel again. "And now, if nobody else has got anything to say, we'll get on with the new business. We—"

"Mr. Chairman, I reckon Jake's got himself a point," Ferdinand Koenig said, "especially on account of the new business you've got in mind."

Bang! "No, sir," Dresser said, angry now. "I said it doesn't matter, and my ruling stands, by Jesus."

"Mr. Chairman, I appeal that ruling to a vote from the floor," Jake said. He hated parliamentary procedure, but he'd started learning it anyhow, even if he did think it was only a way to cheat by the numbers.

"Second," Koenig said.

"Never mind," Dresser said in a low, furious voice. He wasn't ready for a floor vote, then. Jake wasn't nearly sure he was ready for a floor vote, either. When one came, he wanted it to be for all the marbles. Dresser said, "Go ahead, Ernie. Tell 'em what they want to know, so we can get on with things."

Reluctantly, London said, "Some came from dues, some came from contributions from people who heard Featherston's speaking tour."

"How much came from each?" Jake demanded.

Fat as he was, Ernie London looked as if he wished he were invisible. "I don't have the figures showing the split right here with me," he said at last.

"Hell of a treasurer *you* are," Featherston jeered. "All right, let me ask you an easy one: did I bring in more or less than half the week's take? You tell me you don't recollect, I'll call you a liar to your face. Everybody knows bookkeepers like playing with numbers. They don't forget 'em."

Most unwillingly, London said, "It was more than half."

"Thank you, Ernie." Jake beamed at him, then nodded to Anthony Dresser. "Go on ahead, Tony. It's your show for now." He put a small but unmistakable stress on the last two words.

"All right, then." Dresser looked around the room, no doubt gauging his support. Featherston was doing the same. He didn't know how this would come out. He knew how it would come out if there were any justice in the world, but that had been in short supply for a while now. If there were any justice in the world, wouldn't the CSA have won the war? Maybe the same sorts of thoughts were going through Anthony Dresser's mind as he banged the gavel down once more and announced, "New business."

"Mr. Chairman!" Bert McWilliams' voice was more memorable than his face, but not much. When Dresser recognized him, he went on, "Mr. Chairman, I move that we remove Jake Featherston from his position as head of propaganda for the Freedom Party."

"Second!" Ernie London said at once. Jake had expected London to bring the motion and McWilliams to second it; otherwise, he was unsurprised.

"It has been moved and seconded to remove Jake Featherston as head of propaganda," Anthony Dresser said. "I'll lead off the discussion." He rapped loudly with the gavel several times. "And we will have order and quiet from the members, unless they have been recognized to speak. Order!" *Bang! Bang!*

When something not too far from order had been restored, Dresser resumed: "I don't deny Jake has done some good things for the Party—don't get me wrong. But he's done us a good deal of harm, too, and it's not the kind of harm that's easily fixed. He's taken all the great things we stand for and boiled them down to *hang the generals and hang the niggers.* Not that they don't *need* hanging, mind you, but there are so many other things to get the country going again that need doing, too, and he never talks about a one of them. People get the wrong idea about us, you see."

London and McWilliams followed with similar speeches. Out in the hard, uncomfortable seats that filled the hall, the Freedom Party members were silent, listening, judging.

Confidence surged through Featherston. Even here, when they should be doing everything to crush him, his opponents beat around the bush and tried to see all sides of the question. He would never make that mistake. "Mr. Chairman!" he said. "Can I speak for myself, or are you just going to railroad me altogether?"

Warily, Dresser said, "Go ahead, Jake. Have your say. Then we vote."

"Right," Featherston said tightly. He looked out at the crowd. "Now is the time to fish or cut bait," he said. "The reason I'm head of propaganda is that I'm the only man up here people can listen to without falling asleep." That got him a laugh. Anthony Dresser, sputtering angrily, tried to gavel it down and failed. "I'm the one who brings in the money—Ernie said so himself. And I'll tell you why—I keep it simple. That's what propaganda is all about. I make people want to support us. I don't say one thing Monday and another thing Tuesday and something else on Wednesday. Like I say, I keep it simple."

He took a deep breath. "I shake things up. I make the people in high places sweat. That's the other thing propaganda is for, folks—to show people your way is better. So. Here it is: you can go on with me and see how much we can shake loose together, or you can throw me out and spend your time pounding each other on the back, on account of it'll be a cold day in hell before you see any more new members." He rounded on Anthony Dresser. In tones of contemptuous certainty, he said, "Mr. Chairman, I call the question."

Dresser stared, the scales suddenly fallen from his eyes. "You don't want to be head of propaganda," he stammered. "You—You want to head the Party."

Jake grinned, hiding his own unease where Dresser let his show. "I call the question," he repeated.

Licking his lips, Dresser said, "In favor of removing Jake Featherston?" Somewhere between a quarter and a third of the men in the hall raised their hands. In a voice like ashes, Dresser said, "Opposed?" The rest of the hands flew high. So did a great shout of triumph. "The motion is not carried," Dresser choked out.

"Mr. Chairman!" Ferdinand Koenig said, and Dresser was rash enough to recognize the Party secretary. Koenig went on, "Mr. Chairman, I move that you step down and we make Jake Featherston chairman of the Freedom Party."

Another great shout rose. In it were two dozen cries of, "Second!"—maybe more. Featherston and Koenig grinned at each other as Anthony Dresser presided over voting himself out of office. In that glorious moment, Jake felt the world turned only because his hands worked its axis. He had his chance now. He didn't know what he would make of it, not yet, but it was there.

Stephen Douglas Martin looked at his son. "I wish you wouldn't do this," he said, worry in his voice.

"I know," Chester Martin answered. "You've got to understand, though—you have a place. The way the bosses are acting these days, I'll never have one, not unless I take it for myself."

His father pointed to the bulge of the pistol behind his belt. "You won't get it with that."

"I won't get it any other way," Martin said stubbornly. "I don't aim to shoot first—I'm not that stupid—but I'm not stupid enough to stand around and watch my friends on the picket lines get shot down like dogs, either. If there's no trouble, fine. But if those goons start banging away at me, I'm not going to run like a rabbit, not any more."

His father shook his head, a troubled gesture. "You've been lis-tening to the Socialists again. If I never see another red flag, it'll be too soon."

"You don't get it, Pa," Chester said, impatient with the igno-rance of the older generation. "If it weren't for the Socialists, nobody'd make any kind of decent money—the bosses would have it all." Unending labor strife since he'd come home from the war had eroded his lifelong faith in the Democratic Party.

"You're going to end up on a blacklist," his father said gloomily. "Then you won't have any work at all, no matter how the strikes turn out."

"I won't have any steel work, maybe," Chester said with a shrug. "One way or another, though, I'll get along. There's plenty of things I can do if I have to. One of 'em or another is bound to work out. I'm a white man; I pull my weight."

"Aahhh." Stephen Douglas Martin made a disgusted noise. "You're in it for the glory. I remember the red flags flying back in the '90s, too, and the battles, and the blood in the streets. It was all fool-ishness, if you ask me."

"Glory?" Chester Martin laughed bitterly. He unbuttoned his left cuff and rolled the sleeve high to show the scar a Confederate bullet had left on his upper arm. "There's no such thing as glory, near as I can tell. If the machine guns didn't kill it, the artillery did. Teddy Roosevelt promised us a square deal, but I don't see him delivering. If I have to go out into the streets to get it, I'll do that—and to hell with glory."

"Aahhh," his father repeated. "Well, go on, then, since that's what you're bound and determined to do. I only hope you come back in one piece, that's all. You're playing for keeps out there."

Chester nodded. The thought did not bother him, or not unduly. He'd been playing for keeps since his first comrade got hung up on Confederate barbed wire and shot just inside the Virginia line back in August 1914. He said, "What was the war about, if it wasn't about having a better life after it was over? I don't see that, not for me I don't, not without this fight. I'm still here in the old room I had before I went into the Army, for heaven's sake."

"I buried one son, Chester, when the scarlet fever took your brother Hank," his father said heavily. "It tore my heart in two, and what it did to your mother. . . . If I had to do it twice, I don't know how I'd get by afterwards."

Chester Martin slapped his father on the back. "It'll be all right. I know what I'm doing, and I know why I'm doing it." That wasn't the bravado he might have shown in the days before conscription pulled him into the Army. Instead, it was a man's sober assessment of risk and need.

His father said nothing more. His father plainly saw there was nothing more to say. With a last nod, Chester left the flat, went down to the corner, and waited for the trolley that would take him into the heart of Toledo and into the heart of the struggle against the steelmill owners.

The strikers, by now, had their own headquarters, a rented hall a couple of blocks away from the long row of steelworks whose stacks belched clouds of black, sulfurous smoke into the sky. The hall had its own forward guards and then a stronger force of defenders in red armbands closer to it. Most of the strike's leaders had served in the Great War. They understood the need to defend a position in depth.

An unusual number of trash cans and kegs and benches lined the street by the hall. If the Toledo police tried to raid the place, the strikers could throw up barricades in a hurry. They'd already done that more than once, when their struggle with the owners heated up. For now, though, motorcars whizzed past the hall.

For now, too, blue-uniformed police made their way past the strikers' guards. The men in blue strolled along as if they were in full control of the neighborhood. Only a few of them strolled along at any one time, though. A tacit understanding between the leaders of the strike and city hall let the police keep that illusion of control, provided they did not try to turn it into reality. The agreement was not only tacit but also fragile; when things heated up on the picket lines, the cops drew near at their peril.

"What do you say, Chester?" Albert Bauer called when Martin walked into the hall. The stocky steelworker made a fist. "Here's to the revolution—the one you said we didn't need."

"Ahh, shut up, Al," Martin answered with a sour grin. "Or if you don't want to shut up, tell me you were never wrong in your whole life."

"Can't do it," Bauer admitted. "But I'll tell you this: I don't think I was ever wrong on anything this important."

"Teach me to be like you, then," Martin said, jeering a little.

"You're learning." Bauer was imperturbable. "You started out mystified by the capitalists, same as so many do, but you're learning. Before too long, you'll see them like they really are—nothing but exploiters who need to be swept onto the ash heap of history so the proletariat can advance."

"I don't know anything about the ash heap of history," Martin said. "I hope some of them get swept away in the elections. They're only a couple of months off. That would send the country the right kind of message."

"So it would," Bauer said. "So it would. That means we have to send the country the right kind of message between now and election day."

"You mean you don't want me to go out and start taking potshots at the ugly blue bastards who've been taking potshots at us?" Martin said.

"Something like that, yeah." Bauer's eyes went to the pistol concealed—but not well enough—in the waistband of Martin's trousers. "We aren't out to start any trouble now. If the police start it, we'll give them as much as they want, but the papers have to be able to say they went after us first."

"All right." That made sense to Martin. He headed over to the neat rows of picket signs. Choosing one that read A SQUARE DEAL MEANS A SQUARE MEAL, he shouldered it as if it were a Springfield and headed out toward the line the striking steelworkers had thrown up around the nearest plant.

By then, the scabs who kept the plant running had already gone in. Martin was sure they'd gone in under a hail of curses. Perhaps they hadn't gone in under a hail of rocks and bottles today. That was the sort of thing that touched off battles with the police, and everything seemed quiet for the time being, as it had on the Roanoke front when both sides were gearing up to have a go at each other.

Martin marched along the sidewalk. Toledo police and company guards kept a close eye on the strikers. The police looked hot and bored. Martin was hot and bored, too. Sweat ran off him in rivers; the day was muggy, without a hint of a breeze. He kept a wary eye on the company guards. They looked hot, too, but they also looked like Great Danes quivering on the end of leashes, ever so eager to bite anything that came near.

"Scab-lovers!" the strikers taunted them. "Whores!" "Goons!" "Stinking sons of bitches!"

"Your mothers were whores!" the guards shouted back. "Your fathers were niggers, just like the ones who rose up in the CSA!"

"Shut up!" the cops shouted, over and over. "Shut the hell up, all of you!" They didn't want to have to do anything but stand there. Brawling on a day like this was more trouble than it was worth. Chester Martin knew a little sympathy for them, but only a little. He cursed the company guards along with everybody else on the picket line.

Socialist Party workers brought the picketers cheese sandwiches to eat while they marched. In the middle of the afternoon, a picketer and a cop keeled over from the heat within a few minutes of each other. No company guards keeled over. They had all the food and cold water they wanted.

Shift-changing time neared. Chester Martin tensed. The picketers' shouts, which had grown perfunctory, turned loud and fierce and angry once more as the scabs, escorted by guards and police both, left the steelworks.

"Back away!" a policeman yelled at the strikers. Martin had heard that shout so often, he was sick to death of it. The cop shouted again anyhow: "Back away, you men, or you'll be sorry!"

Sometimes the striking steelworkers would back away. Sometimes they would surge forward and attack the scabs regardless of the cops and goons protecting them. Martin had been in several pitched battles—that was what the newspapers called them, anyway. To a man who'd known real combat, they didn't rate the name. Either the reporters had managed to sit out the war on the sidelines or they cared more about selling papers than telling the truth. Maybe both those things were true at once. It wouldn't have surprised Martin a bit.

Today, nothing untoward happened. The strikers jeered and cursed the scabs and called, "Join us!" More than a few former scabs had quit their jobs and started on the picket lines. No one threw a stone or a horse turd this afternoon, though. No one started shooting, either, although Martin was sure he was a long way from the only striker carrying a pistol.

Having been through more gunfire than he'd ever wanted to imagine, he was anything but sorry not to land in it again. He trudged back to the strikers' hall, turned in his sign, and dug a nickel out of his pocket for trolley fare. His father and mother would be glad to see him home in one piece. He wondered about his sister. From some of the stories Sue told, her boss exploited her, too.

As he stood on the streetcorner, he shook his head in slow wonder. "The bosses are too stupid to know it," he murmured, "but they're turning a whole bunch of good Democrats into revolutionaries."

Scipio had hoped he would never hear of the Freedom Party again after that one rally in May Park. He hadn't thought such a hope too unreasonable: he'd never heard of it till that rally. With any luck, the so-called party would turn out to be one angry white man going from town to town on the train. The times were ripe for such cranks.

But, as summer slowly gave way to fall, the Freedom Party opened an office in Augusta. The office was nowhere near the Terry; even had more than a handful of Negroes been eligible to vote, the Freedom Party would not have gone looking for their support. Scipio found out about the office in a one-paragraph story on an inside page of the *Augusta Constitutionalist*.

He showed the story to his boss, a grizzled Negro named Erasmus who ran a fish market that doubled as a fried-fish café. Erasmus, he'd seen, was a shrewd businessman, but read only slowly and haltingly, mumbling the words under his breath. When at last he finished, he looked over the tops of his half-glasses at Scipio. "Ain't such a bad thing, Xerxes, I don't reckon," he said.

"The buckra in this here party hates we," Scipio protested. After close to a year in Augusta, he'd grown as used to his alias as he was to his right name. "They gets anywheres, ain't gwine do we no good."

Erasmus peered at him over those silly little spectacles again. "Most o' the white folks hates us," he answered matter-of-factly. "These ones here, at least they's honest about it. Reckon I'd sooner know who can't stand me than have folks tell me lies."

That made a certain amount of sense—but only, Scipio thought, a certain amount. "The buckra wants to be on top, sure enough," he said. "But these here Freedom Party buckra, they wants to be on top on account o' they wants we in de grave, six feets under de ground."

His boss shook his head. "White folks ain't that stupid. We dead an' buried, who gwine do their for work them? You answer me dat, an then I'll worry 'bout this here Freedom Party."

"Huh," Scipio said. He thought for a little while, then laughed a bit sheepishly. "Mebbe you's right. Cain't you jus' see de po' buckra out in de cotton fields, wid de overseer yellin' an' cursin' at they to move they lazy white backsides?"

"Lawd have mercy, I wish to Jesus I could see me that," Erasmus said. "I pay money to see that. But it ain't gwine happen. White folks ain't about to get their soft hands all blistered an' dirty, an' we's safe enough because o' that." A Negro in overalls came in and sat down at one of the half dozen rickety little tables in front of the counter where fish lay on ice. Erasmus pointed. "Never mind this stupid stuff we can't do nothin' about anyways. Get yourself over there an' see what Pythagoras wants to eat."

"Fried catfish an' cornbread," the customer said as Scipio came up to him. "Lemonade on the side."

"I gets it for you," Scipio answered. He turned to see whether Erasmus had heard the order or he'd have to relay it. His boss had already plucked a catfish from the ice; an empty spot showed where it had been. A moment later, hot lard sizzled as the fish, after a quick dip into egg batter, went into the frying pan.

Scipio poured lemonade and cut a chunk from the pan of moist, yellow cornbread Erasmus had baked that morning. He took the lemonade over to Pythagoras. By the time he got back, Erasmus had slapped the fried catfish onto the plate with the cornbread. He also dipped up a ladleful of greens from a cast-iron pot on the back of the stove and plopped them down alongside the fish.

"He don't ask for no greens," Scipio said quietly.

"Once he sees 'em, he decide he wants 'em," Erasmus said. "He been comin' in here better'n ten years. You reckon I don't know what he wants?"

Without another word, Scipio took the plate over to Pythagoras. He had spent years learning to anticipate Anne Colleton's needs and to minister to them even before she knew she had them. If Erasmus had done the same with his regular customers, how could Scipio argue with him?

And, sure enough, Pythagoras waved to Erasmus and ate the greens with every sign of enjoyment. He ordered a slab of peach pie for dessert. Only after he'd polished that off did he turn a wary eye on Scipio and ask, "What's all that come to?"

"Thirty-fi' dollars," Scipio answered, and waited for the sky to fall.

Pythagoras only shrugged, sighed, and pulled a fat wad of banknotes from a hip pocket. He peeled off two twenties and set them on the table. "Don' fret yourself none about no change," he said as he stood up. "Foe the war, I don't reckon I never had thirty-five dollars, not all at the same time. Money come easy now, but Lord! it sure do go easy, too." He lifted his cloth cap in salute to Erasmus, then went back out onto the street.

"Do Jesus!" Scipio said. "He sure enough right about dat." Erasmus was paying him $500 a week after his latest raise, and feeding him dinner every day besides. Despite what would have looked like spectacular wealth in 1914, Scipio remained just one more poor Negro in the Terry.

Erasmus said, "It ain't all bad. Couple weeks ago, I done took me a thousand dollars down to the bank so I could pay off the note on my house. Should have seen them white bankers fuss an' flop— jus' like a catfish on a hook, they was." His reminiscent grin showed a couple of missing front teeth. "Wasn't nothin' they could do about it, though. Money's money, ain't that right?" He laughed.

So did Scipio. "Money's money," he agreed, and laughed again. These days, the Confederate dollar would scarcely buy what a penny had bought before the war. For anyone in debt, cheap money was a godsend. For those who weren't, it was a disaster, or at best a challenge to make last week's salary pay for this week's groceries.

The eatery got more sit-down trade as afternoon darkened into evening. More women, though, threw down brown banknotes for fish they carried away wrapped in newspaper to fry for their husbands and brothers and children. Scipio watched Erasmus throw the story about the Freedom Party around a fat catfish that a fat woman with a bandanna on her head took off under her arm like a loaf of bread.

He wasn't sorry to see the story go. He wished somebody—God, perhaps—would use the Freedom Party itself to wrap fish. Whatever else you said about the skinny man who spoke for the party, he'd been terribly earnest. He'd believed every word of what he was saying. If that didn't make him all the more frightening, Scipio didn't know what would.

At last, Erasmus said, "Might as well go on home, Xerxes. Don't reckon we's gwine get much more trade tonight. I see you in the mornin'."

"All right." Scipio left the little market and café and headed back to his roominghouse. He kept an eye open as he hurried along. The street lights in the Terry were few and far between; the white men who ran Augusta didn't waste a lot of money on the colored part of town. If anybody was thinking of equalizing the wealth in an altogether un-Marxist way, Scipio wanted to see him before being seen.

No one troubled him on the way to the roominghouse. No one troubled him when he got there, either. "Evenin', Xerxes," the landlady said when he walked up the stairs and into the front hall. "Not so hot like it has been, is it?"

"No, ma'am," Scipio said. He'd been paying the rent regularly for some time now. He was working steady hours, too, which made him a good bet to be able to go on paying the rent. Under those circumstances, no wonder the landlady sounded friendly.

He went on up to his neat little third-floor room, got out of his white shirt and black pants, and threw on a cheap, flimsy cotton robe over his drawers. Then, barefoot, he padded down to the bathroom at the end of the hall. Being butler at Marshlands had left him as fastidious about his person as he was about his surroundings, which meant he bathed more often than most of the people who shared the roominghouse with him.

But when he tried the bathroom door, it was locked. A startled splash came from within, and a woman's voice: "Who's there?"

Scipio's ears heated. Had he been white, he would have blushed. "It's Xerxes, Miss Bathsheba, from up the hall," he said. "I's right sorry to 'sturb you."

"Don't fret yourself none," she said. "I'm just about done." More splashes: he judged she was getting out of the cramped tin tub. He smiled a little, letting his imagination peek through the closed door.

In a couple of minutes, that door opened. Out came Bathsheba, a pleasant-looking woman in her early thirties. Scipio thought she had a little white blood in her, though not enough to be called a mulatto. She wore a robe with a gaudy print, of the same cheap cotton cloth as his. She didn't hold it closed as well as she might have. At Marshlands, Scipio had mastered the art of looking without seeming to. He got himself a discreet eyeful now.

"See you later, Xerxes," Bathsheba said, and headed up the hall past him. He turned his head to watch her go. She looked back at him over her shoulder. Her eyes sparkled.

"Well, well," Scipio murmured. He hurried into the bathroom, ran the tub half full, and bathed as fast as he could. He would have bathed in a hurry anyhow; sitting down in a tub of cold water was a long way from a sensual delight. Now, though, he had an extra incentive, or hoped he did.

He went back to his room almost at a trot, and put on a fresh shirt and a pair of trousers. *Have to take the laundry out soon,* he thought. He started out the door again, then checked himself. When he did leave, he was carrying a flat pint bottle of whiskey. He didn't do a lot of drinking, but there were times . . . He knocked on the door to Bathsheba's room.

"That you, Xerxes?" she asked. When he admitted it, she opened the door, then shut it after him. She was still wearing that robe, and still not bothering to hold it closed very well. She pointed at the whiskey bottle. "What you got there?" Her voice was arch; she knew perfectly well what he had—and why, too.

"Wonder if you wants to take a nip with me," Scipio said.

By way of reply, Bathsheba got a couple of mismatched glasses and sat down at one end of a ratty sofa. When Scipio sat down, too, close beside her, he contrived—or maybe she did—to brush his leg against hers. She didn't pull away. He poured a healthy shot of whiskey into each glass.

They drank and talked, neither one of them in a hurry. After a while, Scipio slipped his arm around her. She leaned her head on his shoulder. He set down his glass, turned toward her, and tilted her face up for a kiss. Then his free hand slid inside her robe. He rapidly discovered she was naked under it.

Bathsheba laughed at what must have been his startled expression. "I was hopin' you might stop by," she said.

"Sweet thing, I ain't stopped," Scipio said. "I ain't hardly even started." He lowered his mouth to a dark-nippled breast. She pressed her hand to the back of his head, urging him on. His breath caught in his throat. He needed no urging.

These days, the Lower East Side in New York City felt strange to Flora Hamburger. That it felt strange was strange itself. She'd lived her whole life there, till she'd gone off to Philadelphia to take her seat in Congress at the start of 1917. Now, as October 1918 yielded to November, she was home again, campaigning for a second term.

But, though she'd visited the Lower East Side several times since, this long campaign swing forcibly brought home to her how much she'd been away. Everything seemed shabby and cramped and packed tighter with people than a tin of sardines was stuffed with little fish. Things surely hadn't changed much in less than two years. But she'd taken them for granted before. She didn't any more.

Her posters—red and black, with VOTE SOCIALIST! VOTE HAMBURGER! in both English and Yiddish—were almost everywhere in the Fourteenth Ward, and especially in the Centre Market, across the street from the Socialist Party headquarters. Her district was solidly Socialist; the Democratic candidate, an amiable nonentity named Marcus Krauskopf, had for all practical purposes thrown in the sponge. The Democrats hadn't been able to win two years before even with an appointed incumbent. Now that Flora held the advantage of incumbency, they looked to be saving their efforts for places where they had a chance to do better.

Flora was not the sort who took anything for granted. She stood on a keg of nails and addressed the people who crowded into the Centre Market, even if many of them were after pickled tomatoes or needles or smoked whitefish, not speeches. "What have we got from our great victory? Dead men, maimed men, men who can't get work because the capitalists care more for their profits than for letting people earn a proper living. That was the war the Democrats gave you. This is the peace the Democrats are giving you. Is it what you want?"

Some people in the market shouted, "No!" About as many, though, went on about their business. Most of them—most who were citizens, at any rate—would vote when the time came. They'd known too much oppression to throw away the chance to have a say in government the United States offered them.

"If you want to help the capitalists, you'll vote for the Democrats," Flora went on. "If you want to help yourselves, you'll vote for me. I hope you vote for me."

Her breath smoked as she talked. The day was raw, with ragged gray clouds scudding across the sky. People sneezed and coughed as they went from one market stall to the next. The Spanish influenza wasn't nearly so bad as it had been the winter before, but it hadn't gone away, either.

When Flora stepped down from the keg of nails, Herman Bruck reached out a hand to help steady her. Bruck was dapper in an overcoat of the very latest cut: not because he was rich, but because he came from a family of master tailors. "Fine speech," he said. "Very fine speech."

He didn't want to let go of her hand. Her being away hadn't made him any less interested in her. It had made her much less interested in him, not that she'd ever been very interested. Next to Hosea Blackford, he was a barely housebroken puppy. Freeing herself, Flora said, "Let's go back to the offices. I want to make sure we'll have all the poll-watchers we'll need out on the fifth." She was confident the Socialists would, but it gave her an excuse to move, and to keep Bruck moving.

The Party offices were above a butcher's shop. Max Fleischmann, the butcher, came out of his doorway and spoke in Yiddish: "I'll vote for you, Miss Hamburger."

"Thank you, Mr. Fleischmann," Flora answered, genuinely touched—the butcher was, or had been, a staunch Democrat. His vote meant a lot to her.

In a slightly different way, it also meant a lot to Herman Bruck. As he went upstairs with Flora, he said, "If people like Fleischmann are voting for you, you'll win in a walk."

"We'll know Tuesday night," Flora said. Inside the office, people greeted her like the old friend she was. A term in Congress slipped away, and for a little while she was just the agitator she had been before Congressman Myron Zuckerman's tragic accidental death made her run to fill his shoes and bring the seat back to the Socialist Party.

Everyone cheered when Bruck reported what Max Fleischmann had said. Maria Tresca remarked, "If we keep on like this, in 1920 the Democrats won't bother to run anybody at all in this district, any more than the Republicans do now." The secretary was a lone Italian in an office full of Jews, but probably the most ardent Socialist there—and, by now, not the least fluent in Yiddish, either.

"Maybe in 1920—*alevai* in 1920 . . . the White House," Herman Bruck said softly. Silence fell while people thought about that. When Teddy Roosevelt rode the crest of the wave after winning the Great War, such dreams from a Socialist would have been only dreams, and pipe dreams at that. Now, with the cost of the war clearer, with the strife that followed—maybe the dream could turn real.

Flora did check the roster of poll-watchers, and suggested some changes and additions. *If you want something done right, do it yourself,* she thought. After everything satisfied her, she headed back to the flat where she'd lived most of her life. The years on the floor of Congress had sharpened her debating; she had no trouble discouraging Bruck from walking along with her.

Coming in through the door reminded her anew of how much her life had changed. The apartment where she lived alone in Philadelphia was far bigger than this one, which housed her parents, two brothers, two sisters, and a toddler nephew, and which had housed her as well. It hadn't seemed particularly crowded before she went away: everyone she knew lived the same way, and sometimes took in boarders to help make ends meet. Now she knew there were other possibilities.

Her sisters, Sophie and Esther, helped her mother in the kitchen. The smell of beef-and-barley soup rising from the pot on the stove mingled with the scent of her father's pipe tobacco to make the odor of home. Her brothers, David and Isaac, bent over a chess board at one corner of the dining-room table. All was as it had been there, too, save for the crutch on the floor by David's chair.

David moved a knight and looked smug. Isaac grunted, as if in pain. Looking up from the board, he consciously noticed Flora for the first time, though she hadn't been particularly quiet. "Hello," he said. "Got my conscription notice today." He was eighteen, two years younger than his brother.

"You knew it was coming," Flora said, and Isaac nodded: everyone put in his two years. Flora quietly thanked the God in Whom her Marxist exterior did not believe that Isaac would serve in peacetime. By the way David's face twisted for a moment, that thought was going through his mind, too.

"How does the leg feel?" she asked him.

He slapped it. The sound it made was nothing like that of flesh: closer to furniture. "Not too bad," he said. "I manage. I only need one leg for a sewing-machine treadle, and it doesn't much matter which." At that, guilt rose up and smote Flora. Seeing it, her brother said, "I didn't mean to give you a hard time. It's just the way things are, that's all."

A fresh puff of smoke rose from behind the *Daily Forward* their father was reading. Abraham Hamburger said, "It's usually not a good idea to say anything that makes you explain yourself afterwards."

"I wish more Congressmen would pay attention to that advice, Father," Flora said, which caused fresh smoke signals to rise from behind the Yiddish newspaper.

Little Yossel Reisen grabbed Flora by the leg and gravely said, "Wowa": the closest he could come to her name. Then he walked on unsteady feet to Sophie and said, "Mama." That he had down solid.

Sophie Reisen stirred the soup, then picked him up. Yossel's father, after whom he was named, had never seen him; he'd been killed in Virginia long before the baby was born. Had he not got Sophie in a family way, they probably wouldn't have been married before he met a bullet.

When supper reached the table, the tastes of home were as familiar as the smell. Afterwards, Flora helped her mother with the dishes. "You will win again," Sarah Hamburger said with calm assurance.

She would have thought the same had Flora reckoned herself out of the running. As things were, Flora nodded. "Yes, I think I will," she answered, and her mother beamed; Sarah Hamburger had known it all along.

Going to sleep that night was a fresh trial for Flora. She'd got used to dozing off in quiet surroundings, queer as the notion would have struck her before she went to Congress. The racket in the apartment, the sort of noise that had once lulled her, now set her teeth on edge because she wasn't accustomed to it any more. Even having to answer Esther's "Good night" struck her as an imposition.

She stumped hard through the last few days of the campaign. On Tuesday the fifth, she voted at Public School 130. The Socialist poll-watcher tipped his cap to her; his Democratic opposite number did not raise his expensive black homburg.

Then it was back to Socialist Party headquarters to wait for the polls to close in the district and across the country. As the night lengthened, telephone lines and telephone clickers began bringing in reports. By the third set of numbers from her district, she knew she was going to beat Marcus Krauskopf: her lead was close to two to one.

Well before midnight, Krauskopf read the writing on the wall and telephoned to concede. "*Mazeltov,*" he said graciously. "Now that you've won, go right on being the conscience of the House. They need one there, believe me."

"Thank you very much," she said. "You ran a good race." That wasn't quite true, but matched his graciousness.

"I did what I could." She could almost hear him shrug over the wire. "But you've made a name for yourself, it's a Socialist district anyhow, and I don't think this is a Democratic year."

As if to underscore that, Maria Tresca exclaimed, "We just elected a Socialist in the twenty-eighth district in Pennsylvania. Where is that, anyhow?"

People looked at maps. After a minute or so, Herman Bruck said, "It's way up in the northwestern part of the state. We've never elected a Socialist Congressman from around there before—too many farmers, not enough miners. Maybe the people really have had enough of the Democratic Party."

"Even if they are finally fed up, it's taken them much too long to get that way," Maria said. As far as she was concerned, the proletarian revolution was welcome to start tomorrow, or even tonight.

The later it got, the more returns came in from the West. The first numbers from Dakota showed Hosea Blackford handily ahead in his district. "A sound man," Herman Bruck said.

"Sound? Half the time, he sounds like a Democrat," Maria Tresca said darkly.

But even her ideological purity melted in the face of the gains the Socialists were making. A couple of districts in and just outside Toledo that had never been anything but Democratic were going Socialist tonight. The same thing happened in Illinois and Michigan and, eventually, in distant California, too.

"Is it a majority?" Flora asked, a question she hadn't thought she would need tonight. She'd been optimistic going into the election, but there was a difference between optimism and cockeyed optimism.

Except, tonight, maybe there wasn't. "I don't know." Herman Bruck sounded like a man doing his best to restrain astonished awe. "A lot of these races are still close. But it could be." He looked toward a map where he'd been coloring Socialist districts red. "It really could be."

Every time Cincinnatus Driver got downwind of the Kentucky Smoke House, spit gushed into his mouth. He couldn't help it; Apicius Wood ran the best barbecue joint in Kentucky, very possibly the best in the USA. Negroes from the neighborhood came to the Kentucky Smoke House. So did Covington's whites. And so did the men who'd come down from the other side of the Ohio since the Stars and Stripes replaced the Stars and Bars atop the city hall. Nobody turned up his nose at food like that.

Lucullus—Lucullus Wood, now that his father Apicius, like Cincinnatus, had taken a surname—was turning a pig's carcass above a pit filled with hickory wood and basting the meat with a sauce an angel had surely brought down from heaven. He nodded to Cincinnatus. "Ain't seen you here for a while," he remarked. "What you want?"

Cincinnatus stretched out his hands in the direction of the pit. For a moment, he wanted nothing more than to revel in the warmth that came from it: the weather outside held a promise of winter. "I want to talk to your pa," he answered as he began to warm up himself.

Lucullus made a sour face. "Why ain't I surprised?"

"On account of you know me," Cincinnatus said. "I'll be damned if I know how you can look like you done bit into a green persimmon when you're takin' a bath in the best smell in the world."

"Only thing I smell when you come around here is trouble," Lucullus said. He never missed a beat in turning the carcass or basting it.

With a bitter laugh, Cincinnatus answered, "That'd be funny, except it ain't. I get into trouble around here, it's trouble your pa put me in. Now"—he let his voice roughen—"can I see him, or not?"

Lucullus Wood was harder to lean on than he had been. He was twenty now, or maybe a year past, and had confidence in himself as a man. Even so, a show of determination could still make him back down. He bit his lip, then said, "That room in back I reckon you know about."

"Yeah, I know about that room." Cincinnatus nodded. "He in there with anybody, or is he by his lonesome?"

"By his lonesome, far as I know," Lucullus said. "Go on, go on. You barged in before. Barge on in again." Had his hands been free, he probably would have made washing motions with them to show that whatever happened next was not his fault. As things were, his expression got the message across.

Ignoring that expression, Cincinnatus went down the hall at the back of the Kentucky Smoke House till he got to the door he knew. He didn't barge in; he knocked instead. "Come in," a voice from within said. Cincinnatus worked the latch. Apicius Wood looked at him with something less than pleasure. "Oh. It's you. Reckoned it might be somebody I was glad to scc."

"It's me." Cincinnatus shut the door behind him.

With a grunt, Apicius pointed to a battered chair. The proprietor of the Kentucky Smoke House looked as if he'd eaten a great deal of his own barbecue. If that was how he'd got so fat, Cincinnatus didn't think he could have picked a better way. "Well," Apicius rumbled, "what we gonna fight about today?"

"Don't want no fight," Cincinnatus said.

Apicius Wood laughed in his face. "Ain't many niggers in this town as stubborn as I am, but you're sure as hell one of 'em. We don't see eye to eye. You know it, an' I know it, too. When we get together, we fight."

Cincinnatus let out a long sigh. "I ain't enough of a Red to suit you, I ain't enough of a diehard to suit Joe Conroy, and I'm too goddamn black to suit Luther Bliss. Where does that leave me?"

"Out on a limb," Apicius answered accurately. "Well, say your say, so I know what we gonna fight about this time."

"What you think of the elections?" Cincinnatus asked.

"What the hell difference it make what I think or even if I think?" Apicius returned. "Ain't like I got to vote. Ain't like you got to vote, neither. Have to wait till after the revolution for that to happen, I reckon."

"Maybe not," Cincinnatus said. "Put 'em together, the Socialists and the Republicans got more seats in the House than the Democrats do. First time the Democrats lose the House in more'n thirty years. They lost seats in the Senate, too."

"Didn't lose a one here in Kentucky," Apicius said. "'Fore they let somebody here vote, they make damn sure they know who he vote for."

Cincinnatus refused to let the fat cook sidetrack him. "How much you work with the white Socialists before the elections?" he asked.

"Not much," Apicius said. "Ain't much to work with. Don't hardly have no homegrown white Socialists, and every one that come over the Ohio, Bliss and the Kentucky State Police got their eye on him. Don't want them bastards puttin' their eye on me any worse than they done already."

"How hard did you try?" Cincinnatus persisted. "Did you—?"

But Apicius wasn't easy to override, either. Raising a pale-palmed hand, he went on, "'Sides, them white Socialists ain't hardly Reds. They're nothin' but Pinks, you know what I mean? They jaw about the class struggle, but they ain't pickin' up guns and doin' anything much."

"What you talkin' about?" Cincinnatus said. "All these strikes—"

Apicius broke in again: "So what? Ain't much shootin' goin' on, not to speak of. When the niggers in the Confederate States rose up, that was a fight worth talkin' about. We'd have done the same thing here, certain sure, if the Yankees hadn't taken us out of the CSA by then. Did do some of it anyways."

That was true, and Cincinnatus knew it. He also knew something else: "Yeah, they rose up, sure enough, but they got whipped. Reds rise up in the USA, they get whipped, too. Got to be more to the class struggle than shootin' guns all the blame time, or the folks with most guns always gonna win."

"Not if their soldiers and their police work out whose side they really ought to be on," Apicius said. This time, he spoke quickly, to make sure Cincinnatus couldn't interrupt him: "Yeah, I know, I know, it ain't likely, not the way things is now. I ain't sayin' no different."

"All right, then," Cincinnatus said. "If it ain't all struggle with guns, we—you—ought to be workin' with the white folks, ain't that right?"

"You ain't been enough of a Red your ownself to tell me what I ought to be doin', Cincinnatus," Apicius said heavily.

"You don't fancy it, you don't got to listen," Cincinnatus returned. "Other thing you ought to be doin' is, you ought to start workin' to get black folks the vote. Ain't impossible, not in the USA."

"Ain't possible, not in Kentucky," Apicius said. "Some of the sons of bitches in the Legislature remember when they used to own us. You was born after manumission. You don't know how things was. When I was a boy, I was a slave. I don't know how to tell you how bad bein' a slave is."

"My pa was a slave," Cincinnatus said. "My ma, too. There's some states in the USA that let niggers vote. If we can't vote, we might as well still be slaves, on account of we ain't got no say in what happens to us."

"Yeah, and you know what states they are," Apicius said with a toss of the head. "They're states that ain't got more than about a dozen niggers, maybe two dozen tops, so havin' 'em vote don't matter one way or the other. Kentucky ain't like that. We got to vote here, we'd have us some say. What that means is, we ain't never gettin' the vote here. White folks won't let it happen."

That held an unpleasant ring of truth. Cincinnatus said, "If we can't win a fight and we can't win the vote, what good are we?"

"Damned if I know what good you are, 'cept to drive me crazy," Apicius said. "What I'm good for is, I make some pretty good barbecue."

Cincinnatus exhaled in exasperation. "If you don't try, how the devil you find out what you can do?"

"I go up on the roof at city hall, I don't need to jump off to know I land in the street," Apicius said. "What you want I should do, hand Luther Bliss a petition to ask him to tell the gov'nor to give us the vote? Not likely!" That *not likely* didn't refer to the orders the chief of the Kentucky secret police might give the governor. But Apicius could never sign such a petition, being unable to read or write.

"This here is one of the United States now," Cincinnatus said stubbornly. "You and me, we're citizens of the United States. We weren't never citizens of the Confederate States. We can try now. Maybe we don't win, but maybe by the time my Achilles grows up, he be able to vote."

"Don't hold your breath," Apicius advised, "or you end up the bluest damn nigger anybody ever seen."

That also sounded altogether too likely to suit Cincinnatus. But he was not a man to give in to trouble if he could get around it. And, as a U.S. citizen, he had more ways to try to get around it than he'd had as a Confederate resident. "I end up bangin' my head against a stone wall here, I can move to one of them states where they do let black folks vote." He didn't know exactly which states allowed Negro suffrage, but a trip to the library would tell him.

He'd succeeded in startling Apicius. "You'd move up to one of them Yankee states?" The barbecue cook seemed to listen to himself, for he laughed. "Hellfire, this here's a Yankee state these days, ain't it?"

"Yeah, except most of the white folks here ain't figured that out," Cincinnatus answered. "So why the hell shouldn't I move? Couldn't be worse'n what I've got now, not in the USA it couldn't"—the Confederate States were a different story altogether, and both men knew it—"so what's keepin' me here? Ought to throw my family in the truck and get on the road."

"I seen that truck," Apicius said. "If it ain't one thing keepin' you here, damned if I know what is. You be lucky to get over the river into Ohio, let alone anywheres else."

"Maybe," Cincinnatus said. "It is a shame and a disgrace, ain't it?" But, even though he chuckled at the barb, the idea of packing up and leaving stayed in his mind. The more he thought about it, the better it seemed. He wouldn't have to worry about Luther Bliss, or Apicius and the Reds, or the diehards. He'd seen that white people from the rest of the USA didn't love Negroes—far from it—but white people in Kentucky didn't love Negroes, either.

He wondered what Elizabeth would say if he proposed pulling up stakes. He wondered what his mother and father would say, too. All of a sudden, finding out didn't seem like the worst idea in the world. He'd never cast a vote in his life. Being able to do that would be worth a lot.

"You got that look in your eye," Apicius said.

"Maybe I do," Cincinnatus answered. "God damn, maybe I do."

V

"There are times when I'm stupid," Jonathan Moss said, "and then there are times when I'm really an idiot."

He looked around. The more he looked, the more this seemed like one of the times when he was really an idiot. Chicago winters were bad. He'd known about them. Winters up in Ontario were worse. He'd known about them, too. He'd shivered his way through three of them during the Great War. Hardly anything was more useless than the pilot of a flying scout in the middle of an Ontario winter.

"I can think of one thing, though," he said, and his breath blew out in a great icy cloud, "and that's a man who comes up here in December after a woman who can't stand him—a married woman who can't stand him, mind you."

If he hadn't done it, though, he would have wondered for the rest of his life. Now, one way or the other, he would know. He had his doubts about whether knowing would make him happy. It would make him sure, though, and that counted, too. So he'd told himself, at any rate, when he left law school.

Coming into the battered little town of Arthur now, he wondered. No town in Ontario through which the front had passed was anything but battered. The Canucks and the British had fought with dreadful intensity for every square foot of ground they'd held. In the end, that had done them no good at all. But the end came much slower and much, much harder than any American had dreamt it would before the war began.

People in heavy coats and fur hats stared at Moss' sturdy Bucephalus as he halted the motorcar in front of the general store. If he'd been driving a lightweight Ford, say, he didn't think he'd have been able to make his way north from Guelph; the road, such as it was, would have defeated him. Here he was, though, and Arthur, Ontario, and Laura Secord would have to make the best of it.

As he got out of the automobile, he wished for the furs and leathers in which he'd flown. He'd lived in them in wintertime. Under canvas, without even a proper roof over his head, they were the only things that had kept him from freezing to death. A cloth coat, even a cloth coat with a fur collar, wasn't the same.

Inside the general store, a potbellied stove glowed a cheery red. The storekeeper was shoveling more coal into it as Moss came inside. He went from being too cold to too warm in the twinkling of an eye.

Setting down the coal shovel, the storekeeper said the same thing any small-town storekeeper in the USA might have said: "Help you, stranger?" Then his eyes narrowed. "No. Wait. You ain't a stranger, or not quite. You were one o' them Yank fliers at the aerodrome outside of town, weren't you?"

"Yes." Moss hadn't expected to be recognized. He didn't know whether that would make things easier or harder. The storekeeper would have been able to tell he was an American before long anyhow. Now the fellow knew which American, or which kind of American, he was. "How are you today, Mr. Peterson?"

"I've been better, but I've been worse, too," the Canuck allowed. He fixed Moss with a flinty stare. "Other thing is, I'm mindin' my business in the town where I've lived all my days. You can boil me for tripe before I figure out why the hell a Yank'd want to come back here. You all of a sudden recollect you left a collar stud over at the aerodrome, or what?"

All at once, Jonathan Moss felt very much alone. No American occupation forces were within miles. The troops had more important places to occupy than a little town in the middle of nowhere like Arthur. If he had an unfortunate accident here, nobody would ever find out anything about it except what the locals revealed. And if it turned out not to be quite so accidental as it looked . . . he would be in no position to explain.

Even so, he decided to grasp the nettle. He'd come here to ask this question. He'd planned on doing it a little later, but he'd seen no plan survive contact with the enemy. Straight ahead, then: "Did Laura Secord's husband come home safe from the war?"

Peterson the storekeeper gave him another long look. "You're *that* crazy Yank," he said at last. "She told me there was one who'd come sniffing around her that was peskier than all the rest. Don't reckon she ever thought you'd be pesky enough to come back here, though."

"You didn't answer my question, Mr. Peterson," Moss said. Peterson went right on not answering it, too. With a sigh, Moss dug in his pocket. He pulled out a twenty-dollar goldpiece. After examining the double eagle for a moment, he let it fall on the counter. It rang sweetly. "You didn't answer my question, Mr. Peterson," he repeated.

The storekeeper studied the coin as if he'd never seen any like it before. Likely he hadn't; not much U.S. gold would have got up here. The eagle in front of crossed swords on the reverse was close to the emblem with which U.S. aeroplanes flew. The legend below held one word: REMEMBRANCE. Peterson scooped up the double eagle and stuck it in his pocket. "She never said you were a *rich* fool of a Yank."

"Thanks so much," Moss replied. "Now will you please answer what I asked you?"

"Nope," Peterson said. For a moment, Moss thought that meant he wouldn't answer. The American wondered if he could get back his goldpiece without killing the storekeeper. As he was making up his mind to try, Peterson slowly went on, "No, Isaac ain't come back. That should make her fall right straight into your arms, don't you reckon?"

"Nope," Moss said, imitating him. What Laura Secord had said the last time he'd seen her still scorched his memory. What *was* he doing here, anyway? Without another word, he spun on his heel and went back out to his automobile.

Winter slapped him in the face as soon as he opened the door to the general store. The sweat the red-hot stove had brought out on his forehead promptly started to freeze. He got into the Bucephalus and stabbed the starter button, silently thanking God he didn't have to stand in the snowy street cranking the engine to life.

He drove out to the aerodrome; it was from there that he knew how to get to the farm Laura Secord had been running. He had some trouble finding the base from which he and his comrades had flown against the Canadians and British. They'd lived under canvas, and the canvas had moved along with the front. But he'd served in these parts through a winter, and so the ground began to look familiar after a while. One field, plainly rutted despite the snow on it, sent chills through him that had nothing to do with the weather. He'd jounced along there any number of times, taking off on missions and coming back afterwards. Now—how strange!—it was only a field again.

It was the field he needed, though. Instead of casting about, he drove confidently once he'd found it. Five minutes later, he pulled off a road even more rutted than the field and up a narrow lane that led to a farmhouse and barn and a couple of smaller outbuildings. The Bucephalus' brakes reluctantly brought him to a halt not far from a stump with a hatchet driven into it. By that, and by the stains on the wood, he guessed it did duty for a chopping block.

He got out of the motorcar. Before he could head for the farmhouse door as he intended, a figure muffled to the eyes walked out of the barn. "Who's coming to see me in a fancy automobile?" The demand was sharp and curious at the same time.

Hearing Laura Secord's voice for the first time in a year and a half sent a shiver through him, as if he'd taken hold of a live electrical wire. The first time he tried to answer, all that came out was a hoarse cough. He felt sixteen years old again, calling on a girl for the first time. His hands and feet couldn't suddenly have grown large and clumsy, but they felt as if they had. He took a deep breath and spoke again: "It's Jonathan Moss, Miss Secord."

He'd forgotten her married name—done his best to blot it from his mind. He wondered if she'd forgotten him altogether. He hadn't seen her that many times, and he'd been far from the only American flier who'd seen her. But her sharp gasp said she remembered. "The mad Yank!" she exclaimed.

"I don't think so," he said, his breath steaming with every word.

"Well, you most certainly are," she said. "Not mad for being a Yank—I don't suppose you can help that—but mad for coming up here again. Why on earth did you? No matter how daft you are, you can't have wanted to see this part of the world again—or can you?"

"No, I didn't come here for that." Moss took another deep breath. He wished he could take a drink, too. "I came up here to see you."

"Oh, dear God," Laura Secord said quietly. She gathered herself. "Didn't you listen to a word I told you the last time you came here? If that's not madness, I don't know what is. You should have stayed wherever you were and gone on doing whatever you were doing."

"I did that," Jonathan Moss said. "For more than a year, I did that. When I couldn't do it any more, I came." He hesitated, then went on, "I heard in Arthur that your husband didn't come home. I'm very sorry, for whatever that may be worth to you."

"You decided to come up here without even knowing that?" she said in open astonishment, and he nodded. Maybe he was mad after all. She remarked, "He would have shot you, you know. He was very good with a rifle even before he went into the Army." Moss didn't say anything. He could think of nothing to say. Had she told him to go then, he would have got back into his motorcar and driven away without another word. Instead, she continued, "Come inside and have a cup of tea. I wouldn't turn out a mongrel dog in this weather before he had a cup of tea."

That did not strike him as the warmest commendation of his personal charms, if any, but it was kinder than anything she'd said to him the last time he was here. He followed her up the stairs and into the farmhouse. The stove was going in the kitchen, but not like the one in Peterson's general store. Laura Secord shoveled in more coal, filled the teapot from a bucket, and set it on the stove. As she busied herself in readying cups and tea, she kept shaking her head. Doing his best to make light of things, Moss said, "I really am a harmless fellow."

"If you really were a harmless fellow, you would have been shot down," she retorted. Then she pointed to a chair by the table. "Sit, if you care to. I can get you bread and butter." He sat and nodded. She served him, then tended to the tea when the pot started whistling.

No matter what he might have expected, the tea wasn't particularly good. It *was* hot. He gulped it, savoring the warmth it brought. It helped unfreeze his tongue, too: he said, "I came to tell you that, if there's ever anything you need—anything at all—let me know, and I'll take care of it."

"A knight in shining armor?" Her eyebrows rose.

Moss shook his head. "I thought of myself like that at the start of the war: a knight of the air, I mean. It didn't last, of course. War's a filthy business no matter how you fight it. But I'll do that for you. So help me God, I will. You're—special to me. I don't know how else to put it." He was more afraid of saying *love* than he had been of facing machine-gun bullets from a Sopwith Pup.

"You'd better go now," Laura Secord said. She wasn't reviling him, as she had the last time he'd come to her, but there was no give in her voice, either. "You mean to be kind; I'm sure you mean to be kind. But I don't see how I can take you up on . . . any part of that generous offer. When I see you, I see your country, too, and your country has destroyed mine. Find yourself an American girl, one who can forgive you for that." She laughed. "Melodramatic, isn't it? But life is sometimes."

He got to his feet. He'd known from the beginning the odds were against him—to put it mildly. "Here." He pulled a scrap of paper and pencil from his pocket and scrawled down three lines. "This is my address. What I said still goes. If you ever need me, let me know." He turned and left as fast as he could, so he wouldn't have to watch her crumple up the paper and throw it away. Soon he was driving back toward Arthur, and then back past Arthur, toward the life he'd done his best to toss out the window. He kept telling himself he was lucky. He had a devil of a time making himself believe it.

"This feels good," Reggie Bartlett said to Bill Foster as the two of them strolled through Richmond. "We haven't done it as much lately as we used to."

"Time has a way of getting on," Foster said, and Reggie nodded. His friend went on, "And we'd stop in a saloon for a beer afterwards, too. When a beer costs twenty-five dollars instead of five cents, stopping in a saloon doesn't seem like such a bully idea any more. My pay's gone up, sure, but it hasn't gone up as fast as prices have."

"It never does," Bartlett said with mournful certainty. This time, Bill Foster nodded. Reggie added, "And you've got to watch your money nowadays. After all, you're going to be a married man this time next month, and Sally's the sort of girl who deserves the best."

"I only hope I'll be able to give it to her." Foster's voice held worry. "How am I supposed to watch my money? All I can do is watch it go away. A dollar I put in the bank at the start of the year isn't worth a quarter now, even with interest."

"Watching money these days means spending it as soon as you get it," Reggie replied. "If you do anything else, you watch it shrink, like you said."

Foster sighed. "Didn't used to be this way. How are we supposed to get on with our lives if we can't even save money? The Freedom Party's right, if you ask me—we've got to put a stop to things before the whole country goes down the water closet."

"Yeah, we've got to put a stop to things," Reggie said. "That doesn't mean the Freedom Party is right. We heard those fellows going on and on when they were new as wet paint, remember? I thought they were crazy then, and I still think they're crazy."

They'd come a long way into the northwestern part of town, to the public square at the corner of Moore and Confederate Street (it had been Federal before the War of Secession). In spite of the chilly weather, somebody was holding a rally in the square: Confederate flags whipped in the breeze, and a gesticulating speaker stood on a platform of fresh yellow pine.

"Is that the Freedom Party again?" Bartlett asked. Then he spotted the signs behind the platform. "No, I see—it's the Radical Liberals. Want to listen, Bill?"

"Sure. Why not?" Foster said. "They have some interesting ideas. If they don't go off the deep end, the way they did when they nominated Arango in '15, I may vote for 'em for president in '21."

"Me, too." Reggie nodded. "That fellow up there, whoever he is, he doesn't look like he's ever gone off the deep end of anything in his whole life."

As he got closer, he noticed a placard identifying the speaker as Congressman Baird from Chihuahua. Waistcoated and homburged, Baird looked more like a banker than a Congressman. "We have to face the facts," he was saying as Reggie and Foster got close enough to hear. "We are not the top dogs any more. Our friends are not the top dogs any more. We can stick our heads in the sand and pretend things still are the way they were in 1914, but that won't do us any good. The war has been over for almost a year and a half, and most of the people in this country don't really understand that things have changed."

Bill Foster looked disgusted. "I take back what I said a minute ago. He wants us to go sucking up to the United States, and I'll see him and everybody else in hell before I lick Teddy Roosevelt's boots."

"We've got to do something," Reggie answered. "If we don't, it's $500 beer next month, or maybe $5,000 beer. They licked us. You going to tell me they didn't?" As if to remind him, his shoulder twinged.

While they were talking, so was Congressman Baird. Reggie started listening to him again in midsentence: "—whole continent, north and south and west alike, might be better off if we dropped our tariff barriers and the USA did the same. I don't say we ought to do that all at once, but I do say it is something toward which we can work, and something liable to lead to greater prosperity throughout America. We share a heritage with the United States; in their own way, the Yankees are Americans, too. We fought a revolution against England, but England became the Confederacy's friend. Even though we have fought wars against the United States, they too may yet become our friends."

"You want to hear any more of this, Reggie?" Foster asked. "If the sign didn't say this fellow was from Chihuahua, I'd reckon he snuck in from California or Connecticut or one of those damnyankee places."

"Damnyankees aren't as bad as all that. They don't have horns and tails," Reggie said. His friend gave him what was plainly meant for a withering look. He didn't wither, continuing, "They doctored me as well as anybody could, when it would have been easier for them to give up and let me die. All you did was fight 'em. They had me in their hands."

Foster was plainly unconvinced. But Congressman Baird got a bigger round of applause than Reggie Bartlett had really expected. Foster looked surprised at that, too. Grudgingly, he said, "Some people here think the way you do. I still don't see it, but I'll listen a while longer."

Buoyed by the cheers, Baird went on, "I don't say for a moment that we should not try to regain as much of our strength as we can. We must be able to defend ourselves. But we must also bear in mind the colossus to our north and west, and that, as I said, our friends have fallen by the wayside. We are on our own, in a world that loves us not. We would be wise to remember as much."

That made good sense to Reggie. The Whigs, who had dominated Confederate politics even more thoroughly than the Democrats had dominated those of the USA, still seemed stuck in the past without any notion of how to face the future. The Freedom Party and others of its ilk wanted to throw out the baby with the bathwater, although they quarreled over which was which. Baird, at least, had some idea of the direction in which he wanted the CSA to go.

His supporters in the crowd raised a chant: "Radical Liberals! Radical Liberals!" Whigs would never have done anything so undignified. But the Whigs didn't have to do anything undignified. They often seemed to think they didn't have to do anything at all. That, Reggie thought, was what holding power for half a century did to a party.

And then, from behind, another chant rose, or rather a furious howl: "Traitors! Filthy, stinking, goddamn traitors!" Reggie spun around. Charging across the yellowed grass were a couple dozen men armed with clubs and bottles and a variety of other improvised weapons. They all wore white shirts and butternut trousers. "Traitors!" they howled again, as they smashed into the rear of Congressman Baird's crowd. They howled something else, too, a word that made Bartlett's hair try to stand on end: "Freedom!"

The Congressman's voice rose in well-modulated indignation: "What is the meaning of this uncouth interruption?"

No one answered him, not in so many words. But the meaning was obvious even so—the newcomers were breaking up his rally, and breaking the heads of the people who'd been listening to him.

"Fight!" Reggie shouted. "Fight these bastards!"

A club whizzed past his ear, swung by a thick-necked, thick-shouldered chap screaming "Freedom!" at the top of his lungs. Reggie kicked him in the side of the knee as he ran past. Then, as the man started to crumple, he kicked him in the belly. He'd learned to fight fair once upon a time, and had to unlearn it in a hurry when he got to the trenches.

He grabbed the muscular goon's club after the fellow lost interest in holding it, then started swinging it at everybody in a white shirt he could reach. Some of the others at the rally were fighting back, too. Most Confederate white men had done a tour in the Army. They'd seen worse fights than this. But the attack force from the Freedom Party had size, ferocity, youth, and surprise on their side. They also had a joyful zest for the brawl unlike anything Reggie had encountered in the trenches.

He knocked two or three of them flat even so. But then somebody hit him from behind. He staggered and fell. A couple of people—one of them was Bill Foster, who was trying, with no luck at all, to play peacemaker—stepped on him, someone else kicked him in the ribs, and he decided to stay down, lest something worse happen to him.

The ruffians had just about completed routing the rally when police at last appeared. Half a dozen men in old-fashioned gray took billy clubs off their belts. Their leader blew a whistle and shouted, "That will be quite enough of that!"

"Freedom!" the goons bawled. All of them still on their feet rushed straight at the cops. They had one other thing Reggie Bartlett noticed only while prone: more than a little discipline. They fought like soldiers after a common goal, not like individual hell-raisers. The startled policemen went down like wheat under the blades of a reaper. Had one of them drawn a pistol . . . Had one of the Radical Liberals drawn a pistol . . . But no one had. The ruffians, or most of them, got away.

Slowly and painfully, Reggie dragged himself to his feet. He looked around for Bill Foster, and spotted him holding a handkerchief to a bloody nose. A couple of the fallen Freedom Party fighters were also rising. Reggie stooped to grab the club, though quick movement hurt. But showing he was ready to fight meant he didn't have to. The goons lifted a comrade who couldn't get up on his own and, with his arms draped over their shoulders, left the public square.

From up on the platform, Congressman Baird kept saying "This is an outrage! An outrage, I tell you!" over and over again. Nobody paid much attention to him. He wasn't wrong. That didn't make what he had to say useful.

"They break your nose, Bill?" Reggie asked.

"Don't think so." Foster felt of it. "No, they didn't. I just got hit, not clubbed or stomped."

"Bastards," Reggie said. That didn't seem nearly strong enough. He tried again: "Goddamn fucking sons of bitches." That didn't seem strong enough, either, but it came closer. He looked around for his hat, and discovered it had got squashed during the brawl. Picking it up, he asked, "Still like what the Freedom Party stands for?"

Foster suggested the Freedom Party do something illegal, immoral, and anatomically unlikely. His hat, when he found it, was in worse shape than Reggie's. Sadly, he dropped it back onto the grass. Then he said, "The thing is, though, plenty of people *will* like it. Damn hard to stomach anybody saying anything good about the United States. A couple of times, I wouldn't have minded walloping Baird myself."

"Thinking about it's one thing," Bartlett said. "Doing it, though . . ." He shook his head. "People won't be able to stomach that. No way in hell will people be able to stomach that." Bill Foster thought it over, then nodded. "People just aren't so stupid," Reggie said, and his friend nodded again.

Lieutenant Colonel Abner Dowling sat at his desk—because of his protruding belly, sat some distance behind his desk—clacking away at a typewriter. He would have starved to death in short order had he had to try to make his living as a secretary, but he was a good typist for an Army officer.

He wished he were out in the field instead of banging out a report no one would ever read here in a War Department office in Philadelphia. He'd wished he were in the field instead of back of the lines at First Army headquarters all through the Great War. He could have commanded a battalion, maybe a regiment—maybe even a brigade, considering how fast front-line officers went down. Of course, he might have gone down himself, but that was the chance you took.

"Dowling!" At the howl from behind him, he made a typographical error. Save that it held the sounds of his name, the howl might have burst from the throat of a trapped wolf.

"Coming, sir." He pushed the chair back far enough to let himself rise, then hurried into the larger, more spacious office behind his own. Sleet beat on the window that gave a blurry view of downtown Philadelphia. Even though it was freezing out there, a steam radiator kept the office warm as toast. Saluting, Dowling asked, "What can I do for you this morning, General Custer?"

Custer stared at him, through him. Dowling had seen that stare before. It meant Custer had been into the bottle he didn't know Dowling knew he had in a desk drawer. No: after a moment, Dowling realized the stare held more than that. Custer's pale, red-tracked eyes roamed the office. Again, he might have been a wild beast in a cage.

"What can I do for you, sir?" his adjutant repeated.

"Do for me?" Custer said slowly; he might have forgotten he'd summoned Dowling in the first place. "You can't do anything for me. No one can do anything for me, no one at all."

Dowling had heard Custer in a great many moods before, but never despairing. "What's wrong, sir?" he asked. "Is there anything I can do to help?"

"No, you can't help me, Major—uh, Lieutenant Colonel." Custer's wits weren't particularly swift, but he hadn't started turning forgetful. As the general continued, Dowling realized that was part of the problem: "I entered West Point in July 1857. July 1857, Lieutenant Colonel: sixty-two years ago come this summer. I have served in the United States Army longer than most men have been alive."

"And served with distinction, sir," Dowling said, which in its own strange way was true. "That's why you have four stars on each shoulder strap, sir; that's why you're here now, still serving your country, at an age when most men"—*are dead,* but he wouldn't say that—"are sitting in a rocking chair with pipe and slippers."

"What do you think I'm doing now, Dowling?" General Custer demanded. "I've been in the army almost sixty-two years, as I say, and in an active command during nearly the whole of that time." He waved a plump, age-spotted hand. "Where is my active command now, pray tell?"

He *was* feeling trapped, Dowling realized. Custer's adjutant picked his words with care: "Sir, there aren't a lot of active commands with the country at peace and our foes beaten. And your assignment here—"

"Is only sound and fury, signifying nothing," Custer broke in. "I have no duties: no duties that matter, at any rate. Evaluate the transmission of orders from corps headquarters to divisions and regiments, they told me. Jesus Christ, Dowling, it's a job for a beady-eyed captain, not for me!"

He had a point, a good point. To try to cheer him up, his adjutant had to ignore it. "No doubt they want the benefit of your long experience."

"Oh, poppycock!" Custer snapped. "Nonsense! Drivel! They've put me out to pasture, Lieutenant Colonel, that's what they've done. They don't give two whoops in hell whether I ever write this goddamn evaluation. Even if I do, no one will ever read it. It will sit on a shelf and gather dust. That's what I'm doing now: sitting on a shelf and gathering dust. They got all they could out of me, and now they've put me on the shelf."

"Everyone is grateful for what you did, General," Dowling said. "Would you have headed last year's Remembrance Day parade if that weren't so?"

"So Teddy Roosevelt was generous enough to toss an old dog one last bone," Custer said, a distinct sneer in his voice. "Ha! If he lives long enough, he'll go into the dustbin of the outmoded, too. And if the election returns from last November are any guide, he may get there faster than I have."

Dowling didn't know what to say to that. He judged Custer was likely to be right. The general formerly commanding First Army did have a makework assignment here in Philadelphia. But what else could he expect? He was going to be eighty at the end of the year. He couldn't very well hope to be entrusted with anything of real importance.

He could. He did. "Barrels!" he said. "That's where I want to be working. Sure as hell, Lieutenant Colonel, the Rebs are plotting ways to make theirs better even as we speak. I know they're not going to be allowed to have any, but they're plotting just the same. We'll fight another round with them, see if we don't. I may not live till then, but you will, I expect."

"Wouldn't surprise me if you were right, sir," Dowling said. No one in the U.S. Army trusted the Confederate States, no matter how peaceful they tried to make themselves seem.

"They need me on barrels," Custer said. "Those chowderheads

didn't know what to do with what they had till I showed them. They won't know how to make barrels better, either, you mark my words."

"Sir, there I don't really know if you're right or not," Dowling said, by which he meant Custer was talking through his hat. "Colonel Morrell is doing good work out in Kansas. I've seen a couple of the analyses he's sent in. They're first-rate. I was very impressed." He meant that. The more he had to do with Morrell, the more he was convinced the former commander of the Barrel Brigade would wear four stars long before his late seventies.

"Oh, Morrell's a sound lad, no doubt about that," Custer said, by which he meant Morrell had given him the victories he'd craved. "But he's only a colonel, and he's only a lad. Will they read his analyses, or will they just shelve them alongside of mine? They aren't soldiers here, Dowling; they're nothing but a pack of clerks in green-gray."

That held enough truth to be provocative, not enough to be useful. Dowling said, "Colonel Morrell will make himself noticed, one way or another."

Custer's thoughts were running down their own track, as they often did. He hardly noticed his adjutant's words. "Nothing but a pack of clerks in green-gray," he repeated. "And now they're making me a clerk, too. How am I supposed to turn into a clerk, Dowling, when I've spent the past sixty years as a fighting man?"

"Sir, I know this isn't your first tour at the War Department," Dowling said. "How did you manage before?"

"God only knows," Custer answered gloomily. "I sat behind a desk, the same as I'm sitting behind a desk now. Then, though, I had an Army to help reform. I had wars to look forward to. I had a purpose that helped me forget I was—stuck here. What have I got now? Only the desk, Lieutenant Colonel. Only the desk." His sigh ruffled his bushy mustache.

Exasperation. Fury. Scorn. Occasional astonished admiration. Horror. Those were the emotions Custer usually roused in Abner Dowling. That he should pity the ancient warrior had never crossed his mind till now. Setting Custer to makework was like harnessing an old, worn-out ex-champion thoroughbred to a brewery wagon. He still wanted to run, even if he couldn't any more.

Quietly, Dowling asked, "Can I get you anything, sir? Anything at all that might make you more comfortable?" Even if Custer told him he wanted an eighteen-year-old blonde—and Custer's asking for something along those lines would not have unduly surprised his adjutant, for he still fancied himself a ladies' man, especially when Libbie wasn't around—Dowling resolved to do his best to get him one.

But the general asked for nothing of the sort. Instead, he said, "Can you get me the president's ear? We still have soldiers in action, enforcing our rule on the Canadian backwaters we didn't overrun during the Great War. Even a command like that would be better than sitting around here waiting to die. And, by God, I still owe the Canucks more than a little. The British bastards who killed my brother Tom rode down out of Canada almost forty years ago. Even so late as this, revenge would be sweet."

Dowling wished he'd kept his mouth shut. He had no great desire to go traipsing up into the great American Siberia, no matter what Custer wanted. But, seeing the desperate hope on the old man's face, he said, "I don't know whether I can get President Roosevelt's ear or not, sir. Even if he hears me, I don't know whether he'll listen to me, if you know what I mean."

"Oh, yes." Custer nodded and looked shrewd. "It might be interesting to find out whether Teddy would enjoy keeping me here under his eye and useless better than he would knowing he's sent me to the ends of the earth. Yes, I do wonder how he'd decide there." Reluctantly, Dowling nodded. Teddy Roosevelt would be making exactly that calculation.

Even more reluctantly, Custer's adjutant telephoned Powel House, the president's Philadelphia residence. He was not immediately put through to Theodore Roosevelt. He hadn't expected to be. He left his name—and Custer's name, too—and how to reach him. If the president decided to call back, he would. If he decided not to . . . well, in that case, Dowling had made the effort.

Two days later, the telephone rang. When Dowling answered, a familiar gravelly voice on the other end of the line said, "This is Theodore Roosevelt, Lieutenant Colonel. What can I do for you and what, presumably, can I do for General Custer?"

"Yes, Mr. President, that's why I called," Dowling said, and explained.

A long silence followed. "He *wants* me to send him up there?" Roosevelt sounded as if he couldn't believe his ears.

"Yes, sir," Dowling answered. "He feels useless here at the War Department. He'd rather be doing something than vegetating. And he wants to rule the Canadians with a rod of iron, you might say, because of what happened to his brother during the Second Mexican

War." Loyally, Dowling refrained from offering his own opinion of a transfer to Canada.

"If Tom Custer hadn't got killed, we probably would have lost the battle by the Teton River, because our Gatling guns would have been wrongly placed," Roosevelt said. "But that's neither here nor there, now, I admit." The president paused. Dowling could almost hear the wheels going round inside his head. At last, he said, "Well, by jingo, if that's what General Custer wants, that's what he shall have. Let no one ever say I put my personal differences with him in the way of fulfilling the reasonable desires of the most distinguished soldier the United States have known since George Washington."

"Thank you, your Excellency, on General Custer's behalf," Dowling said. "You have no idea how pleased he'll be at going back under the saddle again."

"Our old warhorse." Roosevelt chuckled, a sound Dowling wasn't sure he liked. "Tell him to pack his long johns—and you pack yours, too, Lieutenant Colonel."

"Yes, sir." Dowling did his best to sound cheerful. His best, he feared, was far from good enough.

"**L**ies!" Julia McGregor furiously tossed her head. The flames in the fireplace caught the red highlights of her hair and made it seem about to catch fire, too. "The lies the Americans make the teachers tell!"

"What is it now?" her father asked. Arthur McGregor smiled grimly. The harder the Americans tried to indoctrinate his daughters, the more they shot themselves in the foot.

"They call the Tories traitors! They stayed loyal to their own king when everyone around them was rebelling, and for that the Americans call them traitors!" Julia was furious, all right. "I'd sooner be around people who stay loyal even if it costs them than a pack of fools who blow like weather vanes, whichever way the wind happens to catch them."

Maude looked up from her knitting. "She's your daughter," she remarked to her husband.

"That she is," McGregor said with no small pride. "My daughter, my country's daughter—not any American's daughter."

"I should say not," Julia exclaimed indignantly.

Mary shoved aside a piece of scratch paper on which she was practicing multiplication and division. "Pa, do the Yanks lie about nine times eight being seventy-two, too?" she asked, her voice hope-ful. "It would work a lot better if it were seventy-one."

"I'm afraid they're telling the truth there, chick," he answered. "Numbers don't change, no matter which side of the border they're on."

"Too bad," his younger daughter said. "I thought the Ameri-cans would lie about everything under the sun."

"They lie about everything that happened under the sun," Julia said. "But numbers aren't exactly things that happen under the sun. They're real and true all by themselves, no matter how you look at them."

"How does that make them different than anything else?" Mary asked.

Before Julia could answer, one of the kerosene lamps that helped the fireplace light the front room burned dry. The stink of lamp oil spread through the room. McGregor heaved himself up out of his chair and started over to get some kerosene to refill the lamp.

"Don't waste your time, Arthur," Maude said. "We're as near out as makes no difference."

"That's . . . too bad," he said; he did his best not to curse in front of his womenfolk. "Have to ride into town tomorrow and buy some more at Gibbon's general store. Can't go around wandering in the dark."

"Why not, Pa?" Mary said with a wicked smile. "The Yanks do it all the time."

"Hush, you," McGregor said, snorting. "Tend to your cipher-ing, not your wisecracks." Mary dutifully bent her head to the paper. Five minutes later, or ten, or fifteen, she'd come out with something else outrageous. He was as sure of it as of the sun coming up tomorrow morning.

When he drove out in the wagon the next morning, he was only half convinced the sun had come up. A thick layer of dirty gray clouds lay between it and him. In that murky light, the snow cover-ing the ground also looked gray and dirty, though most of it was freshly fallen. Under the wagon's iron tires, the frozen ground was as hard—though by no means as smooth—as if it were macadamized.

As usual, U.S. soldiers meticulously checked the wagon before letting McGregor go on into Rosenfeld. He had nothing to hide, not here: all his bomb-making paraphernalia remained hidden in his barn. After he'd taken his revenge on Major Hannebrink, who'd ordered his son executed, the urge to make his deadly toys had eased.

The Yanks hadn't rebuilt the sheriff's station after he bombed it.

All they'd done was clear away the wreckage. He smiled as he jounced slowly past the bare, snow-covered stretch of ground. It was not enough. Nothing could ever be enough to make up for losing Alexander. But it was something. It was more than most Canadians had, a lot more.

Rosenfeld was a far cry from the big city. It didn't hold even a thousand people. If two railroad lines hadn't met there, it might not have existed at all. Throughout the war, though, Americans had packed it to the bursting point, as it became a staging area and recuperation center for the long, hard campaign against Winnipeg.

Now, with just a small occupation garrison, it seemed much more nearly its old self than it had during the war years. People on the street nodded to McGregor. Why not? No need to bother avoiding his eyes. Alexander was two and a half years dead now: old news, to everyone but his family. No one knew McGregor had had his revenge. Had anyone known, the Yanks would have found out. They would have stood him against a wall, as they'd stood his son, and shot him down, too.

He hitched the horse on the main street in front of the post office. He couldn't have done that during the war; the Yanks had reserved the street for themselves. Digging in his pockets for some change, he went into the post office.

"Hello, Arthur," said Wilfred Rokeby, the postmaster. He was a small, fussily precise man who wore his hair parted in the middle and plastered down to either side with some spicy-smelling oil. "Didn't expect to see you coming into town quite so soon."

"Ran out of kerosene sooner than I thought I would." McGregor set a couple of dimes on the counter. "Long as I'm here, let me have some stamps, too, Wilf."

"I can do that," Rokeby said. He peeled ten red two-cent stamps from a sheet and handed them to McGregor. They were ordinary U.S. stamps, adorned with Benjamin Franklin's fleshy portrait, but had the word MANITOBA overprinted on them in black.

"At least we don't have to pay double any more, to help the singers and dancing girls come up here and perform for the Yankee soldiers," McGregor said, pocketing the stamps. "That was nothing but highway robbery."

"Things *are* settling down a mite," the postmaster said. "I hear some fellow's going to come up from Minnesota and start us a new weekly paper when the weather gets better. Been a long time since that bomb in front of Malachi Stubing's place shut down the old *Register.*"

That bomb had not been one of McGregor's. He hadn't been in the bombing business back then. He had been in Henry Gibbon's general store when the bomb went off. The Americans had almost taken him hostage after the blast. Frowning, he said, "One more way for the Yanks to peddle their lies."

"That's so," Rokeby admitted, "but it'll be good to have the town news, too, and all the advertising. We've missed it. You can't say we haven't, Arthur."

"Well, maybe," McGregor said, but then, as if to rebut himself, he added, "Minnesota." Shaking his head, he turned and walked out of the post office.

The general store was half a block up the street, and on the other side. Henry Gibbon was wiping his hands on his apron when McGregor came inside carrying a large sheet-iron can. A hot stove gave relief from the chill outside. "Didn't expect to see you for another week or ten days, Arthur," the storekeeper said. He raised an eyebrow almost to what would have been his hairline had his hair not long since retreated to higher ground.

"Ran out of kerosene." McGregor set the can on the counter with a clank. "Want to fill me up again?"

"Sure will," Gibbon said, and did so with a large tin dipper. When he was through, he put the top securely back in place and held out his right hand, palm up. "Five gallons makes sixty-five cents."

"Would only have been half a dollar before the war," McGregor said. The fifty-cent piece and dime he gave Gibbon were U.S. coins, the five-cent piece Canadian. More and more of the money in circulation came from the USA these days.

"During the war, you'd have been out of luck if you didn't have your ration book," Gibbon said with a massive shrug. "It's not as good as it was, but it's not as bad as it was, either."

He hadn't had a son killed. He could afford to say things like that. McGregor had, and couldn't. He started to head out the door, then checked himself. Gibbon might not know good and bad from the man in the moon, but he heard all the gossip there was to hear in Rosenfeld. "Has Wilf Rokeby got it straight? Is some fellow coming up from the United States to put out a paper here?"

"That's what I've heard, anyway," Gibbon answered. "Be right good to let folks know every week that I'm still alive and still in business."

"But a Yank," McGregor said. The storekeeper shrugged again. The notion didn't bother him. As long as he got his advertisements in the newspaper, he couldn't have cared less what else went in.

With a grunt, McGregor picked up the can of kerosene and went back out into the cold. He started across the street. A motorcar's horn blared at him. He froze like a deer—he hadn't paid the least attention to traffic. If the automobile hadn't been able to stop in time, it would have run him down.

It halted with its front bumper inches from him. It was a big open touring car, with a U.S. soldier who looked very cold driving and two men in buffalo robes and fur hats in the back seat. One of them looked older than God, with a beaky nose projecting from a wrinkled face. "Jesus Christ, I wanted to see what one of these little towns looked like," he said, his voice American-accented. "I didn't aim to kill anybody while I was doing it."

"Sorry, General Custer, sir," the driver said. His greatcoat didn't offer him nearly the protection from the bitter winter chill that a buffalo robe would have done.

"I think your wife had the right idea, sir," the younger man in back said. He was a porky fellow, porky enough that his blubber probably helped keep him warm. "You might have done better to stay on the train till we got up to Winnipeg."

"I'm supposed to be in charge of things," the old man said querulously. "How can I be in charge of things if I don't see for myself what the hell I'm in charge of?" He shook a mittened fist at McGregor. "What are you standing there for, you damn fool? Get out of the way!"

McGregor unfroze and took a few steps forward. The motorcar shot past him with a clash of gears; its tires spat snow up into his face. He stared after it. He'd learned about General Custer in school. During the Second Mexican War, he'd beaten General Gordon's British and Canadian army down in Montana, beaten it after the USA had agreed to a cease-fire. McGregor had assumed he was long dead till his name started cropping up in war news.

And now he was coming to Canada to be in charge of things? And not just to Canada but to Winnipeg, only a couple of days to the north even by wagon? McGregor hurried back to the wagon. Purpose had indeed leaked out of his life after he'd avenged himself on Major Hannebrink. Now, suddenly, it was back. This time, he wouldn't just be avenging himself. He'd be avenging his whole country.

Nellie Jacobs yawned, right in the middle of business hours. Edna laughed at her. "This is a coffeehouse, Ma," Nellie's daughter said. "If you're sleepy, pour yourself a cup."

"I've been drinking it all day long." Nellie punctuated her reply with another yawn. "I don't want another cup right now." She hesitated and lowered her voice so the couple of customers in the place wouldn't hear: "It hasn't tasted quite right, anyway. Did we get a bad batch of beans?"

"I don't think so," Edna Semphroch answered, also quietly. "Tastes fine to me. Nobody's said anything about it, either, unless somebody went and complained to you."

"No," Nellie admitted. She yawned again. "Goodness! I can't hold my eyes open. If this keeps up, I'm going to have to go upstairs and lie down for a while."

Edna said, "Sure, go ahead, Ma. Leave me with all the work." Maybe she was joking. On the other hand, maybe she wasn't.

In the end, Nellie didn't go upstairs. A few more customers had come in, and sticking Edna with all of them didn't seem fair. She got through the day, though by the end of it she felt as if she had a couple of sacks of cement strapped to her shoulders. "Oh, Lord, I'm beat," she said over the ham steaks and string beans and fried potatoes that made up supper.

"You look it," Hal Jacobs said sympathetically. "What have you been doing, to make yourself so tired?" Her husband looked worried. "Do you think it is something you ought to see the doctor about?"

"I haven't been doing anything special," Nellie answered, "but today—no, the past few days—I've felt like I was moving under water."

"Maybe you *should* go to a doctor, Ma," Edna said. "That ain't like you, and you know it ain't. You've always been a go-getter."

"Doctors." Nellie tossed her head. "They're all quacks. Half the time, they can't tell what's wrong with you. The other half, they know what's wrong but they can't do anything about it."

Neither her daughter nor her husband argued with her. If you had a broken arm, a doctor could set it. If you had a boil, a doctor could lance it. If you needed a smallpox vaccination, a doctor could give you one. But if you had the Spanish influenza, a doctor could tell you to stay in bed and take aspirin. And if you had consumption, he could tell you to pack up and move to New Mexico. That might cure you, or it might not. Doctors couldn't, and the honest ones admitted as much.

Nellie found herself yawning yet again. She covered her mouth with her hand. "Gracious!" she said. "I swear to heaven, I haven't felt this wrung out since I was carrying you, Edna."

The words seemed to hang in the air. Hal Jacobs' eyes widened. Edna's mouth fell open. "Ma," she said slowly, "you don't suppose . . . you don't suppose you're in a family way again, do you?"

"What a ridiculous notion!" Nellie exclaimed. But, when she thought about it, maybe it wasn't so ridiculous as all that. Her time of the month should have been . . . Her jaw dropped, too. Her time of the month should have come a couple of weeks before. She'd never thought of asking Hal to wear a French letter on the infrequent occasions when she yielded him her body. She hadn't even worried about it. She was far enough past forty that she'd figured having a baby was about as likely as getting struck by lightning.

She glanced cautiously up toward the ceiling. That was foolish, and she knew it. If a lightning bolt came crashing through, she'd never know what hit her.

"Are you going to have a child, Nellie?" Hal Jacobs asked in tones of wonder.

"I think—" Try as she would, Nellie had trouble forcing out the words. At last, she managed: "I think maybe I am."

Edna burst out laughing. No matter how tired Nellie felt, she wasn't too tired to glare. A moment later, her daughter looked contrite. "I'm sorry, Ma," Edna said. "I was just thinking that, if you had a baby now, it'd be almost like I had a baby now, and—" She dissolved in more giggles.

Hal looked delighted and awed at the same time. Softly, he said, "With my first wife, I had two children, two little girls. Neither one of them lived to be three years old. Now God has given me another chance, when I never thought He would." He bent his head in thanks.

Nellie wasn't nearly so sure she felt thanks. She hadn't figured on taking care of a child again—not unless Edna had misfortune strike her in the shape of a man (and Nellie could think of no more likely shape for misfortune to assume). And then Nellie started to laugh in the same way Edna had. "It *is* funny," she said. "It's funny now, anyways. Won't be so funny when the baby finally comes. I remember that."

"Oh, yes," Hal said. "I remember, too. It is much work. But you, Nellie, we must take the very finest care of you, to make sure everything goes on in exactly the way it should."

What he meant was, she was getting long in the tooth to have a baby. She couldn't get annoyed about that. For one thing, he'd put it very nicely. For another, she'd thought she was too long in the tooth herself.

Over a gap of half a lifetime, she remembered what bringing forth Edna had been like. Maybe, this time, she'd go to a hospital and have them stick an ether cone over her face. That was one other thing doctors were good for.

"Ma's a tough bird," Edna said with no small pride. She beamed at Nellie. Nellie could hardly recall her beaming before. "Aren't you, Ma?"

Before Nellie could answer, Hal said, "A woman in a delicate condition is in a delicate condition, which means she is . . . delicate, is what it means." He'd talked himself twice round a circle, hadn't said a single, solitary thing, and didn't realize it.

"I'll be all right," Nellie said. "This is something God meant women to do." *And if that doesn't prove God is a man, I don't know what does.* She didn't feel like a tough bird, but she didn't feel delicate, either. What she mostly felt was tired.

Edna said, "If you really are in a family way, Ma, why don't you go on upstairs? I'll do the dishes."

"Why, thank you, sweetheart." Nellie cherished every friendly gesture she got from Edna, not least because she didn't get that many of them. That she'd been watching Edna like a hawk for years never once entered her mind.

When she went upstairs and took off her corset, she sighed with relief. Before too long, she wouldn't be able to wear a corset any more. Her belly would stick out there for all the world to see. But she had a ring on the proper finger—she held up her hand to look at the thin gold circlet—so that was all right.

She sighed again when she lay down on the bed. She felt as if her bones were turning to rubber. She raised an arm and then let it flop limply to the mattress. She wasn't quite ready to fall asleep—though she knew she would be very soon—but she wasn't going anywhere, either.

Her eyes had just started to slide closed when Hal came into the bedroom. "I know we didn't think this would happen, Nellie," he said, "but it will be a blessing in our old age."

"I suppose so," Nellie said, not yet convinced but willing to be. She laughed once more. "I never thought I'd be a mother again at the age I am now."

"And I never expected to be a father," her husband answered. "You made me the happiest man in the world when you said you would be my bride, and you have made me the happiest man in the world since, too." Every hair in his mustache seemed to quiver with joy.

Nellie was a long way from the happiest woman in the world. A million dollars, a fancy house full of servants, and a rich, handsome husband for Edna would probably have turned the trick. But Hal was doing his best to make her happy, and she'd never had anyone do that before. "You're sweet," she told him. "Everything will be fine." Was she talking to herself as well as to her husband? If she was, who could blame her?

Hal said, "I shall have to get more business from the shop across the street."

"How do you aim do to that?" Nellie asked with genuine curiosity. The shoe-repair shop brought in a steady, reliable trickle of money. Building that trickle to anything more struck her as unlikely.

"I know what we need," her husband said: "another war and another invasion." He sighed. "Only the Confederates whose boots I made and mended would probably pay me in scrip, the way they did last time. But even with scrip, I made more from them during the war than from my regular customers before or after."

"I'd sooner be poor," Nellie said. Considering how she felt about money, that was no small assertion.

"So would I," Hal Jacobs said. "The United States have spent my entire life working to get even with the Rebels. Now that we have finally done it, I don't ever want them to have another chance to invade our beloved country. And, of course," he added, "now that our flag flies down to the Rappahannock, the Confederates would have a harder time reaching and shelling Washington than they did in the last two wars."

"I was just a little girl when they shelled the city during the Second Mexican War," Nellie said. "I thought the end of the world had come." Her expression grew taut. "And then I went through 1914, and I was sure the end of the world had come. And then I went through the shellings and bombings during the last few months of the war, and by the time they were through, I was wishing the end of the world would come."

"It was a very hard time," Hal agreed. "But you came through safe, and your lovely Edna, and so did I." He kissed her. "And now this! I never imagined it, but I am ever so glad it has happened."

Nellie wondered how glad he would be when she was bent over a bucket heaving her guts out. She remembered doing that for weeks and weeks when she was carrying Edna. She wondered how glad he would be when she was big as an elephant and couldn't find a comfortable position in which to sleep and had to get up to use the pot every hour on the hour. She wondered how happy he would be with the baby screaming its head off all night long three or four nights in a row.

She would find out. She glanced over at Hal Jacobs, who was gazing fondly at her. He'd made a better husband than she thought he would. Odds were he'd make a good father, too.

Nellie smiled. "If we have a little girl, you're going to spoil her rotten."

"I hope so!" Hal exclaimed. "And if we have a little boy, I expect to spoil him rotten, too. A son!" He blinked. Was he blinking back tears? "I never thought I might have a son. Never. Not for many, many years."

"Well, we don't know if you've got him yet," Nellie said. "We've still got a good many months to go before we find out." She yawned once more, enormously this time. "But I've only got a couple of minutes to go before I'm asleep." She closed her eyes, and discovered she didn't have even that long.

Jefferson Pinkard wished he could walk into a saloon and have himself a cold beer. He didn't feel like getting drunk, or so he told himself. He just wanted one schooner of beer, to take the edge off a bad mood. But Alabama had gone dry before the Great War. All the saloons were either padlocked and ankle-deep in dust or long since converted to some other way of separating a customer from his cash.

That didn't mean a thirsty man had to dry up and blow away. Some beer was sitting back in the icebox in Jeff's cottage. He didn't feel like going back there, though. He'd eyed Emily like a fox eyeing a henhouse ever since he came home from the war. That was more than a year and a half now: heading on toward two years. You couldn't keep watch every livelong minute of every livelong day.

Spring hadn't come to Birmingham yet, but it was on the way. The breezes weren't roaring down out of the freezing USA any more. They might not be very warm yet, but they blew off the Gulf of Mexico, wafting up a hint of Mobile, a hint of the subtropical, even though tree branches remained bare of leaves as skeletons were of flesh and all the grass on the lawns and in the parks was yellow and dead. Somewhere under the bark, somewhere under the ground, new life lurked, and would soon be bursting forth.

Maybe new life lurked somewhere under the ground for the Confederate States, too. If it did, Jefferson Pinkard couldn't sense it as he could the coming spring. He wanted renewal. The country needed renewal. He had no idea where to find it. Nobody else in the CSA seemed to know, either.

Birmingham had been a fine, bustling city before the war. Now it just idled along, like a steam engine running on about a quarter of the pressure it needed. The steel mills remained busy, but most of what they made went north as reparations for the damnyankees. No profit there for the foundry owners. And when they made no profit, the whole town suffered.

Some of the general stores and haberdasheries and furniture stores were recognizable only by the lettering on their windows, being empty, locked shells of their former selves, almost as parched and dead as the deceased saloons with which they shared business blocks. Others still survived. On a Saturday afternoon, though, they shouldn't have been surviving. They should have been thriving, full of steelworkers with money in their pockets to spend on a half-holiday.

Jefferson Pinkard had money in his pockets—more than two hundred dollars. "Hell of a lot of good that does me," he muttered under his breath. The way things were these days, you couldn't even get good and drunk on two hundred dollars. Maybe it was just as well the saloons were all deceased.

A man in a pair of denim pants and a shirt with one sleeve pinned up came out of a secondhand clothing store. Pinkard stopped short. Plenty of men in Birmingham these days had an arm gone above the elbow. But, sure enough, it was Bedford Cunningham, Jeff's best friend once upon a time.

"How are you today, Jeff?" Cunningham asked. He was as tall as Pinkard, and had been as burly when they were both down on the floor at the Sloss Works. Since being wounded, he'd lost a lot of flesh.

"All right," Pinkard answered shortly. He still remembered—he could never forget—what Bedford Cunningham and Emily had been doing when he'd walked into his cottage on leave. But if Bedford was here, he couldn't be back there doing anything with Emily now. That made Jeff somewhat better inclined toward him, enough so to ask, "What you doin' now?"

"I was heading over toward Avondale Park," Cunningham answered. "This new Freedom Party is holding a rally. I want to see what they have to say."

"Christ, Bedford, they're just politicians," Jeff said, now certain he had the excuse he needed not to go along. "You've heard one of 'em, you've heard 'em all. You've heard one of 'em, you've heard too many, too."

"These boys are supposed to be different," Bedford said. "They're the ones who've been banging heads up in Richmond, if you've been reading the papers." He essayed a small joke: "They've been banging heads up in Richmond even if you haven't been reading the papers."

As it happened, Jeff had been reading the papers, though not with so much attention as he might have. "Forgot the name of that outfit," he admitted. "I didn't know they got down here to Birmingham, either." He rubbed his chin. Bristles rasped; he needed a shave. "What the hell? I'll come along with you." Curiosity about the new party outweighed dislike and distrust for his old friend.

People—mostly working-class white men like Pinkard or his shabbier, out-of-work counterparts—straggled into the park and toward a wooden platform bedecked with Confederate flags. In front of the platform stood a row of hard-faced men in what might almost have been uniform: white shirts and butternut trousers.

"Don't reckon you want to pick a quarrel with those boys," Bedford Cunningham said.

"You wouldn't want to do it more than once," Jeff agreed. "They've all been through the trenches, I'll lay—they've got that look to 'em." Cunningham nodded.

On top of the platform prowled a thin man with lank brown hair. He kept looking out at the crowd, as if he wanted to launch into his speech but was making himself wait so more people could hear him. "He's seen the elephant, too," Bedford said. "That's what my grandpappy would call it, anyway."

"Yeah," Pinkard said. "Sure has." Even this long after the war, he usually had little trouble telling a combat veteran from a man who wasn't.

At last, unable to contain himself any more, the skinny man strode to the front edge of the platform. "Aren't you folks proud to be puttin' money in the damnyankees' pockets?" he called in a harsh but compelling voice. "Aren't you glad to be workin' your fingers to the bone so they can put their mistresses in the fancy motorcars they build out of the steel you make? Aren't you glad the fools and the traitors in Richmond blow kisses to the damnyankees when they

send 'em our steel and our oil and our money? They didn't make
those things, so why the devil should they care?"

"He's got something," Bedford Cunningham said.

Pinkard nodded, hardly noticing he was doing it. "Yeah, he
does." He waved a hand. "Now hush up, Bedford. I want to hear
what he has to say for himself."

"Do they remember, up there in Richmond, up there in the
Capitol, up there in that whited sepulcher, do they remember we
fought a war with the United States not so long ago?" the skinny
man demanded. "Do they? Doesn't look like it to me, friends. How
does it look to you?"

"Hell, no!" Jeff heard himself shout. His was far from the only
voice raised from the crowd. Beside him, Cunningham yelled louder
than he did. He grinned at his old friend, the first time he'd done
that since he'd caught him with Emily.

"Up there in Richmond, do they care if we're weak?" the
skinny man asked, and answered his own question: "No, they don't
care. Why should they care? All they care about is getting elected.
Nothing else matters to 'em. So what if the United States kick mud
in our face? We were a great country once, before the traitors in
Congress and the fools in the War Department stabbed us in the
back. We can be great again, if we want to bad enough. Do they
care, up there in Richmond? No, they don't care. Do you care, you
people in Birmingham?"

He could give the same speech in Chattanooga and just drop in
the different place-name and a couple of details. Jeff knew that.
Somehow, it didn't matter. It didn't matter at all. He felt the skinny
man was speaking to him alone, showing him what was wrong,
leading the way toward making it better. "Yes!" he yelled at the top
of his lungs, his voice one among hundreds, all crying the same
word.

"I don't blame the United States for doing what they're doing to
us," the skinny man said. "If I was in Teddy Roosevelt's shoes, I'd
try and do the same thing. But I blame those people up in Richmond
for letting him get away with it—no, by God, for helping him get
away with it. We ought to throw every one of those bastards on the
trash heap for that by itself. Before we stand tall again, we *have* to
throw 'em on the trash heap.

"But we've got more reasons than just that. They sat there sleeping while the niggers plotted and then rose up. And what did they do
after that? They said, fine, from here on out niggers are just as good

as white men. Tell me, friends, you reckon niggers are just as good as white men?"

"No!" roared the crowd, Jefferson Pinkard loud among them. Vespasian wasn't a bad fellow, and he did his job pretty well, but working alongside a white man didn't make him as good as a white man.

"Well, now, you see, you're smarter than they are up in Richmond," the Freedom Party speaker said. "Niggers aren't as good as white men, never were, never will be. Never *can* be, and the liars up in Richmond can't make 'em that way, even if they did give 'em the vote. The vote!" His voice rose to a furious, contemptuous howl. "I've got a donkey back in Richmond. I can whip him from now till doomsday, and he won't ever win a horse race. You can say a nigger's as good as a white man, but that doesn't make it so. Never has. Never will. Can't.

"We've got to give those fools up in Richmond the heave-ho and elect some people who can stand up to the United States and stand up for the white man here. That's what the Freedom Party is all about. We've got Congressional elections coming up this fall. I hope you'll remember us. I'm Jake Featherston. I'll be by again if the money holds out. You'll have somebody on the ballot here who thinks the way I do. Get on over to your polling place and vote for him." He waved to show he was done.

While the applause still thundered, a hat came through the crowd, as if to underscore that *if the money holds out.* Jeff pulled a hundred-dollar banknote out of his pocket and stuck it in the hat. He imagined doing such a thing back in 1914, or tried. He couldn't imagine *having* a hundred-dollar banknote in his pocket back then.

"There's a man who knows what we need," Bedford Cunningham said as the rally began to break up.

"Sure as hell is. Sure as hell does," Pinkard said. His voice was awed, almost as if he'd gone to church and been born again. He felt born again. Listening to Featherston made him believe the Confederate States could pull themselves together again. "I'd follow him a long way."

"Me, too," Cunningham said. "If whoever the Freedom Party runs is even a quarter as good on the stump as this Feathersmith—"

"Featherston," Jeff corrected; he'd listened with great attention to every word the skinny man said. "Jake Featherston."

"Featherston," Cunningham said. "If I like who they're running here, I'll vote for him. I've been a Whig a long time, but I'd change."

"So would I," Jefferson Pinkard said. "This Featherston, he knows what he's talking about. You can hear it in every word he says."

VI

For perhaps the first time in his professional life, Colonel Irving Morrell wished he were back in Philadelphia. Fighting arguments about barrels by way of letters and telegrams from Leavenworth, Kansas, was not getting the job done in the way he would have hoped. Letters and wires were all too easy to ignore.

"What can we do, Colonel?" Lieutenant Jenkins asked when the latest unsatisfactory reply came back from the War Department. "We should have a design ready to build now, and we're not even close."

"Damned if I know, Lije," Morrell answered. He tapped the papers with the tip of his index finger. "I think we would have a design by now, if the budget were what people thought it was going to be when they set up the Barrel Works."

"Miserable Socialists," Jenkins said angrily. "They're trying to take away everything we won on the battlefield."

"They're not making anything easy for us, that's for sure," Morrell said. "I want to make hay while the sun shines, if you know what I mean. You have to figure the Rebs won't stay down forever. The farther ahead of them we are when they do start getting back on their feet, the better I'll like it."

"Yes, sir," Jenkins said. "We'd be a lot better off, sir, if they'd listen to you more. If they don't want to listen to you, why did they send you out here in the first place?"

"To get me out of their hair, for one thing," Morrell answered. "To drive me out of my mind, for another. These days, they're so worried about spending money that they're trying to build barrels on the cheap. I don't know how many times I've explained and explained and explained that the engines in our machines aren't strong enough to do the job, but what sort of answer do I get? What it boils down to is, 'They did the job in the last war, so of course they'll do the job in the next one, too.' " He looked disgusted.

So did Lije Jenkins. "With that kind of thinking, we'd have gone into the Great War with single-shot black-powder Springfields."

Morrell nodded. "You understand that, and I understand that. The War Department understands it can get White truck engines—even the ones built in mirror image to pair with the regular model—in carload lots, cheap as it wants. Coming up with something better won't be anywhere near as cheap. And cheap counts. Right now, cheap counts a lot."

"Are they going to leave our country's safety hanging on nickels and dimes?" Lieutenant Jenkins demanded indignantly. He was still very young, young enough to believe in the tooth fairy, the common sense of Congress, and a great many other unlikelihoods.

"Probably," Morrell said, at which the lieutenant looked as if he'd just watched his puppy run over in the street. Trying not to smile, Morrell went on, "They spent twenty years after the War of Secession tossing the Army nickels and dimes and not much more, remember. They paid for it, too, but that doesn't mean they can't do it again."

"They'd have to be crazy," Jenkins exclaimed.

"No, just shortsighted," Morrell said, shaking his head. "I think it was President Mahan who noted that the biggest trouble republics have is that, over time, the voters are apt to get tired of paying for what their country needs to defend itself. They'd sooner spend the money on bread and circuses, or else not spend it and keep it in their own pockets."

"After everything we've gone through, sir, that would be a crime," Jenkins said.

"You think so, and I think so, and the War Department thinks so, too," Morrell replied, this time with a shrug. "The voters don't think so. They've sent a lot of Socialists to Congress this year. We do what we can with what we have, that's all. If we haven't got much, we do what we can with that. Pharaoh made the Israelites make bricks without straw."

"A crime," Lieutenant Jenkins repeated. He wasn't old enough to recall the cheeseparing the Army had had to put up with during the dark years after the War of Secession. Neither was Morrell, but he'd listened to older soldiers grouse about it ever since he'd put on a green-gray uniform. General Custer, under whom he'd served in Tennessee, had been through it all.

And now, he'd heard, Custer was up in Canada, in charge of the soldiers bringing U.S. authority to a land larger than the United States. He didn't know how the old warhorse would shape in that assignment. It didn't seem to call for the slam-bang drive that characterized Custer's fighting style. On the other hand, Morrell would have preferred it to sitting behind a desk in Philadelphia. No doubt Custer did, too.

Morrell dismissed his former commander from his mind. He glanced over at Lije Jenkins, who still looked unhappy with the world. "The only thing we can do is our best," Morrell said. A cuckoo came out of the clock on the wall and announced six o'clock. Morrell grinned. "The other thing we can do now is head over to the mess hall and get supper. And after that, didn't I hear something about a dance in town tonight?"

"Yes, sir." Jenkins' eyes sparkled. "I'm going over there. You feel like cutting a rug, too, sir?" He eyed Morrell with a certain bemused curiosity.

Morrell had all he could do to keep from laughing out loud. "I'm not a great-grandfather ready for the boneyard yet, Lieutenant," he said. "There's still some juice left in here." He set a hand over his chest and grinned wickedly. "After supper, shall we race over to the dance hall?"

"Uh, no, sir," Jenkins said. "You ran me into the mud out on the practice range. I figure you can probably do the same thing on sidewalks." His grin had a wicked touch, too. "But, sir, there'll be girls there, you know."

"I should hope so," Morrell said. "You don't think I'd want to waltz or foxtrot with an ugly customer like you, do you?" As a matter of fact, Lieutenant Jenkins was a handsome young man. That still didn't mean Morrell wanted to dance with him.

Morrell was heading toward thirty now, and had never come close to acquiring a wife. His eye had always been on the war ahead, as the eyes of the United States had been. But now the war was over and won, and single-minded devotion to duty was looking harder and less desirable not only to the country but also to Irving Morrell.

He did not head for the dance with Lieutenant Jenkins seriously expecting to find a wife the minute he stepped out onto the floor. That would have been unreasonable in the extreme, and he knew it. But if he did find a young lady, a lady he found attractive, he was ready and more than ready to pursue the matter and see where it led. He nodded as he left Fort Leavenworth. He'd never had that kind of determination before, not about anything except the battlefield.

Leavenworth, Kansas, was a town of about twenty thousand people. Not all of them served the fort, by any means. Many mined the large coal deposits in the area, while others worked in flour and lumber mills. But, regardless of whether the locals worked for the Army or not, soldiers got solid respect in Leavenworth. It had been an antislavery settlement back in the days before the War of Secession, when the South tried to make Kansas a slave state. Only the oldest of the old-timers recalled those days now, but the tradition of hatred for the Confederacy ran strong here, as it did in much of Kansas.

Morrell and Jenkins strode past a large bronze statue of John Brown the citizens of Leavenworth had erected after the Second Mexican War. Brown was and always had been a hero to many Kansans. He'd become a national hero during the 1880s, when people in the United States began to see that he'd known what he was doing when he'd attacked the Southerners not only here but also in their own lair down in Virginia.

The dance was at a social hall next to a white-painted Baptist church with a tall steeple, a spare building that might have been transported bodily from New England to the prairie. Sounds of piano and fiddle music drifted out into the night. "That's not the best playing I've ever heard," Morrell said, which was, if anything, a generous assessment, "but they do go right after a tune."

"Yes, sir," Jenkins answered. "Now we just have to hope it's not one of the dances where they've got maybe half a dozen girls and five hundred guys waiting to dance with them. A little bit of that kind goes a long way."

It was chilly outside; a coal stove and the dancers' exertions heated the social hall, so that a blast of warm air greeted Morrell when he opened the door. After looking around, he nodded approval: men did not hopelessly outnumber women. Not all the men were soldiers—close to half wore civilian clothes. Morrell had never feared competition of any sort.

A punch bowl sat on a table at the far end of the hall. He went over to it, got himself a glass, and leaned against the wall, watching couples spin and dip more or less in time to the music. Scouting the terrain before advancing was a good idea in other things besides warfare.

Lije Jenkins, on the other hand, plunged straight into the fray, cutting in on a civilian in a sharp suit. The fellow gave him a sour look as he retired toward the sidelines. Leavenworth might have liked soldiers pretty well, but cutting in like that was liable to start a brawl anywhere.

With a final raucous flourish, the little three-piece band stopped its racket. People clapped their hands, not so much to applaud the musicians as to show they were having a good time. Men and women headed over to the punch bowl. Morrell quickly drained his own glass and, with the empty glass as an excuse, contrived to get to the bowl at the same time as a woman in a ruffled shirtwaist and maroon wool skirt.

He filled the ladle, then, after catching her eye to make sure the liberty would not be unwelcome, poured punch into her glass before dealing with his own. "Thank you," she said. She was within a couple of years of thirty herself, with hair black as coal, brown eyes, and warm brown skin with a hint of blush beneath it. When she took a longer look at Morrell, one eyebrow rose. "Thank you very much, Colonel."

He was, he suddenly realized, a catch: glancing around, he saw a couple of captains, but no soldiers of higher rank. Men were not the only ones playing this game. Well, on with it: "My pleasure," he said. "If you like, you can pay me back by giving me the next dance."

"I'll do that," she said at once. "My name is Hill, Agnes Hill."

"Very pleased to meet you." Morrell gave his own name. The musicians struck up what was no doubt intended to be a waltz. He guided her out onto the dance floor. He danced with academic precision. His partner didn't, but it mattered little; the floor was so crowded, couples kept bumping into one another. Everyone laughed when it happened: it was expected.

They talked under and through the semimusical racket. "My husband was killed in the first few weeks of the war," Agnes Hill said. "He was up on the Niagara front, and the Canadians had lots of machine guns, and—" She shrugged in Morrell's arms.

"I'm sorry," he answered. She shrugged again. Morrell said, "I got shot myself about that time, in Sonora. Only reason I'm here is luck."

His dancing partner nodded. "I've thought about luck a lot the past few years, Colonel. That's all you can do, isn't it?—think, I mean." She whirled on with him for another few steps, then said, "I'm glad you were lucky. I'm glad you are here." As the music ended, Morrell was glad he was there, too.

* * *

Lucien Galtier did not converse with his horse while driving up to Rivière-du-Loup, as he usually did. The horse, a heartless beast, seemed to feel no lack. And Galtier had conversation aplenty, for, instead of going up to the town by the St. Lawrence alone, he had along Marie, his two sons, and the three daughters still living at home with them.

"I can't wait to see the baby," Denise said. She'd been saying that since word came from Leonard O'Doull that Nicole had had a baby boy the evening before.

"I want to see Nicole," Marie said. "Not for nothing do they call childbirth labor." She glared at Lucien, as if to say it was his fault Nicole had endured what she'd endured. Or maybe she was just thinking it was the fault of men that women endured what they endured.

Soothingly, Galtier said, "All is well with Nicole, and all is well with the baby, too, for which I give thanks to the holy Mother of God." He crossed himself. "And I also give thanks that Nicole gave birth with a doctor attending her who was so intimately concerned with her well-being."

"Intimately!" Marie sniffed and slapped him on the leg. Then she sniffed again, on a slightly different note. "A midwife was plenty good for me."

"A midwife is good," Lucien agreed, not wanting to quarrel with his wife. But he did not abandon his own opinion, either. "A doctor, I believe, is better."

Marie didn't argue with him, for which he was duly grateful. She kept looking around, as if she didn't want to miss anything her sharp eyes might pick up. She didn't get off the farm so often as he did, and wanted to make the most of the excursion in every way. After a bit, she said, "Traveling on a paved road all the way to town is very nice. It is so smooth, the wagon hardly seems to be moving."

"Traveling on a paved road all the way to town is even better when it rains," Galtier said. The road had not been paved for his benefit. Paving had been extended as far out from Rivière-du-Loup as his farm only because the Americans then occupying Quebec south of the St. Lawrence had built their hospital on land they'd taken from his patrimony, not least because he hadn't cared to collaborate with them.

And now his daughter had collaborated on a half-American

child. He shook his head. He had not expected that. He had not expected it, but he welcomed it now that it was here.

Clouds drifted across the sky, hiding the sun more often than they let it show through. Snow still lay on the ground to either side of the road. More might fall at any time in the next month. The calendar said it was April, and therefore spring, but the calendar did not understand how far winter could stretch in this part of the world. Lucien and his wife and children were as well muffled as they would have been going out in January, and needed to be.

Here and there, bomb craters showed up as dimples under the snow. British and Canadian aeroplanes had done what they could to harm the Americans after their soldiers were driven north across the river. But now the wounds in the land were healing. The antiaircraft guns that had stood outside of Rivière-du-Loup—guns manned at the end of the war by soldiers in the blue-gray of the new Republic of Quebec—were gone now, stored away heaven only knew where. Lucien hoped they would never come out of storage.

Rivière-du-Loup itself perched on a spur of rock jutting out into the St. Lawrence. Inside its bounds, a waterfall plunged ninety feet from the small river that gave the town its name into the greater one. In the late seventeenth century, when Rivière-du-Loup was founded, it would have been a formidable defensive position. In these days of aeroplanes and giant cannons, Galtier wondered if there were any such thing as a formidable defensive position.

His daughter and son-in-law lived only a couple of blocks from Bishop Pascal's church, not far from the market square. Galtier reckoned that a mixed blessing; the bishop—who had been simply Father Pascal when the war began—had jumped into bed with the Americans so quickly, he had surely endangered his vows of celibacy. There were still times when Lucien had mixed feelings about the way the war had gone. He suspected he would have those times as long as he lived.

The houses on either side pressed close to that of Dr. Leonard O'Doull. "How cramped things are here in the city," Marie said, and clucked in distress. Lucien was inclined to agree with her. Coming into town on market day was all very well, but he would not have cared to live here.

As he was tying the horse to an apple tree in front of the house, Dr. O'Doull opened the door and waved. "Come in, all of you," he called in his ever more Quebecois French. "Nicole can't wait to see you, and of course you will want to see little Lucien."

Galtier froze in his tracks. Slowly, he said, "When you sent word, you said nothing of naming the baby after me."

"When I sent word, we had not yet decided what we would name the baby," his son-in-law returned. "But Lucien O'Doull he shall be." He reached into his pocket and held out cigars. "Come on. Smoke with me. It's the custom in the United States when a man has a son."

If the cigars were anything like the ones O'Doull usually had, Galtier would have been glad to smoke one regardless of whether he had a grandson or not. Shaken out of his startled paralysis, he hurried toward the house.

A coal fire in the fireplace held the chill at bay. Nicole sat in a rocking chair in front of the fire. She was nursing the baby, and did not get up when her family came in. She looked as if she'd been through a long spell of trench warfare: pale and battered and worn. Had Galtier not seen Marie look the same way after her children were born, he would have been alarmed. His other children, who did not remember such things so well, were alarmed. Even Georges had no snide comments ready.

Marie spoke in tones of command: "When he is finished there, hand him to me."

"Yes, Mother. It shouldn't be long." Nicole sounded battered and worn, too.

Lucien Galtier stared at Lucien O'Doull as he nursed. The baby looked very red and wrinkled, its head somewhat misshapen from its passage out into the world. His children exclaimed about that, too. He said, "Every one of you looked the same way when you were born."

Georges said, "Surely I was much more handsome."

"What a pity it hasn't lasted, then," Denise said. She and her sisters laughed. So did Charles. Georges looked something less than amused.

Presently, Nicole lifted the baby from her breast to her shoulder. She patted him on the back. Lucien would have patted harder, but he'd had more practice than his daughter; he realized babies didn't break. After a while, his grandson gave forth with a belch a grown man would not have been ashamed to own.

"Good," Marie said. "Very good. Now he is settled. Now you will give him to me." Nicole held the baby out with great care. Marie took him with an automatic competence she would never lose, supporting his head in her right hand as she shifted him into the crook of her left arm. "He is so small," she murmured, as little Lucien flailed his arms at random. "When you have not had one in the house for a while, you forget how small a newborn baby is."

"He's a good-sized fellow," Leonard O'Doull said. "Almost eight pounds."

"He felt like an elephant when I was having him," Nicole added.

Marie ignored them both. "So small," she crooned. "So small."

"Here, give him to me," Lucien said. His wife gave him a dirty look, but passed him the baby after another minute or so. He discovered he still knew how to hold an infant, too. His tiny namesake stared up at him from deep blue eyes. He knew they would get darker over time, but how much darker might prove an interesting question: Leonard O'Doull had green eyes. Galtier murmured, "What are you thinking, little one?"

"What can he be thinking but, *Who is this strange man?*" Georges said.

"He could be thinking, *Why is this man about to clout his son in the side of the head?*" Galtier returned. He and Georges were both laughing. Had Lucien tried clouting his son in the side of the head, he suspected Georges could and would have made him regret it.

O'Doull said, "He probably *is* thinking, *Who is this strange man?*" Before Galtier could do more than raise an eyebrow, his son-in-law went on, "He is also thinking, *What is this strange world?* Everything must seem very peculiar to a baby: lights and sounds and smells and touch and all the rest. He never knew any of that before, not where he was."

Galtier found it indelicate to mention where the baby had been before he was born. By their expressions, so did both his sons. He reminded himself O'Doull was a doctor, and thought differently of such things.

"Let me hold the baby now, Father," Denise said. As Lucien handed his grandson to her, someone knocked on the front door.

"Who's that?" O'Doull said in some annoyance. Then he laughed at himself. "Only one way to find out, *n'est-ce pas?*" He opened the door.

There stood Bishop Pascal, plump and pink and looking as impressive as a plump, pink man could in miter and cope and cassock. He almost always had a broad smile on his face, and today was no exception. "Did I hear correctly that this house had a blessed event last night?" he asked, and then, seeing little Lucien in Denise's arms, he pointed. "Oh, very good. Very good indeed. I see that I did hear correctly." His eyes twinkled. "I am glad to know that my sources of information remain good."

What he meant was, *I am glad my spies are on the job.* Lucien understood that perfectly well. If O'Doull didn't, it wasn't because Galtier hadn't told him. But Bishop Pascal was not an overt foe to Galtier these days, and had never been a foe to any American: on the contrary. Dr. O'Doull said, "Come in, your Grace, come in. Yes, Nicole had a little boy last night." He handed the bishop a cigar.

"How wonderful!" Bishop Pascal exclaimed. He held out his arms. Denise glanced at Galtier, who nodded ever so slightly. She passed the bishop the baby. He proved to know how to hold him. Beaming, he asked, "And how is he called?"

"Lucien," Leonard O'Doull answered.

"Ah, excellent!" No, Bishop Pascal never stopped smiling. He aimed that large mouthful of teeth at Galtier. "Your name goes on." Lucien nodded. Bishop Pascal turned back to O'Doull. "You should make sure that, as this little fellow grows up, he learns your language as well as the tongue of the Republic of Quebec."

He surely meant it as good advice. It probably was good advice. It made Galtier bristle all the same. Leonard O'Doull answered in a mild voice: "These days, and I expect the rest of my days, the language of the Republic of Quebec *is* my language."

"I meant no offense," Bishop Pascal said quickly. "With the world as it is today, though, knowing English will help a young man throughout his life."

That had been true before the war. It was, as the bishop had said, likely to be even more true now, with Quebec so closely involved with the USA. That didn't mean Lucien had to like it worth a damn, though, and he didn't.

Sylvia Enos lit a cigarette. She sucked smoke down into her lungs, held it there, and blew it out again. Then she took another drag. She didn't feel nearly the exhilaration she had when she'd started the habit, but she did enjoy it. When she couldn't smoke, as on the line at the galoshes factory, she got tense, even jittery. Like so many of the other women working there, she'd taken to sneaking smokes in the restroom. The place always smelled like a saloon.

Then she had to return to the line. Into the can of paint went her brush. She painted a red ring around the top of one of the black rubber overshoes sitting there in front of her, then around the other, working fast so the endless belts of the factory line would not carry them away before she could finish.

Another pair of galoshes, still warm from the mold, appeared before her. She put rings on them, too. Down the line they went. The next girl, armed with knives and shears, trimmed excess rubber from the galoshes. She threw the scraps into a bin under her foot. When the bin filled, the scraps would go back into the hopper along with fresh rubber, to be made into new overshoes. The factory wasted nothing and did everything as cheaply as possible. That was why Sylvia still had a job. Had a man taken it, they would have had to lay out a little more money every week.

After a while, the stink of rubber started to give her a headache. That happened every morning by ten o'clock. It also gave her another reason to wish for a cigarette, or maybe a whole pack. What she'd discovered the first day she lit up got truer the more she smoked: tobacco did blunt her sense of smell.

Frank Best headed her way. She groaned silently; the foreman was carrying an overshoe where she'd missed part of the red line around the top. She knew what he'd say before he said it. That didn't stop him: "Thought you were going to slip this one by, didn't you?"

"I'm sorry, Mr. Best," Sylvia said. She didn't want him to have any kind of hold on her. "Here, give it to me. I'll fix it."

He held on to it. "You know, Sylvia, it really is too bad I have to take one out of a pair like this. It holds up the line and delays everybody. I hope I won't have to do it very often from now on."

He was holding up the line, too, by lecturing her. She didn't say so; she knew a lost cause when she saw one. "I'll do my best not to let it happen again," she said. "Please let me fix it."

At last, Best did. As if she were Leonardo working on the *Mona Lisa,* Sylvia completed the red ring. She handed the rubber overshoe back to Best. *Please,* she thought. *Take it back to wherever you spotted it and leave me alone.* Lectures were one thing, and bad enough. The rest of his routine was worse.

That didn't keep him from trotting it out. "You really should pay more attention to what you're doing," he said. "I would be disappointed, and I know you would be, too, if you made mistakes like this very often. Work is sometimes hard to find these days."

"Mr. Best, I *don't* make mistakes like this very often," Sylvia answered. "You've said so yourself."

He went on as if she hadn't spoken: "If the people above you are happy with you, though, things are liable to go a lot better for you."

She knew how he wanted to be above her: on a bed in some cheap hotel room. She found the idea more appalling than appealing. Now that George was gone, she did have times when she missed a man, sometimes very much. Frank Best, though, was emphatically not the man she missed.

Not understanding him seemed the safest course here. "I'll be extra careful from now on, Mr. Best. I promise I will."

He gave her a sour look. She wondered if he would make himself plainer. If he said, *Sleep with me or lose your job,* what would she do? She'd get up and quit, that was what. Maybe her expression said as much, for he turned and walked away, muttering under his breath.

Sylvia got back to work. She took extra care with the rings all morning long. If Best wanted an excuse to bother her, he'd have to invent one; she didn't want to give him any. She felt his eye on her more than once, but pretended not to notice. At last, the lunch whistle blew.

"Was Frank singing his little be-nice-or-else song at you?" Sarah Wyckoff asked, gnawing on a chicken leg probably left over from supper the night before.

"He sure was." Sylvia took a fierce bite of her own sandwich, which was made from day-old bread and sausage that tasted as if it were about half sawdust. For all Sylvia knew, it was. It cost half as much as a better brand. That mattered.

"He has no shame," May Cavendish said. "None."

"He's a foreman," Sarah said. "Of course he has no shame."

"A foreman at the canning plant where I used to work got one of the girls there in a family way," Sylvia said. Her friends made sad clucking noises and nodded knowingly. "I never found out if he married her afterwards or not—I got fired because I had to take care of my kids when they caught the chicken pox."

She thought Isabella Antonelli would have come and let her know if everything had turned out all right. She hadn't seen the other woman from the canning plant in a long time. That might have meant Isabella was deliriously happy and didn't need her any more. It was more likely to mean the foreman from the canning plant had left her in the lurch. Sylvia wondered if she'd ever find out what had happened. Life didn't tie up every loose end with a neat bow, the way novels did.

"That's just like a man." Sarah Wyckoff studied her own brawny forearm. "Nobody's going to trifle with me, not and keep his teeth he won't."

May sighed. "Men make it so you don't want to live with them, and they make it so you can't hardly make a living by yourself. You don't make as much as a man would doing the same job, and they don't let you do half the jobs anyhow. You tell me what's fair about that."

"If they didn't pay us less than they would a man, we wouldn't have these jobs we've got here," Sylvia said. The other two women nodded.

"And they won't let us vote here in Massachusetts, either," May said bitterly. "They've got to pass a law that says we can, and who's got to pass it? Men, that's who. You think more than half the men over at the New State House are going to vote for women? Hasn't happened yet, and I'm not going to hold my breath, either."

"There are a lot of states where it did happen." Sylvia's voice was wistful. "The world didn't end, either."

"You'd figure it did, the way some men carry on," Sarah said. "May's right. They aren't worth the paper they're printed on."

May ate an apple down to a very skinny core, then took out a pack of cigarettes. She lit one, then blew an elegant smoke ring. "I like a smoke after I eat," she said. "Sort of settles what's in there, if you know what I mean."

"I sure do." Sylvia got out her own cigarettes. The front of the pack showed soldiers in green-gray marching to victory. Nobody ever showed the mangled corpses of soldiers in green-gray and sailors in Navy blue who didn't live to see victory. Sylvia never would have thought that way if she hadn't lost George. Now, deliberately, she turned the pack over so she wouldn't have to see those pink-cheeked soldiers. "Thanks for giving me a cigarette that time, May. I like 'em now."

"Good." May Cavendish had been about to put her cigarettes back into her handbag. She stopped and aimed the pack at Sarah. "Want to try 'em?"

"No, thanks." Sarah shook her head. "I've smoked a couple of times. Never liked it enough to keep up with it. Don't expect I would now, either."

"Have it your own way," May said with a shrug. She did put away the pack.

Sylvia smoked her cigarette with determination. She coughed only once. Her chest was getting used to tobacco smoke, too. And May was right: even without the buzz she'd got when first starting the habit, a smoke after dinner or supper was more enjoyable than just about any other time.

George had liked to smoke after they made love. Sylvia's ears heated as she remembered that. She wondered what taking a deep drag while lazy in the afterglow would be like. *Probably pretty nice,* she thought. Would she ever have the chance to find out?

"There have to be some decent men out there somewhere," she said suddenly.

"A lot of them are dead," Sarah said. "My Martin is." She sighed and looked down at the grimy wood of the floor. "I still can't think about him without wanting to puddle up. I don't even know if I'd ever want to be with anybody else."

"I would, if I could find somebody," May said. "But a lot of the men who are decent are settled down with their wives, on account of that's what decent men do, and a lot of men, whether they're decent or not, don't want anything to do with you if you've got children."

"Oh, there's one thing they want to do with you," Sylvia said. Both her friends laughed at the obvious truth in that. Sylvia went on, "But those aren't the decent ones. Maybe I ought to go to church more often, but Sunday's the only chance I have to rest even a little, not that I can get much with two kids in the house."

"Plenty of men who go to church every livelong Sunday aren't what you'd call decent, either," May said, sounding as if she was speaking with the voice of experience. "They don't go there to pray or to listen to the sermon—they go on account of they're on the prowl."

"That's disgraceful," Sylvia said.

"Sweetheart, there's a whole lot of disgraceful things that go on in this world," Sarah Wyckoff said with authority. "You don't have to look no further than Frank Best if you want to see some."

"Well, heaven knows that's true," Sylvia said with a sigh. "Now that I've told him no, I only hope he leaves me alone and doesn't take it out on me like he said he was liable to."

"All depends," said May, who'd been at the galoshes factory longer than Sylvia. "If he finds somebody who goes along with him before too long, he'll forget about you. If he doesn't, you may not have such a good time for a while."

Sylvia wondered how she ought to feel about hoping some other young woman succumbed to what Best thought of as his fatal charm. It would make her own life easier, no doubt about that. But would she wish the foreman on anyone else? She couldn't imagine disliking anyone enough to hope she suffered such a fate.

When the whistle announcing the end of the lunch hour blew, she headed without enthusiasm back to her position just behind the galoshes molds. She reminded herself to do the best job she could painting rings on the rubber overshoes, to give Frank Best no reason to bother her.

But would he need an excuse? Here he came. That wasn't blood in his eye. Sylvia recognized the expression. George had often worn it when he'd been away at sea for a long time. Frank Best hadn't been, though she would cheerfully have dropped him off a pier. He wore the expression anyhow. Sylvia sighed. The end of the day seemed years away.

Sometimes, Roger Kimball still wished he'd gone to South America. Every so often, the Charleston papers gave tantalizing bits of news about the fighting that continued down there even though the Great War was over everywhere else. The local enmities had started long before the war, and weren't about to disappear because it did. Everybody but Paraguay and Bolivia needed submarine skippers, and they would have if only they'd had coastlines.

But he'd stayed in Charleston almost two years now, and he'd probably stay a while longer. For one thing, he saw Anne Colleton every so often: not so often as he would have liked, not quite so seldom as to make him give up in dismay. He understood how carefully she rationed their liaisons. It would have infuriated him more if he hadn't admired her, too.

And, for another, he'd found, or thought he'd found, a way to help put the Confederate States back on their feet. Clarence Potter, who'd become a friend instead of a barroom acquaintance, thought he was crazy. "I can't believe you've gotten yourself sucked into the Freedom Party," Potter said one evening in Kimball's small furnished apartment. "Those people couldn't start a fire if you spotted them a lit torch and kindling."

"I'm one of those people, Clarence," Kimball said, with only a slight edge to his voice, "and I'll thank you to keep a civil tongue in your head."

"No, you're not," Potter said. "Your deplorable taste in politics aside, you're an intelligent man. Believe me, that makes you stand out from the common herd in the Freedom Party. It makes you stand out from Jake Featherston, too." He held up a hand. "Don't get me wrong—Featherston's not stupid. But he has no more education than you'd expect, and the only thing he's good at is getting up on the stump and making everyone else as angry as he is."

Jack Delamotte took a pull at his whiskey. "I've heard him talk myself now. He even makes me angry, and I'm usually too damn lazy to get mad about anything."

"We *need* to get angry, dammit," Kimball said. "Too much wrong with this country not to get angry about it. The money's still not worth anything, the damnyankees won't let us have a proper Army and Navy, and half the niggers in the country act like they own it. You can't tell me different. You know damn well it's true."

"Featherston has about as good a chance of solving those problems as the man in the moon," Potter said. "Maybe less."

"Clarence is right," Jack Delamotte said. "He's like one of those nigger preachers. He gets folks all hot and bothered, sure as hell, but you look at what he says and you see he doesn't really say anything at all."

"That's all right," Kimball said placidly. Potter and Delamotte both looked startled. Kimball pointed at the former intelligence officer. "Clarence, the first time we met, you were talking about finding a goal for the CSA and getting people to stick to it. You remember that?"

"Of course I do," Potter said. "It was true then, and it's still true now. It's truer than ever now, because we've drifted longer without a rudder."

Kimball chuckled. "Trying to talk like a Navy man, are you? Well, all right, go ahead. But you know this Featherston character, right?" He waited for Potter to nod, then went on, "Like Jack said, he's awful damn good at riling people up. If he doesn't have any kind of education, so what? So much the better, matter of fact. What do you say we get hold of him and give him the kind of ideas the Confederate States need to get back on their feet?"

"You and me and Clarence, saving the country?" Delamotte didn't just seem dubious; he seemed on the point of laughing out loud.

"Somebody's got to," Roger Kimball answered. He wasn't laughing, not now. "Nobody in Richmond knows how, that's for damn sure. What do you say, Clarence? Will Featherston listen to you?"

Potter rubbed his chin. His gray eyes held uncertainty, something Kimball had rarely seen in them. At last, he said, "I don't know for certain. He hated officers in general, but he didn't hate me in particular, because I did him some good turns. But does that mean we'd be able to steer him the way we want him to go? I'm not sure. I'm not sure he's in the habit of listening to anybody, either. He's as stubborn as they come."

Jack Delamotte looked down into his glass, which was empty. "Easy enough to get on a tiger's back," he observed. "How do you get off again?"

"Oh, we'd manage that," Potter said confidently. "Any of the three of us—even you, Jack, no matter how lackadaisical you let yourself get—is a match for Featherston and then some."

"That's settled, then," Kimball said, though it wasn't, not anywhere close. "We'll get hold of Featherston, fill him full of what we figure he ought to say, and get people to pay attention to what really needs doing." He picked up the whiskey bottle from the table, yanked out the cork, and poured fresh drinks for himself and his friends. They solemnly clinked glasses.

As was his way, Kimball wasted no time trying to make what he planned come true. He'd become a familiar fixture at the Freedom Party offices over on King Street, next to the headquarters of the Washington Light Infantry, a unit that, as its name suggested, had fought in the wars of the CSA and the USA since the Revolution. "No, Commander," a fellow there said from behind a typewriter, "I don't know when Sergeant Featherston will be coming into South Carolina again. It shouldn't be too long, though. With Congressional elections this fall, he'll be doing a deal of traveling, I reckon. We aim to send Richmond a message from all across the country."

"That's fine," Kimball said. "That's mighty fine. Thing is, I'd like to send a message to Sergeant Featherston." Having failed to become an officer, the leader of the Freedom Party took an upside-down pride in his noncommissioned rank. Kimball kept his face carefully straight while referring to it. "I just found out a friend of mine served in the Army of Northern Virginia and got to know him pretty well up there. He'd like to have the chance to say hello."

"A lot of people served in the Army of Northern Virginia," the Freedom Party man said. "I did myself, as a matter of fact. And you'd be surprised how many of them say now that they knew Sergeant Featherston then."

"My friend's name is Potter, Clarence Potter," Kimball said patiently. "He told me the name I should mention is Pompey, that Sergeant Featherston would know what it meant." Quite casually, he set a gold dollar, a tiny little coin, on the desk by the typewriter.

The Freedom Party man licked his lips. A gold dollar could buy a couple of thousand dollars' worth of banknotes these days. He made the coin disappear: not hard when it was so small. "I reckon I can arrange a wire up to Richmond. You're right—I know he'd be glad to hear from an old friend, and especially through Party channels."

Kimball could have sent the telegram himself. But how many telegrams did Jake Featherston get every day? Piles, without a doubt. He'd made himself widely known through the CSA. How many of those telegrams got tossed unread? He'd pay more attention to the ones that came from inside his own outfit.

"Thanks, friend," Kimball said, and headed off to a poker game well pleased with himself. He won, too, which left him even more pleased.

When he strolled back into the Freedom Party headquarters a couple of days later, the fellow who'd pocketed the gold dollar held out a pale yellow telegram. Kimball took it with a confidence that evaporated as he read the message: MAJOR POTTER—IF YOU CARED ABOUT SEEING ME, YOU COULD HAVE DONE IT A LONG TIME AGO. FEATHERSTON, SGT., 1ST RICHMOND HOWITZERS.

"He knows your friend, I reckon," the Freedom Party man said, "but it doesn't sound like he's real hot to pay him a visit."

"No, it doesn't," Kimball agreed morosely. "Thanks for trying, anyhow." Now that he knew the man took bribes, he might want to pay him off again, which meant not growling at him now.

But what he really wanted to do was get hold of Jake Featherston. If Potter's name wasn't the key that fit the lock, he needed one that would. As he left the Freedom Party office, he snapped his fingers. Maybe he knew where to find it.

Since he had no telephone in his flat, he went over to the telephone exchange building and placed a call up to St. Matthews. It took a little while to go through. By now, Anne Colleton's brother was used to Kimball calling, even if he didn't quite accept him. But Anne answered the telephone herself. "Hello, Roger!" she said when she found out who was on the other end of the line. "What can I do for you today?"

Kimball had learned to read her tone of voice. It said, *If you're calling because you want to sleep with me, forget about it.* Under other circumstances, that would have angered him. It still did, a little, but he buried that. "What do you think of the Freedom Party?" he asked.

He took her by surprise. There were several seconds of silence up in St. Matthews before she answered, "I haven't really thought much about it one way or the other. It certainly has been making a lot of noise lately, though, hasn't it?" Now she might have been a detective whipping out a magnifying glass. "Why do you want to know?"

He explained what he had in mind for the Freedom Party, finishing, "People are starting to listen to this Featherston. If he says the right things, he might be the one who can haul the country out of the swamp."

"Well," Anne said after another thoughtful pause, "I don't know what I expected you to say when you called, but that wasn't it." She hesitated again. "Why do you think Featherston would listen to me?"

Kimball hadn't wanted Featherston listening to her; he'd wanted the Freedom Party leader listening to what he had to say. Maybe Anne would say the same things he would have, but he had no guarantee about that. Still, she was waiting for an answer, and he gave her a blunt one: "You've got money. You ever hear of a politician—any sort of politician—who didn't need money?"

She laughed. "You're right about that, heaven knows—and so do I, the hard way. I don't know that I want to spend any of my money on the Freedom Party, but I don't know that I don't, either. Let me do some checking around and see if it would be money well spent. If I decide it is, I expect I can find a way to let Featherston know I want to have a talk with him."

She spoke about the Freedom Party as if it were a firm in which she was considering an investment. In a way, that was probably just what it was to her. As far as Roger Kimball was concerned, politics and investments were two separate worlds. Maybe that meant Anne Colleton was the right person to approach Featherston after all. Kimball said, "All right, that's fair enough. Thanks."

When he didn't say anything more, Anne teased him: "No sweet talk, Roger? Have you gone and found somebody else?"

"After you, anyone else'd be boring," he answered. This time, pleasure filled her laugh. He went on, "I just didn't reckon it'd work today, that's all."

"You're a smart man," she said. Getting such praise from her pleased Kimball much more than getting it from Clarence Potter had done.

Tom Colleton looked quizzically at Anne. He asked, "Are you really sure you want to do this?"

"What, meet with Jake Featherston?" she asked. Her brother nodded. She exhaled in some exasperation. "Seeing as he's going to be on the train that gets to St. Matthews in half an hour, don't you think it's a little late to worry about that? If I show him up now, I've made an enemy. I'm liable to have made a dangerous enemy. I don't care to do that, thank you very much."

"I suppose you're right—you usually are." Tom still looked unhappy. "I can't say I much fancy what I've heard about him, though."

"Hush," Anne said absently as she walked over to the closet. "I want to pick out the hat that goes best with this dress." The dress was of orchid cotton voile, with a new-style square collar and with ruffles at the sleeves, waist, hips, and a few inches above the ankle-length hemline. It managed to be stylish and to suit the formidable South Carolina climate at the same time.

The flowered hat she chose had a downturned brim that was also of the latest mode. She didn't know how much attention Featherston paid to fashion. She'd tried to find out what he thought of women; all she'd been able to learn was that he was a bachelor. Not being able to find out more left her obscurely irked.

"Are you sure *you* want to come along, Tom?" she asked. "One thing we do know is that he doesn't love officers."

"Next enlisted man I meet who does love officers will be the first." Her brother pulled out his pocket watch. "We'd better get going, if you aim to meet him at the station."

"Do you expect the train to run on time?" Anne asked, but she went with him.

As it happened, the train did run late, but only by twenty minutes or so: hardly enough time in which to start fuming. It pulled into the battered station—not all the damage from the black uprising had been repaired—with wheels squealing and sparking as the brakes brought it to a halt and with black smoke and cinders belching from the locomotive's stack. Anne brushed soot from her sleeve with a muttered curse that made Tom chuckle and that no one else heard.

Only two people got off the train in St. Matthews. Since one of them was a fat colored woman, figuring out who the other one was did not require brilliance. The lanky white man dressed in butternut trousers, a clean white shirt, and a straw hat looked around for people to greet him, as any traveler might have done.

"Mr. Featherston!" Anne called, and the newcomer alertly swung toward her. His features were pinched and not particularly handsome, but when his eyes met hers, she had to brace herself for an instant. Roger Kimball had been right: whatever else he was, Jake Featherston was not a man to take lightly. She stepped toward him.

"I'm Anne Colleton, Mr. Featherston. Pleased to meet you, and thank you for coming down. This is my brother, Tom."

"Right pleased to meet you both," Featherston said, his Virginia accent not bespeaking any great education. When he shook hands with Anne, his grip was so businesslike, it revealed nothing. He turned to her brother. "You were an officer on the Roanoke front, isn't that right?"

"Yes, that's so," Tom said. *I wasn't the only one doing some checking,* Anne thought. No, Featherston was not a man to be taken lightly, not even a little bit.

He said, "I'll try not to hold it against you." From the lips of most former noncoms, it would have been a joke. Anne and Tom both started to smile. Neither let the smile get very big. Anne wasn't at all sure Featherston was kidding. He asked, "You have a motorcar here, to take us wherever we're going?"

Anne shook her head. "I didn't bother. We're only a couple of blocks from my apartment. This isn't a big town—you can see that. It's an easy walk."

"I'll take your carpetbag there, if you like," Tom added, reaching out for it.

"Don't bother," Featherston said, and did not hand it over. "I've been taking care of myself a long time now. I can go right on doing it." He nodded to Anne. "Lead the way, Miss Colleton. Sooner we're there, sooner we can get down to business."

He was mostly silent as they walked along: not a man with a large store of small talk. As he walked, he studied St. Matthews with military alertness. He studied Anne the same way. His eyes kept coming back to her, but not in the way of a man who looks on a woman with desire. Anne had seen that often enough to be most familiar with it. No, he was trying to size her up. That was interesting. Usually, till they realized she had a brain, men were more interested in trying to feel her up.

Back at the apartment, Featherston accepted coffee and a slice of peach pie. He ate like a man stoking a boiler, emptying his plate very fast. Then he said, "What can I do for you, Miss Colleton?"

"I don't quite know," Anne answered. "What I do know is that I don't like the way the Confederate States have been drifting since the end of the war. I'd like the country to start moving forward again. If the Freedom Party can help us do that, maybe I'd like to help the Freedom Party."

"I can tell you what I want for the CSA," Featherston said. "I want revenge. I want revenge on the damnyankees for licking us. I want revenge on the damnfool politicians who got us into the war. I want revenge on the damnfool generals in the War Department who botched it. I want revenge on the niggers who rose up and stabbed us in the back. And I aim to get it."

Revenge was a word that struck a chord with Anne. She'd spent most of two years getting even with the blacks of the Congaree Socialist Republic after they'd torched Marshlands, killed her brother Jacob, and almost killed her. She dearly wanted to get even with the United States, though she didn't see how the Confederate States would be able to manage it any time soon. Still . . .

"How do you propose to do all that?" she asked.

"You said it yourself: everything in the country seems dead right now," Featherston replied. "The Freedom Party is alive and growing. People see that. They're starting to come over to us. We'll elect Congressmen this year—you just wait and see if we don't. Before too long, we'll elect a president."

He had all the confidence in the world, that was certain. Tom remarked, "You're not running for Congress yourself, are you?"

Featherston shook his head. "That's right—I'm not. Don't want to sit there, for one thing, on account of I can't stand too many who're already in. And for another, I want to be able to go where I want to go when I want to go there. If I had to stay in Richmond too much of the time, I wouldn't be able to do that. So, no, I'm not going to the dance."

"You're going to stay on the sidelines and call the tune," Anne said.

"You might put it that way," Jake Featherston agreed. He had a pretty good poker face, but it wasn't perfect. Anne saw his attention focus on her. It still wasn't the look a man gave an attractive woman: more like the look a sniper gave a target. *Now he's realized I'm no fool,* she thought. *I wonder if I should have let him know so soon. I wonder if I should have let him know at all.*

She also realized Featherston was no fool. Not running for Congress let him pick and choose his issues and what he did about them. It also protected him from the risk of running and losing. She had no feel yet for how smart he was, but he was plenty shrewd.

"What tune are you going to call?" she asked.

"I already told you," he answered. "I don't hide anything I aim to do; I just come right out and say it." An alarm whistle went off in Anne's head: any man who said something like that was almost bound to be lying. She kept her face quite still. Featherston continued, "Platform's pretty simple, like I said. Pay back the USA as soon as we can. Clean out the House and Senate. Clean out the War Department. Put the niggers back in their place. Best place for 'em, you ask me, is six feet under, but I'll settle for less for now. Still and all, this is a white man's country, and I aim to keep it that way."

"What do you propose to do about the black men who got the vote by fighting in the Army?" Tom Colleton asked.

"Most of 'em don't deserve it," Featherston said at once. "Most of 'em ran instead of fighting. I was there. I saw 'em do it. I fired into 'em, too, to make 'em more afraid of me than they were of the damnyankees."

"Some did run," Tom agreed. "I saw that myself. Toward the end of the war, I saw white troops break and run, too." He waited. Slowly, Featherston nodded, looking unhappy about having to do it. Tom went on, "I saw some niggers fight pretty well. They're the ones I'm talking about. How do you take their vote away?"

"Wouldn't be hard, once we got around to it," Featherston replied with breathtaking and, Anne thought, accurate cynicism. "Most decent white folks can't stand 'em anyway. Besides, chances are the ones who fought hard against the USA learned how by fighting against the Confederate States. Pin that on 'em, call it treason, and hang the lousy bastards."

"What do we do if the United States try to stop us from getting strong again?" Anne asked. "That's my biggest worry."

"We walk small as long as we have to," Featherston said. "I hate it, but I don't know what else to tell you. We build up our strength every chance we get, though, and before too long we get to tell the damnyankees to leave us alone unless they want a sock in the nose."

That made sense to Anne. She couldn't see what else the CSA could do, in fact, except become a supine U.S. puppet. She said, "So you want to get the Negroes out of the towns and factories and back to the fields, do you?" Would keeping Marshlands be worthwhile? No, she judged. Featherston had more on the ball than she'd expected, but the Freedom Party remained very new and raw. It sought power; it wasn't about to lay claim to much yet.

Featherston answered, "That's about right, Miss Colleton." He eyed her again. Did he guess the calculation she was making? She wouldn't have been surprised.

Her gaze flicked over to Tom. That did surprise her; she rarely relied on anyone to help her decide. Her brother shrugged, ever so slightly. He was leaving it up to her. He did that more often than not.

She wished he wouldn't have, not here. Featherston waited. He had more patience than she would have thought.

He had more of quite a few things than she'd thought. She wasn't easy to impress, but he'd impressed her. She said, "I think we're traveling in the same direction, Mr. Featherston. I suspect you could use some help along the road, too."

"We sure could," he said. "We sure could. When I joined the Freedom Party, it operated out of a cigar box. We're better off than that now, but not a whole lot." Contempt washed over him, as if poured from a bucket. "Most rich folks don't dare change what made 'em rich. They'll go on sucking up to the Whigs and the Radical Liberals while the country goes down the drain. Always good to find somebody who zigs when most folks zag."

He couldn't have paid her a compliment she appreciated more if he'd tried for a week. "I think I may be able to help some," she said. "How much depends on any number of things."

Featherston got to his feet, as if getting up on the stump. "Put those niggers back in the fields where they belong!" His voice filled the apartment with a raspy thunder that didn't enter it when he was speaking in ordinary tones. That took Anne by surprise again, and for a moment almost took her breath away. She nodded, recognizing the good bargain she'd made. She held out her hand. Jake Featherston shook it. *You give the speeches,* she thought. *Yes, you call the tune—after I whistle it to you.*

Lieutenant Colonel Abner Dowling stared out across the prairie from General Custer's third-story offices in Winnipeg. He'd been there with the general since winter, and the view on a clear day never ceased to astonish him. Today, he managed to put that astonishment into words: "My God, sir, it's flatter than Kansas!"

"It is, isn't it?" Custer agreed. "You can see forever, or if you can't, it certainly seems as though you can. Makes you think God pressed an iron to the countryside hereabouts, doesn't it?"

"Yes, sir." Dowling nodded. "Although, from what I've read, it wasn't an iron at all. It was a great whacking sheet of ice that pressed the land down flat and didn't pull back or melt or whatever it did till not so very long ago."

"I can believe *that*." Custer shivered melodramatically. "By the way the weather felt when we got to this place, I'd say the glacier had been gone about a day and a half—two days, tops."

Dowling laughed. Custer rarely joked. Here, he might well have been kidding on the square. During several days that winter, the temperature never had managed to creep above zero, nor even get very close to it. There was a word for a place more than three hundred miles north of Minneapolis: Siberia.

But people lived here. Before the war, something like 150,000 of them had lived here. In Abner Dowling's considered opinion, they'd been out of their minds. Oh, from May to September the weather was good enough, but that left a lot of time out of the bargain.

Nowhere near so many people were left in Winnipeg now. A lot had fled during the two and a half years in which Canadian and British forces had held the U.S. Army away from the critical rail junctions here. A lot more had fled when they realized the Canucks and limeys could hold the Americans no more. And a lot had died when the city finally fell.

One of the reasons Dowling could see so far was that the building housing Custer's headquarters was one of the few in town to come through the war intact. Had it ever had any taller neighbors, they were rubble now. Nothing got in the way of the view.

A lot of the new houses that were starting to go up in Winnipeg these days were made from the wreckage of older structures. One construction outfit even advertised itself as BEST REBUILDERS IN TOWN. The company had plenty of material with which to work.

Custer said, "I feel as though I can see all the way to the Rockies."

"I wish we could see all the way to the Rockies from here, sir," Dowling said. "It would make our jobs a lot easier—and that's where a lot of our problems lie, anyhow."

"The broom didn't sweep clean," Custer said. "That's what the problem is. That's why they sent me up here to set things to rights."

For as long as Dowling had known him, Custer had had a remarkable gift for revising events so they fit neatly into a scheme of things sometimes existing only in his own mind. The first part of his statement, though, was objectively true. The U.S. broom had *not* swept clean, nor even come close. The USA had conquered Ontario and Quebec, severed eastern Canada from the vast West by—finally—seizing Winnipeg, and struck north into the Rockies to break the rail links with the Pacific. That had been enough to win the war. But it had also left a couple of million square miles unvisited by U.S. troops.

A lot of those square miles, especially in the far north, didn't have enough people on them to make anyone worry. But the cities of the Canadian prairie—Regina and Saskatoon, Calgary and Edmonton—resented having been handed over to the United States when no soldier in green-gray had got anywhere near them during the war. They seethed with rebellion. So did the farms for which they gave markets. So did the logging and mining towns of British Columbia. So did the fishermen of Newfoundland. So, for that matter, did a great many people in the areas the United States had taken by force.

"Confound it, Lieutenant Colonel, how am I supposed to control half a continent without the soldiers I should have lost during one medium-sized battle in the Great War?" Custer demanded. "Every time there's a new little uprising somewhere, I have to rob Peter of troops to pay Paul so Paul can put it down. And then twenty minutes later Peter needs the men back again."

"We have kept the railroads hopping, haven't we, sir?" Dowling shook his head at the understatement. "The way the budget's going in Congress, we ought to count ourselves lucky that we still have as many soldiers up here as we do. It won't get any better next year, either."

"Socialists!" As Custer usually did, he turned it into a swearword. "I tell you, Dowling, the machine gun's most proper use is for shooting down the Socialist blockheads who want to cut our country off at the knees. Blow enough of them to kingdom come and the rest might come to their senses—if they have any sense to come to, which I am inclined to doubt."

"Yes, sir," Dowling said resignedly. He was a rock-solid Democrat himself, but not, he thought with a certain amount of pride, a political fossil like his superior.

Custer said, "If things get any worse, we'll have to start borrowing soldiers from the Republic of Quebec, damn me to hell if I lie."

Dowling started to laugh: for Custer to make two jokes in one day was well-nigh unprecedented. Then he realized Custer wasn't joking. For a moment, he was inclined to scorn. Then, all at once, he didn't feel scornful any more. Every so often, Custer came up with an interesting notion, sometimes without even realizing he'd done it.

"Do you know, sir, I'd bet the Frenchies over there would lend them to us," Dowling said. "And do you know what else? I'd bet the soldiers from Quebec'd have a high old time clamping down on the Englishmen who sat on them for so long. That really might be worth looking into."

"Take care of it, then," Custer said indifferently. No, he hadn't known that was a good idea. He'd just been talking to hear himself talk, something he was fond of doing.

Dowling scribbled a note to himself. "Have to make Quebec pay for the troops they send, too," he said. "That will make Congress happy. It might not make Quebec happy, but I won't lose any sleep over that. If we can't twist Quebec's arm, whose can we twist? If it weren't for the United States, that wouldn't even be a country today." As far as he was concerned, it wasn't much of a country, but nobody in Quebec had gone out looking for his opinion.

"Who cares whether Quebec likes it or not?" Custer said, which meant he'd thought along with Dowling, and which almost set Dowling wondering if he hadn't miscalculated. If Custer agreed with him, he had a good chance of being wrong.

He said, "I think we have managed to put down the latest flare-up outside of Edmonton. That's something, anyhow."

"Putting down flare-ups doesn't get the job done, Lieutenant Colonel," Custer said. "I want to put them down so they don't start again. One of these days, I expect we'll have to raze one of these prairie towns to the ground. It'd serve the bastards right. And after we do that, the other Canucks will get the idea that we mean business."

"Maybe, sir," Dowling said, his tone plainly making that *maybe* a *no*. Sometimes you couldn't be too plain for Custer, so he went on, "If we do that without good reason, the rest of the world will raise a big stink."

"To hell with the rest of the world," Custer said grandly: the philosophy of a lifetime, boiled down to eight words. Through the whole of his long span, Custer had done very much as he pleased. He'd had a good many breaks along the way, but no one could deny he'd made the most of them.

"Will there be anything more, General?" Dowling asked.

"As a matter of fact, there is one other thing." Custer hesitated, which was most unlike him. At last, he resumed: "I'm afraid Libbie and I have had to let our housekeeper go. Could you arrange for the hiring of another one?"

"Wouldn't your wife sooner take care of that for you, sir?" Dowling asked warily. When Elizabeth Custer joined her husband at a posting, she ran their household with a whim of iron.

Custer coughed a couple of times. "This once, Lieutenant Colonel, I'd like you to take care of it. Libbie is a marvelous woman—God never made a finer—but she does have a habit of hiring sour, dried-up sticks with whom I have a certain amount of trouble getting on well. I was hoping you might find a capable woman of cheerier disposition."

"I see." And Dowling did. Libbie Custer hired housekeepers in whom her husband could have no possible interest. That was only common sense on her part, for Custer did have an eye for a pretty woman. Whether anything more than an eye still functioned at his age, Dowling did not know. He didn't want to find out, either. Now that Custer had a real command again, he didn't need some pretty young popsy distracting him.

And Dowling didn't want to anger Custer's wife. Libbie made a far more vindictive, far more implacable foe than her husband ever dreamt of being. If Dowling hired Custer a popsy, she would not be pleased with him.

He had his own coughing fit. "Sir," he said, "I really do think that's something best left to Mrs. Custer's judgment."

"Fiddlesticks!" Custer said. "You handled such arrangements for me plenty of times during the war. Once more won't hurt you a bit."

"Whenever your wife was with you, though, sir, she did prefer to keep such matters in her own hands," Dowling said. "I wouldn't care for her to think I was encroaching on her privileges."

"You're not helping, Lieutenant Colonel," Custer said irritably.

Dowling stood mute. If Custer ordered him to choose a housekeeper, he resolved to find the general the homeliest old crone he could. *Let's see you ask me to do something like that again,* he thought.

But Custer gave no such order. Instead, he let out a long, wheezy sigh. "Here I am, in command of all of Canada," he said, "and I find I'm not even in command of my own household." Dowling wondered how many other famous generals had been defeated by their wives. A good many, was his guess, and he did not think that guess likely to be far wrong.

VII

Scipio was in love, and wondered why in God's name he'd never been in love before. The best answer he could come up with—and he knew it was nowhere near good enough—was that he'd always been too busy. First, he'd had an education forcibly crammed down his throat. Then he'd been butler at Marshlands, which under Anne Colleton was a job to keep any four men hopping. And after that, he'd been swept up into the affairs of the Congaree Socialist Republic.

Now . . . Now, as far as anybody in Augusta, Georgia, knew, he was Xerxes the waiter, an ordinary fellow who did his job and didn't give anybody any trouble. And Bathsheba, he was sure, was the most marvelous creature God had seen fit to set on the face of the earth.

He'd never had any trouble finding a woman to bed when he wanted one. But he'd never understood the difference between making love and being in love, not till now. He stroked Bathsheba's cheek as they lay side by side on the narrow bed in his furnished room. "I is the most luckiest man in the whole wide world," he said—no originality, but great sincerity.

She leaned over and kissed him. "And you are the kindliest man," she said. No one had ever called Scipio anything like that before. He hadn't had many chances to be kindly, either. Now that he did, he was doing his best to make the most of them.

Bathsheba got out of bed and started to dress for the trip back across the hall to her room. "Don't want you to go," Scipio said.

"I got to," she answered. "Got to go clean for the white folks tomorrow mornin'. The work don't never go away."

He knew that. Among the reasons he loved Bathsheba was the

solid core of sense he'd found in her. It wasn't that he wanted to make love with her again that made him want her to stay. Since he'd reached his forties, second rounds didn't seem so urgent as they once had. But he enjoyed talking with her more than with anyone else he'd ever met.

He wished he could recite some of the love poetry he'd learned. The only way he knew it, though, was in the educated white man's accent he'd been made to acquire. Using that accent might—no, would—make her ask questions he couldn't afford to answer.

That was the one fly in the ointment of his happiness: everything he said about his past had to be either vague or a lie. Even the name by which she knew him was false. He counted himself lucky that he quickly got used to the aliases under which he protected his real identity. Back in South Carolina, reward posters with his true name on them still hung in post offices and police and sheriff's stations. Some might even have come into Georgia, though he'd never seen one in Augusta.

As if to flick him on that wound of secrecy, Bathsheba said, "One of these days, I'm gonna know all about you—everything there is to know. And do you know what else? I'm gonna like every bit of it, too."

"I already likes everything there is to know 'bout you," Scipio said, and her eyes glowed. As for him, he was glad of the butler's training that let him think one thing and say another without giving any hint of what was going on behind the expressions he donned like convenient masks.

Bathsheba leaned down over the bed and gave him another kiss. "See you tomorrow night," she said, her voice rich with promise. Then she was gone, gently closing the door behind her.

Scipio rose and put on a light cotton nightshirt. In Augusta in early summer, no one wanted anything more. He picked up a fan of woven straw. He wished the roominghouse had electricity: he would have bought an electric fan and aimed it at the bed as he slept. It got every bit as hot and oppressive here as it did over by the Congaree. He'd heard it got even worse down in Savannah. He found that hard to believe, but you never could tell.

His cheap alarm clock jangled him awake the next morning. He yawned, got out of bed, and started getting dressed. He had his white shirt halfway buttoned before his eyes really came open. Bathsheba's door was closed when he left his room, and everything quiet within her place. She got up earlier than he did, to cram the most work she could into a day.

The fry joint where he worked didn't serve breakfast. He got eggs and grits and coffee at a place that did, and paid for them with a $500 banknote. "Need another hundred on top o' that," the black man behind the counter said.

With a grimace, Scipio peeled off another banknote and gave it to him. "Be a thousand tomorrow, I reckons," he said.

After considering, the counterman shook his head. "Not till next week, I don't think," he answered seriously.

Despite those serious tones, it was funny in a macabre way. Every day, Confederate paper dollars bought less and less. Scipio had just put down six hundred of them on a cheap breakfast. If it was a thousand tomorrow, or a thousand next week at the latest, so what? The printing presses would run off more banknotes with more zeros on them, and another cycle would begin.

The good, sweet smell of baking cornbread filled Scipio's nostrils when he went into Erasmus' fish store and restaurant. The grizzled Negro who ran the place nodded to him and said, "Mornin'."

"Mornin'," Scipio answered. He grabbed a broom and dustpan and started sweeping the floor. He kept his furnished room as neat as he could, and he did the same here, even though Erasmus had given him no such duty.

Erasmus watched him now as he plied the broom. The cook rarely said anything about it. Maybe he didn't know what to make of it. Maybe he was afraid that, if he said anything, Scipio would quit doing it.

A couple of minutes later, Erasmus took the pan of cornbread out of the oven and set it on the counter to cool. Then he said, "Make sure nobody steal the store, Xerxes. I'm gonna git us fish fo' today. The ice man come before I git back, put it in the trays there like you know how to do."

"I takes care of it," Scipio promised.

Erasmus, by now, had good reason to know his promises were reliable. He headed out the door. A fat bankroll made a bulge in his hip pocket. The roll would be considerably thinner after he came back from the riverside fish market. He'd get good value for the money he spent, though. Even in these times of runaway prices, he always did.

Off he went. Left behind to his own devices, Scipio went right on cleaning. The ice man did come in. Scipio stuck some of the slabs of ice in the display trays and put the rest in the damp sawdust underneath those trays so it wouldn't melt before it was needed.

Then he got a hammer and an ice pick and began to break up the ice in the trays from slabs to glistening chunks.

By the time he'd finished dealing with the ice, Scipio wasn't hot any more. His teeth chattered, and he could barely feel his fingers. He wondered if that was what living through a winter up in the USA felt like. He doubted he'd ever find out.

He didn't stay cold for long. Nothing could stay cold very long, not in that weather. He took a little chunk of cracked ice and dropped it down the back of his shirt. It made him squirm and felt good at the same time.

Erasmus came back with a burlap bag slung over his shoulder. He grunted when he saw the ice in the trays. "Come on," he said to Scipio. "Got to clean us these here fish."

He did most of the cleaning himself. He'd long since seen that Scipio knew how, but he was an artist with the knife; had he had a fancy education, he might have made a surgeon instead of a fry cook. Scipio carried fish and set them on ice. He also carried pink, bloody fish guts out to the alley in back of the shop and flung them into a battered iron trash can. He always hosed the can out right after the refuse collectors emptied it. It still stank of stale fish. Flies buzzed around it. Flies buzzed everywhere in Augusta when the weather was warm.

People knew when Erasmus would be getting back with his fish. Within fifteen minutes of his return, housewives started coming in to buy for their husbands and families. When Scipio first started working there, they'd viewed him with suspicion, as people had a way of viewing anyone or anything new with suspicion. By now, they took him for granted.

One woman, carrying away a couple of catfish wrapped in old newspapers, turned back and said to Erasmus, "That Xerxes, he jew me down better'n you ever could, old man."

"It ain't so hard these days, not with money so crazy ain't nobody knows what nothin' supposed to cost," Erasmus answered. The woman took her fish and departed. Scipio glanced over to his boss, wondering if her comments had annoyed him. Erasmus gave no sign of that; catching Scipio's eye, he grinned at him, as if to say the housewife had paid him a compliment.

Business picked up as noon approached. Men started coming in and having their fish fried in the shop for dinner. Erasmus fried potatoes to go with them, too, and a big pot of greens never seemed to go off the stove. A man could leave the table hungry, but it wasn't easy.

And how the money flowed in! Hundred-dollar banknotes, five hundreds, thousands, even a ten-thousand now and then—Scipio felt like a bank cashier as he made change. He would have felt even more like a bank cashier and less like a poor Negro if he hadn't been making $40,000 a week himself. Next week, Erasmus would probably give him fifty or sixty or seventy. However much it was, it would keep food in his belly and a roof over his head, and it wouldn't go a great deal further than that.

One more reason to marry Bathsheba as soon as he could was that then they'd need only one roof over their two heads, and save the cost of the second—not that anyone could save anything much with prices as mad as they were.

Trouble started about half past twelve. The first hint of it Scipio got was an angry shout from not far away: "Freedom!" A moment later, it came again, from a lot of throats: "Freedom!"

"They's buckra!" Scipio exclaimed. "Why fo' buckra come into de Terry carryin' on like dat?"

"Don't know." Erasmus tucked a knife into his belt. "Don't much fancy the notion, neither. They ain't got no business in this part o' town."

Whether they had business or not, here they came, straight up the street past the café: a dozen or so white men, all of them in white shirts and butternut trousers. "Freedom!" they shouted, again and again. As they shouted, they knocked down any Negro in their path, man, woman, or child.

"What we do 'bout dat?" Scipio said. "What *can* we do 'bout dat? I know they's white folks, but they got no call to do nothin' like that. You reckon yellin' fo' the police do any good, Erasmus?"

Erasmus shook his gray head. "Not likely. Two-three of them fellas, they *was* the police." Scipio thought about that for a little while. He thought he'd escaped terror for good when he'd got free from the last wreck of the Congaree Socialist Republic. Now he discovered he'd been wrong.

"**I** never thought I'd live to see the day," Sam Carsten said as the USS *Remembrance* steamed through St. George's Channel. If he looked to starboard, he could see England—no, Wales. Ireland lay to port.

George Moerlein nodded. "I know what you mean," he said. "Pretty damn crazy, us paying a courtesy call in Dublin harbor."

"Only way a U.S. warship would've been able to get into Dublin harbor before the war or during it would've been to kick its way in," Sam agreed. "Of course, Ireland belonged to the limeys then, and we weren't exactly welcome visitors."

"Well, we are now," Moerlein said. "And if England doesn't like it, let her try and start something. She'll get the idea pretty damn quick after we give her a good boot in the ass."

Despite that bravado, he looked east more than a little nervously. The Royal Navy had been beaten in the Great War, but it hadn't been crushed. England hadn't been crushed, not the way the Confederate States and France had been. He had no doubt the USA and the German Empire could crush her if they had to. He also had no doubt they'd know they'd been in a scrap by the time they were through.

A destroyer flying a green-white-orange flag with a harp in the middle of the white led the way for the *Remembrance*. The destroyer had started life as a U.S. four-stacker; dozens much like her had gone into the water during the Great War. Her crew consisted of Irishmen who'd begun their careers in the Royal Navy. Men like that, thousands of them, formed the basis for the Irish Navy.

"I hope they've got a good pilot up there," Carsten said. A moment later, he added, "I hope he's got good charts, too." A moment later still, he made another addendum: "I hope none of the mines from the fields are drifting loose through the Irish Sea."

He thought that covered everything, but his buddy showed him he was wrong. "As long as you're doing all that hoping, hope the limeys haven't snuck out and planted a few of those little bastards right in our path," George Moerlein said.

"That wouldn't be very nice of them, would it?" Sam grimaced. "And they could always say something like, 'Oh, we're very sorry— we didn't have any notion that one was there.' How would anybody prove anything different?"

"You couldn't," Moerlein said. "You wouldn't have a prayer of doing it. Of course, the good thing is that Teddy Roosevelt wouldn't need any proof. If we come to grief here, he'll make England pay. The limeys have to know it, too. I don't think they'll get gay with us."

"Here's hoping you're right." Carsten glanced up at the sky, which was full of thick gray clouds. "Beautiful day, isn't it?"

Moerlein thought he was being sarcastic. "Yeah, if you're moss on a tree," he answered. "I was hoping we'd get sent down to South America myself, to give Brazil a hand against Argentina. That's my kind of weather."

"No, thanks," Carsten said with a shudder. "I burn like a rib roast in the galley after the cooks forgot about it."

When the *Remembrance* came into Dublin harbor, she got a welcome about the size of the one the *Dakota* had enjoyed coming into New York City after the end of the Great War. New York City boasted more people than the whole country of Ireland, but the ones who lined both sides of the River Liffey cheered loud enough to make up for their lack of numbers. As the *Remembrance* drew near its assigned wharf, Sam was bemused by the sight of tens of thousands of people, almost all of them as fair-skinned as he was.

"If you towed this place down to Brazil, you'd give everybody here heatstroke in about a day and a half," he said. No one else paid him any attention. If the other sailors on deck contemplated Irishwomen's skins, as they doubtless did, they had different things on their minds. So, for that matter, did Sam.

A couple of light gray German cruisers were berthed only a few piers over from the *Remembrance*. Sailors aboard them waved toward the aeroplane carrier. Sam and his comrades waved back. Here in Dublin, Americans and Germans were both about the business of giving England a black eye. All the same, Sam sent those cruisers an appraising glance, wondering what going into battle against the squareheads would be like. And officers aboard the German ships were bound to be photographing the *Remembrance* so their bosses in Berlin could figure out how to fight her and whether to build ships like her.

After she'd been made fast, the lord mayor of Dublin and a redheaded fellow in a fancy naval uniform came aboard to welcome her to their country. The lord mayor, who wore a green-white-and-orange sash, made a speech. The admiral studied the *Remembrance* as if wishing he had a dozen of her class under the Irish flag.

"And so," the lord mayor said at last, in an accent that struck Carsten's ear as more nearly British than Irish, "we are proud indeed to welcome this magnificent warship to our port, a symbol of the affection between the United States and Ireland that caused you to aid us in at last regaining our freedom after so many centuries of oppression at the hands of the British Crown."

Along with the rest of the assembled American sailors, Sam dutifully applauded. During the war, the USA would have done anything to help give England a rough time. That, more than affection, had prompted U.S. help for the Irish rebellion. The mayor didn't look stupid; he had to know as much. Politicians looked to be the same on both sides of the Atlantic.

Had the world been a perfect place, an Irishman would have commanded the *Remembrance*. Captain Oliver Roland, though, was a swarthy man of French descent. He said, "The United States are delighted to welcome Ireland into the family of nations. Along with those of Poland and Quebec, her independence shows how the powers of the Quadruple Alliance respect the national aspirations of peoples whom our late foes for too long kept from the freedom they deserved."

The lord mayor bowed in delight. The Irish admiral clapped his hands. Beside Sam, Willie Moore let out a rude but quiet snort. The gun-crew chief proceeded to put words to it: "The Poles get to do what the Germans tell 'em, and the froggies in Quebec get to do what we tell 'em, and the micks have never been any goddamn good at doing what anybody tells 'em."

That was cynical. It was also very likely to be true. A chief gunner's mate could say it to a man in his crew. Had Captain Roland said it to the lord mayor of Dublin, it wouldn't have gone over so well. The skipper had to be, or at least had to act like, a politician here.

"We going to get liberty, Chief?" Sam whispered to Moore.

"I hear we are," Moore whispered back. "Other thing I hear is, anybody picks up a dose of the clap, they're going to cut his balls off so he never, ever gets a chance to do it again. You understand what I'm saying?"

"I sure do," Sam answered in a whispered falsetto.

Willie Moore's eyes opened wide for a moment. Then, in lieu of laughing, he started to cough. "Damn you, Carsten, you sly son of a bitch," he wheezed. He coughed again, and gave Sam a dirty look. Sam did his best to assume a mantle of angelic innocence. By Moore's expression, his best was none too good.

He did get liberty, but not till three days later: this close to England, Captain Roland wanted to keep as near a full crew aboard the *Remembrance* as possible. Maybe officers toured Dublin's cathedrals and other sights. Sam still thought about trying to become an officer himself. He wasn't interested in cathedrals, though. He went into the first bar—pubs, they called them here—he spotted, only a couple of blocks away from the quay on the River Liffey by which the *Remembrance* lay.

GUINNESS IS GOOD FOR YOU! proclaimed a sign in the window. It showed a healthy-looking fellow pouring down a pint of stout. Sam had heard of Guinness, but he'd never drunk any. He couldn't imagine a better place to ease his thirst and improve his education at the same time. In he went.

When he asked for the famous stout, the publican beamed at him. "Indeed and I'm happy to serve a Yank," he declared, sounding much more like an Irishman than had the lord mayor. "If you haven't changed your money, a quarter of a dollar'll do it."

"I'll bet it will," Sam said, not very happily. Back in the States, he could buy five glasses of beer for a quarter. But he wasn't back in the States, and Guinness was supposed to be something special. He dug in his pocket and set a silver coin on the bar.

The Irishman did give him full measure, filling the pint pot to the brim and then using the last drips from the tap to draw a shamrock in the creamy head. Seeing Sam's eye on him, he smiled shyly. "Just showing off," he murmured.

"Thanks," Sam said, and lifted the glass in salute. "Cheers." He sipped at the Guinness. After a moment's thought, he nodded. It might not have been worth a quarter, but it came close. A lot more was going on in that taste than in the pale, watery beers he bought at home. It put him in mind of drinking pumpernickel bread. It packed a wallop, too. He could see where, after three or four pints, he wouldn't be hungry any more and he wouldn't be able to walk, either.

He wasn't ready to get blind. He had something else on his mind first. "You happen to know where I could find me a friendly girl?" he asked.

"I do that," the tapman answered. "You go round the corner here"—he pointed—"then knock at the house with the blue door. Tell 'em Sean sent you, and they'll take a wee bit off the price."

They'd give him his cut for sending trade their way, was what he meant. Sam had got that same answer from a good many bartenders in his time. It didn't bother him. They weren't in business for their health; they wanted to make a buck—no, a pound here—like anybody else.

He drank another pint of Guinness and then, feeling a pleasant buzz, found the house with the blue door. Sean's name got him inside. "*Another* one!" the madam said, seeing his uniform. "Christ, you Yanks are horny devils."

"We've been at sea a long time, ma'am," Sam answered.

Before long, he was happily settled upstairs with a plump blonde who said he could call her Louise. His first round ended almost before it started, as often happened after a long time without. He laid out some more cash and began again. Things were progressing most enjoyably when some sort of commotion broke out down below.

He concentrated on the business at hand till a raucous American-accented voice bellowed, "Any sailors off the *Remembrance* who ain't back aboard in an hour, you're damn well gonna get stranded! We're sailing then!" That blue door slammed shut.

"Jesus!" Sam said, and applied himself. He came in a few strokes. That spoiled things for Louise, who, he thought, had been warming up nicely beneath him. But he didn't have time to worry about her, not any more. She gave him an unhappy look as he scrambled into his clothes. He didn't have time to worry about that, either. He was right behind one American leaving the whorehouse, and right in front of another one.

Panting, he hurried up the gangplank to the *Remembrance*. "What the hell's going on?" he asked as he came aboard.

"Uprising in the north," a sailor answered. "They don't want to cut England's apron strings up there. The Irish have asked us to give 'em a hand with our aeroplanes and guns, and we're going to do it."

"Oh. All right." Sam thought for a moment, then chuckled. "Damn good thing they didn't rise up an hour earlier, that's all I've got to say."

Emily Pinkard said, "I swear to Jesus, Jeff, if I didn't know where you was goin' nights, I'd reckon you had yourself another girl on the side."

"Well, I don't." Jefferson Pinkard gave his wife a severe look. She was the one who'd been unfaithful, and now she had the nerve to think he might be? Emily dropped her eyes. She knew what she'd done. Jeff went on, "The Freedom Party's important, dammit. I don't think there's anything more important in the whole country right now."

What was she doing on nights when he wasn't home? Pinkard worried about that, especially since Bedford Cunningham, however much he'd thought of Jake Featherston's speech, hadn't followed up by joining the Freedom Party. Jeff had, and kept going to Party meetings. Before he'd signed up, everything had seemed pointless, useless. Now his life had a focus. He'd found a cause.

"It's bigger than I am," he said, trying to make Emily understand. "It's more important than I am. But I'm part of it. Things'll get better, and they'll get better partly thanks to me. To me." He jabbed a thumb at his own chest.

Emily sighed. "People carry on too much about politics, I swear they do. You come right down to it, none of that stuff means any-thing anyways."

"Weren't for politics, we wouldn't have fought the war." Jeff gave her a perfunctory kiss, then headed out the door. "I ain't got time to argue tonight. I don't want to be late."

He'd heard that the Freedom Party had started out meeting in a Richmond saloon. Since Alabama was a dry state, the Birmingham Party headquarters couldn't imitate those of the founding chapter. Jeff regretted that; he would have enjoyed sitting around with the new friends he'd made and hashing things out over a couple of schooners of beer or shots of whiskey.

He enjoyed sitting around with his new friends anyway, but doing it in a livery stable wasn't the same. Still, the stable owner was a Party member, and the money he got for renting the place out once a week as a meeting hall helped keep him afloat. With so many peo-ple going from carriages to motorcars these days, he needed all the help he could get.

The chairman of the Birmingham chapter was a beefy, red-faced fellow named Barney Stevens. He'd been a sergeant during the war; Pinkard would have bet he'd been a mean one. At eight o'clock on the dot, he said, "Come on, boys—let's get this show on the road."

Together, they sang "Dixie." The singing wasn't of the best, nor anywhere close. That didn't matter. Roaring out the words to the Confederacy's national hymn reminded Jeff—and everyone else— why they'd banded together. The good times the song talked about could come again. The Freedom Party would make them come again.

After the last notes died, Stevens said, "Boys, the force that will conquer in the end is the fire of our young Confederate manhood. Today new people who claim power are arising in the Confederacy, men who've shed their blood for the Confederate States and know their blood flowed in vain, through the fault of the men who ran the government."

Jeff clapped till his hard-palmed hands were sore. He looked around the stable. A handful of the men there were of solid middle years. Most, though, were like him: men in their twenties and early thirties who'd been through the crucible of war and were ready to be poured into some new shape.

"There are too damned many of us for the government to put down by force," Barney Stevens declared, and his audience applauded again. "We have to wreck what needs wrecking, and by

God there's plenty of it. We have to be hard and tough. The abscess on the body of the country needs cutting out and squeezing till the clear red blood flows. And the blood needs to flow for a good long time before the body is pure again."

"Freedom!" Jeff and the others shouted. The stable, the heavy air inside smelling of hay and horses, echoed to the cry.

"Come this fall," Stevens went on, "you'll need a new chairman here, on account of the Ninth District is going to send me to Congress." More cheers. Through them, he said, "And when I get to Richmond, I'm going to have me a few things to say about—"

"Freedom!" Pinkard shouted again, along with his comrades. He had a hard-on. It made him laugh. Emily had been unfaithful to him with a man. He was being unfaithful to her with the Party.

Stevens said, "Between now and election day, we're going to make people notice us. This Saturday afternoon, I hear tell, the niggers our damnfool government gave the vote to are gonna hold a rally—like they was really citizens, like they deserve to be citizens." Scorn dripped from his words. He wasn't quite so good as the national chairman, but he wasn't bad, either. He grinned out at the crowd. "How many of you boys want to put on white shirts and butternut pants and pay 'em a call?"

Almost every hand shot into the air. One of the men Stevens picked was Jefferson Pinkard. The chairman of the Birmingham chapter said, "Meet me at the corner of Cotton and Forestdale two o'clock Saturday afternoon. We'll have ourselves a good old time, damned if we won't."

"What about the cops?" somebody called from the back of the stable.

"What about 'em?" Barney Stevens said contemptuously. "They ain't gonna do nothin' to hold us off a bunch of uppity niggers." He grinned again. "And besides, a lot of them is us."

Most of the men at the meeting whom Pinkard knew were steel-workers at the Sloss foundries. But there were plenty he didn't know well enough to have learned what they did. He wouldn't have been surprised had some been policemen. Cops needed freedom like everybody else.

On the way out of the meeting, he threw a $500 banknote into the tin hat one of Barney Stevens' friends was holding. Weekly dues would probably go to $1,000 before long. Money didn't seem real any more. It was dying, along with so much of what he held dear. *I'll make it better,* he thought. *I will.*

Emily was still up when he got home. He'd thought she would have gone to bed. "It's late, Jeff," she said. "You're gonna be walkin' around like you was drunk tomorrow, you'll be so tired."

"Don't start in on me," he growled.

"Somebody needs to start in on you," his wife answered. "Dangerous enough out on the foundry floor when you're awake." Her voice rose, shrill and angry and worried, too. "You go out there half asleep, and—"

"Don't start in on me, I said!" He slapped her. She stared at him, her eyes enormous with shock. He'd never raised a hand to her, not even when he'd walked in on her and Bedford Cunningham. *Why the hell not?* he wondered, and found no answer.

He shoved her down the hall toward the bedroom, then picked her up, threw her down, and took her by force. They'd played lots of rough games over the years. This was no game, and they both knew it. Emily fought back as hard as she could. Pinkard was bigger and stronger and, tonight, meaner. After he spent himself and pulled out, she rolled away from him and cried, her face toward the wall. He fell asleep, sated and happy, with her sobs in his ears.

She didn't speak to him the next morning, except to answer things he said to her. But she made him his breakfast and handed him his dinner pail and generally took care not to get him angry. He pecked her on the cheek and walked off to work whistling.

"Mornin', Mistuh Pinkard," Vespasian said when he came onto the manmade hell that was the foundry floor. "Just got here my ownself."

"Good morning, Vespasian," Jeff said cheerfully. Vespasian was the best kind of nigger, sure enough: one who knew his place. Pinkard could hardly wait for Saturday afternoon. He and his buddies would take care of some niggers who didn't know theirs. They'd learn, by God!

He glanced toward Vespasian. In a really proper world, even the best kind of nigger wouldn't be doing any sort of white man's work. He'd be shoveling coal into the furnaces or out in the cotton fields where blacks belonged. Jeff wondered what the Freedom Party would do about that when it got the chance. Something worth doing. He was sure of that.

After he finished his Saturday half-day, he hurried home and changed into a white shirt and trousers the color of the Confederate uniform. When he started toward the door, Emily asked, ever so cautiously, "Where are you going?"

"Out," he answered, and did.

He got to the meeting place in good time. Barney Stevens shook his hand. "Good man," Stevens said, and gave him a two-foot length of thick doweling—as formidable a club as any policeman carried. "We'll teach the niggers they can't get away with putting on airs like they was as good as white folks."

Some of the Freedom Party men brought their own lead pipes or bottles or other chosen instruments of mayhem. With seventy or eighty of them all together, all dressed pretty much alike, they made a formidable force. Jeff's spirit soared at being part of something so magnificent. It soared again when a gray-clad policeman on horseback waved and tipped his cap to the Freedom Party force.

"Let's go," Barney Stevens said, as if they were about to head out of their trenches and over the top. And so, in a way, they were. "Remember, this is war. Hurt the enemy, help your pals, stay together, obey my orders. If I go down and out, Bill McLanahan's next in line. Now—form column of fours." The veterans obeyed without fuss. They'd done it before, countless times. "For'ard— haarch!" Stevens barked.

Magnolia Park, where the Negroes were holding their rally, was only a few blocks away. Their speaker stood on a platform on which Confederate flags fluttered. That made Jeff's blood boil, even more than Birmingham summer did. A dozen or so cops sufficed to keep a couple of dozen white hecklers away from the rally. Those white men weren't organized. The company from the Freedom Party was.

Cries of alarm rose from black throats when the Freedom Party men came into sight. "Double line of battle to the left and right," Barney Stevens shouted, and the men performed the evolution with practiced ease. Stevens pointed with his club as if it were a British field marshal's baton. "Charge!"

"Freedom!" Jeff yelled, along with his friends. A couple of policemen made halfhearted efforts to get between the Freedom Party men and the Negroes. The tough young veterans in white and butternut rolled over them.

Jeff swung his club. It smacked into black flesh. A howl of pain rose. His lips skinned back from his teeth in a savage grin. He swung again and again and again. A few of the black veterans fought back. Far more fled, though. Some few of them might have gained the vote, but a Negro who fought a white man in the CSA fought not just his foe but also the entire weight of Confederate society and history.

Inside five minutes, the rally was broken up, destroyed. Some of the white hecklers had joined the Freedom Party men. None of the cops had made more than a token effort to hold them back. A lot of

Negroes were down with broken heads. Jeff felt as if he'd just stormed a Yankee position in west Texas. He stood tall, the sweat of righteous labor streaming down his face. Just for the moment, he and his comrades were masters of all they surveyed.

The Speaker of the House pointed toward Flora Hamburger. "The chair recognizes the honorable Representative from New York," he intoned.

"Thank you, Mr. Speaker," Flora said. That was more than a mere courtesy; Seymour Stedman of Ohio was himself a Socialist, the first non-Democrat to be Speaker since the first Congress of President Blaine's disastrous term at the start of the 1880s. "Mr. Chairman, I move that the House pass a resolution whose text I have conveyed to the Clerk, deploring and condemning the assaults against law-abiding Negroes now taking place within the Confederate States."

"Mr. Speaker!" Several Congressmen tried to gain Stedman's attention. As had been arranged, he recognized Hosea Blackford. "Second!" Blackford said in a loud, clear voice. He and Flora grinned at each other.

"It has been moved and seconded that we adopt the resolution Miss Hamburger has conveyed to the Clerk," Congressman Stedman said. "The Clerk will now read the resolution for debate."

Read the clerk did, in a deadly drone. As soon as he finished stating the resolution Flora had summarized, hands shot up all around the House chamber. Speaker Stedman said, "The chair recognizes his honorable colleague from Ohio."

"Thank you, Mr. Speaker." William Howard Taft rose ponderously to his feet, then turned toward Flora. "I should like to inquire of the distinguished Representative from New York why she does not include in her resolution the disorders currently taking place in China, Russia, South America, France, and Spanish Morocco, all of those being no less beyond the boundaries of the United States and the purview of the House of Representatives than the events condemned in the Confederate States."

Flora glared at Taft, and there was a lot of him at which to glare. With the Socialists and Republicans holding a slim majority in the House, he no longer chaired the Transportation Committee, and could not use his power there to make her life miserable. He seemed to have trouble realizing that; a lot of Democrats did. They took power for granted, even when it wasn't there.

"I would answer the gentleman from Ohio in two ways," she said. "First, what happens in the Confederate States is vitally important to the United States, because the Confederate States are so close and so closely related to us. And second, the attacks on the Negroes there are fierce, unjustified, and altogether unprovoked."

"They're only niggers, for Christ's sake," somebody called out without waiting to be recognized. "Who the devil cares what the Rebs do to them?"

"Order!" Speaker Stedman slammed down the gavel. "The chair recognizes the honorable Representative from Dakota."

"Thank you, Mr. Speaker," Hosea Blackford said. "That unmannerly fellow gives me the chance to quote Donne, and I shall not waste it: 'No man is an island, entire of itself; every man is a piece of the continent, a part of the main; if a clod be washed away by the sea, Europe is the less, as well as if a promontory were, as well as if a manor of thy friends or of thine own were; any man's death diminishes me, because I am involved in mankind; and therefore never send to know for whom the bell tolls; it tolls for thee.' If the Confederates now permit the terrorizing of their Negroes, as appears to be true from the reports reaching us, who can guess what they may permit a year from now, or five years, or ten?"

"I have two questions for the gentleman from Dakota," said the Democrat who rose to reply to Blackford. "The first is, why do you think the Confederate States will pay any attention to a resolution from this House? The second is, if you Socialists want us to do something the Confederate States *will* pay attention to, why have you taken a meat axe to the War Department budget?"

The second question, in particular, made Flora wince. She'd urged and voted for cutting the military budget, too, and the reasons for which she'd done so—chief among them that the country could no longer afford to keep spending as it had—still seemed good to her. But she had to admit that a warning delivered under credible threat of war would have done far more to deter the thugs who called themselves the Freedom Party than any resolution from the House of Representatives.

As debate went on, she also began to see that even the resolution was going to have a hard time passing. A lot of Democrats proclaimed that they did not care to be seen meddling in the internal political affairs of a neighboring sovereign state. Speaker Stedman countered that one with a sardonic gibe: "As we won't meddle in the affairs of the Republic of Quebec? Had we not meddled in those affairs, there would be no Republic of Quebec."

But the Congressman who'd said, "They're only niggers," had spoken for a great many of his colleagues, whether they would come out and admit it or not. Flora had expected little better from the Democrats. But the Republicans, mostly farm-belt Congressmen from the Midwest, also proved to have little sympathy for the colored man's plight. And even one Socialist stood up and said, "This is not an issue that concerns the people of my district."

"The people of your district don't care about pogroms?" Flora shouted angrily, which made Speaker Stedman bang the gavel against her.

When Stedman called the question, Flora's resolution fell eighteen votes short of passage. "As the hour now nears six, I move that we adjourn for the day," the Speaker said. His motion carried by voice vote, without a single dissenter heard. The House floor emptied rapidly.

Still furious, Flora made no effort to hide it. "What will they do when the bell tolls for them?" she demanded of Hosea Blackford.

"Who can guess, till the time comes?" he answered with a wry smile. "You don't win all the time, Flora. For a lot of years, we hardly won at all. We are on the record, even if the resolution failed. If things go on, we can bring it up again later in the session."

"You take the long view of things," she said slowly.

"I'd better, after all the worthwhile resolutions and bills I've seen die." Blackford flashed that wry grin again. "For now, what sort of view do you take toward supper?"

"I'm in favor of it," Flora admitted. "With luck, someplace where they know how to serve up crow."

"Oh, I think we can do a little better than that," he said, and took her to a chophouse they'd visited a couple of times before. After mutton chops and red wine, the world did seem a less gloomy place. Brandy afterwards didn't hurt, either. Blackford took out a cigar case. He waited for Flora's nod before choosing and lighting a panatela. Between puffs, he asked, "Shall we go out dancing, or to a vaudeville show?"

Flora thought about it, then shook her head. She wasn't *that* happy. "No, thanks. Not tonight. Why don't you just take me back to my flat?"

"All right, if that's what you want." Blackford rose and escorted her out to his motorcar. The ride back to the apartment building where they both lived passed mostly in silence.

They walked upstairs together. The hallway across which their doors faced each other was quiet and dim: dimmer than usual, because one of the small electric light bulbs had burned out. As usual, Blackford walked Flora to her doorway. As usual, he bent to kiss her good-night. The kiss that followed was anything but usual. Maybe Flora was trying to make up for the day's disappointment. Maybe it was just the brandy talking through her. She didn't know, or care.

Neither, evidently, did Hosea Blackford. "Whew!" he said when at last they broke apart. "I think you melted all the wax in my mustache."

Flora's laugh was shaky. Her cheeks felt hot, as if in embarrassment, but she was not embarrassed. Her heart pounded. She turned, wondering if the routine business of unlocking and opening her door would still the tumult in her. It didn't. She reached for the light switch by the door, then looked back to Blackford. "Would you like to come inside?" she asked.

"Good—" he began, responding to the *Good night* she'd always given him before. Then he heard what she'd really said. He asked a question of his own: "Are you sure?"

She leaned forward and stood on tiptoe to kiss him on the end of the nose. He'd never pushed her to go further than she wanted to go. Pushing her would have done no good, as a lot of people, in Congress and out, could have told him. But he hadn't needed telling. He wasn't pushing now. She liked him very much for that . . . and for the feel of his lips pressed against her, his body pressed against her. "Yes," she said firmly.

I could never have done this back in New York, she thought as they sat side by side on the sofa—*not with everyone who lives in our apartment.* But even that wasn't true. When Yossel Reisen was about to go off to war, her sister Sophie had found a way to give him a woman's ultimate gift—and he'd given her a gift in return, a gift that now bore his name, a gift he'd never lived to see. If you wanted to badly enough, you could always find a way.

She'd never dreamt she might want to so badly. When, in an experimental way, Blackford slipped an arm around her, she pinned him against the back of the sofa. This kiss went on much longer than the one in the hallway had, and left her feeling as if she might explode at any moment.

Blackford kissed her eyes, her cheeks; his mouth slid to the side of her neck, then up to her ear. Every time his lips touched her skin, she discovered something new and astonishing and wonderful. He nibbled at her earlobe, murmuring, "You don't know how long I've wanted to do this, darling." She didn't answer, not with words, but left no doubt about what she wanted.

But going into her bedroom with him a few minutes later was another long step into the unknown. She didn't turn on any of the lights in there. No matter how much urgency filled her, the idea of undressing in front of a man left her shaking. Even so, she sighed with relief as she slid off her corset. On a hot, muggy late-summer night, bare skin felt good.

Her bare skin soon felt quite a lot better than good. She was amazed at the sensations Hosea Blackford's hands and lips and tongue evoked from her breasts, and then amazed again when one hand strayed lower. She'd stroked herself now and again, but this was different: every touch, every movement, a startlement. The small, altogether involuntary moan of pleasure she let out took her by surprise.

But that surprise also recalled her partly to herself. She remembered Sophie's horror and panic out on the balcony of the family flat when her sister told her she was pregnant. "I can't have a baby!" she exclaimed.

Blackford hesitated, studying her in the half-light. Had she made him angry? If he got up and left now, she would die of humiliation—and frustration. But, to her vast relief, he nodded. "One of the reasons I care for you so much is for your good sense," he said. "We'll make sure everything is all right." He bent so that his mouth went where his hand had gone before.

Flora had literally never imagined such a thing. She hadn't imagined how good it felt, either. When pleasure burst over her, it made everything she'd done by herself seem . . . *beside the point* was the best way she found to think of it.

If he'd done that for her, she ought to return the favor, though she didn't quite know how. Awkwardly, she took him in her hand. As she drew near, she saw he looked strange. From inadvertencies around the family apartment, she knew how a man was made. Hosea Blackford was made a little differently. *He's not circumcised,* she realized. She'd forgotten that consequence of his being a gentile.

She kissed him and licked him. He needed only a moment to understand she didn't know what she was doing. "Put it in your mouth," he said quietly. She did, though she hadn't imagined that only minutes before, any more than the other. The sound he made was a masculine version of her moan. Encouraged, she kept on.

She didn't need to keep on very long. He grunted and jerked and spurted. It caught her by surprise, and didn't taste very good. She coughed and sputtered and gulped before she could help herself. When she could speak again, she asked, "Was that right?"

He put her hand over his heart, which pounded like a drum. "If it were any more right," he assured her, "I'd be dead." She laughed and lay beside him, still marveling that such pleasure was possible— and ever so relieved that, unlike Sophie, she would not have to worry about consequences nine months later.

"**A**tlanta!" the conductor called, stepping into the car in which Jake Featherston rode. "All out for Atlanta!" He strode down the aisle, making sure no one could doubt the upcoming stop.

Featherston grabbed his carpetbag and sprang to his feet. His seat had been in the middle of the car, but he was one of the first people off it. He was one of the first people to a taxicab, too. "The Kendall Hotel," he told the driver.

"Sure thing," the fellow answered. The hotel proved to be only a few blocks east of Terminal Station. Brakes squealed as the driver stopped in front of the massive brick building with Moorish-looking turrets and ornaments. "That'll be twelve."

"Here you go." Jake handed him a $1,000 banknote and a $500. "I don't need any change." With the taximan's tip, he would have got back only a hundred dollars, two hundred if he wanted to be a cheapskate. He didn't. Anyhow, with currency the way it was these days, you had to be crazy to worry about anything as small as a hundred bucks.

A uniformed Negro porter came up to carry his bag. He gave the black man a hundred dollars. That was what such nearly worthless banknotes were good for. It was also, he thought, what nearly worthless black men were good for.

When Jake gave his name at the front desk, the clerk handed him his key and then said, "I have a message here for you, Mr. Featherston." He plucked an envelope from a pigeonhole and presented it with a flourish.

"Thanks." Featherston pulled out the envelope and unfolded the sheet of paper inside. It read, *Knight got in this morning. If you see this in time, have supper with us at seven tonight in the hotel restaurant. Amos Mizell.* He stuck the note in his pocket. "How do I find the restaurant?" he asked the desk clerk.

"Down that corridor—second doorway on your left—first is the bar," the young man answered. Shyly, he went on, "It's an honor to have you in the Kendall, Mr. Featherston. Freedom!"

"Freedom, yeah." Jake was still getting used to people recognizing his name. It was, he found, very easy to get used to.

Another colored porter carried the bag up to his room, and earned another hundred dollars. Jake snorted, imagining a hundred-dollar tip before the war. He unpacked his clothes, then pulled a watch from his pocket and checked the time. It was half past five.

He didn't feel like sitting in the room for an hour and a half like a cabbage, so he went down to the bar and peeled off a $500 bank-note for a beer. He nursed the one glass till it was time for supper. The last thing he wanted was to go to this meeting drunk, or even tipsy.

When he left the bar and headed over to the restaurant, a professionally obsequious waiter led him to a table in a quiet corner: not the best seating in the place for anyone who wanted to show off, but a fine place to sit and eat and talk. Two other men were already sitting and talking. Featherston would have pegged them both for veterans even had he not known they were.

They got to their feet as he approached. "Featherston?" the taller one asked. Jake nodded. In a twanging Texas accent, the fellow went on, "I'm Willy Knight of the Redemption League, and this here is Amos Mizell, who heads up the Tin Hats."

"Pleased to meet you gents," Jake said, shaking hands with both of them. He wasn't sure how pleased he was to meet Knight; the Freedom Party was growing only slowly west of the Mississippi, not least because the Redemption League spouted similar ideas there. Supper with Amos Mizell was a feather in his cap, though. The Tin Hats were far and away the largest ex-soldiers' organization in the CSA.

Mizell sipped from a whiskey glass in front of him. He was about forty, and missing the little finger on his left hand. He said, "I think all three of us are going in the same direction. I think all three of us want to see the country going in the same direction, too. What we want to do is make sure nobody sidetracks anybody else."

"That's right." Knight nodded. He was blond and handsome and wore an expensive suit, all of which made Jake jealous. "That's just right," he went on. "If we bang heads, the only ones who win are the damnyankees."

"Fair enough." Jake smiled, as he might have smiled over a bad poker hand. Knight reminded him of an officer, which in his book was another black mark against the Redemption League man. "We might have been smarter not to talk till after the Congressional elections, though. Then we'd have a better notion of who's strong and who isn't."

Almost imperceptibly, Willy Knight winced. Featherston grinned at him, the fierce grin of defiance he threw at everyone who got in his way. The Freedom Party was stronger than the Redemption League, at least for now. It had its base in the more populous eastern part of the Confederate States and was reaching west, where only a relative handful of people on this side of the Mississippi belonged to the Redemption League.

Again, Mizell played peacemaker: "One thing certain is, we're stronger together than we are apart." The Tin Hats weren't a political party, so he wasn't a direct rival to either of the men at the table with him. But if he tipped to one or the other of them, his influence would not be small.

They paused when the waiter came up. Knight ordered a beef-steak, Mizell fried chicken, and Jake a ham steak. "I'm shooting for ten Congressmen next session," he said, though he expected perhaps half that many would win seats. "How about you, Knight?"

"We'll win Dallas—I'm pretty sure of that," the leader of the Redemption League said. "They can see the Yankees up in Sequoyah and over in that damned new state of Houston from there. We may take a couple of other seats, too. I'll tell you what we will do, though, by God: we'll scare the Radical Liberals clean out of their shoes."

"No arguments there," Amos Mizell said. He raised the drink to his lips again. "I wish more of the new leaders who think along our lines would have joined us here tonight. The Tennessee Volunteers, the Knights of the Gray, and the Red-Fighters all have ideas we might find worthwhile, and they aren't the only ones."

"There's plenty of people angry with the way things are going now," Jake allowed. "A couple of years ago, the Freedom Party wasn't anything more than a few people sitting around in a saloon grousing." He drew himself up straight with pride. "We've come a long ways since then."

"That you have," Mizell said. Knight nodded once more. Now he looked jealous. The Freedom Party had come further and faster than the Redemption League. Mizell continued, "I know for a fact that a lot of Tin Hats are Freedom Party men, too."

"I never thought we could get away with breaking up the soft parties' rallies," Will Knight said, and looked jealous again. "But you've gone and done it, and you've gone and gotten away with it, too."

"You bet we have," Jake said. "If you reckon the cops love the Whigs and the Radical Liberals and the niggers, you can damn well think again. And"—he lowered his voice a little—"if you reckon the soldiers love the traitors in the War Department, you can damn well think again about that, too."

"Some of the things you've said about the War Department have been of concern to me," Amos Mizell said. "I don't care to bring disrepute down on men who served so bravely against the foe. *Traitor* is a hard word."

Featherston fixed him with that savage grin. "Jeb Stuart III was my commanding officer," he said. "Pompey, his nigger servant, was ass-deep in the rebellion. He shielded that nigger from Army of Northern Virginia Intelligence. His old man, Jeb, Jr., shielded him when it turned out he'd been wrong all the time. If that doesn't make him a traitor to his country, what the hell does it do?"

Before either Mizell or Knight could answer, the waiter returned with their suppers. They ate in silence for a while. Knight was the first to break it. "Suppose what you say is true. If you say it too loud and too often, don't you figure the Army is going to land on your back?"

"I reckon the generals'd love to," Jake answered with his mouth full. "But I don't reckon they'd have an easy time of it, even now, on account of the soldiers who got the orders wouldn't be happy about following 'em. And the longer they wait, the harder it'll be."

"You may be right about the second part of that," Mizell said. "I've got my doubts about the first, I have to tell you. You might be smarter to take a step back every now and then so you can take two forward later on."

"The Freedom Party doesn't back up." Featherston eyed Mizell, but was really speaking more to Knight. "You talk about people who want to straighten out the mess we're in and you talk about us first. Everybody else comes behind us."

"You go on like that, why'd you bother coming down here at all?" Knight asked. "What have we got to talk about?"

That was a good question. Jake did not want to negotiate with the Redemption League. Negotiating implied he reckoned Knight his equal, which he did not care to do. But he did not dare risk antagonizing the Tin Hats. If Amos Mizell started saying harsh things about him and about the Freedom Party, it would hurt. But he was not about to admit that, either.

Picking his words with more care than usual, he replied, "We're on the way up. You want to come with us, Knight, you want to help us climb, that's fine. You want to fight, you'll slow us down. I don't say anything different. But you won't stop us, and I'll break you in the end." That wasn't party against party. It was man against man. The only thing Featherston knew how to do when threatened was push back harder than ever. Knight was a man of similar sort. He glared across the table at Jake.

"We're here to stop these brawls before they hurt all of us," Amos Mizell said. "If we work things out now, we don't have to air our dirty linen in public and waste force we could aim at our enemies. That's how I see it."

"That's how I see it, too," Jake said. "If the Redemption League was bigger than the Freedom Party, I'd ease back. Since it's the other way round—"

"You're the one who gets to talk that way," Willy Knight said. Jake only smiled. He knew he was lying—he would have done anything to get ahead of a rival—but nobody could prove it.

"It appears to me, things being as they are, that our best course is to use the Freedom Party as the spearhead of our movement and the Redemption League and other organizations as the shaft that helps give the head its striking power," Mizell said. "How does it appear to you, Mr. Knight?"

Featherston felt like kissing Amos Mizell. He couldn't have put the leader of the Redemption League on the spot like that himself. Knight looked like a man who'd found a worm—no, half a worm— in his apple. Very slowly, he replied, "I think we can work with the Freedom Party, depending on who's stronger in any particular place."

"That's a bargain," Jake answered at once. "We'll pull a couple of our candidates in Arkansas, where you look to have a better chance, and we'll throw our weight behind you. There are some districts in Alabama and Mississippi and one in Tennessee I can think of where I want you to do the same."

Even more slowly, Knight nodded again. If the Freedom Party outperformed the Redemption League in this election, support would swing Featherston's way, leaving Knight in the lurch. He could see that. He couldn't do anything about it, though.

He'd want a high post if the Redemption League got folded into the Freedom Party. Jake could already tell as much. He'd give Knight a good slot, too. That way, he could keep an eye on him. The CSA, he thought, had been stabbed in the back. He didn't intend to let that happen to him.

Jonathan Moss slid out of his Bucephalus and stumbled toward his Evanston apartment building. He was glad he'd managed to get home without running over anybody. After his last course, he and Fred Sandburg and several other people—he couldn't recall how many right now—had found a friendly saloon and done their best to drink it dry. *Why not?* he thought. It was a Friday night. He wouldn't need his brains again till Monday morning.

His breath smoked. The wind off Lake Michigan blew the smoke away. It was chilly, despite the antifreeze he'd poured into his pipes. "Not as chilly as it would be up in Ontario," Moss said, as if someone had asserted the opposite. He stepped up onto the stairs. "Not half as chilly as Laura Secord's heart."

Fred never had stopped ribbing him about Laura Secord. Even now, after she'd rejected him again, he couldn't get her out of his mind. He'd come home. He'd done well at Northwestern. He hadn't found a girl he cared about, though. He wondered if he ever would. He wondered if he ever could.

He opened the door at the top of the stairs, then quickly shut it behind him. Getting out of the wind felt good. He fumbled for the key to his mailbox. It wasn't easy to find, not when every key on the ring looked like one of twins. He almost gave it up as a bad job and headed for bed. But, figuring he'd probably have trouble finding his apartment key, too, he chose to regard the mailbox key as a test. He made a determined drunk.

"There you are, you sneaky little bastard," he said, capturing the errant key. Making it fit the lock was another struggle, but he won that one, too.

A couple of advertising circulars fell onto the floor. Bending to pick them up made his head spin. He also had a letter from a cousin out in Denver and another envelope with his address written in a hand he didn't recognize. He'd taken two steps toward the stairs before he remembered to go back and shut and lock the mailbox.

He did have a devil of a time finding the key that opened the apartment door, but by luck he got it into the lock on the first try. He flipped on the electric light and tossed the mail down on the table in front of the sofa. He tossed himself down on the sofa and fell asleep.

Next thing he knew, the sun was streaming in the window. A

determined musician pounded on kettle drums inside his head. His mouth tasted the way a slit trench smelled. His bladder was about to explode. He staggered off to the bathroom, pissed forever, brushed his teeth, and dry-swallowed two aspirin tablets. Black coffee would have helped, too, but making it seemed too much like work.

After splashing cold water on his face, he slowly went back out into the front room. He discovered he hadn't thrown out the circulars, so he did that. Then he read his cousin's letter. It had already started snowing in Denver, and David looked likely to get a promotion at the bank where he worked.

"Bully," Moss muttered. His voice sounded harsh and unnaturally loud in his ears. He let the letter lie where he'd left it. Cousin David was not the most interesting man God ever made.

That left the other envelope, the one with the unfamiliar handwriting. It bore no return address. Something about the stamp looked funny. When he peered closely, he saw that Ben Franklin's portrait had the word ONTARIO printed over it.

"No," he said hoarsely. He shook his fist at the window, in the general direction of the Northwestern campus. "God damn you to hell for the practical-joking son of a bitch you are, Fred." He found it much easier to believe that his friend had got hold of some occupation stamps than that anyone in Ontario should write to him. He knew only one person in the conquered Canadian province, and she wished she didn't know him.

But the envelope carried a postmark from Arthur. Could Fred have arranged to have someone up there put it in the mail? Moss knew Fred could have. His friend would go to great lengths to jerk his chain.

"Only one way to find out," he mumbled, and opened the envelope with fingers not all of whose shaking sprang from his hangover. The paper inside was coarse and cheap. He unfolded it. The letter— a note, really—was in the hand that had addressed the envelope.

Dear Mr. Moss, it read, *Now you have the chance to pay me back. I daresay it will be sweet for you. I would sooner do anything than rely on the word of a man to whom I offered nothing but insult, but I find I have no choice. The harvest this year was very bad, and I have no way to raise the $200 I need to keep from being taxed off my farm. So far as I can tell, all my kin are dead. My friends are as poor as I am. Even if you do find it in your heart to send the money, I can make no promise to feel toward you the way you would want me to feel. I would not deceive you by saying anything else. Laura Secord.* Her address followed.

Moss stared. The letter couldn't be anything but genuine. He'd told Fred Sandburg some of what he'd said and done up in Ontario, but he'd never mentioned the promise he'd given Laura Secord. He'd known too well how Fred would laugh.

"What do I do now?" he asked the ceiling. The ceiling didn't answer. It was up to him.

If he threw the letter away, he would have his revenge. The trouble was, he didn't much want revenge. He hadn't been angry at Laura Secord when she turned him down. He'd been disappointed. He'd been wounded, almost as if by machine-gun fire. But what he'd felt for her hadn't turned to hate, though for the life of him he couldn't have said why.

If he sent her the two hundred dollars, he'd be throwing his money away. He knew that. Had he not known it, she'd made it very plain. But, that frozen day up in Arthur, he'd told her that if she ever needed him for anything, all she had to do was ask. Now she'd asked. Was he going to break his promise? If he did, what would that make her think of Americans? What would it make her think of him?

He'd never been a man in whom altruism burned with a fine, hot flame. He was well-to-do, but not so well-to-do that spending two hundred dollars wouldn't hurt—it wasn't as if he were playing with Confederate money.

"What do I do?" he said again. The ceiling still wasn't talking.

He went back into the bathroom and stared at himself in the mirror over the sink. He looked like hell: bloodshot eyes, stubble, hair all awry because he hadn't bothered combing it yet. If he threw Laura Secord's letter into the wastebasket, what would he see the next time he looked in a mirror?

"A lying bastard." That wasn't the ceiling talking. That was him. Did he want to go through life thinking of himself as a liar every time he lathered up with his shaving brush? Some people wouldn't care. Some people would figure rejection made their promise null and void.

But he'd given that promise after Laura Secord had rejected him, in spite of her rejecting him. His headache had only a little to do with the hangover. He sighed, fogging the mirror. That proved he was still alive. He knew what he would do. He'd never tell Fred Sandburg. Fred wouldn't let him live it down if he found out. He'd do it anyway.

It was Saturday morning. The banks would be closed. The post office was open, though. He could send a money order—if he had two hundred dollars in cash. By turning the apartment upside down, he came up with $75.27. He cursed under his breath for a minute, then telephoned Fred Sandburg.

"Hullo?" When Sandburg answered the phone, he sounded as if he'd just been raised from the dead and wished he hadn't been.

"Hello, Fred," Moss said cheerfully—the aspirins were working. "Listen, if I write you a check for a hundred and thirty bucks, can you cash it?"

"Yeah, I think so," his friend answered.

"Good. See you in a few minutes," Moss said. Sandburg started to ask him why he wanted the money right away, but he hung up without answering. Throwing on some clothes, he drove the few blocks to Sandburg's flat.

"What the hell is this all about?" Sandburg asked. He looked like a poor job of embalming; he'd had more to drink than Moss had. "You eloping with some broad and you need to buy a ladder?"

"Got it the first time," Moss told him. He wrote a check and thrust it at his friend. In return, Sandburg gave him two fifties, a twenty, and a gold eagle. "Thanks, pal, you're a lifesaver," Moss said. He headed out, leaving Sandburg scratching his head behind him.

At the post office, Moss discovered he couldn't buy a money order for two hundred dollars. "Hundred-dollar maximum, sir," the clerk said, "but I can sell you two." Moss nodded. The clerk went on, "That will be $200.60—thirty-cent fee on each order." Moss gave him the money. When he got the money orders back, he put them in an envelope he'd already addressed. For another two cents, the clerk sold him a stamp.

After that, he drove home. Now that the deed was done, he wondered how foolish he'd been. *Two hundred dollars foolish,* he thought—*and sixty cents.* When he asked his parents for money, as he'd eventually need to do, they'd want to know where it had gone. They were liable to suspect he'd spent it on a loose woman. He laughed mirthlessly. If only Laura Secord *were* loose, or even a little looser!

He returned to the study of the law on Monday. Every day when he went home, he checked the mail in hope of finding another envelope with an overprinted stamp. Ten days later, he got one. The note inside read simply, *I see there are decent Yanks after all. God bless you.* He read it a dozen times, convinced beyond contradiction that that was the best two hundred dollars he'd ever spent.

VIII

Nellie Jacobs opened her eyes. She was lying on a hard, unyielding bed, staring up into a bright electric light bulb. When she blinked, the bulb seemed to waver and float. It also seemed much farther away than a self-respecting ceiling lamp had any business being.

Hovering between her and the lamp were her daughter and her husband. Hal Jacobs asked, "Are you all right, darling?"

"I'm fine." Even to herself, Nellie sounded anything but fine. What she sounded was drunk. She felt drunk, too, at least to the point of not caring what she said: "Don't worry about me. I was born to hang." She coughed. That hurt. So did talking. Her throat was raw and sore and dry. As she slowly took stock of herself, that was far from the only pain she discovered. Someone had been using her belly for a punching bag.

"Do you know where you're at, Ma?" Edna Semphroch asked her.

"Of course I do," she answered indignantly. That bought her a few seconds in which to cast about through the misty corridors of her memory and try to find the answer. Somewhat to her own surprise, she did: "I'm in the Emergency Hospital at the corner of Fifteenth and D, Miss Smarty-Britches." Recalling where she was made her recall why she was there. "Holy suffering Jesus! Did I have a boy or a girl?"

"We have a daughter, Nellie," Hal said. If he was disappointed at not having a son, he didn't show it. "Clara Lucille Jacobs, six pounds fourteen ounces, nineteen and a half inches—and beautiful. Just like you."

"How you do go on," Nellie said. A little girl. That was nice. Little girls, thank God, didn't grow up to be men.

Someone new floated into her field of view: a man clad all in white, even to a white cloth cap on his head. *A doctor,* she realized, and giggled at being able to realize anything at all. Businesslike as a stockbroker, he asked, "How are you feeling, Mrs. Jacobs?"

"Not too bad," she said. "I had ether, didn't I?" She remembered the cone coming down over her face, the funny, choking smell, and then . . . nothing. The doctor was nodding. Nellie nodded, too, though it made her dizzy, or rather, dizzier. "I had ether, and after that I had the baby." The doctor nodded again. Nellie giggled again. "A lot easier doing it like that than the regular way," she declared. "One hell of a lot easier, believe me."

"Most women say the same thing, Mrs. Jacobs," the doctor answered. Her cursing didn't bother him. He'd surely heard a lot of patients coming out from under ether. He hadn't even noticed. Edna had, and was smirking.

Nellie went on taking stock. She'd felt a lot of labor pains before Hal and Edna brought her to the hospital, and a lot more before the doctors put her under. But she'd missed the ones at the end of the affair, and those were far and away the worst. And she'd missed the process of, as one of her fallen sisters had put it many years before, trying to shit a watermelon. Sure as sure, this was better.

"Would you like to see your daughter, Mrs. Jacobs?" the doctor asked.

"Would I ever!" Nellie said. Smiling, the doctor turned and beckoned. A nurse brought the baby, wrapped in a pink blanket, up to Nellie. Clara was tiny and bald and pinkish red and wrinkled. Edna had looked the same way just after she was born.

"She's beautiful, isn't she?" Hal said.

"Of course she is," Nellie answered. Edna looked as if she had a different opinion, but she was smart enough to keep it to herself.

"If you want to give her your breast now, you may," the doctor said.

What, right here in front of you? Nellie almost blurted. That was foolish, and she figured it out before the words passed her lips. He'd had his hands on her private parts while delivering Clara. After that, how could she be modest about letting him see her bare breast?

But she was. He must have read it in her face—and, of course, he would have seen the same thing in other women, too. He said, "Mr. Jacobs, why don't you step out into the hall with me? I think your wife might have an easier time of it with just the ladies in here with her."

"Oh. Yes. Of course," Hal said. He followed the doctor out of the room, looking back over his shoulder at Nellie as he went.

"Slide down your gown, dearie, and you can give your wee one something good," the nurse said. She was a powerfully built middle-aged woman with the map of Ireland on her face. After Nellie exposed her breast, she set the baby on it. Clara knew how to root; babies were born knowing that. She didn't need long to find the nipple and start to suck.

"Ow," Nellie said, and made a hissing noise between her teeth. She'd forgotten how tender her breasts were and would be till nursing toughened them up.

"She's getting something, sure enough," the nurse said. Nellie heard the gulping noises the baby was making, too. The nurse went on, "You'll be better off if you go right on nursing her, too. Breast-fed babies don't get the bowel complaints that carry off so many little ones, not nearly as often as them that suck a bottle."

"Cheaper and easier to nurse a baby, too," Nellie said. "Nothing to buy, nothing to measure, nothing to boil. I'll do it as much as I can."

Edna watched in fascination. "They know just what to do, don't they?"

"They do that," the nurse said. "If they didn't, not a one of 'em'd live to grow up, and then where would we be?"

"You were the same way," Nellie told Edna. "I reckon I was the same way, too, and my ma, and her ma, and all the way back to the start of time." She didn't mention little Clara's father, nor Edna's father, nor her own father, nor any other man. That wasn't because she assumed they were the same way, too. It was because, as far as she was concerned, men weren't worth mentioning.

After about ten minutes, the baby stopped nursing. Nellie handed her to the nurse, who efficiently burped her. Clara cried for a little while, the high, thin wail of a newborn that always put Nellie in mind of a cat on a back fence. Then, abruptly, as if someone had turned a switch on her back, she fell asleep.

Nellie found herself yawning, too. Not only were the remnants of the ether coursing through her, but she'd also been through labor and delivery: hard work, even if she hadn't felt most of it.

"Rest now, if you want to," the nurse said. "We'll want to keep you here for a week, maybe ten days, make sure you don't come down with childbed fever or anything else." She cast a speculative eye toward Nellie. That *or anything else* no doubt meant *or anything else that's liable to happen to an old coot like you.*

Had Nellie had more energy, she might have resented that. As she was now, without enough get-up-and-go to lick a postage stamp, she simply shrugged. A week or ten days with nothing to do but nurse the baby and eat and sleep looked like heaven to her.

Edna took a different perspective. "A week? Ten days?" she exclaimed in mock anger. "You're going to leave me running things by myself so long, Ma? That's a lot to hand me."

"I've already done a lot," Nellie said. "Besides, the place has to bring in enough to pay for my little holiday here."

It didn't, not really. She and Hal had saved up enough to meet the hospital bill. Hal knew how to sock away money. It wasn't the worst thing in the world. Nellie wished she were better at that. She'd learned some from paying attention to the way her husband handled things. Maybe she could learn more.

Edna stopped complaining, even in fun. Nellie thought she recognized the gleam in her daughter's eye. Hal wouldn't be able to watch Edna the way Nellie had ever since she'd become a woman. Edna wouldn't have a lot of time to get into mischief, but a girl didn't need a lot of time to get into mischief. Fifteen minutes would do the job nicely.

And maybe, nine months from now, Edna would have an ether cone clapped over her face and wake up with a baby hardly younger than its aunt. If she did, Nellie hoped the baby would have a last name.

She yawned again. She was too tired even to worry about that very much. Whatever Edna did in the next week or so—if she did anything—she would damn well do, and she and Nellie and Hal would deal with the consequences—if there were consequences—later. The only thing Nellie wanted to deal with now was sleep. The light overhead and the hard hospital mattress fazed her not at all.

Before she could sleep, though, her husband came back into the room. He bent over her and kissed her on the cheek. "Everything will be fine," he said. "The doctor tells me you could not have done better. You will be well, and little Clara will be well, and every one of us will be well."

"Bully," Nellie said, and then a new word she'd started hearing in the coffeehouse: "Swell. Hal, you're sweet as anything, but will you please get the hell out of here and let me rest?"

"Of course. Of course." He almost stumbled over his own feet, he went out the door so fast. He paused in the doorway to blow her a kiss, and then he was gone. A moment later, Nellie was gone, too.

They woke her in the middle of the night to nurse the baby again. By then, all the anesthetic had worn off. Not to put too fine a point on it, she felt like hell. The night nurse brought her some aspirin. That was sending a boy to do a man's job. She wondered if she'd be able to go back to sleep once they took Clara away again. She did, which testified less to the tablets' effectiveness than to her own overwhelming exhaustion.

When she woke in the morning, she was ravenous. She would have yelled at Edna for serving a customer such greasy scrambled eggs, overcooked bacon, and cold toast. The coffee they gave her with it might have been brewed from mud. She didn't notice till the whole breakfast was gone. While she was eating, she noticed only that it filled the vast, echoing void in her midsection.

After Clara had had breakfast, too, a nurse escorted Nellie down the hall so she could take a bath. It was the first time she'd had a good look at her body since the baby was born. She didn't care for what she saw, not even a little bit. The skin of her belly hung loose and flabby, having been stretched to accommodate the baby who wasn't in there any more. It would tighten up again; she remembered that from the days following Edna's birth. She'd been a lot younger in those days, though. How much would it tighten now?

If Hal wanted her less after she came home . . . that wouldn't break her heart. It would, if anything, be a relief. She resolved to lay in a supply of safes. Now that she knew she could catch, she didn't intend to do it again. If Hal didn't care to wear them— She grimaced. There were other things they could do, things that carried no risk. She hated those things, having had to do them for men who laid coins on the nightstands of cheap hotel rooms, but she hated the notion of getting pregnant again even more.

As it had been on the way to the bathtub, her walk on the way back was not only slow but distinctly bowlegged. She remembered that, too. She'd had a baby come through there, all right. Clara was waiting for her when she returned to her bed. Nellie startled herself with a smile. Another baby, no. This one? "Not so bad," she said, and took her daughter in her arms.

On the night of November 4, Roger Kimball headed over to Freedom Party headquarters on King Street to get the Congressional election returns as fast as the telegraph brought them into Charleston. He'd tried to get Clarence Potter and Jake Delamotte to come along with him. They'd both begged off.

"If your madman friends do win some seats, I'll want to go out and get drunk, and I don't mean by way of celebration," Potter had said. "That being so, I may as well go straight to a saloon now. The company's apt to be better, anyhow."

"I aim to get drunk no matter what happens," Jack Delamotte had echoed. He'd gone along with Potter.

Summer soldiers, Kimball thought. They'd been willing enough to think about using Jake Featherston, but hadn't settled down for the long haul of using Featherston's party. A submersible skipper learned patience. Those who didn't learn ended up on the bottom of the ocean.

Smoke filled the Freedom Party offices when Kimball walked in. As soon as the door closed behind him, he held up a gallon jug of whiskey. A raucous cheer went up, and everybody in the place welcomed him like a long-lost brother. His was far from the only restorative there; several men already seemed distinctly elevated. He laughed. Potter and Delamotte could have got drunk here and saved themselves thousands of dollars—not that thousands of dollars meant much any more.

"We're leading in the fourth district up in Virginia!" somebody at one of the bank of telegraph clickers announced, and more cheers rang out. People had yelled louder for Kimball and his whiskey, though.

He poured himself a glass and raised it high. "Going to Congress!" he shouted, and another burst of happy noise filled the rooms.

It must have spilled out into the street, too, for a gray-uniformed cop poked his head inside to see what the commotion was about. Somebody stuck a cigar in his mouth, as if the Freedom Party had had a baby. Somebody else asked, "Want a snort, Ed?" Before the policeman could nod or shake his head, he found a glass in his hand. He emptied it in short order.

"First votes in from Alabama—we're winning in the Ninth. That's Birmingham," a red-faced Freedom Party man said.

Applause rang out, and a couple of Rebel yells with it. People raised glasses and bottles on high and poured down the whiskey as if they'd never see it again. "Congress is going to be ours!" somebody howled. That set off more applause.

It made Kimball want to laugh or cry or bang his head against the wall. A couple of seats made people think they'd win a majority, which wouldn't, couldn't, come within nine miles of happening. Maybe Clarence Potter was right: maybe the Freedom Party did attract idiots.

From everything Kimball had heard, even Jake Featherston wasn't predicting more than about ten seats ending up with Freedom Party Representatives in them. That didn't make up a tenth part of the membership of the House. And if the leader of a party wasn't a professional optimist before an election, who was? Kimball had figured the night would be a success if the Freedom Party elected *anybody*. By that undemanding standard, things already looked to be going well.

"Here we go—First District, South Carolina. That's us. Quiet down, y'all," somebody at the bank of telegraph tickers called. People did quiet down—a little. The fellow waited for the numbers to come in, then said, "Damn, that Whig bastard is still a couple thousand votes up on Pinky. We're way out in front of the Radical Liberals, though."

Kimball looked around to see if Pinky Hollister, the Freedom Party candidate, was in the office. He didn't spot him. That didn't surprise him too much: Hollister actually lived not in Charleston but in Mount Holly, fifteen miles outside of town. He was probably getting the results there.

"Well, we scared the sons of bitches, anyways," a bald man said loudly. That signaled yet another round of cheers and clapping.

"To hell with scaring the sons of bitches," Kimball said, even more loudly. "We scared the sons of bitches up in the USA, but in the end they licked us. What I want us to do, God damn it to hell, is I want us to *win*."

Another near silence followed that. After a moment, people started to clap and yell and stomp on the floor. "Freedom!" somebody shouted. The cry filled the room: "Freedom! Freedom! Freedom!"

Dizziness that had nothing to do with the whiskey he'd drunk or with the tobacco smoke clogging and thickening the air filled Kimball. He'd known something of the same feeling when a torpedo he'd launched slammed into the side of a U.S. warship. Then, though, the pride had been in something he was doing himself. Now he rejoiced in being part of an entity larger than himself, but one whose success he'd had a hand in shaping.

"Freedom! Freedom! Freedom!" The shout went on and on. It

was intoxicating, mesmerizing. Kimball howled out the word along with everybody else. While he was yelling, he didn't have to think. All he had to do was feel. The rhythmic cry filled him full.

The door out onto the street opened. Kimball wondered if another cop was going to come in and try to make people quiet down. (He hadn't seen the first policeman leave. There he was, as a matter of fact, drinking like a fish.) A good many people must have had the same thought, for the chant of "Freedom!" came to a ragged halt.

But it wasn't a cop standing there. It was Anne Colleton. Not everybody in the office recognized her. Not everybody who recognized her knew she'd helped the Freedom Party. Most of the people who followed Jake Featherston were poor, or at best middle-class. One of the reasons they followed him was the vitriol he poured down on the heads of the Confederacy's elite. And here was an obvious member of that elite—Anne could never be anything else—coolly inspecting them, as if they were in the monkey house at the Charleston zoo.

Kimball started to explain who she was and what she'd done for the Party. Before he could get out more than a couple of words, she took matters into her own hands, as was her habit. "Freedom!" she said crisply.

At that, the chant resumed, louder than ever. Men surged toward Anne, as men had a way of doing whenever she went out in public. If she'd accepted all the drinks they tried to press on her, she would have gone facedown on the floor in short order. After she took one, though, she was vaccinated against taking any more.

Instead of acting like a chunk of iron in the grip of a magnet, Kimball hung back. Anne took her own attractiveness so much for granted, a man who showed he wasn't completely in her grasp often succeeded in piquing her interest by sheer contrariness.

"Hello, Roger," she said when she did finally notice him in the crowd. "I wondered if I'd find you here."

"Wouldn't miss it," he answered. "Best show in the world—this side of the circus, anyhow." She laughed at that. He said, "I didn't expect to see you here, though. If you got out of St. Matthews, I reckoned you'd go on up to Columbia."

"I didn't come down just for the election," Anne said. "I've taken a room at the Charleston Hotel on Meeting Street. The shops in Columbia don't compare to the ones they have here."

"If you say so," Kimball replied.

"I do say so," she answered seriously. "I know what I want, and I aim to get just that, nothing less." She glanced at him out of the corner of her eye. "Some ways, we're very much alike, you and I."

"That's a fact," he said. With a scowl, he went on, "If you're going to tease me, pick another time. I've got a little too much whiskey in me to take kindly to it tonight."

"That's frank enough." She appraised him as frankly. "But I'd already made up my mind that I wasn't going to tease you if I found you tonight: I was going to invite you up to my room. I just told you, I know what I want, and I aim to get it."

He thought about turning her down to prove she couldn't take him for granted. It might make her respect him more. It might also make her furious. And he didn't want to turn her down. He wanted to throw her down on a big soft bed and take her while she clawed his back to ribbons. If she had something like that in mind, he was ready, willing, and able—he hadn't drunk so much as to leave him in any doubts on that score.

"We're ahead in the Seventh in Tennessee," a man at the telegraph tickers announced, which produced a new roar of applause. Through it, the fellow went on, "That's around Nashville. They had the damnyankees occupying them—they got themselves some debts to pay."

Another Freedom Party man was keeping an eye on a different telegraphic instrument. "The Redemption League looks like they're gonna win themselves a seat in Texas," he said. "Ain't as good as if we did it, but it's the next best thing."

"How long do you want to stay here?" Anne asked.

"Up to you," Kimball answered. "We've already done about as much as I reckoned we could, and there's a lot of votes out there waiting to be counted. Maybe we really will get ten seats, the way Featherston said we would."

"That would be remarkable," Anne said. She echoed his own thought: "Most brags before an election turn to wind the second the voting's done." She slipped her arm into his. "Shall we go celebrate, then? My motorcar's a couple of doors down."

She was still driving the spavined Ford she'd got after the C.S. Army commandeered her Vauxhall. That told Kimball she hadn't come all the way back from the financial reverses she'd taken during the war. But then, who in the Confederate States had? He wondered what would have become of him had he not had more than usual skill with a deck of cards.

The Charleston Hotel was a large building of white stucco with a colonnaded entranceway. An attendant took charge of the Ford as if it had been a Vauxhall. The house detective didn't blink an eye as Kimball got into the elevator with Anne.

Their joining was fierce as usual, as much a struggle for dominance as what a lot of people thought of as lovemaking. When it was good, as it was tonight, they both won. Afterwards, they lay side by side, lazily caressing each other and talking . . . politics.

"You were right, Roger," Anne said, the sort of admission she seldom made. "The Freedom Party *is* on the way up, and Jake Featherston *is* someone to reckon with."

"I want to meet him myself," Kimball said. He tweaked her nipple, gently enough to be another caress, sharply enough to be a demand and a warning. "You owe me that, seeing as I was right."

She knocked his hand away and answered with more than a hint of malice: "What makes you think he'd want to meet *you*? You were an officer, after all, and he's not what you'd call keen on officers."

"He's not keen on *rich* officers," Kimball retorted. "You ever saw the farm I grew up on, you'd know I'm not one of those. He'll know it, too."

He saw he'd surprised her by answering seriously. He also saw his answer wasn't something she'd thought of herself. "All right," she said. "I'll see what I can do." She rolled toward him on the broad bed. "And now—"

He took her in his arms. "Now I'll see what I can do."

Cincinnatus Driver wished he didn't keep getting shipments for Joe Conroy's general store. He wished he could stay away from Conroy for the rest of his life. Like so many wishes, that one wasn't granted. He couldn't turn down deliveries to Conroy's. If he started turning down deliveries to one storekeeper, he'd stop getting deliveries to any storekeepers.

He also wished his rattletrap truck had windshield wipers. Since it didn't—he counted himself lucky it had a motor, let alone any fripperies—he drove from the Ohio to the corner of Emma and Blackwell as slowly and carefully as he could, doing his best to peer between the raindrops spattering his windshield. His best was good enough to keep him from hitting anybody, but he clucked to himself at how long he was taking to drive across Covington.

"And when I finally get there, I get to deal with Joe Conroy," he said. He talked to himself a lot while driving, for lack of anyone else with whom to talk. "Won't that just make my day? Sour old—"

But, when he hauled the first keg of molasses into the general store, he found Conroy in a mood not merely good but jubilant. He stared suspiciously at the fat storekeeper; Conroy wasn't supposed to act like that. Conroy didn't usually sign the shipping receipt till Cincinnatus had fetched in everything, but he did today. "Ain't it a beautiful mornin'?" he said.

Cincinnatus looked outside, in case the sun had come out and a rainbow appeared in the sky while his back was turned. No: everything remained as gray and dark as it had been a moment before. Nasty cold drizzle was building toward nasty cold rain; he didn't relish the upcoming drive back to the wharves.

"Tell you straight out, Mistuh Conroy, I've seen me a whole hell of a lot of days I liked the looks of better," he answered, and went back out into the wet to fetch some more of what Conroy had ordered. The sooner he got it all into the store, the sooner he could get away.

When he came inside again, Joe Conroy said, "Didn't say it was pretty out. I said it was a beautiful mornin', and it damn well is."

"I ain't got the time to play silly games." Cincinnatus spoke more rudely to Conroy than to any other white man he knew, and enjoyed every minute of it. "Tell me what you're talkin' about or let it go."

Conroy was in the habit of making noises about what an uppity nigger Cincinnatus was. He didn't even bother with those today. "I'll tell you, by Jesus," he answered. "I sure as hell will tell you. It's a beautiful mornin' on account of the Freedom Party won eleven seats in the Congress down in Richmond, and the Redemption League took four more."

That didn't make it a beautiful morning for Cincinnatus—but then, Cincinnatus, though he'd had to work with the Confederate diehards in Kentucky, wasn't one himself. His considered opinion was that a black man would have to be crazy to want the Stars and Bars flying here again. The Stars and Stripes weren't an enormous improvement, but any improvement, no matter how modest, seemed the next thing to a miracle to him.

Then he thumped his forehead with the heel of his hand. He might not be crazy, but maybe he was stupid. "*That's* how come I've seen 'Freedom!' painted on about every other wall this past couple weeks," he said.

"Sure as hell is," Conroy said. "Those folks is gonna do great things for the country—for *my* country." His narrow little eyes probed at Cincinnatus. Cincinnatus stared back impassively. He didn't want Conroy to know what he was thinking. The storekeeper grunted and went on, "Reckon there'll be a Freedom Party startin' up in Kentucky any day now."

"How do you figure the USA's gonna let you get away with that?" Cincinnatus asked in surprise. "They ain't gonna let there be no party that don't really belong to the United States at all."

Joe Conroy looked sly. He might not have been all that smart, but he was one crafty devil: that much Cincinnatus could not help but recognize. "They let Reds operate in the USA, don't they?" he said. "It's a free country, ain't it? Says it is, anyways—says it out loud, bangin' on a big drum. If the Freedom Party, say, wants to try and get the votes to take Kentucky back into the CSA, how can they stop us from doin' that?"

He looked smug, as if certain Cincinnatus could have no answer. But Cincinnatus did have an answer, and gave it in two words: "Luther Bliss."

"Huh," Conroy said. "We'll handle him, too, when the time comes."

Cincinnatus didn't argue, not any more. Arguing with a fool had always struck him as a waste of time. And Conroy sure as hell wasn't all that smart if he thought he could handle Luther Bliss. Cincinnatus had his doubts about whether Apicius Wood could handle Bliss if he had to. Apicius, he judged, had the sense not to try, but then Apicius really was pretty smart.

"Let me get the rest of your stuff," Cincinnatus said. If he wasn't face-to-face with Conroy, he couldn't possibly argue with him.

The storekeeper wanted to keep on jawing, but Cincinnatus didn't have to play, not today he didn't. With Conroy's receipt in his pocket, all he had to do was finish the delivery and get out. He did exactly that.

As he drove back up toward the river, he really noticed how many walls and fences had FREEDOM! painted on them. The word had replaced the blue crosses and red-white-red horizontal stripes as the diehards' chosen scribble.

He didn't like what he'd heard about the Freedom Party. That put it mildly. The local papers said little about the outfit; these days, they did their best to ignore what went on in the Confederate States. But word drifted up out of the CSA even so, word spread on the black grapevine that ran alongside and occasionally overlapped the one the diehards used. None of that word was good. And now the Freedom Party had done better in the elections than anyone expected. That was not good news, either.

When he got home that evening, he told Elizabeth what he'd heard from Conroy. She nodded. "White lady I clean house for, she was talkin' 'bout the same thing on the telephone. She sound happy as a pig in a strawberry patch."

"I believe it," Cincinnatus said. Kentucky had been taken out of the USA by main force at the end of the War of Secession. It had been dragged back into the United States the same way during the course of the Great War. A lot of Kentuckians—a lot of white Kentuckians—wished the return had never happened. Cincinnatus went on, "The government ever lets people here vote for the Freedom Party, they ain't gonna like the votes they see."

Elizabeth sighed. Part of the sigh was weariness after a long day. Part of it was weariness after living among and having to work for people who despised her the second they set eyes on her. She said, "Reckon you're right. Wish it wasn't so, but it is."

"Pa's right," Achilles said cheerfully. "Pa's right." He didn't know what Cincinnatus was right about. He didn't care, either. He had confidence that his father was and always would be right.

Cincinnatus wished he had that same confidence. He knew all too well how many mistakes he'd made over the years, how lucky he was to have come through some of them, and how one more could ruin not only his life but those of his wife and little son. Slowly, he said, "Maybe we ought to talk some more about pullin' up stakes, Elizabeth. We can do it. Don't need no passbook, not any more."

"We got us a lifetime of roots in this place," Elizabeth said. She'd said the same thing when Cincinnatus brought up the idea of leaving Covington earlier in the year.

He hadn't pressed her very hard then. Now he said, "Sometimes the only thing roots is good for is gettin' pulled out of the ground. Sometimes, if you don't pull 'em out, they hold you there till somethin' cuts you down."

Instead of answering directly, Elizabeth retreated to the kitchen. Over her shoulder, she said, "Go set yourself down. Smells like the ham is just about ready."

Sit himself down Cincinnatus did, but he didn't abandon the subject, as his wife plainly hoped he would. "I been thinkin' about this," he said. "Been thinkin' about it a lot, even if I ain't said much. If we leave, I know where I'd like us to go. I been lookin' things up, best I can."

"And where's that?" Elizabeth asked, resignation and fear mingling in her voice.

"Des Moines, Iowa," he answered. "It's on a river—the Des

Moines runs into the Mississippi—so there'll be haulin' business off the docks. Iowa lets black folks vote. They let women vote for president, too."

"I reckon they got women there," Elizabeth allowed. "They got any black folks there at all?"

"A few, I reckon," he answered. "There's a few black folks in just about every good-sized town in the USA. Ain't any more than a few very many places, though." He held up a hand before his wife could say anything. "Maybe that's even for the best. When there ain't very many of us, can't be enough for the white folks to hate us."

"Who says there can't?" Elizabeth spoke with the accumulated bitter wisdom of her race. "And Jesus, how far away is this Des Moines place? It'd be like fallin' off the edge of the world."

"About six hundred miles," Cincinnatus said, as casually as he could. Elizabeth's eyes filled with horror. He went on, "Reckon the truck'll make it. They got a lot o' paved roads in the USA." He pursed his lips. "Have to pick the time to leave, make sure everything's all good and dry."

"You aim on bringin' your ma an' pa along?" Elizabeth asked. Her own parents were both dead.

"They want to come, we'll fit 'em in some kind of way," Cincinnatus answered. "They don't—" He shrugged. "They're all grown up. Can't make 'em do nothin' they don't take a shine to."

"I don't take no shine to this myself." Elizabeth stuck out her chin and looked stubborn.

"You take a shine to livin' here in Kentucky if that Freedom Party starts winnin' elections?" Cincinnatus asked. "Somethin' like that happen, you'll be glad we got somewheres else to go."

That hit home. "Maybe," Elizabeth said in a small voice.

Something else occurred to Cincinnatus: if the Freedom Party started winning elections in the Confederate States, what would the Negroes there do? They couldn't run away to Iowa. They'd already tried rising up, tried and failed. What did that leave? For the life of him, Cincinnatus couldn't see anything.

Stephen Douglas Martin's eyes went from his daughter to his son and back again in something that looked like pleased bemusement. "You don't have to do this on account of me, you know," he said. "If you want to go out and paint the town red, go right on out and do it."

Chester Martin grinned at his father. "You already say I'm too much of a Red. I don't even want to go out and paint the town green."

"We just want to spend New Year's Eve with you and Mother, that's all," Sue Martin said, nodding vigorously. Chester's kid sister looked a lot like him, with sharp nose, green eyes, and sandy hair. She thought a lot like him, too, on labor matters and on a lot of other things as well.

"Besides, Pa," he added, "where the devil could I go in Toledo to paint the town red even if I wanted to? This isn't exactly Philadelphia or New York City." Toledo also didn't boast the multitude of saloons and brothels that sprang up behind an army's lines to cater to the needs—or at least the desires—of soldiers briefly free from the trenches.

"Well, you've got me there," his father answered. "Yes, sir, you've got me there. Once upon a time, I used to know where all the hot joints were, but that was a while ago now. Don't look so much to go out and get rowdy, like I used to before I hooked up with your mother and settled down."

From the kitchen, Louisa Martin called, "What are you blaming me for now, Stephen?" Dishes rattled as she put them back into the cabinet. "I'm almost finished in here. Whatever you're trying to pin on me, in a minute I'll be out there and you won't be able to do it."

She was as good as her word. Her husband said, "What I was trying to pin on you, dear, was settling me down. If you don't think you've done it, I'll go out and get drunk and leave you home with the kids." His eyes twinkled. "I'll probably beat you when I get back, too, the way I always do."

"I don't know why you haven't quit yet," Louisa Martin said with a pretty good martyred sigh. "I'm all over bruises, and the police keep dragging you down to the station every other day."

They both started laughing. Sue looked from one of them to the other, as if astonished her parents could act so absurd, and about something that would have been very serious had they been serious themselves. Chester said, "Well, Ma, that's better work for the cops than most of what they do, believe me."

"Hold on there." His father held out his hand like a cop halting traffic. "If we're going to have a happy New Year's Eve, let's see if we can manage not to talk politics. Otherwise, we'll just start arguing."

"I'll try," Chester said, knowing his father was likely to be right. He let out a wry chuckle before going on, "Doesn't leave me much to talk about but my football team, though."

"I wish you wouldn't talk about that, either," his mother said. "It's just as dangerous as going out there on the picket line."

"Not even close." Chester shook his head. "The fellows on the teams we play hardly ever carry guns, the way the cops and the company goons do."

"What did I say a minute ago?" Stephen Douglas Martin asked rhetorically. "If you want to turn out editorials, son, go work for a newspaper."

"All right," Chester said.

His father looked at him in some surprise, evidently not having expected such an easy victory. The older male Martin arose with a grunt from the chair in which he'd been ensconced since suppertime. He went into the kitchen and came out with a bottle of whiskey and two glasses.

"Well, I like that," Sue said with annoyance only partly affected. "Are you going to leave Mother and me thirsty?"

"I only have two hands." Her father set the whiskey and the glasses on the side table by his chair, then held up the members in question. "Count 'em—two." He returned to the kitchen and brought out two more tumblers.

Chester wondered if his father had intended to include Sue and his mother in the drinking. If he hadn't, nobody could prove it now. Whiskey gurgled into four glasses. Chester raised his. "To 1920!" he said.

"To 1920!" his sister and his parents echoed. They all drank. Chester sighed as the whiskey ran down his throat. It wasn't the smoothest he'd ever drunk, but it wasn't bad, either. Some of the rotgut he'd had in back of the lines—and, every once in a while, in a canteen or jug smuggled up to the forward trenches—had been like drinking liquid barbed wire.

His father stood to propose a toast. "To the 1920s—may they be a better ten years than the ten we've just gone through." Everyone drank to that, too. Stephen Douglas Martin said, "Now we ought to all pitch our glasses into the fireplace. Only trouble with that is, you go through a lot of glasses."

Sue looked at the clock on the mantel over the fireplace. "Three hours till midnight, less a couple of minutes. Will starting a new calendar really make a difference? It'd be nice to think it would."

"We always hope it will," her mother said wistfully. She sighed. "And we usually end up looking back and saying, 'Well, that's another year down.' "

"This wasn't too bad a year," Chester said. "I've had work through most of it, anyway, and that's more than I can say for the rest of the time since I got out of the Army."

He left it at that. Had he said more, he and his father would have got to arguing politics. He was convinced the factory owners had settled with the steelworkers because of the 1918 election returns. Whatever else you might say about them, big capitalists weren't stupid. When handwriting went up on the wall, they could read it. If they didn't come to terms with the people who worked for them, Congress would start passing laws they didn't fancy.

His mother sat down at the tired old upright piano and began to play. Her choice of tunes made him smile. After a little while, he said, "I'm not in the Army any more. You don't have to give me one Sousa march after another." He stomped up and down the room as if on parade.

"I like playing them, Chester," Louisa Martin said. "They make me want to go marching—except I can't, not while I'm playing." She swung into a spirited if not technically perfect rendition of "Remembrance and Defiance."

"She'll do as she pleases, son," Stephen Douglas Martin said. "If you haven't learned that about her by now, how long is it going to take you?"

"If she's playing them for herself, that's fine," Chester said. "If she's doing them for me, though, she's wasting her time. I never was so glad as the last time I took that uniform off."

"You went through a lot," Sue said. "I remember the hard time you gave that military policeman in the park when you were home on convalescent leave. It was like you'd seen a lot of things he never had, so you didn't think he had any business bothering you."

"That's just what I was thinking, Sis," he answered. "He behaved like he thought God had sent him down in a puff of smoke. The people who really went through the mill don't act that way."

"I've seen that with the younger fellows I work with," his father said. "One of 'em won the Medal of Honor, but you'd never hear it from him."

"That's the way it ought to be," Martin said. "We didn't go out there to blow our own horns or to have a good time—not that there were any good times to have in the trenches. We went out there to win the war, and we did that." He tossed down the rest of his whiskey. "And you know what? I wonder if what we bought is worth what we paid for it."

"We licked the Rebs," his father said. "Along with Kaiser Bill, we licked everybody. We've paid people back for everything they ever did to us."

"That's so," Chester said, "but there are—what? a million? something like that—say a million men who won't ever see it. And Lord only knows how many there are on crutches and in wheelchairs and wearing a hook instead of a hand." He touched his own left arm. "I'm one of the lucky ones. All I got was a Purple Heart and some leave time—a hometowner, we called a wound like that. But it was just luck. It wasn't anything else. A few inches to one side and I wouldn't be here now. I wouldn't be anyplace. I was a good soldier, but that's not why I came out in one piece. Nothing but luck."

The Sousa march Louisa Martin was playing came to a ragged halt. "You've upset your mother," Stephen Douglas Martin said, and then, to his wife, "It's all right, dear. He *is* here. He's fine. If he weren't here and fine, he wouldn't be spouting such nonsense, would he?"

"No," Chester's mother said in a small voice. "But I don't like to think about . . . about things that might have been."

Chester poured his glass full of whiskey again. He didn't like to think about things that might have been, either. Most of them were worse than the way things had really turned out. Some of them still made him wake up sweating in the night, even though the war had been over for two and a half years. He drank. If he got numb, he wouldn't have to think about them.

His mother got herself another drink, too. He raised an eyebrow at that; she didn't usually take a second glass. Maybe she had things she didn't want to think about, too. Maybe he'd given her some of those things. All at once, he felt ashamed.

"I'm sorry," he mumbled.

His father got up and clapped him on the shoulder. "You'll make a man yet," he said. "I think that's the first time I ever heard you say you were sorry and sound like you meant it. Kids say it, too, but they don't say it the same way. 'I'm sorry.' " Stephen Douglas Martin did a good imitation of a nine-year-old apologizing lest something worse happen to him.

Sue said, "Here's hoping we don't need to say we're sorry at all—well, not much—next year."

"I'll drink to that," Chester said, and he did.

Every time he looked at the clock on the mantel, it got a bit later. He found that pretty funny, which was a sign he'd taken a little too much whiskey on board. He'd have a headache in the morning. He was glad he wouldn't have to go in to the steel mill. That would have made his head want to fall off.

A few minutes before midnight, firecrackers started going off. They alarmed Chester; they made him think of gunfire. They alarmed all the dogs in the neighborhood, too. Along with bangs and pops, Toledo ushered in 1920 with a chorus of canine howls and frantic barks and yips.

"Happy New Year!" Chester said when both hands on the clock stood straight up. "Happy New Year!" He wondered if it would be. Then he wondered something else, something perhaps not altogether unrelated: who would be running for president?

Arthur McGregor stood in front of the stove in the kitchen, soaking in warmth as a flower soaked in sunlight. He had no idea why he thought of flowers: they weren't likely to appear in a Manitoba January. He turned so he'd cook on all sides.

Maude said, "When you came inside, you had frost on your eyebrows."

"I believe it," he answered. "If I wore a mustache, I'd have icicles hanging down from it, too. It's that kind of day. But if I don't get out there and take care of the stock, who's going to do it, eh?"

His wife's mouth tightened. Alexander should have been there to help. But Alexander was gone, except in the picture on the wall. McGregor moved away from the stove for a moment to go over and slip an arm around Maude. Her mouth fell open in surprise. Neither of them was greatly given to open displays of affection.

"I'm not doing as much as I should," he said discontentedly.

"You hush," Maude told him. "You've done plenty. You don't need to worry about not doing more. If you want it to be enough, it can be enough."

"But I don't," he said. "I have to do this, don't you see? I have to—and I can't." Of themselves, his hands folded into fists of frustration.

Maude set a consoling hand on his shoulder. "You went up to Winnipeg, Arthur. You looked around. And then you came home and said the thing couldn't be done." That was as close as she would come to talking out loud about his bombs. "If it can't be done, it can't, that's all."

"*Damn* the Yanks!" he said fiercely. "They keep too many soldiers around Custer's headquarters, and around the house he's stolen, too."

Looking back on it, blowing up Major Hannebrink had been fairly easy. The Yanks' euphoria at winning the war had helped; everyone in Rosenfeld that night had been celebrating as if joy would turn illegal the second the sun came up again. And Hannebrink was only a major, and not nearly so valuable to the Americans as their commander for all of Canada.

They knew General Custer would make a target for Canadians, as Archduke Franz Ferdinand had made a target for the Serbs. A Serb bomber had killed Franz Ferdinand and touched off the Great War. The Americans didn't intend to let Custer go the same way. They kept swarms of soldiers around him. McGregor had had no chance whatever to plant a bomb anyplace where it might do any good.

He might have flung one into Custer's motorcar, as the Serbs had flung one into Franz Ferdinand's carriage. The Serbian nationalist who flung his bomb had been shot dead a moment later. McGregor wanted to live. Even killing Custer was not revenge enough to satisfy him. He wanted more later, if he ever got the chance.

"Maybe he'll come down here to Rosenfeld again," Maude said.

She sounded consoling, the way she did when one of the girls was sad after breaking a toy. McGregor was sad—and furious, too—because he couldn't break his toy. If you looked at that the right way, it was grimly funny.

"Not likely," he said. "It isn't much of a town, when you get right down to it." He scowled. "There's just no chance for a man working by himself."

Maude asked the question that had stymied him over and over again: "Who can you trust?"

"Nobody." That was the answer he always reached. "Too many people up here have their hands in the Yanks' pockets. Too many people spy on their neighbors. Too many people would just as soon turn into Yanks—and you can't always tell who they are, not till you find out the hard way you can't."

His wife nodded. "I don't know what you can do, then, except get on with things here."

"I don't, either." McGregor felt like a lone wolf looking to pull down the biggest bull moose in an enormous herd. That was, when you thought about it, a crazy thing to want to do. Part of him knew as much. No: all of him knew as much. It was just that most of him didn't care. Slowly, he said, "The trouble is, there are too many hours in the day in the middle of winter—too much time to sit around and think."

Farm work was harder and made a man keep longer hours than

any town job. There were times, especially around the harvest, when he wished he could stay awake for a couple of weeks at a stretch so as not to waste any precious time. When snow lay deep on the ground, though, what a man could do diminished. After he tended the stock and made repairs around the house and barn, what was left but coming inside and sitting around and brooding?

Maude had an answer: "You might help me with some of my chores. They don't go away when the weather gets cold. Just the opposite, as a matter of fact."

He stared at her. Did she think he was going to put on an apron and do women's work? If she did, she had another think coming. He intended to let her know as much, too, in great detail.

Then he saw her eyes sparkle. He'd drawn in his breath for an angry shout. He let it out in a gust of laughter instead. "You're a devil," he said. "You really are. You had me going there."

"I hope so," his wife answered. "It's good to see you smile, Arthur. I haven't seen it often enough, not since—" She stopped. No one in the family had smiled much since Alexander got shot. Gamely, she went on, "We can't stay gloomy all the time. Life is too short for that. In spite of everything, life is too short for that."

"I suppose not," he said, nowhere near sure he supposed anything of the sort. To keep from having to decide whether he did or not, he pointed toward the ceiling. "What are the girls doing?"

"As much schoolwork as they can, I hope," Maude said. "If it doesn't snow again, they ought to be able to start going again tomorrow or the day after. They want to go back." A smile twisted only one corner of her mouth. "I hope they can. I won't be sorry to have them out of the house for a while. They've been snapping at each other a lot the past few days."

"I've noticed." McGregor ruefully shook his head. "I can still heat up Mary's backside, but that doesn't work with Julia any more." His older daughter was a woman, which still bemused him. "Have to talk sense to her, and sometimes she doesn't want to listen to sense."

"And where do you figure she gets that?" his wife murmured. He pretended not to hear. Knowing when not to hear struck him as not the least important part of a happy marriage.

What he did say was, "Fix me up a cup of tea, will you? I think I've warmed up enough so that it won't turn into a lump of ice in my belly now."

He was sipping it when Julia came downstairs dramatically

rolling her eyes and demanded, "Who will do something about my nuisance of a little sister?"

McGregor laughed again—twice in one morning. "You remind me of Henry II saying 'Who will rid me of this turbulent priest?'— and that was the end of Thomas à Becket," he said.

Julia looked so angry, he thought for a moment she wanted someone to rid her of Mary. But she was angry about something else: "They don't teach the history of England in school any more, except how the mother country was so wicked, the Americans had to have a revolution to get away."

"I'm not surprised," McGregor said. "I'm not happy, mind you, but I'm not surprised. The Yanks are doing everything they can to make us the same as they are, and they try to pretend they invented everything they borrowed from the mother country. The less youngsters know about England, the easier it is for the Americans to get away with their lies."

"That's right." Julia seemed about to burst into tears. "And there's nothing we can do about it, either, is there?"

Hearing that, McGregor knew he would have to try again to bomb General Custer. Maybe Custer's death would spark an uprising throughout Canada. Even if it didn't, it would remind his countrymen that they had a country of their own, that they weren't Yanks who happened to live in a cold climate and speak with a slightly strange accent.

And, with her fury against the United States, Julia had forgotten to be furious at her little sister. Or so McGregor thought, till Julia said, "And Mary keeps humming in my ear until it drives me to distraction. She's being annoying on purpose."

"If you'd been born a boy, you'd know how to take care of that," McGregor said. "You'd tell her to stop. If she didn't, you'd wallop her. If you want to go back upstairs and pretend you're a boy for a bit, that's all right with me."

Julia went, the light of battle in her eyes. A few minutes later, McGregor heard a thump. He waited for Mary to come down and complain about what a beast Julia was being. Nothing of the sort happened. There were several more thumps, interspersed with shouts and a couple of thuds, as of one body, or perhaps two, suddenly landing on the floor.

He chuckled. "That sounds cheery, doesn't it?"

"I hope they don't hurt each other," Maude said worriedly. "Julia's bigger, but I don't think Mary knows how to quit."

"If she goes up against somebody who's bigger and who means business, she'll learn how to quit after a little while," McGregor said.

His wife looked at him—caught and held his eye—without saying anything. For a moment, he wondered why. Then he realized that what he'd said about his younger daughter could apply to Canada's struggle against the United States. His own face showed that realization, but Maude kept staring at him. Again, he wondered why, and started to get angry.

But then he saw that what he'd said about his younger daughter could also apply to his own struggle against the United States. The United States were enormously bigger than he was, and they meant business about holding on to his country. He didn't care whether they meant business or not. He intended to go on fighting them.

"They haven't licked me yet, Maude," he said. "I've hit them a few licks, but they haven't licked me."

"All right," was the only thing his wife said. She wanted him to be careful in what he was doing, but she didn't want him to stop. Or, if she did want him to stop, she didn't let him know it, which amounted to the same thing.

Somebody was coming downstairs: Mary, by the sound of the footsteps. McGregor waited to console her. But, when his younger daughter came into the kitchen, triumph glowed on her face. "Julia got mean," Mary said. "I guess she won't try *that* again in a hurry."

Maude gaped in astonishment. So did McGregor. This time, he caught and held his wife's eye. If Mary could triumph against long odds, why couldn't he? That bomb still lay in the barn, hidden below the old wagon wheel. In spite of everything, he might find the chance to place it. He didn't need to do that right this minute. He had time.

Colonel Irving Morrell stood in the Fort Leavenworth, Kansas, train station, waiting for the special from Pontiac, Michigan, to come in. His green-gray overcoat held the worst of the cold at bay, though he wished he'd put on a fur hat instead of an ordinary service cap. Soot-streaked snow covered the ground. By the look of the mass of dirty-gray clouds building in the northwest, more would be coming before too long.

Beside him, Lieutenant Lije Jenkins stirred restlessly. "Everything's gone slower than it should have, sir, I know," he said, "but we're finally going to get the prototype for the new model."

"No, not the prototype." Morrell shook his head. "Just a test model, to see how some of the ideas we sent the War Department work out. Most of the parts come from the barrels we used in the Great War, so the test model will run maybe half as fast as it ought to." He sighed, blowing out a small cloud of vapor. "Getting the real McCoy built will run half as fast as it ought to, too."

"When I think what we could have had—" Jenkins angrily shook his head. "When I think what we should have had by now—the war will have been over three years this summer, and the new model still isn't anywhere near ready to go into production."

"We're living on borrowed time," Morrell said. "Ask any soldier, and he'll tell you the same thing. You can live on borrowed time for a while, but then you have to pay it back—with interest."

Jenkins stared north and east, across the Missouri. He pointed. "Don't I see exhaust there, sir? Time's right for that to be the special."

"So it is," Morrell agreed. "We'll know pretty soon, I expect." He glanced around, then nodded in satisfaction. "Ah, good. The station boys are on the ball. They've got the heavy ramp ready to unload the barrel from its flatcar. They've helped take barrels off trains before, so they'll know the drill."

Coal smoke billowing from the stack, the special crossed the Missouri, rolled through Leavenworth, and came north again to the Fort Leavenworth station. It was about the shortest train Morrell had ever seen, consisting of a locomotive, a tender, and one flatcar, on which perched a large shape covered by green-gray tarpaulins to shield it from the weather and from prying eyes.

When the train stopped, an officer jumped out of the locomotive and came up to Morrell. "Colonel Irving Morrell?" he asked. Morrell admitted he was himself. The officer nodded briskly, then saluted. "Very pleased to meet you, sir. I'm Major Wilkinson; I've ridden down with this beast from Pontiac. As soon as I get your John Hancock on about sixty-eleven different forms here, I can put it into your hands and let you start finding out what it can do."

Morrell signed and signed and signed. By the time he was through, the signatures on the forms hardly looked like his any more. After he gave the last sheet of paper back to Major Wilkinson, he said, "Why don't you take the wrapping off so I can see what's in the package?"

"I'll be glad to, sir. If you and Lieutenant—Jenkins, was it?—will come along with me, you can see just what's in there." Nimble as a monkey, he swung himself up onto the flatcar and untied the ropes that held the tarps in place. Morrell and Jenkins ascended more sedately. They helped him pull away the heavy cloth covering the new barrel.

"Bully," Lije Jenkins said softly when he got his first look. "If that's not a machine for the 1920s, I'll be darned if I know what is. Compared to what we had in the Great War, that's a machine from out of the 1930s, by God."

"Yeah, it's pretty on the outside," Morrell said, "but what it reminds me of is a homely girl with a lot of paint and powder on." He started to rap the barrel's hull with his knuckles, but checked himself; it was cold enough that he'd lose skin on the metal. He contented himself with pointing. "That's just mild steel, not armor plate, and it's thin mild steel to boot. That makes the barrel lighter, so the one White engine they threw in there can give it even a halfway decent turn of speed. But you couldn't take it into combat; it's not even proof against rifle fire, let alone anything else."

But even as he spoke, his eyes caressed the test barrel's lines as they did Agnes Hill's whenever he saw her. Here, in metal, was the shape he'd sketched not long after coming to the Barrel Works. The turret cannon and machine gun stared at him. So did the machine gun mounted in the front of the hull.

"It doesn't look as . . . as busy as one of our regular barrels," Lieutenant Jenkins said.

"No, I suppose not," Morrell said, "but I hope it'll keep the enemy busier than one of the regular sort. And we won't need to put a whole regiment of soldiers inside here when we go into action, either." He strode to the rear of the flatcar. "Hurry up with that ramp, if you please, gentlemen."

"We're just about ready, Colonel," one of the soldiers replied. A couple of minutes later, he said, "All right, sir, everything's in place."

"Do you want to back it off the car, Major?" Morrell asked.

"I will if you want me to, sir," Wilkinson answered, "but go right ahead if you'd rather do the honors."

Morrell needed no more urging. He opened the hatch in the top of the hull that led down into the driver's compartment, then wriggled inside. The controls were identical to those of the older barrels. He'd learned the driver's art since coming to the Barrel Works, but had applied himself to it as he applied himself to everything that caught his interest. His finger stabbed the electric-starter button.

Behind him, the White engine grunted, coughed, and came to life. It was loud. It was not, however, deafening, as the engines in old-style barrels were. That wasn't because the test model had only one, where normal machines needed two. It was because, instead of sitting right there in the middle of the barrel's interior, the engine had a compartment of its own, separated from the crew by a steel bulkhead.

He wished he didn't have to back the barrel down the ramp to get it off the flatcar. Even with his head out of the hatch, even with the rearview mirror the manufacturer had thoughtfully provided (a little bonus that might possibly last thirty seconds in combat), he couldn't see behind himself for beans. That was something he hadn't thought about when he decided on a turret-mounted cannon.

Well, that was what the test model was for: to discover all the things he hadn't thought of, and nobody else had, either. With luck, he'd be able to get rid of them before the new model went into production. He knew perfectly well that he wouldn't find them all; he was human, and therefore fallible. But he'd do the best job he could.

He'd do the best job he could of getting this beast off the flatcar, too. All he had to do was back straight. If he looked ahead, he ought to be able to judge how well he was doing that. And he couldn't keep sitting up here forever. His left foot came down on the clutch. He threw the shift lever into reverse and gave the barrel a little gas.

It was peppier than the ones in which he'd fought the Great War: not peppy like a fancy motorcar, not peppy enough to suit him, but peppier. It went down the ramp faster than he'd expected. Almost before he knew it, he was on the ground. From the flatcar, Major Wilkinson waved and Lieutenant Jenkins gave him a thumbs-up.

"Come on!" he shouted to Jenkins over the rumble of the engine—which seemed a lot louder with his head out the hatch. The lieutenant jumped down from the train, clambered up the side of the barrel, and scrambled into the turret through a hatch on the roof.

"There's no ammunition in here," he said indignantly. Morrell snorted—as if anyone would be crazy enough to put ammunition in a barrel that would be traveling by train. Accidents didn't happen very often, but who would take the chance on sending an expensive test model up in smoke? Then Jenkins went on, "I wanted to shoot up the landscape as we drove along," and Morrell snorted again, this time on a different note. His subordinate was just acting like a kid again.

Morrell put the barrel into the lowest of its four forward speeds. It rattled over the railroad tracks and off toward the muddy prairie northwest of Fort Leavenworth. He built up to full speed as fast as he could. If the speedometer wasn't lying, he was doing better than ten miles an hour, more than twice as fast as a Great War barrel could manage on similar ground. The power-to-weight ratio of the test model was supposed to be the same as that of the eventual production machine. If so, these barrels would do tricks their ancestors had never imagined. They still weren't fast enough to suit him.

"Hell of a ride!" Jenkins shouted, sounding as exhilarated as a skilled horseman on a half-broken stallion. "*Hell* of a ride! Now we've got the cavalry back again, by Jesus!"

"That's part of the idea," Morrell said. Men on horseback had been poised throughout the Great War, ready to exploit whatever breakthroughs the infantry could force. But infantry alone hadn't been able to force breakthroughs, and cavalry melted under machine-gun fire like snow in Death Valley summer. The old barrels *had* broken through Confederate lines, but hadn't always been swift enough to exploit to the fullest the breaches they made.

Maybe these machines would, even in their present state. In his mind's eye, Morrell saw barrels clawing at the flank of a foe in retreat, shooting up his soldiers, wrecking his supply lines, keeping reinforcements from reaching the field, pushing the front forward by leaps and bounds, not plodding steps.

It was a heady vision, so heady it almost made Morrell see with his mind's eye to the exclusion of the pair at the front of his head. Had he not paid attention to the gauges in front of him, he would have missed noting how little fuel the test model carried in its tank. Stranding himself out on the prairie was not what he had in mind when it came to getting acquainted with the new machine. Reluctantly, he steered for the muddy field where half a dozen survivors of the Great War sat.

He turned off the engine, climbed out of the hatch, and got down off the test model. Lije Jenkins came down beside him. The youngster looked from the new barrel to the old ones. "It's like stacking the first Duryea up against an Oldsmobile, isn't it, sir?" he said.

"Something like that, anyway," Morrell said. "Of course, there is one other difference: there really are Oldsmobiles, but this baby"—again, he remembered in the nick of time not to rap his knuckles on the hull—"is just pretend, for now."

"I hope we don't take twenty years to get the real ones, sir," Jenkins said.

"So do I, Lieutenant, with all my heart. We may need them sooner than that," Morrell said. He started off toward the barracks. Jenkins tagged along after him.

As Morrell walked, he wondered what he could tell Agnes Hill about his new toy. She knew, in a general way, what his duties were. Being a soldier's widow, she also knew not to ask too many questions about what exactly he did. But the next time he saw her, he was going to be excited. He wanted to share that excitement. He also needed not to talk too much. He was awfully glad he'd gone to that dance with Jenkins. He wanted to go right on being glad. The only place where taking chances was a good idea was on the battlefield.

IX

A fat man with a nasty cough came up to the counter of the drugstore where Reggie Bartlett worked. "Help you?" Reggie asked.

"Hope to God you can," the man answered, hacking again. "If I don't shake this damn thing, it's going to drive me right up a tree." He pulled out a pack of cigarettes and tapped one in the palm of his hand.

"Here you go." Reggie handed him a box of matches with HAR-MON'S DRUGS printed on the top—good advertising. He waited till the man lit up, then went on, "I can give you a camphorated salve to rub on your chest and under your nose. And we've got a new cough elixir in. It's got a kind of denatured morphine in it—not nearly as strong, and not habit-forming, but it does the job."

"Give me some of the salve, and a bottle of that stuff, too," the sufferer said. He coughed some more and shook his head. "This is killing me. I can't even enjoy my smokes any more."

"Another thing you can do is, you can set a pot of water on the stove to boil, put in some of the salve, and breathe in the steam," Bartlett said. "That'll help clear out your lungs, too."

"Good idea," the fat man answered. His face took on a kind of apprehension that had nothing to do with his ailment. "Now—what do I owe you?"

"Two thousand for the salve," Reggie said. The customer nodded in some relief. Reggie continued, "The elixir, though, it's new stuff, like I said, and it's expensive: $25,000."

"Could be worse," the fat man said. He took three $10,000 banknotes from his wallet and shoved them across the counter at

Bartlett. Reggie gave him three $1,000 banknotes in change. As the fat man tucked them away, he shook his head in wonder. "It's like play money, ain't it? Reckon I'm a millionaire, and a whole hell of a lot of good it's doing me." He coughed again, then picked up the squat blue bottle of salve and the taller one of the elixir. "Much obliged to you, young fellow, and I hope these here give me some relief." As he headed for the door, he called a last word over his shoulder: "Freedom!"

Bartlett started violently. He had all he could do to hold his tongue, and indeed to keep from running after the fat man and screaming curses at him. "Christ!" he said. His hands were trembling.

Jeremiah Harmon looked up from the tablets he was compounding. "Something troubling you, Reggie?" He was in his late forties, with a brown mustache beginning to go gray, and so quiet Bartlett was always straining to hear him. That wasn't bad, not so far as Reggie was concerned. He'd walked out on McNally, his previous employer, because the man wouldn't stop riding him.

"Yes, sir," he answered. "That fellow who just left used the Freedom Party salute when he went out the door. I don't fancy those people, not even a little I don't."

"Can't say I do, either," Harmon said, "but I doubt they're worth getting very excited about." As far as he was concerned, nothing was worth getting very excited about.

"Lord, I hope you're right, but I just don't know," Bartlett said. "I watched their goons bust up a rally. They almost busted me up, too. That's not the only brawl they've gotten into—not even close. And now Richmond's got a Freedom Party Congressman. Makes me sick to my stomach."

"Bicarbonate of soda will do the trick there," Harmon remarked; he was a druggist down to the tips of his toes. After a moment, though, he realized Reggie had used a figure of speech. With a shrug, he went on, "My guess is, they're a flash in the pan. Having a few of them in Congress is probably a good thing. Once they show they're nothing but a pack of noisy windbags, people will wise up to them pretty fast."

Bartlett grunted. "I hadn't thought about it like that. Maybe you've got something there." He didn't take the Freedom Party seriously even now. When more people had a chance to see it in action, how could they take it seriously, either? "Sometimes the best thing you can do is let a fool prove he is one."

"That's right," Jeremiah Harmon said. A customer came into the store. Harmon bent to his work again. "Why don't you see to Mrs. Dinwiddie there?"

"All right. Hello, Mrs. Dinwiddie," Reggie said. "What can I get for you today?" He thought he knew, but he might have been wrong.

He was right: Mrs. Dinwiddie answered, "I need a bottle of castor oil. My bowels have been in a terrible state lately, just a terrible state, and if I don't get something to loosen them up, well, I swear to Jesus, I don't know what I'll do. Explode, I reckon."

She went on in that vein for some time. She bought castor oil every other week; the purchases were regular as clockwork, even if her bowels weren't. Every time she bought it, she gave the same speech. Bartlett was sick of listening to it. So, no doubt, was Jeremiah Harmon. Since Harmon was the boss, he had the privilege of avoiding Mrs. Dinwiddie. Reggie didn't.

By the time she ran down, he was on much more intimate terms with her lower bowel than he'd ever wanted to be. "Well, I won't keep you any more," she said, having already kept him too long. She opened her handbag. "What do I owe you?"

"That's $15,000, ma'am," Reggie answered.

"It was only ten the last time I came in," she said sharply. He shrugged. If she didn't like the way prices jumped, she could take that up with Harmon. He figured out how much to charge. But, after grumbling under her breath, Mrs. Dinwiddie gave Bartlett a pair of $10,000 banknotes. He returned her change and the bottle of castor oil.

So the day went. It was something less than exciting, but it put money in his pockets. It put tens of thousands of dollars in his pockets. Those tens of thousands of dollars left him somewhat worse off than he had been before the war started, when he'd been making two dollars a day. Inflation made a bitter joke of everything he'd thought he knew about money.

He supposed that was one reason people voted for the Freedom Party and other outfits like it. They loudly proclaimed they had the answers to all the problems bedeviling the Confederate States. Proclaiming they had the answers was the easy part. Really having them, and making them work—that looked harder. That looked a hell of a lot harder to him. But some people would buy castles in the air because they were short of beans on the ground.

When six o'clock rolled around, he said, "See you tomorrow, Mr. Harmon."

The druggist looked up in vague surprise. "Oh, yes, that will be fine." He made no move to leave himself. Reggie was just hired help, and could come and go as he pleased—so long as he pleased to be on time most of the time. The drugstore belonged to Harmon. He worked as long as he thought he had to.

Reggie put on his overcoat and went out into the cold. It wasn't too bad—no snow lay on the ground—but it wasn't anything he enjoyed, either. He walked quickly, his feet clicking along the sidewalk. As long as he kept moving, he didn't feel the chill too badly. And Bill Foster's flat, where he had a supper invitation, lay only a few blocks away.

Sally Foster opened the door. "Hello, Reggie," she said. "Come in, get warm, make yourself at home. How are you today?"

"I've been worse," he answered, and heaven only knew that was true.

"Bill, hon," Sally called, "Reggie's here." She was a short, slightly pudgy blonde in her mid-twenties. For reasons Bartlett couldn't quite fathom, she thought well of him. He'd wondered if he would keep Bill Foster as a friend after Bill and Sally got married; a lot of men gave up their bachelor friends after they stopped being bachelors themselves. But Sally had gone out of her way to be cordial, and so the friendship stayed warm.

"Hello, Reggie," Bill Foster said. Married life plainly agreed with him; he'd put on ten pounds, easy, since Sally started cooking for him. "Can I get you a little something to light a fire inside?"

"Thanks. I wouldn't mind," Reggie answered.

Foster took down a whiskey bottle and a couple of glasses. "Do you want water with that?" he asked. Sometimes Reggie did, sometimes he didn't.

Tonight, he didn't. "Pipes are rusty enough already," he said. Sally laughed. Maybe she hadn't heard it before. It was an old joke in the trenches, though, as Foster's resigned chuckle showed. When Reggie had the glass in his hand, he raised it and said, "Here's to a long walk off a short pier for Jake Featherston."

"Lord knows I'll drink to that," Bill said, and he did. So did Bartlett. Sure enough, the whiskey warmed him nicely. Foster said, "I'll drink to that any day, and twice on Sunday, as a matter of fact. But what made you come out with it just then?"

Reggie told him about the fat man with the cough who'd called out the Freedom Party's one-word slogan, and finished, "When he walked out, I was standing there wishing I'd given him rat poison instead of his cough elixir."

"I've heard it, too," Bill Foster said. "It makes the hair stand up on the back of my neck, same as the noise of a shell coming in. You'd reckon people had better sense, but a lot of 'em don't."

"The other thing I wondered was whether he was just somebody who voted for the Freedom Party, or if he was one of the tough guys who put on white and butternut and go out looking for heads to break," Bartlett said. "He didn't look like the type, but you never can tell."

"They don't need very many ruffians," Foster said. "As long as folks think the fellows with the clubs are doing the right thing, they won't try and stop 'em. And that worries me more than anything."

It gave Reggie something new to worry about, too: "We can't even write our Congressman and complain. He'd likely send goons right to our door."

"What you can do," Sally said, "is come and sit down and have supper. Once you get some food in your bellies to go along with the whiskey you're pouring down, the world won't seem like such a rotten place."

Ham and applesauce and canned corn and string beans cooked with a little salt pork might not have changed the world, but Sally was right: they did improve Reggie's opinion of it. Peach pie improved it even more. He patted his stomach. He had no trouble understanding how Bill had put on weight. "You don't happen to have a sister, do you?" he asked Sally, knowing she didn't.

He'd pleased her, though; he saw it in her eyes. "You should have got married a long time ago," she told him.

He shrugged. "My mother says the same thing. She wants grandchildren. I never met a girl I felt like marrying." He shook his head. "No. That's not so. Before the war, I was sweet on a girl. But she wasn't sweet on me. She wasn't sweet on anybody, not back then she wasn't. I heard she finally married some Navy man after the war. Now, what was his name? I heard it. It's going to bother me if I can't remember." He paused, thinking hard. "Brantley? Buckley? No, but something like that . . . Brearley! That's what it was, Brearley. I knew I'd come up with it."

"Now, if you could just come up with a girl," Sally said.

"If I wanted to listen to my mother, I'd have gone to visit my mother," Reggie said. Everybody laughed. He held out his glass to Bill Foster. "You want to get me another drink? I know good and well my mother wouldn't." Everyone laughed again.

*   *   *

Sylvia Enos smoked in short, savage puffs. "That man!" she said.

Neither Sarah Wyckoff nor May Cavendish needed to ask about whom she was talking. "What did Frank do now?" Sarah asked.

"Felt me up," Sylvia snarled. "He hadn't bothered me for weeks, but this morning, all of a sudden, he grew more arms than an octopus. He came back to where I was working and he felt me up like I was a squash he was buying off a pushcart. I almost hauled off and belted him."

"You should have," Sarah said. "I would. I'd have knocked him into the middle of next week, too." With her formidable build, she could have done it.

May said, "He's been sniffing around Lillian for a while. He's probably been doing more than sniffing, too; she's a little chippy if I ever saw one." She sniffed herself, then went on, "But I haven't seen Lillian for the past couple days, and—"

"She quit," Sylvia said. "I heard one of the bookkeepers talking about it. She's moving out to California. It's good for your lungs out there."

"Well, if she quit, then Frank is going to be on the prowl for somebody new," May said. "We've watched it happen often enough now."

"Often enough to be good and sick of it," Sylvia said. "And I wish to heaven he wouldn't come sniffing around me. If he doesn't know by now that I don't feel like playing games, he's an even bigger fool than I think he is."

"He couldn't be a bigger fool than I think he is," Sarah Wyckoff said.

Sylvia took a big bite of her egg-salad sandwich. She wished she were a gigantic carnival geek, biting the head off of Frank Best instead of a chicken. Then she shook her head in bemusement. He really had to be on her nerves, or she would never have come up with such a bizarre mental image.

She said, "I wish I could find another job. But how am I even supposed to look for one when I'm here five and a half days a week? And jobs aren't easy to come by, not like they were during the war."

"It's a nasty bind to be in, dearie," May said. "I hope it turns out all right for you."

"The worst he can do is fire me," Sylvia said. "Then I will have time to look for a new job. When he gets to be like this, I almost wish he would fire me. You girls are dears, but I wouldn't mind getting out of this place."

"What makes you think it would be different anywhere else?" May asked. "You'd still have a man for a boss, and you know what men are like."

"Careful," Sarah said in a low voice. Frank Best strolled past and waved to the women at their dinner break. He doubtless thought his smile was charming. As far as Sylvia was concerned, it was so greasy, it might have been carved from a block of lard.

She lit a new cigarette. The foreman favored her with another oleaginous smile when he returned from wherever he'd gone. "Almost time to get back to the line," he said.

"Yes, Mr. Best." Sylvia looked forward to returning to work about as much as she looked forward to going to the doctor to have a carbuncle lanced. Sometimes, though, she had to go to the doctor. And, when the whistle blew, she had to go back and paint red rings on galoshes.

Frank Best left her alone for twenty minutes after that, which was about fifteen minutes longer than she'd expected. Then he came back toward her with a pair of rubber overshoes in his hand. The rings on them were perfect. Sylvia had made a point of painting perfect rings since he'd started bothering her again, to give him as little excuse as she could.

But, being the foreman, he didn't necessarily need an excuse. Sylvia dipped her brush in the can of red paint by the line and painted two more perfect rings on the galoshes in front of her.

"Tried to slip these by on me, did you, Sylvia?" Best asked. He thrust the overshoes in his hand at her.

"I don't see anything wrong with them," Sylvia said.

That turned out to be a mistake—not that she had any right course. "Here. Take a closer look," Best said, and stepped up right alongside her. He brushed her breast with his arm as he brought the galoshes up and held them under her nose. That might have been an accident—had he not been bothering her all morning.

She took half a step back—and knocked over the can of red paint so that most of it spilled on his shoes. That might have been an accident—had he not been bothering her all morning.

"Oh, Mr. Best!" she exclaimed. "I'm so very sorry!" *I'm so very sorry I didn't think of that a long time ago.*

He jumped and hopped and used language no gentleman would have employed in the presence of a lady. He'd already proved he was no gentleman by treating Sylvia as if she were no lady. "You'd better watch yourself!" he said when something vaguely resembling coherence returned to his speech. "You'd better clean this mess up, and you'd better make sure nothing like it ever happens again, or you'll be out on the sidewalk so fast, it'll make your head spin."

"Yes, Mr. Best. I'm terribly sorry, Mr. Best," Sylvia said. The foreman stomped off, leaving a trail of red footprints.

Sylvia soaked up as much of the red paint in rags as she could. She got some on her hands, but none on her dress or shirtwaist—she was careful about them, where she hadn't cared at all about Best's shoes. She opened another can of paint and went right on giving galoshes red rings, too. If she hadn't done that, Best would have got another reason to come back and have a word with her.

As things worked out, he didn't speak to her for the rest of the day. That suited her fine. Women from all along the production line found excuses to come by and say hello, though. Under their breath, they found considerably more than hello to say, too. She got more congratulations than she'd had on any one day since Mary Jane was born. If any of the women had a good word to say about Frank Best, nobody said it where she could hear.

Sarah Wyckoff said, "That was even better than knocking his teeth down his throat, on account of it made him look like the fool he is."

May Cavendish added, "Now all the girls will be bringing paint to work, Sylvia, and it's your fault, nobody else's."

"Good," Sylvia said. May giggled.

When the closing whistle blew, Sylvia left the galoshes factory with a spring in her step that hadn't been there at quitting time for quite a while. She got her children off the school playground, and was far from the only mother doing so. The school didn't take care of children in the classrooms after teaching was done for the day, as it had during the war. But it did let kids play in the yard till their parents could pick them up. That was something, if not much.

"I'm frozen, Ma," George, Jr., said.

"Me, too," Mary Jane added. Half the time, she agreed with whatever her big brother said. The other half, she disagreed—violently. Sylvia never knew in advance which tack she would take.

"We'll be home soon," Sylvia said. "We've got the steam radiator, and I'll be cooking on the stove, too, so things will be nice and toasty. The more time you spend complaining here, the longer it'll be before you're back."

For a wonder, the kids got the message. In fact, they ran to the trolley stop ahead of her. She might have had a spring in her step, but they were children. They didn't need to spill paint on anybody to feel energetic.

After they all got back to the apartment, Sylvia boiled a lot of cabbage and potatoes and a little corned beef for supper. The vegetables were cheap; the corned beef wasn't. The children loved potatoes and ate cabbage only under protest. Sylvia had been the same way when she was small.

As long as she was boiling water for supper, she also heated some for the bathroom down at the end of the hall. The children were old enough now that she couldn't bathe them together any more. That meant going down the hall first with Mary Jane, then with George, Jr., and last by herself. By the time she got to use the tub, she could hardly tell any hot water had ever gone into it.

That meant she bathed as fast as she could. Then she got out, threw on a robe, wrapped her wet hair in a towel, and hurried back to her flat. It was just as well that she did; she found the children doing their best to kill each other. Size favored George, Jr., ferocity and long fingernails Mary Jane.

"Can't I leave the two of you alone for five minutes?" Sylvia demanded, despite the answer obviously being *no*. She did her best to get to the bottom of what had started the brawl. The children told diametrically opposite stories. She might have known they would. She *had* known they would. This time, she couldn't sort out who was lying, or whether they both thought they were telling the truth. With fine impartiality, she whacked both their bottoms.

"I hate you!" Mary Jane screamed. "I hate you even worse than I hate *him*." She pointed to George, Jr.

Ignoring his sister, he told Sylvia, "I'm never going to speak to you again as long as I live." He'd made that threat before, and once made good on it for a solid half hour: long enough to unnerve her.

She went into the bedroom and looked at her alarm clock. "It's after eight," she said. "You both need to get ready for bed." That produced more impassioned protests from the children; George, Jr., abandoned silence so he could squawk his head off. It did him no good. In fifteen minutes, he and Mary Jane were both in bed, and asleep very shortly after that.

Sylvia sat down on the couch with a weary sigh. She would have to go to bed pretty soon herself. When she got up, all she had to look forward to was another day at the galoshes factory. Life was supposed to be better than that, wasn't it?

Life would have been better—she was sure of it—had George lived. Then he would have been going out to sea, true, and complaining about the drudgery when he was back on land. But, no matter how hard the work was, he'd liked it. Sylvia wouldn't have liked making galoshes even had Frank Best not bothered her whenever he wasn't bothering someone else. It was only a job, something she did to keep food on the table. She wished she could quit.

She sighed again. She was trapped. The only difference between her and a mouse in a trap was that her back wasn't broken . . . yet.

"If I had that limey submersible skipper here," she said, "I'd shoot him right between the eyes. What the *hell* was he doing in that part of the Atlantic?" She didn't own a pistol; George hadn't kept one in the flat. She would gladly have learned to shoot one, though, if she could have avenged herself on that Englishman. She shook her head. For all she knew, the King of England had pinned a medal on him. If there was any justice in the world, she had a devil of a time seeing where.

A nasty wind blew snow into Lucien Galtier's face. He pulled down his hat and yanked up the collar of his coat as he made his slow way from the farmhouse to the barn. His way had to be slow; because of the snow, he could hardly tell where the barn lay. But his feet knew.

He accepted Quebec winter with the resignation of a man who had never known and scarcely imagined anything different. Moving to a warmer climate had never crossed his mind. Quebec boasted no warmer climates. Besides, moving would have taken him off the land his family had farmed since the seventeenth century. He was less likely to leave his patrimony than he was to leave his wife, and never once in all the years since the priest joined them together had he had any thought of leaving Marie.

When he got to the barn, he let out a sigh of relief. The horse snorted, hearing him come in. It was not a snort of friendly greeting, in spite of all the hours of conversation that had passed between the two of them as they traveled the roads around the farm. No, the only thing that snort meant was, *Where's my breakfast, and what kept you so long?*

"Compose yourself in patience, greedy beast," Galtier said. The horse snorted again. It was not about to compose itself in patience, or any other way. It wanted hay and it wanted oats and it wanted them right this second.

He fed all the livestock and cleaned up the muck. By the time he was done with that, the muscles in the small of his back were complaining. *Why didn't you send out Georges or Charles?* was what they were complaining. He did do that a lot of the time, but they were busy elsewhere this morning.

"And," he said, speaking to his muscles as if they were the horse, and therefore incapable of talking back, "I am not in my dotage. If I cannot do this work, what good am I?" But it was not that he couldn't do the work. It was that doing the work exacted its price these days, and the price went up with the years.

He went back out into the cold, back to the farmhouse. Once he got close to it, he whistled in surprise. Dr. Leonard O'Doull's Ford was parked by the house. Even though his son-in-law worked at the hospital on Galtier land, he didn't come to visit all that often. Lucien picked up his pace, to see why O'Doull had come today.

"Bonjour, mon beau-père," O'Doull said, rising to shake his hand. Marie had already given the young doctor a cup of coffee and a sweet roll.

"Bonjour," Lucien said. "My daughter and my grandson, I trust they are well?"

"Yes," O'Doull said, and Marie nodded: she must have asked the same question. The American went on, "I have come, as I was beginning to tell your wife before you got here, to ask a favor of you."

"Vraiment?" Lucien said in some surprise. O'Doull was an independent fellow, and the favors he asked few and far between. Galtier waved his arms. "Well, if you came here to do that, you'd better get on with it, don't you think?"

"Yes, certainly." But O'Doull hesitated again before finally continuing, "My mother and father have decided they would like to come up to Quebec to see their first grandson. You know our house, and know that it is not of the largest. Is it—would it be—possible that you might put them up here for a few days' visit? If it cannot be done, you must know I will understand, but it would be good if it could."

Before answering, Galtier glanced toward Marie. The farmhouse was her province. He knew there would be disruption, but she was the one to gauge how much. Only after she gave him a tiny nod did he answer in effusive tones: "But of course! They would be most welcome. When would they be traveling up to see you?"

"In a couple of weeks, if that's all right," O'Doull answered. "They're so looking forward to meeting Nicole and seeing little Lucien and to meeting all of you, for your doings have filled the pages of our letters."

"I hope we are not so bad as you will have made us out to be," Galtier said.

While Leonard O'Doull was still figuring out how to take that, Marie asked, "Is it that your mother and father speak French?"

"My father does, some," O'Doull replied. "He is a doctor himself, and studied French in college. My mother has been trying to learn since I decided to live here, but I do not know how much she has picked up."

"We will get along," Galtier said in his rusty English. Then he had to translate for his wife. Marie nodded, though she had almost no English of her own.

"I thank you very much," O'Doull said with a nod of his own that was almost a bow. "I will wire them and tell them it is arranged. Truly, they do want to meet you. I will also, naturally, let you know when I hear just when they will arrive in Rivière-du-Loup." With one more nod, he went back to his motorcar and then back to the hospital.

After the door closed behind him, Lucien and Marie looked at each other. They both raised eyebrows and then both started to laugh. Galtier said, "Well, this will be something out of the ordinary, at the very least."

"Out of the ordinary, yes," Marie agreed. "And the work we will have to do to be ready in time will be out of the ordinary, too." She drew herself up straight with pride. "But we will do it. We will not shame ourselves before Leonard's rich American parents."

Doctors weren't necessarily rich, but Lucien didn't bother contradicting his wife. Contradicting Marie rarely did any good. Besides, she was in essence right. Galtier too wanted to put on the best show he could for his son-in-law's parents.

Over the next couple of weeks, a tornado might have passed through the house. Doing spring cleaning and the laundry that went with spring cleaning while snow lay on the ground wasn't easy, but Marie and her daughters managed, with help from Lucien and the two boys whenever they could be roped into it. Denise, who'd had the room she'd once shared with Nicole to herself since her sister's wedding, was bundled off to sleep with Susanne and Jeanne to give the guests a room of their own.

"Why have we no electricity?" Marie moaned. "Why have we no piped water?"

"Why does not matter for these things," Galtier said with a shrug. "We do not have them, and we cannot have them before the O'Doulls arrive. Save your worries for things we can help."

"They will think we are backwards," Marie said.

"They will think we live on a farm." Galtier looked around. "As best I can see, they will be right." She wrinkled her nose at him. Shrugging again, he added, "I have heard from our son-in-law that it is the same on farms in the United States as it is here."

That quieted Marie for the time being. She got nervous a dozen more times before Leonard O'Doull, having met his parents at the train station in Rivière-du-Loup, brought them and Nicole and little Lucien down to the farmhouse. By then, the suits Lucien and Charles and Georges wore had been aired long enough that they no longer smelled of mothballs.

Harvey O'Doull looked like a shorter, older, more weathered version of his son. Rose, his wife, resembled nothing so much as a suet pudding, but her eyes, green like Leonard's, were kind. "I was pleased to meet your lovely daughter at last, and I am pleased to meet all of you," Harvey said, his accent about two-thirds American, one-third Parisian. "I am glad to have you in our family, and to be in yours."

"*Moi aussi,*" his wife said. Her accent was considerably worse than his, but she made the effort to speak at least a little French.

Because she did, Lucien answered in his own creaky English: "And I am glad also to meet you. Please to come inside, where it is more hot."

Harvey O'Doull's eyes had been flicking back and forth around the farm, as if they were a camera taking snapshots. His face showed a good deal of knowledge; how many farms had he seen in the course of his practice? A lot, probably. When he said, "This is a good place," he spoke with authority.

"This is precious!" Rose said in English when they did go inside. It wasn't quite the word Galtier would have used to describe the house where he lived, but it was meant as praise, and he accepted it in the spirit offered.

Leonard O'Doull carried in suitcases. His father opened one and rummaged through it. "I have here for the baby many toys," he said in his rather strange French, "and one also for you, M. Galtier." With the air of a man performing a conjuring trick, he held up a large bottle of whiskey.

"Since I cannot drink all that by myself—at least not right away—I will share it with anyone who would like some," Galtier said. "Denise, run into the kitchen and fetch glasses, would you?"

There was plenty of whiskey to go around. There would be enough to go around several times. "To Lucien O'Doull!" Harvey

O'Doull said loudly. Everyone drank. It was, Lucien Galtier discovered, not only abundant whiskey but excellent whiskey as well.

Lucien O'Doull, without whom the gathering would not have taken place, drank no whiskey. He kept pulling himself up to a stand, letting go, and falling on his bottom. His cries were much more of indignation than of hurt. He knew he was supposed to get up there on his hind legs, but he didn't quite know how.

Dinner featured roast chicken and sausage and mashed potatoes and buttered turnips and Marie's fresh-baked bread. Nothing was wrong with either senior O'Doull's appetite, and they both praised the food in two languages. The first awkward moment came when Rose asked in careful French, *"Où est le W.C.?"*

"Il n'y a pas de W.C.," Galtier answered, and then, in English, "No toilet." With resigned regret, he pointed outside. One small advantage of cold weather was that the outhouse was less ripe than it would have been in summer.

Rose O'Doull blinked, but wrapped herself in her thick wool coat and sallied forth. When she came back, she was, to Lucien's surprise, smiling. "I haven't been on a two-holer since Hector was a pup," she said in English. Lucien didn't know exactly what that meant, but he had a pretty fair notion.

Rose also insisted on going back and helping the Galtier women with the dishes. Harvey proved to have brought a box of cigars to go with the fine whiskey. After the menfolk were puffing happy clouds, he said, "I hope, M. Galtier, we do not put you to too much trouble."

"Not at all," Lucien said. "It is our pleasure."

"All except Denise's," the incorrigible Georges murmured.

Fortunately, Harvey O'Doull either did not hear or did not understand. He went on with his own train of thought: "I know how much work a farm is. I was a child on a farm. To have guests is not easy for a man with much work to do."

"When the guests are the other grandparents of my grandson, they are, in a way, of my own flesh and blood," Galtier replied.

Harvey O'Doull nodded. "You are very much as my son has written of you in his letters. He says you are the finest gentleman he ever met."

The key word was in English, but Galtier understood it. He glared at Leonard O'Doull and spoke fiercely: "See what lies you have been spreading about me!"

Harvey O'Doull started to explain himself, thinking Lucien had misunderstood and really was insulted. Leonard O'Doull, who knew his father-in-law better, wagged a forefinger at him, a thoroughly French gesture for an Irishman to use. "If I had not heard the words come from your lips, I would have thought Georges had spoken them."

"*Tabernac!*" Galtier exploded. "Now I *am* insulted!"

"So am I," Georges said. They all laughed. Lucien had not thought his meeting with these Americans would begin so well. But then, he reflected, he had not thought his meetings with any Americans would go so well as they had. Occasionally—*but only occasionally,* the stubborn peasant part of him insisted—surprises were good ones.

Scipio stood in line outside the Augusta, Georgia, city hall with more worry in his heart than he let his face show. The queue of black people stretched for blocks. Every so often, a white passing by would offer a jeer or a curse. Gray-clad policemen kept the whites from doing anything worse, if they'd intended to.

Bathsheba squeezed his hand. "Hope none o' them Freedom Party buckra come to raise a ruction."

He nodded. "Me, too." That was indeed one of the worries he was doing his best to conceal. As those worries went, though, it was only a small one.

Bathsheba cheerfully went on, "Passbooks won't be *so* bad. Did well enough with 'em before, an' I reckon we can again. Just a nuisance, is all."

"I hopes you's right," Scipio said. He had his doubts. The Freedom Party men in Congress were the ones who'd introduced the law tightening up the passbook system in the CSA, which had fallen to pieces during the Great War. He distrusted anything that had anything to do with the Freedom Party. But that worry wasn't at the top of his list, either.

The line slowly snaked forward, not toward the front entrance to the city hall—whites wouldn't have stood for blacks' impeding their progress that way—but toward a side door. Negroes newly issued passbooks went out the back way. Some of them came around to talk with friends still in line.

"Look like a police station in there," one of them said. "They got wanted posters up for every nigger ever spit on the sidewalk."

A couple of blacks, hearing that, suddenly found other things to do than stand in line just then. Scipio felt like finding something else to do, too. But, from what he read in the papers, he was more likely to get in trouble without a passbook later than he was to be recognized now. Maybe a poster with his name—his real name—on it would be hanging there with all the rest. Nobody in Georgia wanted him except Bathsheba, and he was glad she had him. Everything he'd done for the Congaree Socialist Republic had been over in South Carolina. He was perfectly happy to have people beating the bushes for him there; he never intended to set foot in the state again.

Up the worn stone steps leading to the side door he and Bathsheba went. "Glad we ain't doin' this in the summertime," he said. "We melt jus' as fas' as the ice under the fish over at Erasmus' place."

"For true," Bathsheba agreed. When they got inside, she looked along the hallway. "That fellow weren't lyin'. Who would have thought there was so many bad niggers in this here town?"

Scipio scanned the wanted posters. Sure as hell, there was a faded one with his name on it. The poster, though, bore no picture. He'd been photographed only a couple of times in his life, and those images had gone up in smoke when Marshlands burned. He'd never had any brushes with the police, as had the men and women whose photos adorned most of the fliers. On the other hand, if caught for his political crimes, he'd face the gallows or a firing squad.

At last, he came before a sour-faced white clerk. "Name?" the fellow asked.

"Xerxes," Scipio answered, and then had to spell it for the clerk, who'd started it with a Z instead of an X.

Being corrected by a black man made the clerk's face even more sour, but he made the change. "Residence address?" he said, and Scipio gave him the address of the roominghouse over in the Terry. The clerk didn't have any trouble getting that down on paper. Then he asked, "Birthplace?"

"I were borned on a plantation over in South Carolina." Scipio hoped his sudden tension didn't show. He hadn't expected that question.

But the clerk only nodded. "You talk like it," he said, and wrote SOUTH CAROLINA on the passbook and on the form that would record its new owner. He asked about Scipio's age (on general principles, Scipio lied five years off it), his employer, and his employer's address. After taking all that down, he said, "State the time and reason your previous passbook was lost."

"Suh, it were 1916, I reckons," Scipio said, "an' I were gettin' the hell out o' where I was at, on account of I didn't want to git kilt. Didn't take nothin' but de clothes on my back."

The clerk grunted. "Another patriotic nigger running away from the Reds," he said. "If I had a dime—a real silver dime, I mean—for every time I've heard that one the past couple days, I'd be a hell of a rich man." But he was just blowing off steam in general; he didn't seem to disbelieve Scipio in particular. When Scipio didn't flinch, the clerk grunted again. "Raise your right hand."

Scipio obeyed.

"Do you solemnly swear that the information you have given me in regard to this book is true and complete, so help you God?" the white man droned.

"Yes, suh," Scipio said.

Still droning, the clerk went on, "The penalty for perjury in regard to this book may be fine or imprisonment or both, as a court of law may determine. Do you understand?" Scipio nodded. The clerk looked miffed, perhaps at finding a black man who didn't need the word *perjury* explained to him. Thrusting the new passbook at Scipio, he said, "Keep this book in your possession at all times. It must be shown or surrendered on demand of any competent official. If you move or change jobs in Augusta, you must notify city hall or a police station within five days. You must have the proper stamp in the book before you travel outside Richmond County. Penalty for violating those provisions is also fine or imprisonment or both. Do you understand all *that*?"

"Yes, suh," Scipio repeated.

"All right, then," the clerk said, as if washing his hands of him. "Go down that hall and into one of the rooms on the left. Get yourself photographed. A copy of the photograph will be sent to you. It must go into your passbook, on the blank page opposite your personal information. If you do not receive it within two weeks, come back here to be photographed again. Next!"

Bathsheba, who'd gone to the clerk next to the one who'd dealt with Scipio, was waiting when he finished. Together, they went to get their pictures taken. The photography room was full of flash-powder smoke, as if soldiers with old-fashioned weapons had fought a battle in there.

Foomp! A photographer set off more flash powder. Scipio's eyes watered at the blast of light. "Do Jesus!" he exclaimed. A blowing green-purple spot danced at the center of his vision before slowly fading.

"That was just like lookin' into the sun," Bathsheba said as the two of them made their blinking way to the back door and out of the Augusta city hall.

"Sure enough was," Scipio said. He put the passbook in the pocket of his dungarees. If he couldn't leave the county without getting the book stamped, Confederate authorities were tightening up with a vengeance. And yet, oddly, that bothered him only a little. Now he had an official document to prove he was Xerxes of Augusta, Georgia. That made it much harder for Anne Colleton—or anyone else, but he worried most about Miss Anne—to accuse him of ever having been Scipio the bloodthirsty Red.

He spotted Aurelius in the line of men and women waiting to get passbooks, and waved to the waiter with whom he'd worked at John Oglethorpe's restaurant before the white man let him go. Aurelius waved back. "How you is?" Scipio called.

Aurelius waggled his hand back and forth. "Same as always." He looked from Scipio to Bathsheba and back again. "You look like you's doin' pretty good for yourself," he said with a smile.

"This here my intended," Scipio answered proudly. He introduced Bathsheba and Aurelius, then asked, "How Mistuh Oglethorpe' doin'?"

"He don't change," Aurelius said. "Tough as rocks on the outside, sof' as butter underneath."

Scipio nodded. That described his former boss very well. He was about to say so when a shout from farther up Greene Street made him whip his head around. The shout was one he'd heard before: "Freedom!" It seemed to come from a great many throats.

All up and down the queue, Negroes looked at one another and up the street in alarm. No one with a dark skin thought of the Freedom Party with anything but dread. "Freedom!" That great shout was closer now. Scipio glanced at the policemen who'd been keeping the line orderly. He'd always seen the white police as a tool for keeping Negroes in their place. Now he hoped they could protect him and his people.

Past the line of Negroes came the Freedom Party marchers. Scipio stared at them in dismay: hundreds of men tramped along in disciplined ranks. They all wore white shirts and butternut pants. Many of them had steel helmets on their heads. The men in the first rank carried the Stars and Bars and Confederate battle flags. The men in the second rank bore white banners with FREEDOM printed on them in angry red letters, and others that might have been Confederate battle flags save that they featured a red St. Andrew's cross on blue, not blue on red.

"Freedom!" the marchers roared again. Had they turned on the Negroes in line outside the city hall, the handful of policemen could not have hoped to stop them. But they just kept marching and shouting their one-word slogan. That showed discipline, too, and frightened Scipio almost as much as an attack would have done.

He looked from the marchers back to the police. Not only were the policemen outnumbered, they also seemed cowed by the Freedom Party's show of force. It was almost as if the marchers represented the Confederate government and the police were civilian spectators.

"Them bastards is bad trouble," Aurelius said, speaking in a low voice to make sure he gave the white men no excuse to do anything but march.

"Every time the Freedom Party do somethin', mo' poor buckra join they than the time befo'," Scipio said. "That go on, they gwine end up runnin' this here country one fine day. What they do then?"

"Whatever they please," Bathsheba said. "They do whatever they please."

"Ain't nothin' we can do about it, anyways," Aurelius said.

Scipio suddenly felt the weight of the passbook in his pocket. It might have been the weight of a ball and chain. For the very first time, he truly sympathized with the Red uprising in which he'd played an unwilling part. This march was what Cassius and Cherry and the other Reds had feared the most.

But their uprising had helped spawn the Freedom Party—Scipio understood the dialectic and how it worked, even if he didn't think of it as revealed truth. And the black uprising had failed, as any black uprising was bound to do: too few blacks, too few weapons. What did that leave for Negroes in the CSA? Nothing he could see.

"We's trapped," he said, hoping Bathsheba or Aurelius would argue with him. Neither of them did, which worried him more than anything.

Sam Carsten slammed a shell into the breech of the five-inch gun he served aboard the USS *Remembrance*. "Fire!" Willie Moore shouted. Carsten jerked the lanyard. The cannon roared. The shell casing fell to the deck with a clang of brass on steel. One of the shell-jerkers behind Sam handed him a fresh round. Coughing a little from the cordite fumes, he reloaded the gun.

Moore peered out through the sponson's vision slit. "I think we've got to bring it down a couple hundred yards to drop it just where we want it," he said, and fiddled with the elevation screw to achieve the result he wanted. When he was satisfied, he nodded to Sam. "Give 'em another one."

"Right, Chief." Sam yanked the lanyard again. The gun bellowed. Carsten said, "Christ, by the time we're through with Belfast, there won't be anything left of it."

"Damn stubborn crazy micks," Moore said. "The ones who want to stay part of England, I mean, not the ones who aim to put all of Ireland into one country. They're damn stubborn crazy micks, too, but they're on our side."

Overhead, two aeroplanes roared off the deck of the *Remembrance*, one on the other's heels. "They'll give the Belfasters something to think about," Sam said.

"That they will," the commander of the gun crew agreed. "No doubt about it." He peered through the slit again. "Sons of bitches!" he burst out. "The bastards are shooting back. One just splashed into the water a few hundred yards short of us."

One of the shell-jerkers, Joe Gilbert—like most in his slot, a big, muscular fellow—said, "Goddamn limeys must have smuggled in some more guns."

"Yeah," Carsten said. "And if we call 'em on it, they'll say they never did any such thing—their pet micks must've come up with the guns and the shells under a flat rock somewhere, or else made 'em themselves."

Officially, Britain recognized Ireland's independence. She'd had to; the United States and the German Empire had forced the concession from her. The Royal Navy never ventured into the Irish Sea to challenge the *Remembrance* or any other U.S., German, or Irish warship.

But hordes of small freighters and fishing boats smuggled arms and ammunition and sometimes fighting men into the loyalist northeastern part of Ireland. The British Foreign Office blandly denied knowing anything about that. However many ships stood between Ireland on the one hand and England and Scotland on the other, the gun runners always found gaps through which they could slip.

Willie Moore said, "The damn micks—*our* damn micks, I mean—had better start doing a better job of patrolling, that's all I've got to tell you. It's their goddamn country. If they can't hang on to it all by their lonesome, I can tell you we ain't gonna hang around forever to pull their chestnuts out of the fire." He adjusted the elevation screw again. "Let 'em have the next one now."

"Aye aye." Sam fired the five-inch gun again. He had to step smartly to keep the casing from landing on his toes.

Joe Gilbert passed him another shell. He was bending to load it into the breech when a shell from the shore slammed into the sponson. That he was bending saved his life. Most of the shell's force was spent in penetrating the armor that protected the sponson, but a fragment gutted Willie Moore as if he were a muskie pulled from a Minnesota lake. Another one hissed over Sam's head and into Gilbert's neck. The shell-jerker fell without a sound, his head almost severed from his body. Moore screamed and screamed and screamed.

Sam could look out through the hole the shell had torn and see the ocean and, beyond it, burning Belfast. He wasted only a tiny fraction of a second on that. What to do when the sponson got hit had been drilled into him during more than ten years in the Navy. No fire—he checked that first. Inside the sponson, it was just bare metal, with no paint to burn. That didn't always help, but it had this time. The ammunition wouldn't go up.

Next, check the gun crew. Joe Gilbert was beyond help. Blood dripped from Sam's shoes when he picked up his feet. Calvin Wesley, the other shell-hauler, hadn't been scratched. He gaped at Gilbert's twitching corpse as if he'd never seen one before. He was a veteran—everybody aboard the *Remembrance* was a veteran—so that was hard to imagine, but maybe it was so.

Willie Moore kept shrieking. One glance at what the shell had done told Sam all he needed to know. He opened the aid kit on the wall of the sponson; a shell fragment had scarred the thick metal right beside it. From the kit, he drew two syringes of morphine. One might have been enough, but he wanted to make sure.

He stooped beside Moore. "Here, Chief, I'll take care of you." He gave the gunner's mate all the morphine in both syringes. After a very little while, Moore fell silent.

"That's too much," Wesley said. "It'll kill him."

"That's the idea," Sam said. He watched Moore's chest. It stopped moving. Like a man waking up from a bad dream, Carsten shook himself. "Come on, God damn it. We've got this gun to fight. You know how to load, right?"

"I better," Wesley answered. "I seen you guys do it often enough."

"All right, then. You load and fire, and I'll aim the damn gun." Sam had seen that done often enough, too, and practiced it himself when he got the chance during drills. The hit had torn the left side of the sponson too badly for the gun to track all the way in that direction. Otherwise, though, he was still in business. "Fire!"

Calvin Wesley sent on its way the shell Sam had been loading when they were struck. He was setting the next round into the breech when someone out in the passage pounded on the dogged hatch. A shout came through the thick steel: "Anybody alive in there?"

"Fire!" Sam said, and the gun roared. That should have answered the question, but the pounding went on. He nodded to Wesley. "Undog it."

"Aye aye." The shell-jerker obeyed.

Half a dozen men spilled into the sponson, Commander Grady among them. "Two dead, sir," Carsten said crisply, "but we can still use the gun."

"So I gather." Grady looked at the bodies. His rabbity features stayed expressionless; he'd seen his share of bodies before. After a moment's thought, he nodded briskly. "All right, Carsten, this is your gun for the time being. I'll get you shell-heavers. We'll clean up this mess and get on with the job."

Another shell from the shore splashed into the Irish Sea, close enough to the *Remembrance* to send some water through the hole the hit had made in the sponson's armor. Sam said, "Sir, if we can use a couple of aeroplanes to shoot up that gun and its crew, our life will get easier."

Even as he spoke, one of the Wright fighting scouts buzzed off the deck of the aeroplane carrier, followed a moment later by another and then another. Commander Grady said, "You aren't the only one with that idea, you see."

"Never figured I would be," Sam answered, not altogether truthfully. All his time in the Navy had taught him that officers often had trouble seeing things that should have been obvious.

Grady pointed to two of the ratings with him. "Drinkwater, you and Jorgenson stay here and jerk shells. Carsten, can Wesley cut the mustard as a loader?"

"Sir, if we fired with a two-man crew, we'll sure as hell do a lot better with four," Sam answered. Calvin Wesley shot him a grateful glance. Loader would be a step up for Wesley, as crew chief was a step up for Sam. Sam wished he hadn't earned it like this, but, as was the Navy way, nobody paid any attention to what he wished.

Grady pointed to the dead meat that had been Willie Moore and Joe Gilbert. "Get these bodies out of here," he ordered the men he hadn't appointed to the gun crew. "We've already spent too much time here."

As the sailors dragged the corpses out of the sponson, Sam took what had been Willie Moore's spot. The chief of a gun crew had an advantage denied the rest of the men—he could see out whenever he chose: through the vision slit, through the rangefinder, and now through the hole that would, when time allowed, no doubt have a steel plate welded over it.

Sam peered southwest, toward the shore half a dozen miles away. The fighting scouts the *Remembrance* had launched were buzzing around something. A flash told Carsten it was the gun that had fired on his ship. The shell fell astern of the aeroplane carrier.

He twisted the calibration screw on the rangefinder and read out the exact distance to the target: 10,350 yards. Willie Moore had known without having to think how far to elevate the gun for a hit at that distance. Sam didn't. He glanced at a yellowing sheet of paper above the vision slit: a range table. Checking the elevation, he saw the gun was a little low, and adjusted it. Then he traversed it ever so slightly to the left.

"Fire!" he shouted. He'd given the order before, with only Calvin Wesley in the sponson with him, but it seemed more official now. If he fought the gun well, it might be his to keep.

Wesley let out a yelp as the shell casing just missed mashing his instep. But when one of the new shell-heavers handed him the next round, he slammed it home in good style.

"You want to mind your feet," Sam said, traversing the gun a little farther on its track. "You can spend some time on crutches if you don't." He turned the screw another quarter of a revolution. "Fire!"

He spied another flash in the same instant as his own gun spoke. The shell the pro-British rebels launched was a near miss. At the range at which he was fighting, he could not tell whether he'd hit or missed. But the gun on the shore did not fire again. Either his shell had silenced it, one from a different five-incher had done the trick, or the aeroplanes from the *Remembrance* had exterminated the crew.

He didn't waste time worrying over which was so. As long as the Irish rebels couldn't hurt the *Remembrance* any more, he was free to go back to what his gun had been doing before the ship came under fire: pounding Belfast to bits. Sooner or later, the rebels would figure out they couldn't win the war against their more numerous opponents—and against the might of Germany and the United States. If they needed help figuring that out, he would gladly lend a hand.

The shell-heavers were just hired muscle, big men with strong backs. Calvin Wesley did his new job well enough, though Sam knew he'd done it better himself. He shrugged. Willie Moore would have handled the gun better than he was doing it. Experience counted.

"Only one way to get it," he muttered, and set about the business of acquiring as much as he could.

Roger Kimball's heart thumped with anticipation as he knocked on the hotel-room door. He'd met Anne Colleton this way whenever she'd let him. Once, she'd opened the door and greeted him naked as the day she was born. Her imagination knew no bounds. Neither did his own appetites.

With a slight squeak, the door opened. The figure in the doorway was not naked. It was not Anne Colleton, either. Kimball's heart kept pounding just the same. Vengeance was an appetite, too, as Anne would have agreed in a flash. "Welcome to Charleston, Mr. Featherston," Kimball said.

"Thank you kindly, Commander Kimball," Jake Featherston answered. The words were polite enough, but he didn't sound kindly, not even a little bit. And he bore down on Kimball's title in a way that was anything but admiring. But, after he stood aside to let Kimball come in, his tone warmed a little: "I hear tell I've got you to thank for whispering my name into Miss Colleton's ear. It's done the Party good, and I won't say anything different."

That was probably why he'd agreed to see Kimball. Did he recall the dismissive telegram he'd sent down to Charleston? He must have; he had the look of a man who remembered everything. Kimball didn't intend to bring it up if Featherston didn't. As for whispering Featherston's name into Anne Colleton's ear ... well, mentioning it on the telephone was one thing, but when Anne let him get close enough to whisper in her ear, he had other things to say.

"Want a drink?" Featherston asked. When Kimball nodded, the leader of the Freedom Party pulled a bottle out of a cabinet and poured two medium-sized belts. After handing Kimball one glass, he raised the other high. "To revenge!"

"To revenge!" Kimball echoed. That was a toast to which he'd always drink. He took a long pull at the whiskey. Warmth spread from his middle. "Ahh! Thanks. That's fine stuff."

"Not bad, not bad." Jake Featherston pointed to a chair. "Set yourself down, Kimball, and tell me what's on your mind."

"I'll do that." Kimball sat, crossed his legs, and balanced the whiskey glass on his higher knee. Featherston seemed as direct in his private dealings as he was on the stump. Kimball approved; nobody diffident ever commanded a submersible. "I want to know how serious you are about going after the high mucky-mucks in the War Department."

"I've never been more serious about anything in my life." If Featherston was lying, he was damn good at it. "They made a hash of the war, and they don't want to own up to it." Something else joined the anger that filled his narrow features, something Kimball needed a moment to recognize: calculation. "Besides, if the Freedom Party Congressmen keep asking for hearings and the Whigs and the Radical Liberals keep turning us down, who looks good and who looks bad?"

Slowly, Kimball nodded. "Isn't that pretty?" he said. "It keeps the Party's name in the papers, too, same as the passbook bill did."

"That's right." The calculation left Featherston's face. The anger stayed. Kimball got the idea that the anger never left. "Niggers haven't gotten half of what they deserve, not yet they haven't. And even the nigger-loving Congressmen up in Richmond now won't stop us from giving it to 'em."

"Bully." Roger Kimball's voice was savage. "When the uprising started, they kept my boat, the *Bonefish*, from going out on patrol against the damnyankees. Instead, I had to sail up the Pee Dee and pretend I was a river gunboat so I could fight the stinking Reds."

"I knew they were going to rise up," Featherston said. "I knew they were going to try and kick the white race right in the balls. And when I tried to warn people, what did I get? What did the goddamn War Department give me? A pat on the head, that's what. A pat on the head and a set of stripes on my sleeve they might as well have tattooed on my arm, on account of I wouldn't get 'em off till Judgment Day. That's what I got for being right."

His eyes blazed. Roger Kimball was impressed in spite of himself, more impressed than he'd thought he would be. He'd known how Featherston could sway crowds. He'd been swayed in a crowd himself. He'd expected the force of the Freedom Party leader's personality to be less in a personal meeting like this. If anything, though, it was greater. With all his heart, he wanted to believe everything Jake Featherston said.

Kimball had to gather himself before he could say, "You don't want to throw the baby out with the bathwater, though. The War Department could do the country some good, once the dead wood got cleared out."

"Yeah, likely tell," Featherston jeered. "Best thing that could happen to the War Department would be blowing it to hell and

gone. And anybody who says anything different is just as big a traitor as the lying dogs in there."

"That's shit," Kimball said without raising his voice. Featherston's eyes opened very wide. Kimball grinned; he got the idea
nobody had spoken that way to Featherston in quite a while. Grinning still, he went on, "Without the War Department, for instance,
how are we going to get decent barrels built? You'd best believe the
damnyankees are working to make theirs tougher, same as they are
with aeroplanes. Don't you reckon we ought to do the same?"

"Barrels. Stinking barrels," Featherston muttered under his
breath. He'd stopped jeering. Now he watched Kimball as a man
might watch a rattlesnake in the shocked instant after its tail began
to buzz. No, he hadn't had a supporter talk back to him for a while.
It threw him off stride, left him startled and confused. But he rallied
quickly. "Well, yes, Christ knows we'll need new barrels when we
fight the USA again. But where the hell are they? Are we working on
them? Not that I've ever heard, and I've got ears in all sorts of funny
places. We've got people—mercenaries—using some old ones down
south of the border, but new ones? Forget it. Proves what I told you,
doesn't it?—pack of damn traitors in the War Department."

When we fight the USA again. Featherston's calm acceptance of
the next war took Kimball's breath away, or rather made it come
fast and hard, as if Anne Colleton had greeted him in the doorway
naked. He wanted that next war, too. He hadn't wanted to give up
on the last one, but he'd had no choice. Seeing how much Featherston longed for it made him forget their disagreement of a moment
before.

When he didn't answer back right away, the sparkle returned to
Featherston's eye. The Freedom Party leader said, "Reckon you were
just sticking up for the officers in Richmond, seeing as you were one
yourself."

"Screw the officers in Richmond," Kimball said evenly. "Yes, I
was an officer. I fucking earned being an officer when I won an
appointment at the Naval Academy in Mobile off a lousy little
Arkansas farm. I earned my way through the Academy, too, and I
earned every promotion I got once the war started. And if you don't
like that, Sarge"—he laced Featherston's chosen title with scorn—
"you can go to hell."

He thought he'd have a fight on his hands then and there. He
wasn't sure he could win it, either; Jake Featherston had the hard,
rangy look of a man who'd cause more than his share of trouble in a

brawl. But Featherston surprised him by throwing back his head and laughing. "All right, you were an officer, but you ain't one of those blue-blooded little goddamn pukes like Jeb Stuart III, that worthless sack of horse manure."

"Blue-blooded? Me? Not likely." Kimball laughed, too. "After my pa died, I walked behind the ass end of a mule till I figured out I didn't want to do that for a living any more. I'll tell you something else, too: it didn't take me real long to figure *that* out, either."

"Don't reckon it would have," Featherston said. "All right, Kimball, you were an officer, but you were my kind of officer. When I'm president, reckon I can find you a place up in Richmond, if you want it."

When I'm president. He said that as calmly as he'd said, *When we fight the USA again.* He said it as surely, too. His confidence made Kimball gasp again. A little hoarsely, the ex-submersible skipper said, "So you are going to run next year?"

"Hell, yes, I'll run," Featherston answered. "I won't win. The people here aren't ready yet to do the hard things that need doing. But when I run, when I tell 'em what we'll have to do, that'll help make 'em ready. You know what I'm saying, Kimball? The road needs building before I can run my motorcar down it."

"Yeah, I know what you're saying." Kimball knew he sounded abstracted. He couldn't help it. He'd thought about guiding Jake Featherston the way a rider guided a horse. After half an hour's conversation with Featherston, that seemed laughable, absurd, preposterous—he couldn't find a word strong enough. The leader of the Freedom Party knew where he wanted to go, knew with a certainty that made the hair stand up on the back of Kimball's neck. Whether he would get there was another question, but he knew where the road went.

Far more cautiously than he'd spoken before, Kimball said, "I'm not the only officer you could use, you know. You shouldn't be down on all of us. Take Clarence Potter, for instance. He—"

Featherston cut him off with a sharp chopping gesture. "You and him are pals. I remember that. But I haven't got any real use for him. There's no fire in the man; he thinks too damn much. It's not the fellow who thinks like a professor who gets a pile of ordinary working folks all het up. It's somebody who thinks like them. It's somebody who talks like them. He'd just piss and moan about that, on account of he can't do it himself."

Recalling Potter's Yale-flavored, Yankee-sounding accent and his relentless precision, Kimball found himself nodding. He said, "I bet you would have had more use for him, though, if he'd come over to the Party right away."

"Hell and blazes, of course I would," Featherston said. "But I can see him now, lookin' down his nose, peerin' over the tops of his spectacles"—he gave a viciously excellent impression of a man doing just that—"and reckoning I was nothing but a damn fool. Maybe he knows better nowadays, but maybe it's too late."

Kimball didn't say anything at all. Featherston's judgment of Clarence Potter was close to his own. Clarence was a fine fellow—Kimball wouldn't have gone so far in denigrating him as Featherston had—but he did think too much for his own good.

"We're on the way up," Featherston said. "We're on the way up, and nobody's going to stop us. Now that I'm here, I'm damn glad I came down to Charleston. I can use you, Kimball. You're a hungry bastard, just like me. There aren't enough of us, you know what I'm saying?"

"I sure do." Kimball stuck out his hand. Featherston clasped it. They clung to each other for a moment, locked in the alliance of the mutually useful. The president of the Confederate States, Kimball reflected, was eligible for only one six-year term. If Jake Featherston did win the job, who would take it after him? Roger Kimball hadn't known any such ambition before, but he did now.

Excitement built in Chester Martin as winter gave way to spring. Before long, spring would give way to summer. When summer came to Toledo, so would the Socialist Party national convention.

"Not Debs again!" he said to Albert Bauer. "He's run twice, and he's lost twice. We've got to pick somebody new this time, a fresh face. It's not like it was in 1916, or in 1912, either. We've got a real chance to win this year."

"In 1912 and 1916, you were a damn Democrat," Bauer returned, stuffing an envelope. "What gives you the right to tell the Party what to do now?"

Martin's wave took in the local headquarters. "That I *am* here now and wouldn't have been caught dead here then. Proves my point, doesn't it?"

His friend grunted. "Maybe you've got something," Bauer said grudgingly. After a moment, though, he brightened. "This must be how the real old-time Socialists felt when Lincoln brought so many Republicans into the Party after the Second Mexican War. It was nice having more than half a dozen people come to meetings and vote for you, but a lot of the new folks didn't know a hell of a lot about what Socialism was supposed to mean."

"Are you saying I don't know much?" Martin asked, amusement in his voice.

"Tell me about the means of production," Albert Bauer said. "Explain why they don't belong in the hands of the capitalist class."

"I don't have to sit still for examinations: I'm not in school any more, thank God," Martin said. "I don't know much about the means of production, and I don't give a damn, either. What I do know is, the Democrats have jumped into bed with the fat cats. I want a party to jump into bed with me."

"You're voting your class interest," Bauer said. "Well, that's a start. At least you know you have a class interest, which is a devil of a lot more than too many people do. You wouldn't believe how much trouble we've had educating the proletariat to fulfill its proper social role."

"Yeah, and one of the reasons why is that you keep talking so fancy, nobody wants to pay any attention to you," Martin said. "You keep on doing that, the Socialists are going to lose this election, same as they've lost all the others. And God only knows when we'll ever have a better chance."

By the way Bauer winced and grimaced, he knew he'd struck a nerve, maybe even struck it harder than he'd intended. "What do you think?" Bauer asked, shifting the subject a little. "Will TR run for a third term?"

"Nobody ever has before," Martin answered, but that wasn't the question Bauer had asked. At length, he said, "Yeah, I think he will. What's he going to do, dust off his hands and walk away? Go hunt lions and elephants in Africa? You ask me, he likes doing what he's doing. He'll try and keep doing it." He held up a forefinger. "Here's one for you, Al: if Teddy *does* run again, will that make things easier or harder for us?"

"I'm damned if I know," Bauer replied, his voice troubled. "Nobody knows. Maybe people will remember he fought the war and won it. If they do, they'll vote for him. Or maybe they'll remember how many men died and all the trouble we've had since. If they do that, they won't touch him with a ten-foot pole."

"The war will have been over for almost three and a half years by the time the election rolls around," Martin said.

"That's a fact." Albert Bauer sounded glad it was a fact, too. "People don't remember things very long. Of course"—he didn't seem to want to be glad about anything—"the Great War is a big thing to forget."

"Losing two elections in a row is a big thing to forget, too, and that's what Debs has done," Martin said. "If we do run him again, what'll our slogan be? 'Third time's the charm'? I don't think that'll work."

"He walks in and he knows all the answers." Bauer might have been talking to the ceiling; since he spoke of Martin in the third person, he wasn't—quite—talking to him. But then he was once more: "All right, all right, maybe not Debs. But if we don't run him, who do we run? He's the one fellow we've got who has a following across the whole damn country."

"You pick somebody," Chester Martin said. "You're always going on about how you're the old-time Red, so you have to know all these people. I'm nothing but a damn recruit. That's what you keep telling me, anyway."

"Go peddle your papers," Bauer said. A little less gruffly, he continued, "Go on, take the rest of the day off. It's Sunday, for Christ's sake. Don't you have anything better to do with your time?"

"Probably." Martin got up from the table where he and his friend had been preparing fliers for mailing. "But if too many people find better things to do with their time than work for the Party, the work won't get done. Where will we be then?"

"Up the same old creek," Bauer admitted. "But the Rebs won't capture Philadelphia if you have yourself a couple of beers or something."

"Twist my arm," Martin said, and Bauer did, not very hard. Martin groaned anyway. "Aii! There—you made me do it. See you later."

When he stepped outside, spring was in the air. While he'd fought in the Roanoke Valley, it had arrived sooner and more emphatically than it did here by the shore of Lake Erie. That was the one good thing he could say about Virginia. Against it, he set filth and stench and horror and fear and pain and mud and lice. They sent the scales crashing down against the place.

How many veterans would weigh what they'd been through in the same fashion? Was what they'd done worth it? Could anything have been worth three years of hell on earth? He didn't think so, especially not when he reckoned in the trouble he'd had after the war was over. Would the rest of the millions who'd worn green-gray—those of them left alive, anyhow—feel as he did? If so, Teddy Roosevelt faced more trouble than he guessed.

Red flags flew above the Socialists' building. Toledo cops still prowled past. Martin no longer carried a pistol in his pocket. Something like peace had returned to the labor scene. He wondered how long it would last. The answer supplied itself: *till the day after the election.*

One of the policemen in brass-buttoned dark blue flashed Martin a thumbs-up. Martin was so surprised to get it, he tripped on a crack in the sidewalk and almost fell. During the great wave of strikes, that cop had undoubtedly broken workers' heads along with his goonish chums. Did he think he could turn into a good

Socialist with one simple gesture? If he did, he was an ever bigger fool than the usual run of cop.

Or maybe he was a straw, blowing in the wind of change. If a cop found it a good idea to show somebody coming out of the Socialist hall that he wasn't hostile, who held the power? Who was liable to hold it after March 4, 1921? Maybe the policeman was hedging his bets.

"Won't do you any good," Martin muttered under his breath. "We'll still remember you bastards. Hell, yes, we will."

He listened to himself. That was when he began to think the party that had wandered so long in the wilderness might have a chance to come home at last. The Democrats had ruled the roost for a long time. They wouldn't be happy about clearing out, not after all these years they wouldn't.

"Too damn bad," Martin said.

Red Socialist posters were plastered on every wall and fence and telegraph pole. They shouted for freedom and justice in big black letters. For once, more of them were up than their red-white-and-blue Democratic counterparts. Those showed the U.S. eagle flying high over a burning Confederate flag, and bore a one-word message: VICTORY!

As poster art went, the Democrats' handbills were pretty good. The only drawback Chester Martin found in them was that they bragged about old news. As Bauer had said, people forgot things in a hurry.

Martin walked over to the trolley stop and rode back to the apartment building where he and his parents and sister lived. They were playing hearts three-handed. "About time you got home," his father said. "This is a better game when the cards come out even when you deal 'em."

"See what you get for starting without me?" Martin said, drawing up a chair.

"Dad wants to throw in this game because he's losing," his sister said. But Sue's grin said she didn't mind throwing it in, either.

"My own flesh and blood insult me," Stephen Douglas Martin said. "If I'd told *my* father anything like that—"

"Gramps would have laughed his head off, and you know it," Martin said. He gathered the cards and fanned them in his hand. "Draw for first deal." He ended up dealing himself. After generously donating the ace of spades and a couple of hearts to his mother, who sat on his left (and receiving a similar load of trash from his sister, who sat on his right), he called, "All right, where's the deuce?"

Out came the two of clubs. As the hand was played, his father asked, "Did you get the whole world settled, there at the Socialist meeting hall?"

"Sure as heck did," Martin said cheerfully. "The revolution of the proletariat starts next Wednesday, seven o'clock in the morning sharp. You'd better step lively, Pop—you don't want to be late." He took a trick with the ace of diamonds, then led the ten of spades. "Let's see where the queen's hiding."

"Ask a stupid question, get a stupid answer," his father said. As Chester's mother had done, he ducked the spade. So did Sue. Stephen Douglas Martin went on, "Do people want it to be that rabblerousing fool of a Debs again?"

"Some people do," Martin answered. "I think we'd have a better chance with somebody else." Since the ten of spades had failed to flush out the queen, he led the nine. "Maybe this'll make her show up."

His mother pained and set out the ace of spades. His father grinned and tucked the king under it. His sister grinned even wider and dropped the queen, sticking his mother with thirteen points she didn't want. "There you go, Ma," Sue said sweetly.

"Thank you so much," Louisa Martin said. She turned to her son. "When the revolution comes, will the queen only be worth one point, to make her equal with all the hearts in the deck?"

"Don't know about that one, Ma," Chester said. "I don't think there's a plank that talks about it in the Socialist Party platform."

"Is there a plank that explains why they think we need anybody but bully old Teddy?" Stephen Douglas Martin inquired.

"I can think of two," his son replied. "First one is, nobody's ever had three terms. If TR decides to run again, he shouldn't, either. And even if the Democrats run somebody else, they have to explain what we got for all the men who got killed and maimed during the war, and why they've been in the trusts' pocket ever since."

When he was around Albert Bauer, he sounded like a reactionary. When he was around his parents—who were, in his view of things, reactionaries—he sounded as radical as Bauer did. The more he thought about that, the funnier it seemed.

The quitting whistle's scream cut through the din on the floor of the Sloss Works like a wedge splitting a stump. Jefferson Pinkard leaned on his crowbar. "Another day done," he said. "Another million dollars."

He wasn't making a million dollars a day, but he was making better than a million a week. Next month, probably, he'd be up over a million a day. It didn't matter. What the CSA called money was only a joke, one that kept getting funnier as the banknotes sprouted more and more zeros. The bottom line was, he'd lived better before the war than he did now. That was so for almost everybody in the Confederate States.

"See you in the mornin', Mistuh Pinkard," Vespasian said.

"Yeah," Jeff answered. "See you." He didn't make his voice cold on purpose; it just came out that way. The more he went to Freedom Party meetings, the less he cared to work alongside a black man. Vespasian turned away and headed for the time clock to punch out without another word. Pinkard wasn't in the habit of bragging about going out on Freedom Party assault squadrons, but he wouldn't have been surprised had Vespasian known about it. Blacks had funny ways of finding out things like that.

Too damn bad, Jeff thought. Tired and sweaty, he headed toward the time clock himself.

Going into and out of the Sloss foundry, whites had always hung with whites and Negroes with Negroes. That hadn't changed. What had changed, lately, was how men from one group eyed those from the other. Blacks seemed warier than they had been during the war. Whites seemed less happy about having so many colored men around, doing jobs they wouldn't have been allowed to do before the war started. Pinkard understood that down to the ground. It was how he felt himself.

He didn't stop sweating just because he'd stopped working for the day. Spring had come to Birmingham full of promises about what the summer would be like. If those promises weren't so many lies, summer would be hotter than hell, and twice as muggy. Summer in Birmingham was usually like that, so the promises probably held truth.

When he got close to home, Bedford Cunningham waved to him. Bedford was sitting on his own front porch, with a glass of something unlikely to be water on the rail in front of him. "Come on over after supper, Jeff," he called. "We'll hoist a few." He hoisted the one sitting on the rail.

"Can't tonight," Pinkard answered. "Got a meeting."

"Man alive." Cunningham shook his head, back and forth, back and forth. By the way he did it, that one on the rail wasn't the first he'd hoisted. "Never reckoned you'd dive into the Freedom Party like a turtle diving off a rock into a creek."

It was, when you got down to it, a pretty fair figure of speech. Jeff felt a lot happier swimming in the river of the Party than he did out on a rock by his lonesome. He said, "Maybe you ought to come along, give yourself somethin' to do besides gettin' lit up."

"I like getting lit up," Cunningham said. "What the hell better have I got to do, anyhow? Can't hardly work, not shy an arm. I'll vote Freedom, sure as hell I will, but I don't fancy sitting around and listening to people making speeches."

"It's not like that," Jeff protested, but Bedford Cunningham was hoisting his glass again. With a shrug, Pinkard went up the walk and into his own house.

"Hello, dear," Emily said. She tilted up her face for a kiss. He gave her one, rather a perfunctory job. She didn't try to improve it. "I know you got your meeting tonight," she went on when he let her go, "so supper'll be on the table for you in two shakes of a lamb's tail." She went back into the kitchen to dish it out. She didn't shake her own tail, as she would have not so long before.

Jeff paid no attention to the change. "Good thing you remembered," he told her. "Barney Stevens is back in town from Richmond, and he's going to let us know what those bastards in Congress are up to. I don't want to be late, not for that."

"You won't be," Emily promised, her voice floating out through the hall. "Come on and set yourself down."

He did, then shoveled chicken and dumplings into his face with the single-minded dedication a stoker might have shown in shoveling coal into a steam engine's firebox. Then, after bestowing another absentminded kiss on his wife, he headed over to the closest trolley stop for the ride to the livery stable where the Freedom Party still met.

He felt at home there, more even than he did in the cottage he'd shared with Emily since the days before the war. Almost all the men who'd joined the Party were veterans, as he was; they'd fought the damnyankees in Virginia, in Kentucky, in Arkansas, in Sequoyah, in Texas, in Sonora. And most of them had put on white shirts and butternut pants these past few months and gone charging forth to break up rival parties' rallies and to remind the blacks of Birmingham where in the scheme of things they belonged.

"Freedom!" he said every time he shook somebody's hand or slapped somebody else on the back. And men also reached out to clasp his hand and slap his back and hailed him with the one-word greeting that was also a battle cry. He might have been a Freemason or an Odd Fellow: everyone in the livery stable with him was his brother.

Along with everyone else, he stamped and whistled and clapped when Barney Stevens, massive and impressive in a black suit, strode to the front of the open area. "Freedom!" Stevens—now Congressman Stevens—called.

"Freedom!" his audience roared back. Jefferson Pinkard felt different when he used the slogan along with his comrades. It took on a power then that it lacked when it was simply a greeting. It became a promise, and at the same time a warning: anyone who didn't care for the Freedom Party's ideas needed to get out of the way, and in a hurry, too.

"Boys, we've got a power of work to do, and that's a fact," Barney Stevens said. "Nobody's mucked out that big barn they call the Capitol in a hell of a long time. Most of the folks, they've been there since dirt, or else their pappies were there since dirt, and they're taking over after the old man finally upped and dropped dead. Damn fancy-pants bluebloods." Stevens fluttered his hand on a limp wrist. The Freedom Party men howled laughter. He went on, "But we're starting to get things moving, to hell with me if we're not. This business with passbooks was just the first shell in the bombardment. Let me tell you some of what I mean . . ."

After a while, Jeff found himself yawning. Stevens wasn't a bad speaker—far from it. But Jeff hadn't joined the Freedom Party to pay close attention to the nuts and bolts of policy. He'd joined because he'd felt down in his bones that something had gone dreadfully wrong with his country and he thought Jake Featherston could fix it.

Exactly how it got fixed didn't matter so much to him as getting together every week with other people who followed Featherston and going out with them every so often to bust the heads of people who didn't. That brought back the sense of camaraderie he'd known in the trenches: about the only good thing he'd known in the war.

And so, when Barney Stevens went on and on about hearings and taxes and tariffs and labor legislation, Jeff slipped from the middle of the open area in the livery stable toward the back. "Sorry, Grady," he whispered after stepping on another man's toes. He noticed he wasn't the only fellow moving toward the back of the stable, either. Everybody was glad to have Stevens in Congress, but he'd lost part of his audience tonight. He'd been elected to take care of the details, not to bore everybody with them.

Pinkard wasn't the first one to slide out the door. "My wife's a bit poorly," he whispered to the two burly guards as he left. They nodded. Odds were, they knew he was lying. He shrugged. He'd been polite—and he'd thrown half a million dollars into the big bowl by the door. As long as he was both polite and paid up, the guards didn't care if he left early.

Since he was leaving early, Emily would probably still be awake. Maybe they'd make the mattress creak when he got home. For some reason, she'd acted kind of standoffish toward him lately. He'd take care of that, by God. Horning it out of her was the best way he knew—he'd enjoy it, too.

He took the trolley to the edge of Sloss company housing, then walked to his cottage. A few people still sat on their front porches, enjoying the fine night air. He wondered if he'd see Bedford Cunningham on his, drunk or passed out. But Bedford must have gone inside to bed, because he wasn't there.

Pinkard's own house was also dark, so he figured Emily had gone to bed, too. Well, if she had, he'd damn well wake her up. He turned his key in the lock. The door didn't squeak as it swung on its hinges. He'd oiled them after he came home from the war, and quietly kept them oiled ever since. He'd caught Emily cheating on him once, and wanted a fair chance to do it again if she stepped out of line. She hadn't, not that he knew of, but. . . .

The hinges didn't squeak, but something in the house was squeaking, squeaking rhythmically. He knew what that noise was. It came from the bedroom. Rage filled him, the same rage he knew when he put on white and butternut and went off to break heads, but focused now, as if with a burning glass.

"God damn you, Emily, you little whore!" he bellowed, and stomped down the hall toward the bedroom.

Twin cries of horror greeted him, one Emily's, the other a man's. They were closely followed by scrabbling noises, a thump, and the sound of running feet. Whoever'd been in there with Emily hadn't wanted to face Jeff. As Jeff stormed in, his feet caught on something, then kicked something else: a man's tangled trousers and his shoe. Whoever the fellow was, he'd departed too quickly to bother retrieving his clothes.

"Jeff, honey, listen to me—" Emily spoke in a quick, high, desperate voice.

"Shut up," he said, and she did. She hugged the blanket to herself. The moonlight sliding in through the window—the window through which her lover had fled—showed her arms pale and bare against the dark blue wool.

He yanked the blanket off her. She was naked under it. He'd known she would be. Breathing hard, he lashed out and slapped her twice, forehand and backhand, fast as a striking snake. She gasped, but made no other sound. If he killed her on the spot, no jury would convict him. She had to know as much.

When he'd caught her the first time, she'd used all her bodily charms to mollify him. It had worked, too, even if he'd felt filthy and used as he traveled back to the front in west Texas. Now he aimed to use his body to take revenge. He undid his trousers, let them fall to the floor, and flung himself upon her.

She endured everything he did without a whimper, without a protest. In other circumstances, he might have admired that. Now he just wanted to break her, as if she were a wild horse. When his imagination and stamina ran out at last, he got up from the bed and lit the gas lamp above it. Having spent himself again and again, he was prepared to go easy—and too worn to do anything else.

Or so he thought, till he saw that the shirt on the floor had the left sleeve pinned up. "Bedford," he whispered in a deadly voice. Emily's face went pale as skimmed milk, which only made the bruises he'd given her look darker.

He pulled up his pants, then yanked her out of the bed and slung her over his shoulder. She squealed then, squealed and kicked. Ignoring everything she did, he carried her out of the cottage and dumped her, still naked, on the walk. Then he went back inside and locked the door behind him.

When she came up crying and wailing, he shouted, "Go to hell. You made your choice. Now you pay for it." He'd made his choice, too. *I'll live with it,* he thought. He went back to the bedroom, lay down, and fell asleep right away.

Arthur McGregor worried every time he left the room he'd taken in the cheap Winnipeg boardinghouse. He worried while he was in the room, too. That wasn't because inside his trunk sat a wooden box containing the largest, finest bomb he'd ever made. He worried about the bomb when he left the room: he worried that someone would discover it, and that he wouldn't be able to use it.

When he was in the sparsely furnished room, he worried about the farm. He worried about whether Maude and Julia and Mary could do everything that needed doing without his being there. He also occasionally worried about whether the story he and his family had put about—that he'd gone to visit cousins back in Ontario— would hold up under close scrutiny. If some bright Yank added two and two and happened to come up with four . . .

But the Yank likeliest to do that, Major Hannebrink, was dead. McGregor had made sure of that, and he'd got away with it. Now he was going to make sure of General Custer's demise, too, and he thought he could get away with that. And, if he couldn't, he was willing if not eager to pay the price.

"Strike a blow for freedom," he muttered under his breath as he went downstairs for breakfast.

He wasn't used to eating anyone's cooking but Maude's. The eggs here were fried too hard, while the bacon felt rubbery between his teeth. Morning chatter flowed around him. Apart from a "Good day" or two and a couple of polite nods, he added nothing to it.

Off he went, for all the world as if he had a job to which he didn't want to be late. His landlady thought he did have a regular job. He'd made certain she thought that. If she thought anything different, the Yanks were liable to hear about it. That was the last thing he wanted.

Almost three years after the end of the Great War, Winnipeg presented an odd mixture of rubble and shiny new buildings, as if a phoenix had risen halfway from the ashes. In another few years, McGregor thought, it might turn into a handsome city again. The rubble would be forgotten. So would the buildings and the hopes from which that rubble had been made. The new Winnipeg would be an American city, not a Canadian one.

HORNE'S HOUSE PAINTS, said a sign on Donald Street. 37 COLORS AVAILABLE. If Horne had been in business before 1914, if he wasn't a johnny-come-lately Yank, his sign would have advertised 37 COLOURS then. Even spelling changed under U.S. rule.

McGregor scowled. To him, COLORS looked clipped, unnatural . . . American. He stepped off the curb—and almost got clipped himself, by an American motorcar. An angry blast from the Ford's horn sent him leaping back onto the sidewalk. "Watch out, you goddamn hayseed!" the driver screamed, in an accent unmistakably from the USA. "Ain't you never seen an automobile before?" He stepped on the gas and whizzed away before McGregor could say a single word.

"Christ!" McGregor wiped his forehead on his sleeve. "That'd be all I need, stepping out in front of one of those damn things when

I'm carrying . . ." He let his voice trail away. He did not intend to mention out loud what he might be carrying. He wouldn't have come so close had he not just come close to getting killed.

Had so many motorcars scurried through the streets of Winnipeg before the Great War? McGregor had come up to the city only a couple of times in those days, so he couldn't be sure, but he didn't think so. It might end up prosperous as well as handsome.

He didn't care. He would sooner have been poor under King George than rich under the Stars and Stripes. The Yanks had taken his country away from him. If they expected him to be happy about it, they were in for a disappointment.

As a matter of fact, if they expected him to be happy about it, they were in for a *big* disappointment. He chuckled grimly—so grimly that a fellow in a business suit edged away from him. He didn't notice. He wanted to make sure their disappointment was as big as possible.

He crossed the Donald Street bridge over the Assiniboine and strolled past a three-story building that had somehow come through the war intact. Soldiers in green-gray with pot-shaped helmets stood guard around the building in sandbagged machine-gun nests that gave it a formidable defensive perimeter. He didn't linger. The U.S. guards asked pointed—or sometimes blunt—questions of people naive enough to linger around General Custer's headquarters.

They would, without a doubt, ask even more pointed—or perhaps blunt—questions of anyone foolhardy enough to try to leave a wooden box anywhere in the neighborhood. McGregor had seen as much on his last trip to Winnipeg.

There was a park not far away. It didn't even boast children's swings. All it had were grass and a few benches. McGregor sat down on the grass and waited for noon. He'd done that a good many times by now, and come to know the park well. The earth here was not smooth, but full of round depressions of different sizes and depths. A narrow zigzag strip of low ground, partly obliterated by the depressions, ran across the park from east to west. The troops defending Winnipeg had made a stand here. McGregor grunted. They'd failed, damn them.

He wasn't the only one out on this fine, mild day. Boys and girls frolicked where shells had burst and men had bled. An unshaven man in a filthy Canadian Army greatcoat and tattered khaki trousers lifted a bottle to his lips. He set it down slowly and reluctantly, as if its opening were the mouth of his beloved. In a drunken way, that was bound to be so.

McGregor killed time till the bells of the St. Boniface Cathedral, across the Red River, chimed twelve. He got up and ambled back by Custer's headquarters. He'd timed it perfectly. He'd just gone past the building when a chauffeur-driven Packard—the motorcar that had almost run him down in Rosenfeld when Custer was on his way up to Winnipeg—pulled away from the front of the place. He kept on walking, hardly looking at the automobile, and turned west, away from the Red River.

After a little while, he went up Kennedy. Sure as the devil, there in front of a chophouse called Hy's sat the Packard. The chauffeur remained on the front seat, eating a sandwich. General Custer and his aide, a tubby officer who seemed to accompany him everywhere, had gone inside.

McGregor smiled to himself. Custer dined at Hy's every Monday, Wednesday, and Friday. He was reliable as clockwork. He ate his dinner somewhere else—McGregor hadn't been able to find out where—on Tuesdays and Thursdays. So far as McGregor could tell, no swarm of guards surrounded him here.

Luck had had very little to do with McGregor's discovering his weekday routine, or at least three-fifths of it. The embittered farmer had taken to tramping the streets of Winnipeg during the dinner hour, looking for that Packard. Patience paid, as patience has a way of doing. McGregor walked past the motorcar on the other side of the street. The driver paid him no attention whatever. Had he suddenly turned around and gone back the way he'd come, that might have drawn the fellow's notice to him.

He couldn't have that, not when he was so close. He made his way back to the park, though he didn't go past Custer's headquarters this time. "Now they shouldn't see me at all," he said as he sat down on the grass once more. No one heard him. The children were gone. The ex-soldier had passed out. His bottle lay empty beside him.

A little past five, McGregor returned to the boardinghouse. He ate the landlady's frugal supper without complaint. Afterwards, he went up to his room and read *Quentin Durward* till he grew sleepy. Then he turned off the electric lamp and, so far as he knew, didn't stir till morning.

Since the next day was Thursday, Custer wouldn't be dining at Hy's. McGregor walked in, went over to the bar, and ordered himself a Moosehead. As he drank the beer, he studied the place. He couldn't very well plant the bomb among the seats; he had nowhere to conceal it there. But a lot of tables were close to the bar, and he'd packed a lot of dynamite and a lot of tenpenny nails for shrapnel into the wooden case he'd brought up from the farm. If he could hide it under the bar somewhere, that stood a good chance of doing the trick. The blast might even bring down the whole building . . . if the detonation worked as it should.

He worried about that, too. He'd known from his earlier trip to Winnipeg that he'd have to set this bomb and leave it. To make it go off when he wanted it to, he'd brought up an alarm clock, which he would set while he was planting the bomb. When it rang, the vibrating hammer and bells would set off the blasting caps he'd pack around them, which would in turn set off the dynamite. So he hoped, at any rate. But he knew the method was less reliable than a tripwire or a fuse.

"It will work," he whispered fiercely. "It *has* to work."

He got out of bed at two the next morning and sneaked out of the boardinghouse. He carried the bomb on his back with straps, as if it were a soldier's pack. In one pocket of his coat were caps, in the other a small electric torch and a pry bar.

Winnipeg remained under curfew. If a patrolling U.S. soldier spotted him, he was liable to be shot then and there. If he got shot, he was liable to go straight to the moon then and there, in fragments of various sizes. He was taking any number of mad chances with this venture, and knew it. He didn't care, not any more. Like a soldier about to go over the top, he was irrevocably committed.

An alley ran behind Hy's. Motion there made his heart spring into his mouth, but it was only a cat leaping out of a garbage can. He wondered if the restaurant had a burglar alarm. He would find out by experiment. He let out a long, happy sigh when the back door yielded to the pry bar almost at once.

Tiptoeing through the kitchen, he came out in back of the bar, as if he were the greasy-haired gent who tended it. Only when he crouched behind it did he turn on the torch. He felt like cheering on seeing not only plenty of room under the bar to stash the bomb but also a burlap bag with which to hide it.

He wound the alarm clock and set it for one, then pried up the lid to the bomb, set the clock in place, and, handling them very carefully, packed the blasting caps by the bells. Then he replaced the lid, covered the box with the burlap sack, and left by the route he'd used to come. He closed the door behind him, risking the torch once more to see if the pry marks were too visible. He grinned: he could hardly see them at all. Odds were, no one else would even notice he'd come and gone.

He reentered the boardinghouse as stealthily as he'd left. Going back to sleep was hard. Getting up to appear to go to work was even harder. When he departed after breakfast, he didn't pass by Custer's headquarters, but used the next street over to head for the park. He settled himself on the grass to wait.

St. Boniface's bells chimed the hours. After they rang twelve times, he began to fidget. Time seemed to crawl on hands and knees. How long till one o'clock? Forever? No. Before the bells chimed one, a far greater and more discordant blast of sound echoed through Winnipeg. Arthur McGregor sprang to his feet, shouting in delight. He frightened a few pigeons near him. Other than the pigeons, no one paid him the least attention.

Lieutenant Colonel Abner Dowling eyed General Custer with a sort of sad certainty. The old boy was having altogether too much fun for his own good. When his wife noticed how much fun he'd been having—and Libbie would; oh yes, she would—she would have some sharp things to say about it.

For the moment, though, Custer was doing the talking. He liked nothing better. "All in the line of duty," he boomed, like a courting prairie chicken. "All in the line of duty, my dear."

The reporter's pencil scratched across the notebook page, filling it with shorthand pothooks and squiggles. "Tell me more," Ophelia Clemens said. "Tell me how you happened to decide the War Department was using barrels the wrong way and how you came up with one that proved more effective."

"I'd be glad to," Custer said with a smile broad enough to show off all the coffee-stained splendor of his store-bought teeth.

I'll bet you would, Dowling thought. He wouldn't have minded having Ophelia Clemens interview him, either. She was a fine-looking woman—somewhere between forty and forty-five, Dowling guessed—with red-gold hair very lightly streaked with gray, and with an hourglass figure that had yielded nothing (well, next to nothing) to time.

Instead of answering her question, as he'd said he would, Custer asked one of his own: "How'd a pretty lady like you get into the newspaper business, anyhow? Most reporters I know have mustaches and smoke cigars."

Miss Clemens—she wore no wedding band—shrugged. "My father was in the business for fifty years, till he died ten years ago. He taught me everything I know. For whatever it may be worth to you, he wore a mustache and smoked cigars. Now, then—" She repeated the question about barrels.

She's sharp as a tack behind that pretty smile, Abner Dowling judged. Custer hadn't figured that out yet; the pretty smile was all he noticed. His answer proved as much. He didn't quite say God and a choir of angels had delivered the new doctrine for barrels to him from on high, but he certainly implied it.

Ophelia Clemens tapped the unsharpened end of her pencil against the spiral wire that held her notebook together. "Isn't another reason the fact that you've been known for headlong attacks straight at the foe ever since the days of the War of Secession, and that barrels offered you the chance to do that again, except in a new way?"

Dowling wanted to kiss her for reasons that had nothing to do with the way she looked. She *was* sharp as a tack, by God. Custer had done nothing but go straight at the enemy all through the Great War. First Army had suffered gruesomely, too, sending attack after attack straight into the teeth of the Rebs' defensive positions. If not for barrels, Custer would probably still be banging heads with his Confederate opposite numbers down in Tennessee.

Now he said, "What was that, Miss Clemens? My ears aren't quite what they used to be, I'm afraid." Dowling had seen him use that selective deafness before. He wasn't too hard of hearing, not considering how old he was. But he was, and always had been, ever so hard of listening.

Patiently, Ophelia Clemens repeated the question, changing not a single word. As she did so, the bells of St. Boniface's Cathedral, over on the east side of the Red River, announced the noon hour.

Custer had no trouble hearing the bells, even if he managed to miss the question again. He said, "Perhaps you'll take luncheon with my adjutant and me, Miss Ophelia. There's a very fine chop-house not ten minutes away that I visit regularly: in fact, I have a motorcar laid on that should be pulling up in front of this building right about now."

"I'd be delighted," the reporter said, "provided we can keep working through it. That way, my editors won't mind picking up the tab for me."

"Oh, very well," Custer said with poor grace. He'd no doubt wanted to use the luncheon as a breather from her astute questions. But Ophelia Clemens wasn't half bad at getting her own way, either.

When they boarded the chauffeured Packard, Custer got his way, placing himself between Dowling and Miss Clemens. The seat was crowded for three: both he and his adjutant took up a good deal of space. Had Custer been so tightly squeezed against another officer, he would have had something rude to say about Dowling's girth. As things were, he didn't complain a bit.

"Hy's, Gallwitz," Dowling said, realizing the general was otherwise occupied.

"Yes, sir." The chauffeur put the Packard in gear.

At the chop house, Custer got himself a double whiskey and tried to press the same on Ophelia Clemens. She contented herself with a glass of red wine. Dowling ordered a Moosehead. Say whatever else you would about them, the Canucks brewed better beer than they did down in the States.

Custer ordered a mutton chop and then, his glass having somehow emptied itself, another double whiskey. Dowling chose the mutton, too; Hy's did it splendidly. Miss Clemens ordered a small sirloin—likely, Dowling thought, to keep from having to match Custer in any way.

The second double vanished as fast as the first had done. Custer began talking a blue streak. He wasn't always perfectly clear, but he wasn't always perfectly clear sober, either. Even after the food arrived, Ophelia Clemens kept taking notes. "Tell me," she said, "from the viewpoint of the commanding general, what is the hardest thing about occupying Canada?"

"There's too much of it, and I haven't got a quarter of the troops I need," Custer answered. Drunk or sober, that was his constant complaint, and one with a good deal of truth to it, too. He cut a big bite off his chop and continued with his mouth full: "Not a chance in . . . blazes of getting the men I need, either, not with the . . . blasted Socialists holding the purse strings in their stingy fists."

"You would favor a third term for TR, then?" Miss Clemens asked: a shrewd jab if she knew of the rivalry between Roosevelt and Custer, as she evidently did.

I'm a soldier, and shouldn't discuss politics, would have been the discreet answer. But Custer had already started discussing politics, and was discreet only by accident. He'd just put another forkful of mutton into his mouth when he got the question, and bit down hard on it, the meat, and the fork, all at the same time.

He bit down hard literally as well as metaphorically. Too hard, in fact: Dowling heard a snapping noise. Custer exclaimed in dismay: "Oh, fow Jeshush Chwisht'sh shake! I've bwoken my uppuh pwate!" He raised his napkin to his mouth and removed the pieces.

"I'm terribly sorry, General," Ophelia Clemens said. Her green eyes might have sparkled. They definitely didn't twinkle. Dowling admired her self-control.

He went over to the bartender and got the name and address of a nearby dentist. "He'll have you fixed up in jig time, sir," Dowling said, and then, "I'm sorry, Miss Clemens, but it looks like we're going to break up early today."

"That'sh wight," Custer said, nodding. "I'm showwy, too, Mish Ophewia, but I've got to get thish fikshed."

"I understand." Ophelia Clemens kept on taking notes and asking questions. Dowling wondered if Custer's embarrassment would become news from coast to coast. *If so, too bad,* Dowling thought. Custer had always courted publicity. That usually paid handsome dividends. Every once in a while, it took a bite out of him.

When they got out to the automobile, Dowling told Gallwitz where to take Custer. Ophelia Clemens got in, too. No matter how mushy Custer sounded, she wanted to finish the interview. "Yes, sir," the chauffeur said, stolid as always. He started the engine; the Packard rolled smoothly down Kennedy Street.

He'd just turned right onto Broadway, where the dentist had his office, when the world blew up behind the motorcar. The roar sounded like the end of the world, that was for sure. Windows shattered on both sides of the street, showering passersby with glass. The Packard's windshield shattered, too. Most of the glass it held, luckily, blew away from the chauffeur. Gallwitz shouted anyway, in surprise and maybe fright as well. Dowling could hardly blame him.

And Custer shouted, "Shtop the automobiwe! Tu'n awound! Go back! We've got to shee what happened and what we can do to he'p!" He should have sounded ridiculous—an old man with no teeth, real or false, in his upper jaw, bellowing like a maniac. Somehow, he didn't.

"Yes, sir," Gallwitz said, and spun the motorcar through a U-turn that would have earned him a ticket from any traffic cop in the world.

"My God," Dowling said when he saw the devastation on Kennedy. "My God," he repeated when he saw where the devastation centered. "That's Hy's. I mean, that was Hy's." Only rubble remained of the chophouse, rubble from which smoke and flames were beginning to rise.

"A bomb," Ophelia Clemens said crisply. "A bomb undoubtedly meant for you, General Custer. What do you make of that?" She poised pencil above notebook to record his answer.

"Cowa'd'sh way to fight," he said, as if he'd almost forgotten she was there—most unusual for Custer with a journalist, especially a good-looking female journalist, in range. "Canucksh have awwaysh been cowa'd'sh." Even now, Custer got in a dig at the country from which the men who'd killed his brother had come. He pounded Gallwitz on the shoulder. "Shtop!" Gallwitz did, as close as he could get to the shattered Hy's. Custer sprang out of the Packard. "Come on, Dowwing! Let'sh shee if we can weshcue anybody!"

Dowling came. Men and women were spilling out of the shops and houses and offices around Hy's, some bleeding and screaming, others looking around for someone to lead them into action. Custer did just that, and people hastened to obey his orders even if his voice did sound mushy or maybe drunk. With a plain problem set right in front of his face, he was a world-beater.

"Buwwy!" he cried when Dowling and a fellow in a barber's white shirt and apron dragged a groaning, smoke-blackened man from the ruins of Hy's. "Now—have we got a docto'? We need a bucket bwigade to keep the fwamesh down unti' a fiwe engine getsh heah. You, you, and you! Find wunning watuh! We've got to do what we can!"

"He's in his element, isn't he?" Ophelia Clemens said to Dowling.

"Yes, ma'am," Custer's adjutant answered. Loyally, he went on, "You see what a fine commander he is."

"Oh, poppycock," she said. "These are the talents of a captain or a major, not the talents of a four-star general. The evidence that he *has* the talents of a four-star general is moderately thin on the ground, wouldn't you say?"

"No, ma'am," Dowling replied, loyal still, though he thought Miss Clemens had hit the nail right on the head. With someone pointing his battalion at an enemy strongpoint and saying *Take it*, Custer would go right at it, ahead of all his men, and take the position or die trying. During the Great War, an awful lot of his men had died trying, because smashing through was all he'd ever known.

Here, for one brief shining moment, fate—and the luck of a broken dental plate—had put him back in his element. Was he enjoying himself? Looking at him, listening to his insistent commands, Dowling could not doubt he was.

A woman stuck a box of arrowroot cough lozenges into her handbag. "Thank you kindly," she told Reggie Bartlett. "Freedom!"

Reggie grimaced, as he did whenever he heard that salutation. "Those people are crazy, and there's more of them every day," he said to his boss.

Jeremiah Harmon shrugged. "Their money spends as good as anybody else's," he said, and then gave a thumbs-down. "Which is to say, not very." He laughed. So did Reggie. He'd charged the woman a quarter of a million dollars for her lozenges, and wasn't sure whether the drugstore had made or lost money on the transaction.

A tall, rather pale man about his own age came up to the counter and set down a jar of shaving soap. He looked vaguely familiar, though Bartlett couldn't recall where he'd seen him before. "Good to hear somebody who can't stand the Freedom Party lunatics and isn't afraid to come out and say so," he remarked.

When he spoke, Reggie knew him. "You're Tom, uh, Brearley. You married Maggie Simpkins after she showed me the door."

"So I did, and happy I did it, too," Brearley answered. He looked at Reggie out of the corner of his eye, as if wondering whether the druggist's assistant were about to grab a stove lifter and try to brain him with it.

Reggie harbored no such intentions. He wanted to talk about the Freedom Party, was what he wanted to do. Instead of a stove lifter, he brandished a newspaper at Brearley. "Ten thousand people for a rally down in Charleston the other day, if you can believe it. Ten thousand people!" He opened up the paper and went hunting for the quotation he wanted: " 'Party district manager Roger Kimball told the cheering crowd, "This is only the beginning." ' "

"Jesus Christ!" Brearley started violently, then checked himself. "Doesn't surprise me one damn bit that he ended up in the Freedom Party," he said. "He would, as a matter of fact. As bloodthirsty a son of a bitch as ever hatched out of his egg."

"You know him?" Reggie asked, as he was surely supposed to.

"I was his executive officer aboard the *Bonefish* for most of the last two years of the war—till the very end." Brearley looked as if he'd started to add something to that, but ended up holding his peace.

"That's a real kick in the head." Bartlett shuffled through the newspaper again. "Other thing it says here is that a gal named Anne Colleton's been pumping money into the Party down in South Carolina. 'We have to put our country back on its feet again,' she says."

He'd surprised Brearley again. "You know Anne Colleton?" the former Navy man asked.

"If I knew a rich lady, would I be working here?" Bartlett asked. From the back of the drugstore, his boss snorted. Brearley chuckled. Reggie went on, "On the Roanoke front, though, I had a CO name of Colleton, Tom Colleton. He was from South Carolina, too. Her husband, I bet, or maybe her brother."

"Brother." Brearley's voice held certainty. "She's not married. Roger knows her, any way you want to take the word. Every time he'd come back to the boat after a leave, he'd brag like a fifteen-year-old who just laid his first nigger whore."

"Small world," Reggie said. "You know him, I know her brother, they know each other." He blinked; he hadn't intended to burst into rhyme.

"I wonder how well they know each other," Brearley said in musing tones. He caught the gleam in Reggie's eye and shook his head. "No, not like that. But Roger's done some things that don't bear bragging about. You'd best believe he has."

"Oh, yeah?" Reggie set his elbows on the countertop and leaned across it. "What kind of things?"

But Brearley shook his head in a different way. "The less I say, the better off I'll be, and the better off you're liable to be, too. But if I could tell my story to Anne Colleton, that might drive a wedge between 'em, and that couldn't help hurting the Party."

"Anything that hurts the Freedom Party sounds good to me." Reggie leaned forward even more. "How about this? Suppose I write a letter to Tom Colleton? I'll tell him you want to talk to his sister because you know something important."

"He's liable to be in the Freedom Party up to his eyebrows, too," Brearley said.

"If he is, I'm only out a stamp," Bartlett answered. "What's ten grand? Not worth worrying about. But his name isn't in the paper, so maybe he's not."

"All right, go ahead and do it," Brearley said. "But be mysterious about it, you hear? Don't mention my name. Just say you know somebody. This really could be my neck if these people decide to come after me, and they might."

"I'll be careful," Bartlett promised. He wondered if Brearley was in as much danger as he thought he was, or if he was letting his imagination run away with him. Had Reggie cared more about losing Maggie Simpkins, he might have thought about avenging himself on the ex–Navy man. As a matter of fact, he did think about it, but only idly.

Brearley took out his wallet. "What do I owe you for this?" he asked, pointing to the almost forgotten shaving soap.

"Four and a quarter," Reggie said. "Good thing you got it now. If you came in here next week, you can bet it'd cost more."

"Yeah, that's not as bad as I thought." Brearley handed Reggie a crisp, new $500,000 banknote. Reggie gave him a $50,000 banknote, two $10,000 notes, and one valued at a minuscule $5,000. As he made change, he laughed, remembering when—not so very long before—the idea of a $5,000 banknote, let alone one worth half a million dollars, would have been too absurd for words.

"I will write that letter," Reggie said. "I saw this Jake Featherston on a stump not long after the war ended—so long ago, you could still buy things for a dollar. I thought he was crazy then, and I haven't seen anything since to make me want to change my mind."

"Roger Kimball's not crazy, but he can be as mean as a badger with a tin can tied to its tail," Brearley said. "Not the sort of fellow you'd want for an enemy, and not the sort of fellow who's got a lot of savory friends."

"Maybe we'll be able to bring both of 'em down, or help, anyway," Reggie said. "Here's hoping." He paused. "If you care to, give my best to Maggie. If you don't care to, I'll understand, believe me."

"Maybe I will and maybe I won't." Brearley picked up the shaving soap and walked out of the drugstore. Bartlett nodded at his back. He hadn't expected anything much different. Then he nodded again. Anything he could do to sidetrack the Freedom Party struck him as worthwhile.

Jeremiah Harmon came up and set a bottle full of murky brown liquid on the shelf below the counter. "Here's Mr. Madison's purgative," the druggist said. "If this one doesn't shift him, by God, nothing ever will. I reckon he'll be by after he gets off at the bank."

"All right, boss," Bartlett said. "I'll remember it's there."

"That's fine." Harmon hesitated, then went on, "You want to be careful what you get yourself into, Reggie. I heard some of what you and that fellow were talking about. All I've got to say is, when a little man gets in the prize ring with a big tough man, they're going to carry him out kicking no matter how game he is. You understand what I'm telling you?"

"I sure do." Reggie took a deep breath. "Other side of the coin is this, though: if nobody gets in the ring with a big tough man, he'll go and pick fights on his own." That didn't come out exactly the way he'd wanted it to; he hoped Harmon followed what he'd meant.

Evidently, the druggist did. "All right, son," he said. "It's a free country—more or less, anyway. You can do as you please. I wanted to make sure you didn't do anything before you thought it through."

"Oh, I've done that," Reggie assured him. "My own government sent me out into the trenches. The damnyankees shot me twice and caught me twice. What can the Freedom Party do to me that's any worse?"

"Nothing, maybe, if you put it like that," Harmon allowed. "All right, then, go ahead—not that you need my permission. And good luck to you. I've got the feeling you're liable to need it." He went back to his station at the rear of the store and began compounding another mixture.

In due course, Mr. Madison did appear. Reggie's opinion was that his bowels would perform better if he lost weight and got some exercise. Like most people, Madison cared nothing for Reggie's opinion. Studying the bottle, he said, "You're sure this one is going to work?"

"Oh, yes, sir," Reggie said. "Mr. Harmon says it's a regular what-do-you-call-it—a depth charge, that's it. Whatever's troubling you, it won't be."

"Christ, I hope not." As Mrs. Dinwiddie had done before, as people had a habit of doing, the bank clerk proceeded to tell Bartlett much more about the state of his intestinal tract than Reggie had ever wanted to know. After far too long, Madison laid down his money, picked up the precious purgative, and departed.

Reggie paid less attention to his work the rest of that day than he should have. He knew as much, but couldn't help it. His boss overlooked lapses that would have earned a dressing-down most of the time. Harmon had no great love for the Freedom Party, even if he declined to get very excited about it.

At last, Reggie got to go home. The bare little flat where he lived wasn't anything much. Tonight, it didn't need to be. He found a clean sheet of paper and wrote the letter. Then—another triumph—he found an envelope. He frowned. How to address it?

After some thought, he settled on *Major Tom Colleton, Marshlands Plantation, South Carolina.* He had no idea whether the plantation was still a going concern; he'd been in a Yankee prisoner-of-war camp when the black rebellion broke out in the CSA. With that address, though, the letter ought to get to the right Tom Colleton. He was just glad he'd managed to recall the name of the plantation; he couldn't have heard it more than a couple of times.

He licked a stamp and set it on the envelope. The stamp didn't have a picture of Davis or Lee or Longstreet or Jackson or a scene of Confederate soldiers triumphing over the damnyankees, as most issues up through the war had done. It said C.S. POSTAGE at the top. The design, if it deserved such a name, was of many concentric cir-

cles. Printed over it in black were the words TEN THOUSAND DOL-
LARS.

His important work done, Reggie read the *Richmond Examiner* and then a couple of chapters of a war novel written by someone who didn't seem to have come close to the front. Reggie liked
that sort better than the realistic ones: it gave him something to
laugh at. The way things were, he took laughter wherever he could
find it.

The next morning, he woke up before the alarm clock did its
best to imitate a shell whistling down on his trench. He hadn't done
that in a while. After frying himself some eggs, he carried the letter
to the mailbox on the corner and dropped it in. He nodded, well
pleased, as he headed toward Harmon's drugstore. If he'd dawdled
for a week, the cost of a stamp would probably have gone up to
$25,000.

He looked back over his shoulder at the mailbox. "Well," he
said, "let's see what that does."

Jonathan Moss turned the key in his mailbox. Since he was sober, he
had no trouble choosing the proper key or getting it to fit. Whether
the mail would be worth having once he took it out of the box was
another question. The bulk of what he got went straight into the
trash.

"There ought to be a law against wasting people's time with so
much nonsense," he said. He knew perfectly well that such a law
would violate the First Amendment. Faced with a blizzard of advertising circulars, he had trouble caring about free-speech issues.

Then he saw the envelope franked with a two-cent stamp with
an ONTARIO overprint. His heart neither fluttered nor leaped. He let
out a resigned sigh. He wouldn't throw that envelope into the wastebasket unopened, as he would a lot of others, but he'd learned better
than to get too excited about such things.

When he got up to his apartment, he slit the envelope open. It
held just what he'd expected: a postal money order and a note. The
money order was for $12.50. The note read, *Dear Mr. Moss, With
this latest payment I now owe you $41.50. I hope to get it all to you
by the end of the year. The crops look pretty good, so I should have
the money. God bless you again for helping me. Laura Secord.*

She'd been sending him such money orders, now for this
amount, now for that, since the middle of winter. He'd written her
that it wasn't necessary. She'd ignored him. The only thing he'd

managed to do—and it hadn't been easy—was persuade her she didn't owe him any interest.

"Lord, what a stiff-necked woman," he muttered. He'd realized that when he was up in Canada during the war. She hadn't bent an inch in her animosity toward the Americans.

He'd made her bend to the extent of being polite to him. He hadn't made her bend to the extent of wanting to stay obligated to him one instant longer than she had to. As soon as she'd paid off the last of what she owed, she could go back to pretending he didn't exist.

He couldn't even refuse to redeem the money orders. Oh, he could have, but it wouldn't have made things any easier for Laura Secord. She'd already laid out the cash to buy the orders. Not redeeming them would have been cutting off his nose to spite his face.

"Haven't you done enough of that already?" he asked himself. Since he had no good answer, he didn't try to give himself one.

He cooked a little beefsteak on the stove, then put some lard in with the drippings and fried a couple of potatoes to go with it. That didn't make a fancy supper, but it got rid of the empty feeling in his belly. He washed the plate and silverware and scrubbed the frying pan with steel wool. His housekeeping was on the same order as his cooking: functional, efficient, uninspired.

Once he'd taken care of it, he hit the books. Bar examinations would be coming up in the summer. Much as he'd enjoyed most of his time at the Northwestern law school, he didn't care to wait around another semester to retake the exams after failing.

A tome he studied with particular diligence was titled, *Occupation Law: Administration and Judicial Proceedings in the New American Colonial Empire.* The field, naturally, had swollen in importance since the end of the Great War. Before the war, it had hardly been part of U.S. jurisprudence at all, as the United States, unlike England, France, and Japan, had owned no colonial empire. How things had changed in the few years since! Occupation law was said to form a large part of the examination nowadays.

Moss told himself that was the only reason he worked so hard with the text. Still, if he decided to hang out his shingle somewhere up in Canada, it behooved him to know what he was doing, didn't it? He didn't think about hanging out his shingle anywhere near Arthur, Ontario . . . not more than a couple of times, anyway.

He realized he couldn't study all the time, not if he wanted to stay within gibbering distance of sane. The next morning, he met his friend Fred Sandburg at the coffeehouse where they'd whiled away—wasted, if one felt uncharitable about it—so much time since coming to law school.

"You've got that look in your eye again," Sandburg said. Moss knew he was a better legal scholar than his friend, but he wouldn't have wanted to go up against Fred in a courtroom: Sandburg was ever so much better at reading people than he was at reading books. He went on, "How much did she send you this time?"

"Twelve-fifty," Moss answered. He paused to order coffee, then asked, "How the devil do you do that?"

"All in the wrist, Johnny my boy; all in the wrist." Sandburg cocked his, as if about to loose one of those newfangled forward passes on the gridiron. Moss snorted. His friend said, "No, seriously—I don't think it's something you can explain. Sort of like card sense, if you know what I mean."

"Only by hearing people talk about it," Jonathan Moss confessed sheepishly. "When I played cards during the war, I lost all the damn time. Finally, I quit playing. That's about as close to card sense as I ever got."

"Closer than a lot of people come, believe me," Fred Sandburg said. "Some of the guys I played with in the trenches, it'd take inflation like the damn Rebs are having to get them out of the holes they dug for themselves."

Up came the waitress. She set coffee in front of Moss and Sandburg. Sandburg patted her on the hip—not quite on the backside, but close—as she turned away. She kept walking, but smiled at him over her shoulder. Moss was gloomily certain that, had he tried the same thing, he'd have ended up with hot coffee in his lap and a slap planted on his kisser. But Fred had people sense, no two ways about it.

Moss decided to put his pal's people sense to some use and to change the subject, both at the same time: "You think Teddy Roosevelt can win a third term?"

"He's sure running for one, isn't he?" Sandburg said. "I think he may very well, especially if the Socialists throw Debs into the ring again. You'd figure they'd have better sense, but you never can tell, can you? As a matter of fact, I hope Teddy loses. Winning would set a bad precedent."

"Why?" Moss asked. "Don't you think he's done enough to deserve to get elected again? If anybody ever did, he's the one."

"I won't argue with you there," Sandburg said. "What bothers me is that, if he wins a third term, somewhere down the line somebody who doesn't deserve it will run, and he'll win, too."

"All right. I see what you're saying," Moss told him, nodding. "How many other people will worry about that, though?"

"I don't know," Sandburg admitted. "I don't see how anybody could know. But I'll bet the answer is, *more than you'd think*. If it weren't, we'd have elected someone to a third term long before this."

"I suppose so." Moss sipped his coffee. He watched people stroll past the coffeehouse. When a man with only one leg stumped by on a pair of crutches, he sighed and said, "I wonder how the fellows who didn't come through the war would vote now if they had a chance."

"Probably not a whole lot different than the way our generation will end up voting," Sandburg said. Moss nodded; that was likely to be true. His friend continued, "But we're in the Half Generation, Johnny my boy. Every vote we cast will count double, because so many of us haven't even got graves to call our own."

"The Half Generation," Moss repeated slowly. "That's not a bad name for it." He waved for the waitress and ordered a shot of brandy to go with the coffee. Only after he'd knocked back the shot did he ask the question that had come into his mind: "Did you ever feel like you didn't deserve to come back in one piece? Like fellows who were better than you died, but you just kept going?"

"Better fighters? I don't know about that," Fred Sandburg said. "Harder to tell on the ground than it was in the air, I expect. But I figured out a long time ago that it's just fool luck I'm still breathing and the fellow next to me caught a bullet in the neck. I don't guess that's too far from what you're saying."

"It's not," Moss said. For that matter, Sandburg had caught two bullets and was still breathing. No doubt luck had a great deal to do with that. Moss wished there were something more to it. "I feel I ought to be living my own life better than I am, to make up for all the lives that got cut short. Does that make any sense to you?"

"Some, yeah." Sandburg cocked an eyebrow. "That's why you're still mooning over this Canuck gal who sends you rolls of pennies every couple of weeks, is it? Makes sense to me."

"God damn you." But Moss couldn't even work up the energy to sound properly indignant. His buddy had got him fair and square. He defended himself as best he could: "You don't really have much say about who you fall in love with."

"Maybe not," Sandburg said. "But you're not quite ready to be a plaster saint yet, either, and don't forget it."

"I don't want to be a plaster saint," Moss said. "All I want is to be a better person than I am." This time, he caught the gleam in Fred's eye. "You tell me that wouldn't be hard and I'll give you a kick in the teeth."

"I wasn't going to say anything of the sort," Sandburg answered primly. "And I'll be damned if you can prove anything different."

"You're not in court now, Counselor," Moss said, and they both laughed. "But what the devil are we going to do—the Half Generation, I mean, not you and me—for the rest of our lives? We'll always be looking over our shoulders, waiting for the other half to come up and give us a hand. And they won't. They can't. They're dead."

"And you were the one who just got through saying Teddy Roosevelt deserved a third term," Sandburg pointed out. "And I was the one who said I couldn't argue with you. God help us both."

"God help us both," Jonathan Moss agreed. "God help the world, because there's hardly a country in it that doesn't have a Half Generation. With the Canucks, it's more like a Quarter Generation."

"Italy came through all right," Sandburg said. "The Japs didn't get hurt bad, either, damn them."

"Yeah, we'll have to have a heart-to-heart talk with the Japs one day, sure enough," Moss said. "They're like England, only more so: they don't really know they were on the losing side." He thought for a moment. "The only thing worse than going through the Great War, I guess, would have been going through the Great War and losing. Roosevelt saved us from that, anyway."

"So he did." Sandburg's whistle was low and doleful. "Can you imagine what this country would be like if the Rebs had licked us *again*? We'd have had ourselves another revolution, so help me God we would. I don't mean Reds, either. I just mean people who'd have wanted to hang every politician and every general from the nearest lamppost they could find."

"Like this Freedom Party down in the CSA," Moss said, and Sandburg nodded. Moss went on, "You know, maybe TR really does deserve a third term. Even if he didn't do anything else, he spared us that." His friend nodded again. Moss discovered he still had a couple of drops of brandy in the bottom of the shot glass. He raised it again. "To TR!" he said, and drained them.

XI

"**D**own with TR! Down with TR! Down with TR!" Along with everyone else in the great hall in Toledo, Flora Hamburger howled out the chant. The air was thick with tobacco smoke. It was also thick with an even headier scent, one never caught before at a Socialist Party national convention: the smell of victory.

"We can do it this time." Flora didn't know how often she'd heard that since coming to Toledo. Whether it was true or not remained to be seen. True or not, though, people believed it. Scarred and grizzled organizers who'd been coming to conventions since long before the turn of the century were saying it, and saying it with wonder in their voices and on their faces. They'd never said it before.

"Mr. Chairman! Mr. Chairman!" Half a dozen people here on the floor clamored for the attention of the august personage on the rostrum.

Bang! The gavel came down. "The chair recognizes the leader of the delegation from the great state of Indiana."

"Thank you, Mr. Chairman," that worthy bellowed. The chairman rapped loudly once more, and kept rapping till something a little quieter than chaos prevailed. The leader of the Indiana delegation spoke into it: "Mr. Chairman, in the interest of victory and unity, the state of Indiana shifts twenty-seven votes from its own great patriot and statesman, Senator Debs, to the next president of the United States of America, Mr. Sinclair! We so act at the specific request of Senator Debs, who understands that the interests of the Party should, indeed must, come ahead of all personal concerns."

Flora had never been on the battlefield. If the roar that went up at that announcement didn't match that of a great cannonading, though, she would have been astonished. More men, including the chairman of the delegation from New York, waved hands or hats or banners to attract the chairman's attention. After five indecisive ballots, the Socialists had their presidential nominee. Someone moved that the nomination be made unanimous; the motion passed by overwhelming voice vote. That done, the proud and happy delegates voted to adjourn till the next day.

But they did not want to leave the floor. As if they had already won the election, they milled about in celebration, meeting old friends, making new ones, and having themselves a terrific time.

Being taller than most of the men at the convention, Hosea Blackford was easy for Flora to spot as he made his way from the small Dakota delegation to the large one from New York. "It's done," he said. "The first part of it's done, anyhow, and done well." When he grinned, he shed years. "Ain't it bully, Flora?"

"Yes, I think so," she answered. "And the second part—who knows what the second part may be?" She wanted to take him in her arms. She couldn't, not in public. She couldn't, even in private, not while the convention was going on: no privacy in Toledo was private enough. "When you find out the second part, please let me know, whenever it is you happen to hear."

"Whether it goes one way or the other, I will do that," Blackford promised solemnly. "Shall we have supper now?"

"Why not?" Flora said. They left the hall and went back to the hotel where they were both staying. Neither of them minded being seen in public with the other; their friendship was common knowledge in Philadelphia. That they were anything more than friends, they kept to themselves.

They were working their way through indifferent beef stew when an excited-looking young man in a brightly checked jacket approached the table and said, "Congressman Blackford?"

"That's right," Blackford answered. The young man in the gaudy jacket glanced toward Flora. Understanding that glance, Blackford said, "Do I understand that you come from Mr. Sinclair?" The newcomer nodded. "Speak freely," Blackford urged him. "You may rely on Congresswoman Hamburger's discretion no less than my own."

"Very well." The eager youngster tipped his bowler to Flora. "Pleased to meet you, ma'am." He gave his attention back to Blackford. "Mr. Sinclair says I am to tell you that you are his first choice. It's yours if you want it."

Flora clapped her hands together. "Oh, Hosea, how wonderful!" she exclaimed.

"Is it?" Blackford said, more to himself than to anyone else. "I wonder. If I take it and lose, I go home. If I take it and win, I go into the shadows for four years, maybe for eight. It's not a choice to be made lightly."

"You can't turn it down!" Flora said. "You *can't*, not this year."

"Can't I?" Blackford murmured. She looked alarmed. The young man in the loud jacket didn't. Pointing to him, Blackford smiled and said, "You see? He knows there are plenty of other fish in the lake." Flora sputtered angrily. Smiling still, Blackford went on, "But no, I don't suppose I can, not this year. Yes, sir: if it pleases Mr. Sinclair to have my name placed in nomination for the vice presidency, I shall be honored to run with him and see if we can't tie a tin can to Teddy Roosevelt's tail and send him yapping down the street."

"Swell!" The youngster stuck out his hand. Blackford shook it. "My principal will be delighted, and I already am. This time, by thunder, we're going to lick 'em." He waved and departed.

"We're going to lick them," Blackford repeated. His smile was wide and amused. "Well, by thunder, maybe we are. What I'm afraid of is that tomorrow you're going to have to listen to nominating speeches telling the convention what a saint I am, and you'll laugh so loud, you'll get yourself thrown out of the hall."

"I would never do such a thing!" With a mischievous twinkle in her eye, Flora added, "Not right out loud, I wouldn't."

And, indeed, she sat beaming with pride as speaker after speaker stood up to praise Hosea Blackford the next day. A couple of other names were also placed in nomination, but Blackford won on the first ballot. Flora clapped till her hands were red and sore, and she was far from the only one who did.

But, even in the nominating convention, the would-be vice president yielded pride of place to the man heading the ticket. A runner went to summon Hosea Blackford (custom had forbidden him from being in the hall while the nomination proceedings went on). The chairman of the convention said, "And now, my friends"—no *ladies and gentlemen*, not in the Socialist camp—"I have the privilege of presenting to you the next president of the United States, Mr. Upton Sinclair of New Jersey!"

More applause followed, louder and more prolonged than that which had announced Hosea Blackford's nomination. Sinclair bounded up to the platform. Both his stride and the white summer-weight suit he wore proclaimed his youthful energy: Flora couldn't remember whether he was forty-one or forty-two. Set against the six-tyish Roosevelt, he seemed boyish, bouncy, full of spit and vinegar.

He knew it, too. "My friends, it's time for a change!" he shouted in a great voice, and cheers went up like thunder. Sinclair held up his hands, asking for quiet. Eventually, he got it. "It's time for a change," he repeated. "It's time for a change in ideas, and it's time for a change in the people who give us our ideas, too." Flora, to whom even Sinclair was not all that young, clapped hard again.

"What this convention has done here in Toledo marks the first step in that great and necessary change," Sinclair said. "This convention has passed the torch to a new generation, a generation born since the War of Secession, tempered by our troubles, disciplined by the harsh peace our neighbors forced upon us, and eager for the freedom and justice and equality of which we have heard so much and seen so little. Tell me, my friends: are you willing to witness or permit the slowing of those freedoms to which this nation has always been committed?"

"No!" Flora shouted, along with everyone else in the hall.

"Neither am I! Neither is the Socialist Party!" Upton Sinclair cried. "And I also tell you this, my friends: if our free country cannot help the men who are poor, it surely cannot—and should not—save the few who are rich!" Every time Flora thought the next round of applause could be no louder than the last, she found herself mistaken. When silence returned, Sinclair went on, "Now that we have suffered so much in the struggle against our nation's foes, let us struggle instead against the common enemies of mankind: against oppression, against poverty, and against bloody-handed war itself!"

He went on in that vein for some time. It seemed more an inaugural address than an acceptance speech. No Socialist presidential candidate had ever spoken not only to the Party but also to the country with such easy confidence before. Upton Sinclair sounded as if he took it for granted that he might win. Because he took it for granted (or sounded as if he did), would not the rest of the country do the same?

And then, at last, he said, "And now, my friends, I have the pleasure and the honor of introducing to you the next vice president of the United States, Congressman Hosea Blackford of the great state of Dakota."

Blackford got more than polite applause. Flora's contribution was as raucous as she could make it. As the tumult died away, Blackford said, "I too am of the generation born after the War of Secession, if only just. And I am of the generation that learned of Socialism from its founders: in my case literally, for Abraham Lincoln pointed out to me the need for class justice and economic justice on a train trip through Montana—the Montana Territory, it was then—and Dakota."

Lincoln's name drew a nervous round of applause, as it always did: half pride in the role he'd played in making the Socialist Party strong, half fear of the contempt that still clung to him because he'd fought—and lost—the War of Secession. Flora hoped that, with victory in the Great War, the country would not dwell on the War of Secession so much as it had in earlier days.

"I stand foursquare behind Mr. Sinclair in his call for freedom and in his call for justice," Blackford said. "The Socialist Party, unlike every other party in the USA, is committed to economic freedom and economic justice for every citizen of the United States. Others may speak of a square deal, but how, my friends, how can there be a square deal for the millions of workers who cannot earn enough to buy a square meal?"

That won him solid cheers, in which Flora joined. Possessive pride filled her: that was *her* man up there, perhaps—*no, probably,* she thought, defying a generation and a half of Democratic tenure in the White House—the next vice president, as Upton Sinclair had said. Hard on the heels of pride came loneliness. If Blackford was to become the next vice president, he'd be crisscrossing the country between now and November 2. They wouldn't have many chances to see each other till the election.

More solid applause followed Blackford's speech: the sort, Flora thought, a vice-presidential candidate should get. Blackford had spoken ably, but hadn't upstaged Sinclair. "On to victory!" the chairman shouted, dismissing the delegates and formally bringing the convention to a close.

On the street outside the hall, a sandy-haired fellow in the overalls and cloth cap of a steelworker called Flora's name. "Yes? What is it?" she asked.

"I wanted to ask how your brother's getting along, ma'am," the man said. "I was his sergeant, the day he got hurt. Name's Chester Martin." He took off the cap and dipped his head.

"Oh!" Flora exclaimed. "He spoke well of you in his letters, always. You know he lost the leg?"

"I thought he would—I saw the wound," Martin answered. "Please say hello for me, next time you see him."

"I will," Flora answered. "He's doing as well as he could hope on the artificial leg. With it and a cane, he gets around fairly well. He's working, back in New York City."

"That's all good news, or as good as it can be," Martin said.

"He's a Democrat," Flora added, as if to say all the news wasn't good.

"I used to be, but I'm a Socialist now," Martin said. "It evens out. And I think, with Sinclair running, we may win the election this time, ma'am. I really do."

"So do I," Flora whispered—she didn't want to say it too loudly, for fear Something might hear and put a jinx on it. "So do I."

Anne Colleton gave her brother an annoyed look. "I still don't see exactly why you think I ought to meet this person."

"Because I remember very well the soldier who wrote to me about him," Tom Colleton replied. "If Bartlett says something is important, you can take it to the bank." He looked sheepish. "These days, as a matter of fact, Bartlett's word is a damn sight better than taking something to the bank."

"I think you want me to meet this Brearley because you're still trying to get me out of the Freedom Party," Anne said.

"If the big wheels in the Party aren't just the way you think they are, isn't that something you ought to know?" her brother returned.

If Roger Kimball isn't just the way you think he is, isn't that a reason to stop your affair with him? That was what Tom meant. Kimball could have been a Baptist preacher, and Tom would have disapproved of the affair. That Kimball was anything but a Baptist preacher made the disapproval stick out all over, like the quills on a porcupine.

Her brother did have a point, though. Anne was not so blindly devoted to either the Freedom Party or to Roger Kimball as to be blind to that. "He's coming. I can't stop him from coming. I'll hear him out," she said.

"So glad you're pleased." Tom grinned impudently. "Seeing as his train gets into St. Matthews in twenty minutes, I'm going to head over toward the station. Want to come along?"

"No, thank you," Anne answered. "This is your soldier and your soldier's pal. If you want to deal with him, go right ahead. You invited him down without bothering to ask me about it, so you can bring him here on your own, too."

"All right, Sis, I will," Tom said. "See you soon—or maybe not quite so soon, depending on how late the train is today." He grabbed a hat off the rack and went out the door whistling. Anne glared at his back. If he knew she was doing it, he didn't let on.

Anne resolved to be as poor a hostess as rigid notions of Confederate hospitality allowed. But, when her brother returned with the stranger, her resolution faltered. She hadn't expected the fellow to look like such a puppy. Out came a peach pie whose existence she hadn't intended to admit. She put on a fresh pot of coffee. "Your name is Brearley, isn't that right?" she said, knowing perfectly well it was.

"Yes, ma'am," he answered. "Tom Brearley, ex–C.S. Navy. Through most of the war, I was Roger Kimball's executive officer aboard the *Bonefish*."

"Of course," Anne said. "I knew the name sounded familiar." It hadn't, not really; Kimball had mentioned his exec only a couple of times, and in less than flattering terms. Anne had an excellent memory for names, but Brearley's had slid clean out of her head. He hadn't wanted to give it before coming down, either; only her and Tom's flat refusal to meet with a mystery man had pried it out of him.

Brearley said, "Up in Richmond, I saw in the papers that you were working for the Freedom Party, and that he is, too."

Tom Colleton raised an eyebrow. Anne ignored it, saying, "Yes, that's right. The war's been over for three years now. That's far past time for us to get back on our feet again, but the only people who want this country to do things and not just sit there with its head in the sand are in the Party, seems to me."

"I don't think that's so, but never mind," Brearley said. "I didn't come down here to argue politics with you. Getting somebody to change politics may be easier than getting him to change his church, but it isn't a whole lot easier."

"Why did you come down here, then?" Anne asked. "In your last letter, you said you knew something important about Roger Kimball, but you didn't say what. I'm not sure why you thought it would matter to me at all, except that both our names happened to end up in the same newspaper story."

Kimball hadn't talked much about Brearley to her. How much had Kimball talked about her to Brearley? Men bragged. That was one of their more odious characteristics, as far as she was concerned. She'd thought Kimball relatively immune to the disease. Maybe she'd been wrong.

She couldn't tell, not from reading Brearley's face. He still looked like a puppy. But he didn't sound like a puppy as he answered, "Because if what he did ever came out, it would embarrass the Freedom Party. For that matter, if what he did ever came out, it would embarrass the Confederate States."

"You don't talk small, do you?" Tom Colleton remarked.

"My granddad would have called it a sockdologer, sure enough," Brearley said, "and he'd have been right, too. Let me tell you what happened aboard the *Bonefish* right at the end of the war." He detailed how Kimball, fully aware the war was over and lost, had nonetheless stalked and sunk the USS *Ericsson*, sending her to the bottom without, so far as Brearley knew, a single survivor.

"That's it?" Anne said when her visitor fell silent. Tom Brearley nodded. "What do you expect me to do about it?" she asked him.

She was asking herself the same question. Kimball had certainly kept this secret from her. She wasn't surprised. The more people who knew about the *Ericsson*, the more dangerous the knowledge got. She made a point of not looking over at her brother. She knew how he was likely to use it: not in any way that would make her comfortable.

Tom Brearley said, "What I do with it doesn't matter. I'm nobody in particular. But you're involved in the Freedom Party, same as Roger Kimball is. How do you feel about working side by side with a cold-blooded murderer?"

Anne gnawed the inside of her lower lip. No, Brearley didn't talk like a puppy. He minced no words at all, as a matter of fact. She decided to match his bluntness: "If you really want to know, Mr. Brearley, it doesn't bother me one bit. If I'd been in position to hit the Yankees one last lick, I'd have done it, and I'd have done it regardless of whether the war was supposed to be over or not. What do you think of that, sir?"

Now Brearley looked like a horrified puppy. He coughed a couple of times before blurting, "No wonder you back the Freedom Party!"

"The United States worked for fifty years to get their revenge on us," Anne said. "I don't know how long I'll have to wait for my turn. I hope it isn't that long. However long it takes, I think it'll come sooner from the Freedom Party than from anybody else out there right now."

Tom Colleton said, "Mr. Brearley's right about one thing, though: if the United States ever get word of what the *Bonefish* did, they can put us in hot water on account of it. If Roosevelt wins a third term, he'll do it, too."

"Then we have to see that the United States don't find out about it," Anne said, doing her best to put Brearley in fear with her expression.

It didn't work. She should have realized it wouldn't work, not if he'd gone through the war in a submersible. He said, "If you want to make sure the story gets to the United States, arranging an accident for me is the best way to go about it. I didn't come here without taking the precautions a sensible man would take before he stuck his head in the lion's mouth."

"I didn't threaten you, Mr. Brearley," Anne said: a technical truth that was in fact a great, thumping lie.

"Of course not," Brearley said—another lie.

Anne wondered if she ought to offer to pay him to keep the secret of the *Bonefish* from reaching the United States. After some thought, she decided not to. If he wanted money in exchange for silence, let him bring it up. If he wanted Confederate paper money in exchange for silence, he was a bigger fool than he'd shown himself to be.

Her brother said, "Mr. Brearley, you do understand that, whatever score you may want to settle with Mr. Kimball, you're liable to hurt the whole country if this story gets told too widely." Anne looked at him now, in nothing but admiration. She hadn't been able to come up with anything nearly so smooth.

Brearley nodded. "Of course I do. That's why I've kept quiet for so long. You may call me a great many things, but I love my country. If you'll forgive me, I love my country too well to want to see it fall into the hands of the Freedom Party."

"I'll forgive you for that," Tom Colleton said. "Whether my sister will is liable to be a different question."

Brearley glanced at Anne. She looked back, bland as new-churned butter. "I don't agree, but Mr. Brearley didn't come down here for me to change his politics, either," she said.

Brearley looked relieved. Anne almost laughed in his face. One thing he plainly didn't understand about the Freedom Party was that so many people joined it because they wanted revenge: revenge against the United States, revenge against the Negroes in the Confederate States, and revenge against the government and Army that had failed to live up to the CSA's long tradition of victory. Hunger for revenge had led Anne into the Party. Now she had one more piece of revenge to attend to, as opportunity arose: revenge against Tom Brearley.

He said, "I'll leave it at that, then. I do thank you kindly for hearing me out. Next train north doesn't come in till tomorrow, does it?"

"No," Tom Colleton said. "St. Matthews isn't the big city. You'll have seen that for yourself, I reckon. If you want to come along with me, we'll see whether the hotel has an empty room." He snorted. "Let's see if the hotel has any rooms that aren't empty besides the one you'll be in. Come on."

As soon as her brother took Tom Brearley out of the flat, Anne tried to get a telephone connection through to Richmond. She didn't want to put anything down in writing, which eliminated both the telegraph and a letter. Telegraphers weren't supposed to pay any attention to what they sent, but they did, or they could. Letters could go astray, too.

And so could telephone connections. "Sorry, ma'am," the operator reported. "Don't look like you can get there from here today." She laughed at her own wit.

Anne didn't. Anne was not—was emphatically not—amused. She snarled something wordless but potent and hung up the telephone with a crash. She hoped it rattled the operator's teeth. Who could guess where the trouble lay? Storms knocking down wires? Squirrels gnawing through insulation and shorting out the line? Anything was possible—anything except getting through to Richmond.

Her brother came in a couple of minutes later. "Well, what do you think of Kimball now?" he asked.

"The same as before," Anne answered, to Tom's evident disappointment. "Like I told that fellow, if I'd been in the *Bonefish*, I'd have torpedoed that destroyer, too."

"My fire-eating sister," Tom said, more admiringly than not.

"That's right," Anne said. "That's exactly right. And anybody who forgets it for even a minute will be sorry the rest of his livelong days."

Cincinnatus Driver looked back at the house in which he'd lived his whole married life. He looked around at the Covington, Kentucky, neighborhood in which he'd lived his whole life. There was a last time for everything, and this was it.

He cranked the engine. The shabby old Duryea truck thundered into life. It didn't give half the trouble it usually did, as if it too were glad to shake the dust of Kentucky from its tires. Cincinnatus hurried back to the cab.

There sat Elizabeth, Achilles on her lap. "We ready?" Cincinnatus asked as he slid in behind the wheel. In one way, it was a foolish question: everything they owned and aimed to take along was behind them in the bed of the truck. In another way, though, it was *the* question, and Cincinnatus knew it. He still didn't know whether he and his family were ready to abandon everything they'd ever known in the hope for a better life.

Ready or not, they were going to do it. Elizabeth nodded. Achilles yelled "Ready!" at the top of his lungs. Cincinnatus put the truck in gear. He waited for the engine to die or for something else dreadful to happen. Nothing did. Smooth as if it were ten years newer, the Duryea began to roll.

As Cincinnatus turned out of Covington's colored district and onto Greenup, Elizabeth said, "I do wish your ma and pa decided to come along with us."

"I do, too," he answered. "But they're set in their ways, like folks can get. I ain't gonna worry about it much. Once we find a place, you wait and see if they don't come after us."

"Maybe they will," his wife said. "I hope they do. Won't be so lonesome if they do, that's for sure."

"Yeah." If Cincinnatus had let his hands drive the truck for him, he would have gone on to the waterfront. He'd been heading there, walking or taking the trolley or driving the truck, since the early days of the war. But he wasn't going to head there any more. Instead, he took the suspension bridge north across the Ohio River and over into Cincinnati.

"The United States," Elizabeth said softly.

Cincinnatus nodded. Oh, Kentucky was one of the United States these days, but in many ways Kentucky still seemed as it had when it belonged to the Confederacy. That was the biggest reason Cincinnatus had decided to better his luck and his family's elsewhere. He wasn't going to wait around holding his breath till he got the vote and other privileges whites in Kentucky took for granted.

Back in the days before the war, he'd spent a lot of time looking across the Ohio. Negroes didn't have it easy in the USA. He knew that. Had he not known it, he would have got his nose rubbed in it during the war. A lot of men down from the United States thought they had to act like slave drivers to get any kind of work out of Negroes. But not all of them did, and laws restricting what blacks could do were milder in the USA than in the CSA: he didn't have to worry about a passbook any more, for instance.

One reason for such mildness, of course, was that blacks were

far thinner on the ground in the United States than in the Confederate States. That did worry Cincinnatus. He'd always spent most of
his time among his own kind. That would be much harder now.
Covington hadn't had a huge colored community, but what would
he do in a town with only a handful of blacks?

Down off the bridge, down into Cincinnati, went the truck. The
waterfront on the northern bank of the Ohio didn't look much different from the one with which Cincinnatus was so familiar. But
Elizabeth noted one difference right away: "Look at all the white
folks doin' roustabouts' work. Wouldn't never seen nothin' like that
in Covington. Wouldn't never see nothin' like that nowhere in the
CSA. White folks doin' nigger work?" She shook her head.

"This here's what I been tellin' you, honey," Cincinnatus said.
"Ain't no such thing as nigger work in the USA, or not hardly. Ain't
enough niggers to do all the dirty work that needs doin', so the white
folks have to lend a hand. A lot of 'em is foreigners, I hear tell, but
not all of 'em, I don't reckon."

"What's a foreigner, Pa?" Achilles asked.

"Somebody who's in a country he wasn't born in," Cincinnatus
replied.

His son thought about that, then asked, "How do you tell a foreigner from somebody who ain't?"

"A lot of times, on account of he'll talk funny—they don't talk
English in a lot of them foreign places," Cincinnatus said. By that
standard, though, a foreigner's son, somebody who went to school
in the USA, would turn into an American indistinguishable from any
other. If Achilles ended up as educated and eloquent as Teddy Roosevelt, he still wouldn't be an American indistinguishable from any
other. That struck Cincinnatus as unfair.

He shrugged. It *was* unfair, no two ways about it. His hope was
that Achilles would find things less unfair elsewhere in the USA than
in Kentucky.

People were looking at him: people on the sidewalk, people in
motorcars, even a couple of men who stopped painting a sign to
stare. They were all white. Cincinnati had some Negroes; Cincinnatus knew as much. But he saw none on the streets. That was a
change, a jolting change, from the way things were back in Covington, over on the other side of the river.

A fat, red-faced policeman held up his hand. Cincinnatus
stopped in front of him, as he should have done. He was very
pleased at how well the spavined old Duryea was behaving. He'd

spent a lot of time getting the truck into the best shape he could, but the only thing that would really have cured its multifarious ills was a new truck, and he knew it.

The expression of distaste on the cop's face was broad enough for him and the truck both. The fellow jerked a thumb toward the curb. "Pull over that wagon," he said in gutturally accented English. "I will with you speak."

"Is he a foreigner, Pa?" Achilles asked excitedly. "He talks funny, like you said."

"Reckon he might be," Cincinnatus answered. "They do say Cincinnati's chock full of Germans."

"Real live Germans?" Achilles' eyes were enormous. The USA's European allies were folk to conjure with, just as Frenchmen had been in the CSA . . . until the war came, and France lost.

When Cincinnatus stopped the truck by the curb, the policeman strutted over. "You are from where?" he demanded.

"Covington, Kentucky, suh—just the other side of the river," Cincinnatus answered. He wouldn't have got uppity with a Covington cop, and he wasn't so rash as to think the police would be much friendlier on the north side of the Ohio.

"What do you do here?" the policeman asked. "Why don't you stay on the other side of the river where you belong?"

"I ain't plannin' on settling down in Cincinnati, suh," Cincinnatus said hastily. "My family and me, we're just passin' through."

"Where are you going to?" the policeman inquired.

"Headin' for Iowa," Cincinnatus told him. "Des Moines, Iowa."

"This is a good long way from Cincinnati," the cop said, as much to himself as to Cincinnatus. "You will the worry of the people in Iowa be, not the worry of the people here. Very well. You may go on." He even condescended to stop traffic and let Cincinnatus pull out once more. Cincinnatus would have been more grateful had it been less obvious that the policeman was getting rid of him.

"Welcome to the United States," Elizabeth remarked. "Welcome—but not very welcome."

"I was thinking that myself, not very long ago," Cincinnatus said. "Better here than if we'd headed down to Tennessee."

His wife didn't argue about that. He went back to concentrating on his driving. He knew where he was going, but he wasn't completely sure how to get there. Road maps left a lot to be desired. He'd studied as many as he could at the Covington library, so he knew how far from perfect they were. He also mistrusted road signs. Oh, roads in towns had names and numbers; he could rely on that. But he'd seen during the war that roads between towns might change names without warning or might never have had names in the first place. That made traveling more interesting for strangers.

He managed to get out of Cincinnati, and congratulated himself on that. Only after he'd been out of town for a while did he realize he was going due north, not northwest toward Indianapolis.

"Don't fret yourself about it none," Elizabeth said when he cursed himself for fourteen different kinds of a fool. "Sooner or later, you'll come across a road that runs into the one you should have used. Then everything'll be fine again."

"Sure, I'll come across that blame road," Cincinnatus snarled, "but how the devil will I know it's the right one? It won't look no different than any other road, and it won't have no sign on it, neither." He felt harassed.

He felt even more harassed a couple of minutes later, when one of the truck's inner tubes blew out with a bang that would have put him in mind of a gunshot had he not heard more gunshots than he'd ever wanted to hear the past few years. He guided the limping machine to the side of the road and began the slow, dirty business of repairing the puncture.

Motorcars and trucks kept rolling past him as if he weren't there. Every one of them—every one he noticed, anyhow—had a white face behind the wheel. Most, no doubt, wouldn't have stopped to help a white man, either. But would all of them have sped past a strange white without more than a single hasty glance? Maybe. On the other hand, maybe not, too.

At last, when he was wrestling the wheel back onto the axle, a Ford did pull up behind the truck. "Give you a hand?" asked the driver, a plump blond fellow in a straw hat and overalls.

"Just about done it now," Cincinnatus said. "Wish you'd come by a half hour ago; I don't mind tellin' you that."

"Believe it," the white man said. "Where you bound for?"

"Des Moines," Cincinnatus answered, and held up a filthy hand. "Yeah, I know I'm on the wrong road. I missed the right one down in Cincinnati. You know how I can get back to it from here?"

"Go up . . . lemme see . . . four crossings and then turn left. That'll put you heading toward the highway to Indiana," the white man said. He cocked his head to one side. "You got family in Des Moines?"

"No, suh," Cincinnatus said. "Just lookin' for a better place to live than Kentucky." He waited to see how the white man would take that.

"Oh. Good luck." The fellow climbed into his automobile and drove away.

"Thanks for the directions," Cincinnatus called after him. He couldn't tell whether the white man heard. He shrugged. The man had stopped, and had given him some help. He couldn't complain about that—even if, worn as he was, he felt sorely tempted. "Des Moines," he said. He'd be on the road again soon.

"Come on," Sylvia Enos said impatiently to George, Jr., and Mary Jane as they made their way across the Boston Common toward the New State House. "And hold on to my hands, for heaven's sake. If you get lost, how will I find you again in this crowd?"

U.S. flags fluttered from the platform that had gone up in front of the New State House. Red-white-and-blue bunting wreathed it. Although President Roosevelt wasn't scheduled to start speaking for another hour, the crowd was already growing rapidly. Most of the people gathering around the platform were men. Why not? They enjoyed the right to vote.

Even though Sylvia didn't, she wanted to hear what Roosevelt had to say for himself. She wanted to see him, too, and to have the children see him. They'd remember that for the rest of their lives.

Mary Jane, at the moment, had her mind on other things: "The dome sure is shiny, Ma!" she said, pointing. "It's as shiny as the sun, I bet."

"That's because it's gilded, silly," George, Jr., said importantly.

"What's *gilded* mean, Ma?" Mary Jane asked.

"It means *painted with gold paint*," her big brother told her.

"I didn't ask you, Mr. Know-It-All," Mary Jane said. "Besides, I bet you're making it up, anyway."

"I am not!" George, Jr., howled. "I ought to pop you a good one, is what I ought to do."

"I'll pop both of you if you don't behave yourselves," Sylvia said. What ran through her mind was that she'd remember this day for the rest of her life, but not because she'd seen the president.

"You tell Mary Jane that I do so know what *gilded* means," George, Jr., said. "I learned it in school. And there's a wooden codfish inside there somewhere, and it's gilded, too. They call it the Sacred Cod." He frowned. "I don't know what *sacred* means."

"It means *holy*," Sylvia said. "And your brother's right, Mary Jane. *Gilded* does mean *painted with gold paint*. And I'll thank you not to call him names. You're supposed to know better than that."

"All right, Ma," Mary Jane said in tones of such angelic sweetness, Sylvia didn't believe a word of it. The face Mary Jane made at George, Jr., a moment later said her skepticism had been well founded.

Sylvia worked her way as close to the platform as she could. It wasn't close enough to satisfy her children, who set up a chorus of, "We can't see!"

At the moment, there wasn't anything to see. Sylvia pointed that out, but it did nothing to stem the chorus. She finally said, "When the president starts to speak, I'll pick both of you up so you can see him, all right?"

"Will you pick both of us up at the same time?" Mary Jane sounded as if she liked the idea.

"No!" Sylvia exclaimed. "If I do that, you and your brother can pick me up afterwards and carry me home." She thought that might calm them down. Instead, it got them jumping around with excitement. George, Jr., did try to pick her up, and kept trying till she had to smack him to get him to quit.

After what seemed like forever, people started coming out of the New State House and going up onto the platform. They had the same look to them: plump men, middle-aged and elderly, many with big drooping mustaches, all of them in somber black suits with waistcoats. Most wore top hats; a few of the younger ones contented themselves with homburgs. They might have been rich undertakers. In fact, they were Democratic politicians.

They buried more men in the Great War than undertakers could in a hundred years, Sylvia thought bitterly. One of them stepped forward. "Hurrah for Governor Coolidge!" somebody shouted, which told her who the fellow was.

"You didn't come here to listen to me today," Coolidge said. "I'm going to step aside for President Roosevelt." With a bow, he did just that. "Mr. President!"

"Thank you, Governor Coolidge." Theodore Roosevelt matched the rest of the men up there in age and build and dress, but he had enough energy for four of them, maybe six. He bounded to the front of the platform, almost running over the governor of Massachusetts in his eagerness to put himself in the public eye. "Ladies and gentlemen," he cried in a huge voice, "this is the greatest nation in the history of the world, and I am the luckiest man in the history of the world, to have had the privilege of leading her for the past eight years."

"No third term! No third term!" The cry broke out in several places around Sylvia at the same time. She suspected that was not an accident. She also suspected Roosevelt would be hearing the same cry everywhere he went up till election day.

He must have suspected the same thing. He bared his mouthful of large, square teeth and growled, "Ah, the Socialists are barking already. If they'd had their way, we would have sat on the sidelines while the greatest struggle the world has ever known was decided without us. I submit to you, ladies and gentlemen, that a great nation does not let others choose its destiny for it. A great nation makes its own fate: that is the mark of greatness."

He got a round of applause. But the hecklers sent up another chant: "How many dead? How many dead?" That one hit Sylvia hard. Had Roosevelt sat on the sidelines, her husband would have been alive today. Maybe the USA wouldn't have been so strong. Sylvia would have made that trade in a heartbeat, if only she could have, if only someone would have asked her.

"How many would have died had we waited?" Roosevelt returned. "How many would have died if we'd let England and France and Russia and the Confederate States gang up on our allies? After the Entente powers beat down our friend Kaiser Bill, how long do you think it would have been before our turn came around again? They piled onto us in the War of Secession, didn't they? They piled onto us in the Second Mexican War, didn't they? Don't you think they would have piled onto us in the Great War, too? By jingo, I do! We're young and virile and up-and-coming, just like the German Empire. The countries that had the power didn't care to share it with the countries that wanted it, the countries that deserved it. Well, if they wouldn't yield us a place in the sun, we had to go and take one. And we did. And I'm proud that we did. And if you're proud, too, you'll vote the Democratic ticket in November."

That earned him more applause, with only a thin scattering of boos mixed in. *How many dead?* still echoed inside Sylvia Enos as she lifted first her son and then her daughter to see Theodore Roosevelt. The president was a master of the big picture; he made her see the whole world turning in her hands. But that still counted for less with her than a husband who had not come home.

And the hecklers hadn't given up, either. "No third term!" they called again. "No third term!"

Roosevelt stuck out his chin. The sun flashed from the lenses of his spectacles, making him look as much like a mechanism as a man. "Because George Washington decided he would not seek a third term, is it Holy Writ that every succeeding president must follow suit?" he thundered. "We are speaking of the United States of America here, ladies and gentlemen, not a hand of auction bridge." He pounded fist into palm. "I refuse to reckon my actions bound by those of a slaveholding Virginian a hundred and twenty years dead. Vote for me or against me, according to whether you think well or ill of me and what I have done in office. This other pernicious nonsense has no place in the campaign."

"Four more years! Four more years!" Roosevelt had friends in the crowd, too: many more friends than foes, by the number of voices urging a third term for the president. With so much support, Sylvia didn't see how he could fail to be reelected. Maybe it wouldn't be so bad. He probably wouldn't find any excuse to start a new war between now and 1924.

"Capitalist tool! Capitalist tool!" The Socialists started a new jeer.

Roosevelt had been talking about the vote for women, which, rather to Sylvia's surprise, he professed to favor. "I am the tool of no man!" he shouted, meeting the hecklers as combatively as he had throughout the speech. "I am the tool of no man, and I am the tool of no class. Let me hear Mr. Sinclair say the same thing, and I will have learned something. A dictatorship of the proletariat is no less a dictatorship than any other sort."

George, Jr., tugged at Sylvia's skirt. "What's the pro—prole—prolewatchamacallit, Ma?"

"Proletariat. It means the people who do all the work in factories and on farms," Sylvia answered. "Not the rich people who own the factories."

"Oh." Her son thought about that. "People like us, you mean."

"That's right, people like us." Sylvia smiled. Painting red rings on galoshes was about as proletarian a job as you could get. If she didn't come in tomorrow, the foreman could replace her with just about anyone off the street. And, the day after that, Frank Best would no doubt be trying to get the new ring-painter into bed with him.

Up on the platform, concerned with bigger things, Theodore Roosevelt was winding up his speech: "I love this country. I have served this country all my adult life, and with every fiber of my being. If it please you, the citizens, that I continue to serve the United States, that will be the greatest honor and privilege you have in your power to grant me. I hope it will. I pray it will. Let us go forward together, and make the twentieth century be remembered forevermore as the American century. I thank you."

"Is he finished?" Mary Jane asked as the crowd applauded. Sylvia nodded. Her daughter found another question: "Can we go home now?"

"All right, dear." Sylvia didn't quite know how to take the question. She wondered whether Mary Jane really would remember the day as long as she'd hoped. As they were heading toward the trolley stop, she asked, "What did you think of the president?"

"He talked for a long time." By the way Mary Jane said it, she didn't mean it as a compliment.

"He had a lot of things to talk about." Sylvia gave credit where it was due, even if she didn't care for all the things Roosevelt had said. "Running the country is a big, complicated job."

"Huh," Mary Jane said. "I bet more people would vote for him if he didn't talk so much." Sylvia tried to figure out how to answer that. In the end, she didn't answer at all. Her best guess was that Mary Jane had a point.

Jake Featherston had never imagined he'd end up working out of an office. He had one now, though, paid for with Freedom Party dues. He had a secretary, too, whose pay came from the same source. Without Lulu endlessly tapping away on the typewriter, he wouldn't have got done a quarter of what needed doing. As things were, he got done half of what needed doing, sometimes even more.

Lulu couldn't handle everything by her lonesome. Featherston studied the snapshot on his desk. It showed a British- or Confederate-style rhomboidal barrel in the middle of some dry, rough-looking country. The letter that had come with the photo was from a Party member fighting for the Emperor of Mexico against rebels who had Yankee backing.

We're not really here at all, the letter read. *Neither is our friend.* The friend in question was the barrel. *Only a couple of us ever used these critters in the war against the USA. Now we all know how to handle them. Some of us are going to try and see if we can't get some stronger engines, too, so they'll go better. You bet we'll bring home what we're learning. Freedom!*

Slowly, Featherston nodded to himself. The Confederate States weren't allowed to have barrels of their own. So the United States said, and the United States were strong enough to make their word stick. But Confederate mercenaries in Mexico, in Peru, and in Argentina were getting practice fighting in barrels and in aeroplanes and on the sea, and were figuring out improvements for the machines they used. A lot of those mercenaries belonged to the Freedom Party. Jake figured he knew as much about clandestine Confederate military affairs as the War Department did—and the War Department didn't know how much he knew.

Lulu stopped typing. She came into his private office: a thin, gray-haired woman, competent rather than decorative. "Mr. Kimball is here to see you, Mr. Featherston."

"Bring him right on in," Jake said. "We've got some things to talk about, sure enough." His secretary nodded, left, and returned a moment later with Kimball. Jake rose and shook his hand. "Good to see you. Glad you could get up to Richmond."

"I hadn't planned to," Roger Kimball answered, "but things have a way of coming up when you don't expect them, eh?"

Featherston nodded. After Lulu went out and started typing again, he said, "Just when you thought you had everything sunk down out of sight for good, you find out you were wrong. That fellow who went and saw Anne Colleton isn't by any chance lying, is he?"

Kimball looked as if he wanted to say yes, but in the end he shook his head. "I sank the Yankee bastard, all right. So the war was over? Too damn bad." He glared at Jake, defying him to make something of it.

"Good," Jake said. Kimball stared. Featherston went on, "I fought the damnyankees up to the very last second I could. You think I care if you waited till the cease-fire went into effect before you gave 'em one last lick? In a pig's ass, I do. What matters to me is whether it'll make trouble for the Party and trouble for the country. If I decide it will, I'm going to have to cut you loose."

He waited to see how Kimball would take that. The ex–submersible skipper said, "I'll kill that son of a bitch of a Brearley if it's the last thing I ever do. I knew he was a weak reed right from the start."

"You will not," Jake Featherston said. "You *will* not, do you hear me?" He waited to see how Kimball would take the flat order.

Kimball took it just the way he'd expected him to: he blew his stack. "The hell I won't," he snarled, going brick red. "I told that bastard I'd murder him if he ever started running his big mouth. He damn well has, and I damn well will."

"Then I damn well will cut you loose right this minute," Featherston said. "Forget what I told you down in Charleston. I don't want a man who can't do what he's told in the Freedom Party. I don't want somebody who's liable to blow up behind my back in the Party. If you want to kill Brearley after I told you not to, you can kindly wait till you don't have any connection to me. Do whatever you please on your own hook. Don't embarrass the Party."

He waited again. What would Kimball do? He'd been an officer. Would he get shirty about taking orders from an ex-sergeant? A lot of fellows who'd worn fancy uniforms couldn't stomach anything like that. Or would he remember that, in the Freedom Party, he was still a mid-ranking officer and Jake was commander-in-chief?

Kimball started to blow his stack once more. Featherston could see it begin ... and, a moment later, could see Kimball ease off again. Jake eyed the former Navy man with respect he hoped he concealed. Not everybody could go into a rage and then clamp down on it. The people who could were apt to be very useful indeed.

Slowly, Roger Kimball said, "All right, Sarge, suppose I let the son of a bitch live for a while? That means you've got a line on giving him what he deserves some other way, right?"

"Not yet, it doesn't," Featherston answered. Yes, Kimball was worth keeping around, all right—he'd got one step ahead of Jake, which didn't happen every day. "I'm not saying I will yet, either. Have to cipher out how I want to do it, if I decide to do it. Do I want it to look like the Party didn't have anything to do with it? Or do I want the job to say, *You screw around with the Freedom Party and you'll end up good and dead?*"

All at once, instead of taking it personally, Kimball started looking at it as a tactical problem. Jake saw the change in his eyes. He smiled to himself, but only to himself—he didn't want Kimball to know he could read him.

"That's a nice question, isn't it?" Kimball said. "I guess the one to ask right afterwards is, If we let the world know the Freedom Party got rid of Brearley, can we do it without having anybody go to jail?"

"There are places we could," Jake answered. "South Carolina's one of 'em, I reckon: Anne Colleton has big chunks of that state sewed up tight for us."

"I haven't done too bad my own self, you don't mind my saying so," Kimball replied. Was that touchiness in his voice?

It was, Jake decided. Was Kimball jealous of Anne Colleton? Damned if he wasn't. *That* was a useful thing to know. Featherston filed it away. He couldn't use it now, but that didn't mean he wouldn't be able to somewhere down the line. For the moment, he needed to stick to the business at hand: "I'm not so sure about Richmond. We've got a lot of cops in the Party here, same as most places, but they've got city hall and the state government and the Confederate government all sitting over 'em. They might have to go after us, whether they really want to or not."

"I can see that." Kimball raised an eyebrow. He was cool and collected again. Yes, he would have made a formidable submarine skipper. Nothing fazed him for long. Jake could easily picture him stalking and sinking that U.S. destroyer after the war ended, and banking on success to keep him out of hot water. He went on, "The Whigs and the Radical Liberals don't fancy the Freedom Party much these days, do they?"

"If they did, I'd reckon I was doing something wrong," Featherston said. "Pack of damn fools, want to keep on doing things the same old way. That's real sly, ain't it? That's how we got into the mess we're in. That's how we'll get into more messes, too, sure as the devil."

"I don't reckon you're wrong there." Kimball leaned forward, Brearley almost forgotten. "What the hell are you going to do about the niggers if we ever get the chance?"

"Smack 'em down and make sure they don't have the chance to get back up on their feet and stab us in the back again," Jake answered: the reply he usually gave. He had more in mind, but he still didn't know if he could do, if anybody could do, everything he really wanted. What he'd told Kimball would suffice for the time being. "Let's get back to this business here. There's no paper, nothing in your log or anything, that says you sank this Yankee ship too late, right?"

To his relief, Kimball nodded. "I made sure there wouldn't be. Brearley can't prove anything like that. But I didn't sink the *Ericsson* all by myself, either. If the rest of the crew start blabbing, they could give me a hell of a hard time."

"Would they do that?" Jake asked.

"Most of 'em wouldn't, I'm sure of it," Kimball said, again the reply Featherston wanted to hear. "They were howling like a pack of wolves when we sent that damn destroyer to the bottom. But even on a little boat like the *Bonefish*, there's a couple dozen sailors. I can't tell you nobody would chime in with my exec, because I don't know that for a fact."

"All right." Jake scratched his head and thought for a while. "Here's what we're going to do for now: sit tight and see what happens. If Brearley goes to the papers, he damn well does, that's all. I don't reckon it hurts the Party. You weren't in the Party during the war, on account of there wasn't any Party *to* be in during the war."

"Fair enough," Kimball said: yes, he was ready to take orders. "What do we do if he does go to the papers?"

"*You* don't do anything," Featherston said, "not to him, anyhow. You go back down to South Carolina and stay there. If reporters start asking questions, tell 'em . . . tell 'em you can't talk about it, that's what you say." He grinned. "You got to remember, Roger, our only *big* worry is getting the USA riled at us when we're not strong enough to hit back. Most of the people in the CSA—hell, in your shoes, they'd've done the same thing."

"By Jesus, they would've. You're right about that. You're dead right about that, Sarge," Kimball said. "I'll do just like you say. I'll tell the snoops I can't talk about it. And if they ask why I can't, I'll tell 'em I can't talk about that, either."

"There you go," Jake said, nodding. "Make it sound mysterious as all get-out. That'll drive the whole raft of reporters crazy, same as a girl who plays hard to get drives the guys crazy. Reporters are used to people who put out. Most folks love to talk—nothin' they love better. You keep your mouth shut and you're a long ways ahead of the game." He studied Kimball. "You reckon you can do that?"

"I can do it," the ex–Navy man said, and Jake thought he could. Kimball went on, "Be kind of fun, matter of fact, leading 'em around by the nose."

As far as Jake was concerned, very little was more fun than leading reporters around by the nose. Much more often than not, reporters wrote the stories he wanted them to write about the Freedom Party. They usually thought they were slamming the Party—but they were slamming it the way he wanted them to, a way that let them feel clever about themselves but at the same time made the Party look appealing to a lot of their readers.

He didn't tell Kimball that. Maybe Kimball was smart enough to figure it out for himself. If he was, he also needed to be smart enough to keep it to himself.

"Anything else on your mind?" Jake asked him.

"I don't reckon there is," Kimball said after a little thought. "We've got things squared away here, don't we?"

"Yeah, we do," Featherston said. "I'm right glad you came up— glad we had the chance to talk about a few things." He was even gladder Kimball had proved sensible, but the other man didn't need to know that, either. Having used the stick before, Jake threw him a carrot now: "Looks to me like you're going places in the Freedom Party. I've said that before, haven't I? Still looks like it's so."

"I aim to," Kimball said. "Yes, sir, I aim to." Jake studied him again. How high did he aim? The trouble with ambitious men was their nasty habit of aiming straight for the top.

But Jake was aiming for the top, too, for a different top, one high above anything to which he thought Roger Kimball could aspire. If everything went perfectly, he'd get there next year. He hadn't imagined he could win even a couple of months before. Now he thought he just might. And if things went wrong, he'd take longer, that was all. Either way, he aimed to do it. "I'm glad we've got you settled," he said, "on account of I don't want anything getting in the way of that run for president when 1921 rolls around."

"No, sir!" Kimball said, and his eyes glowed.

Colonel Irving Morrell and Agnes Hill hurried across Wallman Park toward yet another statue of John Brown—they seemed to be everywhere in Leavenworth. Decked with bunting as this one was, it looked far more festive than the dour old warrior for freedom had ever been in truth.

"Everyone in town will be here today." Agnes Hill pointed to the throngs of people crossing the foot bridges over Threemile Creek.

"Everyone in town *should* be here today," Morrell said. "Upton Sinclair drew a good crowd when he spoke a couple of weeks ago. Only right the president should draw a bigger one."

Agnes nodded. They shared a common faith in the Democratic Party. They shared a lot of things, including a great deal of pleasure in each other's company. Morrell laughed at himself. He'd gone to that dance not intending to fall in love with the first woman he set eyes on, and here he'd gone and done it. And, by all appearances, she'd fallen in love with him, too.

Not only was President Roosevelt a potent magnet for the crowd, but the day itself seemed to be summoning people outdoors. With September running hard toward October, the summer's muggy heat had broken. The sun still shone brightly, and the oaks and elms and chestnuts in the park still carried their full canopies of leaves to give shade to those who wanted it. The blight spreading among the chestnuts back East hadn't got to Kansas yet; Morrell hoped it never would. The air felt neither warm nor crisp. In fact, he could hardly feel the air at all.

"Perfect," he said, and Agnes Hill nodded again.

A lot of the men in the crowd wore green-gray like Morrell's, Fort Leavenworth lying just north of the town whose name it shared. That helped Agnes and him advance through the crowd: soldiers who spotted his eagles made way for his companion and him. "This is swell!" she exclaimed when they ended up only three or four rows from the rostrum at which Roosevelt would speak.

"It is, isn't it?" Morrell said, and squeezed her hand. They grinned at each other, as happy as if alone together rather than in the middle of the biggest crowd Leavenworth had seen for years (Morrell did hope the crowd was bigger than the one Sinclair had drawn, anyhow).

People whooped like red Indians when President Roosevelt ascended to the rostrum. Off to one side, a brass band blared away at "The Stars and Stripes Forever." Morrell wished the band had picked a different tune; that one rattled around in his head for days whenever he heard it, and it made noisy company.

Roosevelt said, "By jingo, it's always a pleasure for me to come to Kansas. This state was founded by men and women who knew a Southern viper when they saw one, even before the War of Secession." He glanced back at the statue of John Brown. "There is a man who knew who the enemy was, and a man who hit our country's enemies hard even when they still pretended to be friends. For that, I am proud to salute him." He doffed his homburg and half bowed toward the statue.

Morrell clapped till his hands ached. Beside him, Agnes Hill blew Roosevelt a kiss. "Should I be jealous?" Morrell asked her. She stuck out her tongue at him. They both laughed.

"People say—newspapers say—I'm in the fight of my political life," Roosevelt went on. "I say, bully!" He reveled in the new round of applause washing over him from the friendly crowd. "Maybe they'll drag this old Democratic donkey down," he shouted, "but if they do, I tell you this: they'll know they've been in a fight, too."

"You won the war, Teddy," somebody called. "You can win this fight."

Roosevelt, Morrell happened to know, did not care to be called Teddy. On the campaign trail, though, he endured it. His grin looked friendly, not forced. And then somebody else yelled, "The country needs you, Teddy!"

"I don't know whether the country needs me personally or not," Roosevelt said, "but I do know for a fact that I take enormous pride in having served the country. And I also know for a fact that the country needs a Democrat in Powel House or the White House, and I seem to be the one the Democratic Party is putting forward this year.

"Here is something I want you to think about, ladies and gentlemen: in the years since 1852, the Democratic Party has won every presidential election save two. Every schoolchild knows that, but I am going to take a moment of your time to remind you of it once again. In 1860, the voters sent Abraham Lincoln to Washington, and he saddled us with a war, and a losing war to boot. Twenty years later, having forgotten their lesson, the people elected James G. Blaine, who gave us another war—and another loss.

"When war came around yet again, the United States were ready for it. Democratic presidents had made this country strong. Democratic presidents had found us allies. And, thanks to the people, we had a Democratic president at the helm of the ship of state." He preened to remind his audience who that Democratic president was.

"We won the Great War, with God's help. We paid back half a century and more of humiliation of the sort no great nation should ever have had to endure. And now, the editorial writers say, now the people are grown tired of the Democratic Party. They say we were good enough to win the war, but aren't good enough to govern in time of peace. They say the Socialists deserve a turn, a chance."

Roosevelt looked out over the crowd. "Well, let them say whatever they please. It's a free country. Thanks to the Democratic Party, it's stayed a free country—and, I might add, a victorious country as well. And now I am going to tell you what I say. Ladies and gentlemen, I say that, if you elect a Socialist president in 1920, the mischief he will do the United States will make Lincoln and Blaine's mischief look like what a couple of skylarking boys might do."

"That's right!" Morrell shouted at the top of his lungs. The whole enormous crowd was shouting, but Roosevelt caught Morrell's voice and then caught his eye. They'd met several times in Philadelphia, and had always got on well: two aggressive men who both believed in taking the fight to the enemy.

"Here in Leavenworth, you've already seen how the Socialists have gone after the War Department budget with a meat axe," Roosevelt said. "They've done the same thing to the Navy Department, too. If they control the presidency as well as Congress, we'll be lucky to *have* a War Department and a Navy Department by the time we can vote them out of office. Here in front of me, I see one of our nation's most distinguished soldiers, Colonel Irving Morrell, *the* leading exponent of barrel warfare in this country. I know the pittance on which Colonel Morrell has had to operate since the election of 1918. Like a good patriot, he soldiers on as best he can with what he is allotted, but I know, as you must know, he could do far more if only he had more with which to do it. Isn't that the truth, Colonel?"

"Yes, sir, that is the truth," Morrell said loudly. Agnes stared at him with sparkling eyes. She might have imagined a great many things when coming to hear Roosevelt, but surely she hadn't imagined the president would praise Morrell for everyone to hear. Morrell hadn't looked for any such thing himself.

Roosevelt said, "There you have it, ladies and gentlemen, straight from the horse's mouth. If you want to keep the United States strong, vote for me. If you don't care, vote for Sinclair. I thank you."

He got another ovation as he stepped down from the platform. Then, to Morrell's further surprise, Roosevelt beckoned to him. "How's that test model doing, Colonel?" the president asked.

"Sir, it's a great improvement over the barrels we used to fight the war," Morrell answered. "It would have been better still if we'd been able to build a real barrel to that design, not a lightweight machine armored in thin, mild steel."

"You will have such a machine, Colonel," Roosevelt boomed. "If I have anything to say after this November about how the War Department spends its money, you will have it."

"That would be wonderful, Mr. President," Morrell said, and then, "Sir, I'd like to introduce to you my fiancée, Agnes Hill."

"I'm very pleased to meet you, Miss Hill." Roosevelt bowed over her hand. "I want you to take good care of this man. The country will need him for a long time to come."

"I'll do my best, your Excellency," she said. "It's a great honor to meet you."

"Fine, fine." The president smiled at her, then turned away to talk to someone else.

Agnes had stars in her eyes. "How about that?" Morrell said, grinning. He hadn't really expected to get a chance to talk with Roosevelt, nor to be able to introduce Agnes to him. Because of his previous acquaintance with the president, he'd hoped something along those lines might happen, but he'd spent enough time playing poker to understand the difference between hope and likelihood. Every so often, though, you got lucky.

"How about that?" Agnes echoed. "I didn't know you were such an important fellow." She studied Morrell. "But even the most important fellows, from everything I've heard, ask a woman if she'd like to be their fiancée before they introduce her that way."

"Oops," Morrell said, which made Agnes burst into laughter. Gulping a little, he went on, "I guess the only way I can make amends is by asking later instead of sooner: *would* you like to be my fiancée, Agnes?"

"Of course I would," she answered. "You've taken your own sweet time getting around to finding out, but I didn't worry about it too much, because I always figured you would."

"Always?" Morrell asked, still nervous but happy, too. "How long is always?"

"Ever since we met at that first dance," Agnes Hill said. "I thought you were a catch, and I figured I ought to be the one who caught you." She raised an eyebrow. "Now what are you snickering about?"

"Only that I've had my eye on you since that dance where we met, too," he said. "That comes out fair and square, doesn't it?"

"It sure does," Agnes said. "I think everything will work out fine."

"You know what?" Morrell said, and she shook her head. "I do, too," he told her. He meant every word of it. She knew what being a soldier's wife was like, and knew it the best possible way: she'd been one. She'd been through the worst that could happen to a soldier's wife—she'd been through it, she'd come out the other side, and she was willing to try it again. What more could he ask for?

Only after all that went through his mind did he stop to wonder what sort of husband he was liable to make. Agnes might know what she was doing heading into this marriage, but he didn't. He had no clue; marriage wasn't part of the curriculum at West Point. *Maybe it should be,* he thought. It might not produce better officers, but was very likely to produce happier ones.

XII

Lucien Galtier looked up into the heavens. He got a glimpse of the sun, which he rarely did these days. It scurried along, low in the south, and soon ducked behind the thick gray clouds that were the dominant feature of the sky as October gave way to November.

Drizzle started spattering down. Soon, he judged, it would be turning to sleet, and then to snow. "Do your worst," he said. "Do your worst, or even a little worse than that. You did not do it during the harvest, and you cannot hurt me now. Go ahead. I could not care in the least."

"Do you always talk to the clouds, Papa?" asked Georges, who must have come out of the barn while Lucien was mocking the weather for missing its chance.

"Always," Lucien replied solemnly. "It is, I am convinced, my best hope of getting an intelligent answer around these parts."

"Truly?" Georges glanced toward the farmhouse. "Could it be that I should tell my *chère maman* of your view in this matter? I am sure she would be most interested to learn."

"I am sure that, if you breathe even a word of it to her, I will break open your head to see if it is altogether empty or just almost," Lucien said. "If I had to guess, I would say you have nothing at all in there, but I could be wrong: you might have some rocks. No sense, certainly."

"*Mais non, certainement pas,*" Georges said. "And do I take after you or after my mother in my senselessness?"

"I will take after you in a moment—with a hatchet, by choice," Galtier said. "Have you done everything with the livestock that wants doing?"

"Oh, no, not at all," his son answered. "I am always in the habit of quitting work when it is but half done."

"What you are in the habit of is driving me mad," Lucien said. Georges bowed, as if at a considerable compliment. Just then, a motorcar came to a halt beside the farmhouse. Lucien laughed. "Look—here is your brother-in-law. See if you can drive him mad. You have not done it yet, and not from lack of trying."

Dr. Leonard O'Doull seemed to unfold like a carpenter's rule as he got out of the Ford. Seeing Lucien and Georges, he waved to them and came sauntering over. If the cold, nasty drizzle bothered him, he gave not a sign. "How does it go?" he called around the cigar in his mouth.

"It goes well," Lucien answered. "And with you, how does it go?"

"Well enough," his son-in-law said. "Today is Saturday, so I have only a half day to put in at the hospital. I thought I would stop by and say good day before I drove up to town, to Nicole and little Lucien."

"And I am glad to give you good day as well," Lucien said. He glanced toward Georges. They both nodded, ever so slightly. No day on the farm was a half day. Leonard O'Doull was a first-rate fellow. The longer Galtier knew him, the more he thought of him. But one thing O'Doull was not and could never be: a farmer. He did not understand—by the nature of things, he could not understand—how hard the folk of his family by marriage worked.

Georges obliquely referred to that: "With but a half-day's work today, how can it go only 'well enough' for you?"

"Well, for one thing, what does the last day of October mean to you?" O'Doull asked.

Georges scratched his head. So did Lucien Galtier. At last, Lucien said, "It is the even of All Saints Day: all very well, but not a holiday to speak of alongside Easter or the festival of our Lord's birth."

"The Eve of All Saints Day." O'Doull nodded. "We call it *Halloween* in English. We have a custom of celebrating it with costumes and masks and carved pumpkins and parties—and sometimes pranks, too. It is a jolly time, a time of pretended fright."

"We do not do this here in Quebec," Georges said.

"I know," O'Doull said. "I miss it."

"Halloween." Galtier let the English word roll off his tongue. "I remember, when I was in the Army, the English-speakers had this holiday. But Georges is right: we do not do this in Quebec. I would be amazed if I had thought of it three times in all the years since I came home to my farm."

O'Doull looked unhappy. "Last year, I carved a pumpkin into a jack-o'-lantern"—another English word—"and put it in the window with a candle inside. I won't do that again. All my neighbors thought I was a pagan. It's a good thing Bishop Pascal knows about the custom, or there would have been a lot bigger stink than there was."

"You did not tell me about this then," Lucien said. "Nicole did not speak of it, either."

"I think we both felt foolish about it," O'Doull said. "And it was my own fault."

"I know men who go their whole lives without ever saying those words," Lucien remarked.

"They aren't doctors." His son-in-law spoke with great assurance. "Every doctor in the world knows he has buried patients he should have saved."

"It could be so," Galtier said. "If it is so, why would any man want to become a doctor?"

"Because we also save patients who would be buried without us," Leonard O'Doull said. With what sounded like considerable effort, he changed the subject: "And Tuesday is also a day different here from what it will be in the United States."

"And why is that?" Lucien's acquaintance with American holidays had begun only with the U.S. occupation of Quebec. He knew it remained incomplete.

"Because on Tuesday, we will vote for our president," O'Doull replied, "and, for the first time in longer than I have been alive, I think the election will be very close." He kicked at the dirt. "And here I am, a resident alien in the Republic of Quebec. All I can do is wait to see what my country does."

"How can the Americans not elect Roosevelt again?" Georges asked. "Behind him, they won the war. Without him, who knows what might have happened?"

"You have reason," O'Doull said. "But the war has been over almost three and a half years now. For me, the war was very fortunate, for without it I would not have met Nicole—nor any of you other fine Galtiers, I make haste to add. But many were hurt, and many who now can vote lost loved ones in the fighting. And there has been endless labor strife since. People may vote for Roosevelt, certainly. But then again, they may not. And no one has ever won a third term as president of the United States."

"For whom would you vote, if you were back in the United States?" Galtier inquired.

"I am not really sure," O'Doull said slowly. "With Roosevelt, I know exactly what the country would be getting. If the Socialists had run Debs again, I would also know what we were getting. But with Sinclair, it is harder to tell. He has the energy of a young man, and, from what I can tell from up here in Quebec, a lot of people think he would lead the United States in a new direction. Maybe that would be good. As I say, it is hard to be sure."

"It will be as it will be," Galtier said with a shrug. "However it is, the United States will still be a large country and the Republic of Quebec a small one. I hope you are not unhappy, having left your country to make your home here."

"Unhappy?" O'Doull shook his head. "It was only a lifetime ago that my ancestors left Ireland for the United States. We have pulled up stakes before, the O'Doulls. I have done it again, that's all."

Galtier scratched his head. His ancestors had lived not merely in Quebec but on the ground on which he stood since the seventeenth century. Even having his daughter remove to Rivière-du-Loup seemed an uprooting. He could not comprehend how O'Doull talked about one place as if it were good as the next. For him, that would have been a manifest—indeed, an unimaginable—untruth. His son-in-law took it for granted, as a fact of life.

O'Doull said, "Well, I had better head back to town, or Nicole will wonder what has become of me. I hope you get the chance to come up before too long, before the weather gets too bad." He touched the brim of his fedora, then hurried back to his automobile. It roared to life. He drove away.

"American politics," Georges said with a shrug. "I care very little for American politics."

"Had you said this in 1910, you might have shown some sense," his father replied. "In 1910, I knew very little of American politics, but they were important to us even then. Saying it now . . . well, I chaffed you before for senselessness. If American politics were different, would we have had a war? If American politics were different, would we be living in the Republic of Quebec? If American politics were different, would you have the nephew you have?"

"If American politics were different, I would still have a father who lectures me more than the schoolmasters ever did," Georges said. Lucien made an exasperated noise, but then started to laugh. Georges was as he was. The right wife might whip him into shape, but, on the other hand, he was liable to stay as he was even married to the most somber girl in the neighborhood.

Not that Lucien and Marie intended saddling Georges with the most somber girl in the neighborhood. For one thing, Béatrice Rigaud would bring only a small bridal portion with her. And, for another, Lucien did not think it right to do such a thing to his fun-loving younger son. That reason, though, ran in second place behind the other.

Halloween came and went, unremarked, uncelebrated. Galtier wondered whether Dr. Leonard O'Doull carved a pumpkin for his own family. He would not put it in the window this year—he'd made that very plain.

Two days later, the American elections also came and went. They produced no fanfare that reached Galtier's farm. Had Lucien not had an American son-in-law, he would not have known on which day they took place. Eventually, he would find out who won: if the news hadn't got to his farm before then, he'd learn when he went into town.

Marie said, "I have heard that not all American women can vote: it is for them, poor dears, as it was for us in the days before the Republic."

"I do not know anything about whether American women can vote," Lucien replied. He remained unconvinced that granting the franchise to the women of Quebec had been the best idea in the history of the world. But he'd discovered that saying as much to his wife landed him in hotter water than anything this side of announcing he'd taken a mistress. He knew several men who *had* taken mistresses, none of them rash enough to announce it.

"I hope the Americans elect the Socialist," Marie said. "They will be calmer if they do."

"I think they will return Roosevelt," Lucien declared. "Even if he is a Protestant, he is a very great man. And Socialists, from everything I have heard, do not believe in *le bon Dieu* at all."

He thought that would change his wife's mind; she cared far more for the trappings of piety than did he. But she said, "Perhaps *le bon Dieu* believes in them," a reply so oracular, Galtier had not the faintest idea how to respond to it.

Hal Jacobs said, "What was that song Lord Cornwallis' band played when he had to surrender to the Americans at Yorktown?"

"I haven't the faintest notion," Nellie Jacobs answered. Her schooling had stopped early. Not only that, Clara was trying to twist out of her arms and land on her head on the bedroom floor. That kept Nellie from thinking as clearly as she might have done.

"Now it will bother me," Hal said. "It is something I used to know, and I am not such an old man that I should be forgetting things." He smiled at Clara. "If I were such an old man, I would not have a little daughter now."

Nellie had not expected he would have a little daughter now. Even more to the point, she hadn't expected she would have a little daughter now. Had she expected such a thing, she would have taken precautions. She admitted to herself, though, that she did enjoy having Clara around.

Hal snapped his fingers, which made Clara stop wiggling and look to see where the funny noise came from. " 'The World Turned Upside Down'!" he exclaimed.

"What, when we had the baby?" Nellie said. "It sure did."

"No, no, no," he answered. "I mean, yes, it did, but no, that is not what I meant." He paused, by all appearances having confused himself. After a moment, he went on, "What I meant was, 'The World Turned Upside Down' is the song Cornwallis' band played at the surrender."

"Oh," Nellie said. "Well, why didn't you say that, if it's what you meant? And why are you bothering your head about Corn-what's-his-name in the first place?"

"I wasn't thinking about Cornwallis so much," Hal said. "I was trying to remember the name of the song. You must admit, it fits the news of the last couple of days."

"Oh," Nellie said. "The election." It hardly seemed real to her: she was disenfranchised not because she was a woman but because she lived in Washington, D.C. Hal hadn't voted on Tuesday, either, and couldn't have.

"Yes, the election." He clicked his tongue between his teeth. "When the Democrats lose for the first time since 1880, the world *has* turned upside down. And when the Socialists win for the first time ever, it has *really* turned upside down."

"I suppose it has." Nellie shook her head. "Doesn't seem right, turning President Roosevelt out of a job after he went and won the war for the United States. I can't name anybody else who could have done that."

"Dada," Clara said. She said *mama*, too, and *Eh-uh*, which was intended as the name of her half sister.

"How about it, Hal?" Nellie asked. "Do you think you could

have won the war for the United States?" After a moment, she went on, "As a matter of fact, you did go a long way toward winning the war for the USA, at least as far as Washington goes."

Hal waved a hand. He was, Nellie had seen, as modest and self-deprecating a man as had ever been born. That had helped keep her from noticing his many good qualities for longer than she should have. He said, "For one thing, I had the very best of help, of which you were no small part."

"Pooh!" Nellie said.

"Pooh!" Clara echoed. She gurgled and laughed, liking the sound she'd just imitated.

"Pooh!" Nellie repeated, which made Clara laugh again. Nellie continued, "I got a medal I didn't especially deserve, and you deserved one and never got it."

Hal Jacobs shrugged. "I know what I did. My country knows what I did. I do not need any medals. And besides, if anyone should have won a medal, it was Bill Reach. I was far from the only man who reported to him. He was the one who put everything together and got most of it out. I know you did not much like him, but it is very sad that he did not live to see our victory."

"You've said that before," Nellie replied, and dropped it there. She was the only person in the world who knew what had happened to Bill Reach, and she intended to take the secret to the grave with her. As far as she was concerned, he deserved everything she'd given him. But Hal still thought well of him, so she'd kept her own remarks to the fewest she could get away with.

"President Upton Sinclair." Hal, to her relief, went back to the world turning upside down. He shrugged again. "It does not sound like a name that belongs to a president. Presidents are named John or Thomas or Andrew or Theodore. Upton?" He shook his head. "It sounds like a name for a butler, not a president."

"Well, so it does," Nellie said. "We've got four years to get used to it, though. By the time 1924 rolls around, it'll seem natural enough."

"I suppose it may," Hal admitted. "By then, I hope the country will be sick of it, and will vote him out of office and put in a good Democrat with a nice, ordinary name."

"Maybe it won't be so bad." Nellie slid a finger under the edge of Clara's diaper. "Oh, good—you're dry." She sat down at the edge of the bed and began to bounce the baby gently up and down. "Come on, sweetheart, time for you to go to sleep."

"Time for you to go to sleep so your mother and father can go to sleep," Hal added. He yawned. "I had forgotten how much sleep you lose when a baby is small."

"So had I," Nellie said. "And the other thing is, I need sleep more now than I did when Edna was little. I'm not as young as I used to be, and boy, does Clara let me know it." She glanced warily down at her daughter, whose eyelids were fighting a losing battle against sliding shut. "Shh. I think she is going to drop off."

Only after Nellie had put the baby in the cradle that made the bedroom crowded did Hal say, "You are still young and beautiful to me, my dear Nellie. You always will be."

"Pooh!" Nellie said once more. She knew why men talked that way: to get women to go to bed with them. Any woman who believed such blandishments was almost enough of a fool to deserve what she would assuredly get. So a hard lifetime of experience had taught Nellie. But living with and listening to Hal were giving her occasional second thoughts.

She was too tired to indulge in second thoughts now, or even first ones. She let herself collapse onto the bed. Had she lain there for even a couple of minutes, she would have fallen asleep without changing into nightclothes. She'd done that a couple of times, on days when Clara was teething or sick or just ornery. Falling asleep in a corset was impressive proof of what exhaustion could do.

Tonight, though, she decided she wanted to be free of lacing and steel rods. With a weary sigh, she got to her feet, took off her skirt and shirtwaist, and escaped from the corset. A wool flannel nightgown went over her like a friendly, comfortable tent. Hal put on not only a nightshirt only a bit shorter than her gown but also a wool nightcap with a tassel. No cold breezes would take him by surprise.

"Good night," he said as he and Nellie crawled under the covers. "I hope little Clara will let us sleep till morning."

She did. She did more often than not these days, a blessed relief from the first few weeks after she'd come home from the hospital. Still, the nights when she didn't were appalling enough to make up for a lot of the ones when she did.

But she woke the next day so smiling and cheerful, Nellie smiled, too, even before she'd had breakfast or, more important, coffee. She gave Clara her breast. The baby was taking cereal these days, and other solid food as well, but still enjoyed starting the day at the same old stand.

Nellie changed her—she emphatically needed it now—slapped powder on her bottom with a puff, and took her downstairs after getting dressed herself. She let Clara crawl and toddle around while she built up the fire in the stove and got the first pot of coffee going. She and Hal and Edna would split that one; customers got what came afterwards.

"Quiet night, thank God," Edna said when she came down a few minutes later. Living across the hall from a baby wasn't that much different from living in the same room as one. Edna started toasting bread, and melted butter in a frying pan to do up eggs for herself and her mother and stepfather. In another pan, she fried ham steaks in bacon grease left over from the day before. Hal Jacobs came down in time to eat before anything got cold, but too late to keep Nellie and Edna from teasing him about dawdling.

He was about to go across the street and open up his shoe-maker's establishment when a fancy motorcar pulled to a stop in front of the coffeehouse Nellie ran. The driver hurried to open the door for his passenger, a portly gentleman of late middle years. The fellow headed for the coffeehouse door.

"Lord, Ma," Edna breathed, "will you look at that? It's the president. He's coming here again."

Nellie snatched up Clara, who howled in outrage at not getting the chance to eat the tasty-looking piece of dust she'd picked up. "Hush, you," Nellie whispered sternly, which did no good at all.

In came Theodore Roosevelt. "Good morning, Miss Sem-phroch," he said, bowing to Edna. He turned to Nellie. "And good morning to you, Mrs.—Jacobs. Ha! I got it right, by jingo!" He looked pleased with himself. "Good morning to you, too, Mr. Jacobs," he told Hal. "You have a lovely daughter here. Congratula-tions."

"Thank you, your Excellency," Nellie and Hal said together. Hal went on, "A great shame the election went against you, sir."

"The people have spoken," Roosevelt said. "It's another case of what Austria told Russia after the Russians saved their bacon in 1848: 'We shall astonish the world by our ingratitude.' Astonish it they did, by not helping the Czar in the Crimean War. Now we have a similar example on our own side of the Atlantic. But the country will survive it—I have great faith in the United States—and I shall, too."

"What will you do?" Nellie asked.

"I don't precisely know," Roosevelt answered. "Hunt big game, perhaps, or fly an aeroplane—maybe I shall hunt big game *from* an aeroplane. That might be jolly. But it's not why I came here today."

Edna gave him a cup of coffee. "Why did you come today, sir?" she asked.

Today, Roosevelt was without bodyguards. No—Nellie corrected herself. Today, the guards had not come into the coffeehouse. A couple of them paced outside, watchdogs in homburgs and fedoras. Roosevelt reached into his waistcoat and pulled out a small, felt-covered box. "I have here a token of appreciation for the signal service Mr. Jacobs rendered his country during the late war. This is a Distinguished Service Medal—I pulled some strings to get the War Department to issue it, since Mr. Jacobs was not formally in the Army during the war. But they humored me in this matter: one of the few advantages of lame-duckhood I have as yet discovered."

Nellie clapped her hands together in delight. So did Edna. Hal Jacobs turned red. He said, "Mr. President, I thought I made it perfectly clear I wanted no special recognition for any small things I may have done."

"You did," Roosevelt said. "I'm ignoring you. There—another advantage of lame-duckhood: I don't have to listen to anyone if I don't feel like it, not any more. You'll take your medal and you'll be a hero, Mr. Jacobs, and if you don't happen to care for it, too bad. What do you think of that?"

"He thinks it's splendid!" Nellie exclaimed. Hal Jacobs gave her a dirty look. She didn't care. She didn't care a bit. If a wife couldn't speak for a husband when he needed speaking for, what good was she? None at all, as far as Nellie could see.

Arthur McGregor shooed a hen off her nest and grabbed the egg she had laid. The hen's furious squawks and flutterings said she was convinced he'd murdered part of her immediate family. She was right—he had, or would as soon as Maude got around to cooking the egg. McGregor had had a member of his immediate family murdered, too. It gave him some sympathy for the hen . . . but not enough to keep him from robbing her nest.

He slipped a china egg in there and let the hen return. She kept on fussing for a moment or two. Then she discovered the substitute. Her clucks changed from outrage to contentment. She settled down and began to brood an egg that would not hatch even on Judgment Day.

A scowl on his face, McGregor went on to the next nest. No one had given him any kind of substitute for Alexander. He wished he were as stupid as a chicken, so that a photograph might fool him into thinking he still had a son. Unfortunately, he knew better.

All he could hope for was revenge. The scowl grew deeper. "I couldn't even get that," he growled, knocking the next hen out of her nest with a backhand blow that almost broke her fool neck. She had no eggs in the nest, so he might as well have done her in.

"Dentures!" What a word to make into a curse! But if Custer hadn't broken his false teeth, he'd still have been sitting in Hy's when McGregor's bomb went off. As things were, McGregor had killed more than a dozen innocent people without getting the man he really wanted. He felt bad about that, and worse because they were all Canadians, victims of the U.S. occupation no less than he.

But Alexander had been innocent, and Alexander had been a victim, and nothing would ever bring him back to life. As far as McGregor was concerned, the war against the United States went on. Canadian forces might have surrendered (though rebellion did still simmer here and there, especially in parts of the Dominion the U.S. Army hadn't reached before the Great War ended). The mother country might have yielded. Arthur McGregor kept fighting, whenever he saw the chance.

He finished gathering the eggs and installing china pacifiers under the hens. As he headed back toward the farmhouse, he thought again how much easier life would have been had the U.S. issued him a china son, and had he been stupid enough to reckon it the same as the real thing.

Winter and reality slapped him in the face as soon as he left the barn. The wind cut like a knife. The sky was clear and blue, a blue that put him in mind of a bruise. If he stayed outside very long, he'd start turning blue, too. He'd never met a U.S. soldier who'd taken Manitoba winters in stride. The USA just didn't manufacture weather like this.

"So why the devil did the Yanks want to come up here and take this away from us?" he asked. The snarling wind blew his words away. That didn't matter. The question had no good answer, save that the Americans were as they were.

When he opened the kitchen door, the blast of heat from the stove was a blow hardly less than the one the freezing wind had given him. Where he'd been shivering an instant before, now sweat started out on his forehead. He shed his hat and heavy coat as fast as he could.

Maude looked up from the carrots she was peeling. "How many eggs have you got there?"

"Seven." McGregor looked in the basket. "No, I take it back—eight."

"Not bad," his wife said. He shrugged. He didn't want to look on the bright side of anything right now. Maude went on, "If things keep going the way they have been, we'll come through this winter in better shape than we have since before the war."

"We won't ever be in the kind of shape we were before the war," McGregor answered, his voice colder than the weather outside.

Maude bit her lip. "You know what I mean," she said. He did, too. It didn't help. Had Alexander been there with him, a year where he didn't end up broke might not have looked so bad, even under U.S. occupation. As things were, every year showed a loss to him, even if he made money.

"If only—" he began, but he let that hang in the air. He still hadn't exactly told his wife about his bombs. She knew he'd gone to Winnipeg, of course, and she knew what had happened while he was there. But they both still pretended that was nothing but coincidence.

"You know the Culligans are putting on a dance next week if we don't get a blizzard between now and then, and maybe even if we do," Maude said.

"No, I didn't know." McGregor looked at her in some surprise. "You want to go dancing?" She hadn't shown any interest in that sort of thing since before the Great War. He shrugged. "If you do, I'll take you. I'll be switched if I think I remember the steps, though."

Maude shook her head. "I don't care one way or the other. But Julia and Ted Culligan have known each other since they were little, you know, and I think she'd enjoy dancing with him more than a bit."

"Do you?" McGregor made automatic protest: "But she's just a—" He stopped, feeling foolish. Julia wasn't just a baby any more. She'd be eighteen in a few weeks. He'd been engaged to Maude when she was eighteen. He coughed a couple of times. "I never paid any attention to Ted Culligan one way or the other. Does he matter that much to Julia?"

"He might," Maude said. "I don't know if she's serious, and I really don't know if he's serious—you men." McGregor only blinked at that blanket condemnation of his half of the human race. When he did nothing more, Maude shrugged and went on, "They could be serious, I think. We have to decide if we want them to be serious. The Culligans aren't bad folks."

"No, they're not. They mind their own business—they're not like any of the people who got Alexander into trouble." McGregor made up his mind. "All right, we'll go to this dance."

Go they did. It was snowing, but not hard. Julia chattered excitedly as McGregor drove the wagon toward the Culligans'. Mary chattered even more excitedly; it was her very first dance (actually, it wasn't quite, but she'd been too little to remember going to any of the others).

People had come from miles around, including the families of a couple of the boys who'd named Alexander as their fellow plotter. McGregor held his face still when he saw the McKiernans and the Klimenkos. He'd been holding his face still for years. Doing it now wasn't that much harder than any other time.

Ted Culligan's ears stuck out. Other than that, he seemed a nice enough kid. He wasn't good enough for Julia; that was obvious. But it was also obvious no one else could be good enough for Julia, either.

A handful of American families had come up and taken over deserted farms around Rosenfeld. McGregor had wondered if the Culligans would invite them to the dance. Keeping his face still would have been harder then. But he didn't see them, and didn't hear any American accents, either.

A pair of fiddlers, a fellow with a concertina, and a man who pounded a drum with more enthusiasm than rhythm provided the music. The tunes were all old ones, and all safe ones. The little band stuck to love songs. McGregor would have loved to hear some of the regimental ballads he'd learned in the Army, but understood why the musicians fought shy of them; word would surely have got back to the U.S. authorities in town, which would have brought trouble on its heels.

McGregor danced a couple of dances with Maude. She did recall the steps better than he; he was content to let her lead. He noticed he wasn't the only farmer whose wife did the steering, either. That made him laugh, something he rarely did these days.

After those first few dances, McGregor was content to stand on the sidelines and drink punch. His eyebrows rose at the first taste of it. The Culligans hadn't stinted on the whiskey. A cup or two, and a man would think he could stay warm outside without coat and hat. He might even prove right. He was more likely to freeze to death.

Julia danced with other boys besides Ted Culligan. That helped ease McGregor's mind. His daughter was having a good time, which made him feel good. He danced a dance with Mary, whose head, he realized in surprise, came almost to the top of his shoulder. When had she grown so big?

There stood Julia, talking with Ted over a cup of the potent punch. Suddenly, McGregor didn't mind the weather at all. In the summertime, courting couples might slip out to a barn for a while. Doing that now invited frostbite, not romance.

McGregor shook hands with Ted Culligan's father when it was time to go home. He pretended not to see Ted kiss Julia on the cheek. That wasn't easy, not when she turned the color of a red-hot stove.

"I had a wonderful time," she said over and over on the drive back to the farm. "Simply wonderful." She was young enough to forget for a while what had happened to her family and her country, and to enjoy the moment. McGregor wished he could do the same.

Back at the farmhouse, he lit a lamp in the kitchen. His wife and daughters went yawning upstairs to bed. He brought the lamp outside and set it on the wagon while he unhitched the horse. Then he picked up the lamp again and carried it in his left hand while leading the horse to the barn.

He put the beast in its stall and started out of the barn again. But he stopped after a couple of steps: stopped and held the lantern high, peering around in all directions. No, he wasn't wrong. Someone had been in the barn while the McGregors were at the dance.

Fear and fury warred inside him. At first, fear was uppermost. Whoever had pawed through his things hadn't bothered trying to conceal his presence. Tools weren't where they should have been. A couple of drawers under McGregor's work table were open; he knew he'd left them closed, for he always did.

Heart hammering in his throat, he went over to the old wagon wheel beneath which he hid his bomb-making paraphernalia. Holding the lamp close, he tried to see if the snooper had tampered with it. As far as he could tell, it was undisturbed. His secret remained safe.

When he realized that, fury overtook fear. "God damn those sons of bitches," he said softly. "They do still figure I might be a bomber." He was, if anything, more indignant than if he'd been innocent. The Yanks had paid—no, the Yanks had seemed to pay—no attention to him the past couple of years. He'd thought they'd forgotten about him. He'd been wrong.

But they hadn't found anything. They'd have been waiting here for him if they had. "They're trying to rattle me," he murmured. "That's got to be it." They couldn't prove he'd planted bombs, so they were showing their cards, trying to force him into a mistake. He shook his head. He didn't intend to oblige them.

By the time he went back to the farmhouse and upstairs to his bedroom, Maude was sound asleep. He shrugged. Even if she'd been awake, he wouldn't have said a word. He got ready for bed himself.

* * *

Before the presidential election, a lot of firms had put printed messages in their workers' pay envelopes. The one Chester Martin got had read, *If Upton Sinclair is elected on Tuesday, don't bother showing up for work Wednesday morning.* The capitalists had tried to the very end to keep the proletariat from voting its conscience and its class interest.

They'd tried those games before, too, though not so aggressively: up till this election, they hadn't been so worried about losing. Well, they'd lost anyhow. Martin laughed every time he thought about it. Come March 4, it would be out with the old and in with the new, and the United States would have their first Socialist president. He could hardly wait.

Here it was late December, too, and he hadn't been fired. He didn't expect to be fired any time soon, either, not unless he hauled off and punched his foreman or something of that sort. His foreman was an idiot. Everyone on the foundry floor knew as much. The foreman's boss didn't, though, and his was the only opinion that mattered. But work went on as usual, in spite of there being a Socialist president-elect.

"Did you really expect anything different?" Albert Bauer asked when Martin remarked on that one day at the Socialist hall near the steelworks.

"I don't know that I *expected* anything different," Martin answered. "I will say I wondered."

"Mystification," Bauer said scornfully. "That's all it is—nothing but mystification. The capitalists tried to intimidate us, and tried to make us believe they had the power to get away with intimidating us. It didn't work, and now they'll have to learn how to walk a lot smaller."

"Yeah," Martin said, and then, "How much do you think Sinclair will be able to do once he gets in?"

"Don't know," Bauer answered. "We've got a majority in the House, and I *think* the Socialists and Republicans and progressive Democrats make a majority in the Senate. The courts are full of reactionaries. They'll give us trouble."

"If they give too much trouble, we'll stop listening to them," Martin said. "Let's see them get their way if everybody ignores them. Or let's see them get their way if the worst reactionaries start having accidents."

Bauer laughed at him. "This from the man who used to be a Democrat? I've heard people who've been revolutionaries since before you were born who didn't sound half as fierce as you do."

"In for a penny, in for a pound," Chester Martin said, shrugging. "Besides, nobody who's been through the trenches is going to fuss about killing a judge or two. Once you've had practice, killing looks pretty easy."

"Something to that, I shouldn't wonder." Bauer looked thoughtful. "The capitalists might not have realized what they were doing when they started the war, but they helped create opponents who wouldn't back away from meeting force with force when they had to."

Martin nodded. "After artillery and poison gas and machine guns, cops are nothing special," he said, a thought he'd had before. He paused, then asked, "What do you think of this Freedom Party down in the CSA, Al? They're another bunch that doesn't seem like it's afraid of mixing things up with anybody they don't like."

"Reactionary maniacs," Bauer said with a toss of the head. "They want to turn back the clock to the way things were before the Great War. You can't turn back the clock, and you have to be a fool to think you can."

"That's about what I thought," Martin said. "You believe the papers, though, a lot of people like what they're saying. Stupid damn Rebs."

"Stupid damn Rebs," Bauer agreed. "But if we'd lost the war, imagine how fouled up our politics would be. There'd be a bounty on Socialists now. You'd better believe there would—they'd be hunting us in the streets. And they'd go on electing Democrats president for the next fifty years. So maybe we shouldn't blame the Rebs—too much—for being stupid."

"Hmp," was all Chester Martin said to that. He'd spent three years with the Confederates shooting at him. Hell, they hadn't just shot *at* him—they'd shot him. He had the Purple Heart to prove it, and the note of sympathy signed by Theodore Roosevelt, too. Even with the war almost three and a half years behind him, he wasn't inclined to feel charitable toward the former enemy.

Bauer slapped him on the back. "Go on, get out of here. Go home. Go Christmas shopping. Go somewhere. I keep having to tell you that. You've got a case of the mopes, looks like to me. You won't do yourself any good till you get over 'em. You won't do the Party any good, either, so go on. Scram."

Martin didn't argue with him. He buttoned his overcoat and headed out of the Socialist hall. The trolley stop was a couple of blocks away. His breath smoked around him. The one thing he envied the Confederate States was their mild winter weather. Summer in Virginia, on the other hand, was a pretty fair approximation of hell. Of course, summer in Toledo wasn't all that far removed from hell, either.

Shops shiny with tinsel and bright with electric lights beckoned to people walking past them on the street. BIG SALE! signs in the window shouted. Some of them might even have meant it. But Martin had gone into more than a few shops, and had yet to see much in the way of price cutting. The signs were just a come-on, like the tinsel and the bright lights.

He would have to get presents for his father and his mother and his sister. He wanted to get something for Albert Bauer, too, though Bauer was the least sentimental man he'd ever known off the battlefield. *Maybe some shaving soap,* he thought. That would be thoughtful and useful at the same time.

"Shaving soap," he said several times. A woman walking past gave him an odd look. He didn't care, or not too much. Saying something out loud helped him remember it.

Coins jingled in his trouser pocket: only a faint noise through the thick wool of his coat. He wasn't broke, as he had been through the labor strife after the war. With a Socialist administration, maybe there wouldn't be any more labor strife. That had been his hope as he'd made an X in the square beside the names of Upton Sinclair and Hosea Blackford. The capitalists had had everything their way for a long time. *Now,* he thought, *it's labor's turn.*

He unbuttoned his coat long enough to grab a nickel. A bum came up to him while he waited for the trolley. The fellow whined for change. He stank of unwashed hide and stale beer. Martin knew he'd just buy another mug with a nickel, but tossed him the coin anyway. "Merry Christmas, pal." He dug another five cents out of his pocket.

"God bless you, mister," the bum said. Martin waved impatiently, wanting him to get out of there before he regretted his own generosity. The bum had had practice at what he did. He faded away.

Up rattled the trolley, almost fifteen minutes late. Martin grumbled as he threw his nickel in the fare box. He grumbled some more when he saw he'd have to stand for a while: the car was full, with a lot of passengers festooned with packages. He did the best he could, positioning himself next to a pretty girl who also had no place to sit. She glanced over toward him once, a look colder than the weather outside. When she left a few blocks later, he was more relieved than anything else.

He eventually did land a seat for himself; more people got off than on as the trolley rolled up to Ottawa Hills. Not for the first time, he thought about renting a place of his own as he walked to the apartment he shared with his parents and sister. He could afford it—as long as the work stayed steady, he could afford it. But his paycheck helped his folks pay the rent here, and they'd carried him when he was out on strike, carried him even though they'd disagreed with his stand. He didn't have to do anything in a hurry.

When he walked in the front door, his father was draping the Christmas tree with tinsel. A fresh, piney scent fought the usual odors of tobacco smoke and cooking. "That's a good one, Dad," Martin said. "You haven't found such a nice, round, plump one in a long time."

"Haven't gone looking for nice, round, plump ones, not since I married your mother," Stephen Douglas Martin answered. Ignoring his son's half-scandalized snort, he went on, "I am pretty happy with it, though. Found it at a little lot round the corner; I jewed 'em down to four bits for it."

"That's a good price," Martin agreed. "You recall where you hid the star and the other ornaments after last Christmas?"

"I didn't hide them," his father said with dignity. "I put them away safe." About every other year, he had to turn the apartment upside down because he'd put the decorations away so securely, he hadn't the faintest idea where they were.

This time, though, he came up with them and gave his son a superior look that Chester did his best to ignore. They hung the ornaments together. "Are we going to have candles on the tree this year?" Chester asked.

"Unless you really want 'em, I'd say no," Stephen Douglas Martin answered. "Every year, you read in the paper about some damn fool"—his eyes went toward the kitchen as he made sure Louisa Martin hadn't heard him swear—"who burns down his house and burns up his family on account of those things. I don't aim to be that kind of fool, thank you very much."

"All right," Martin said. After bombs and barrels and shell fragments in the trenches, after cops and goons with pistols and clubs, candles struck him as a silly thing to worry about. But his father wasn't wrong; people and houses did go up in flames every Christmas. Martin supposed that, absent big fears, small ones pushed their way to the fore.

Sue came in while they were still decorating. She scaled her broad-brimmed flowered hat across the room as if it were an aeroplane and said, "I get to put the star on top. After the day I had today, I've earned it."

"What happened today?" Chester asked.

"Everyone wanted everything typed at the same time, and it was all stupid," his sister answered. "And everyone yelled at me because I couldn't do sixteen different things at the same time. If half the people in the office would have thought for even a couple of seconds before they started piling stuff onto me, everything would have been fine. But throwing things at me and then yelling their heads off was easier, so they did that instead."

She took the gilded glass star and impaled it on top of the Christmas tree. Then she glared at her brother and her father, defying them to tell her she had no business getting angry. Chester was not about to take his life in his hands. He said, "Why don't you go get a bottle of Schmidt's out of the icebox?"

Sue didn't usually drink beer. Tonight, she nodded briskly. "I'll do that. Thank you, Chester." Off toward the kitchen she went. Chester Martin grinned at Stephen Douglas Martin. He might have been trained as a soldier, but he'd just served the cause of peace.

Scipio seldom saw snow. Because he seldom saw it, he enjoyed it when he did. So did everyone else in Augusta. Pickaninnies made snow angels and threw snowballs. So did their parents. So did their grandparents, some of whom had hair as white as that snow.

Because of the clogged, slippery streets, he got to Erasmus' later than he should have, and with his hat askew on his head. More and more boys played football Yankee-style these days, which meant more of them threw the ball, which meant they had practice they used to good effect with snowballs.

Erasmus' eyes glinted with amusement, but all he said was, "Mornin', Xerxes. How you be today?"

"Cold," Scipio answered. "This here nothin' but damnyankee weather. Far as I is concerned, it kin stay up there wid they."

"Fish keep longer," Erasmus said. "Don't got to buy so much ice from that thief of an ice man for a couple days. Outside o' dat, I ain't gwine argue with you."

Scipio had just started his morning sweeping when the first breakfast customer came in. Erasmus had found he made money serving breakfast, so he'd started. The customer shouted for hot coffee. Scipio didn't blame him. He had to pry himself away from the nice, warm stove to bring the fellow the steaming cup, and then the fried eggs and grits that followed.

After pouring down several steaming cups and shoveling in his food, the black man got to his feet, stuck a hand in the pocket of his dungarees, and looked a question toward Scipio. Even if it was wordless, Scipio understood it. "A million and a half," he said.

"Was only a million last week," the customer said with a sigh. He gave Scipio two crisp, new $1,000,000 banknotes, with Robert E. Lee's portrait on one side and a picture of Jefferson Davis taking the oath of office as provisional president in Montgomery on the other. Scipio handed him five $100,000 banknotes (older and more worn, because they'd been in circulation longer) for change. As he'd hoped, the customer left a couple of hundred thousand dollars' tip when he went on his way.

"When was the last time you seen silver or gold money?" Erasmus asked, his voice wistful. "I ain't even seen no pennies in a hell of a long time."

"Me neither," Scipio said. "Not since the war jus' over. Somebody put down a dime or a qua'ter, reckon I fall over. Somebody put down a Stonewall, I *knows* I fall over."

"How much paper you reckon a Stonewall buy these days?" Erasmus' lips moved silently as he made his own calculation. "Somewheres around twenty, twenty-five million, I reckon. What you think?"

"Sound about right," Scipio agreed. Erasmus had no formal education, but he was shrewd with figures. Scipio added, "Ain't bad fo' fi' dollars in gold."

"Sure ain't," Erasmus said, and said no more. Scipio wouldn't have been the least bit surprised to find out his boss had a nice pile of Stonewalls hidden away somewhere. If he needed them, they'd come out. If times ever got better, so that money stopped stretching like India rubber, they'd come out then, too. Scipio wished he had his own pile.

He wondered how many goldpieces Anne Colleton had these days. He was willing to bet she had a good many. She'd always been one to land on her feet. And, if the papers didn't lie, she'd been pumping money into the Freedom Party. That worried Scipio. His former boss didn't back losers. He'd seen as much, time and again.

But if the Freedom Party was a winner, every black man and woman in the CSA lost. What the men in the white shirts and butternut trousers had already done in Augusta made that crystal clear.

If it hadn't been for Bathsheba, he wouldn't have worried so much. He'd always been able to take care of himself. Even after the Congaree Socialist Republic collapsed in blood and fire, he'd taken care of himself. Taking care of somebody else, though, somebody he loved—that was different. It was harder, too: he didn't dare take risks for Bathsheba that he would have cheerfully taken for himself.

Another Negro came in, asking for flapjacks and eggs. He wore a ribbon on his jacket. After a moment, Scipio recognized what it was: the ribbon for a Purple Heart. Pointing to it, he asked, "Where you git that?"

"Up in Virginia," the man answered. "Some damnyankee shot me in the leg. I was damn lucky, let me tell you. All he did was blow off a chunk o' meat. Bullet didn't hit no bone or nothin', or I reckon I'd be walkin' around with a peg leg."

Listening to somebody talk about how lucky he'd been to get shot struck Scipio as strange, but he'd heard white veterans go on the same way. He said, "So you fit the war and done everything the gummint want?" The customer nodded. Scipio hurried back to get his breakfast and bring it to him, then asked, "And now you is a citizen? Now you kin vote an' do like the buckra all kinds o' ways?"

"Can't marry no white woman." The veteran shrugged. "Don't want to marry no white woman—like the colored gal I got. But yeah," he went on with quiet pride, "I's a citizen." He reached into his pocket and displayed an elaborately printed form attesting to his service in the war. "I carry this here 'stead of a passbook."

Scipio hadn't thought about the aspect of citizenship. He was deeply and sincerely jealous of the veteran, who enjoyed a liberty he was unlikely ever to know. "Freedom Party give you trouble?" he inquired. He didn't know why he asked the question: was he trying to ease his own mind about what the Freedom Party could do, or was he hoping to make the veteran feel bad in spite of the privilege he'd earned?

The man's mouth tightened. His eyes narrowed. A vertical groove appeared between them, and other lines by the edges of his lips. "Them bastards," he said quietly. "You know any niggers don't get trouble from them?"

"Sure enough don't," Scipio answered. "I was hopin' you did."

"Ain't none." The Negro veteran spoke with assurance. "Ain't nothin' we can do about it, neither, nothin' I can see. Yeah, I'm a citizen. I punch one o' them sons o' bitches for callin' me names or givin' me some other kind o' hard time, what happen then? White folks' jury send me to jail for about twenty years. That Freedom Party man kick me in the balls, what happen *then*? White folks' jury say he didn't do nothin' wrong." He didn't try to hide his bitterness.

"But you kin vote against they," Scipio said. "Most black folks can't do nothin' a-tall."

"I can vote." The veteran nodded. "I went an' did it last election, an' I'll do it again come November. But so what? So what, God damn it? Ain't but one o' me, an' all them Freedom Party white folks. Even if all the niggers in the country could vote, wouldn't be enough of us. White folks can do what they want, near enough. Why shouldn't they let me vote? They can afford it."

He got up, laid two million dollars on the table, and stamped out without waiting for change.

"Hope you didn't ride Antiochus so hard, he don't come back," Erasmus said. "That ain't good business."

"Sorry," Scipio answered, which was true in the business sense if in no other. "You hear what he say?" He waited for Erasmus to nod, then went on, "You still reckon we ain't got nothin' to fear from no Freedom Party?"

Erasmus nodded again. "I keeps tellin' you an' tellin' you, the white man ain't gwine do the work hisself. If he ain't gwine do it hisself, he ain't gwine do us no harm—or no worse'n usual, anyways. You show me them Freedom Party fellas out in the cotton fields at pickin' time, then I commence to worry. Till then—" He shook his head.

Scipio wished he could take matters in stride the way his boss did. Rationally, everything Erasmus said made sense. That should have sufficed for Scipio, himself a man rational by inclination and education both. It should have, but it didn't.

The past few years had been hard on rationality. If the Negro uprising of 1915 hadn't been an exercise in romanticism, he didn't know what was. The Reds hadn't had a chance, but they'd risen anyhow. He didn't think the Freedom Party had a chance of restoring the *status quo ante bellum*, either. That didn't stop whites from flocking to its banners. Most whites liked the way things had been before the war just fine.

And there were, as the Negro veteran had said, a lot of whites. If they got behind the Freedom Party, Jake Featherston and his pals might win. How far could they turn back the clock? Finding out would be as big a romantic folly as the Red uprising. But nothing had stopped Cassius and the other Red leaders, and likely nothing would stop Featherston, either.

Scipio sighed. "Life ain't easy, and at the end you can't do nothin' but up and die. Don't seem right."

Erasmus busied himself making a fresh pot of coffee. When he was through, he said, "So tell me then, you gwine kiss your lady friend good-bye? You gwine lay in bed by your lonesome, waitin' for to drop dead?"

" 'Course not," Scipio said angrily. Then he stopped and stared at Erasmus. The fry cook had pierced his gloomy pretensions as neatly as any white man with a fancy degree in philosophy might have done—and with a tenth, or more likely a hundredth, as many words. Instead of angry, Scipio felt foolish, to say nothing of sheepish. "Got to get on with your reg'lar 'fairs," he mumbled.

"That there make a deal more sense'n what you was spoutin' a minute ago, don't you reckon?" Erasmus demanded.

"Yes, suh," Scipio said. So far as he could recall, he'd never called a black man *sir* before in his life. Whites got the title because they had the whip hand in the CSA. He gave it to Erasmus because—*because he deserves it,* was the thought that ran through Scipio's mind.

Erasmus noticed, too. His head whipped around sharply. Scipio would have bet several million dollars—maybe even a Stonewall—nobody'd ever called him *sir* before that moment, either. "Just get back to work, will you?" he said, his voice gruff. He didn't know how to respond to being treated with respect.

Why should he? Scipio thought. *It's altogether likely no one has ever shown him any.* With that, Scipio came closer to understanding why the Reds had rebelled against the Confederate government than he ever had before. Was being treated like a human being worth fighting and dying for? Maybe it was.

What do I know about being treated like a human being? he thought. *I was only a butler.* He didn't think in the dialect of the Congaree, but in the precise, formal English he'd had drilled into him. Sometimes that helped him: it gave him a wider, more detailed map for his world than he would have had if he'd gone to the cotton fields. Sometimes it left him neither fish nor fowl. And sometimes it made him angry at what the Colletons had done to his mind, to his life. They hadn't done it for his sake, either. They hadn't cared at all about him, except as a thing. They'd done it for their own convenience.

"Just got to get through the day and not worry about nothin' you can't change anyways," Erasmus said. Scipio nodded. The fry cook was pursuing the thought he'd had a little before. But Scipio's thought had veered in a different direction. *How can a black man make life worth living in the Confederate States?* he wondered. The question was easy to ask. Finding an answer, though . . .

"Here is the latest report, sir." Lieutenant Colonel Abner Dowling set the document on General Custer's desk.

"Well, let's have a look at it." The electric lights in the overhead fixture glittered off Custer's reading glasses as he picked up the report and started to go through it. Abner Dowling waited for the explosion he guessed would not be long in coming. He was right. The commander of U.S. forces in Canada slammed the typewritten sheets on the desk. "Poppycock!" he shouted. "Twaddle! Hare-brained idiocy! Who was the idiot who produced this nonsense?"

"Sir, Captain Fielding, our operative in Rosenfeld, is one of the best we have anywhere in this country," said Dowling, who had read the report before giving it to Custer. "If he says there's no evidence this McGregor planted the bomb in Hy's chop house, you can rely on it."

"If he says there's no bloody goddamn evidence, he can't see the nose in front of his face," Custer snarled. "Christ on His cross, McGregor blew up this brilliant operative's"—Custer's sarcasm stung—"predecessor. Otherwise, this imbecile wouldn't have the job in the first place. Look at McGregor's photograph. Does that shifty-eyed devil look like an honest man to you?"

"There's no evidence for that, either, sir," Dowling said patiently. "They've searched McGregor's farmhouse and barn and grounds any number of times, and they haven't found a thing to suggest he's the bomber."

"Which only proves he's not an imbecile, very much unlike our own people down there," Custer said with a sneer that displayed the fine white choppers in his new upper plate. "The chap who was there during the war ordered McGregor's son shot, didn't he?"

"Among a good many other executions, yes," Dowling answered with a sigh he barely tried to hide. He'd been certain ahead of time Custer would take this line. Custer was irresistibly attracted to the obvious.

And, sure enough, Custer charged ahead as if he hadn't spoken: "Other bombs around Rosenfeld, too. All of them either had to do with families that got his brat in trouble or with people connected to that other operative down there, the one who got himself blown sky high the night the war ended. Coincidence? Are you telling me it's coincidence?"

"Sir, *someone's* been making bombs, yes," Dowling said. "But it's no more likely to be McGregor than anyone else down there. Major Hannebrink—the operative who's dead now—had to hold down the countryside during the war, and he didn't use a light hand. No one used a light hand during the war, sir."

Again, Custer might not have heard him. He went right on with his own thoughts, such as they were: "And was this McGregor down on his farm when Hy's was bombed? He was not. You know he was not."

"I know where he was, too: visiting kin in Ontario," Dowling said. "He didn't make a secret of where he was going. His farm was checked after the bombing, and then again a little before Christmas, in the hope he might have gotten careless. I don't think he could have gotten careless, sir, because I don't think he had anything to get careless about."

"Ought to haul him in," Custer said. "Ought to haul him in, give him a blindfold and a cigarette, and stand him up against a wall and give him the same his son got."

"Sir!" Dowling exclaimed in real alarm. "Sir, the country's been pretty quiet lately. Do you want to give the Canucks a martyr? If you execute a man when you can't prove he's done anything, you're asking for trouble. Don't you think it's better to let sleeping dogs lie?"

"That dog of a McGregor lies, all right, but he's not asleep," Custer retorted. "He's wide awake and laughing at us, that's what he's doing. And as for asking for trouble . . ." He looked sly, always a dangerous sign. "With the damned Socialists coming into power in another five weeks, I'd love to see the Canucks turn fractious. It might remind the Reds in Philadelphia why we have soldiers up here."

That was devious. Dowling wondered how a soldier who'd gained his reputation by charging straight at the foe—regardless of whether the situation called for it—had acquired such a byzantine sense of politics. It might even be a clever move . . . if you didn't stop and think about what it meant to this Arthur McGregor and what was left of his family.

Dowling said, "Sir, this fellow's already lost his son. If you shoot him, you leave a widow and a couple of orphaned daughters. That's pretty hard, sir. If he were the bomber, he would have conspired with somebody, wouldn't he? There's nothing to show he's done that. I mean nothing at all, sir. No claims, no circumstantial evidence—zero. He hasn't done it, period."

"Lone wolf," Custer said, but he didn't sound so cocksure as he had a moment before. Lone-wolf mad bombers weren't that easy to believe in, even for Custer.

Pressing his advantage, Dowling went on, "So you see, sir, it really isn't that bad a report. I know it would be more satisfying if they could tie up the bomber with a pretty pink ribbon, but there are millions of Canucks and millions of square miles in this miserable icebox of a country. Catching the stinking bastard isn't easy."

"Bah," Custer said—a sign of weakening. Then, as if it proved something, he added, "He almost blew you up, too."

"Believe me, sir, I know that," Dowling said fervently. Nobody cared enough about him personally to want to do him in. But if Custer went, he was liable to go, too. He'd make one line in the fourth paragraph of the newspaper stories. *The commanding general's adjutant also perished in the blast*—all the obituary he'd ever get.

He sighed. His name and photograph wouldn't make it into the encyclopedias or the history books. If he ever wrote his memoirs, the only reason they might find a publisher would be that people had an endless appetite for stories about Custer. Dowling coughed. He could tell stories about Custer, all right, stories that would curl the hair of anybody with an ounce of sense.

He did not think he was boastful in reckoning himself smarter than the senior soldier in the U.S. Army. Custer had graduated dead last in his West Point class—hardly a shining example, save perhaps of what not to do. Whenever Custer had been right, all through his enormously long military career, he'd been right for the wrong reasons. The shouting match he'd got into with Teddy Roosevelt about how and why they'd used their Gatling guns in Montana Territory the way they had proved how far back that went.

And yet, for all his failings, Custer was, and deserved to be, famous. He might have been right for the wrong reasons, but he'd been right at the right times. That counted for more. And Custer, whatever else you said about him, never did anything by halves. That counted for a lot, too.

Flaws and all—and Dowling, from long exposure to them, knew how massive they were—Custer would live in the country's memory for generations to come. And, when authors got around to writing historical novels about him, they would have to invent a character to play his adjutant, because no one would remember that perfectly competent but uninspired lieutenant colonel, Abner Dowling, whose only measurable defect was measurable indeed, in his uncommon and ever-increasing girth. It hardly seemed fair.

No doubt it wasn't fair. But then, life wasn't fair. Some people were smarter than others. Some were handsomer than others. Some—Custer sprang to mind—were pushier than others. You did what you could with what you had. And, even if no one would recall the contributions of an obscure officer named Dowling, Custer had done more than he might have otherwise because he'd had that obscure officer at his side and guarding his back.

Testily, Custer said, "Oh, very well, Dowling—have it your way. If you think this McGregor is pure as the driven snow"—a comparison that hardly required a poetic spirit in Winnipeg in January—"we'll leave him alone. On your head be it. And if he sets off another bomb, on your head it will be."

"You already pointed that out, sir." Dowling sounded on the testy side himself. "I would point out to you in return that this is not merely my opinion. It is the opinion of the expert on the spot. If we pay no attention to the opinion of the expert on the spot, where are we?"

He'd meant it for a rhetorical question. Custer answered as if it were literal: "In the General Staff offices in Philadelphia." That jerked a startled snort of laughter out of Dowling. Custer went on, "But if we fall down and worship the expert on the spot, where are we then? With the Israelites who fell down and worshiped the Golden Calf, that's where."

Dowling thought the second comparison far-fetched. What Custer meant was that he wanted the liberty to do as he damn well pleased. That was all Custer had ever wanted. Since he was eighty-one years old and still hadn't learned the difference between liberty and license, he wasn't likely to gain that knowledge in however much time he had left.

"I do think you're doing the right thing by letting this McGregor alone," Dowling said. "The whole country has been noticeably calmer lately than it was when you first took over."

"I put the fear of God in the Canucks, that's why, and I had my own good reasons for doing it," Custer said. There might even have been some truth in his words, though Dowling thought the Canadians' despair over a cause obviously lost had more to do with it. "We will make a desert if we have to, and we shall call it peace."

"Yes, sir," his adjutant said resignedly. No use expecting Custer to become a decent Latin scholar at his age, either (more hope that he might become a scholar of indecent Latin). When Tacitus had said the Romans made a desert and called it peace, he was condemning them. Custer took it for praise.

"I don't care if they hate us," Custer added, "as long as they're afraid of us." That was another Latin tag. Custer probably knew as much; having thought of the one, coming up with the other would have been easier for him. But did he remember the phrase came from Caligula's lips? *Not likely,* Dowling judged. He glanced over at Custer. Would Caligula have been like this if he'd lasted to eighty-one? Dowling's shiver had nothing to do with the subzero cold outside. He couldn't recall the last time he'd had such a frightening thought.

He said, "Now that they *are* quiet, sir, I really do think it's best not to stir them up."

"So you've said—over and over and over," Custer said. "So everyone says. Well, I have something to say to you, too: you and everyone else had better be right, or the United States are going to end up with egg on their face. And what do you think of that?"

"I think you're right, sir." Dowling didn't see what good pointing out Custer's unfailing gift for the obvious would do.

XIII

Jefferson Pinkard's alarm clock went off with a sound like doom. The steelworker thrashed and writhed and finally managed to turn the bloody thing off. He wished he could thump himself in the head and get rid of his headache the same way. Alabama was a dry state, but that didn't mean he and his Freedom Party buddies couldn't lay their hands on some whiskey after meetings when they set their minds to it.

"Ought to know better than to go into work hungover," he said. He did know better. He'd learned better the hard way. He hadn't headed for the Sloss Works hurting in years—not till he threw Emily out of the house after catching her whoring with Bedford Cunningham a second time. Since then . . . since then, he knew he'd been drinking more than he should, but knowing and stopping were two different critters.

He built up the fire in the stove and got a pot of coffee going. Then he went back to the bathroom and dry-swallowed a couple of aspirins. He lathered his face and shaved. As he was toweling himself dry afterwards, he wondered why he hadn't cut his own throat. It wasn't the first time that question had occurred to him.

After a cup of strong black coffee, after the aspirins started to work, the world looked a little less gloomy. He ate a big chunk of bread and ham and cut off a piece of last night's partly cremated ham steak to toss into his dinner pail. Since he'd thrown Emily out, he'd discovered just what a lousy cook he was. "Ain't starved yet," he declared, and headed out the door. The place was an unholy mess, but he lacked the time, the energy, and the skill to do anything about it.

He had to walk past Bedford Cunningham's cottage on the way to the foundry. He looked straight ahead. He didn't want to see Bedford, even if he was there. He didn't want to see Fanny Cunningham, either. He blamed her, too. If she'd kept her husband happy in bed, he wouldn't have had to go sniffing around Emily.

More steelworkers, white and black, crowded the path leading to the Sloss Works. Greetings filled the air: "Hey, Lefty!" "Mornin', Jeff." "How you is, Nero?" "What's up, Jack?" "Freedom!" Pinkard heard that a couple-three times before he got to the time clock and stuck in his card to start the day. As the aspirins and coffee had done, the slogan made him feel better.

He winced only a little when he stepped out onto the foundry floor. Once he was out there, he knew he'd make it through the day. If he could stand the clangor now, he wouldn't even notice it by the time afternoon rolled around.

Vespasian came onto the floor only a minute or so after he did. "Mornin', Mistuh Pinkard," the Negro steelworker said.

"Morning," Pinkard answered. Every time he thought about it these days, the idea of working with a black buck graveled him more. But Vespasian had been out on the foundry floor since 1915, and he wasn't even slightly uppity. He gave Jeff's anger no place to perch. That in itself was infuriating.

They had no time for light conversation, not this morning. The big crucible swung down and poured a fiery load of molten metal down onto the sand of the foundry floor. Steam rose in hissing, stinking clouds. The steel seemed as determined to get free of the mold as any house cat was to get outdoors.

Whatever else Pinkard thought of Vespasian, he had to allow that the big Negro knew his way around steel. Vespasian made as good a partner as Bedford Cunningham ever had, and he wasn't likely to try and sleep with Emily.

Or maybe he is, Jeff thought. *Who the hell knows? Emily's liable to be taking on niggers these days.* He didn't know what the woman he'd married, the woman he'd loved, was doing these days, not for certain. He'd finally let her back into the house so she could put on some clothes and gather up whatever she could carry in her arms. Then he'd thrown her out again. She hadn't come round the place since. He wouldn't have let her in if she had.

Maybe she was working in a factory somewhere downtown. Maybe she was standing on a streetcorner, shaking her ass whenever a man walked by and hoping he'd give her five or six million dollars for a fast roll in the hay.

"I don't care what she's doing," Pinkard said, quickly, fiercely. Vespasian shouldn't have been able to hear that low-voiced mumble. But the Negro had been on the foundry floor a long time. He'd got as good as anybody could get at hearing under the racket and picking up talk. He knew about Emily. Everybody at the Sloss Works knew about Emily, sure as hell. Just for a second, he looked at Pinkard with pity in his eye.

Jeff glared back, and Vespasian flinched as if from a blow. The last thing in the world Jeff wanted was a black man's pity. "Work, God damn you," he snarled. Vespasian did work, his face as blank of expression now as a just-erased blackboard.

Before Pinkard had been conscripted, he wouldn't have talked to Vespasian that way. He'd thought the Negro a pretty good fellow then. He might not have talked to Vespasian that way before he first heard Jake Featherston speak. He might as well have been blind before. But Featherston had opened his eyes, all right.

"Joining the Freedom Party was the best thing I ever did," he said. If Vespasian heard that, he pretended he didn't.

It was true, though. The Freedom Party gave him a family, a place to go, things to do. If he hadn't been active in the Party, he might have gone clean round the bend when Emily took off her dress for Bedford Cunningham that second time. That Emily might not have done any such thing if he hadn't so immersed himself in the Freedom Party never once entered his mind.

What he did think about was that several of his Party buddies had had their marriages go to hell and gone in the past few months. None of the other blowups had been quite so spectacular as his, but having pals who understood what he was going through because they were going through the same thing made life easier. None of his friends had been able to figure out why they and their wives had broken up. Trying gave them something to talk about at Party meetings and when they got together betweentimes.

The only place where he didn't think that much about the Freedom Party was out on the foundry floor. If you thought about anything but what you were doing out there, you were asking for a trip to the hospital if you were lucky and a trip to the graveyard if you weren't. He'd learned that early on, and relearned it when he came back to the Sloss Works after the war. Work came first. That was a matter of life and death.

At last, work ended for the day. As the screech of the steam whistle faded, Pinkard turned to Vespasian and said, "See you tomorrow. Freedom!"

Vespasian's lips had started to shape the word *see*. But he didn't say anything at all. He showed expression now: the expression was pain. Jeff had seen it on Yankees' faces as he drove home the bayonet. Vespasian turned away from him and stumbled off to clock out as if he too had taken a couple of feet of sharpened steel in the guts. He might have had a pretty good notion of Jeff's politics beforehand, but now he was left in no possible doubt. Jeff laughed out loud. The future was on his side. He felt it in his bones.

He clocked out and hurried home to his cottage. Fanny Cunningham sat out on the front porch of hers next door. Jeff leered at her, wondering if this was how Bedford had looked at Emily. It didn't draw Fanny into his arms. She fled back into the house. He laughed again. His hot, burning laughter filled the street, as molten steel filled its mold.

He took some sausages out of the icebox and burned them for supper. His suppers, these days, were of two sorts: burnt and raw. He ate bread with them, and gulped down a glass of homebrew that was no better than it had to be. The dishes sat in the sink, waiting. As far as he was concerned, they could go right on waiting, too. He had a Freedom Party meeting tonight. That was a hell of a lot more important than a pile of goddamn dishes.

"Freedom!" The greeting filled the livery stable. It wasn't a challenge here, nor a shout of defiance: it was what one friend said to another. The men who filled the stable—filled it almost to overflowing; before long, like it or not, the Birmingham chapter would have to find a new place to meet—*were* friends, colleagues, comrades. Those who'd been in the Party longer got a little more respect than johnny-come-latelys, but only a little. Jeff had joined long enough ago to deserve some of that respect himself.

With Barney Stevens up in Richmond, a skinny little dentist named Caleb Briggs led the meetings and led the Party in Birmingham. "Freedom!" he shouted, his voice thin and rasping—he'd been gassed up in Virginia, and wouldn't sound right till they laid him in his grave.

"Freedom!" Pinkard shouted with the rest of the men who'd come together to find, to build, something larger and grander than themselves.

"Boys, I'm not telling you anything you don't already know when I say that Jake Featherston's going to be running for president this year." Briggs paused to suck more air into his ruined lungs—and to let the Party members cheer till they sounded almost as hoarse as he always did. Then he went on, "We've done a little bit of brawling every now and again, but it's not a patch on what we're going to be doing, let me tell you that!"

More cheers erupted. Jeff pumped his fist in the air. Brambles and thorns in his throat, Briggs went on, "The Whigs will be holding rallies here in town. The goddamn Radical Liberals will be holding rallies here in town." He shook his head. Lamplight reflected wetly from his eyes. "That's not right. Those traitor bastards will try and hold rallies here in town. Are we going to let 'em?"

"No!" Jeff shouted, along with most of the Freedom Party men. The rest were shouting "Hell, no!" and other, coarser, variations on the theme instead.

"That's right." Caleb Briggs nodded now, which made his eyeballs glitter in a different way. Jeff could not have said how it was different, but it was. Briggs went on, "That's just right, boys. This is a war we're in, same as the one we fought in the trenches. We would have won that one, only we got stabbed in the back. This time, we hit the traitors first."

Jeff applauded till his hard, horny hands were sore. Somebody not far away pulled out a flask of moonshine and passed it around. Pinkard took a swig. "Son of a bitch!" he said reverently, his vocal cords for the moment nearly as charred as Briggs'. He passed the flask along, half sorry to see it go, half relieved it was gone.

Someone started singing "Dixie." Jeff roared out the words, a fiery fury in him that had surprisingly little to do with the whiskey he'd just drunk. The Freedom Party sang "Dixie" at every meeting. Then someone else began "Louisville Will Be Free." That one dated from just after the Second Mexican War, and recounted the greatest fight of that war. With Louisville forced back into the USA in the Great War, it took on a poignancy now that it hadn't had then.

Tears ran down Jefferson Pinkard's face. They took him by surprise. He wondered if he was weeping for ravaged Louisville or for himself. A great determination filled him. Like his country, he'd paid for doing what he remained convinced was right. Sooner or later, everyone else would pay, too.

"Freedom!" he cried at the top of his lungs. "Freedom! Freedom!"

Reggie Bartlett nodded in some surprise when Tom Brearley came into Harmon's drugstore. He hadn't seen much of Brearley since the ex–Navy man went down to South Carolina to talk with Anne Colleton. Reggie had been waiting for fireworks to spring from that meeting. He was still waiting.

Evidently, Brearley was getting tired of waiting. He said, "All right, Mr. Bartlett, what's your next great idea for blowing the Freedom Party out of the water?"

"I haven't got another one," Reggie admitted. "Wish to heaven I did."

"Well, I've got another one." Brearley looked very determined. Reggie could easily picture him peering through a periscope at a U.S. cruiser. Oddly, he also looked much younger than he had before sticking out his chin. He said, "If I can't get those bastards fighting among themselves, I'll just have to take the story to the newspapers."

"Jesus," Reggie said. "Are you sure you want to do that? I wouldn't, not unless I had my life-insurance premiums all paid up."

"As a matter of fact, I do," Brearley said, doing a determined and pretty good best to sound unconcerned. "I made sure they were before I went down to talk to Tom Colleton's sister, because I wasn't sure I'd be coming back. But by now Kimball has to know I've talked. He has to figure I'll talk more. That means he'll try and kill me sooner or later—likely sooner. I'm kind of surprised he hasn't tried it yet—him or some of the Freedom Party apes up here. I want to make sure the word gets out before he does." He didn't sound unconcerned any more: just matter-of-fact, a man tackling a job he knew was dangerous.

Reggie understood that. He wouldn't have, not before the war. Going through the trenches—coming out of the trenches on command to attack—changed a man forever. He knew he would be afraid again, many times in his life. But fear would never paralyze him, as it might have done before. He had its measure now.

He said, "If you're bound and determined to do it, you'd better think hard about which paper you go to. You don't want to head for the *Sentinel*, because—"

"Don't teach your grandpa to suck eggs," Brearley said with a wry grin. "Do I look that stupid? Half the time, I reckon Jake Featherston puts that rag out himself. Shame and a disgrace, the garbage it prints."

"Why don't I just shut up?" Reggie said to nobody in particular.

"I don't want you to shut up," Brearley told him. "You go to political rallies for fun. You really think about this stuff, a lot more than I do. So I want your advice: you reckon I should talk to the *Whig* or the *Examiner*?"

"Go with the Whigs or the Radical Liberals?" Reggie stroked his chin. After a minute or so of silent thought, he said, "That's an interesting one, isn't it? The Freedom Party's probably giving the Whigs a harder time—they were the ones who ran the country during the war. But I think the Radical Liberals are more afraid of Featherston and his gang, don't you? For one thing, they're farther away from the stand he takes, where some of the right-wing Whigs might as well start yelling 'Freedom!' themselves. And for another, the Rad Libs are running scared. If they don't get a break, the Freedom Party'll be number two in the country after this fall's election. You give them some dirt, they'll run with it."

Tom Brearley looked at him as if he'd never seen him before. "You're wasting your time shoving pills across a counter, Bartlett. You should have been a lawyer, something like that. You think straight. You think real straight."

"Maybe I do," Reggie said. "You're the one who's not thinking straight now, I'll tell you that. Where the devil am I going to get the money to study law? Where am I going to get the money to get the education I'd need so I could study law? If I'd had a million dollars *before* the war, it might have been a different story."

Brearley shrugged. "If you want something bad enough, you can generally find a way to get it. What I want right now is to torpedo the Freedom Party. I tried one way. It didn't work. All right—I'll try something else. The *Examiner* it'll be. Thanks, Bartlett." He sketched a salute and left.

Jeremiah Harmon came up from the back of the drugstore. "I overheard some of that," he said, sounding apologetic—astonishing in a boss. "None of my business, but anybody who goes up against a machine gun without a machine gun of his own is asking for a whole peck of trouble. You ask me, the *Examiner*'s a popgun, not a machine gun. Wish I could say different, but I can't."

"Where do you find a machine gun to fight the Freedom Party?" Reggie asked.

"Haven't the foggiest notion," the druggist replied. "Don't know if there is any such animal. But if I didn't have one, I think I'd stay down in my dugout and hope no big shell caved it in."

He hadn't been to the front. He'd passed the war in Richmond, making pills and salves and syrups. He never pretended otherwise. But the vocabulary of the trenches had come to be part of everyone's day-to-day speech in the CSA. An awful lot of men had passed through the fire. Reggie wasted a moment wondering if expressions from the front line filled the sharp-sounding English of the United States, too.

Harmon went back to whatever he'd been doing when Tom Brearley came into the drugstore. He didn't waste a lot of time banging a drum for what he thought. If you agreed with him or decided he had a point, fine. If you didn't, he wouldn't lose any sleep over it.

And it wasn't just an interesting discussion to Reggie Bartlett. He'd signed his name to the letter that had gone down to Tom Colleton. If Freedom Party thugs came after Tom Brearley, they were liable to come after him, too.

All at once, he wished he'd told Brearley to keep the hell away from newspapers. Part of him wished that, anyhow. The rest realized such worries came far too late. The cat had been out of the bag ever since he touched pen to paper.

He started watching the newspapers, especially the *Richmond Examiner*, like a hawk. Day followed day with no banner headline about a U.S. destroyer sunk after the Confederate States asked for quarter. Maybe Brearley had got cold feet and hadn't bent a reporter's ear after all. In a way, that disappointed Reggie down to the depths of his soul. In another way, one that left him ashamed, it relieved him. Maybe Brearley had talked, and the reporter hadn't believed him. Reggie almost hoped that was so. It would have given him the best of both worlds.

And then one day with March approaching, and with it the first inauguration of a Socialist president of the USA, that banner headline did run in the *Examiner*: WAR CRIMINAL HIGH IN FREEDOM PARTY CIRCLES! For a moment, Reggie hoped the story under the headline would be about some other war criminal; he wouldn't have been surprised to learn the Freedom Party sheltered battalions of them under its banner.

But it wasn't. The reporter didn't name Tom Brearley—citing concerns for his informant's safety—but he did name Roger Kimball, the *Bonefish*, and the USS *Ericsson*. Reggie hadn't known exactly what kind of secret Brearley was keeping. Now he did. Now everybody did. He nodded to himself. Brearley hadn't been stretching things—it was a big one.

The reporter made it sound as if several members of the submersible's crew had confirmed what Brearley said, too. Maybe that was camouflage, to make the story seem more authoritative and to take some of the heat off Brearley. Maybe he really had checked with other crewmen, and that was why the story had waited so long to run.

However that worked, the story made the Freedom Party hopping mad. The very next day, a blistering denunciation ran in the *Sentinel*. What it amounted to was that the damnyankees had had it coming, and that anyone betraying a Confederate officer who'd done his duty as he saw it deserved whatever happened to him. It didn't quite declare open season on Tom Brearley, but it didn't miss by much. Reggie was glad he didn't figure in the piece in any way.

Jeremiah Harmon said, "Now your friend gets to find out what sort of whirlwind he reaps."

"He's not my—" Reggie stopped. He'd been about to say that Brearley was no friend of his. The only reason they knew each other was that the ex–Navy man had married an old flame of his. But they shared a common foe: the Freedom Party. That might not make them friends, but it did make them allies.

Harmon noted Reggie's pause, nodded as if his assistant had spoken a complete sentence, and went back to work. A customer came into the drugstore, marched up to the counter, and demanded a ringworm salve. Reggie sold him one, knowing the best the store offered were none too good. Doctors and researchers had got pretty good at figuring out what caused a lot of ailments. Doing anything worthwhile about them was something else again.

Tom Brearley came by a couple of days later. He grinned a skeletal grin at Reggie. "Still here," he said in sepulchral tones.

Reggie made shooing motions. "Well, get the hell out of *here*," he hissed. "You think I want to be seen with you?"

His acting was too good; Brearley turned and started to leave. Only the laughter Reggie couldn't contain stopped him. "Damn you," Brearley said without heat. "You had me going there. Freedom Party's still screaming about traitors. Seems to be the only song they know."

"Anybody give you any real trouble?" Reggie asked.

Brearley shook his head. "Not yet, thank God. The only people in the Freedom Party who know what I look like live down in South Carolina. But they know my name. They can find out where I live." He patted the waistband of his trousers. His coat concealed whatever he kept there, but Reggie had no trouble figuring out what it was. Brearley said, "They want to try and give me a hard time, I'm ready for 'em."

"Good." Reggie hesitated, then asked, "How's Maggie doing?"

"Pretty well," Brearley answered. "She doesn't take the whole business as seriously as I do. She hasn't paid that much attention to politics, and she doesn't really know what a pack of nasty . . . so-and-so's join the Party."

Reggie wasn't sure he took the whole business as seriously as Brearley did, either. Then he recalled his relief at not getting into the newspaper. Maybe—evidently—he took things seriously after all.

Unable to stomach his own cooking, he stopped in a greasy spoon for supper. He regretted it shortly thereafter; the colored fellow sweating at the stove knew less about what to do there than he did. When he got home, he gulped bicarbonate of soda. That quelled the internal rebellion, but left him feeling gassy and bloated. He read for a while, found himself yawning, and went to bed.

Bells in the night woke him. He yawned again, enormously, put the pillow over his head, and very soon went back to sleep. When morning came, he was halfway through breakfast before he remembered the disturbance. "Those were fire bells," he said, and then, "Good thing the fire wasn't next door, I reckon, or I'd be burnt to a crisp right about now."

Somebody had been burnt to a crisp. Newsboys shouted the story as they hawked their papers. "Liar's house goes up in smoke! Read all about it!" a kid selling the *Sentinel* yelled.

A cold chill ran through Reggie Bartlett. He didn't buy the *Sentinel*; that would have been the same as putting fifty thousand dollars in the Freedom Party's coffer. Two streetcorners farther along, he picked up a copy of the *Examiner* and read it as he walked the rest of the way to Harmon's drugstore.

He shivered again as he read. The paper reported that Thomas and Margaret Brearley had died in "a conflagration that swept their home so swiftly and violently that neither had the slightest chance to escape, which leads firemen to suspect that arson may have been involved." It talked about Brearley's naval career in general terms, but did not mention that he'd served aboard the *Bonefish*.

Jeremiah Harmon had a newspaper in his hand when Reggie walked into the drugstore. Reggie didn't need to ask which story he was reading. "You see?" the druggist said in his mild, quiet voice.

"Oh, yes," Reggie answered. "I see. God help me, Mr. Harmon, I sure do."

Sylvia Enos sank into the trolley seat with a grateful sigh. She didn't often get to sit on her way to the galoshes factory. And, better yet, the seat had a copy of the *Boston Globe* there for the grabbing. She snatched up the paper before anyone else could. Every penny she didn't spend on a newspaper could go to something else, and she needed plenty of other things, with not enough pennies to go around.

Most of the front page was filled with stories about the inauguration of President Sinclair, which was set for day after tomorrow. Sylvia read all of them with greedy, gloating interest; she might not be able to vote herself, but the prospect of a Socialist president delighted her. She didn't quite know what Upton Sinclair could do about Frank Best, but she figured he could do something.

Another prominent headline marked the fall of Belfast to the forces of the Republic of Ireland. No wonder that story got prominent play in Boston, with its large Irish population. "Now the whole of the Emerald Isle is free," Irish General Collins was quoted as saying. The folk of Belfast might not agree—surely did not agree, else they wouldn't have fought so grimly—but no one on this side of the Atlantic cared about their opinion.

Sylvia opened the paper to the inside pages. She picked and chose there; the factory was getting close. A headline caught her eye: REBEL ACCUSER PERISHES IN SUSPICIOUS FIRE. Most of the story was about the death of a man whose name was spelled half the time as Brierley and the other half as Brearley. *He had drawn the wrath of the Freedom Party, a growing force in the CSA,* the *Globe's* reporter wrote, *by claiming that a leading Party official in one of the Carolinas was, while in the C.S. Navy, responsible for deliberately sinking the USS* Ericsson *although fully aware that the war between the United States and Confederate States had ended. The Freedom Party has denied this charge, and has also denied any role in the deaths of Brierley and his wife.*

The trolley came to Sylvia's stop. It had already started rolling again before she realized she should have got off. When it stopped again, a couple of blocks later, she did get off. She knew she should hurry back to the factory—the implacable time card would dock her for every minute she was late, to say nothing of the hard time Frank Best would give her—but she couldn't make herself move fast, not with the way her mind was whirling.

Not a British boat after all, she thought. *It was the Rebs. They were the ones George worried about, and he was right. And they did it after the war was over, and the fellow who did it is still running around loose down there.* She wanted to scream. She wanted to buy a gun and go hunting for the submarine skipper. Why not? He'd gone hunting for her husband.

"Are you all right, dearie?" May Cavendish asked when Sylvia came in and put her card in the time clock. "You look a little peaked."

"I'm—" Sylvia didn't know how she was, or how to put it into words. She felt as if a torpedo had gone off inside her head, sinking everything she thought she'd known since the end of the war and leaving nothing in its place. Stunned and empty, she went into the factory.

Frank Best greeted her, pocket watch in hand. "You're late, Mrs. Enos."

Most days, she would have apologized profusely, hoping in that way to keep him from bothering her too much. Most days, it would have been a forlorn hope, too. Now she just looked at him and nodded. "Yes, I am, aren't I?" She walked past him toward her station near the molds. If he hadn't quickly stepped out of the way, she would have walked over him. He stared after her. She did not look back over her shoulder to see.

After a while, he came up to her carrying a pair of rubber overshoes. "Thought you could slip these by me, did you?" he said: his usual opening line.

She looked at the galoshes. The red rings around the top looked fine to her, which meant they'd look fine to a customer, too. "They're all right, Mr. Best," she said, brushing a wisp of hair back from her eyes with the sleeve of her shirtwaist. "I really don't have time to play games today. I'm sorry."

He stared at her again, in complete astonishment. "I could have you fired," he said. "You could be on the street in fifteen minutes."

"That's true," she said calmly, and bent to paint a couple of overshoes coming down the line at her.

"Have you gone out of your mind?" the foreman sputtered.

"Maybe." Sylvia considered it for a moment. "I don't think so, but I rather wish I would."

"You're kid—" Frank Best began. He studied Sylvia. She wasn't kidding. That must have been obvious, even to him. He started to say something else. Whatever it was, it never passed his lips. He walked away, shaking his head. He was still carrying the galoshes about which he'd intended to give her a hard time.

So that's the secret, she thought. She'd been drunk only a few times in her life, but she had that same giddy, headlong, anything-can-happen feeling now. *Act a little crazy and Frank will leave you alone.*

But she hadn't been acting. She didn't just feel drunk. She felt crazy. The world had turned sideways while she wasn't looking. Everything she thought she'd known about who'd killed George turned out to be wrong. Now she was going to have to grapple with what that meant.

As she painted red rings on the next pair of overshoes, she suddenly wished Upton Sinclair hadn't won the election after all. Sinclair, when he talked about dealings with other countries, talked about reconciliation and improving relations with former foes. That had sounded good during the campaign. Now—

Now Sylvia wished Teddy Roosevelt were going to be inaugurated again come Friday. With TR, you always knew where he stood. Most of the time, Sylvia had thought he stood in the wrong place. But he would have demanded that Confederate submersible skipper's head on a silver platter. And, if the Rebs hesitated about turning him over, TR would have started blowing things up. He wouldn't have stopped blowing things up till the Confederates did what he told them, either.

Sylvia sighed. *So much for Socialism,* she thought. As soon as she wanted the United States to take a strong line with their neighbors, she automatically thought of the Democrats.

That's why they ran things for so long, she realized. Lots of people had wanted the United States to take a strong line with their neighbors. As soon as people thought they didn't need to worry about the CSA and Canada, England and France, any more, they threw the Democrats out on their ear. She'd wanted to throw the Democrats out on their ear, too. Maybe she'd been hasty.

How am I going to get revenge with Upton Sinclair in the Powel House or the White House or wherever he decides to live? she wondered. *He won't do it. He's already said he wouldn't do things like that. Will I have to do it myself?*

She laughed, imagining herself invading the Confederate States singlehanded. What would she wear? A pot helmet over her shirtwaist and skirt? A green-gray uniform with a flowered hat? And how would she get rid of the Reb who'd killed her husband? With a hatpin or a carving knife? Those were the most lethal weapons she owned. She had the feeling they wouldn't be enough to do the job.

She kept on doing her job, as automatically as if she were a machine. The factory owners hadn't figured out how to make a machine to replace her. The minute they did, she'd be out of work. Millions of people, all over the country, were in that same boat. That was another reason Sinclair had beaten TR.

When the dinner whistle blew, Sylvia jumped. She couldn't

decide whether she thought it came too soon or too late. Either way, it shouldn't have come just then. It snapped her out of a haze: not the haze of work, but the haze of a mind far away—in the Confederate States, in the South Atlantic, and back in her apartment with her husband.

Still bemused, she picked up her dinner pail and went out to meet her friends. "What in the world did you say to Frank?" Sarah Wyckoff demanded. "He's been walking around all morning like he just saw a ghost."

"And the way he's been looking at you," May Cavendish added, taking a bite from a pungent sandwich of summer sausage, pickles, and onions. "Not like he wants to get his hands inside your clothes, the way he usually does, but more like he's scared of you. Tell us the secret."

"I don't know," Sylvia said vaguely. She remembered talking with the foreman not long after the shift started, but hardly anything of what had passed between them. Most of what had gone on since she'd seen that story in the *Boston Globe* was a blur to her.

"You all right, dearie?" May asked.

"I don't know," Sylvia said again. She realized she had to do better than that, and did try: "I'm having a lot of trouble keeping my mind on my work—on much of anything—this morning."

"Well, I know all about *that*," Sarah said. "This isn't the most exciting place they ever built, and that's the Lord's truth." May nodded while lighting a cigarette.

Sylvia lit one, too. The surge of well-being that went with the first couple of puffs penetrated the fog around her wits. In thoughtful tones, she asked, "May, what would you do if you could find the soldier who killed your husband? I mean *the* soldier, the one who fired the machine gun or rifle or whatever it was."

"I don't know," May Cavendish answered. "I never thought about that before. For all I know, he's already dead." Her eyes went flat and hard. When she spoke again, her voice was cold as sleet: "I hope he's already dead, and I hope he took a long time to die, too, the stinking son of a bitch." But then, after a savage drag on her cigarette, she sounded much more like her usual self, saying, "But how could you ever tell? With so many bullets flying around, nobody knew who shot people and who didn't. Herbert always used to talk about that when he came home on leave." Now she sighed and looked sad, remembering.

"I suppose you're right," Sylvia said. She'd forgotten the differences between the wars the Army and the Navy fought. She knew the name of her husband's killer: Roger Kimball. She knew he lived down in South Carolina and agitated for the Freedom Party. She had no idea whether the Freedom Party was good, bad, or indifferent.

"What would you do, Sylvia?" Sarah asked. "If you knew?"

"Who can say?" Sylvia sounded weary. "I like to think I'd have the gumption to try and kill him, but who can say?" The whistle blew, announcing the end of the dinner break. "I like to think I'd have the gumption to try and kill Frank Best, too, but it hasn't happened yet," Sylvia added. Chuckling, she and her friends went back to work.

Flora Hamburger remembered the last presidential inauguration she'd attended, four years before. *That long?* She shook her head in wonder. So much had changed since 1917. She'd been brand new in Congress then, unsure of herself, unsure of her place in Philadelphia. Now she was starting her third term. The war had still raged. Now the United States were at peace with the world. And she'd gone to the inauguration of a Democrat then. Now—

Now half the bunting that decorated Philadelphia was the traditional red, white, and blue. The other half was solid red, symbol of the Socialists who had come into their own at last.

A lot of people in Philadelphia were going around with long faces. Being the home of the federal government since the Second Mexican War, it had also been the home of the Democratic Party since the 1880s. Now President Sinclair would be choosing officials ranging from Cabinet members down to postmasters. A horde of Democrats who'd thought they owned lifetime positions were discovering they'd been mistaken and would have to go out and look for real work.

President-elect Sinclair had chosen to hold the inauguration in Franklin Square, to let as large a crowd as possible see him. He'd thought about going down to Washington, D.C., but the *de jure* capital remained too war-battered to host the ceremony. Philadelphia it was. "We are the party of the people," he had said a great many times. "Let them know how they are governed, and they will ensure they are governed well."

Before Sinclair took the presidential oath, Hosea Blackford would take that of the vice president. Flora shook her head again. In March 1917, she'd had a mild friendship with the Congressman from Dakota. Now . . . *Now I am the mistress of the vice president–elect of the United States.*

The title should have left her feeling sordid and ashamed—and it did, sometimes. What, after all, was *mistress* but a fancy word for *fallen woman*? But she also knew she'd never been so happy as in the time since she and Blackford became lovers. Did that make her depraved? She didn't think so—most of the time, she didn't think so—though no doubt others would if they knew.

Whatever she was, it didn't show on the outside. Dressed in a splendid maroon wool suit (Herman Bruck would have approved) and a new hat, she had one of the best seats for the ceremony. Why not? She was a Socialist member of Congress. Then she wondered, *Is it a matter of rank? Is this what we get? Will we become part of the ruling class, the way the Democrats did?*

She hoped not. The people had elected Upton Sinclair to prevent that kind of thing, not to promote it. Then all her thought about anything but the immediate present blew away. A rising hum from the enormous crowd behind her announced the arrival of the motor-cars full of dignitaries who would go through the ceremony that marked the changing of the guard for the United States.

People clapped and cheered to see them. In the lead, behind an honor guard of soldiers and Marines, strode Chief Justice Oliver Wendell Holmes. He was a little thinner, a little more stooped, than he had been when Flora first saw him four years before, but he still moved like a much younger man.

Behind him came Vice President McKenna, an amiable nonentity who was almost as fat as Congressman Taft. In white tie and tails, he looked like a penguin that had swallowed a beach ball. And behind McKenna walked Theodore Roosevelt, also in white tie and tails. As he moved toward the raised platform on which President Sinclair would take the oath of office, Senators and Representatives got to their feet and began to applaud him. Democrats rose sooner than Socialists and Republicans, but soon, regardless of party, members of both houses of Congress stood and cheered the man who had led the United States to victory in the Great War.

Roosevelt did not seem to have expected such a tribute. He doffed his stovepipe hat several times. Once, he took off his spectacles for a moment and rubbed at his eyes. Had he got a cinder in them, or was he wiping away a tear? Flora had trouble believing that of an old Tartar like TR. Then, spotting her among the crowd of nearly identical-looking men, the outgoing president waved and blew her a kiss. He could hardly have astonished her more if he'd turned a cartwheel.

She stayed on her feet after he passed, as did all the other Socialists, most of the Midwestern corporal's guard of Republicans, and the more courteous Democrats—about half. Here came Hosea Blackford, about to make the change from vice president–elect to vice president. He too wore formal attire. He didn't look like a penguin, not to Flora. He looked splendid.

Flora called his name while she was applauding. He smiled at her, but he was smiling at everybody. He hurried after Roosevelt toward the platform.

And behind him—in front of another honor guard, this one of sailors and soldiers—walked the man of the hour, Upton Sinclair. Craning her neck to look back at him, Flora saw a sea of red flags waving in the crowd. Her heart slammed against her rib cage in excitement and delight. As the dialectic predicted, the people had at last turned to the party that stood for their class interests.

Up on the platform, Theodore Roosevelt shook Sinclair's hand, a formal gesture, and then slapped him lightly on the back, one much less so. The president that was and the president that would be grinned at each other. Flora remembered how Senator Debs had stayed personally cordial toward TR even after losing two presidential elections to him.

Whatever Roosevelt and Sinclair said to each other, they were too far away from the microphone for it to pick up their words. Chief Justice Holmes stood by it, a Bible in his hand. He beckoned to Hosea Blackford. When Blackford took the vice-presidential oath, the electric marvel let the whole enormous crowd hear him do it.

Then Justice Holmes summoned the president-elect to the microphone. His amplified oath filled the vast, echoing silence in Franklin Square: "I, Upton Sinclair, do solemnly swear that I will faithfully execute the Office of President of the United States, and will to the best of my ability, preserve, protect and defend the Constitution of the United States."

"Congratulations, Mr. President," Oliver Wendell Holmes said. As Roosevelt had done, he reached out to shake Sinclair's hand. What had been quiet erupted into a vast roar of noise: the noise of almost forty years of Socialist struggle finally rewarded with victory.

Upton Sinclair lifted up his hands. As if he were a magician, silence returned. Into it, he said, "It's time for a change!"—the same theme he'd used in Toledo, the theme the Socialists had used through the whole campaign. "We've been saying that for a long time, my friends, but now the change is here!"

More fervent applause followed, as did scattered shouts of,

"Revolution!" Sinclair raised his hands again. This time, quiet was slower in coming.

At last, he got it. He said, "We are at peace, and I hope and expect we shall remain at peace throughout my term." That drew more cheers, and a jaundiced look from Theodore Roosevelt. Sinclair went on, "And we shall have peace here at home as well, peace with honor, peace with justice, peace at last. We shall have not the peace of the exploiter who rules his laborers by force and fear, but the peace of the proletariat given its rightful place in the world."

The crowd roared its approval. Theodore Roosevelt looked like a thunderstorm about to burst. But all he could do was frown impotently. Upton Sinclair had the microphone. Upton Sinclair had the country.

He said, "If the capitalists will not give the workers their due, this administration will see to it that the rights and aspirations of the laboring classes are respected. If the capitalists will not heed our warnings, this administration will see to it that they heed our new laws. If the capitalists go on thinking that the means of production are theirs and theirs alone, this administration will prove to them that those means of production belong in the hands of the people, which is to say, the hands of the government. For too long, the trusts have had friends in high places. Now the people have friends in high places."

The red flags dipped and waved. The crowd in Franklin Square screeched itself hoarse. The Democratic minority in the House and Senate listened to President Sinclair in stony silence. So did Chief Justice Holmes. Flora noticed that, even if Sinclair did not. Sinclair might propose laws, Congress might pass them . . . and the Supreme Court might strike them down.

But that would be later. Now there was only the headiness of victory. Flora felt it, too, and applauded loudly when President Sinclair made an eloquent call for equity among nations. *If we'd had equity among nations all along,* she thought, *my brother would walk on two legs.*

But even pain and bitterness could not last, not today. After President Sinclair's speech ended, the celebrating began. Every saloon in Philadelphia had to be packed. So did every ballroom. Not every Socialist had proletarian tastes in amusement—far from it.

Flora went to a reception at Powel House for the Socialist Congressional delegation. She met the president and his wife, a vivacious redhead named Enid who was wearing an off-the-shoulder green velvet gown that would have caused multiple heart attacks on the Lower East Side; Flora's district was radical politically but not when it came to women's clothes.

Sinclair was also dashing in the clawhammer coat he still wore. "I want you to go right on being the conscience of the House," he told Flora.

"I'll do my best, Mr. President," she said.

Senator Debs came up then, and shook the president's hand. "Congratulations, Upton," he said graciously. "You've done what I couldn't do. And now that you have done it, I've got a question for you." He waited till Sinclair nodded, then asked, "What do you propose to do about the claims this Confederate submarine sank one of our ships after the war was over?"

"Examine them. Study them," the new president answered. "Not go off half-cocked, the way TR would. The Confederates are having their own political upheavals. The claims may have more to do with those than with the truth. Once I know what's what, I'll decide what I need to do."

Debs nodded, but said, "That Freedom Party down there could do with some slapping down. It's reaction on the march"—a sentiment with which Flora agreed completely.

"Once I know what's what, I'll decide what I need to do," President Sinclair repeated. Flora had hoped for more, but had to be content with that.

The reception went on for a very long time. Flora had grown more used to late hours in Philadelphia than she'd ever been in New York City, but she was yawning by the time it got to be half past one. Hosea Blackford—Vice President Hosea Blackford—said, "I'm heading home, Flora. Can I give you a ride?" He grinned. "I get a housing allowance, but no house—shows where the vice president fits into the scheme of things. So why should I move?"

"That would be very kind, your Excellency," Flora said with a smile that made Blackford snort. The vice president's nondescript Ford seemed out of place among the fancy motorcars around Powel House. In companionable silence, he drove Flora back to the apartment house where they both lived.

No matter how tired she was, she invited Blackford into her flat. He cocked an eyebrow. "Are you sure?"

"Of course I am." Flora stood on tiptoe to whisper in his ear: "I've never done this with a vice president before."

He laughed out loud, and was still laughing when he stepped inside. After Flora closed the door behind him, he said, "I should hope not! Walter McKenna would have squashed you flat." Flora squeaked in outrage. Then she started to laugh, too. He took her in his arms. She forgot she was tired. She knew she'd be reminded in the morning, but for now—she forgot.

Cincinnatus Driver and his family had never lived in an apartment house before moving to Iowa. One thing he hadn't been able to investigate at the Covington, Kentucky, public library was how much houses cost in Des Moines. It was a lot more than it had been down in Covington, either to buy or to rent. The two-bedroom flat he'd found was much more in his price range, even if none of the rooms was big enough to swing a cat. But the flat had electricity, which went some way toward making up for that. He'd never lived in a place with electricity before. He liked it. Elizabeth liked it even better.

The apartment house was in the near northwestern part of town, west of the Des Moines River and north of the Raccoon. It was as close as Des Moines came to having a colored district, although only a little more than a thousand Negroes were hardly enough to constitute a real district in a city of over a hundred thousand. The Drivers shared their floor with two other black families and one white; the proprietor of a Chinese laundry lived upstairs. Nobody was rich, not in that neighborhood. People got by, though. As far as Cincinnatus could tell, they got by rather better than they had in Covington.

"I want to go to school, Pa," Achilles yelled to Cincinnatus when he came home worn from a day's hauling one evening. "Some of my friends go to school. I want to go to school, too."

"You'll go to school in the fall," his father told him. "You turn six then. We'll put you in this kindergarten they have here."

In Covington, white children had kindergartens. Black children hadn't had any formal schooling till the USA took Kentucky away from the CSA. Cincinnatus was unusual in his generation of Negroes in the Confederate States in being able to read and write; he'd always had a restless itch to know. Having that kind of itch was dangerous in a country where, up until not long before he was born, it had been not merely difficult but illegal for blacks to learn their letters.

"What can I get for you, dear?" Elizabeth asked, coming out of the kitchen. "How did it go today?"

"Got plenty of hauling business," Cincinnatus answered. "Folks was right—the Des Moines runs high in the springtime, even more so than the Ohio does, and boats get up here that can't any other time of year. Won't have so much to do in the summertime. Last summer, when we got here, I wondered for a while if we was goin' to starve."

"We made it." Elizabeth's voice was warm with pride.

"Sure enough did," Cincinnatus agreed. "I want to see if we can get ourselves a little bit ahead of things while the river's high. Always good to have some money socked away you don't have to spend right now."

"Amen," Elizabeth said, as if he'd been a preacher making a point in the pulpit.

"Amen," Achilles echoed; he liked going to church of a Sunday morning.

Cincinnatus smiled at his son. Then he looked back to his wife. "What I'd like me right now is a bottle of beer. I knew Iowa was a dry state, but I didn't reckon folks here'd take it so *serious*. Down in Kentucky, folks always preached against the demon rum, but that didn't stop 'em from drinkin' whiskey. Didn't even hardly slow 'em down none. People round these parts mean it."

"Most of 'em do, uh-huh." Elizabeth nodded. Her eyes sparkled—or maybe it was a trick of the sun-bright electric bulb above her head. She turned and went back into the kitchen. Her skirt swirled around her, giving Cincinnatus a glimpse of her trim ankles. Some of the white women in Des Moines were wearing skirts well above the ankle—scandalously short, as far as he was concerned. He would have something to say if Elizabeth ever wanted to try that style.

She opened the icebox, then came back into the living room. In her hand was a tall glass of golden liquid with a creamy white head, on her face a look of triumph. Cincinnatus stared at the beer. "Where'd you get that?"

"Chinaman upstairs makes it," Elizabeth answered.

"I'll be." He shook his head in wonder. "I didn't even know Chinamen drank beer, let alone made it." He took the glass from Elizabeth, raised it to his mouth, and cautiously sipped. He smacked his lips, pondering, then nodded. "It ain't great beer, but it's beer, sure enough."

"I know." Now Elizabeth's eyes definitely twinkled. "Had me some before I'd pay the Chinaman for it. Don't drink that all up now—why don't you bring it to the table with you? Beef stew's just about ready."

Spit jumped into Cincinnatus' mouth. "I'll do that." Beef was cheap here, and plentiful, too, compared to what things were like in Kentucky. He ate his fill without worrying about whether he'd go broke on account of such lavish meals. He still ate a lot of pork, but now more because he liked it than because he couldn't afford anything better.

After supper, while Elizabeth washed dishes, Cincinnatus got out a reader and went to work with Achilles. The boy had known for some time the alphabet and the sounds the letters made; up till just a couple of weeks before, he'd had trouble—trouble often to the point of tears—combining the sounds of the letters into words. Cincinnatus, who had learned to read a good many years later in life, vividly remembered that himself.

Now, though, Achilles had the key. "Ban," he read. "Can. Dan. Fan. Man. Pan. Ran. Tan. Bat. Cat. Fat. Hat. Mat. Pat. Rat. Sat. Den. Fen . . . What's a fen, Pa?"

"Dunno. Let's find out." Cincinnatus had a dictionary. Because of the catch-as-catch-can way he'd become literate, his vocabulary had holes. He used the dictionary to fill them. Riffling through it now, he answered, "A fen is like a swamp. Go on, Achilles. You're doin' swell."

"Hen. Men. Pen. Ten. Wen." That one made the dictionary open again, as did *yen*. Achilles beamed. "I can *read*, Pa!"

"You're gettin' there," Cincinnatus agreed. "We'll keep at it." He figured Achilles would have to work twice as hard at school to get half the respect he deserved. That was what life handed you along with a black skin. People would call Achilles a damn nigger, sure as the sun would come up tomorrow. But nobody would call Achilles a damn dumb nigger, not if Cincinnatus had anything to do with it.

"I want to read stories like the ones you read to me," Achilles said.

"You're gettin' there," Cincinnatus said again. "Now let's work on this a little while longer, and then you'll get to bed." Achilles liked learning to read any time. Faced with the choice between trying to read some more and going to bed, he would have read till four in the morning had his father let him. Cincinnatus didn't let him, because he wanted—and needed—to get some sleep himself. Achilles squawked, but was soon breathing heavily; when he did yield to sleep, he yielded deeply and completely.

So did Cincinnatus, because he was very tired. He slept through the alarm clock; Elizabeth had to shake him awake. A couple of cups of coffee and some scrambled eggs got him moving. He jammed a cloth cap onto his head, kissed Elizabeth, and went downstairs to fire up the Duryea.

He felt more affection for the truck than he ever had down in Covington. It had run very well since the overhaul he'd given it before moving to Iowa. He wished he'd overhauled it sooner; it would have served him better in Kentucky. He climbed in and drove to the wharves along the Des Moines.

At the high-water season, steamboats were tied up at almost all the piers. Some of the haulers who took their goods to merchants and warehouses were black like him; most were white. Despite his color, he had no trouble getting work. The sheer volume of unloading had something to do with that. But he'd also established a reputation for dependability. He hoped that would give him a boost when the river went down and jobs grew scarcer.

After hauling dry goods to several general stores, a cargo of plates and bowls to a china shop, and a truckful of reams of paper to the State Capitol over on the east side of the Des Moines, he came back to the wharves to eat his dinner. A couple of other colored drivers, Joe Sims and Pete Dunnett, pulled their trucks up alongside of his within five minutes of each other. They carried their dinner pails over to the bench where he was eating.

"Business is bully," said Sims, a stocky, very black man in his mid-forties. "Here's hoping it lasts."

Dunnett was thinner, young, and paler; he might have had a quarter portion of white blood in his veins. "That's right," he said. He and Sims both spoke with an accent Cincinnatus found peculiar. It had some of the rhythms of the black speech with which he was familiar, but only some. It was also heavily tinted by the sharp, nasal, almost braying speech of white Iowans. Because the Negroes of Des Moines were such a small minority, the white sea around them diluted their dialect.

Cincinnatus said, "Sure enough would be good if it did. Ain't nothin' wrong with money, nothin' *a*-tall."

Dunnett and Joe Sims looked at each other. After a moment, Sims said, "First time we heard you talk, Cincinnatus, we thought you were a dumb nigger, you lay on that *ain't* stuff so thick. We know better now, but you still talk the way my great-grandpa did."

"I talk like I talk. Can't hardly help it," Cincinnatus said with a shrug. In Covington, his accent had passed for a mild one among Negroes.

Pete Dunnett added, "That fancy handle you've got didn't help, either."

"What's wrong with my name?" Now Cincinnatus really was peeved. "When I came up here and found out all the U.S. niggers had names like white folks, I reckoned that was like oatmeal without sugar or salt or butter or milk or nothin'."

"I'd rather have me a boring name than sound like I was named after a city," Dunnett retorted.

"The city's named after me, not the other way round," Cincinnatus said. "I mean, the city and me both got named for the same fellow from back in ancient days."

"Still sounds funny," Joe Sims said. "And what's your kid's name?"

"Achilles," Cincinnatus said. "He was a hero." He paused a little while in thought, then went on, "You niggers up here in the USA, they let you-all have last names. They let you have plenty of stuff, too—down in Covington, you-all'd be a couple of really rich niggers. When it was the Confederate States down there, most of us hardly had nothin' but our one name. We had to pack everything we could into it."

Sims and Dunnett glanced at each other again. "We've had hard times, too," Dunnett said. He sounded a little defensive. Cincinnatus didn't answer. Dunnett had reason to sound defensive. White men had patrolled the Ohio to keep blacks from the Confederate States out of the USA. Nobody had ever needed to patrol the Ohio to keep blacks from the United States out of the CSA. Blacks in the USA knew perfectly well the distance between the frying pan and the fire.

Sam Carsten would sooner not have had the new stripe on his sleeve that showed he was a petty officer second class. He hadn't lost his ambition—far from it. But he'd earned that stripe by doing a good job as head of his gun crew after Willie Moore got killed. It had blood on it, as far as he was concerned.

The USS *Remembrance* steamed west across the Atlantic toward Boston harbor. Sam didn't have to worry about taking shellfire here. He didn't have to worry about renegade Confederate submersibles, either. What he'd learned about the C.S. boat that had sunk the U.S. destroyer after the war was over filled him with rage. Under that rage lay terror. A Rebel boat could have stalked his old battleship, the USS *Dakota*, just as readily.

A deck hand jerked the prop on a Wright fighting scout. The two-decker's engine thundered to life. The prop blurred into invisibility. The *Remembrance*'s steam catapult hurled the fighting scout into the sky.

"Bully," Sam said softly. Launching aeroplanes had fascinated him even aboard the *Dakota*. The fascination had changed to urgency when land-based aeroplanes bombed his battleship off the Argentine coast. He'd imagined air power on the sea then. He lived it now, and still found it awe-inspiring.

Behind him, a dry voice spoke: "I wonder how long we'll be able to keep them in the air."

Sam turned. If Commander Grady had wanted to stick a KICK ME sign on him, he stood close enough to do it. "What do you mean, sir?" Sam asked, thinking he knew and hoping he was wrong.

"How much longer will we be able to keep them in the air?" the gunnery officer repeated. "You're not stupid, Carsten. You understand what I mean. Will the Socialists put enough money into the Navy to keep this ship operating? Right now, your guess is as good as mine."

"Yes, sir," Sam said dully. His guess was that the Socialists would shut down as much as they could. Except when the war dragged some into the Navy, Socialists were thinly scattered aboard warships: almost as thinly scattered as colored people in the USA. He didn't know a great deal about what Socialist politicians thought, except that they didn't think much of the Navy or the Army.

He looked at Commander Grady. Grady had always been as proud of the *Remembrance* as if he'd designed her himself. Now, looking from the flight deck to the conning tower, his eyes were dull, all but hopeless: the eyes of a man who expected a loved one to die. Sighing, he said, "It was a good idea, anyhow. It still is a good idea."

"It sure as hell is, sir," Carsten said hotly. "It's a swell idea, and anybody who can't see that is a damn fool."

"Lot of damn fools running around loose in the world," Grady said. "Some of them wear fancy uniforms. Some of them wear expensive suits and get elected to Congress or elected president. Those fools get to tell the ones in the fancy uniforms what to do."

"And the ones in the fancy uniforms get to tell us what to do." Sam's laugh was harsh as salt spray. "It's the Navy way." He couldn't think of another officer to whom he would have said such a thing. Grady and he had been through a lot together.

"Damn it," Grady said in a low, furious voice, "we proved what this ship can do. We proved it, but will we get any credit for it?"

"No way to tell about that, sir," Carsten answered, "but I wouldn't bet anything I cared to lose on it."

"Neither would I," Grady said. "But I tell you this: we *did* show what the *Remembrance* can do. Congress may not be watching. President Upton goddamn Sinclair may not be watching. You *can* bet, though, the German High Seas Fleet was watching. The Royal Navy was watching. And if the Japs weren't watching, too, I'd be amazed. Plenty of countries are going to have squadrons of aeroplane carriers ten years from now. I hope to God we're one of them." Before Sam could say anything to that, Grady wheeled and rapidly strode away.

Carsten tried to figure out where he'd be ten years down the line. Likeliest, he supposed, was chief petty officer in charge of a gun crew. He could easily see himself turning into Hiram Kidde or Willie Moore. He'd just have to follow the path of least resistance.

If he wanted anything more, he'd have to work harder for it. Mustangs didn't grow on trees. And, if he aimed at becoming an officer, he'd have to get lucky, too. He wondered how much he really wanted that kind of luck. What was good for him might turn out to be anything but good for other people. He thought of Moore again, Moore writhing on the floor with his belly torn open.

The steam catapult hissed like a million snakes, hurling another fighting scout into the air. The crew of the *Remembrance* kept honing their skills. They were, at the moment, the best in the world at what they did, whether Congress appreciated it or not. They were also, at the moment, the only ones in the world who did what they did. Sam wondered how long that would last. He remembered the German sailors in Dublin harbor staring and staring at the aeroplane carrier. Kaiser Bill's boys built better aeroplanes than the USA did; the Wright two-deckers were Albatros copies. Could the Germans build better aeroplane carriers, too?

One of the Wright machines roared low over the flight deck. Had it shot up the deck, Sam would not have cared to be standing there. On the other hand, the flight deck bristled with machine guns and one-pounders. Had that fighting scout been painted with the Stars and Bars instead of the U.S. eagle in front of crossed swords, it would have got a warm welcome.

It zoomed above the *Remembrance* again, this time even lower and upside down. A couple of the sailors on deck saluted the pilot with upraised middle fingers. Sam didn't, but he felt like it. He hadn't had a whole lot to do with the pilots aboard the aeroplane carrier: they were officers, and pretty much kept to themselves. But what he had seen made him wonder if their marbles had spilled out of their ears as they flew, because they didn't seem to give two whoops in hell whether they lived or died.

Staring after the fighting scout after it finally rolled back to right side up, Sam decided that made a certain amount of sense. The rickety contraptions the pilots flew had a habit of falling out of the sky by themselves. The pilots had to take them into harm's way, and had to land them on the rolling, pitching deck of a warship. You probably needed to be crazy to want to do any of that. And, if you weren't crazy when you started doing it, you'd get that way after a while.

As if to prove the point, the pilot of the other fighting scout dove out of the sky on the *Remembrance* like a sparrowhawk swooping on a field mouse. In an impossibly short time, the aeroplane swelled from buzzing speck to roaring monster. It seemed to be heading straight for Sam. He wanted to dig a hole in the deck, dive in, and then pull the planking and steel over himself: an armored blanket to keep him safe and warm. A couple of sailors started to run. Their comrades screamed curses at them. He understood why, but had to work to hold his own feet still.

At the last possible instant, the Wright two-decker pulled out of the dive. Sam couldn't help ducking; he thought one wheel of the landing gear would clip him. It wasn't quite so close as that, but he did have to snatch at his cap to keep it from blowing off his head and perhaps into the sea. Had it gone into the drink, the price of a new one would have come out of his pay.

The two-decker almost went into the drink, too, off to port of the *Remembrance*. Carsten would have sworn its lowest point was lower than the aeroplane carrier's deck. The landing gear didn't quite touch the wavetops, but a flying fish might have leaped into the cockpit. Then the Wright started to gain altitude again, much more slowly than it had shed it.

"That bastard's nuts," somebody said, shaken respect in his voice.

"That bastard's nuts almost got cut off him," somebody else said, which was also true, and made everybody who heard it laugh to boot.

A fellow with bright-colored semaphore paddles strode out near the edge of the deck to guide the aeroplanes in to the controlled crash that constituted a landing aboard ship. His wigwagged signals urged the pilot of the first fighting scout up a little, to starboard, up a little more . . . Sam had learned to read the wigwags, just as he'd picked up Morse as a kid.

Smoke spurted from the solid rubber tires as they slammed against the deck. The hook under the fuselage caught a cable. The aeroplane jerked to a halt. Watching it, Carsten understood why the fighting scouts had needed strengthening before they came aboard the *Remembrance.*

As the pilot took off his goggles and climbed out of the aeroplane, his face bore an enormous grin. What was he thinking? *Lived through it again,* probably. Sailors hauled the two-decker out of the way so the other fighting scout could land.

Here he came, chasing the aeroplane carrier from astern. As before, the semaphore man stepped out and signaled to the approaching flying machine. Sam wondered why he bothered. That fellow had pulled out of his dive without help. If he couldn't land the same way . . .

Up, the man with the paddles signaled, and then *Up* again, more emphatically. The bow of the *Remembrance* slid down into a trough; the stern rose. Sam kept his balance as automatically as he breathed. So did the signalman. He had the paddle raised, urging more altitude, when the aeroplane slammed into the carrier.

The pilot almost got it onto the ship. That made things worse, not better. He still killed himself, and debris from the aeroplane scythed along the deck, cutting down the fellow with the semaphore paddles and half the crew waiting to take the aeroplane to the hydraulic lift and stow it belowdecks.

Sam sprinted forward, dodging blazing fuel and oil like a halfback dodging tacklers in the open field. He skidded to a stop beside a sailor who was down and moaning and clutching his thigh. Blood was soaking his trouser leg and puddling on the deck under him. He couldn't keep losing it that fast for long. Sam unhooked his belt, yanked it off, and doubled it around the man's leg above the wound for a tourniquet.

"It hurts!" the sailor moaned. "Christ, it hurts!"

"Hang on, pal," Sam said. More sailors came running across the deck, some with stretchers. Sam waved to draw their eyes. The sailor might live. As for the pilot . . . His head lay about ten feet away, still wearing goggles. Carsten looked down at the planking. Yeah, flyboys earned the right to be crazy.

XIV

Jake Featherston liked riding the train. When he rode the train, he was getting somewhere. He associated travel on foot with the long, grinding retreat through Pennsylvania and Maryland and Virginia. Then he'd been going where the damnyankees made him go. Now he was—mostly—on his own.

The train rattled through the Mississippi cotton country, bound for New Orleans. Featherston smiled to see Negroes working in the fields. Their hoes rose and fell as they weeded. The red and blue bandannas the women wore added splashes of color to the green, green fields. Jake nodded to himself in his Pullman car. That was where Negroes belonged.

The splendid car was where he belonged. He hadn't known luxury till lately. He figured he was entitled to a little, after so long without. He did wish he weren't going to New Orleans. He brought a fist down on his knee. Even the leader of the Freedom Party couldn't get everything he wanted, not yet.

Amos Mizell of the Tin Hats had strongly urged him to hold the Party's national convention on the banks of the Mississippi, to show it was a party for all the Confederate States. Willy Knight, who headed the Redemption League, said the same thing. Their arguments made sense, especially since Jake wanted to draw the League all the way into the Freedom Party.

He hadn't particularly wanted to hold a convention at all; he knew, and everybody else knew, who the Party's candidate would be. But the notion of having him simply declare his candidacy and point a finger at a running mate had horrified everyone around him. So here he was, on his way to a convention, on his way to New

Orleans. He slammed his fist down again, this time hard enough to make himself jump and curse.

"Well, where the hell else could I go?" he demanded of the empty air around him. If he brought the convention to the Mississippi, New Orleans was the only logical choice. Little Rock was the middle of nowhere. Going to Dallas would have been asking for trouble from Willy Knight, who wanted to run for vice president; the Redemption League was stronger than the Party in Texas. Chihuahua? Featherston laughed without humor. "The greasers down there would love me, wouldn't they?"

And so, to prove the Freedom Party's national appeal, he'd had to bring the convention to the one Confederate city least friendly to him and his message. New Orleans not only had rich niggers with their own high society, it had a whole great raft of white men who didn't care. The latter offended Jake even more than the former.

He felt better when the train pulled into the station. A company of men in white shirts and butternut trousers stood waiting for him on the platform. Some carried Freedom Party flags, others the Confederate battle flag with reversed colors that the Party also used. "Sarge!" they shouted when he left his car. "Sarge! Sarge! Sarge!"

"Good to be here," Jake lied. "Now, on to victory!" The Freedom Party stalwarts cheered lustily. Some of the other people on the platform, New Orleans natives by the look of them, raised eyebrows and curled lips in Gallic disdain at the raucous display. Featherston hardly noticed. He was among his own again—the dispossessed, the rootless, the angry—and so back where he belonged.

When he got to the hotel, he felt as if part of Richmond had been transplanted to this alien soil. He might have been back at Party headquarters, to judge by the deference he got. That from Party members was genuine, that from the hotel staff—both white and black—professionally perfect. *Whores,* he thought. *Nothing but whores.* But, like whores, they made him feel good.

He spotted Roger Kimball across the gorgeously rococo lobby. Kimball spotted him, too, and hurried over. He could have done without that. "Good to see you, Sarge," Kimball said, shaking his hand. "Say, are they going to try those fellows they arrested for burning down Tom Brearley's house?"

Brearley and his wife had burned, too; Jake was wryly amused Kimball hadn't mentioned that. He answered, "Reckon they are, yeah." Lowering his voice, he added, "Don't reckon any jury's gonna convict 'em, though. That's how it looks from here, anyway."

"Bully," Kimball said, and then, "I won't keep you. You've got to get settled in, I reckon." He drifted away. That was a smoother performance than Featherston had looked for from him. Thoughtfully, Jake rubbed his chin. If Kimball could be smooth as well as ferocious, he might end up making himself very valuable indeed.

After unpacking, Jake walked the couple of blocks to the convention hall, a huge marble wedding cake of a building that had gone up on Esplanade, just outside the French Quarter, a few years before the Great War. He was standing on the rostrum, looking out over the great hall, when Amos Mizell walked down the center aisle toward him. Willy Knight came in a couple of minutes later, before Jake and Mizell could do much more than say hello. Featherston was irked, but only a little; both men would have had spies in the hotel, and maybe back at the train station, too.

All the greetings were warier than they would have sounded to anyone who didn't know the men involved. At last, Mizell said, "The Tin Hats will throw their weight behind you, Jake. You're what this country needs this year, no two ways about it."

Suddenly, Featherston was awfully damn glad he'd come to New Orleans. He'd met Mizell halfway, and now the head of the veterans' organization was coming through for him in a big way. Willy Knight looked as if he'd just bitten down hard on the sourest lemon ever picked. He'd been threatening that if Jake didn't tap him for vice president, he'd run for the top spot himself on an independent Redemption League ticket. That would have hurt, and hurt bad, especially in the West. He could still do it. But if the Tin Hats were loudly backing the Freedom Party, his bid would look like nothing but an exercise in spite.

Now, still sour, he asked, "You think you have any real chance of winning, Featherston?"

"Don't know for certain," Jake said easily. "The Party would have a better shot if TR had won up in the USA. Everybody down here hates him just as much as he hates us. Those Red bastards they've got up there now are bending over backwards so far, it's hard to get people riled up at 'em the way they ought to be."

"You ought to count your blessings, Jake," Mizell said. "If Roosevelt had been president of the United States for longer than a couple of days after the news about your fellow down there in South Carolina broke, he'd have had his head on a plate—either that or he'd have blown Richmond to hell and gone."

"Yeah, I was lucky there," Featherston admitted. Knight sent him another hooded glance, as if to say, *If I were a little luckier, I'd be wearing your shoes now.* He was probably right. It did him no good.

"Picked a running mate yet?" Mizell asked, casual as if wondering about what Jake intended to have for supper. Maybe he was just idly curious, the way he sounded. And maybe Jake would flap his arms and fly to the moon, too.

"Yeah," he answered, and let it go at that.

"It isn't me." Knight's voice was flat, uninflected.

"No, Willy, it isn't you." Jake looked him over. "And if you want to raise a stink, go right ahead. You can run your own little outfit, do whatever you want. Would you sooner be a general in a little tinpot army or a colonel in a real one?"

He waited. He didn't know how he'd answer that question himself. Knight glared at him, but finally said, "I'll stick." He didn't add, *Damn you,* not quite. His eyes said it for him.

Jake didn't care. From that moment on, he seemed to hold the world in his hands and turn it as he desired. The convention—the convention he hadn't wanted—went smooth as silk, slick as petroleum jelly. The platform called for ending reparations to the USA, restoring a sound currency, punishing the people who'd botched the war, putting Negroes in their place, and making the Confederate States strong again (by which Jake meant rearming, but he remained too leery of the United States to say so openly). It passed by thunderous voice vote; Jake hoped it would grab lots of headlines.

The next day was his. People made speeches praising him. He'd helped draft some of them. His nomination went forward as smoothly as the Confederate advance on Philadelphia should have gone at the start of the Great War. No one else's name was raised. He became the Freedom Party's choice on the first ballot.

He let it be known he wanted Ferdinand Koenig to run with him. The Freedom Party secretary had backed him when he needed it most, and deserved his reward. That didn't go quite so smoothly as the first two days of the convention had. Willy Knight let his name be placed in nomination, and his followers made fervent speeches about balancing the ticket geographically. Having made their speeches, they sat down—and got steamrollered. Knight sent Jake a note saying he hadn't known they would do it. It might possibly have been true. Jake wouldn't have bet a postage stamp on it.

On the night after the convention nominated Koenig, Featherston stood on the stage at the front of the smoke-filled hall and stared out at the throng of delegates calling his name. The hair at the nape of his neck tried to stand up. Three and a half years before, he'd climbed up on a streetcorner crate to take Anthony Dresser's place because the founder of the Freedom Party wasn't up to speaking to even a couple of dozen people. Thousands waited for Jake's words now. Millions—he hoped—would vote for him come November.

"We're on the way!" he shouted, and the hall erupted in cheers. He held up his hands. Silence fell, instantly and completely. God must have felt this way after He made the heavens and the earth. "We're on the way!" Jake repeated. "The Freedom Party is on the way—we're on the way to Richmond. The Confederate States are on the way—they're on the way back. And the white race is on the way—on the way to settling accounts with the coons who stabbed us in the back and kept us from winning the war. And we should have won the war. You all know that. We should have won the war!"

Not even his upraised hands could keep the Freedom Party delegates from yelling their heads off. He basked in the applause like a rosebush basking in the sun. When he began to speak again, the noise cut off. "The Whigs say vote for them, everything's fine, nothing's wrong, nothing's really changed a bit." Jake's guffaw was coarse as horsehair. "Bet you a million dollars they're wrong." He pulled a $1,000,000 banknote from his pocket, crumpled it up, and threw it away.

Laughter erupted, loud as the cheers had been. Jake went on, "The Rad Libs say everything's fine, and all we need to do is cozy on up to the USA." He looked out at the crowd. "You-all want to cozy on up to the USA?" The roar of *No!* almost knocked him off his feet.

"And the Socialists—*our* Socialists, not the fools in the United States—say everything will be fine, and all we need to do is cozy on up to the niggers." He paused, then asked the question everyone waited for: "You-all want to cozy on up to the niggers?" *No!* wasn't a roar this time, but a fierce and savage howl. Into it, through it, he said, "If we'd have gassed ten or fifteen thousand of those nigger Reds at the start of the war and during the war, how many good clean honest white Confederate soldiers would we have saved? Half a million? A million? Something like that. And the ones who did die, by God, they wouldn't have died for nothing, on account of we'd have won.

"But the dirty cowards in Richmond, the corrupt imbeciles in the War Department, didn't have the nerve to do it. So the niggers rose up, and they dragged us down. But like I said before, we're on the way again. This time, nobody stops us—nobody, do you hear me? Not the Congress. Not the jackasses in the War Department. Not the niggers. Not the USA. Nobody! Nobody stops us now!"

He suddenly realized he was dripping with sweat. He'd got the crowd all hot and sweaty, too. They were on their feet, screaming.

He saw a sea of glittering eyes, a sea of open mouths. He had a hard-on. He didn't just want a woman. He wanted the whole country, and he thought he might have it.

Once upon a time, the town had been called Berlin. Then, when the Great War broke out, the Canadians rechristened it Empire, not wanting it to keep the name of an enemy's capital. Jonathan Moss had flown over it then, as the U.S. Army pounded it to pieces and eventually overran it during the long, hard slog toward Toronto. Now it was Berlin again. And now he was back, a brand-new lawyer with a brand-new shingle, specializing in occupation law.

He had himself a brand-new office, too. The Canadians and British had defended Empire as long as the last man who could shoot still had cartridges for his rifle. By the time the Americans forced their way into the town, hardly one stone remained atop another. The Romans could only have dreamt of visiting such destruction on Carthage. All the buildings that stood in Empire were new ones.

Arthur, Ontario, lay about thirty miles to the north. Jonathan Moss told himself over and over that that wasn't why he'd decided to set up his practice in Berlin. Sometimes he even believed it. After all, he hadn't hopped into his Bucephalus and driven up to Arthur, had he? Of course he hadn't. That meant he didn't have Laura Secord on his mind, didn't it? It did, at least some of the time.

But when days were slow, he had too much time to sit in his brand-new office and think. On days like that, he welcomed visitors not so much for the sake of the business they might bring as for their distraction value.

And so, now, he was happy to set a cigarette in the brass ashtray on his desk and greet the skinny man in the faded, shiny suit of pre-war cut who came through the door and said, "Mr. Moss, is it?"

"That's right." Moss' swivel chair squeaked as he rose from it. He stuck out his hand. "Very pleased to meet you, Mr.—?"

"My name is Smith. John Smith." The skinny man sighed. "Save the question, sir: yes, that really is my name. I can prove it if I have to. There are a lot of Smiths, and my father and his father were both Johns, so . . ." He sighed again. "It's almost as much trouble as being named something like Cyrus Mudpuddle, or I think it must be, anyhow."

"You're likely right, Mr. Smith," said Moss, who'd taken his share of ribbing about his name over the years. "Why don't you sit down, have a smoke if you care to, and tell me what you think I can do for you." He glanced at that shabby suit again. "No fee for the first consultation." Smith was hungrier than he.

"Thank you, sir. You're very kind." Smith sat, then made a show of patting his pockets. "Oh, dear, I seem to have left my cigarettes at home."

"Have one of mine." Moss extended the pack. He'd half expected something like this. He lit a match for Smith, wondering whether he'd ever see any money from the man if he undertook to represent him. After the Canadian had taken a couple of drags, Moss repeated, "What can I do for you?"

For a moment, he didn't know if he'd get an answer. John Smith seemed entranced with pleasure at the tobacco smoke. Moss wondered how long he'd gone without. After a few seconds, though, Smith seemed to recall he hadn't come into the office just to cadge a smoke. He said, "I wish your assistance, sir, in helping me regain a piece of property taken from me without good reason."

"Very well." A lot of Moss' business was of that sort. He slid a pad toward himself and took a fountain pen from the middle drawer of his desk. "First, the basics: did you serve in the Canadian Army during the Great War?"

"No, sir," Smith said. "I am badly ruptured, I'm afraid, and was not fit for duty. I have a doctor's certificate."

"Good enough." Moss scribbled a note. "Next obvious question: have you taken the oath of loyalty to the occupation authorities?"

"Yes, I did that—did it not long after the war ended, as soon as I had the chance," Smith answered. "I am a peaceable man. I would not tell you a falsehood and say I am glad your country won the war—you *are* an American, I take it?" He waited for Moss to nod, then went on, "Because I am a peaceable man, all I can do is make the best of things as I find them."

"That's sensible, Mr. Smith." Moss noted he'd taken the oath. "All right. I may be able to help you. If you'd answered *no* to either of those questions, I couldn't possibly, and neither could any lawyer. Some would take your money and tell you they could work miracles, but they'd be lying. I make no promises yet, you understand, but you do meet the minimum criteria for pursuing a claim. Now—what piece of property are we talking about?"

Smith coughed apologetically. "This one, sir."

"What?" Moss stared.

"This one, sir." John Smith looked even more embarrassed.

"Before the war, sir, my house stood right about"—he pronounced it *aboat*, as a Canadian would—"here, instead of this fine big building where you have your office."

"You want me to help you make me move out of my office?" Moss had judged Smith a man without any nerve. Now he revised his opinion. If that wasn't gall, Julius Caesar had never seen any.

With or without nerve, Smith remained a quiet, apologetic fellow. "It's not so much that I want to, sir," he said, "but this property was—is—almost the only thing I own. I've not had an easy time of it since . . . since the war." Maybe he'd been on the point of saying something on the order of, *Since you Yankee robbers came up here.* But maybe not, too. Maybe he'd just stumbled over a word. He seemed the type to do a good deal of that.

Jonathan Moss started to laugh. He quickly held up a hand. "I'm not laughing at you, Mr. Smith—really, I'm not," he said. "But this is absurd, and I don't think you can argue with me there."

"I wouldn't think of it," Smith said, and Moss believed him. The Canadian got to his feet. "I am sorry to have troubled you."

"Don't go away!" Moss sprang to his feet, too, quick as if he'd been turning his fighting scout onto the tail of a Sopwith Pup. "I didn't say I wouldn't take your case. Let me see your documents, Mr. Smith, and I'll see what I can do for you."

"Really?" John Smith's hangdog expression vanished, to be replaced by astonishment. "But you work here!"

"It's not like I own the building." Moss corrected himself: "It's not like I *think* I own the building." He wondered what he would have done in his landlord's shoes. Probably thrown Smith out so hard he bounced. But the Canuck could always have found another lawyer. Plenty of eager young hotshots had come up from the United States, and some Canadians were also jumping into occupation law.

"I—I don't know what to say," Smith told him. "Thank you very much, sir." He coughed and looked embarrassed again. "I'm also afraid I'll have some trouble paying you."

One look at his suit had warned Moss that was likely. The way Smith had "forgotten" his cigarettes warned him it was as near certain as made no difference. He shrugged. "What the hell, Mr. Smith," he said—not proper legal language, but at the moment he didn't care. "We'll see what you can afford. If you can't afford much, I'll do it for a lark. I want to see the look on my landlord's face when I serve him the papers."

"Oh, that's good. That's very good." For a moment, Smith, who had to be close to fifty, looked about fifteen. "What they call a practical joke, isn't it?"

"Isn't it just?" Moss leaned forward in his chair. "Now—let's find out exactly how practical a joke it is. Show me these documents."

"I haven't got everything with me, I'm afraid," Smith said. Moss exhaled through his nose. He hadn't been practicing long, but he'd already seen that unprepared clients were the bane of an attorney's life. Blushing, Smith went on, "I left most of the papers I still have back at my flat, because I didn't really believe you'd be interested in helping me."

"Show me what you've—" Moss stopped. "The papers you still have?" he asked sharply. "What happened to the ones you used to have?"

John Smith showed a touch of temper for the first time. "What do you think happened to them?" he snapped. "You Yanks, that's what. I stayed in Empire—in Berlin—till the shells started falling. When I got out, it was with the clothes on my back and one carpetbag. You try stuffing your whole life in one carpetbag, sir, and see how well you do."

Before coming to Berlin, Moss hadn't thought much about how civilians on the losing side felt about the war. He was getting an education in quiet bitterness. "All right," he said. "What have you got?"

Smith reached into his breast pocket and pulled out the two documents he'd already mentioned. He'd have needed the doctor's certificate as he fled the advancing Americans. Without it, the Canadians would have stuck a rifle in his hands and sent him to the trenches, rupture or no rupture. They might have done that anyhow, but he had the paper that said they wouldn't have. He also had the paper that said he'd made his formal peace with the U.S. occupiers. No Canadian could work without that one.

And he had a photograph of himself—a younger version of himself—standing in front of a clapboard house that bore the same address as this big brick office building. A plain woman in a black dress and a frumpy hat stood beside him. "Your wife?" Moss asked.

"That's right." Smith paused, then went on, "Some Yank pilot shot us up as we were leaving—shot up the road, I mean, for the sport of it. He killed my Jane and left me without a scratch—and ever since, I've wished it had been the other way round."

Moss didn't know what to say to that. He'd shot up refugee columns. It was part of war: it disrupted the enemy. He hadn't thought much about the consequences of what he did. He resolutely tried not to think about those consequences now.

"Besides this photograph," he managed at last, "what sort of title can you show to this property? Have you got a deed? Have you got bank records?"

"Haven't got a deed," Smith said. "Used to be bank records—in the bank. Isn't any bank any more. I hear tell Yank soldiers blew the vault open and stole everything inside—everything they wanted, anyway."

That wouldn't have surprised Moss. Among other things, armies were enormous robber bands. He said, "You do understand, lacking the proper papers will make your claim much harder to establish."

"I should hope I understand that," John Smith said. "If I'd reckoned it would be easy, I'd have tried it myself."

"All right," Moss said. "Go through your effects. Whatever you can bring that's evidence you own this land, I want to see it. No matter how unlikely you think it is, I want to see it. If you know people who can testify they know you owned this land, I want to hear from them. I won't kid you, though. We've got our work cut out for us."

"I'll do my best," Smith promised.

When Lucien Galtier saw the green-gray motorcar coming down the road from Rivière-du-Loup toward his farmhouse, he took it for granted at first. He had seen an infinitude of green-gray motorcars and trucks coming down that road, and another infinitude going up it.

Then, after he'd already started turning away, he spun back and stared at the Ford with eyes that wanted to narrow in suspicion and widen in surprise at the same time. He had not seen a green-gray motorcar in some time. The U.S. Army painted its motorcars that color. But the U.S. Army had not occupied the Republic of Quebec since the end of the war—well, since a little after the end of the war.

The Ford pulled off the road and parked beside the farmhouse, as Leonard O'Doull's automobile more commonly did these days. Lucien sighed and walked toward it. "I might have known," he muttered under his breath. "A man may think he has escaped troubles, but troubles never escape a man."

Two men got out of the motorcar. Galtier recognized Bishop Pascal first, more by his vestments than by his own tubby form. His companion, the driver, was whipcord lean and, sure enough, wore a U.S. Army uniform. Seeing Lucien approach, he waved. *"Bonjour!"* he called in excellent Parisian French. "It is good to see you once more, M. Galtier."

"Bonjour . . ." As Galtier drew near, he saw that Jedediah Quigley wore eagles on his shoulders, not oak leaves of either gold or silver. He'd been a major when Galtier first made his acquaintance. Now— *"Bonjour,* Colonel Quigley. You have come up in the world since I saw you last."

"He is the military liaison officer between the United States and the Republic of Quebec," Bishop Pascal said. Hearing the bishop speak ahead of Colonel Quigley surprised Lucien not at all; Pascal had always found the sound of his own voice sweeter and more intoxicating than communion wine.

"An important man indeed," Galtier said. "And how and why does a simple farmer deserve a visit from not only the military liaison officer between the United States and the Republic of Quebec but also the illustrious and holy bishop of Rivière-du-Loup?"

Bishop Pascal had no ear for irony. Colonel Quigley did. One of his eyebrows quirked upward. "It is a matter concerning the hospital," he said.

"What about the hospital?" Galtier demanded, suddenly apprehensive. He saw Marie peering out the kitchen window, no doubt wondering what was going on. He'd been about to ask Quigley and Bishop Pascal to come into the farmhouse so she could serve them tea—or something stronger—and some of the cinnamon buns she'd baked the day before. Now, he was not nearly so sure they were welcome in his house.

"The hospital, of course, is built on land taken from your patrimony," Bishop Pascal said. The plump bishop always looked out for himself first. He had embraced the Americans with indecent haste. Galtier would not have cared to turn his back on him for an instant. But he did understand the way a Quebecois farmer's mind worked.

Colonel Quigley, despite having been in Quebec since 1914, didn't. "And we've been paying you a good rent for it, too," he said gruffly.

"It is my land," Galtier replied with dignity. "And"—his own eyebrow rose—"for some long stretch of time, you paid not a cent of rent. You simply took it, because you had men with guns."

"We suspected your loyalty." Quigley was blunt in a way no Quebecois would have been. "Once we didn't any more, we paid what we owed you."

"If you steal land from a man's patrimony, you are liable to make him disloyal," Galtier said. "Indeed, you are fortunate this did not happen with me." He still marveled that it hadn't. He'd been disloyal after the Americans invaded Quebec. He clearly remembered that. But Nicole had gone to work at the hospital, she and Leonard O'Doull had fallen in love, Quigley had agreed to pay rent, and the Americans had not treated him so badly after all. He'd thrived since they came. Quebec had prospered, too. And he had a half-American grandson. Sure enough, he was at peace with Americans now.

Bishop Pascal said, "Naturally, my son, you can comprehend that it is awkward for this fine hospital to rest on land where, if the owner so desires, he may, at a whim, order it to leave so he might seed the soil with lettuces."

"Lettuces?" Galtier said. "Certainly not. That is wheat land, and wheat land of the first quality, I might add."

Jedediah Quigley seemed to need both hands to hold on to his patience. "Whatever you raised on it is beside the point," he said. "The point is, the Republic of Quebec wants to buy that land from you, so no troubles of the sort Bishop Pascal is talking about can arise. I'm involved here because I am the one who took that land from you in the first place."

"You wish me to *sell* part of my patrimony?" Galtier knew he sounded as if Colonel Quigley had asked him to sell one of his children. He didn't care. That was how he felt—even if, at times, he wouldn't have minded getting rid of Georges.

"Money can be part of your patrimony, too," Quigley said, which only proved he did not completely understand the folk of Quebec.

"It would be an act of Christian charity, for the sake of the people of Rivière-du-Loup and the surrounding countryside," Bishop Pascal said. "And, unlike most acts of charity, my son, it would not only be good for your soul but would bring money into your pocket rather than having it flow out."

"And not just money," Colonel Quigley added. "You know the hospital makes its own electricity. As part of the bargain, we would have the hospital make electricity for this farm as well."

They were eager to make a deal. They were showing how eager they were. Against a canny peasant like Lucien Galtier, they were begging to be skinned. He knew now, he would sell the land. Marie would skin him if he let the chance to get electricity escape. But he intended to make the bishop and the colonel sweat first. "It is my patrimony," he growled. "One day, my grandson's grandson will grow wheat on that land."

Colonel Quigley rolled his eyes. "Damn stubborn frog," he muttered under his breath in English. Galtier smiled. He didn't think he was supposed to hear, or to understand if he did. *Too bad,* he thought. He *was* a damn stubborn frog, and they would have to make the best of it.

"My son, have you not seen in these past few years how things can change, and change unexpectedly and quickly?" Bishop Pascal asked. "Would you not like to see this change be for the better?"

"By better, your Grace, you mean doing as you wish." Galtier did not want to lose the chance he had here. Gruffly, grudgingly, he said, "Very well. Let us speak of this further, since you insist. Come inside. We may as well sit down."

When he brought them into the farmhouse, Marie fussed over them, as he'd known she would. Once she had them settled with tea and buns, she asked, "How is it that we have such distinguished visitors?"

Before either visitor could speak, Lucien kept right on growling: "They seek to purchase some of our patrimony. Along with money, they even offer electricity." He curled his lip, as if to show how little he cared for electricity. "They do not comprehend the importance of a man's patrimony."

"Mme. Galtier, I am sure you can make your husband see reason here," Colonel Quigley said.

"I leave these matters to him. He is the man, after all," Marie said primly. A single flashing glance toward Galtier sent quite another message, but neither Quigley nor Bishop Pascal saw it. After that glance, Marie retreated to the kitchen.

In tones of gentle reason, Bishop Pascal said, "You have not even inquired what the Republic and the United States—we will share the expense, our two countries—might pay for your parcel of land."

"You haven't said what you want for it, either," Quigley said.

"I have not said I would take any amount of money for it," Galtier replied. "But, if you must, you may name a price." Quigley had invited him to set his own price when he'd started getting rent for the land on which the hospital stood. He'd named the highest price he dared, and Quigley had paid without a blink. Lucien knew he could have gone higher, but not how much. This time . . . If Quigley mentioned any sum less than five hundred dollars, maybe he really wouldn't sell the piece of property.

"The United States are prepared to pay you one thousand dollars for that tract, M. Galtier," Colonel Quigley said.

"And the Republic of Quebec will add one thousand dollars to that sum," Bishop Pascal put in.

Galtier's ears rang. Two thousand dollars? And electricity? "You are not serious," he said, meaning he could not believe they would pay so much.

Thanks to his bold front, Bishop Pascal and Quigley thought he meant they weren't offering enough. The American looked sour, the bishop piously resigned. Colonel Quigley said, "Oh, very well, then. Fifteen hundred from us, another fifteen hundred from the Republic, and not a dime more."

Three thousand dollars? Lucien could buy a motorcar. He could buy a tractor. He would be a man to reckon with for miles around. He smiled at his guests. "Two thousand dollars from the United States, another two from the Republic, and not a dime less."

Colonel Quigley and Bishop Pascal both looked alarmed. Galtier felt alarmed—had he pushed it too far? The bishop and Quigley put their heads together. After a couple of minutes, Bishop Pascal said, "In the interest of concord, we will split the difference with you— one thousand seven hundred and fifty dollars from Quebec and a like amount from the United States. Is it agreeable to you?"

"And electricity?" Galtier demanded.

"And electricity," Colonel Quigley said. "I told you that beforehand."

"It is better to have everything certain than to leave anything in doubt." Galtier sighed with reluctance he did not feel. "Very well. Let it be as you say. For one thousand seven hundred and fifty dollars from each of your governments—and electricity—I will sell this land, but only, mind you, in the interest of concord, as the holy bishop says."

"God will surely bless you, my son," Bishop Pascal said, beaming.

"Do you think so?" Lucien said interestedly. "That would be good, too."

Bishop Pascal didn't know what to make of that. He scratched his head. Colonel Quigley knew exactly what to make of it. He looked even more sour than he had while they were dickering. *Why should he care?* Galtier thought. *It isn't his money.* However sour Quigley looked, the bargain was sealed. The money would be Galtier's—soon, he hoped.

* * *

Edna Semphroch came back into the coffeehouse. Nellie Jacobs gave her daughter an unhappy look, even though midafternoon business was slow. Truth to tell, business had never got back to what it was during the war, when Confederate officers from the force occupying Washington had kept the place hopping morning, noon, and night. Nellie didn't miss the Rebs, not even a little bit, but she did miss their cash.

"Took you long enough, didn't it?" Nellie said sourly. "I reckon I could have looked at every skirt between here and St. Louis in the stretch of time you've been gone. And you didn't even buy anything. Can't you make up your mind?" People who joked about women's indecision had never met Nellie.

"Nope, didn't buy anything," Edna agreed. She eyed her mother with an odd mix of amusement and apprehension. "Didn't even go looking at skirts, as a matter of fact."

Nellie had no fancy education. She was, most ways, shrewd rather than really clever. But when Edna said something like that, her mother didn't need a road map to figure out what she'd say next. "You've been sneaking around behind my back," Nellie said, and could have sounded no more outraged if she'd been reading a philandering husband the riot act.

She would have had an easier time accepting a philandering husband. Men got it where they could. That was part—too large a part, as far as she was concerned—of how they were made. Women, though . . . She'd known for a long time that Edna burned hot. Her daughter had seemed calmer the past couple of years, so Nellie had dared hope she'd got it out of her system. No such luck, evidently.

"I've been trying to have a life, Ma," Edna said. "God knows you don't make it easy for a girl." But the unbearably smug look on her face said she'd had her desire fulfilled—and had something else filled full, too, more than likely.

"You little hussy," Nellie hissed. She wished Clara, who was taking a nap upstairs, would pick that moment to wake up. Otherwise, she'd be locked in a fight with her older daughter of the sort they'd had during the war, the sort they hadn't had since Nellie married Hal Jacobs.

Again, no such luck. Edna tossed her head. "Hussy? Huh! Takes one to know one, I guess." Had Nellie had a knife in her hand, she might have used it. Fortunately, she'd been washing cups and saucers. Edna ignored her furious squawk. Edna seemed inclined to ignore just about everything. She went on, "But none of that matters, anyhow. He asked me to marry him today."

"Did he think about asking you to get an abortion instead?" Wounded, Nellie wanted to hit back any way she could.

Her daughter shook her head. "I ain't in a family way, Ma. And I ought to know, too, I felt so lousy last week." She laughed. "Turned out you were the one who ended up in a family way. I still think that's the funniest thing in the whole wide world."

If she'd had to find out for sure she wasn't pregnant, she'd been doing things that left doubt in her mind. "At least I was married," Nellie said.

"And I'm going to be," Edna said. "Whether you like it or not, I'm going to be. I ain't getting any younger, you know. I'm sick and tired of you watching me the way Teddy Roosevelt watched the damn Rebs."

Edna *wasn't* getting any younger, Nellie realized. She was closer to thirty than twenty, as Nellie was closer to fifty than forty. Even better than three years of marriage to Hal Jacobs hadn't come close to making Nellie understand why a woman would marry for the sake of bedroom pleasures; for her, bedroom pleasures were at most rare accidents that brought as much embarrassment as release. But Edna wasn't like that, however much Nellie wished her daughter were.

"Who is this fellow?" After Nellie asked the question, she realized it should have been the first one out of her mouth.

Her daughter seemed surprised she'd asked it at all. In less snippy tones than she'd been using, Edna answered, "His name is Grimes, Ma, Merle Grimes. He's right my age, and he's a clerk for the Reconstruction Authority."

"If he's right your age, how come he hasn't got a wife already?" Nellie asked, wondering if in fact he had one Edna didn't know about.

But Edna said, "He had one, but she died of the Spanish influenza a couple-three years ago. He showed me a snapshot once. I asked him to. She looked a little like me, I think, only her hair was darker."

That took some of the wind out of Nellie's sails. When she asked "What did you tell him about Lieutenant Kincaid?" she didn't sound mean at all.

"I've told him I was engaged during the war, but my fiancé got killed," Edna said. "I didn't tell Merle he was a Reb, and I'll thank you not to, neither."

"All right," Nellie said, and Edna looked surprised. Nellie guessed Merle Grimes would eventually find out, and there would be trouble on account of it. Too many people knew about the late

Nicholas H. Kincaid for the secret to keep. His death at what would have been Edna's wedding had even made the newspapers, though a clerk for the U.S. government wouldn't have been in Washington then.

Bill Reach and me, we can keep a secret, Nellie thought. *If anybody else knew* . . . But no one else did, not Edna, not Hal, no one. No one ever would.

"He's a nice man, Ma," Edna said. "He's a *good* man. You'll like him when you meet him, swear to God you will."

If he was such a nice man, if he was such a good man, what was he doing sticking it into Edna before he put a ring on her finger? Nellie started to ask that very question, but caught herself. For one thing, it would make Edna mad. For another, this Grimes had offered to put a ring on her finger. Nellie found a different question to ask: "How did you meet him?"

Edna giggled. "The first couple times were right here in the coffeehouse. I don't reckon you'd recall him"—which was certainly true—"but he was here, all right. He doesn't live too far away. We ran into each other at the greengrocer's one time, and then again a week later. After that, one thing sort of led to another."

I'll bet it did, Nellie thought. But, regardless of whether she thought Edna was a fool, she couldn't deny Edna was also a grown woman. "All right," Nellie said again. "If he wants to marry you, if you want to marry him, the only thing I can say is, I hope you don't end up sorry on account of it."

"I don't think we will, Ma," Edna said. A few years before, she'd been unshakably certain she and Confederate Lieutenant Kincaid would live happily ever after. Maybe she really was growing up as well as grown—even if she did have more trouble keeping her legs together than she should have. Edna was thinking about such things, too, but in a different way, for she asked, "Wouldn't you like to have a little grandbaby?"

"With Clara around, it feels like I've already got one," Nellie said. "If you had a baby, the biggest difference would be that I wouldn't have to keep an eye on the kid every single second of the day and night. I hope you'll be happy, Edna. I wish you didn't think you had to sneak around to meet somebody, and to see him."

Edna didn't answer that, which was probably just as well. Nellie had done everything but shove her daughter into a chastity belt to keep her from meeting and seeing anybody. Nellie had been sure—was still sure—she'd done the right thing, but Edna'd finally managed to get around her. Now she had to make the best of it.

Her husband was very little help. "High time she gets married, if that is what she wants," Hal said. "If she is unhappy afterwards, she will have no one to blame but herself. But I hope and pray she will not be unhappy."

"So do I," Nellie said. "If she is, though, I bet she blames me."

"We will see what we will see when we meet the young man," Hal said. "He may turn out to be very nice." Nellie was inclined to doubt that on general principles—hardly any young men, in her estimation, were very nice—and on specifics—had this Merle Grimes been very nice, he wouldn't have yanked Edna's drawers down till after they were married, and not too often then, either. By that standard, Hal Jacobs was very nice.

After Edna's announcement, Nellie didn't want to let her leave the coffeehouse for any reason whatever. With Edna a woman grown, that wasn't easy. It was, in fact, impossible. And one day, about a week after Edna's bombshell, she did go out. When she came back, she came back arm in arm with a man. "Ma," she said proudly, "this here's my intended. Merle, this is my mother. She's Nellie Jacobs now; like I told you, my pa's been dead a long time."

"I'm very pleased to meet you at last, Mrs. Jacobs," Grimes said.

"Pleased to meet you, too," Nellie said grudgingly. She'd intended to limit herself to a simple *hello*. But Grimes wasn't what she'd expected. For one thing, he walked with a cane, and wore the ribbon for the Purple Heart in a buttonhole. For another, he didn't look like a practiced seducer. He seemed serious and quiet; his long, rather horsy face and gold-framed spectacles might have belonged to a lawyer, not a clerk.

Nellie knew that didn't necessarily prove anything. Some of the men she recalled from her own sordid past had seemed ordinary enough on the outside. But she didn't hate Grimes on sight, as she'd thought she would.

He said, "I think I'm the luckiest man in the world. Edna may have told you, ma'am, I lost my wife to the influenza. I never thought I'd fall in love with another woman again till I met your daughter. She showed me I was wrong, and I'm ever so glad she did."

Edna looked as if she would have lain down on the floor for him then and there if Nellie hadn't been in the coffeehouse. Nellie did her best to hide her disgust. Grimes *had* asked Edna to marry him. He hadn't got her in a family way, either, as Edna's father had before he married Nellie.

"Where are your people from, Mr. Grimes?" Nellie asked. "What do they do?"

"I was born in New Rumley, Ohio, Mrs. Jacobs," Grimes answered, "the same town that saw the birth of the great General Custer. My father runs the weekly newspaper there: the *New Rumley Courier*. His father ran it before him; I reckon my brother Caleb'll take it on when the time comes."

"Why aren't you still back there yourself?" What Nellie meant was, *If you were still back there, you wouldn't be rumpling my daughter's clothes.*

Merle Grimes could hardly have missed that, but it didn't faze him. He said, "I wanted steady work. The newspaper business is a lot of things, but it's not steady. You go to work for the U.S. government, you know you've got a paycheck for the rest of your days. I won't get rich, but I won't go hungry, either."

Nellie didn't know what sort of answer she'd thought she would get, but that wasn't it. "You seem a steady enough young fellow," she said, an admission she hadn't looked to make.

"I try to be," Grimes said—steadily.

"Isn't he the bulliest thing in the whole wide world, Ma?" Edna said.

She was thinking with her cunt, a phrase that hadn't come to Nellie's mind since her days in the demimonde. But Merle Grimes did look to be a much better bargain than Nellie had expected. "He may do," she said. "He just may do."

Engine roaring, the barrel bounded across the Kansas prairie north of Fort Leavenworth. Colonel Irving Morrell stood head and shoulders out of the turret, so he could take in as much of the battlefield as possible. The test model easily outran and outmaneuvered the Great War machines against which it was pitted.

Morrell ducked down into the turret and bawled a command to the driver in the forward compartment: "Halt!" And the driver halted, and it was not divine intervention. With the engine separated from the barrel's crew by a steel bulkhead, a man could hear a shouted order. In a Great War barrel, one man could not hear another who was screaming into his ear.

At Morrell's order, the gunner traversed the turret till the cannon bore on the barrel he had chosen. The old-style machines were trying to bring their guns to bear on him, too, but they had to point themselves in the right direction, a far slower and clumsier process than turning the turret.

"Fire!" Morrell yelled. The turret-mounted cannon roared. A shell casing leaped from the breech as flame spurted from the muzzle. It was only a training round, with no projectile, but it made almost as much noise as the real thing, and getting used to the hellish racket of the battlefield was not the least important part of training. The loader passed a new shell to the gunner, who slammed it home.

An umpire raised a red flag and ordered the barrel at which Morrell had fired out of the exercise. Morrell laughed. This was the fifth or sixth lumbering brute to which he'd put paid this afternoon. The Great War barrels hadn't come close to hurting him. Had it been a prizefight, the referee would have stopped it.

But, in the ring or on the battlefield, he who stood still asked to get tagged. Morrell ducked down again and shouted, "Go! Go hard! Let's see how many of them we can wreck before they make us call it a day."

He laughed. This was as close to real combat as he could come. He might have enjoyed going up to Canada with a few companies of barrels, but he knew General Custer didn't really need his services. The Canucks had been pretty quiet lately. The Confederate States were still licking their wounds, too. So he would pretend, as he'd pretended before the Great War, and have a dandy time doing it, too.

The barrel up ahead had the name PEACHES painted on its armored flanks. That made Morrell laugh, too. Since the earliest days of barrels, men had named them for girlfriends and wives and other pretty women. Peaches belonged to Lieutenant Jenkins; Morrell could see him standing up in the cupola. He saw Morrell, too, and sent him a gesture no junior officer should ever have aimed at his superior. Morrell laughed again.

Jenkins tried to keep him off by opening up with his rear and starboard machine guns. They fired blanks, too. Not only was that cheaper, but live ammunition would have torn through the thin steel of the test model's superstructure. This time, Morrell's chuckle had a predatory ring. It wouldn't do Jenkins any good. This machine was assumed to be armored against such nuisances.

But an umpire raised a flag and pointed at Morrell. Morrell started to shout a hot protest—sometimes the umpires forgot they were supposed to pretend his barrel was properly armored. But then he realized the officer was pointing not at the barrel but at himself. He could not argue about that. His own body was vulnerable to machine-gun fire, even if that of the barrel was supposed not to be.

It was, in fact, a nice test of his crew. He bent down into the turret one last time. "I'm dead," he said. "You're on your own. I'll try not to bleed on you." He started to tell them to nail Jenkins' barrel, but decided he'd used up enough "dying" words already.

The men made him proud. His gunner, a broad-shouldered sergeant named Michael Pound, said, "If you're dead, sir, get the hell out of the way so I can see what I'm doing." As soon as Morrell moved, Pound peered out of the turret and then started giving orders with authority a general might have envied. They were good orders, too, sensible orders. Maybe he couldn't have commanded an entire brigade of barrels, but he sounded as if he could.

And he went straight after the barrel that had "killed" his commander. Morrell knew he couldn't have done a better job himself. In short order, Pound shelled Jenkins' machine from the side: fire to which its main armament could not respond. An umpire soon had to raise a flag signaling the Great War barrel destroyed.

"Bully!" Morrell shouted, and smacked Pound on his broad back. "How did you learn to command so well?"

"Sir, I've been listening to you all along," his gunner answered, "and keeping an eye on you, too. I copied what you'd do and what you'd say."

"At least you didn't copy my accent," Morrell said. Pound laughed. His voice had a northern twang to it that made him sound almost like a Canadian. Morrell went on, "It's still your barrel, Sergeant. What are you going to do next?"

Sergeant Pound went barrel hunting as ferociously as Morrell could have wanted. When the umpires finally whistled the exercise to a halt, one of them approached the test model. "Colonel, you were supposed to have been killed," he said in the fussily precise tones that failed to endear umpires to ordinary soldiers.

"Captain, on my word of honor, I did and said nothing at all to fight this barrel after your colleague signaled that I'd been hit," Morrell answered. He climbed out onto the top of the turret, then called down into it: "Sergeant Pound, stand up and take a bow." Pound did stand up. When he saw the captain with the umpire's armband, he came to attention and saluted.

As if doing him a favor he didn't deserve, the captain returned the salute. Then he gave Morrell a fishy stare. "I have a great deal of trouble believing what you just told me, Colonel," he said.

That was the wrong tack to take. "Captain, if you are suggesting that I would lie to you on my word of honor, I have a suggestion for you in return," Morrell said quietly. "If you like, we can meet in some private place and discuss the matter man to man. I am, I assure you, at your service."

U.S. Army officers hadn't dueled since before the War of Secession. Morrell didn't really have pistols at sunrise in mind. But he would have taken a good deal of pleasure in whaling the stuffing out of the officious captain. He let that show, too. As he'd expected, the captain wilted. "Sir, I think you may have misunderstood me," he said, looking as if he wished he could sink into the churned-up prairie.

"I hope I did," Morrell said. "I also hope Sergeant Pound's outstanding achievement will be prominently featured in your reports of the action. He deserves that, and I want to see him get it."

"He shall have it," the umpire said. "You may examine the report as closely as you like." He wasn't altogether a fool, not if he realized Morrell would be reading that report to make sure he kept his promise. He still came too close to being a perfect fool to make Morrell happy.

Pound said, "Thank you very much, sir," as Morrell climbed down into the turret once more.

"Don't thank me," Morrell said. "You're the one who earned it. And now, let's take this beast back to the barn. We keep showing them and showing them that we can run rings around every other barrel in the United States. If that won't make them build more like this one, I don't know what will."

Odds were, nothing would make the Socialists build new, improved barrels. The political fight back in Philadelphia at the moment had to do with old-age pensions, not the War Department. Morrell was convinced he'd have a better chance of living to collect an old-age pension if the Army got better barrels, but he had no friends in high places, not in President Sinclair's administration.

After the barrel returned to the shed that sheltered it from the elements—and at whose expense the quartermasters had grumbled—Morrell climbed out and headed for the Bachelor Officer Quarters. Then he stopped, did a smart about-face, and went off in the other direction. As he went, he shook his head and laughed at himself. He'd been married only a little more than a month, and the habits he'd acquired over several years died hard.

The cottage toward which he did go resembled nothing so much as the company housing that went up around some factories. It was small and square and looked like the ones all around it. It was also the first time Irving Morrell had had more than a room to himself since joining the Army more than half a lifetime before.

Agnes Hill—no, Agnes Morrell; the habit of thinking of her by her former name died hard, too—opened the door when he was still coming up the walk. "How did it go today?" she asked.

He kissed her before waggling his hand and answering, "So-so. We blew a bunch of Great War barrels to smithereens, the way we always do, but I got shot in the middle of the exercise."

To his surprise, Agnes looked stricken. She needed a few seconds to realize what he meant. Even when she did, her laugh came shaky. "An umpire decided you got shot," she said, sounding as if she needed to reassure herself.

Morrell nodded. "That's right. See? No blood." He did a neat pirouette. When he faced Agnes again, she still wasn't smiling. Now he had to pause to figure out why. When he did, he felt stupid, not a feeling he was used to. Her first husband had died in combat; was it any wonder she didn't find cracks about getting shot very funny? Contritely, Morrell said, "I'm sorry, dear. I'm fine. I really am."

"You'd better be." Agnes' voice was fierce. "And now come on. Supper's just about ready. I've got a beef tongue in the pot, the way you like it—with potatoes and onions and carrots."

"You can spend the rest of the night letting out my trousers, the way you feed me," Morrell said. Agnes laughed at that with real amusement. However much Morrell ate—and he was a good trencherman—he remained skinny as a lath.

After supper, Morrell stayed in the kitchen while his wife washed dishes. He enjoyed her company. They chatted while she worked, and then while she read a novel and he waded through reports. And then they went to bed.

Though he'd hardly been a virgin before saying "I do," Morrell's occasional couplings with easy women had not prepared him for the pleasures of the marriage bed. Every time he and his wife made love, it was as if they were getting reacquainted, and at the same time learning things about each other they hadn't known before and might have been a long time finding out any other way. "I love you," he said afterwards, taking his weight on elbows and knees while they lay still joined.

"I love you, too," Agnes answered, raising up a little to kiss him on the cheek. "And I love—this. And I would love you to get off me so I can get up and go to the bathroom, if that's all right."

"I think so," he said. Agnes laughed and poked him in the ribs. When she came back to bed, he was nearly asleep. Agnes laughed again, on a different note. She put on her nightgown and lay down beside him. He heard her breathing slow toward the rhythms of sleep, too. Feeling vaguely triumphant at staying awake long enough to notice that, he drifted off.

Anne Colleton had always fancied that she had a bit of the artist in her. Back before the war, she'd designed and arranged the exhibition of modern art she'd put on at the Marshlands mansion. Everyone had praised the way the exhibit was laid out. Then the world went into the fire, and people stopped caring about modern art.

Now Anne was working with different materials. This Freedom Party rally in Columbia would be one of the biggest in South Carolina. She was bound and determined it would also be the best. She'd done her best to get permission to hold the rally on the grounds of the State House, but her best hadn't been good enough. The governor was a staunch Whig, and not about to yield the seat of government even for a moment to Jake Featherston's upstarts. She'd hoped for better without really expecting it.

Seaboard Park would do well enough. Neither the governor nor the mayor nor the chief of police could ban the rally altogether, though they would have loved to. But the Confederate Constitution guaranteed that citizens might peaceably assemble to petition for redress of grievances. The Freedom Party wasn't always perfectly peaceable, but it came close enough to make refusal to issue a permit a political disaster.

Tom Colleton touched Anne's arm. "Well, Sis, I've got to hand it to you. This is going to be one devil of a bash."

"Nice of you to decide to come up from St. Matthews and watch it," Anne replied coolly. "I didn't expect you to bother."

"It's my country," Tom said. "If you remember, I laid my life on the line for it. I want to see what you and that maniac Featherston have in mind for it."

"He's not a maniac." Anne did her best to hold down the anger in her voice. "I don't deal with maniacs—except the ones I'm related to."

"Heh," her brother said. But then he surprised her by nodding. "I suppose you're right—Featherston's not a maniac. He knows what he wants and he knows how to go after it. You ask me, though, that makes him more dangerous, not less."

Anne wondered and worried about the same thing herself. Even so, she said, "When he does win, whether it's this year or not, he'll set the Confederate States to rights. And he'll remember who helped him get to the top." Tom started to say something. She shook her head. "Can't talk now. The show's about to start."

Gasoline-powered generators came to life. Searchlights began to glow all around Seaboard Park. Their beams shot straight up into the air, making the park seem as if it were surrounded by colonnades of bright, pale light. Anne had come up with that effect herself. She was proud of it. Churches wished they made people feel the awe those glowing shafts inspired.

More electric lights came on inside the park. Tom caught his breath. They showed the whole place packed with people. Most of the crowd consisted of the ordinary working people of Columbia in their overalls and dungarees and cloth caps and straw hats, with a sprinkling of men in black jackets and cravats: doctors and lawyers and businessmen, come to hear what the new man in the land had to say.

At the front, though, near the stage a team of carpenters had spent the day running up, stood neat, military-looking ranks of young men in white shirts and butternut trousers. Many of them wore tin hats. If the Whigs and the Radical Liberals tried imitating Freedom Party tactics and assailing the rally, the protection squads would make them regret it.

The foremost rows of Party stalwarts carried flags—some Confederate banners, some C.S. battle flags with colors reversed, some white banners blazoned with the red word FREEDOM. The tall backdrop for the flag-draped stage was white, too, with FREEDOM spelled out on it in crimson letters twice as tall as a man.

"You don't need to worry about investing money," Tom said. "You could make billions designing sets for minstrel shows and vaudeville tours. Christ, you might make millions even if Confederate dollars were really worth anything."

"Thank you, Tom," Anne Colleton said. She wasn't altogether sure whether he offered praise or blame, but took it for the former. "Look—here comes Featherston." Her own vantage point was off to the right, beyond the edge of the crowd, so she could see farther into the left wing than any of the regular audience. She tensed. "If those spotlight men have fallen asleep on the job, God damn them, they'll never work in this state again."

But they hadn't. As soon as Jake advanced far enough to be visible to the crowd, twin spotlight beams speared him. One of the Freedom Party bigwigs from Columbia rushed to the microphone and cried, "Let's hear it for the next president of the Confederate States, Jaaake *Featherston*!"

"Free-*dom*! Free-*dom*! Free-*dom*!" The rhythmic cry started among the stalwarts in white and butternut. At first, it had to compete with the unorganized cheers and clapping and the scattered boos from the larger crowd behind them. But the stalwarts kept right on, as they'd been trained to do. And, little by little, the rest of the crowd took up the chant, till the very earth of Seaboard Park seemed to cry out: "Free-*dom*! Free-*dom*! Free-*dom*!"

The two-syllable beat thudded through Anne. She'd orchestrated this entire performance. Thanks to her, Jake Featherston stood behind the microphone, his hands raised, soaking up the adulation of the crowd. Knowing what she knew, she should have been immune to what stirred the thousands of fools out there. But, to her own amazement and rather to her dismay, she found she wasn't. She wanted to join the chant, to lose herself in it. The excitement that built in her was hot and fierce, almost sexual.

She fought it down. The farmers and factory hands out there didn't try. They didn't even know they might try. They'd come to be stirred, to be roused. The ceremony had started that work. Jake Featherston would finish it.

He dropped his hands. Instantly, the Freedom Party faithful in white and butternut stopped chanting. The cries of "Freedom!" went on for another few seconds. Then the people in the ordinary part—much the bigger part—of the crowd got the idea, too. A little raggedly, the chant ended.

Jake leaned forward, toward the microphone. Anne discovered she too was leaning forward, toward him. Angrily, she straightened. "God damn him," she muttered under her breath. Tom gave her a curious look. She didn't explain. She didn't want to admit even to herself, let alone to anyone else, that Jake Featherston could get her going like that.

"Columbia," Jake said. "I want you all to know, I'm glad—I'm proud—to set foot in the capital of the first state of the Confederacy." He talked in commonplaces. His voice was harsh, his accent none too pleasing. Somehow, none of that mattered. When he spoke, thousands upon thousands of people hung on his every word. Anne was one of them. She knew she was doing it, but couldn't help herself. Featherston was formidable in a small setting. In front of a crowd, he was much more than merely formidable.

Through cheers, he repeated, "Yes, sir, I'm proud to set foot in the capital of the first state of the Confederacy—because I know South Carolina is going to help me, going to help the Freedom Party, give the Confederate States back to the people who started this country in the first place, the honest, hard-working white men and women who make the CSA go and don't get a dime's worth of credit for it. Y'all remember dimes, right? That'd be a couple million dollars' worth of credit nowadays, I reckon."

The crowd laughed and cheered. "He's full of crap," Tom said. "The people who started this country were planters and lawyers, just about top to bottom. Everybody knows that."

"Everybody who's had a good education knows that," Anne said. "How many of those folks out there do you figure went to college?" Before Tom could answer, she shook her head. "Never mind now. I want to hear what he's going to say."

"Now I know the Whigs are running Wade Hampton V, and I know he's from right here in South Carolina," Featherston went on. "I reckon some of you are thinking of voting for him on account of he's from here. You can do that if you want to, no doubt about it. But I'll tell you something else, friends: I thought this here was an election for president, not for king. His Majesty Wade Hampton the Fifth." He stretched out the name and the number that went with it, then shook his head in well-mimed disbelief. "Good Lord, folks, if we vote him in, we'll be right up there with the Englishmen and George V."

"He *is* good," Tom said grudgingly as the crowd exploded into more laughter. Anne nodded. She was leaning forward again.

"Now, Hampton V means well, I don't doubt it for a minute," Jake said. "The Whigs meant well when Woodrow Wilson got us into the war, too, and they meant well when a War Department full of Thirds and Fourths and Fifths fought it for us, too. And you'd best believe they meant well when they stuck their heads in the sand instead of noticing the niggers were going to stab us in the back. If you like the way the war turned out, if you like paying ten million dollars for breakfast—this week; it'll be more next Wednesday—go right ahead and vote for Wade Hampton V. You'll get six more years of what we've been having.

"Or if you want a real change, you can vote for Mr. Layne. The Radical Liberals'll give you change, all right. I'll be . . . switched if they won't. They'll take us back into United States, is what they'll do. Ainsworth Layne went to Harvard, folks—Harvard! Can you believe it? It's true, believe it or not. And the Rad Libs want him to be president of the *CSA*? I'm sorry, friends, but I've seen enough damnyankees come down on us already. I don't need any home-grown ones, thank you kindly."

That drew more laughter and applause than his attack on Wade

Hampton had done. The Radical Liberals, though neither very radical nor very liberal, had always been weak in hard-line South Carolina. Were Hampton not a native son, Anne would have thought Jake Featherston the likely winner here. Even with things as they were, she thought he had a decent chance to take the state.

Featherston went on, "The Whigs and the Rad Libs both say we have to learn from the war, to take what the Yankees dish out on account of we're not strong enough to do anything else. What I say is, we have to learn from the war, all right. We have to learn that when we hit the United States, we have to hit 'em hard and we have to keep on hitting 'em till they fall down! They've stolen big chunks of what's ours. I give you my word, friends—one fine day, it's going to be ours again!"

The crowd exploded. Anne caught herself shouting at the top of her lungs. She thirsted for revenge against the USA. She glanced over toward her brother. Tom was shouting, too, his fist pumping the air. Whatever he thought of Jake Featherston and the Freedom Party, he wanted vengeance on the United States, too. That yen for revenge brought together people in the CSA who had nothing else in common. With luck, it would bring them together under the Freedom Party banner.

"Free-*dom*! Free-*dom*! Free-*dom*!" The stalwarts began the chant as Jake stepped back from the microphone. It swelled until the whole huge crowd bellowed the word as if it came from a single throat. Anne looked at Tom again. He was shouting it, too. She'd been shouting it till she made a deliberate effort of will and stopped. All of Columbia could hear that furious roar. By the time November came, all of the Confederate States would hear it.

XV

Roger Kimball whistled cheerfully as he tucked his white shirt into a pair of butternut trousers. A lot of Freedom Party leaders didn't care to join in the brawling that had marked the Party's rise. Kimball shrugged. He'd never backed away from a fight, and he'd gone toward a good many. And Ainsworth Layne was speaking in Charleston tonight, or thought he was.

"I need a tin hat," Kimball said, buttoning his fly. A helmet was useless aboard a submersible. It was a handy thing to have with clubs and rocks flying, though.

He picked up his own club and headed for the door. He was about to open it when somebody knocked. He threw it wide. There stood Clarence Potter. The former intelligence officer eyed him with distaste. "If you don't agree with what I have to say, you could simply tell me so," Potter remarked.

"I don't agree with what you have to say," Kimball snapped. "I don't have time to argue about it now, though. Can't be late."

Potter shook his head. "When we first got to know each other, I thought better of you. You were a man who wanted to build up his country, not a ruffian tearing down the fabric of the republic. We used to talk about riding Jake Featherston. Now he rides you—and you're proud of it."

"He doesn't ride me," Roger Kimball said. "We're both going the same way, that's all."

"Toward riot and mayhem." Potter pointed to the stout bludgeon in Kimball's hand. Then he added, "Toward murder, too, maybe."

"Clarence, I had nothing to do with Tom Brearley going up in smoke," Kimball said evenly. "I don't miss him, but I didn't have anything to do with it. Far as I know"—he carefully hadn't asked Featherston any questions—"the Freedom Party had nothing to do with it, either. The jury found those fellows up in Richmond innocent."

"No, the jury found them not guilty, which isn't close to the same thing," Potter answered. "And if the jury had found anything different, how many out of those twelve do you suppose would be breathing today?"

"I don't know anything about that. What I do know is, maybe you'd better not come around here any more." Kimball hefted the club.

Potter had very little give in him. Kimball had seen as much when they first met in a saloon. The club didn't frighten him. "You needn't worry about that," he said. Slowly and deliberately, he turned his back and walked away.

Kimball pulled his watch out of his pocket. Good—he wasn't late yet. He frowned, then set the watch on a table by the door. Some of the Radical Liberals were liable to have clubs, too, and that could be hard on a timepiece.

He passed a policeman on his way to Freedom Party headquarters. The gray-clad cop inspected him. He wondered if the man would give him trouble. But the cop called "Freedom!" and waved him on his way. Kimball raised the club in salute as he hurried along.

Freedom Party stalwarts spilled out onto the sidewalk and into the street around the headquarters. They'd drawn a few policemen on account of that. "Come on, fellows, you don't want to block traffic," one of the policemen said. The men in white and butternut took no special notice of him. Yes, he had a six-shooter, but there were more than a hundred times six of them, combat veterans all, and some no doubt with pistols of their own tucked into pockets or trouser waistbands.

"Form ranks, boys," Kimball called. The Freedom Party men did. They didn't just spill into the street then: they took it over, in a long, sinewy column that put Kimball in mind of the endless close-order drill he'd gone through down at the Naval Academy in Mobile. The comparison was fitting, because the stalwarts—mostly ex-soldiers, with a handful of Navy men—had surely done their fair share of close-order drill, too.

"You can't do that!" a cop exclaimed. "You haven't got a parade permit!"

"We are doing it," Kimball answered. "We're out for a stroll together—isn't that right, boys?" The men in butternut and white howled approval. Kimball waited to see if the policeman would have the nerve to try arresting him. The cop didn't. Grinning, Kimball said, "On to Hampton Park! Forward—march!"

The column moved out, the stalwarts raising a rhythmic cry of "Freedom!" Kimball had all he could do not to break into snickers. Here he was, leading Freedom Party men to attack Radical Liberals in a park named for the family of the Whigs' presidential candidate. If that wasn't funny, what was?

Hampton Park lay in the northwestern part of Charleston, across town from Freedom Party headquarters. The column of stalwarts was ten men wide and a hundred yards long; it snarled traffic to a fare-thee-well. Some automobilists frantically blew their horns at the men who presumed to march past them regardless of rules of the road. More than a few, though, shouted "Freedom!" and waved and cheered.

"What do you aim to do?" a nervous policeman asked Kimball as the stalwarts strode up Ashley toward Hampton Park. By then, a couple of dozen cops were tagging along with the Freedom Party men. Tagging along was all they were doing; they seemed shocked to find themselves such a small, shadowy presence.

In Hampton Park, a couple of searchlights hurled spears of light into the sky. The Rad Libs hadn't adopted the glowing cathedral Anne Colleton had come up with, but they were doing their best to keep pace. Kimball pointed toward the searchlights. "We aim to have a talk with those folks yonder." The cop spluttered and fumed. He knew the Freedom Party aimed to do a hell of a lot more than that. But knowing it and being able to prove it were two different critters.

Ainsworth Layne had provided himself with a microphone, too. His amplified voice boomed out from the park. "—And so I say to you, people of the Confederate States, that with goodwill we can be reconciled to those with whom we have known conflict in the past: with our American brethren in the United States and with the colored men and women in our own country." He sounded earnest and bland.

"Are you listening to that crap, boys?" Roger Kimball asked. "Sounds like treason to me. How about you?" A low rumble of agreement rose from the men marching behind him. He asked another question: "What does this country really need?"

"Freedom!" The thunderous answer put Layne's microphone to shame. The Freedom Party men advanced into the park.

Dark shapes rushed out of the night to meet them. The Radical Liberals had a cry of their own: "Layne and liberty!"

"Freedom!" Kimball shouted, and swung his club. It struck flesh. A Rad Lib howled like a kicked dog. Kimball laughed. If the other side felt like mixing it up, he and his comrades were ready.

Dozens of searchlights marked Freedom Party rallies these days. The Radical Liberals used only a couple. The Radical Liberals incompletely imitated the Freedom Party when it came to assembling a strong-arm force, too. They'd recruited a few dozen bullyboys: enough to blunt the first charge of the men in white and butternut, but nowhere near enough to halt them or drive them back.

"Layne and liberty!" A Radical Liberal swung at Roger Kimball's head. Kimball got his left arm up in time to block the blow, but let out a yip of anguish all the same. He shook the arm. It didn't hurt any worse when he did that, so he supposed the Rad Lib hadn't broken any bones—not from lack of effort, though. Kimball swung his own club. His foe blocked the blow with an ease that bespoke plenty of bayonet practice. But the Radical Liberal couldn't take on two at once. Another Freedom Party man walloped him from behind. He fell with a groan. Kimball kicked him, hard as he could, then ran on. "Freedom!" he cried.

Ainsworth Layne must have caught the commotion at the back of the park. "And now, I see, the forces of unreason seek to disrupt our peaceable assembly," he boomed through the microphone. "They pay no heed to the rights enumerated in the Confederate Constitution, yet they feel they have the right to govern. We must reject their violence, their radicalism, for we—"

"Freedom!" Kimball shouted again. Only a few of the Radical Liberals' muscle boys remained on their feet. Kimball smashed one of them down. Blood ran dark along his club. He guessed he'd fractured a skull or two in the fight. He hoped he had.

"Freedom!" the Party stalwarts roared as they crashed into the rear of the crowd. Some people tried to fight back. Others tried to run. They had a devil of a time doing it, with Layne's partisans so tightly packed together. Men and women started screaming.

"Freedom!" It was not only a war cry for Kimball and his comrades, it was also a password. They did their best to maim anyone who wasn't yelling their slogan.

They had fury on their side. They had discipline on their side, too. As they'd done in the trenches, they supported one another and fought as parts of a force with a common goal. The men in the crowd of Radical Liberals might have been their matches individually, but never got the chance to fight as individuals. The Freedom Party men mobbed them, rolled over them, and plunged deep into the heart of the crowd, aiming straight for the platform from which Ainsworth Layne still sent forth unheeded calls for peace.

Kimball stepped on someone. When she cried out, he realized her sex. He refrained from kicking her while she was down. Thus far his chivalry ran: thus far and no further. Swinging his club, he pressed on toward the platform.

Through the red heat of battle, he wondered what he and the rest of the Freedom Party men ought to do if they actually got there. Pull Layne off it and stomp him to death? A lot of the stalwarts would want to do that. Even with his blood up, Kimball didn't think it would help the Party. Some people would cheer. More would be horrified.

When the shooting started, it sounded like firecrackers on the Fourth of July. Roger Kimball didn't know whether a stalwart or a man in the crowd first pulled out a pistol, aimed it at somebody he didn't like, and squeezed the trigger. No sooner did one gun come out, though, than a dozen or more on each side were barking and spitting furious tongues of fire.

What had been chaos turned to a panicked stampede. All the people in the crowd tried to get away from the Freedom Party men—and from the gunfire—as fast as they could. If they trampled wives, husbands, children . . . then they did, and they'd worry about it later. The only thing they worried about now was escape.

"Let us have peace!" Ainsworth Layne cried, but there was no peace.

Kimball saw a Freedom Party man taking aim at Layne. "No, dammit!" he shouted, and whacked the revolver out of the stalwart's hand with his club. The fellow snarled at him. He snarled back. "We've got to get out of here!" he yelled. "We've done what we came to do, but every cop in Charleston's going to be heading this way now. Time to go home, boys."

He thought the stalwarts might be able to take on the whole Charleston police force and have some chance of winning. He didn't want to find out, though. If the Freedom Party won here, the governor would have to call out the militia. Either the citizen-soldiers would slaughter the stalwarts or they'd mutiny and go over to them, in which case South Carolina would have a revolution on its hands less than a month before the election.

Jake Featherston would kill him if that happened. It was no figure of speech, and Kimball knew as much. "Out!" he yelled again.

"Away! We've done what we came for!" Discipline held. The Freedom Party men began streaming out of Hampton Park. Even they forgot about Ainsworth Layne.

November 8 dawned chilly and drizzly in Richmond. Reggie Bartlett got out of bed half an hour earlier than he usually would have, so he could vote before going to work at Harmon's drugstore. Yawning in spite of the muddy coffee he'd made, he went downstairs and out into the nasty weather. It wasn't raining quite hard enough for an umbrella. He pulled his hat down and his coat collar up and muttered curses every time a raindrop trickled along the back of his neck.

A big Confederate flag flew in front of the house that served as his polling place. A couple of policemen stood in front of the polling place, too. He'd seen cops on election duty before. They'd always looked bored. Not this pair. Each of them had a hand on his pistol. After the riots that had ripped through the CSA in the weeks leading up to election day, Bartlett couldn't blame them.

"Freedom! Freedom!" Four or five men in white shirts and butternut trousers chanted the word over and over again. They held placards with Jake Featherston's name on them, and stood as close to the polling place as the hundred-foot no-electioneering limit allowed. The cops watched them as if they were enemy soldiers.

So did Reggie Bartlett. He carried a snub-nosed .38 revolver in his trouser pocket these days. A jury might have acquitted the Freedom Party goons who'd burned down Tom Brearley's house around him, but Reggie knew—along with the rest of the world—who'd done what, and why. He'd signed his name on the letter that introduced Brearley to Tom Colleton. That presumably meant the Freedom Party knew it. No one had yet tried to do anything to him on account of it. If anyone did try, Reggie was determined he'd regret it.

As he walked past the policemen, they gave him a careful once-over. He nodded to them both and went inside. The voting officials waiting in the parlor all looked like veterans of the War of Secession. Reggie nodded to them, too; the next young voting official he saw would be the first.

They satisfied themselves that he was who he said he was and could vote in that precinct. Then one of them, a fellow with splendid white mustaches and a hook where his left hand should have been, gave Bartlett a ballot and said, "Use any vacant voting booth, sir."

Reggie had to wait a couple of minutes, for none of the booths was open. A lot of men were doing their civic duty before heading for work. At last, a fellow in overalls came out of a booth. He nodded to Bartlett and said "Freedom!" in a friendly way. The voting officials glared at him. So did Reggie. The man didn't even notice.

In the voting booth, Bartlett stared down at the names of the candidates as if they'd lost their meaning. That didn't last long, though. As soon as he saw Featherston's name, he wanted to line through it. *Hampton or Layne?* he wondered. Wade Hampton surely had the better chance against the Freedom Party, but he liked Ainsworth Layne's ideas better.

In the end, he cast defiant ballots for Layne and the rest of the Radical Liberal ticket. If Jake Featherston took Virginia by one vote, he'd feel bad about it. Otherwise, he'd lose no sleep.

He came out of the voting booth and handed his ballot to the old man with the hook. The precinct official folded it and stuffed it into the ballot box. "Mr. Bartlett has voted," he intoned, a response as ingrained and ritualistic as any in church. Secular communion done, Reggie left the polling place and hurried to the drugstore.

"Good morning," Jeremiah Harmon said as he came in. "You vote?" He waited for Reggie to nod, then asked, "Have any trouble?"

"Not really," Reggie answered. "Some of those Freedom Party so-and-so's were making noise outside the polling place, but that's all they were doing. I think the cops out front would have shot them if they'd tried anything worse, and I think they'd have enjoyed doing it, too. How about you?"

"About the same," the druggist said. "I wonder if Featherston's boys aren't shooting themselves in the foot with all these shenanigans, I truly do. If they make everyone but a few fanatics afraid of them, they won't elect anybody, let alone the president of the Confederate States."

"Here's hoping you're right," Bartlett said, and then, "You don't mind my asking, boss, who'd you vote for?"

"Wade Hampton," Harmon answered evenly. "He's about as exciting as watching paint dry—you don't need to tell me that. But if anybody's going to come out on top of Featherston, he's the man to do it. Layne's a lost cause. He's never been the same since that brawl down in South Carolina, and his party hasn't, either." He raised a gray eyebrow. "I suppose you're going to tell me you voted for him."

"I sure did," Reggie said with a wry chuckle. "Why should I worry about lost causes? I live in the Confederate States, don't I?"

"That's funny." Harmon actually laughed a little, which he rarely did. "It'd be even funnier if it weren't so true."

"We'll find out tonight—or tomorrow or the next day, I suppose—just how funny it is," Reggie said. "If Jake Featherston gets elected, the joke's on us."

"And isn't that the sad and sorry truth?" his boss replied. "Whoever wins, though, the work has to get done. What do you say we do it? After all, if we don't make a few million dollars today, we'll have to beg for our suppers."

That would have been funnier if it weren't so true, too. Reggie dusted the shelves with a long-handled feather duster. He put out fresh bottles and boxes and tins to replace the ones customers had bought. He kept track of the prescriptions Harmon compounded, and set them under the counter to await the arrival of the people for whom the druggist made them. When customers came in, he rang up their purchases and made change.

Ringing things up wasn't so easy. The cash register, a sturdy and massive chunk of gilded ironmongery, dated from before the Great War. It was a fancier machine than most of that vintage, and could handle a five-dollar purchase with the push of but one key. Had Reggie had to do all the pushing he needed to ring up something that cost $17,000,000—and a lot of things did this week, give or take a couple of million—he would have been banging that five-dollar key from now till doomsday.

Everyone wanted to talk politics, too. Women couldn't vote, but that didn't stop them from having opinions and being vociferous about them. "Isn't Mr. Featherston the handsomest man you ever saw in your life?" asked a lady buying a tube of cream for her piles.

"No, ma'am," Reggie answered. In the back of the drugstore, Jeremiah Harmon raised his head. He didn't want to lose customers, regardless of Reggie's own politics and opinions. Reggie thought fast. "Handsomest man I ever saw was my father," he told the woman. "Pity I don't take after him."

She laughed. Bartlett's boss relaxed. Reggie felt some small triumph. Even if he'd sugarcoated what he said, he hadn't had to take it back.

He tried to gauge the shape of the election from conversations with customers. That wouldn't prove anything, and he knew it. He kept trying anyhow. From what he saw and heard, Jake Featherston had a lot of support. So did Wade Hampton V. Only a few people admitted to backing Ainsworth Layne and the Radical Liberals. Reggie hadn't expected anything different. He was disappointed just the same.

When six o'clock rolled around, he said, "Boss, I think I'm going to get myself some supper somewhere and then head over to the *Richmond Examiner*. I reckon they'll be posting returns all night long."

"I expect they will," Harmon answered. "While you're there, do try to recall you're supposed to come in to work tomorrow." The druggist's voice was dry; he had a pretty good idea that Reggie was liable to be up late.

Supper was greasy fried chicken and greasier fried potatoes, washed down with coffee that had been perking all day. Reggie's stomach told him in no uncertain terms what it thought of being assaulted in that fashion. He ignored it, shoved a few banknotes with a lot of zeros on them across the counter at the cook, and hurried on down Broad Street to the *Examiner*'s offices, which were only a few blocks from Capitol Square.

Like the *Whig* and the *Sentinel* and the other Richmond papers—like papers across the CSA—the *Examiner* was in the habit of setting up enormous blackboards on election night and changing returns as the telegraph brought in new ones. When Reggie got there, the blackboards remained pristine: the polls were still open throughout the country. Because of that, only a few people stood around in front of the offices. Reggie got an excellent spot. He knew he might have to defend it with elbows as the night wore along, but that was part of the game, too.

A man came up, loudly unhappy that all the saloons were closed on election day. "Bunch of damn foolishness," he said. "Fools we've got running this year, we need to get drunk before we can stand to vote for any of 'em." By his vehemence, he might already have found liquid sustenance somewhere.

At half past seven, a fellow in shirtsleeves and green celluloid visor came out with a sheaf of telegrams in his hand. He started putting numbers from states on the eastern seaboard in their appropriate boxes. Earliest returns showed Hampton ahead in South Carolina and Virginia, Jake Featherston in North Carolina and Florida, and the Radical Liberals—Reggie clapped his hands—in Cuba. The numbers meant hardly more than the blanks they replaced. He was glad to have them anyhow.

More numbers went up as the hour got later. Hardly any of them made the people who awaited them very happy. The *Examiner* leaned toward the Radical Liberals, and it soon became abundantly clear that, whatever else happened, Ainsworth Layne would not be the next president of the Confederate States.

That would have disappointed Reggie more had he thought going in that Layne enjoyed any great chance of winning. The Radical Liberals always did best on the fringes of the Confederacy; they were liable to win Sonora and Chihuahua, too, when results finally trickled out of the mountains and deserts of the far Southwest.

But the real battle would be decided between Texas and Virginia. Returns also came in slowly from the Confederate heartland. They hadn't seemed so slow during the last Congressional election, nor the one before that. Bartlett had been in no position to evaluate how fast the returns for the last presidential election came in, not in November 1915 he hadn't. Back in 1909, he hadn't cared; he hadn't been old enough to vote then.

"Hate to say it, but I'm pulling for Wade Hampton," a man about his own age said not far away. "I've voted Radical Liberal ever since I turned twenty-one, and I'd get into screaming fights with Whigs. But you look around at what the other choice is—" The fellow shivered melodramatically.

"I voted for Layne," Reggie said. "I'm not sorry I did, either. I'm just sorry more people didn't."

Off in the distance, somebody shouted, "Freedom!" But the Freedom Party muscle boys did not wade into the crowd outside the *Examiner* building. They would have paid for any attack they made; Reggie was sure he wasn't the only Radical Liberal packing a revolver in case of trouble from goons.

More and more numbers went up. By midnight or so, they started to blur for Reggie. Strong coffee at supper or not, he couldn't hold his eyes open any more. Things weren't decided, but he headed back toward his flat anyway. He was glad the election remained up in the air. Only when he'd got very close to home did he realize he should have been sorry Jake Featherston hadn't been knocked out five minutes after the polls closed.

Jake Featherston yawned so wide, his jaw cracked like a knuckle. He hadn't been so tired since the battles of the Great War. It was half past four Wednesday morning, and he'd been up since first light Tuesday. He'd voted early, posed for photographers outside the polling place, and then headed here to the Spottswood Hotel at the corner of Eighth and Main to see what he would see. He'd wanted the Ford Hotel, right across the street from Capitol Square, but the Whigs had booked it first.

He looked down at the glass of whiskey in his hand. Yawning again, he realized he might not have felt so battered if he hadn't kept that glass full through the night. He shrugged. Too late to worry about it now. He wasn't in the habit of looking back at things he'd done, anyway.

Somebody knocked on the door to his room. He opened it. As he'd expected, there stood Ferdinand Koenig, his backer when the Freedom Party was tiny and raw, his vice-presidential candidate now that the Party was a power in the land . . . but not quite enough of a power. Koenig held the latest batch of telegrams in his left hand. His face might have been a doctor's coming out of a sickroom just before the end.

"It's over, Jake," he said—like Roger Kimball and only a handful of others, he talked straight no matter how bad the news was. "Our goose is cooked. We won't win it this time."

Featherston noticed he was still holding that whiskey. He gulped it down, then hurled the glass against the wall. Shards sprayed every which way, like fragments from a bursting shell. "Son of a bitch," he snarled. "*Son* of a bitch! I really reckoned we might pull it off."

"We scared 'em," Koenig said. "By God, we scared 'em. You're still outpolling Ainsworth Layne. We took Florida. We took Tennessee. We took Texas. We've got—"

"We've got nothing," Jake said flatly. "God damn it to fucking hell, we've got nothing. During the war, we killed a million Yankees. Didn't do us one damn bit of good. We lost. I didn't want to scare Wade Hampton the goddamn Fifth. I wanted to whip the Whigs out of office like the cur dogs they are."

Koenig stared, then shook his head in rueful admiration. "You never did aim to do anything by halves, did you?"

"Why do you think we are where we're at?" Jake returned. "Anybody who settles for what he reckons is good enough deserves whatever happens to him. I want the whole damn shootin' match. Now I have to wait till 1927 to try again. That's a goddamn long time. What the hell's going to happen to the country from now till then? Christ, we aren't going to hell in a handbasket, we're already there."

"You can come down off the stump for a few minutes, anyway," Ferdinand Koenig said. "The election's over, even if the reporters are waiting downstairs to hear what you've got to say."

"Goddamn vultures," Featherston muttered. *The election's over* meant nothing to him. His life was a seamless whole; he could not have told anyone, himself included, where Jake Featherston the man stopped and Jake Featherston the Freedom Party leader began. He wished he had another glass to shatter. "All right, I'll go down. Maybe they'll all be passed out drunk by then, and I won't have to make a speech after all."

Koenig was still trying to look on the bright side of things: "We picked up four, maybe five seats in Congress, not counting the Redemption League. Florida gave us a Senator; looks like we'll pick up the governor's spot in Tennessee, and maybe in Mississippi, too."

"That's all fine and dandy, but it's not enough, either." Even now, worn and half drunk and sorely disappointed, Jake knew he'd be happier in a few days. The Freedom Party had done very well. It just hadn't done well enough to suit him. He'd have to start building on what it had done, and to start looking ahead to see what it could do for 1923. He made a fist and slammed it into his own thigh several times. The pain was oddly welcome. "The reporters are waiting, eh? Let's go, by Jesus. Let's see how they like it."

Now his running mate looked faintly—no, more than faintly—alarmed. "If you want to get a couple hours' sleep, Jake, those bastards won't care one way or the other. Maybe you should grab the chance to freshen up a touch," Koenig said.

"Hell with it," Featherston replied. "Might as well get it over with." He headed for the stairway. Had Koenig not jumped aside, Jake would have pushed him out of the way.

Down in the lobby of the Spottswood, the victory celebration for which the Freedom Party had hoped was a shambles now. A few young men in white shirts and butternut trousers remained on their feet and alert. They'd been detailed to keep order, and keep order they would. The task was easier than Jake had thought it would be when he assigned it. *Six more years of waiting.* The thought was as bitter as yielding to the damnyankees had been.

More Freedom Party men sprawled snoring on couches and chairs and on the floor, too, some with whiskey bottles close at hand, others simply exhausted. A lot of reporters, by the look of things, were already gone. Watching the Freedom Party lose an election so many thought it might win had been story enough for them. But half a dozen fellows in cheap but snappy suits converged on Jake when he showed himself.

"Do you have a statement, Mr. Featherston?" they cried, as if with a single voice.

"Damn straight I have a statement," Featherston answered.

"Jake—" began Ferdinand Koenig, who had followed him downstairs.

"Don't you worry, Ferd. I'll be fine," Jake said over his shoulder. He turned back to the reporters. "Reckon you boys are waiting for me to say something sweet like how, even though I wish I was the one who'd gotten elected, I'm sure Wade Hampton V will make a fine president and I wish him all the best. That about right? Did I leave anything out?"

A couple of the reporters grinned at him. "Don't reckon so, Sarge," one of them said. "That's what we hear from the Radical Liberals every six years."

"To hell with the Radical Liberals," Featherston said. "And to hell with Wade Hampton V, too." The reporters scribbled. Jake warmed to his theme, despite Koenig's dark mutterings in the background: "To hell with Wade Hampton V, and to hell with the Whig Party. They led us off a cliff in 1914, they don't have the slightest scent of a notion of how to turn things around, and now they've got six more years to prove they don't know what the devil they're doing."

"If they're such a pack of bums, why'd you lose the election?" a reporter called.

"Don't you think you ought to ask, 'How'd you do so well the first time you tried to run anybody for president?' " Jake returned. No matter how he felt in private, in public he put the best face on things he could. "Christ, boys, in 1915 there was no Freedom Party. We didn't elect anybody to Congress till two years ago. And now, our first time out of the gate, we get more votes than the Radical Liberals, and they've been around forever. And what do you ask? 'Why'd you lose?' " He shook his head. "We'll be back. As long as Hampton and the Whigs leave us any kind of country at all, we'll be back. You wait and see."

"You really have it in for Hampton, don't you?" a man from the *Richmond Whig* asked.

Jake bared his teeth in what was not a smile. "You bet I do," he said. "He's part of the crowd that's been running the Confederate States since the War of Secession: all the fancy planters, and their sons, and *their* sons, too. And he's part of the War Department crowd, like Jeb Stuart, Jr., and the other smart folks who helped the damnyankees lick us. When I look at Wade Hampton and the Whigs, I look at 'em over open sights."

He'd let his journal by that name slip when the Freedom Party began to climb; the furious energy that had gone into the writing came out in Party work instead. Now, for the first time in a while, he might have some leisure to put his ideas down in paper. *Have to look back over what I did before,* he thought. *Pick up where I left off.*

"If you don't work with the other parties, why should they work with you?" the reporter from the *Whig* asked.

"We'll work with our friends," Jake said. "I don't have any quarrel with folks who want to see this country strong and free. People who want us weak or who try and sell us to the USA had better steer clear, though, or they'll be sorry."

"Sorry how?" Two men asked the question at the same time. The man from the *Richmond Whig* followed it up: "Sorry the way Tom Brearley's sorry?"

Though half loaded himself, Jake knew a loaded question when he heard one. "I don't know any more about what happened to that Brearley than I read in the papers," he answered. That was true; he'd also made a point of not trying to find out any more. "I do know a jury didn't convict the people the police arrested for burning down his house."

"They were all Freedom Party men." This time, three reporters spoke together.

"They were all acquitted," Jake said. The reporters looked disappointed. Jake smiled to himself. Did they think he was stupid enough to carry ammunition to their guns? Too bad for them if they did. He went on, "A lot of people like the Freedom Party these days—not quite enough to win me the election, but a lot."

"Are you saying you can't be responsible for all the crazy people who follow you?" The fellow from the *Whig* wouldn't give up.

"There's crazy people in every party. Look in the mirror if you don't believe me," Jake replied. "And I'll say it again, on account of you weren't listening: the jury acquitted those fellows from the Freedom Party. I don't know *who* burned Brearley's house, and neither do the cops. No way to tell if it was Freedom Party men or a bunch of riled-up Whigs."

"Not likely," the reporter said.

Privately, Featherston thought he was right. Publicly, the Freedom Party leader shrugged. "Anything else, boys?" he asked. None of the reporters said anything. Jake shrugged again. "All right, then. We didn't win, but we don't surrender, either. And that's about all I've got to say." The newspapermen stood scribbling for a bit, then went off one by one to file their stories.

When the last one was out of earshot, Ferdinand Koenig said, "You handled that real well, Jake."

"Said I would, didn't I?" Jake answered. "Christ, I spent three years under fire. Damn me to hell if I'm going to let some stinking newspapermen rattle me."

"All right," Koenig said. "I was a little worried, and I don't deny it. Hard loss to take, and you are sort of lit up." Again, he told Featherston the truth as he saw it.

"Sort of," Jake allowed. "But hell, you think those fellows with the notebooks are stone cold sober? Not likely! They've been drinking my booze all night long."

Koenig laughed. "That's true, but nobody cares what they say. People do care what you say. What do you say about where we go from here?"

"Same thing I've been saying all along." Jake was surprised the question needed asking. "We go straight ahead, right on down this same road, till we win."

As she did any evening she was at her apartment by herself, Flora Hamburger waited for a knock on the door. All too often, the quiet, discreet knock didn't come. There were times these days—and, especially, these nights—when she felt lonelier than she had when she'd first got to Philadelphia almost five years before. That it was a few days before Christmas only made things worse. The whole city was in a holiday mood, which left her, a Jew, on the outside looking in.

She sat on the sofa, working her way through President Sinclair's proposed budget for the Post Office Department. It was exactly as exciting as it sounded. Did the president really need to revise the definitions for third- and fourth-class post offices? At the moment, she hadn't the faintest idea. Before long, though, the bill would come to a vote. She owed it to her constituents—she owed it to the country—to make her vote as well informed as she could.

Someone knocked on the door: the knock she'd been waiting for, the knock she'd almost given up expecting.

She sprang to her feet. Pages of the Post Office budget flew every which way. Flora noticed, but didn't care. She hurried to the door and threw it open. There stood Hosea Blackford. "Come in," Flora said, and the vice president of the United States did. She closed the door behind him, closed it and locked it.

Blackford kissed her, then said, "You'd better have something to drink in this place, dear, or I'll have to go across the hall and come back."

"I do," Flora said. "Sit down. Wait. I'll be right back." She went into the kitchen, poured him some whiskey, and then poured herself some, too.

"You are a lifesaver," he said, and gulped it down.

Flora sat down beside him. She drank her whiskey more slowly. "You look tired," she said.

To her surprise, Blackford burst into raucous laughter. "God knows why. All I do is sit in a corner and gather dust—excuse me, preside over the Senate. There's not much difference between the two, believe me. I've spent most of my life in the middle of the arena. Now . . . now I'm a $12,000-a-year hatrack, is what I am."

"You knew this would happen when Sinclair picked you," Flora said.

"Of course I did. But there's a difference between knowing and actually having it happen to you." Blackford sighed. "And I wanted it when he picked me. The first Socialist vice president in the history of the United States! I'll go down in history—as a footnote, but I'll go down." His laugh was rueful. Flora thought he'd ask for another whiskey, but he didn't. All he said was, "I feel like I've already gone down in history—very ancient history."

"If you have so little to do, why haven't you stopped by here more often?" Flora's question came out sharper then she'd intended. After she'd said it, though, she was just as well pleased she'd said it as she had.

He raised an eyebrow. "Do you really want me here crying on your shoulder every night? I can't believe that."

"Of course I do!" she exclaimed, honestly astonished. And she'd astonished him—she saw as much. She wondered if they really knew each other at all, despite so much time talking, despite lying down together in her bedroom.

"Well, well," he said, and then again, in slow wonder: "Well, well." He reached out and brushed the backs of his fingers against her cheek. She didn't know whether to pull away or clutch him to her. Deciding she was lonelier than angry took only a moment. She reached for him at the same time as he reached for her.

Later, in the bedroom, she moaned beneath him, enclosed in the circle of his arms, his mouth hot and moist and urgent on her nipple. His hand helped her along as he drove deep into her. Her pleasure was just beginning to slide down from the very peak when he gasped and shuddered and spent himself.

He kissed her again, then got off her and hurried into the bathroom. From behind the door came a plop as he tossed the French letter he'd been wearing into the toilet. He was careful not to leave them in the wastebasket for the maid to find. Usually, that wet plop made her laugh. Tonight, it only reminded her how wary they had to be. She was a mistress, after all, not a wife.

Usually, she managed not to think about that. Tonight, piled onto everything else, it hit her hard, harder than it ever had before. What had she done to her life, not even realizing she was doing it? While Blackford loosed a long stream into the toilet, she rolled over onto her belly and softly began to cry.

"I've been thinking," he said, and punctuated that by flushing. Flora didn't answer. He opened the door, turned out the light, and stood there for a moment while his eyes got used to dimness again— or maybe his ears caught her quiet sobs first. He hurried over to the bed and set a hand on her back. "What on earth is the matter, dear?"

"Nothing!" Flora shrugged the hand away. She tried to stop crying, but discovered she couldn't.

"I've been thinking," Blackford repeated, and then, this time, went on: "I've been thinking we ought to figure out where we're going."

"Where *are* we going?" Flora asked bitterly. "Are we going anywhere?" She didn't want to roll back over. She didn't want to look at him.

"Well, that doesn't just depend on me. That depends on both of us," Blackford said. He waited for Flora to reply. When she didn't, he shrugged; she felt the mattress shake. He spoke again: "We can't very well get married, for instance, unless you want to marry me, too."

Flora's head jerked up. She swiped at her eyes with her arm— she didn't want to see Blackford, or what she could see of him in the near darkness, through a haze of tears. Gulping to try to steady her voice, she said, "Married?"

Hosea Blackford nodded. She both saw and felt him do that. "It seems to be the right thing to do, don't you think?" he said. "Heaven knows we love each other." He waited for Flora again. She knew she had to respond this time, and managed a nod. That seemed to satisfy Blackford, who went on, "All over the world, you know, when people love each other, they do get married."

"But—" The objections that filled Flora's head proved she'd been in Philadelphia, in Congress, the past five years. "If you marry me, Hosea, what will that do to your career?" She didn't just mean, *If you marry me.* She also meant, *If you marry a Jew.*

He understood her. One of the reasons she loved him was that he understood her. With another shrug, he answered, "When you're vice president, you haven't got much of a career to look forward to, anyhow. And I don't think the party will ever nominate me for president—Dakota doesn't carry enough electoral votes to make that worthwhile. So after this term, or after next term at the latest, I'm done."

"In that case, you go back to Dakota and take your old seat back," Flora declared. "Or you could, anyhow. Could you do it with a Jewish wife?"

"I don't know that I particularly want my old seat back. It seems in pretty good hands with Torvald Sveinssen, and he'll have had it for a while by the time I'm not vice president any more," Blackford said. He reached out and put his hand on her bare shoulder. This time, she let it stay. He went on, "All you've done is talk about me. What about you, Flora? How will people in New York City like it if you came home with a gentile husband?"

"I don't think it would bother them too much—the Fourteenth Ward is a solidly Socialist district," she answered. "And you wouldn't be just any gentile husband, you know. You're a good Socialist yourself—and you're the vice president."

"It could be," Blackford said. "I can see how it could be that that would do well enough for your district. But I don't have a lot of family back in Dakota. What will your family think if you go home and tell them you're marrying a gentile?"

Flora rejected the first couple of answers that sprang to mind. Her family might indeed be delighted she was marrying at all, but Hosea didn't have to know that. And her father, an immigrant tailor, might indeed be so awed she was marrying the vice president that he wouldn't say a word even if her fiancé were a Mohammedan—but she doubted that. Abraham Hamburger wasn't so outspoken as either Flora or her brothers and sisters, but he never had any trouble making his opinions known.

And the question Blackford had asked cut close to the one she was asking herself: *how do I feel about marrying a gentile?* Somehow, she'd hardly given that a thought while they were lovers. She wondered why. Because being lovers was impermanent, something she wouldn't have to worry about forever? She didn't think that was the whole answer, but it was surely part.

She ended up answering the question in her own mind, not the one Blackford had asked: "When we have children, I want to raise them as Jews."

"Children?" Blackford started, then laughed wryly. "I'm getting a little long in the tooth to worry about children. But you're not; of course you'll want to have children." Much more to himself than to Flora, he muttered, "I won't be sorry not to wear a sheath any more, that's for sure." After a few seconds' thought, he spoke to her again: "Your faith has a stronger hold on you than mine does on me; I've been a pretty pallid excuse for an Episcopalian for a long time now. If I'm not shooting blanks after all these years, I suppose it's only fair we bring up the children your way."

That was as rational an approach to the irrational business of religion as Flora could imagine. She'd seen in Congress that Blackford approached problems in a commonsense way. She'd seen he did the same in his private life, too, but this was an important proof. She said, "I think my father and mother will get along with you just fine."

"Does that mean you'll marry me, then?"

"I think it does." Flora knew she shouldn't sound surprised at a moment like that, but couldn't help herself.

"Bully!" Blackford said softly. He took her in his arms. She felt his manhood stir a little against her flank, and tried her best to revive him. Her best turned out not to be good enough. He made a joke of it, saying, "See? This is what's liable to happen when you have an old man for a husband." Under that light tone, though, she could tell he was worried.

"It's all right," she said, but it plainly wasn't all right. She cast about for a way to reassure him, and finally found one, even if it meant coming out with the most risqué thing she'd ever said in her life: "Your tongue never gets tired." She was glad the only light came from a single lamp in the front room; he couldn't possibly see her blush.

"Yes, some parts do still work better than others," Blackford said, doing his best not to sound as if he were taking things too seriously. But, however hard saying that had been, Flora was glad she'd done it. She knew she'd eased his mind.

"I didn't really expect—this," she said, and then, "I didn't expect any of this, not when I first came down from New York City. I was green as paint."

"I didn't know what to expect, either, when I met you at the Broad Street station," Blackford answered. "Lord knows I didn't expect this—but then, I didn't expect any of the wonderful things you turned out to be, in Congress or out of it."

Nobody else said things like that about Flora. She didn't know how to take them. "Thank you," she whispered. She said it again, on a slightly different note: "Thank you." The day had been long and boring. The night had been even longer, and lonely. Going to sleep was the most she'd had to look forward to. Now, in the space of an hour, her whole world had changed. That had happened once before, when she was elected to Congress. She looked forward to these changes even more.

Judge Mahlon Pitney slammed down the gavel. He looked every inch a jurist: a spare, erect, handsome gray-haired man in his early sixties, his gray eyes clear and alert. "Here is my verdict in the action *Smith* v. *Heusinger*," he said, with a glance toward the court clerk to make sure that worthy was ready to record the verdict. "It is the decision of this court that title to the property at issue in the above-entitled action does rightfully rest with the plaintiff, John Smith, who has shown right of possession sufficient to satisfy the court."

Letting out a whoop would have been undignified, unprofessional. That very nearly didn't stop Jonathan Moss, who instead reached out and shook hands with his client. John Smith looked more nearly amazed than delighted.

On the other side of the courtroom in Berlin, Ontario, Paul Heusinger stared daggers at Moss. Well he might have: Moss had just shown Judge Pitney he did not have good title to the land on which he'd built his office building—the building in which Moss had his law office. "You're gone," Heusinger mouthed. Moss nodded. He'd known he was gone whichever way the case went. At least he was going out a winner.

John Smith tugged at Moss' sleeve. "Will he appeal?" the mousy little Canadian whispered.

"Can't say for sure now," Moss whispered back. "I'd guess not, though. I think we have a solid case here—and appeals are expensive."

Back in the spectators' seats, a couple of reporters scribbled furiously. They'd been covering the case since it first showed up on the docket; occasional man-bites-dog stories appeared in the *Berlin Bulletin* and, Moss supposed, some other papers as well. He didn't mind—on the contrary. The stories had already brought him three or four clients much more able to pay his usual fees than John Smith was.

But for the reporters, the spectators' gallery was empty. As far as Moss could tell, Heusinger had not a friend in town. Smith probably had had friends here, but those who weren't dead were scattered. The war had been hard on Berlin.

One of the reporters asked, "Now that you have your property back, Mr. Smith, what do you aim to do with it?"

Smith looked amazed all over again. "I don't really know. I haven't really thought about it, because I didn't believe the Yanks would play fair and give it back to me. I don't suppose they would have without Mr. Moss here."

"No, that's not true, and I don't want anyone printing it," Moss said. "Americans respect the law as much as Canadians do. It wasn't a judge who said Mr. Smith has good title to that land. It was the law. And the law would have said the same thing regardless of whether Mr. Smith's attorney came from the United States or Canada."

The reporters took down what he said. If they didn't believe him, they were too businesslike to show it on their faces. John Smith, less disciplined, looked highly dubious. Moss felt dubious himself. One of the things he'd already discovered in his brief practice was that judges were not animate law books in black robes. They were human, sometimes alarmingly so.

After a little more back-and-forth with the reporters, Moss reclaimed his overcoat, hat, and galoshes from the cloakroom. In a pocket of the overcoat were mittens and earmuffs. He put them on before venturing outside. Even so, the cold tore at him. The coat that had been better than good enough for winter in Chicago was just barely good enough for winter in Ontario. He wished for a nosemuff to go with the earmuffs.

He also wished for taller rubber overshoes. As he kicked his way through the new-fallen snow toward his apartment, some of the freezing stuff got over the red-ringed tops of the galoshes and did its best to turn his ankles into icicles. He wished he would have driven his motorcar over to the courthouse. If he had, though, it was only about even money the Bucephalus would have started after sitting so long unprotected in the snow.

The people of Berlin took the weather in stride in a way even Chicagoans didn't. When it stayed this cold this long, people in Chicago complained. Complaining about the weather was as much Chicago's sport as football was America's. People up here simply went about their business. Moss didn't know whether to admire them for that or to conclude they hadn't the brains to grumble.

He hurled coal into the stove when he got into his flat, then stood in front of the black iron monstrosity till he was evenly done on all sides. He didn't have a whole lot of room to stand anywhere in the apartment. Ever since he'd started the action against his landlord, he'd been moving crates of books out of his office, anticipating that Paul Heusinger or his own client would give him the bum's rush.

"Tomorrow," he said, having picked up the habit of talking to himself down in Chicago, "tomorrow I get to find myself some new digs. Then maybe I'll be able to turn around in this place again."

He took some pork chops out of the icebox, dipped them in egg and then in flour, and fried them in a pan on the hot stove. He fried potatoes in another pan at the same time. Practice had made him a halfway decent cook—or maybe he just thought so because he'd got used to eating what he turned out.

He didn't go office hunting the next day, nor the several days after that, either. The blizzard that roared through Berlin kept even the locals off the streets. It was the sort of blizzard that sent Americans running back over the border. Moss didn't think of leaving— not more than a couple of times, anyhow—but he was damn glad he had plenty of coal in the scuttle.

"Have to start burning books if I run out," he said. He had enough books in the flat for . . . He looked around. "Eight or ten years, is my guess."

Despite the dreadful weather, he did get some work done. He'd already seen that the Canadians were good at keeping telegraph and telephone lines up and functioning in the teeth of the worst winter could do. The telephone in his flat rang several times a day. Somehow, the newspapers had gone out, and with them word of his victory for John Smith. Other Canadians with similar problems wanted him to give them a hand, too.

He had just headed for the bathroom to dispose of some used coffee when the telephone jangled yet again. He thought about ignoring it—anyone who really wanted him would call back—but duty defeated his bladder. Stepping over a crate, he went back to the telephone. "Jonathan Moss, attorney at law."

"Hello, Mr. Moss. I called to congratulate you for getting Mr. Smith what belongs to him."

"Thank you, ma'am." He wondered where the woman was calling from. The line had more clicks and pops on it than he would have expected from a call placed inside Berlin, but the storm might have had something to do with that, too. He waited for the woman to say more. When she didn't, he asked, "Can I do anything else for you?"

"I don't think so," she answered. "I've already found out that you aren't what I thought you were during the war. No—you may be what I thought you were, but you're more than that, too."

Moss almost dropped the telephone earpiece. "Laura," he whispered.

He didn't know if Laura Secord would hear him, but she did. "Yes, that's right," she said. "When I found out what you had done, I knew I had to come into Arthur to ring you up and say thank you."

He hadn't stirred out of doors since coming home from winning the case. Did that say she was hardier than he, or just that she was out of her tree? Moss couldn't make up his mind. Whatever else it said, it said she'd very badly wanted to telephone him. "How are you?" he asked.

"Well enough," she said. "As well as I can be with my country occupied. I'd heard you'd set up in Empire"—she would be one not to call it Berlin—"but I didn't know what sort of practice you had, and so I didn't think it right to speak to you. From the way you lent me money, I thought you were a decent man, and I am glad to see you proved me right when you had nothing else on your mind."

"Ah," he said. Then he shrugged. She could hardly have helped knowing what he'd felt about her. He'd gone up to Arthur in weather almost this bad—Christ, had it been three years ago?—to tell her so. And she'd told him to get lost.

He noticed how he thought about that as if it were in the past tense. And, he realized, some of it was. He'd been surprised—hell, he'd been flabbergasted—to have her call, but some of what he'd felt, or thought he'd felt, was missing. That flabbergasted him, too. Where did it go? *Into the place where everything that doesn't work out goes,* he thought.

Now she'd been waiting for him to say something more, and seemed nonplussed when he didn't. "When the weather gets better, maybe you could come up for a picnic, if you care to," she said. "We haven't seen each other in a long time."

Moss didn't know whether to laugh or to weep. Had she said that in 1919, he would have driven his Bucephalus through fire, never mind ice, to go to her side. But it was 1922. He'd got over some of his infatuation without quite noticing he was doing it. While he was doing that, had she grown interested in him? So it seemed.

"I'll see what I can do," he said, which was polite, even friendly sounding, and committed him to nothing.

"All right," Laura Secord said. "I hope to see you. I'd better go now. Good-bye." She hung up. The line went dead.

Slowly, Moss set the earpiece back on its cradle. He stood staring at the telephone for a long moment before his body reminded him of what he'd been about to do before the phone rang. He took care of that, then went into the kitchen, which wasn't so overrun with books and crates as the rest of the apartment. To make up for that, it did contain several bottles of whiskey. He picked one, yanked out the cork, and looked around for a glass.

He didn't see one. "Hell with it," he said, and took a long pull straight from the bottle. He coughed a couple of times, drank again—not so much—and set the bottle down. He started to pick it up once more, but changed his mind. Instead, he shoved in the cork and put it back in the cupboard, where it would be out of sight.

"Laura Secord," he said. "My God." He started to giggle, which was surely the whiskey working. "That telephone call would shut Fred Sandburg up forever all by itself."

He didn't need Fred to tell him he'd been foolish to fall so hard. He'd figured it out all by himself. And now, if he wanted to, he had the chance to make his dreams turn real. To how many men was that given? Of them, how many would have the sense to steer clear?

He laughed out of the side of his mouth. He wasn't nearly sure he would have the sense to steer clear, or even that it was sense. As the snowstorm howling through Berlin attested, picnic weather was a long way away. Now his mind would start coming back to Laura Secord, the way his tongue kept coming back to a chipped front tooth. It hardly seemed fair. Just when he'd thought he was over her at last . . .

He'd known Arthur wasn't that far from Berlin when he started his practice here. He'd figured the John Smith case would draw wide notice. Had he hoped Laura Secord would be one of the people who noticed it? Maybe he had. He shook his head. He knew damn well he had, even if he hadn't admitted it to himself.

She'd been in his mind for five years. Now he was in hers. "What the hell am I going to do?" he muttered. "What the *hell* am I going to do?" His tongue found that chipped tooth again. He got very little work done the rest of the day.

Scipio hardly thought of himself by the name he'd been born with these days. His passbook called him Xerxes. His boss called him Xerxes. His friends called him Xerxes. Most important of all, his wife called him Xerxes. Bathsheba had no idea he'd ever owned another name.

Bathsheba knew very little about his life before he'd come to

Augusta. One day, she asked him point-blank: "Why don't you never come out an' say where you was from and what you was doin' when you was there?"

He wondered how she'd react if he answered her in the accent of an educated white, the accent he'd had to use while serving Anne Colleton at Marshlands. He didn't dare find out. He didn't dare tell her of his days on the plantation, or of the blood-soaked time in the Congaree Socialist Republic that had followed. As long as only he knew, he was safe. If anyone else found out—anyone—he was in trouble.

And so he answered as he usually did: "I done what I done, is all. Never done nothin' much." He tried to soften her with a smile. "You is the best thing I ever done."

It worked—to a degree. Eyes glinting, Bathsheba said, "I bet you done ran away from a wife an' about six children."

Solemnly, Scipio shook his head. "No, ma'am. Done run away from three wives an' fo'teen chilluns."

Bathsheba stared. For a moment, she believed him. Then, when he started to laugh, she stuck out her tongue. "You are the most aggravatin' man in the whole world. Why won't you never give me no straight answers?"

Because if I did, I might end up standing against a wall with a blindfold on my face. I wonder if they would waste a cigarette on a nigger before they shot him. As usual, he heard his thoughts in the educated dialect he'd been made to learn. He sighed. That was a straight answer, but not one he could give Bathsheba. He tried jollying her once more instead. Batting his eyes, he said, "I gots to have some secrets."

His wife snorted and threw her hands in the air. "All right," she said. "All right. I give up. Maybe you done crawled out from under a cabbage leaf, like folks tell the pickaninnies when they're too little to know about screwin'."

"Mebbe so," Scipio said with a chuckle. "My mama never tol' me no different, anyways. Don't matter where I comes from, though. Where I's goin' is what count."

Bathsheba snorted again. "And where you goin'?"

"Right now, sweet thing, I believe I's goin' to bed." Scipio yawned.

In bed, in the darkness, Bathsheba grew serious again. "When the Reds rose up, what did you do then?" She asked the question in a tiny whisper. Unlike so many she'd asked earlier in the evening, she knew that one was dangerous.

But she didn't know how dangerous it was. Scipio answered it seriously without going into much detail: "Same as mos' folks, I reckons. I done my bes' to hide a lot o' the time. When de buckra come with the guns, I make like I was a good nigger for they, an' they don' shoot me. Wish the whole ruction never happen. Do Jesus! I wish the whole ruction never happen." There he told the complete truth. He set a hand on her shoulder. "What you do?" If she was talking about herself, she couldn't ask about him.

He felt her shrug. "Wasn't so much to do here. A couple-three days when folks done rioted and stole whatever they could git away with, but then the white folks brung so many police and sojers into the Terry, nobody dared stick a nose out the door for a while, or they'd shoot it off you."

"Damn foolishness. Nothin' but damn foolishness," Scipio said. "Shouldn't never've riz up. The buckra, they's stronger'n we. I hates it, but I ain't blind. If we makes they hate we, we's sunk."

Bathsheba didn't say anything for a while. Then she spoke two words: "Jake Featherston." She shivered, though the February night was mild.

Scipio took her in his arms, as much to keep himself from being afraid as to make her less so. "Jake Featherston," he echoed quietly. "All the buckra in the Freedom Party hates we. They hates we bad. An' one white man out o' every three, near 'nough, vote fo' Jake Featherston las' year. Six year down de road, he be president o' de Confederate States?"

"Pray to Jesus he ain't," Bathsheba said. Scipio nodded. He'd been able to pray when he was a child; he remembered as much. He wished he still could. Most of the ability had leached out of him during the years he'd served Anne Colleton. The Marxist rhetoric of the Reds with whom he'd associated during the war had taken the rest. Marx's words weren't gospel to him, as they had been to Cassius and Cherry and Island and the rest. Still, the philosopher had some strong arguments on his side.

Outside, rain started tapping against the bedroom window. That was a good sound, one Scipio heard several times a week. He wished he hadn't been thinking about the Red rebellion and the Freedom Party tonight. He couldn't find any other reason why the raindrops sounded like distant machine-gun fire.

"The Freedom Party ever elect themselves a president, what we do?" Bathsheba asked. Maybe she was having trouble praying, too.

"Dunno," Scipio answered. "Maybe we gots to rise up again." That was a forlorn hope, and he knew it. All the reasons he'd spelled out for the failure of the last black revolt would hold in the next one, too. "Maybe we gots to run away instead."

"Where we run to?" his wife asked.

"Ain't got but two choices," Scipio said: "the USA an' Mexico." He laughed, not that he'd said anything funny. "An' the Mexicans don't want we, an' the damnyankees *really* don't want we."

"You know all kinds of things," Bathsheba said. "How come you know so many different kinds of things?"

It wasn't what he'd said, which was a commonplace, but the way he'd said it; he had, sometimes, a manner that brooked no contradiction. Butlers were supposed to be infallible. That he could sound infallible even using the Congaree dialect, a dialect of ignorance if ever there was one, spoke well of his own force of character.

"I knows what's so," he said, "an' I knows what ain't." He slid his hand under the hem of Bathsheba's nightgown, which had ridden up a good deal after she got into bed. His palm glided along the soft cotton of her drawers, heading upwards. "An' I knows what I likes, too."

"What's that?" Bathsheba asked, but her legs drifted apart to make it easier for his hand to reach their joining, so she must have had some idea.

Afterwards, lazy and sated and drifting toward sleep, Scipio realized he'd found the best way to keep her from asking too many questions. He wished he were ten years younger, so he might use it more often. Chuckling at the conceit, he dozed off. Bathsheba was already snoring beside him.

The alarm clock gave them both a rude awakening. Scipio made coffee while Bathsheba cooked breakfast. Erasmus trusted Scipio with the coffeepot, but not with anything more. Scipio occasionally resented that; he could cook, in a rough and ready way. But both Erasmus and Bathsheba were better at it than he was.

When he got to Erasmus' fish market and fry joint, he found the gray-haired proprietor uncharacteristically subdued. Erasmus was never a raucous man; now he seemed to have pulled into himself almost like a turtle pulling its head back into its shell. Not until Scipio pulled out the broom and dustpan for his usual morning sweep-up did his boss speak, and then only to say, "Don't bother."

Scipio blinked. Erasmus had never encouraged him to keep the place tidy, but he'd never told him not to do it, either. "Somethin' troublin' you?" Scipio asked, expecting Erasmus to shake his head or come back with one of the wry gibes that proved him clever despite a lack of education.

But the cook and fish dealer nodded instead. "You might say so. Yeah, you just might say so."

"Kin I do anything to he'p?" Scipio asked. He wondered if his boss had been to a doctor and got bad news.

Now Erasmus shook his head. "Ain't nothin' you can do," he answered, which made Scipio think he'd made a good guess. Erasmus continued, "You might want to start sniffin' around for a new place to work. I be goddamned if I know how much longer I can keep this here place open."

"Do Jesus!" Scipio exclaimed. "Ain't nothin' *a*-tall the doctor kin do?"

"What you say?" Erasmus looked puzzled. Then his face cleared. "I ain't sick, Xerxes. Sick an' tired, oh yes. Sick an' disgusted, oh my yes. But I ain't sick, not like you mean." He hesitated, then added, "Sick o' white folks, is what I is."

"All o' we is sick o' the buckra," Scipio said. "What they do, make you sick this time?"

"After you go home las' night, these four-five white men come in here," Erasmus said. "They tell me they's puttin' a special tax on all the niggers what owns business in the Terry here. Now I know the laws. I got to know the laws, else I find even more trouble'n a nigger's supposed to have. An' I tell these fellers, ain't no such thing as no special tax on nigger businesses."

Scipio had the bad feeling he knew what was coming. He asked, "These here buckra, they Freedom Party men?"

"I don't know yes and I don't know no, not to swear," Erasmus answered. "But I bet they is. One of 'em smile this mean, chilly smile, an' he say, 'There is now.' Any nigger don't pay this tax, bad things gwine happen to where he work. He still don't pay, bad things gwine happen to him. I seen a deal o' men in my day, Xerxes. Don't reckon this here feller was lyin'.."

"What you do?" Scipio said.

Erasmus looked old and beaten. "Can't hardly go to the police, now can I? Nigger complain about white folks, they lock him in jail an' lose the key. Likely tell they beat him up, too, long as he there. Can't hardly pay this here tax, neither. I ain't gettin' rich here. Bastards want to squeeze a million dollars out of every three million I make. That don't leave no money for me, an' it sure as hell don't leave no money to pay no help. You work good, Lord knows. But I don't reckon I can keep you."

"Maybe you kin go to the police," Scipio said slowly. "Freedom Party done lose the election."

"Came too close to winning," Erasmus said, the first time he'd ever said anything like that. "An' besides, you know same as I do, half the police, maybe better'n half, spend their days off yellin' 'Freedom!' loud as they can."

It was true. Every word of it was true. Scipio wished he could deny it. He'd been comfortable for a while, comfortable and happy. As long as he had Bathsheba, he figured he could stay happy. If he lost this job, how long would he need to get comfortable again? He hoped he wouldn't have to find out.

XVI

Abner Dowling went into General Custer's office. The commander of U.S. forces in Canada was scribbling changes on a report Dowling had typed. Some of them, Dowling saw, reversed changes he'd made in an earlier report. Usually, that would have infuriated Custer's adjutant—not that Dowling could do anything about it. Today, though, he felt uncommon sympathy for his vain, irascible superior.

"Sir?" he said. Custer didn't look up. Maybe he didn't hear. Maybe he didn't want to hear. Dowling could hardly have blamed him were that so. But he had to make Custer notice him. "Sir!"

"Eh?" With surprise perhaps genuine, perhaps well feigned, Custer shoved the papers aside. "What is it, Dowling?"

Either he'd entered his second childhood the night before or he knew perfectly well what it was. Dowling didn't think senility had overcome the old coot as suddenly as that. He said, "Sir, Mr. Thomas is here to see you. He's from the War Department." He added that last in case Custer *had* gone around the bend in the past twenty-four hours.

Custer sighed, his wrinkled features drooping. He knew what that meant, all right. "No reprieve, eh?" he asked, like a prisoner who would hang in the morning if the governor didn't wire. Dowling shook his head. Custer sighed again. "Very well, Lieutenant Colonel. Bring him in. If you care to, you may stay and listen. This will affect you, too."

"Thank you, sir. By your leave, I will do that." Dowling tried to recall the last time Custer had been so considerate. He couldn't. He

428 AMERICAN EMPIRE: BLOOD AND IRON

went out to the anteroom and said, "Mr. Thomas, General Custer will see you now."

"Good." N. Mattoon Thomas got to his feet. He was a tall, long-faced man in his late thirties, and looked more like a preacher than Upton Sinclair's assistant secretary of war. He walked with a slight limp; Dowling knew he'd taken a machine-gun bullet in the leg during the Great War.

When they'd gone down the short hallway to Custer's sanctum, Dowling said, "Mr. Thomas, I have the honor to present to you General George Custer. General, the assistant secretary of war." Being one of the civilians overseeing the Army, Thomas took precedence over Custer in the introductions.

"Pleased to meet you, sir," Custer said: a palpable lie. He waved to the chair in front of his desk. "Please—sit down. Make yourself comfortable." As Thomas did so, Abner Dowling also took a seat. He tried to be unobtrusive, which wasn't easy with his bulk. N. Mattoon Thomas' blue eyes flicked his way, but the assistant secretary of war only nodded, accepting his presence.

Custer would have said something more then, but the words seemed stuck in his throat. He sent Dowling a look of appeal, but it wasn't Dowling's place to speak. He was here only as an overweight fly on the wall.

Before the silence could grow too awkward, Thomas broke it, saying, "General, I wish to convey to you at the outset President Sinclair's sincere appreciation for the excellent service you have given your country in this difficult and important post."

"That's kind of him," Custer said. "Very kind of him. I'm honored to have him send someone to deliver such a generous message in person. You came a long way to do it, sir, and I'm grateful."

He was going to be difficult. Dowling would have bet he'd be difficult, but hadn't looked for him to be quite so gracefully difficult. Maybe Libbie had coached him. She was even better at being difficult than her husband.

N. Mattoon Thomas gave him the look of a preacher who'd had the collection plate come back with thirty-seven cents and a subway token on it. "In view of your long career in the U.S. Army, General, the president feels it is time for you to come home to well-deserved thanks and to rest on your laurels hereafter," he said.

"Mr. Thomas, I have no desire to rest on my laurels," Custer replied. "I am as hale and spry as a man of my years can be, and I do not believe those years have adversely affected my ability to reason clearly and to issue appropriate orders. I have been in the saddle a long time. I should like to continue."

"I am afraid I must remind you, General, that you serve at the pleasure of the president of the United States." Thomas was less than half Custer's age. But he had the power in this situation, and also had the ruthlessness that came naturally to many young men given power over their elders.

Dowling saw that, and pitied Custer. Custer saw it, too, and grew angry. He dropped his polite mask as if he'd never donned it. "Christ, I despise the notion of taking orders from that Socialist pipsqueak," he growled.

"Which is one reason the president takes a certain pleasure in giving them to you," Thomas replied easily. "Would you prefer to retire, General, or to be sacked? Those are your only choices now."

"Teddy Roosevelt could sack me and not worry about what happened next," Custer said. "He was a soldier himself—not so good a soldier as he thought he was, but a soldier nonetheless. President Sinclair will have a harder time of it: the papers will hound him for months if he dismisses me, for he has not the prestige, the authority—call it what you like—to do so without reminding people of his own inexperience in such matters."

That all made excellent political sense to Abner Dowling. Custer the political animal had always been far more astute than Custer the soldier. Dowling glanced toward Thomas, wondering how Upton Sinclair's assistant secretary of war would take such defiance.

It fazed him not at all. He said, "General Custer, the president predicted you would say something to that effect. He told me to assure you he was determined to seek your replacement, and that he would dismiss you out of hand if you offered difficulties. Here is his letter to you, which he instructed me to give you if it proved necessary." Thomas reached into his breast pocket and took out an envelope, which he passed across the desk to Custer.

The commandant of U.S. forces in Canada had taken off his reading glasses when Thomas came in. Now he put them back on. He opened the envelope, which was not sealed, and drew forth the letter inside. It must have been what Thomas said it was, for his cheeks flushed with rage as he read.

"Why, the arrogant puppy!" he burst out when he was through. "I saved the country from the limeys when he was still making messes in his drawers, and he has the impudence to write a letter like this? I ought to let him sack me, by jingo! I can't think of anything else likely to do the Socialists more political harm."

"General—" Dowling began. Custer had a large—indeed, an enormous—sense of his own importance. Much of that was justified. Not all of it was, a fact to which he sometimes proved blind.

N. Mattoon Thomas held up a large, long-fingered hand. "Let General Custer decide as he will, Lieutenant Colonel," he said. "If he prefers being ignominiously flung out of the Army he has served so well for so long to being allowed to retire and to celebrate his achievements as they deserve, that is his privilege."

Dowling sucked in a long breath. President Sinclair had sent the right man up to Winnipeg to do this job. Thomas could be smooth, but under that smoothness he had steel, sharp steel. Dowling had not realized it till that moment. Like so many professional soldiers, he'd assumed any Socialist had to be soft.

Custer, evidently, had assumed the same thing. Hearing the cool contempt in Thomas' voice, he was discovering he'd made a mistake. He could hardly have looked more horrified. "Mr. Thomas . . ." he began.

"Yes, General?" Once again, Thomas was the picture of urbanity.

"Perhaps I was a mite hasty, Mr. Thomas," Custer said. He'd never willingly retreated in battle, but he was backpedaling now.

"Perhaps you were." The assistant secretary of war let the slightest hint of scorn show in his agreement. Dowling eyed him with respect verging on alarm. He was a formidable piece of work, was N. Mattoon Thomas.

"Could—Could we arrange it so that I need not retire immediately?" Custer asked. Now he was grasping at straws. Soldiers in the USA had political power only when politicians chose to acknowledge it. By refusing to do that, Sinclair and Thomas left Custer nowhere to stand.

And Thomas, now that he'd won, was willing to let Custer have a straw. "We could indeed," he said. "President Sinclair has instructed me that your retirement may take effect as late as the first of August—provided you give me a letter announcing your intention to retire before I leave this room."

"Damn you," Custer muttered. Thomas pretended not to hear. Dowling knew he was pretending, because he himself had no trouble hearing at all. The general pulled a piece of paper from a desk drawer and wrote rapidly—and furiously, if the way the pen scratched over the paper gave any clue. When he was done, he thrust the sheet at Thomas. "There!"

The assistant secretary of war read it carefully before nodding. "Yes, this appears to be satisfactory," he said. "I will announce it directly on my return to Philadelphia." He folded it and put it into the envelope in which he'd brought President Sinclair's letter to Custer. "And, now that the retirement is in order, you may, as I said before, mark it in any way you like. If you want to stop at every town between here and the U.S. border and parade through it with a brass band, go right ahead. When you reach Philadelphia, the president will lead the cheers for you."

"Of course he will—it'll make him look good." Now that the deed was done, Custer bounced back fast. He leaned forward across the desk toward N. Mattoon Thomas. "And I'll tell you why he won't let me retire after August first, either—because he knows damn well it'll raise a stink, and he wants to make sure the stink dies down before the Congressional elections this fall."

"It could be," Thomas answered. "I'm not saying it is, mind you, but it could be." He got to his feet. "Whether it is or not, though, is neither here nor there. No, no need to escort me out, Lieutenant Colonel Dowling. Now that I have what I came for, my driver will take me back to the train station, and then I can return to my duties in Philadelphia. A very good day to you both, gentlemen." Away he went, young, confident, powerful.

George Custer let out a long sigh. "Well, Dowling, I think it may at last be just about over. I squeezed a couple of more years of active duty out of Teddy Roosevelt, and got what I really wanted from him, too, but you can't win all the time."

"There can't be many who had a longer run, sir," Dowling answered. He did his best to sound consoling while he wondered what his own career would look like once he finally got free of Custer.

He'd said the right thing. Custer nodded. "Only one I can think of is Wilhelm I, Kaiser Bill's grandfather. He fought under Napoleon—imagine it!—and he was still German Kaiser when I licked Gordon in 1881, and for six or seven more years after that, too. He was up over ninety when he finally gave up the ghost."

"That's . . . quite something, sir." Dowling could easily imagine Custer up over ninety. He wouldn't go till they came and dragged him away—and neither would Libbie, come to that.

And now Custer was scheming again. "A brass band in every

town, that damn Red told me," he said. "I'll take him up on it, too—and if he thinks I aim to head straight south for the border from here, he can damn well think again, and so can Upton goddamn Sinclair. I aim to have the bulliest farewell tour in the history of the world."

"Yes, sir," Dowling said, knowing full well who would have to plan that tour.

"A good morning to you, Arthur," Wilfred Rokeby said as Arthur McGregor walked into the post office in Rosenfeld, Manitoba.

"Morning to you, too, Wilf," McGregor answered. He thrust a hand into the pocket of his overalls. Coins jingled. "Need to buy a mess of stamps."

"That's what I'm here for," Rokeby said. "This have to do with Julia and Ted Culligan? Congratulations. I expect they'll be happy together."

"Hope so," McGregor said. "The Culligans are nice folks, and Julia's so happy, she thinks she invented Ted. If she still feels that way ten years from now, they'll have done it up right. For now, though, Maude and me, we've got invitations to write."

"You can have some of your kinfolk come out here for a change," Rokeby said, "instead of you going back to Ontario."

"That's right," McGregor said. Since he hadn't been in Ontario as Rokeby thought, that was liable to get awkward, but he figured he could slide through it. And he wasn't about to give the postmaster any hint that he'd actually been in Winnipeg. He didn't think Wilf Rokeby told the Yanks things they didn't need to know, but he didn't want to find out he was wrong the hard way.

He bought a dollar's worth of stamps, about as many as he'd bought at one crack in his life. "Thank you kindly," Wilfred Rokeby said. Maybe because McGregor had been such a good customer, he slid a copy of the *Rosenfeld Register* across the counter to him. "You can have this, too, if you like. I'm done with it."

"Thanks, Wilf. That's nice of you." Because an American was putting out the new *Register*, McGregor didn't like to buy it. He'd read it, though, if he got the chance. As it had in the old days, the *Register* reserved the top right part of the front page for important news from out of town. The headline leaped out at McGregor. He pointed to it. "So Custer's finally going back to the USA, is he? Good riddance." He didn't mind saying that to the postmaster; most Canadians would likely have said worse.

Rokeby nodded so emphatically, a lock of hair flopped down on his forehead despite the spicy-scented oil he used to plaster it down. The smell of that hair oil was to McGregor, as to other folks for miles around Rosenfeld, part of the odor of the post office.

"He's celebrating more triumphs than imperial Caesar while he's doing it, too," Rokeby said. "Just have a look at the story there."

McGregor did. The more he read, the longer his face got. "He'll be parading through every town where his train stops?" he said, shaking his head in wonder. "He doesn't think he's imperial Caesar, Wilf. He thinks he's God Almighty."

"He's a vain old man," the postmaster said. "Pretty soon he'll meet God Almighty face-to-face, and I guarantee you'll be able to tell the difference between the two of them."

"That's the truth," McGregor said. Had he had any luck at all, the devil would already be roasting Custer over a slow fire. He wondered if Custer would parade through Rosenfeld on his way back to the United States, and made a silent vow: if the American general came into town, he wouldn't go out again.

Wilfred Rokeby sighed. "Wish to Jesus I could go back to selling stamps with the portrait of the King, God bless him, but it doesn't look like it's going to happen. You have to get along the best way the big fish let you if you're only a little fish yourself."

"I suppose you're right," McGregor said. The big fish—the big Yank fish—hadn't let him get along. But he could still bite. He'd show them he could still bite. His features revealed none of that. Nodding to the postmaster, he went on, "Thanks for the stamps, and thanks for the paper, too."

"Any time, Arthur," Rokeby said. "And congratulations again for your daughter. She's a nice gal; I've always thought so. She deserves to be happy."

She'd have been a lot happier if the Yanks hadn't come up over the border. But McGregor kept that to himself. He'd kept a lot of things to himself since Alexander was shot. With a last nod to the postmaster, he headed across the street to Henry Gibbon's general store.

Snow crunched under his boots. The calendar said it would be spring any day, but the calendar didn't know much about Manitoba. As he walked, he thought hard. If Custer came to Rosenfeld . . . If Custer paraded through Rosenfeld . . . If he did, McGregor was going to try to kill him, and that was all there was to it.

He could see only one way to do it: toss a bomb into Custer's motorcar. That was how the Serbs had touched off the Great War. McGregor couldn't see doing it and getting away with it. The prospect of not getting away with it had held him back in the past. He looked deep into himself. No, he really didn't care any more. If he paid with his life, he paid with his life. He'd never have the chance to strike another blow like this against the Yanks. The next commandant they appointed would probably be some faceless functionary whose own mother had never heard of him. If someone like that got blown to smithereens, so what? But Custer had been famous for more than forty years. Killing him would mean something. The USA didn't have an Archduke Franz Ferdinand, but Custer came close.

Murder on his mind, McGregor walked right past the general store. He turned around, shaking his head, and went back. Henry Gibbon nodded from behind the counter. "Morning, Arthur," he said. "What can I do for you today?"

"I've got a list here somewhere," McGregor said, and went through his pockets till he found it. Handing it to the storekeeper, he went on, "It's Maude's stuff, mostly: canned goods and sundries and such. We need kerosene, too, and there's a couple of bottles of cattle drench on there for me, but it's mostly for the missus."

Gibbon ran his finger down the list. "Reckon I can take care of just about all of this." He looked up. "Hear tell your daughter's going to tie the knot. That's a big day, by heaven. Congratulations."

"Thank you, Henry," McGregor said. He pointed to Gibbon. "I bet the Culligans came into town in the last couple of days. Mercy, even Wilf Rokeby's heard the news."

"You know it's all over creation if Wilf's heard it, and that's a fact," Henry Gibbon said with a chuckle. He turned to the shelves behind him. "This'll take a little bit. Why don't you grab a candy cane—or a pickle, if one'd suit you better—and toast yourself by the stove while I rustle up what you need?"

"I don't mind if I do." McGregor reached into the pickle barrel and pulled a likely one out of the brine. It crunched when he bit into it, the way a proper pickle should.

"I'm going to give you a crate," Gibbon said. "Bring it back and I'll knock a dime off your next bill."

"All right. I would have brought one with me this time, only I didn't think."

"I noticed that. It's why I started knocking a dime off the bill," the storekeeper answered. "Plenty of people who won't think about anything else will remember money."

McGregor would have been one of those people before the Great War. He would have been one of those people up until 1916. Now the only thing he remembered was revenge. "What do I owe you?" he asked when Gibbon set the last can in the crate.

"Well, when you bring in the kerosene can and I fill it, everything put all together comes to $8.51," Gibbon said. "You did bring the kerosene can, I reckon?" By his tone, he reckoned no such thing.

"Yeah, I did." McGregor shook his head in dull embarrassment. "Lucky I remembered to hitch the horse to the wagon. I'll go get the can."

"You'd have been a mite longer getting here, Arthur, if you'd forgotten about the horse," McGregor called after him as he left.

He didn't answer. He would have walked back to the wagon for the kerosene can before going to the general store had Rokeby not given him a copy of the *Register*. Seeing that Custer was leaving Canada, seeing that Custer was going to celebrate while here, realizing that Custer might come through Rosenfeld, had taken everything else from his mind. He wanted to go back to the farm. He wanted to go back into the barn and get to work on a bomb he could throw.

He would have forgotten the crate of groceries had Henry Gibbon not reminded him of it. The storekeeper laughed as he carried it out toward the wagon. McGregor was glad he didn't own an automobile. He wasn't altogether sure he recalled how to get back to the farmhouse. The horse, thank heaven, would know the way.

When he carried the crate indoors, the *Rosenfeld Register* was stuck on top of the cans and jars. Naturally, Maude grabbed it; new things to read didn't come to the farm often enough. As naturally, McGregor's wife noticed the story about Custer right away. "Is he going to parade through Rosenfeld?" she asked.

"I don't know," McGregor answered.

"If he does parade through Rosenfeld, what will you do?" Sharp fear rode Maude's voice.

"I don't know that, either," McGregor answered.

Maude set a hand on his arm. His eyes widened a little; the two of them seldom touched, except by accident, outside the marriage bed. "I don't want to be a widow, Arthur," she said quietly. "I've already lost Alexander. I don't know what I'd do if I lost you, too."

"I've always been careful, haven't I?" he said, coming as close as he ever did to talking about what he did besides farming.

"You go on being careful, do you hear me?" Maude said. "You've done what you had to do. If you do anything more, it's over

and above. You don't need to do it, not for me, not for Alexander."
She wasn't usually so direct, either.

"I hear you," McGregor said, and said no more. He was the
only one who could judge what he had to do. He was the only one
who could judge how much revenge was enough for him. Now, he
was the only one who could judge how much revenge was enough
for Alexander. As far as he was concerned, he might kill every Yank
north of the border without it being revenge enough for Alexander.

"Maybe he won't come through Rosenfeld," Maude said. Did
she sound hopeful? Without a doubt, she did.

"Maybe he won't," McGregor said. "But maybe he will, too.
And even if he doesn't, don't you think the newspapers will print
where he's going to be and when he's going to be there? If he's having parades, he'll want people to turn out. I suppose I can go meet
him somewhere else if I have to."

"You don't have to," Maude said, as she had done before. "Will
you please listen to me? You don't have to, not any more."

"Do you think Mary would say the same thing?" McGregor
asked.

Maude's lips shaped two silent words. McGregor thought they
were *Damn you*. He'd never heard her curse aloud in all the years
he'd known her. He still hadn't, but only by the thinnest of margins.
When she did speak aloud, she said, "Mary is a little girl. She
doesn't understand that dying is forever."

"She's not so little any more, and if she doesn't understand that
after the Yanks murdered Alexander, when do you suppose she
will?" McGregor asked.

Maude spun away from him and covered her face with her
hands. Her shoulders shook with sobs. McGregor stamped past her,
back out into the cold. When he strode into the barn, the horse
snorted, as if surprised to see him again so soon.

He didn't pick up the old wagon wheel and get out the bomb-
making tools he hid beneath it. Time enough for that later, when he
knew exactly what sort of bomb he needed to build and where he'd
have to take it. For now, he just stood there and looked. Even that
made him feel better. Slowly, he nodded. In a sense more important
than the literal, he knew where he was going again.

Colonel Irving Morrell slammed his fist against the steel side of the
test-model barrel. "It's not right, God damn it," he ground out. He
couldn't remember the last time he'd been in such a temper. When

the doctors said his leg wound might keep him from going back to active duty in the early days of the Great War? Maybe not even then.

"What can we do, sir?" Lieutenant Elijah Jenkins said. "We're only soldiers. We haven't got anything to do with deciding which way the country goes."

"And I've always thought that was how things should be, too," Morrell answered. "But when this chowderhead—no, this custard-head—of a Socialist does something like this . . . I ask you, Lije, doesn't it stick in your craw, too?"

"Of course it does, sir," Jenkins said. "It's not like I voted for the Red son of a bitch—uh, beg pardon."

"Don't bother," Morrell said savagely. "That's what Upton Sinclair is, all right: a Red son of a bitch." He seldom swore; he was not a man who let his feelings run away with his wits. Today, though, he made an exception. "That he should have the gall to propose canceling the rest of the reparations the Rebs still owe us—"

"That's pretty low, all right, sir," Jenkins agreed, "especially after everything we went through to make the CSA have to cough up."

But he'd put his finger on only part of Morrell's fury. "Giving up the reparations is bad enough by itself," Morrell said. "But he wants to throw them away—however many millions or billions of dollars that is—and he won't spend the thousands here to build a proper prototype and get the new-model barrel a step closer to production."

"That's pretty damn stupid, all right," Jenkins said. "If the Rebs can start putting money in their own pockets again instead of in ours, they'll be spoiling for a fight faster than you can say Jack Robinson."

"That's the truth," Morrell said. "That's the whole truth and nothing but the truth, so help me God. Why can't Sinclair see it? You can't get along with somebody who's bound and determined not to get along with you." He did his best to look on the bright side of things: "Maybe Congress will say no."

"Socialist majority in each house." Jenkins' voice was gloomy. He kicked at the dirt. "After the Confederates licked us in the War of Secession and the Second Mexican War, they weren't dumb enough to try and make friends with us. They knew damn well we weren't their friends. Why can't we figure out they aren't our friends, either?"

"Why? Because workers all across the world have more in common with other workers than they do with other people in their own country." Morrell wasn't usually so sarcastic, but he wasn't usually so irate, either. "What happened in 1914 sure proved that, didn't it? None of the workers would shoot at any of the other workers, would they? That's why we didn't have a war, isn't it?"

"If we didn't have a war, sir, where'd you get that Purple Heart?" Jenkins asked.

"Must have fallen from the sky," Morrell answered. "Pity it couldn't have fallen where Sinclair could see it and have some idea of what it meant."

"Why don't you send it to him, sir?" Jenkins asked eagerly.

"If I did, I'd have to send it in a chamber pot to show him how I felt," Morrell said. "And I'll bet I could fill that chamber pot with medals from men on just this base, too." For a moment, the idea of doing just that held a potent appeal. But then, reluctantly, he shook his head. "It wouldn't do. I'd throw my own career in the pot along with the medal, and somebody has to defend the United States, even if Sinclair isn't up to the job."

"Yes, sir, I suppose so." Jenkins was a bright lad; he could see the sense in that. He was still not very far from being a lad in the literal sense of the word, though, for his grin had a distinct small-boy quality to it as he went on, "It would have been fun to see the look on his face when he opened it, though."

"Well, maybe it would." Morrell laughed. He knew damn well it would. He slapped Jenkins on the back. "See you in the morning." Jenkins nodded and hurried away toward the officers' club, no doubt to have a drink or two or three before supper. In his bachelor days, Morrell might—probably would—have followed him, even if he would have been sure to stop after the second drink. Now, though, he was more than content to hurry home to Agnes.

She greeted him with a chicken stew and indignation: she'd heard the news about Sinclair's proposal to end reparations down in Leavenworth. "It's a disgrace," she said, "nothing but a disgrace. He'll throw money down the drain, but he won't do anything to keep the country strong."

"I said the same thing not an hour ago," Morrell said. "One of the reasons I love you is, we think the same way."

"We certainly do: you think you love me, and I think I love you," Agnes said. Morrell snorted. His wife went on, "Would you like some more dumplings?"

"I sure would," he answered, "but I'll have to run them off one day before too long." He still wasn't close to fat—he didn't think he'd ever be fat the way, say, General Custer's adjutant was fat—but now, for the first time in his life, he wondered if he'd stay scrawny forever. Agnes' determination to put meat on his bones was starting to have some effect. He was also past thirty, which meant the meat he put on had an easier time sticking.

"You served under General Custer," Agnes said a little later. With a mouth full of dumpling, Morrell could only nod. His wife continued, "What do you think about him taking a tour through Canada before he finally comes home for good?"

After swallowing, Morrell said, "I don't begrudge it to him, if that's what you mean. He did better up there than I thought he would, and he's the one who really broke the stalemate in the Great War when he saw what barrels could do and rammed it down Philadelphia's throat. He may be a vain old man, but he's earned his vanity."

"When you're as old as he is, you'll have earned the right to be just as vain," Agnes declared.

Morrell tried to imagine himself in the early 1970s. He couldn't do it. The reach was too far; he couldn't guess what that distant future time would be like. He couldn't guess what he'd be like, either. He could see forty ahead, and even fifty. But eighty and beyond? He wondered if anybody in his family had ever lived to be eighty. He couldn't think of anyone except possibly one great-uncle.

He said, "I hope I don't have the chance to get that vain, because I'd need another war, maybe another couple of wars, to come close to doing all the things Custer's done."

"In that case, I don't want you to get old and vain, either," Agnes said at once. "As long as you have the chance to get old, you can stay modest, for all of me."

"I suppose that will do," Morrell answered. Agnes smiled, thinking he'd agreed with her. And so he had . . . to a point. Old men, veterans of the War of Secession, talked about seeing the elephant. He'd seen the elephant, and all the horror it left in its wake. It *was* horror; he recognized as much. But he'd never felt more intensely alive than during those three years of war. The game was most worth playing when his life lay on the line. Nothing felt better than betting it—and winning.

He had a scarred hollow in the flesh of his thigh to remind him how close he'd come to betting it and losing. Agnes had a scarred hollow in her heart: Gregory Hill, her first husband, had laid his life on the life—and lost it. Morrell knew he ought to pray with all his heart that war never visited the borders of the United States again. He *did* pray that war never visited again. Well, most of him did, anyhow.

The next morning, he put on a pair of overalls and joined the rest of the crew of the test model in tearing down the barrel's engine. They would have done that in the field, too, with less leisure and fewer tools. The better a crew kept a barrel going, the less time the machine spent behind the lines and useless.

Morrell liked tinkering with mechanical things. Unlike the fluid world of war, repairs had straight answers. If you found what was wrong and fixed it, the machine would work every time. It didn't fight back and try to impose its own will—even if it did seem that way sometimes.

Michael Pound looked at the battered engine and sadly shook his head. "Ridden hard and put away wet," was the gunner's verdict.

"That's about the size of it, Sergeant," Morrell agreed. "It does a reasonably good job of making a White truck go. Trying to move this baby, though, it's underpowered and overstrained."

"We ought to build something bigger and stronger, then," Pound said. "Have you got the three-sixteenths wrench, sir?"

"Matter of fact, I do." Morrell passed it to him. He grinned while he did it. "You always make everything sound so easy, Sergeant—as if there weren't any steps between *we ought to* and doing something."

"Well, there shouldn't be," Pound said matter-of-factly. "If something needs doing, you go ahead and do it. What else?" He stared at Morrell with wide blue eyes. In his world, no steps lay between needing and doing. Morrell envied him.

Izzy Applebaum, the barrel's driver, laughed at Pound. "Things aren't that simple, Sarge," he said in purest New York. His eyes were narrow and dark and constantly moving, now here, now there, now somewhere else.

"Why ever not?" Pound asked in honest surprise. "Don't you think this barrel needs a stronger engine? If it does, we ought to build one. How complicated is that?" He attacked the crankcase with the wrench. It yielded to his straightforward assault.

Morrell wished all problems yielded to straightforward assault. "Some people don't want us to put any money at all in barrels," he pointed out, "let alone into better engines for them."

"Those people are fools, sir," Pound answered. "If they're not fools, they're knaves. Hang a few of them and the rest will quiet down soon enough."

"Tempting, ain't it?" Izzy Applebaum said with another laugh. "Only trouble is, they make lists of people who ought to get hanged, too, and we're on 'em. The company's better on their list than on ours, but none of them lists is any goddamn good. My folks were on the Czar's list before they got the hell out of Poland."

"Down south of us, the Freedom Party is making lists of people to hang," Morrell added. "I don't care for it, either."

Michael Pound was unperturbed. "Well, but they're a pack of wild-eyed fanatics, sir," he said. "Go ahead and tell me you don't think there are some people who'd be better off dead."

"It *is* tempting," Morrell admitted. He had his mental list, starting with several leading Socialist politicians. But, as Applebaum had said, he was on their list, too. "If you ask me, it's just as well nobody hangs anybody till a court says it's the right and proper thing to do."

"Have it your way, sir," Pound said with a broad-shouldered shrug, and then, a moment later, another one. "It's the law of the land, I suppose. But if I were king—"

"If you was king, I'd get the hell out of here faster than my old man got out of Poland," Izzy Abblebaum broke in.

The gunner looked aggrieved. He no doubt thought he'd make a good king. He'd done a fine job of commanding one barrel after Morrell got "killed." That didn't mean he could run roughshod over the world leading a brigade of them, even if he thought it did. Checking a gasket, Morrell reflected that nobody could do too much roughshod running in the USA; the Constitution kept such things from happening. If it sometimes left him frustrated . . . he'd just have to live with it. "This lifter is shot," he said. "We have a spare part?"

"With this budget?" Applebaum said. "Are you kidding? We're lucky we've got the one that doesn't work." Morrell spent a long time pondering that, and never did straighten it out.

Nellie Jacobs felt harassed. Once Edna got Merle Grimes to pop the question, she hadn't wasted a minute. She'd said, "I do," and moved out. That meant Nellie had to try to run the coffeehouse and keep track of Clara—who at two was into everything—all by herself. Either one of those would have been a full-time job. Trying to do both at once left her shellshocked.

Every once in a while, when things got more impossible than usual, she'd take Clara across the street to Hal's shop to let her husband keep track of the kid in between half-soling shoes and occasionally making fancy boots. On those days, she ended up tired and Hal exhausted instead of the other way round.

"Now I know why God fixed it up so that young people have

most of the babies," she groaned after one particularly wearing day. "Folks our age don't have the gumption to keep up with 'em."

"I wish I could tell you you were wrong," Hal answered. He looked more like a tired grandfather than a father. He wasn't Nellie's age; he was better than ten years older. Having Clara around seemed to be making both her parents older still at a faster rate than usual.

"Shall I make us some more coffee?" Nellie asked. "It's either that or prop my eyelids up with toothpicks, I reckon."

"Go ahead and make it," Hal said. "You always make good coffee. But I do not think it will keep me awake. I do not think anything will keep me awake, not any more." He sighed. "And she sleeps through the night so well now, too."

"I know." Nellie would have groaned again, but lacked the energy. "If she didn't, I wouldn't just be tired—I'd be dead."

"I do love her—with all my heart I love her," Hal said. "But you are right—she can be a handful. Two handfuls, even. I will be very glad when she stops saying no to everything we tell her."

"You mean they stop saying no?" Nellie exclaimed in surprise more or less mock. "Hard to tell, if you go by Edna."

"Edna is fine," Hal said. "There is nothing wrong with Edna. You worry about her too much."

"I don't think so," Nellie said in a flat voice. "If you knew what I've been through—if you knew what I've put myself through for her . . ."

"They are not the same thing," Hal said.

"Huh!" was the only answer Nellie gave to that. After a while, she went on, "Merle's going to find out about Nicholas Kincaid. You wait and see. That kind of thing won't stay under the rug."

Her husband shrugged. "You are probably right. I cannot blame Edna for not wanting to talk about it, though."

"Not fair to tell lies," Nellie said. Then she remembered Bill Reach, almost five years dead now. She remembered how the knife had felt going into him. And she remembered Hal could not, must not, find out how he'd died. The only difference between her case and her daughter's was that she had a better chance of keeping her secret.

"It is not a lie that intends to hurt," Hal said, and Nellie had to nod, for that was true. She let him win the argument, which she didn't always do by any means.

The next morning, the past rose up and bit her. She should have expected such a thing, but somehow she hadn't. A ruddy, handsome fellow in an expensive suit came in, looked around, and said, "Well, you've done the place up right nice, Widow Semphroch. Likely looked like a tornado went through it at the end of the war, but you've done it up right nice." His Confederate accent was thick enough to slice—she guessed he hailed from Alabama, or maybe Mississippi.

"Should I know you, sir?" she asked, her voice cool but resolutely polite: business wasn't so good that she could afford to anger any customer, even a Rebel.

"Name's Alderford, ma'am—Camp Hill Alderford, major, CSA, retired," he answered. "You might not recognize me out of uniform, and I used to wear a little chin beard I've shaved off on account of I've gotten a lot grayer since the war. But I had some of my best times in Washington right here in this coffeehouse, and that's a fact. Now that I'm in town again, I figured I'd stop by and see if you and the place made it through in one piece. Right glad you did."

"Thank you." Nellie didn't remember him at all. A lot of Confederate officers had spent a lot of time in the coffeehouse. She wondered if more of them would start paying visits. *If they do, they'd better have U.S. money,* she thought. Since she didn't want this one to go without spending some cash, she said, "Now that you're back in town, Mr. Alderford, what can I get you?"

"Cup of coffee and a ham sandwich," he answered. He must have been thinking along with her, for he added, "I won't pay in scrip, and I won't pay with Confederate banknotes, either."

"All right." She got him what he'd ordered. While she was serving him, she asked, "What are you doing in Washington now?"

"Selling cottonseed oil, ma'am, cottonseed oil and cottonseed cake," Alderford said. "Cottonseed oil brings a dollar a gallon, near enough—a U.S. dollar, I mean, and a U.S. dollar brings enough Confederate dollars to choke a mule. Two mules, even." He bit into his sandwich. "That's good. That's mighty good. You always had good grub here, even when things were lean."

That was to keep you Rebs coming in so I could spy on you. Nellie almost said it aloud, to see the look on his face. Reluctantly, she kept quiet. Word would get around, down in the CSA. If more ex-officers stopped by, she wanted them in a mood to spend money, not to burn down the coffeehouse.

Clara had been amusing herself in what had been a storeroom before Nellie filled it with toys and a cot to keep the toddler either busy or resting. Camp Hill Alderford smiled to see her. "That your granddaughter, ma'am?" he asked. "Reckon your pretty daughter found somebody else after what happened to poor Nick. That was a hard day, a powerful hard day."

"Mama," Clara said, and ran to Nellie. She was shy of strangers, especially men with their deep voices.

Alderford's eyebrows rose. Nellie nodded. "She's my daughter, too," she said. "I got married again after the war." *And I got a surprise not so long after I did.* "And yes, Edna finally did get married, just a few months ago." She started to add that Merle Grimes was a veteran, too, but didn't bother. Men of the proper age who weren't veterans were few and far between.

"Well, I'm happy for you," Alderford said. He beckoned to Clara with a crooked index finger. "Come here, sweetheart. I've got a present for you."

"You can go to him, Clara," Nellie said. But Clara didn't want to go anywhere. She clung to Nellie's skirt with one hand. The thumb of the other was in her mouth.

"Here, I'll give it to your mama," Camp Hill Alderford told her. She watched with round eyes as he reached into his hip pocket, pulled out his wallet, and extracted a brown Confederate banknote. "Here y'are, ma'am."

It was beautifully printed: more handsome than U.S. paper money. That wasn't what made Nellie gape. She'd never seen, never imagined, a $50,000,000 bill. Gasping a little, she asked, "What's this worth in real money?"

"About a dime." Alderford shrugged. "Five cents next week, a penny the week after that." He paused. "Maybe we'll be able to start setting our house in order again if we get to stop sending you-all reparations. If we don't, Lord knows what we'll do."

"I haven't got anything to do with that," Nellie said. She hoped Congress wouldn't let President Sinclair cut off Confederate reparations. As far as she was concerned, the weaker the Rebs stayed, the better. What was the first thing they were likely to do if they ever got strong again? As far as she could see, *head straight for Washington* was the best bet.

"I know you don't," Camp Hill Alderford answered. He held out his cup. "If you'd fill that up for me, I'd be obliged."

"I sure will," Nellie said, and did, after detaching Clara from her skirt. Alderford was the only customer in the place; of course she'd get another nickel out of him. She kept looking at all the zeros on the bill he'd given her for Clara. A sigh escaped her. If only it were U.S. green instead of C.S. brown!

The bell above the door chimed. Nellie looked that way with a smile of greeting on her face—someone else to spend money. But it wasn't: it was her son-in-law. Alarm ran through her. "Merle!" she exclaimed. "What are you doing here this time of day? Why aren't you at work?" *Why did you have to come in when this goddamn Reb's here?*

"Edna just telephoned me from the doctor's office," Merle Grimes answered. "Since you don't have a telephone, I figured I'd come over and tell you the news—you're going to be a grandmother."

"Oh," Nellie said, and then, "Oh," again. She would have been more excited about the news if she hadn't been afraid Camp Hill Alderford would start running his mouth. "Won't you get in trouble for leaving your job in the middle of the morning?" she asked, hoping to get Grimes out of the coffeehouse as fast as she could.

But he shook his head. "My boss said it was all right. We're pals—we were in the same company during the war. Small world, isn't it?"

"Isn't it just?" Nellie said tonelessly.

"Congratulations, ma'am," Alderford said. He turned to Merle Grimes. "And to you, too, sir. Children make everything worthwhile."

"Er—thank you," Grimes said. He couldn't help realizing Alderford was a Confederate—and probably couldn't help wondering why a Confederate spoke as if he knew Nellie so well.

Nellie decided to take that bull by the horns: "Mr. Alderford was Major Alderford during the war, and used to stop by here a good deal."

"Oh," Grimes said, not in surprise, as Nellie had, but more for the sake of saying something. He had a way of holding his cards close to his chest. Nellie had trouble telling what he was thinking.

"That's right," Alderford said. Nellie sent him a look of appeal to keep him from saying any more. She hated that; she hated asking any man for anything. And she feared the ex–Rebel officer wouldn't even notice, or would notice and decide to pay back some damnyankees for winning the war.

But Alderford never said an untoward word. He set coins—U.S. coins—on the table and went on his way. Nellie let out a quiet sigh of relief. She'd got by with it. But if more Confederates came to visit, could she keep on getting by with it? *One more thing to worry about,* she thought, as if she didn't have enough already.

* * *

Lucien Galtier reached out and pressed the starter button on the dashboard of his Chevrolet. He'd bought the automobile in large measure because it had a Frenchman's name on it; a Ford would have been easier to come by.

The engine coughed before coming to noisy life. The motorcar shuddered under him, then settled into a steady vibration different even from the motion of a railroad car, the closest comparison he could find.

His feet were still clumsy on gas and clutch and brake. Charles and Georges had taken to driving more readily than he, which infuriated him. "I *will* learn to do this, and to do it well," he muttered. He did not talk to the automobile, as he had to the horse. He was talking only to himself. He knew it, and felt the lack.

He stalled the motorcar the first time he tried to shift from neutral up into low gear. Naturally, Georges had taken the moment before to come out of the barn. As naturally, Lucien's younger son laughed at his father's fumbles, and did not even try to keep that laughter to himself. Galtier called the automobile several names he would not have used on the horse even in the worst of moods. Then, still wishing he had not bought the machine, he started it once more and succeeded in driving away.

As he drew near Rivière-du-Loup, he came up behind a horse-drawn wagon—one very much like that which he had driven himself up till a few weeks before. The cursed thing crawled along at a snail's pace. Galtier squeezed the horn bulb again and again. The stupid farmer sitting up there like a cowflop might have been deaf. He refused either to speed up or to pull over.

At last, seizing an opportunity, Lucien shot around him. "*Mauvaise calisse!*" he shouted, and eked out the malediction with gestures. The other farmer smiled a smile that, to Galtier, proved his feeblemindedness. "Some people have no consideration," Galtier fumed. "None whatsoever." He never once thought how he had behaved when driving a wagon rather than a motorcar.

Traffic in Rivière-du-Loup was far heavier than he recalled from the days before the war. Automobiles had been rare then, with most people traveling by wagon or carriage or on horseback. Now everyone seemed to have a motorcar, and to drive it with a Gallic disdain for consequences that matched Galtier's own. He cursed. He shouted. He waved his arms. He blew his horn, and blew it and blew it. He fit right in.

Finding a parking space was another adventure, one made worse because the streets of Rivière-du-Loup had not been designed with the automobile in mind. A good many motorcars were parked with two wheels in the road, the other two up on the sidewalks—sidewalks were none too wide, either. At last, Lucien imitated that example.

When he got out, money jingled in his pockets. Some of the coins were from the USA, a few from the Canada of before the war, and some from the Republic of Quebec. As they were all minted to the same standard, merchants took one lot as readily as another. A newsboy was hawking papers on a street corner. Galtier gave him a couple of pennies—one, a U.S. coin, said ONE CENT on the reverse; the other, an issue of Quebec, featured the fleur-de-lys and announced its value as UN SOU—and took a newspaper.

FRANCE IN CHAOS! shouted the headline. He read the accompanying story as he walked back to the automobile. Police and soldiers had turned machine guns on rioters in Paris furious about the worthless currency and about the country's forced subservience to the German Empire.

The reporter didn't seem to know what tone to take. Germany was the USA's ally, and so was also the ally of the Republic of Quebec. But the Quebecois sprang from French stock, and nothing would ever change that. The ambiguity made the writer take almost no tone at all, but set forth what he'd learned from the cable as baldly as if it were going down in a police blotter.

Galtier sighed. He didn't know how to feel about France's troubles, either. He wished she were not having such troubles. But if the only way for her not to have troubles was for her to have won the war . . . Galtier shook his head. "Too high a price to pay," he murmured.

He would not have said that during the war. He shrugged. He'd had the same thought many times before, in many different contexts. The world had changed, too. Taken all together, the changes pleased him. He would not have said that during the war, either.

When he knocked on the door to the house where Nicole and Leonard O'Doull lived, his daughter answered almost at once. Tagging along behind her was little Lucien. Staring gravely up at Galtier, he asked, "Candy?"

"No, no candy today, I regret," Galtier answered.

His grandson clouded up and got ready to cry. "You know you aren't supposed to do that," Nicole said, and, for a wonder, little Lucien didn't. Nicole smiled at Galtier. "And what brings you here today, Papa?"

"Nothing much," he said grandly. "I was just out for a drive in my Chevrolet, and I thought I would stop in." Was that how a gentleman of leisure should sound? He didn't know. He'd never met a gentleman of leisure.

"Ah," Nicole said. "You have the motorcar here, then?"

"Here in Rivière-du-Loup, yes. Here in my pocket"—Galtier peered into it, as if to make sure—"here in my pocket, no."

Nicole wrinkled her nose. "It certainly isn't hard to see sometimes where Georges comes by it," she remarked.

"Comes by what?" Galtier demanded. He was perhaps a sixteenth part as annoyed as he pretended to be.

His daughter knew as much. "Will you let me drive your new motorcar, Papa?" she asked.

"What's this?" Now Galtier's surprise was genuine. "How is it that you, a girl, a woman"—he added that last with the air of a man granting a great concession—"can drive a motorcar?"

"Leonard showed me, Papa," Nicole answered, very much a woman and very much a woman of the new century. "It isn't very hard. I've driven our Ford any number of times. It's a handy thing to know, don't you think?"

"What if you have a puncture, and your husband is not there?" Lucien asked.

"I fix it," she answered calmly. "I've done it once. It's a dirty job, and not an easy job, but I know I can do it again."

"Do you?" Galtier muttered. Nicole hadn't yet mentioned her driving to Marie or to Denise. He knew that for a fact. If she had, his wife and his next eldest daughter would have been nagging him to learn to drive, too. With Charles and Georges always wanting to go courting or just gallivanting around in the machine, where would he ever find time to use it himself if his womenfolk were taking it, too?

"Yes, I do." Nicole answered the question he hadn't quite aimed at her, and answered it with arrogant confidence a man might have envied. "And so, may I drive your automobile?"

Thus directly confronted, Lucien found no choice but to yield. "Very well," he said, "but I will thank you to be careful of the delicate machine—and of your delicate father as well."

Nicole laughed, for all the world as if he'd been joking. She reached down and took little Lucien's hand; evidently, she was not afraid to trust his life to what she knew behind the steering wheel. Galtier's heart had not pounded so since the war crossed the St. Lawrence. Nonetheless, he led her to his mechanical pride and joy.

She slid into the driver's seat, but then stopped in consternation.

"Everything is different, Papa!" she exclaimed. "On the Ford, the spark knob is on the left side of the steering column, the throttle on the right. I have a lever on the floor to my left for the emergency brake and clutch release and the pedals on the floor seem different from these, too. On the Ford, they are the high- and low-speed clutch, the reverse pedal, and the foot brake."

"Here, they are the clutch, the brake, and the gas pedal," Galtier said gravely. "And this lever here shifts the gears. I did not know motorcars were so different, one from another. I do not think you had better drive the Chevrolet after all."

"I don't, either." Nicole looked so unhappy, he reached out and touched her hand. She went on, "Leonard told me Fords were— *eccentric* was the word he used. I did not know how eccentric they were." She brightened. "You must teach me to drive this motorcar, too, so I will be able to use whatever sort there is. I already know how to steer; everything else should be easy enough."

"Should it?" Galtier said. He still found it hard himself; he hadn't got used to it, as he had to managing a horse. But Nicole seemed to have been driving longer than he had. He wondered why she hadn't told him. She probably hadn't wanted him to feel bad when he had no automobile of his own. Maybe she also hadn't wanted him to know she could do anything so unladylike.

They traded places in the Chevrolet; Nicole took charge of little Lucien. Galtier started the motorcar and bounced it down off the curb and onto the street. "Tell me what you are doing while you do it," Nicole said. She was trying to watch his hand on the gearshift and his feet on the pedals at the same time.

Galtier did explain as he drove. He thought he might have trouble doing that, but he didn't. He'd learned so recently, everything was still fresh in his mind, and came bubbling forth like a spring from out of the ground. After a while, he said, "You will want to try for yourself, eh?"

"Of course," Nicole replied.

And it was indeed *of course*; Galtier would have been astonished to hear any other answer. He said, "In that case, I will drive out of town before I let you back behind the wheel. Better you should learn where there are fewer targets."

"The idea, Papa, is to *miss* the other automobiles and the wagons," Nicole said.

"Oh, yes. I understand. And the people and the walls, also," Lucien said. "But if you are learning, you do not yet hold the idea firmly in your mind." He almost ran down a pedestrian, proving he did not yet hold the idea firmly in his mind, either. The man jumped back and to one side, then shouted angrily at him.

Nicole said nothing at all. She would have been bound to when she was living back at the farm. *Has marriage taught her restraint?* Galtier wondered. It hadn't done any such thing for Marie . . . or had it? Better not to think about that, perhaps.

Once he got out into the countryside again—not a long drive, Rivière-du-Loup being anything but a metropolis—he stopped the Chevrolet, shut off the engine, and got out. Nicole slid slowly and carefully across the front seat to take her place behind the wheel, then, when he got in on the passenger side, handed him little Lucien, who had fallen asleep in her lap. The boy stirred and muttered, but did not wake.

"Now—to start I have only to press this button?" Nicole said, and hit the starter. Sure enough, the engine awoke. "This is easier than with the Ford. Next, I let out the clutch and put the motorcar in gear." Nicole stalled a couple of times before she managed to get the automobile moving, and her shift from low to second was abrupt enough to wake up Galtier's grandson, but Galtier praised her anyhow. Why not? He too had stalled, not long before. And she did know how to steer; once she got going, she piloted the Chevrolet with confidence.

"Very good," Galtier said after she'd churned up dust along several miles of country road. "You were not fooling me after all. You really can drive."

"Of course I can," Nicole said. She was shifting gears a bit more smoothly now, learning to ease off the gas pedal as she came down on the clutch. "And this car is easier in nearly every way than Leonard's Ford. I see no reason at all why Mama and Denise should not also learn."

"Oh, you don't?" Galtier said, and Nicole shook her head, defying him to make something of it. She wouldn't have done that when she was living at home, either. Leonard O'Doull, Lucien thought, kept too loose a rein on her now. But she *had* shown she could drive. If she could, were Marie and Denise too ignorant? They would never let him forget it if he thought so. With a shrug that made little Lucien giggle, Galtier added, "It could be that you have reason," and then, "It could even be that I will tell them you have reason."

"Oh, Papa," Nicole said fondly, and Galtier was reduced to mumbling. *Tabernac!* he thought. *She is a wife now, and so she sees right through me.*

* * *

Sylvia Enos didn't go down to T Wharf nearly so often these days as she had in the past. For one thing, her connections with the fishermen and the folk who worked in the fish markets had slipped with the passage of time. For another, going down to the wharf where George had worked tore open old wounds.

But all her old wounds had been torn open when she found out that that Confederate submersible skipper had fired the torpedo that sank the USS *Ericsson*. She knew her husband's killer's name: Roger Kimball. Even though he'd attacked the U.S. destroyer after the war was over, he still walked free down in the CSA.

President Sinclair had done no more than issue a tepid protest. That ate at Sylvia, too. Lots of people still sang the Socialists' praises. Sylvia supposed they had done good things for the workers of the USA. But they hadn't done what she most wanted. Had she had a vote, Upton Sinclair would have lost it.

With the old wounds already bleeding again, going to T Wharf couldn't make them hurt any worse. After Sylvia got off work from her Saturday half day, she gathered up George, Jr., and Mary Jane and took them down by the sea. They enjoyed it; they kept exclaiming over the raucous gulls and over all the fishing boats tied up to the wharf.

"Sure does stink, Ma," Mary Jane said, more admiringly than not.

"It's supposed to smell this way," Sylvia answered. Tar and salt air, horse manure and old fish—without them, T Wharf would have been a different, a lesser, place.

Seeing the boats made Sylvia want to exclaim, too, but for a different reason from that of her children. The fishing fleet had changed while she wasn't looking, so to speak. Before the war, most of the boats had been steamers, with some still relying on sail. Now diesel- and gasoline-powered boats were driving steam from the scene. They changed one element of the wharf's familiar smell, and not to the better in her mind. She far preferred coal smoke to the stink of diesel exhaust.

She walked along the wharf, looking into the boats for men she knew, men from whom she might buy some choice fish before they ever got to market. That sort of business was highly unofficial, but went on all the time. Fishermen needed extra cash in their pockets enough to make them anything but shy about taking it from the pockets of the boat owners.

Sylvia was discovering to her dismay that the fishermen were almost as unfamiliar as the boats they took to sea when, from behind her, someone called, "Mrs. Enos!"

She turned. So did her children. George, Jr., asked, "Who's the spook, Ma?"

Fortunately, he kept his voice down. "You hush your mouth," she told him. "Charlie White isn't a spook; he's a very nice man. He used to be the cook on the *Ripple* when your father sailed in her." She waved to White, who was coming up the wharf toward her. "Hello, Charlie. It's been a long time. You stayed in the Navy, I see."

He brushed a hand across the front of his dark blue uniform tunic. "I surely did, Mrs. Enos. Work's not near as hard, and that's a fact. In the Navy, all I've got to do is cook." His accent was two parts Boston, one part something that put Sylvia in mind of the CSA. He looked at George, Jr., and Mary Jane. "Good God, but they've grown! Fine-looking children, Mrs. Enos."

"Thank you," Sylvia said, her voice shaky. Seeing an old friend of her husband's—and Charlie had been a friend, even if he was colored—here at this place where George had worked left her close to tears.

White solemnly nodded, perhaps understanding some of what was going through her mind. He said, "I was right sorry when I found out George didn't come home from the war, ma'am."

"Thank you," Sylvia said again, even more softly than before. But then fury filled her, and she asked, "Did you find out George was aboard the *Ericsson*?"

She didn't have to explain that to the Negro cook. No doubt she wouldn't have had to explain it to any Navy man. "No, ma'am," he said. "I didn't know that. I think it's a crying shame we ain't going after the dirty rotten coward who sank that ship a . . . lot harder than we are."

"So do I," Sylvia said grimly.

"The president is lily-livered," Mary Jane declared. She was just echoing her mother, but Sylvia didn't want her views aired in public. No, on second thought, maybe she did.

"Weren't a lot of people in the Navy who voted for Sinclair," Charlie White said. "Must have been an awful lot of people on dry land who did, though."

"Yes," Sylvia said. Then she remembered her manners. "How's your family, Charlie? Everyone well?"

"Sure are, and praise the Lord for that," the colored man

answered. "Got me a new little boy since I saw you last, I think. Eddie's going to turn two in a couple weeks."

"Good for you," Sylvia said. She and George might have had more children by now, if only . . . She pulled back from that. "What are you doing on T Wharf now?"

"Same thing you are, I bet," White said: "buying fish. I'm chief cook on the *Fort Benton*—big armored cruiser. Sailors eat like pigs, you know that?"

"They're men," Sylvia said, and Charlie White laughed. Sylvia wasn't sure she'd said anything funny. Men had appetites; women satisfied them. That was the way the world had always worked. Nobody'd ever bothered asking women what they thought of it. Men had power, too.

"Well, well, what have we got here?" someone said. "Looks like old home week, or I'm a Chinaman."

Sylvia knew that voice. "Hello, Fred," she said, turning. "It's been a while." Fred Butcher had been first mate aboard the *Ripple*. When Sylvia got a good look at him, she had to fight to keep her face straight. He was up in his fifties now, and his hair and Kaiser Bill mustache had gone snowy white. He'd put on weight, too, which shocked her even more: he'd always been skinny and quick-moving, like a lizard. Only his eyes, clever and knowing, were as she remembered. Fixing on them let her say, "Good to see you," and sound as if she meant it.

"Anything I can do for you folks?" Butcher asked, shaking hands with Charlie White. He'd always known the angles; a first mate who didn't know them couldn't do his job. "You need fish, talk to me. I'm not going to sea any more; I'm a factor with L.B. God-speed and Company. If I can't get it for you better and cheaper than anybody else on T Wharf, I'll eat my straw boater."

"That would be funny," Mary Jane said, and Butcher took off the hat and made as if to do it. She laughed. So did George, Jr.

"Godspeed's a good outfit," Charlie White said seriously. "They've been in business since not long after the War of Secession, haven't they?"

"That's right—used to be called Marston and Company," Butcher said. "So what can I do for you, Charlie? Cod? Halibut?"

"Five hundred pounds of each, for delivery to the *Fort Benton* at the Navy Yard," White said. They haggled hard over the price. White gave Butcher no special deference either because of his race or from old association; business was business.

Sylvia's children were fidgeting by the time Fred Butcher said, "All right, Charlie; that's a deal. Jesus, the way you jewed me down, anybody'd reckon you were spending your own money, not Uncle Sam's."

"Things are tight these days," White answered. "My own boss'll be all over me if I don't watch every dime."

"Well, you've done that, by God," Butcher said. "I'm liable to catch the dickens for giving you such a good deal." Charlie White grinned proudly. Sylvia didn't believe Butcher for a minute; he'd never hurt himself or his firm. Nodding to her, Butcher asked, "How about you, Mrs. E? You want a thousand pounds of fish, too? I'll give you the same deal I gave Charlie." He winked at her.

"Give me the same price per pound for five pounds of good cod as you gave Charlie for five hundred, then," Sylvia said at once.

Instead of winking, Fred Butcher looked pained. "Come on, Mrs. E, have a heart. He gets a discount for quantity." Then he seemed to listen to what he'd said a moment before. "All right, already. We won't go broke over five pounds of cod. Come on down to Number Sixteen and I'll take care of you. You want to come, too, Charlie, see what you're getting?"

"You bet I do," the Negro said. "And if what you deliver ain't what I see now, Godspeed'll have some talking to do with the U.S. Navy. Like I say, it's a good company, but things like that can happen. I want to make sure ahead of time they don't."

"I'll make sure of it," Butcher promised. Charlie nodded, as if to say he'd check anyway. His ex-shipmate, unfazed, led him and Sylvia and her children along the wharf to Number 16. Sylvia got first choice, and picked a couple of fine young cod. When she started to open her handbag, Butcher waved for her not to bother. "Now that I think about it, these are on the house."

Sylvia couldn't have been more astonished if he'd burst into song. "You don't have to do that, Fred," she said. "You were doing me a favor when you gave me a good deal. This is too much."

"No, no, no." The quick, decisive way Butcher shook his head reminded Sylvia of the dapper man he'd been only a few years before. "I just recalled—George was on the *Ericsson*, wasn't he?" He waited for Sylvia to nod, then went on, "Take 'em, then, and don't say another word about it. Times can't be easy for you."

"They aren't," Sylvia admitted. "God bless you, Fred." She dipped her head to Charlie White. "Remember me to your wife, please." As he promised to do that, she steered her children out of the Godspeed & Co. shop.

"That was nice of that man, Ma," George, Jr., said.

"He used to sail with your father," Sylvia answered. "Now we'll have some good suppers with this fish." And her budget, which was always tight, would have a little more stretch to it during the coming week. That was as well, because . . . "There's one more thing I want to get while we're out. Come on, you two. We're going to Abie's."

"Hurray!" Sylvia couldn't tell whether George, Jr., or Mary Jane cheered louder. They both loved going to the pawnshop. Anything in the world—anything from anywhere in the world—was liable to be there. Sylvia remembered seeing a set of false teeth smiling at her from the front window one day. Next to that, who could get excited about something as mundane as a stuffed owl?

Abie Finkelstein, the proprietor of the pawnshop, looked rather like a frog. "Hello, Mrs. Enos," he said in a thick, not quite German accent. "Vot can I do for you today? If your little children a piece candy from the bowl there on the counter take, I do not think I even notice." At Sylvia's nod, George, Jr., and Mary Jane helped themselves. Finkelstein looked a question at Sylvia.

"I don't want any candy, thanks." But that wasn't all of what he'd asked, not even close. She pointed to the items hanging on brackets on the wall behind him. "Let me have that one, please."

"All right." He got it down. "Everybody needs these days to be safe."

"Yes," Sylvia said. "Everybody does."

XVII

Cincinnatus Driver pulled into the Des Moines railroad yard well before six in the morning, well before sunup. Most of the year, he'd found, business there was better and steadier than along the riverfront. He missed going over by the river; he'd been doing it for a long time, both down in Covington and since moving to his new home here. But he didn't miss an empty wallet, not even a little he didn't.

Early as he was, several other trucks were already waiting for the Chicago and North Western Railroad Line train to pull into the yard. Three or four others came in while he drank lukewarm coffee from a flask Elizabeth had given him. He sat in the cab of the Duryea and yawned. It wasn't so much that he hadn't got enough sleep the night before: more that he was always busy and always tired.

The train pulled into the yard at 6:35, right on time. Then the drivers scrambled to make deals with the conductor, who did the same job as a steamboat clerk and had the same cold blood in his veins.

For a while, Cincinnatus had had trouble getting any work at all from these hard-eyed gentlemen. That was partly because he'd been new to Des Moines and even more because he had a dark skin. He knew as much. He'd expected nothing more.

But he was still here. He'd got his foot in the door, he'd proved he was reliable . . . and now he was dickering with a conductor over a load of rolled oats for one of the last few livery stables in town. "Have a heart, Jerry," he said, putting a hand over his own heart. "You wouldn't pay that low if I was white."

Jerry rolled his eyes. "You're a Hebe in blackface, Cincinnatus, that's what you are. You want me to see if I can get somebody else to haul the stuff for that price?"

"Go ahead," Cincinnatus said. "Somebody else wants to lose money on gasoline and wear and tear on his truck, that's his affair. You don't pay me another dollar, it ain't worth my time and trouble."

"You *are* a Hebe," the conductor said. "All right, dammit, another four bits."

"Six bits," Cincinnatus said. "Six bits and I break even, anyways."

"What a damn liar you are. Tell me you don't sandbag when you play poker." Jerry puffed out his cheeks, then exhaled. "Awright, six bits. The hell with it. Deal?"

"Deal," Cincinnatus said at once, and went to get his hand truck to move the barrels of oats.

When he got to the livery stable, the proprietor, a big, ruddy, white-haired man named Hiram Schacht, said, "Stow the barrels in that corner there." He pointed.

"Will do, Mistuh Schacht," Cincinnatus answered. From everything he'd seen, Schacht didn't treat him any worse because he was colored. The stable owner approved of anyone who helped him care for his beloved horses. The trouble was, he had fewer horses to care for every month. People kept buying automobiles.

As Cincinnatus rolled barrel after barrel past the old man, Schacht sighed and said, "Getting harder and harder to stay in business. Back before the war, I'd have gone through an order this size in a week. Now it'll last me two, maybe three." He scratched at his bushy mustache. "Pretty soon, I won't need to order any oats at all. That'll cut down on my overhead, now won't it?" His laugh held little mirth.

"Well, suh, you don't see me bringin' you these oats in a wagon with a team pullin' it, now do you?" Cincinnatus said. "Automobiles and trucks, they're the coming thing."

"Oh, I know, I know," Schacht said, unoffended; they'd had this conversation before. "But I'm heading toward my threescore and ten, as the Good Book says. Up till a couple years ago, I was sure the stable would last out my lifetime, and I was damn glad of it, too: I'm just flat-out crazy about horses. Motorcars have no soul to 'em, and they smell bad, too. Anyway, though, I ain't so sure now. I'm lasting longer than I reckoned I would, and more people are getting rid of their horses faster than I reckoned they would."

"Can't blame me for that," Cincinnatus said as he trundled the dolly back out to the Duryea for another barrel of oats. "Never had me a horse—never could afford one—before I got the chance to buy my truck. By then, I figured a truck'd do me more good."

"Do your wallet more good, anyway," Schacht said, and Cincinnatus nodded; that was what he'd meant, all right. The stable owner went on, "A horse'd do your spirit more good, though. You can make friends with a horse—oh, not with all horses; some of 'em are stupid as fenceposts and a hell of a lot meaner, and God knows I know it—but with some horses, anyways. What can you feel about a truck? When it breaks down, all you want to do is kill it, but you can't even do that, on account of the son of a bitch is already dead."

Having had the urge to murder the Duryea a good many times since buying it, Cincinnatus could only nod. He did say, "Man's got to eat."

"Oh, no doubt about it," Schacht said. "I don't begrudge folks their autos and their trucks—well, not much I don't, anyways. But back when you were a pup, everybody had horses—near enough everybody, I guess I ought to say—and motorcars were toys for rich men. By the time you get as old as I am, it'll be the other way round, I bet: everybody'll have himself a motorcar, but only rich folks'll be able to keep horses."

"Could be so," Cincinnatus agreed. In fact, he found it very likely, and likely to happen sooner than Schacht had predicted, too. He wouldn't have been surprised to find out that the livery-stable man thought the same thing.

"You take care of yourself, Cincinnatus," Schacht said after he'd brought in the last barrel of oats, "and take care of that rattle-trap contraption you drive."

"Thank you kindly, Mistuh Schacht." Cincinnatus touched the brim of his cloth cap in salute. "Hope it's me bringin' your oats next time you need some."

"I wouldn't mind." Schacht scratched at that walrus mustache again; he didn't bother waxing it up into a stylish Kaiser Bill. As Cincinnatus fired up the Duryea, the stable owner added, "By the time you get as old as I am, folks will be trading in their autos for flying machines—but rich folks'll still keep horses." He shouted to make himself heard over the thunderous roar of the engine.

"Flying machines," Cincinnatus said to himself. All he knew about them was that he didn't want to go up in one; the miserable things were too likely to fall out of the sky, with gruesomely fatal results the newspapers liked to play up. Maybe they'd solve all the problems by the time Achilles was an old man. Maybe they wouldn't, too. Either way, it would be for his son to worry about.

He picked up another hauling job when he went back to the railroad yard, and then another one. That one took him through his own neighborhood—right past the school where Achilles went. The kindergarten classes were just letting out as he drove by: sure enough, there was Achilles along with his schoolmates, who included blacks, whites, and the daughter of the Chinese laundryman upstairs. In Kentucky, Cincinnatus would never have dreamt that his son would go to a school whites also used. Iowans seemed to take it for granted.

Cincinnatus squeezed the bulb of the Duryea's raucous horn. All the little kids looked his way. "That's my pa!" Achilles squealed, loud enough for Cincinnatus to hear him over the Duryea's motor.

"Wow! What a swell truck!" a white boy exclaimed, also loudly. Cincinnatus laughed, waved, and drove on. Only to a six-year-old would this truck have seemed swell. Had the kid said *funny-looking* or *beat-up*, he would have been closer to the mark. But Cincinnatus had succeeded in impressing one of his son's pals, so swinging by the school had been all to the good.

"Pals." Cincinnatus spoke the word he'd just thought. Could a Negro boy in Des Moines have real white friends? He'd probably have to be able to, if he expected to have more than a handful of friends: there wouldn't be enough other colored boys to go around. But, for a Negro from Covington, it was a strange and troubling notion. Cincinnatus would have been willing to bet it was a strange and troubling notion for a lot of whites from Des Moines, too.

When he got home that evening, Achilles was still bubbling over with pride. "Louie Henderson and Joey Nichols both said that was the swellest truck they ever saw," he reported.

"That's good," Cincinnatus said. He paused and listened again in his mind to what his son had just told him. When he'd been Achilles' age, back before the turn of the century, he would surely have said *they ever seen*. He still said things like that every now and then, or maybe more often than every now and then. Achilles had said them, too, till he started going to school: he'd listened to his mother and father and, while they were still down in Covington, to his grandmother as well. Now he listened to his teacher and to the boys and girls in class with him.

"Yeah, he's learnin' to talk like a Yankee, all right," Elizabeth said when Cincinnatus remarked on it over supper. "I seen that myself." She didn't notice her own slip. To her, it wasn't a slip: it was just the way she talked. It had been the same for Cincinnatus, too, but it wasn't any more. The more like a white he talked, the less likely people here—even other Negroes here, he'd seen—were to reckon him a dumb nigger. Not being thought of that way usually worked to his advantage.

After supper, Achilles read aloud from his primer and Cincinnatus read to him from an abridgement of *Robinson Crusoe* he'd picked up for a dime in a secondhand store. The sentences in the primer and the story of the castaway both used white folks' grammar—they used it rather better than a lot of the white folks with whom Cincinnatus did business. The more of those kinds of sentences Achilles read and had read to him, the more natural they would seem, and the more he would likely end up sounding like a white man himself. Up here, that couldn't help but be useful.

After Achilles had gone to bed, Cincinnatus sat on the sofa and read ahead in *Robinson Crusoe*; he was enjoying the tale himself. Elizabeth mended clothes on a chair under the other electric lamp. She'd sew a few stitches along a seam, yawn, and then sew a few more stitches.

Cincinnatus set down his book. "You know," he said, "we've done a lot better for ourselves up here than I figured we would 'fore we left Covington. Things keep going good a little while longer, maybe we can think about buyin' us a house here." He spoke hesitantly; he wasn't used to getting even a little ahead of the game.

Elizabeth yawned again. "You reckon Achilles asleep yet?" she asked.

Despite the yawn, Cincinnatus thought he knew why she asked that question. "Hope so," he answered, a large, male grin on his face. "Sure do hope so."

His wife would usually make a face of her own in response to that grin. Tonight, she ignored it. "Didn't want to say nothin' where he can hear it," she told Cincinnatus, "not yet—too soon. But I reckon I'm in the family way again."

"For true?" he said, and Elizabeth nodded. He thought about that, then started to laugh.

His wife's eyes flashed. "What's funny? Don't you want another baby?"

"Don't have much choice, do I?" Cincinnatus said, but that wasn't close to the right answer. He tried to improve it: "Just when you think you get up on things, life goes and hands you another surprise. This one, though, it sure enough is a nice surprise." He waited anxiously, then thought of something better to do: he walked over and kissed Elizabeth. Even without words, that did turn out to be the right answer.

Jefferson Pinkard put on his white shirt and butternut trousers. Both were freshly laundered and pressed. Ever since throwing Emily out of his cottage, he'd grown careless about the shirts and overalls and dungarees he wore to work. When he donned the white and butternut, though, he wasn't just himself: he was part of the Freedom Party. If he didn't look sharp, he let the Party down.

He went into the bathroom, examined himself in the streaky mirror there, and frowned. He rubbed some Pinaud's brilliantine into his hair, washed the greasy stuff off his hands, and combed out a nice, straight part. "That's more like it," he said. He grabbed his club off the sofa in the front room and headed out the door.

Bedford Cunningham sat on his front porch, enjoying the warm June Sunday afternoon. By the glass at his side and by the way he sprawled, he'd been enjoying it for quite a while. Pinkard raised the club as he walked by. His neighbor, his former friend, cringed. That was what he'd wanted to accomplish. He kept walking.

He wasn't the only man in Party regalia who'd come to the trolley stop by the Sloss Works company housing. Three or four of his comrades greeted him as he came up: "Freedom!"

"Freedom!" he answered, and grinned a fierce grin. "Reckon we're going to teach Wade Hampton V a thing or two about sticking his nose in where it's not welcome, ain't we, boys?"

"That's right. That's just right," the other Freedom Party men said, almost in chorus. Jeff was glad to have the reassurance, though he didn't really need it. Hampton might have won the election, but he had a lot of damn nerve to go barnstorming around the country making speeches and trying to pump up the Whigs. Who did he think he was, Jake Featherston or somebody?

Nobody sat near the men in white and butternut as the trolley rattled through the streets of Birmingham all the way out to the Alabama State Fairgrounds at the west edge of town, where Hampton would speak. When Negroes got on or off, they edged past the Freedom Party men and made their way to or from the back of the trolley car as if afraid they would be set upon at any moment. They had reason to fear; such things had happened before.

"State Fairgrounds! End of the line!" the trolley driver announced, and loudly clanged his bell.

"End of the line for Wade Hampton, all right," Pinkard said, and the other Freedom Party men laughed wolfishly.

Caleb Briggs, the dentist who headed the Freedom Party in Birmingham, was marshaling his forces at the edge of the fairgrounds. "Won't be easy this time, boys," he rasped in his gas-ruined voice. "Goddamn governor got wind of what we had in mind and called out the goddamn militia. Anything we want, we're going to have to take."

Pinkard looked west across the rolling, grassy countryside to the platform from which President Hampton would speak. Sure enough, there were men in butternut and old-fashioned gray uniforms along with those in shirtsleeves or black civilian coats. The sun glinted off bayonets. He'd seen that too many times in Texas to mistake it for anything else.

Suddenly, the club in his hand didn't seem such a wonderful weapon at all. He asked, "We move on those sons of bitches, they going to open up on us?"

"I don't know," Briggs answered. "Only one way to find out, though, and that's what we're going to do." He raised his voice: "Anybody who hasn't got the balls to go forward, run along home to mama. The rest of us, we'll see if those summer soldiers mean it or if they'll fold when we come at 'em. Nobody's stopped us yet. My bet is, nobody can. Let's go."

Everybody advanced. Pinkard's mouth was dry, as it had been when he came up out of the trenches, but he kept going. It wasn't that he lacked fear: far more that he feared letting his comrades know he was afraid. If they didn't feel the same way, he'd have been astonished. On they came, through the ankle-high grass, past the little groves of shade trees planted here and there on the fairgrounds. The muggy heat accounted for only some of the sweat on Jeff's face.

The militiamen deployed to meet the Freedom Party stalwarts. They were outnumbered, but they had the rifles and the bayonets and the helmets. Pinkard didn't like the way they moved. Their manner said they were not about to give way for anything or anybody.

To applause from the smallish crowd in front of him, President Hampton began to speak. Pinkard paid scant heed to his amplified words. Why bother? They'd be full of lies anyhow. The major moving out ahead of the militiamen was more important. The fellow held up a hand. "You men halt right there," he said. "This is your first, last, and only warning."

"Hold up, boys," Caleb Briggs said, and the Freedom Party men obeyed him, not the militia major. He spoke to the officer: "Who are you to tell us we can't protest against the so-called policies of the government in Richmond?"

"You can stay right here," the major answered. "You can shout your fool heads off. I don't give a damn about that. If you take one step forward from where you stand now, I will assume you are attempting to riot, not to protest, and I will order you shot down like dogs. Those are my orders, and I shall carry them out. So will my men. If you think we are bluffing, sir, I invite you to try us."

Jeff didn't think the major was bluffing. The soldiers behind him looked ready, even eager, to open fire. The governor had picked with care the troops he'd activated. Caleb Briggs came to the same conclusion. "You'll pay for this, Major, when the day comes," he hissed.

"If you take that step, sir, you'll pay for it now," the major told him. "Your ruffians have gotten away with too many things for too long. You will not get away with anything today, by God. You may do what the law allows. If you do even a single thing the law does not allow, you will pay for it."

The stalwarts jeered him and hooted at him and cursed him. He seemed to worry about that no more than a man with a good slicker and a broad-brimmed hat worried about going out in the rain. And not one of the Freedom Party men took the step forward that would have made the officer issue his fatal order.

"All right, boys," Briggs said. "Maybe we won't give Hampton the tyrant what-for today in person. But we can let him know what we think of him, right? This here country still has freedom of speech."

"Freedom!" was the chant they raised, a loud and mocking chant. Jefferson Pinkard bellowed out the word as ferociously as he could, doing everything in his power to drown out the president of the Confederate States. As far as he was concerned, Jake Featherston should have been up on the platform a few hundred yards away. He would have told the truth, not the bland lies Wade Hampton V spewed forth. The bland crowd ate them up, too, and cheered Hampton almost as if they had true spirit.

"Freedom! Freedom! Freedom!" All the stalwarts were roaring, doing their best to show Hampton and show the world the militia hadn't cowed them. *Maybe next time we'll bring rifles, too,* Pinkard thought. It had almost come to that during the presidential campaign. After fighting the damnyankees, he did not shy away from fighting his own government. "Freedom! Freedom! Freedom!"

When the first shot rang out from the grove of hackberry trees off to the right of the Freedom Party men, Jeff didn't hear it. But he saw Wade Hampton V stagger on the platform and clutch at his chest. He did hear the second shot. That second bullet must have caught Hampton in the head or the heart, for he stopped staggering and went down as if all his bones had turned to water.

A few of the stalwarts whooped when the president of the Confederate States fell. Most, though, Pinkard among them, stared in the horrified silence that filled the crowd of Hampton's backers. Men dashed across the platform to the president's side. Jeff didn't think they'd be able to do much for him. He'd seen too many men go down in that boneless way during the Great War. Hardly any of them ever got up again.

From the hackberry grove came a wild, exultant shout: "Freedom!"

"Sergeant Davenport! Sergeant Sullivan!" the militia major rapped out. "Take your troops in among those trees and bring that man to me. I don't care whether he's breathing or not, but bring him to me."

Two squads of militiamen trotted toward the hackberries. Another shot rang out. A man fell. Another shot from the trees—this one a miss, the bullet whining past not far from Pinkard. Without conscious thought, he threw himself flat. A lot of Freedom Party men and a lot of militiamen did the same. The advancing militiamen opened fire on the grove.

Caleb Briggs stayed on his feet. More than gas roughened his voice as he said, "That man is not one of ours, Major. My God, I—"

One of the dignitaries on the platform walked up to the microphone. "President Hampton is dead." He sounded astonished, disbelieving.

Jeff understood that. He felt stunned and empty himself. He'd been ready—he'd been eager—to fight for the Freedom Party, but this . . . No one had murdered—*assassinated,* he supposed was the proper word—a president in the history of the Confederate States, or in the history of the United States before the Confederacy seceded.

Drawing his pistol, the militia major aimed it at Briggs. More shots came from the hackberries. Another militiaman went down with a shriek. But some of the others were in among the trees. The major ignored that action. Infinite bitterness filled his voice: "Not one of yours, you say? He shouts your shout. He uses your methods. Politics was not war till the Freedom Party made it so."

"Now listen here—" Briggs began.

Triumphant cries rang out from the hackberry grove. Through them, the major said, "No, sir. You listen to me. Get your rabble out of here by the count of five, or I will turn my men loose on them and we will have a massacre the likes of which this country has never seen. Maybe it's one we should have had a couple of years ago—then things wouldn't have come to this. One . . . two . . . three—"

"Go home, boys," Caleb Briggs said quickly. His face was gray. "For the love of God, go home. There's been enough blood spilled today."

"Too much," the militia major said. "Far too much. You disappoint me, Mr. Briggs. I would have liked to shoot you down."

Briggs stood silent, letting himself be reviled. As Jefferson Pinkard got to his feet, militiamen came out of the hackberry grove. They were dragging a body by the feet. The corpse wore butternut trousers and a green shirt, now soaked with blood. The gunman must have been almost invisible in among the trees. Jeff stared at his long, pale, sharp-nosed face. He'd seen that face at Party meetings, not regularly, but every so often. The fellow was named Grady . . . Grady Something-or-other. Jeff knew he'd talked with him, but couldn't remember his surname.

From the appalled looks on other Party stalwarts' faces, he knew they also recognized the assassin. The militia major saw that, too. "Not one of yours, eh?" he repeated. "Another lie. Get out of my sight before I forget myself."

Briggs went. Jeff stumbled after him, along with his comrades. Someone close by was moaning. After a moment, he realized it was himself. *What do we—what do I—do now?* he wondered. *Sweet suffering Jesus, what do I do now?*

Anne Colleton was frying chicken for supper when her brother came into the kitchen of the large apartment they still shared. She started to greet him, then got a good look at his face. She hadn't seen that kind of dazed, horrified expression since the war. Above the cheerful crackling of the chicken, she asked, "My God, Tom, what's gone wrong?"

By way of answer, he held up the copy of the *Columbia South Carolinian* he carried under his arm. The headline was enormous and very, very black:

PRESIDENT MURDERED IN BIRMINGHAM!!!

Under it, a half-page subhead said, FREEDOM PARTY ASSASSIN SHOT DEAD AT ALABAMA STATE FAIRGROUNDS.

"My God," Anne said again. "Oh, my God." Mechanically, she kept turning the floured chicken in the hot fat.

"I think you'd better do the same with your investments in the Freedom Party as you did with your Confederate investments right after the war," Tom told her, "and that's get rid of 'em. This time tomorrow, Jake Featherston's going to be worth less than a Confederate dollar, and that's saying something."

She shook her head. "Featherston would never order that kind of thing."

"I didn't say he did, though I wouldn't put it past him if he thought he could get away with it," Tom replied. "But that hasn't got anything to do with it. You think what he ordered or didn't order matters? Only thing that matters is, one of his people pulled the trigger. Who's going to vote for a party that blows the head off the president if they don't care what he's up to?"

"No one," Anne said dully. Tom was right. She wasn't so naive as to pretend otherwise. She'd been riding the crest of the Freedom Party wave up and up and up. She'd been sure she could ride it all the way into the president's residence in Richmond. And so she could have. She remained certain of that. But now . . . "The son of a bitch," she whispered. "The stupid son of a bitch."

"Who? The late Grady Calkins?" Tom said. "You bet he was a stupid son of a bitch. But who built a whole party out of stupid sons of bitches? Who aimed 'em at the country and fired 'em off, first with bare knuckles and then with clubs and pistols? You know who as well as I do, Sis. Is it any wonder one of 'em picked up a Tredegar and decided to go president hunting?"

Anne had never thought, never dreamt, such a thing might happen. That didn't necessarily mean it was any wonder, though, not when you looked at it the way her brother suggested. "What do we do now?" she said. She rarely asked for advice, but her mind remained blank with shock.

Tom didn't have a lot of help to offer. "I don't know," he said. "You burned a lot of bridges when you went with Featherston. How the devil do you propose to get back across them?"

"I don't know, either," Anne said. "Maybe things will straighten out somehow." Even to herself, she didn't sound as if she believed that. Hot lard splashed up and bit the back of her hand. She swore with a fervor that wrung a couple of embarrassed chuckles from her brother.

The chicken was ready a few minutes later. In the years since Marshlands burned, she'd turned into a pretty fair cook. Before then, she'd have had trouble boiling water. But she took no pleasure in crispy skin or moist, juicy, flavorsome flesh. She hardly noticed what she ate, as a matter of fact: the chicken was bones and the baked potato that went with it reduced to its jacket without any apparent passage of time.

After supper, Tom pulled a bottle of whiskey from the shelf where it sat. That, Anne noticed. "Pour me a slug, too, will you?" she asked.

"I sure will." He did. Anne wanted to drink to the point of oblivion, but refrained. Far more than most in the Confederate States, she appreciated the value of a clear head. But oh, the temptation!

As she drank the one drink she allowed herself, she read the newspaper Tom had brought home. Grady Calkins was an out-of-work veteran who'd belonged to the Freedom Party. Past that, the reporters hadn't found out much about him. That was plenty. That was more than plenty.

"He shouted 'Freedom!' after he shot Hampton down," Tom said, as if to rub salt in the wound.

"Yes, I read that," Anne answered. "It's a disaster. I admit it. I don't see how I can deny it. It's a disaster every way you look at it."

"It sure is," Tom said. "God only knows what kind of president Burton Mitchel will make."

"I don't think anybody outside of Arkansas knows anything about Burton Mitchel, maybe including God," Anne said. Tom let out a startled snort of laughter. Anne went on, "The Whigs plucked him out of the Senate to balance the ticket; Featherston would have done the same thing if he'd chosen Willy Knight. All Mitchel was supposed to do was sit there for the next six years."

"He'll do more than that now," her brother said. "Christ, a backwoods bumpkin running the country till 1927. Just what we need!"

"Look on the bright side," Anne told him.

"I didn't know there was any bright side *to* look on," Tom answered.

"Of course there is. There always is," Anne said. "The bright side here is: how could things get any worse?"

"That's a point," Tom acknowledged. "The other side of the coin is, now we get to find out how things get worse."

Anne opened the *South Carolinian* to the inside page on which the story of President Hampton's assassination was continued. She read aloud: "'After taking the oath of office, President Mitchel declared a week of national mourning and lamentation. The new president prayed for the aid of almighty God in the difficult times that lie ahead, and said he would do his best to promote internal order, establish good relations with foreign neighbors, and put the currency on a sound basis once more.'" Her lip curled. "And while he's at it, he'll walk across the James River without getting his trouser cuffs wet."

"What's he supposed to say?" her brother asked, and she had no good answer. Tom continued, "Those are the things that need doing, no doubt about it. I haven't any idea whether he can do them, but at least he knows that much. And after this"—Tom took a deep breath—"after this, maybe people will back off and give him room to move in for a while."

"Maybe," Anne said. "I don't know if that will help, but maybe." She shoved the newspaper to one side. "And maybe everything I've done since the end of the war to try to set the CSA to rights went up in smoke with a couple of shots from that maniac's gun. If the militiamen hadn't killed that Calkins, I'd be glad to do it myself—but I think I'd have to stand in line behind Jake Featherston."

"Probably," Tom agreed. "Calkins may have killed the Freedom Party along with a Whig president. Featherston has to know that—he isn't stupid. But he's the one who raised the devil. He's got no business being surprised if it ended up turning on him."

"That isn't fair," Anne said, but even in her own ears her voice lacked conviction. Tom said nothing at all, leaving her with the last word. She'd never been so sorry to have it.

When she walked to the tailor's the next morning, people in the streets of St. Matthews, white and black alike, fell silent and stared at her as she went by. They'd been talking about the assassination. They started talking about the assassination again as soon as she passed. While she was close by, they would not talk. Some of them moved away from her, as if they didn't want her shadow to fall on them. She'd been the dominant force in this part of South Carolina for more than a decade. People had always granted her the deference she'd earned. By the way they acted now, she might have just escaped from a leper colony.

Going into Aaron Rosenblum's shop felt like escaping. *Clack, clack, clack* went the treadle of his sewing machine. The clacking stopped when the bell above his door rang. He looked up from the piece of worsted he'd been guiding through the machine. "Good morning, Miss Colleton," he said, polite but no more than polite.

He got to his feet. "I have ready the skirt you asked me to make for you."

"Good. I hoped you would." As was often her way, Anne chose to take the bull by the horns. "Terrible about President Hampton yesterday."

"Yes." The little old tailor looked at her over the tops of his half-glasses. "A very terrible thing. But what can you expect from a party that would sooner fight than think?"

Rosenblum had to know she backed the Freedom Party. She'd made no secret of it—on the contrary. If he thought he could rebuke her like this . . . If that was so, the Party was in as much trouble as she'd feared. In a tight voice, she said, "The Freedom Party is trying to make the Confederate States strong again."

"Oh, yes. Of course." The tailor had a peculiar accent, half lazy South Carolina Low Country, the other half Yiddish. "And I, I am a lucky man to live now in the Confederacy. In Russia, where I am from, parties that try to make the country strong again go after the Jews. Here, you go after black people instead, so I am safe. Yes, I am a lucky man."

Anne stared at him. She knew sarcasm when she heard it. And Rosenblum's words held an uncomfortable amount of truth. "That isn't all the Freedom Party does," Anne said. The tailor did not answer. What hung in the air was, *Yes, you also shoot the president.* Twice now in two days, she would sooner not have been left with the last word. She attempted briskness: "Let me see the skirt, if you please."

"Yes, ma'am." He gave it to her, then waved her to a changing room. "Try it on. I will alter it if it does not suit you."

Try it on she did. The gray wool skirt fit perfectly around the waist; she might be irked at Rosenblum, but he did good work. And the length was in the new mode, as she'd requested: it showed off not only her ankles but also several inches of shapely calf. Tom would pitch a fit. Too bad for Tom. Roger Kimball would approve, though he'd sooner see her naked altogether.

She changed back into the black skirt she'd worn, then paid Rosenblum for the new gray one: a bargain at two billion dollars. "Thank you very much," he said, tucking the banknotes into a drawer.

"You're welcome," she said, and then, "I *am* sorry the president is dead. I don't care whether you believe me or not."

"If you didn't care, you wouldn't say you didn't care," Rosenblum answered. While she was still unraveling that, he went on, "I do believe you, Miss Colleton. But now you believe me, too: a party that shouts and shoots for freedom is not a party that really wants it."

Another paradox. Anne shook her head. "I haven't got time for riddles today. Good morning." The new skirt folded over her arm, she stalked out of the tailor's shop.

Chester Martin sat down in a folding chair at the Socialist Party hall near the Toledo steel mill where he worked. "What did you call the Freedom Party down in the CSA?" he asked Albert Bauer. "Reaction on the march? Was that it? You hit the nail right on the head."

"Yeah, even for a reactionary party, shooting a reactionary president dead because he's not reactionary enough to suit them takes a lot of doing," Bauer allowed. "They'll be sorry, too, you mark my words."

"They're sorry already, I'll bet," Martin said. "It'll be a cold day in hell before they come so close to winning an election again."

"They'll be sorrier, too," Bauer predicted. "They've done something I wouldn't have bet they could: they've made people in the United States feel sorry for the Confederate States."

"They've even made me feel that way, and some Rebel bastard shot me," Martin said. "But shooting a president—" He shook his head. "Nobody's ever done that before, there or here. What is the world coming to?"

"Revolution," Bauer answered. "And the reactionaries in the CSA just gave the progressive forces here a leg up. Before, President Sinclair couldn't have gotten ending reparations through Congress if his life depended on it. Now, though, I think he may just have the votes to pull it off."

"Do you?" Martin wasn't so sure he liked the idea. "As far as I can see, we'd be better off if the Confederates stayed broke and weak."

"Sure we would, in the short run," Bauer said. "But in the long run, if the Confederate States keep going down the drain, who does that help? That Featherston lunatic almost won the election last year because the Rebs were in such bad shape. What happens if they get worse?"

"Well, they aren't going to have a revolution—not a Red one, anyway," Martin said. He got up, went over to a coffeepot that sat on top of an iron stove, and poured himself a cup. After he set it down on the table, he lit a cigarette.

Bauer waited patiently till he'd puffed a couple of times, then nodded. "No, they won't have a Red revolution, not right away. It's a conservative country, and Marxism is tied to the black man there, which means the white man has, or thinks he has, a strong extra reason to hate it. But the Confederates' time is coming, too. Sooner or later, all the capitalist countries will have their revolutions."

He spoke with the certainty of a devout Catholic talking about the miracle of transubstantiation. Chester Martin's faith in Socialism was newer, more pragmatic, and neither so deep nor so abiding. He said, "Maybe so, Al, but there's liable to be a hell of a long time hiding in that *sooner or later.*"

"The dialectic doesn't say how fast things will happen," Bauer answered calmly. "It just says they *will* happen, and that's enough for me."

"Maybe for you," Martin said. "Me, I'd sort of like to know whether a revolution's coming in my time or whether it's something my great-grandchildren will be waiting for—if I ever have any." He wasn't so young as he had been. There were times when he wished he'd found a girl as soon as he came home from the war, or maybe even before then. But work in the foundry and work for the Socialist Party left little time for courting, or even thinking about courting.

Back when he'd been a Democrat, he'd thought Socialist girls were loose, without a moral to their name. People said it so often, he'd been sure it was true. Now, rather to his regret, he knew better. A lot of the women in the Socialist Party were married to Socialist men. A lot of the ones who weren't might as well have been married to the Party. That left . . . slim pickings.

Albert Bauer said, "Even if we don't get a revolution in the CSA any time soon, we don't want the reactionaries in charge down there. That would turn the class struggle on its head. As far as I'm concerned, keeping the Freedom Party down is reason enough to let reparations go."

"Well, maybe," Martin said. He wouldn't say any more than *maybe*, no matter how his friend tried to argue him around. He was sorry the Confederates had had their president shot. He wouldn't have wished that even on the CSA. But not wishing anything bad on the Confederate States didn't necessarily mean he wished anything good on them, either.

After he got home that evening, the topic came up again around

the supper table. He'd expected it would; the newsboys were hawking papers by shouting about reparations. "What do you think,
Chester?" Stephen Douglas Martin asked. "You were the one who
was doing the fighting."

"Hard to say, Pa," Martin answered. "I used to think that, if I
ever saw a Reb drowning, I'd toss him an anvil. Now—I just don't
know."

"Can't we let the war be over at last?" Louisa Martin said.
"Haven't both sides been through enough yet? When can we be satisfied?"

"Might as well ask the Mormons out West, Ma," her daughter
Sue said. "They just took some shots at a couple of Army trucks—
did you see that in the newspaper? They don't forget we beat them.
You can bet the Confederates haven't forgotten we beat them. So
why should we forget it?"

"It goes both ways, though," Chester said. "It's not an easy
question. If we keep holding the Rebs down, they'll hate us on
account of that. They did it to us for years and years, after the War
of Secession and then after the Second Mexican War. Do we want
them thinking about nothing but paying us back, the way we
worked so hard to get even with them and with England and
France?"

"You sound like a Socialist, all right," his father said, laughing.
"Pass the peas, will you, you lousy Red?"

Chester laughed, too, and passed the bowl. "Talking to you and
Mother, I sound like a Socialist. When I talk to people down at the
Socialist hall, I sound like a Democrat half the time. I've noticed that
before. I'm stuck in the middle, you might say."

"People who can see both sides of the question usually are," his
mother told him. "It's not the worst place in the world to be."

Sue Martin looked curiously at Chester. "With that Purple
Heart in your bedroom, I'd think you'd be the last one to want to let
the Confederates up off the floor."

He shrugged. "Like Mother says, maybe it's time for the war to
be over and done with. Besides, the one thing I don't want to do is
have to fight those . . . so-and-so's again." Talking about a new war
almost made him slip back into the foul language of the trenches. "If
they can settle down because they're not paying reparations any
more, that might not be too bad."

"You make good sense, son," Stephen Douglas Martin said. His
wife nodded. After a moment, so did Sue. Martin's father went on,

"Now, what are the odds that anybody in Congress would know common sense if it flew around Philadelphia in an aeroplane?"

"There's a Socialist majority," Martin said. But that didn't prove anything, and he knew it. "We'll just have to wait and see, won't we?"

Out of the blue, Sue asked, "How do you think that Congresswoman you met would vote? You know the one I mean—the one whose brother got wounded while he was in your squad?"

"Flora Hamburger," Martin said. "Yeah, sure, I know who you mean. That's a good question. She usually does what's right. I don't really know. We'll have to keep watching the newspapers, I guess."

"Flora Hamburger." Louisa Martin snapped her fingers. "I know where I saw that name. She's the one who got engaged to the vice president a little while ago." She looked from her son to her daughter and back again, as if to say getting engaged would satisfy her: catching a vice president was unnecessary.

"Mother," Sue said in warning tones.

"She's just giving you a rough time," Martin said. That got his sister and his mother both glaring at him. He forked up some peas, freshly conscious of the dangers peacemakers faced when they stepped between warring factions.

When Chester looked up from the peas, he found his father eyeing him with more than a little amusement. Stephen Douglas Martin had the good sense to stay out of a quarrel he couldn't hope to influence.

Over the next few days, the debate about reparations stayed in the newspapers, along with the reprisals the Army was taking against the perennially rebellious Mormons in Utah. The collision of two aeroplanes carrying mail elbowed both those stories out of the headlines for a little while, but the excitement about the crash died quickly—though not so quickly as the two luckless pilots had.

When Flora Hamburger came out in favor of ending reprisals, the papers carried the news on the front page. "Conscience of the Congress says yes!" newsboys shouted. "Reparations repeal seen as likely!"

Martin was less impressed with the announcement than he would have been before Congresswoman Hamburger got engaged to Vice President Blackford. In a way, that made her part of the administration proposing the new policy. But then again, from what he knew of her, she wasn't so easy to influence. Maybe she was speaking her mind after all.

"I think the bill will pass now. I hope it works out for the best, that's all," Martin said when Sue asked him about it that night over oxtail soup. "Can't know till it happens."

"When you do something, you can't know ahead of time what will come of it," his father said. "Politicians will tell you they do, but they don't. Sometimes, you just go ahead and do things and see where they lead."

"That's how the war happened," Martin said. "Nobody imagined it would be so bad when it started. When it started, people cheered. But we locked horns with the Rebs and the Canucks, and for the longest time nobody could go forward or back. I hope this doesn't go wrong the same way, that's all."

"Sometimes being afraid of what could go wrong is a good reason not to do anything," Stephen Douglas Martin observed.

"You're a Democrat, all right," Chester said.

"Well, so I am," his father agreed. "Upton Sinclair's been in for more than a year now, and I'm switched if I can see how he's set the world on fire."

Louisa Martin said, "We already set the world on fire once, not very long ago. Isn't that enough for you, Stephen?"

"Well, maybe it is, when you put it like that," her husband said. "If letting the Confederates off the hook means we don't have to fight another war, I suppose I'm for it. But if they start spending the money they would have given us on guns and such, that'll cause trouble like you wouldn't believe." He raised his mug of beer. "Here's hoping they've learned their lesson." He sipped the suds.

"Here's hoping," Chester Martin echoed. He drank, too. So did his mother and sister.

Roger Kimball was drunk. He'd been drunk a lot of the time since Grady Calkins shot President Wade Hampton V. Staring down into his glass of whiskey, he muttered, "Stupid bastard. Stupid *fucking* bastard." Calkins might as well have taken his Tredegar and shot the Freedom Party right between the eyes.

The whiskey, Kimball decided, was staring back at him. He drank it down so it wouldn't do that any more. *Any old excuse in a storm,* he thought. He poured himself a fresh glass. Maybe this one would be more polite. Whether it was or not, he'd drink it.

He did a lot of his own pouring these days. Too many people recognized him on the streets and in the saloons of Charleston. A few weeks before, a lot of those people would have greeted him with

a wave and a cheery call of "Freedom!" Now they glared. Sometimes they cursed. One man had threatened to kill him if he saw him
again. Kimball wasn't too alarmed—he knew how to take care of
himself—but he spent more time in his flat than he had.

That meant his bankroll shrank with every day's inflation. He
didn't get into so many card games as he had, which was too damn
bad, because they'd been what kept him afloat. Without them, the
millions that paid the rent one week bought a sandwich the next
week, a cigar the week after that, and were good only as pretty
paper the week after that.

"God *damn* Grady Calkins," he said, and drank some of the
polite whiskey. It wasn't fair. The more whiskey he drank, the more
obviously it wasn't fair. The Freedom Party still stood for exactly the
same things as it had before the madman shot the president. Kimball
still thought those things were as important as he had then. A couple
of weeks before, people had applauded him and applauded Jake
Featherston. Now they wouldn't give the Freedom Party the time of
day. Where was the justice in that?

Tears came into his eyes, a drunk's easy tears. One rolled down
his cheek—or maybe that was just a drop of sweat. Charleston in the
summer, even early in the summer, taught a man everything he
needed to know about sweating and then some.

Kimball knocked back the rest of his drink. At last, instead of
leaving him furious or maudlin, it did what he wanted it to do: it hit
him over the head like a rock. He staggered into the bedroom, took
off his shoes, lay down diagonally across the bed, and passed out
before he could undress.

Sunlight streaming in through the bedroom window woke him
the next morning. It seemed so hot, so bright, so molten, he thought
for a moment he'd died and gone to hell. He squinted his eyes down
to narrow slits so he could come close to bearing the glare. When he
rolled away from it, his head pounded like a submersible's diesel
running at full throttle.

His mouth tasted as if too many people had stubbed out too
many cigars in there. Greasy sweat bathed his body from aching
head to stockinged feet. He thought about getting up and taking a
small nip to ease the worst of the pain, but his stomach did a slow,
horrified loop at the mere idea.

Eventually, he did get up. "Only proves I'm a hero," he said,
and winced at the sound of his own voice even though he hadn't
been so rash as to speak loudly. He staggered into the bathroom,
splashed his face with cold water, and used more cold water to wash

down some aspirins. His stomach let out another loud shout of protest when they landed, as if it were a submarine under heavy attack from depth charges. He wondered if they'd stay down. He gulped a few times, but they did.

He brushed his teeth, which got rid of the worst of the cigar butts. Then he ran a tub full of cold water, stripped off his sweat-soaked clothes, and gingerly stepped in. It felt dreadful and wonderful at the same time. After he'd toweled himself dry and put on a shirt and trousers that didn't smell as if he'd stolen them from a drunk in the gutter, he felt better. Before too long, he might decide he wanted to live after all.

Showing stern military discipline, he walked past the whiskey bottle on the coffee table in the front room and into the kitchen. Black coffee was almost as painful to get down as the aspirins had been, but made him feel better. After some thought, he cut a couple of thick slices of bread and ate them. They sank to his stomach like rocks, but added ballast once there.

He went back into the bathroom and combed his hair in front of the mirror. Only red tracks across the whites of his eyes and a certain general weariness betrayed his hangover to the world. He would do. Donning a straw hat to help shield his eyes from the slings and arrows of outrageous sunbeams, he left the apartment. However much he might have wanted to, he couldn't stay indoors all the time.

Newsboys selling the *Courier* and the *Mercury* both shouted the same headline: "United States end reparations!" The boys with stacks of the *Mercury*, the Whig outlet, added, "President Mitchel says Confederate currency will recover!"

"I'll believe that when I see it," Kimball sneered: both newspapers cost a million dollars. But, if enough people believed it, it might happen. The prospect made him less happy than he would have thought possible. The shrinking—hell, the disappearing—Confederate dollar had helped fuel the Freedom Party's rise.

A cop strode up the street toward Kimball, twirling his billy club in a figure-eight. He recognized the ex–Navy man, and aimed the nightstick at him like a Tredegar. "I catch you and your pals going around making trouble like you used to, I'll run y'all in, you hear? Them's the orders I got from city hall."

"Oh, for Christ's sake, Bob," Kimball answered wearily, "tell me you didn't vote for Featherston and I'll call you a liar to your face."

"That don't have nothing to do with nothing." The policeman brushed a bit of lint from the sleeve of his gray tunic. "Word is, we got to be tough on keeping public order. We ain't messin' around with you boys no more, you hear?"

"I hear you," Kimball said, and went on his way. He would have made sure the Freedom Party walked small for a while, anyway—only sensible thing to do. But getting orders from a fairweather friend rankled.

And, when he opened the door to the Freedom Party's Charleston offices, he realized the orders had been unnecessary for a different reason. The way things were right now, he would have had a devil of a time raising trouble even had he wanted to. The headquarters that had bustled all the way through the presidential campaign and afterwards felt more like a tomb now. Only a few people sat at their desks, none of them doing anything much. *Damn that Calkins,* Kimball thought again.

"God damn it," he said loudly, "it isn't the end of the world."

"Might as well be." Three people, one in the front of the office, one in the middle, and one at the back, said the same thing at the same time.

"No! Jesus Christ, no," Kimball said. "If we were right before that miserable son of a bitch of a Hampton got his head blown off, we're still right now. People *will* see it, so help me God they will."

One of the men who'd said *Might as well be* replied, "I had a rock chucked through my front window the other night. Had a note tied round it with a string, just like in the dime novels."

"The dime novels that cost millions nowadays," Kimball broke in.

As if he hadn't spoken, the Freedom Party functionary went on, "Said my neighbors would whale the tar out of me if I ever went out wearing white and butternut again, or else burn my house down." He gave Kimball as hard a look as he could with his round, doughy face.

Kimball glared back. The leftover pain of his hangover made his scowl even fiercer than it would have been otherwise. "God damn you to hell, Bill Ambrose, I didn't have a thing to do with burning down Tom Brearley's house. I don't do things like that. I might have shot the bastard—Lord knows I wanted to—or I might have beat him to death with a two-by-four, but I wouldn't have done that. It's a coward's way out, like throwing a rock through a window. I go straight after what I don't like. You understand me?"

Bill Ambrose muttered something. Kimball took two swift strides toward him. Feeling the way he did, he was ready—more than ready—to brawl. Ambrose wasn't, though he'd been bold enough when the stalwarts marched. Hastily, he said, "I understand you, Roger."

"You'd damn well better," Kimball growled. "We've got to walk small for a while, that's all. Yeah, some of our summer birds have flown south. Yeah, the cops are going to give us a rough time for a bit. But Jake Featherston's still the only man who can save this country. He's still the only man who has a prayer of licking the United States when we tangle with 'em again. All right, getting to the top won't be as easy as we hoped it would. That doesn't mean we can't do it."

He knew what he sounded like: a fellow at a football game when his team was down by two touchdowns more than halfway through the fourth quarter. If they only tried hard enough, they could still pull it out. If they gave up, they'd get steamrollered.

Looking around the office, he thought a lot of the men still there were on the point of giving up. They'd drift away, go back to being Whigs, and try to pretend their fling with the Freedom Party never happened, as if they'd gone out with a fast woman for a while and then given her up for the homely, familiar girl next door.

"Don't quit," he said earnestly. "That's all I've got to tell you, boys: don't quit. We *are* making this country what it ought to be. We never would have seen passbook laws with teeth if there hadn't been Freedom Party men in Congress. That bastard Layne might have won the election if it hadn't been for us."

Some of the men looked happier. Kimball knew he wasn't the only true-blue Party man here. But somebody behind him said, "Maybe things'll get better anyhow, now that we're not stuck with reparations any more."

That was Kimball's greatest fear. To fight it, he loaded his voice with scorn: "Ha! I know about Burton Mitchel, by God—I'm from Arkansas, too, remember? Only reason he got into the Senate is that his daddy and granddad were there before him—he's another one of those stinking aristocrats. You ask me, if he does anything but sit there like a bump on a log, it'll be the biggest miracle since Jesus raised Lazarus."

A few people laughed: not enough. Kimball spun on his heel and stalked out of the Freedom Party offices. He'd never been aboard a slowly sinking ship, but now he had a good notion of what it felt like.

And he got no relief out on King Street, either. Up the sidewalk toward him came Clarence Potter and Jack Delamotte. Potter's face twisted into a broad, unpleasant smile. "Hello, Roger. Haven't seen you for a while," he said, his almost-Yankee accent grating on Kimball's ears. "I expect you're pleased with the pack of ruffians you chose. By all accounts, you fit right in."

Kimball's hands balled into fists. "First time I ever heard your whiny voice, I wanted to lick you. Just so you know, I haven't changed my mind."

Potter didn't back away, not an inch. And Delamotte took a step forward, saying, "You want him, you've got us both."

Joyously, Kimball waded in. The tiny rational part of his mind said he'd probably end up in the hospital. He didn't care. Potter's nose bent under his fist. As long as he got in a few good licks of his own, what happened to him didn't matter at all.

Sam Carsten was sick to death of the Boston Navy Yard. As far as he could see, the USS *Remembrance* might stay tied up here forever. He expected to find cobwebs hanging from the hawsers that moored the aeroplane carrier to its pier.

"There's nothing we can do, Carsten, not one damn thing," Commander Grady said when he complained about it. "The money's not in the budget for us to do anything but stay in port. We ought to count ourselves lucky they aren't cutting the ship up for scrap."

"They're fools, sir," Sam said. "They're nothing but a pack of fools. There's enough money in the budget for them to let the goddamn Confederates off the hook. But when it comes to us, when it comes to one of the reasons the Rebs had to pay reparations in the first place, a mouse ate a hole in the Socialists' pockets."

"If it makes you feel any better," Grady said, "the Army's feeling the pinch as hard as we are."

"It doesn't make me feel better, sir," Carsten answered. "It makes me feel worse."

"What kind of a Navy man are you, anyway?" the gunnery officer demanded in mock anger. "You're supposed to be happy when the Army takes it on the chin. Besides"—he grew serious once more—"misery loves company, doesn't it?"

"I don't know anything about that," Carsten said. "All I know is, I want us strong and the CSA weak. Whatever we need to do to make sure that happens, I'm for it. If it goes the other way, I'm against it."

"You do have the makings of an officer," Grady said thoughtfully. "You see what's essential, and you don't worry about anything else."

"Long as we are tied up here, sir, I've been trying to hit the books a little harder, as a matter of fact." Sam scratched his nose. His fingertips came away white and sticky from zinc-oxide ointment. A wry grin twisted up one corner of his mouth. "Besides, the more I stay belowdecks, the less chance I get to sunburn."

"Nobody can say you're not a white man," Grady agreed gravely. "With that stuff smeared all over your face, you're about the whitest man around."

"I only wish it did more good," Sam said. "I put it on just like the pharmacist's mate says, or even thicker, but I still toast. Hell, most of the time I look more like a pink man than a white one. I even burned over in Ireland."

"I remember that. It wasn't easy," Grady said. "They should have given you some kind of decoration for it."

"I guess they figured me turning red was decoration enough, even if I didn't think it was real pretty," Carsten said, which wrung a strangled snort from Commander Grady. Sam went on, "Sir, do you think we'd have more to do and more to do it with if Lieutenant Sandes hadn't flown his aeroplane into the stern when we were coming back across the Atlantic?"

"Nope," Grady answered. "We'd had accidents and battle damage before then. This business of flying aeroplanes off ships may be important, but it sure as hell isn't easy. The *Remembrance* doesn't carry as much armor as a battleship, either."

Remembering the shell that had struck his gun position, Sam nodded. "All right," he said. "I did wonder."

"I think we could have come through without any damage or accidents and still wound up right here," Grady said. "The problem isn't how we fought, because we fought well. The problem is politics." He made it a swearword.

"Yes, sir," Carsten said resignedly. He raised one of his pale eyebrows. "Can you think of any troubles that aren't politics, when you get down to it?"

Commander Grady rocked back on his heels and laughed. "No, by God, or not many, anyhow." He slapped Sam on the back, then pulled out a pad and a fountain pen and wrote rapidly. He pulled the top sheet off the pad and handed it to Carsten. "And here's a present for you: twenty-four hours' liberty. Go on across the river into Boston and have yourself a hell of a time."

"Thank you very much, sir!" Sam exclaimed.

He wanted to charge off the *Remembrance* then and there, but Grady held up a hand. "Just don't come back aboard Sunday afternoon with a dose of the clap, that's all. You do and I'll tear your stupid shortarm off and beat you over the head with it."

"Aye aye, sir," Sam said. "I promise." There were ways to make that unlikely to happen even if he didn't put on a rubber, though not all the girls in any house cared to use their mouths instead of doing what they usually did. If he had to pay a little extra for his fun, he would, that was all. He usually preferred a straight screw himself, but he hadn't expected to get this liberty and sure didn't want to end up in trouble on account of it. And the other was a hell of a lot of fun, too.

Several houses operated on the narrow streets across the Charles from the Navy Yard. *Go where the customers are* was a rule as old as the oldest profession. Sam got what he wanted—got it twice in quick succession, in fact, from an Italian woman about his own age who was as swarthy as he was fair. "Thanks, Isabella," he said, lazy and happy after the second time. He ran his hand through her hair. "And here's an extra dollar you don't have to tell anybody about."

"I thank you," she said as she got to her feet. "My little girl needs shoes. It will help." He hadn't thought about whores having children, but supposed it was one of the hazards of the trade.

A lot of the businesses near the south bank of the Charles that weren't brothels were saloons. Sam had himself a couple of schooners of beer. He thought about getting drunk—Commander Grady hadn't told him not to do that. But, after he'd emptied that second glass, he wiped his mouth on his sleeve and walked out of the dingy dive where he'd been drinking. He'd had his ashes hauled, he'd drunk enough to feel it, and nothing in the whole wide world seemed urgent, not even getting lit up. If he felt like doing it later, he would. If he didn't . . . well, he still had most of a day left without anyone to tell him what to do. For a Navy man, that was a pearl of great price.

He sauntered through the streets of Boston, thumbs in the pockets of his bell-bottomed trousers. He wasn't used to sauntering. When he went somewhere aboard the *Remembrance*, he always went with a purpose in mind, and he almost always had to hurry. Taking it easy was liberty of a sort he rarely got.

Half by accident, half by design, he came out onto the Boston Common: acres and acres of grass intended for nothing but taking it easy. If he wanted to, he could lie down there, put his cap over his eyes, and nap in the sun.

"No, thanks," he said aloud at that thought. If he napped in the sun, he'd roast, sure as pork would in the galley ovens of the

Remembrance. But there were trees here and there on the Common. Napping in the shade might not be so bad.

He headed for a good-sized oak with plenty of drooping, leafy branches to hold the sun at bay. Also heading for it from a different direction were a girl of nine or so, a boy who looked like her older brother, and, behind them, a woman with a picnic basket. Seeing Sam, the girl started to run. When she got to the shade under the oaks, she said, "This is our tree. You can't have it."

"Mary Jane, there's plenty of room for us all," the woman said sternly. "And don't you dare be rude to a sailor. Remember, your father was a sailor."

"Ma'am, if it's any trouble, I'll find another tree," Sam said.

The woman shook her head. "It's no trouble at all—or it won't be, unless you make some. But if you made a lot of trouble, you wouldn't have said you'd go someplace else like that."

"I'm peaceable," Sam agreed. If he hadn't paid a call on the house where Isabella worked, he might have felt like making some trouble: she was a pretty woman, even if she looked tired. And she'd said the girl's—Mary Jane's—father *was* a sailor, which probably made her a widow. Sometimes widows missed what their husbands weren't there to give them any more. As things were, though, Sam just sat down on the grass near the tree trunk, in the deepest part of the shade.

In a rustle of wool, the woman sat down, too, and took a blanket from the basket and spread it out on the grass. She started putting bowls of food on the blanket. While she was doing that, her son asked Sam, "Sir, did you know anybody who sailed aboard the USS *Ericsson?*"

"Can't say that I did," Carsten answered. Then his eyes narrowed as he remembered where he'd heard the name. "*That* ship! Was your father on her, sonny?"

"Yes, sir," the boy said. "And the stinking Rebs sank her after the war was over. That's not right."

"It sure as . . . the dickens isn't," Sam said, inhibited in his choice of language by the presence of the woman and little girl. "I'm awfully sorry to hear that. My ship got torpedoed once, by the Japs out in the Pacific. We didn't sink, but I know we were just lucky."

"And the Confederate skipper who sank the *Ericsson* is still walking around free as a bird down in South Carolina," the woman said. "He murdered my husband and more than a hundred other men, and no one cares. Even the president doesn't care."

"If Teddy Roosevelt had won his third term, he'd have done

something about it," Carsten said. "If the Rebs didn't hand that . . . fellow over, TR would have walloped the Confederate States till they did."

"I think so, too," the woman said. "If women had the vote in Massachusetts, I would have voted for Sinclair when he got elected. I've changed my mind since I found out about the *Ericsson*, though."

"I bet you have," Sam said. "One thing you have to give Teddy—he never took any guff from anybody."

"No." The woman pointed to the food. "Would you like some fried chicken and ham and potato salad? I made more than we can eat, even if these two"—she pointed at her children—"do put it away like there's no tomorrow."

"Are you sure, ma'am?" Carsten asked. If she was a widow, things were liable to be as tough for her as for the whore who'd gone down on her knees in front of him—tougher, maybe. But she nodded so emphatically, turning her down would have been rude.

He ate a ham sandwich and a drumstick and homemade potato salad and pickled tomatoes, and washed them down with lemonade that made him pucker and smile at the same time. Even though her children did eat like starving Armenians, the woman tried to press more on him.

"Couldn't touch another bite," he said, which wasn't quite true, and, "Everything was terrific," which was. "Haven't sat down to a spread like that since I was a kid." That was true, too.

"I'm glad you enjoyed it," she said, and seemed happy for a moment. She took a pack of cigarettes from her handbag. He got out a box of matches and lit the smoke for her. But as she drew on it, she frowned. "*He's* probably walking around down there in Charleston, puffing a big fat cigar. *Damn* him."

Sam had heard women swear before, but never with that quiet intensity. He didn't know what to say, so he didn't say anything. He watched the children play for a while, then got to his feet. "Obliged, ma'am—much obliged," he said. "Good luck to you." She nodded, but didn't speak. He went on his way. Only after he'd crossed half the Common did he realize he hadn't learned her name.

XVIII

Arthur McGregor stared down at the copy of the *Rosenfeld Register* he'd just set on the kitchen table. The headline stared back at him: RETIRING GENERAL CUSTER TO VISIT ROSENFELD NEXT WEEK.

His wife eyed the newspaper, too: eyed it as she might have eyed a rattlesnake coiled and ready to strike. "Please let it go, Arthur," she said. "Please let him go. The debts are paid, and more than paid. Let it go."

"I'll do what I have to do." McGregor didn't feel like quarreling, but he knew what that would be.

So did Maude. "Let it go," she said again. "If you won't do it for my sake, do it for the sake of the children you have left."

That hurt. McGregor had to mask his feelings against his wife now, as he'd had to mask them so often against the outside world. When he answered, his voice was steady: "Ted Culligan will take care of Julia, I expect. Shall we ask Mary whether she wants to see George Custer go on breathing?"

Maude bit her lip. Like her husband, her younger daughter had never come close to reconciling herself to what the Americans had done to Canada or to Alexander. But Maude replied, "Shall we ask Mary whether she wants to see you go on breathing?"

"I'll be fine," McGregor answered easily.

His wife glared at him, her hands on her hips. "I don't see how."

"Well, I will," he said. He even meant it. The bomb he intended for Custer had been sitting under the old wagon wheel in the barn since not long after he'd learned the U.S. commander in Canada would make a last gloating tour of the country he'd held down.

With any kind of luck, McGregor thought he could make Custer pay and get away clean.

Instead of arguing any more, McGregor went out into the farmyard. He'd set a large, empty wooden keg in the middle of the yard, not far from the chopping block where hens spent their last unhappy moments on earth. A few feet away from the barrel lay a gray rock. He picked it up and hefted it. It weighed the same as the bomb he'd made, within an ounce or two. He'd checked them both on Maude's kitchen scale, one night after she went to bed.

He paced off fifteen feet from the keg, tossing the rock up and down as he walked. If he stood at the back of the crowd watching General Custer, that was about how far away he'd be. He'd have no trouble seeing the general in his motorcar; he had several inches on most people. Custer's automobile wouldn't be moving very fast. The U.S. commander wouldn't hold a parade if he didn't want people gaping at him.

McGregor threw the rock. It thudded down into the keg. He strode over, bent down to pick it up, then paced off fifteen feet again. His next throw thudded home, too. He'd been practicing for weeks, and had got to the point where he could drop it in about eight times out of ten. If he could do that with a small-mouthed keg, he'd have no trouble landing a bomb in Custer's motorcar.

He kept practicing for about twenty minutes, making sure each toss was slow and relaxed. He wouldn't need to hurry. He didn't want to hurry. When he finally threw the bomb, time would seem to stretch out, as if he had forever. He didn't want to do anything foolish like heaving too hard. He'd get only one chance. *Do it right,* he told himself. *You've got to do it right.*

And then, as quietly and inconspicuously as he could, he'd slip away. When the bomb went off, people wouldn't pay attention to him. They'd pay attention to Custer's funeral pyre. With a little luck, nobody would notice he'd flung the nail-encased sticks of dynamite.

Maude watched him from the kitchen window. Her face was pale and set. He'd never said a word about why he kept throwing a rock into a keg. She'd never asked him, either; that wasn't her way. But they'd been married a long time. Maude knew him well. She'd understand. He knew her well, too. She was no fool.

Her lips shaped a word the kitchen-window glass made silent. He could read her lips anyhow: "Please," she was saying. He pretended he didn't see her, and turned away. When he looked toward the farmhouse again, she wasn't standing at the window any more.

What if he didn't slip away? What if the Yanks caught him? They'd shoot him or hang him. He could figure that out for himself. But Julia, married to Ted Culligan, would be all right. Maude had grit and to spare. She'd get by. And Mary? She was his youngest, his chick, so of course he worried about her. But she was also his firebrand. She'd grieve for him. He wanted her to grieve for him. But she would understand why he had to do this. She would understand it better than Maude seemed able to do.

"Alexander," McGregor said. Were his son at his side, he might have accepted Yankee rule. Not now. Never again. "Not as long as I live," he said.

He went to the barn and did some chores—even though he'd been contemplating his own death, life had to go on in the meanwhile. After a bit, he'd done everything that needed doing. He stayed out anyhow; if he went back to the farmhouse, he'd have another row with Maude. He knew he'd be having rows with Maude till Custer, like imperial Caesar, made his triumphal procession through Rosenfeld. After that, one way or another, they'd end. He looked forward to saying, *I told you so*.

When he finally went back inside, his wife wasn't in the kitchen, but the wonderful smell of baking bread filled it. McGregor smiled before he knew what he was doing. Life still held pleasure for him. He didn't want to throw it away. But he was ready, if that turned out to be what he had to do.

In the parlor, he found Mary reading the copy of the *Register* he'd brought back from Rosenfeld. She looked up at him, her eyes enormous. "He's coming here," she said. "He really is."

McGregor didn't have to ask who *he* was. He nodded. "He sure is," he answered.

"He shouldn't," Mary said. "He's got no business doing that. Even if they won the war, do they have to go and brag about it?"

"That's how Yanks are," McGregor said. "They like to boast and show off." So it seemed by his self-effacing Canadian standards, anyhow.

"They shouldn't," Mary said, as if stating a law of nature. "And *he* shouldn't have a parade through the middle of our town." Something sharp and brittle as broken glass glinted in her pale eyes. "Something ought to happen to him if he does."

She's my daughter, McGregor thought. *Flesh of my flesh, soul of my soul.* He almost told her something just might happen to the famous Yank general, George Armstrong Custer. But no. Proud of her though he was, he kept his plans to himself. Custer might be a showy American. McGregor was no American, and glad not to be one. He held his secrets close.

"Something ought to happen to him," Mary repeated, looking straight at McGregor. She knew what he'd done over the years. She had to know even if he'd said far less to her and to Julia than to Maude. So she knew what she was saying now. She wanted Custer blown sky high.

"Your mother thinks there's nothing more to be done," McGregor said, to see how Mary would take that.

His daughter hissed like an angry cat. She said, "Till we're free again, there's always more to be done."

"Well, maybe so," McGregor answered, and said no more. He wondered if Mary knew how risky throwing a bomb at Custer's motorcar was. He couldn't ask her. He couldn't tell her, either. But he'd been right when he told Maude that Mary loved Custer as much as he did. Maybe he'd get to say *I told you so* twice.

Thoughtfully, Mary asked, "What would Alexander do now?"

"Why, he'd—" McGregor broke off. He realized he didn't know what his son would do. Alexander had always denied to the American authorities that he'd had anything to do with the kids who were sabotaging the railroad track. If that was so, the Yanks had shot him for nothing—but he might agree with Maude when she said, *Enough is enough.* If, on the other hand, he'd been lying, he'd be all for trying to blow up Custer now—but the Americans would have had some reason for standing him against the wall. The more McGregor thought about it, the more confused he got.

Mary wasn't confused; she had the clear, bright certainty of youth. "He'd want us to be free, too," she said, and her father nodded. That, no doubt, was true.

Day inexorably followed day. When McGregor took care to note time passing, it seemed to crawl on hands and knees. When he didn't note it, when he busied himself with farm chores as he had to do, it sped by. Faster than he'd looked for it came the day when Custer would parade through Rosenfeld.

At breakfast that morning, Maude said, "Maybe we could all go into town and watch the show." Her smile pasted gaiety over stark fear.

McGregor paused with a bite of home-cured bacon halfway to his mouth. Tonelessly, he said, "I don't think that would be a good idea."

"Why not?" Maude said, determined to force the issue. "It would be jolly." She waited for Mary to clamor to be allowed to go into town, as she usually did. But Mary just sat, toying with her breakfast. She looked from her mother to her father and said not a word.

Into the silence, McGregor repeated, "I don't think that would be a good idea." He ate a couple more forkfuls of bacon and eggs, emptying his plate, then got to his feet. "I'm going out to the barn and hitch up the wagon. I don't want to be late, not today."

Mary nodded at that, not looking up at McGregor, still not saying a word. Before McGregor could get out the door, Maude ran to him and took him in her arms. "Come home," she whispered fiercely.

"I intend to," McGregor answered, which was true. He disentangled himself from his wife and went to the door.

The day was mild, not too warm, so the coat with big pockets he wore wouldn't particularly stand out. His one worry was that the U.S. Army might have set up security checkpoints around Rosenfeld, as the Yanks had done during the Great War. He'd built a false bottom to his seat to leave a space in which he could conceal the bomb, but he didn't want to have to rely on it, and it would make life more difficult even if it worked. But the Americans seemed sure all their Canadian subjects were cowed. He had no trouble getting into Rosenfeld.

He hitched the wagon on a side street well away from the post office and general store; he didn't want Wilf Rokeby or Henry Gibbon spotting him, not today. Then he casually took a place from which he'd be able to see the parade. Before long, people started filling the space in front of him. He didn't mind. He could still see well enough.

Custer's train pulled into Rosenfeld right on time and started disgorging all the trappings of the U.S. commandant's triumphal procession: soldiers, a marching band, and the Packard limousine McGregor had seen up in Winnipeg.

And here came the band, blaring out "The Star-Spangled Banner." Some people were shameless enough to cheer. McGregor's hand went into his pocket. He took out the bomb and held it by his side. No one noticed. He pulled out a match, too, and palmed it.

Here came the limousine behind the band, a gaudily uniformed Custer standing in it to receive the plaudits of the crowd. Nearer, nearer . . . Custer's eyes went wide—he recognized McGregor. McGregor smiled back at him. He hadn't expected this, but it only made things sweeter. He scraped the match on the sole of his shoe and touched it to the bomb's fuse. Smiling still, McGregor threw the bomb. All that practice paid off. The throw, straight for Custer, was perfect.

Down the track toward Rosenfeld rattled the train. In his fancy Pullman car, General George Armstrong Custer whipped a long-barreled Colt revolver out of his holster and pointed it not quite far enough away from Lieutenant Colonel Abner Dowling.

"Sir, will you please put that . . . thing away?" his adjutant asked. Dowling commended himself for not modifying *thing* with a pungent adjective, or perhaps even a participle. The pistol, he knew, was loaded. Fortunately, the retiring U.S. commandant in Canada wasn't.

With a grunt, Custer did set the revolver back in the holster, only to yank it out again a moment later. This time, he did point it at Dowling. His adjutant yelped. "Don't you turn into an old woman on me," Custer said peevishly. "You never know when an assassin may strike."

Dowling couldn't even tell him that was nonsense, not after the bomb in Winnipeg the summer before, and especially not after Wade Hampton V had been gunned down only a couple of months earlier. Custer's adjutant did say, "I think you'll be safe enough in a sleepy little town like Rosenfeld, sir."

"Oh, you do, do you?" Custer sneered. "Have you forgotten that blackguard Arthur McGregor makes his home just outside this sleepy little town?"

As a matter of fact, Dowling had forgotten that till Custer reminded him of it. "Sir," Dowling answered, taking a firm grip on his patience, "there really is no evidence this McGregor is a blackguard, or anything but a farmer. The experts are all convinced he's an innocent man."

"Experts?" Custer rolled his rheumy eyes. "The experts were all convinced we should use barrels by dribs and drabs, too. What the devil do experts know, except how to impress other experts?" He holstered the revolver again, then took out the report the experts had compiled on Arthur McGregor and flipped through it till he found a photograph of the man. "Here!" He thrust it at Dowling. "If this isn't the face of a villain, what is it?"

Relieved that that miserable pistol wasn't aimed at his brisket any more, Dowling studied the photograph of McGregor for the first time in several months. He reached the same conclusion now as he had then. "Sir, he just looks like a farmer to me."

"Bah!" Custer snatched back the report. "All I can say is, you are no judge of the imprint character makes on physiognomy."

All I can say is, you're an old fraud starting at shadows, Dowling thought. And he couldn't even say that, not really. Pretty soon, Custer would at last officially step down as the longest-serving soldier in the history of the U.S. Army. And then, perhaps, just perhaps, Abner Dowling would get an assignment where he could use his talents as something other than a nursemaid.

Iron wheels squealed against iron rails as the train began to slow outside of Rosenfeld. Custer pulled out the revolver yet again. He had the fastest draw Dowling had ever seen in an eighty-two-year-old man. Since he was the only eighty-two-year-old man Dowling had ever seen draw a pistol, that proved less than the tubby lieutenant colonel might have liked.

Dowling was convinced that, were an assassin lurking in Rosenfeld, Custer was unlikely to hit him with a pistol shot. The retiring general had a far better chance of nailing an innocent bystander or two, or himself, or Dowling. He had a better chance still of forgetting he wore the revolver. But, since no assassin would be lurking, Dowling didn't have to worry about any of that . . . too much.

Libbie Custer ignored them both. She lay in her Pullman berth, gently snoring. She was down with a bad cold, or maybe the grippe. Combined with the medicine she'd taken for it—like most such nostrums, almost as potent as brandy—the sickness had knocked her for a loop. She would not be parading today.

And now, evidently, Custer had done all the practicing he intended to do. After putting the pistol back into the holster, he clapped on a black felt cocked hat gleaming with gold braid, adjusted it to a jaunty angle with the help of the mirror atop the walnut sideboard, and then turned back to Dowling to ask, "How do I look?"

"Magnificent," his adjutant answered. Custer was a spectacle, no two ways about it. He'd always worn a uniform as splendid as regulations allowed, and then a little more besides. Now that no one could possibly criticize him for his outfits, he'd stopped even pretending to pay attention to the regulations. He looked something like a South American emperor, something like God on a particularly tasteless afternoon. Dowling found another fancy word: "Refulgent, sir."

"Thank you very much," Custer said, even though Dowling hadn't meant it altogether as a compliment. Dowling glanced out the

Pullman car's window. The sun was going in and out behind clouds. With a little luck, the medals and gold cords on Custer's tunic and the gold stripes down each trouser leg wouldn't blind too many of the spectators.

The train pulled into the Rosenfeld station. By this time, the people who formed Custer's procession worked together as smoothly as circus acrobats, and a good deal more smoothly than most of the forces under his command had done during the Great War. "Here comes your motorcar, sir," Dowling said as the limousine descended from the flatcar on which it rode.

"And about time, too," Custer said—nothing ever satisfied him. He looked around. "What a miserable excuse for a town this is. The only reason I can think of for scheduling a parade through it is that it is on the railroad line."

"Do you want to cancel the parade and go on, sir?" Dowling asked. If Custer did that, he'd stop worrying about the bomber who, his adjutant remained sure, was a bomber only in the retiring general's mind.

Custer's mind was certainly full of the fellow. "And let McGregor think he's frightened me away?" he demanded haughtily. "Never!" He looked around again. "We stopped here once before, didn't we? On the way up to Winnipeg, I mean. We drove through the streets then, too, and almost ran over some yahoo who'd probably never seen a motorcar before in his life."

"Why, so we did, sir." Dowling had forgotten that. Custer was an old man, but his memory hadn't slipped. He still vividly recalled slights he'd suffered during the War of Secession, and had never forgotten his quarrels with Teddy Roosevelt during the Second Mexican War—even if TR didn't remember things the way he did.

"I thought as much." Now Custer sounded complacent. He knew his memory still worked, and delighted in showing off. He pulled from a trouser pocket that photograph of Arthur McGregor, which he'd removed from the report. "And if we run into this fellow, I'll be ready, by thunder."

To Dowling's relief, he didn't demonstrate his fast draw. By then, the members of the marching band were forming up in front of the Packard limousine. They wore uniforms far more ornate and colorful than those of the platoon of ordinary soldiers who were taking their places behind the automobile, but were moons beside the sun compared to Custer.

"One good thing," Custer said as his chauffeur got out of the

Packard and opened the door so he and Dowling could go up into the back seat: "at least this will be a short procession. Then I'll be able to get back to Libbie."

He really did love her, Dowling realized with some reluctance. He wasn't always faithful to her—or, at least, he did his best to be unfaithful when he saw the chance—but she mattered to him. After almost sixty years of marriage, Dowling supposed that was inevitable.

Dowling sat in the motorcar. Custer stood erect and proud. "Are we ready, Captain?" he called to the bandleader.

"Let me see, sir." The young officer checked his watch. "It still lacks a couple of minutes of one, sir."

"Very well," Custer said. "Commence precisely on the hour. Let the people know they can expect absolute certainty from the rule of the United States."

Absolute certainty Custer had—*enough for a regiment, let alone one man,* his adjutant thought. Sometimes that had led to great disasters. Sometimes it had led to great triumphs. It always made the retiring general hard to deal with.

At one on the dot—or so Dowling assumed, for he did not take his own watch out of his pocket—the bandleader raised his hands. The musicians in his charge struck up "The Star-Spangled Banner." They began to march. The chauffeur put the limousine in low gear and followed them. Custer's honor guard, in turn, followed the automobile.

Rosenfeld might not have been a big city, but people lined both sides of the short, narrow main street to get a good look at General Custer. Some of them applauded the band. That didn't happen in every Canadian town; sometimes spectators received the U.S. national anthem in stony silence.

Here, though, most of the men and women seemed to accept that they had been conquered and that the United States were here to stay. Dowling saw smiles, he saw waves . . . and then, beside him, he saw Custer stiffen. "There!" Custer said, his eyes wide. "Right there. That's McGregor!"

Dowling's head swung to the right. He had a brief moment to recognize the Canadian, an even briefer moment to think that, even if McGregor was here, it meant nothing—and then the Canuck threw something in the direction of the motorcar. *How embarrassing*—he was sure it was his last thought—*the old boy was right all along.*

Custer didn't whip out his pistol, as he'd been practicing. The bomb—Dowling saw the sizzling fuse—flew straight toward him. He caught it as a U.S. footballer might have caught a forward pass, then underhanded it back the way it had come.

Very clearly, Dowling saw the astonishment on Arthur McGregor's face. He lacked the time to feel any astonishment of his own. The bomb landed at McGregor's feet and blew up. Dowling felt a sudden, sharp pain in his left arm. He looked down and discovered he had a torn sleeve and was bleeding.

So was Custer, from a wound on the outside of his thigh. If he noticed the injury, he gave no sign of it. "Stop the car!" he shouted to the chauffeur, and then, to the soldiers behind him, "See to the wounded." Now he drew his revolver. "And you and I, Dowling, we shall see to Mr. Arthur McGregor."

"I think, sir, you may have done that already." Dowling was astonished at how steady he sounded. He squeezed the fingers of his left hand. They worked. Like Custer, he'd taken only a minor wound. The men and women standing between McGregor and the motorcar had borne the brunt of the bomb and shielded the Americans from the worst.

Some of those people were down and screaming and thrashing, blood pouring from them. Blood poured from others, too, men and women who would not get up again. And there, flung against a wall like a bundle of rags, lay Arthur McGregor. His eyes were set and staring, his belly and groin a shredded, gory mass. Custer thrust the pistol back into his holster. "I don't need this—he did it to himself."

"No, sir." Abner Dowling spoke more humbly than he ever had in his life. "You did it to him. You were ready for anything."

Custer shrugged. "He cut his fuse just a bit too long—otherwise, we'd look like that now." His tone was one of dispassionate criticism of another man's work. "He had a good run, but no one man can lick the United States of America. Sooner or later, his luck had to give out. And I've paid Tom back, too, by God—in person."

"Yes, sir." Dowling said what needed saying: "How does it feel to be a hero—again?"

Custer drew himself up as straight as he had stood in the limousine. The dramatic pose he struck came straight out of the nineteenth century. "Dowling, it feels bully!"

Summer in Ontario wouldn't last much longer. Jonathan Moss knew that very well. Before long, the idea of sitting out on the grass with an attractive woman would have been an absurdity. Better, then, to enjoy such times while they lasted and not to worry about the snow surely only weeks away.

Laura Secord didn't make that easy. In all the time he'd known her, Laura Secord had never made anything easy. Now she said, "I wish that brave man had managed to blow your famous General Custer higher than the moon."

"I don't suppose I should be surprised," Moss answered. "If you want to know what I think, though, somebody who hides bombs or throws them and doesn't care if he kills innocent bystanders isn't much of a hero. Pass me that plate of deviled eggs, will you? They're good."

"I'm glad you like them." But, after she'd passed him the eggs, she returned to the argument: "I think anyone who keeps up the struggle against impossible odds is a hero."

"If the odds are impossible, anyone who keeps up the struggle against them is a fool," Moss returned.

"Canada still has a few fools left," Laura Secord said. She leaned forward and picked up a deviled egg herself.

"One fewer now." Law school and his practice had sharpened Moss' wits and made his comebacks quicker than when he'd been here as a pilot.

"We won't just turn into pale copies of Americans and of the United States," Laura said. "We *won't*."

Moss nodded. "That's easy enough to say. I don't know how easy it will be to do. The fellow who threw the bomb at General Custer thought the same way you do. Now he's dead. There's no revolution up here. And you're feeding a Yank a picnic lunch. Have I told you that you make really good pickles?"

She glared at him. "If you keep going on like this, I won't ask you to come back."

"I'm still not sure I should be coming up here at all," Moss answered. "For me, coming to picnics with you is what going to an opium den is for somebody who can't shake the poppy." He spoke lightly, which didn't mean he wasn't telling the truth.

Laura Secord raised an eyebrow. "Is that a compliment or an insult?"

"Probably," he answered, which startled a laugh out of her. Maybe he would have done better to stay down in Berlin and meet some nice girl there. But he hadn't met any girls there—or women, either, as Laura was unquestionably a woman—who'd struck his fancy. And so, still with the fragments of what was, without a doubt, an obsession left over from the Great War, he'd started driving up to

Arthur. He didn't know what would come of this. He didn't know if
he wanted anything to come of it.

She waved her hand, a wave encompassing the farm she'd stubbornly kept going on her own. "I don't know whether I ought to be
inviting you here, either," she said, her voice troubled. "It feels a lot
like giving aid and comfort to the enemy. But you were the one who
aided me, after all." Was she trying to convince herself, as Moss
tried to convince himself coming here was all right?

He said, "I don't know about aid, but I'm certainly comforted."
He lay back on the grass. A couple of cows grazing twenty or thirty
yards away looked at him with their large, dark eyes, then went
back to their own lunches. He thumped his belly to show how comforted he was. The waist of his trousers felt pleasantly tight.

"I'm glad of that." Laura reached for a pewter pitcher. "More
tea?"

"All right," Moss answered. "One thing I will say for tea: it
makes a better cold drink than coffee does."

"It makes a better hot drink than coffee does, too," she said.
Moss shrugged. She made as if to pour the pitcher over his head
before filling his tumbler. "You Yanks have no taste."

"I suppose not," he said, watching puffy white clouds drift
across the blue sky. The weather wouldn't stay good that much
longer. He thought about how bad it could get. That made him
smile, and then laugh.

"And what's so funny?" Laura Secord asked. "That you Yanks
have no taste?"

"As a matter of fact, yes." He sat up and sipped at the tea she'd
given him. "I was just thinking about the snowstorm I drove
through three years ago to come up here and visit you. If that
doesn't prove I've got no taste, I don't know what would."

She made a face at him. "The only thing it proves is that you're
mad. I'd already had a pretty fair notion of that from the way you
behaved during the war."

"Mad about you," he said, which made her blush and look
down at the grass. Jonathan Moss knew—had known for years—
that was metaphorically true. He'd also wondered a good many
times if it was literally true, in the alienist's use of the word *mad*.

"My mad Yank." Laura Secord spoke with a curious mixture of
affection and bemusement. "Till you stood up for that poor fellow
done out of his property—done out of the property where you had
your office—I didn't think I should ever want to see you again."

Maybe it would have been just as well for both of us if you hadn't, Moss thought. Here he was, when he would have been almost anywhere else with almost anyone else. All his friends from down in Chicago—a lot of his friends from down in Berlin—would have called him a fool. He called himself a fool a lot of the time. He kept coming back here.

"Would you like anything else here?" Laura Secord asked him. He finished the glass of tea she'd given him, then shook his head. "All right," she said, and started loading things back into the picnic hamper. As he always did when he came up to her farm, he tried to help. As she always did, she refused to let him. "You'll just make a hash of things."

"Roast-beef hash, by choice," Moss said.

With a snort, Laura got to her feet. Moss stood up, too. As she always did, she consented that he carry the hamper back to the farmhouse. She rubbed that in, too: "I really would have no trouble with it, you know. It's not nearly as heavy as a bale of hay, and I haul those all the time."

"Well, up till you said that, I did feel useful," Moss confessed. "But don't worry about it—you've cured me."

She muttered something under her breath. Moss thought it was *Mad Yank* again, but couldn't be sure. She hurried on ahead of him and opened the kitchen door. He set the picnic basket on the counter next to the tin sink, which was full of water. She put the dirty dishes and bowls and glasses in the water, saying with her back to him, "They'll be frightful to clean if I let them dry."

"All right," he answered; that was also part of her routine.

When the picnic basket was empty, she turned and took a step toward him. He took a step toward her, too, which brought him close enough to put his arms around her. She was reaching for him, too, her face tilted up, her mouth waiting for his.

The first time that had happened, he'd taken her right there on the kitchen floor. They'd both been mad then. He was sure he'd hurt her, ramming home like a pile driver, again and again. She hadn't acted as if it hurt, though. She'd clawed his back to ribbons and yowled like a cat on a back fence and finally screamed out his name loud enough to rattle the windows. She'd gone without for a long time, and had done her best to make up for it all at once.

They weren't quite so frantic now, but they were hurrying when they went to her bedroom, hurrying when they undressed, hurrying when they lay down together. His hand closed on her breast. He teased her nipple with his thumb and forefinger. She sighed and pulled his head down to follow his fingers. Her breath sighed out. "Oh, Jonathan," she whispered.

She took him in hand, more roughly than any other woman he'd ever known. "Careful there," he gasped, both because he was afraid she'd hurt him and because he'd spurt his seed out onto her breasts and belly if she didn't ease up.

His own hand slid down to the joining of her legs. She was already wet and wanton, waiting for him. A few picnics hadn't come close to fully sating her, not when she hadn't seen her husband since early in the war. He wondered what he would have been like after abstaining for so long. He couldn't imagine. He couldn't come close. He knew women were different, but even so . . .

She pulled him over onto her. It wasn't the wild bucking and plunging of the first time they'd joined, but it was a long way from calm and sedate and gentle. She bit his shoulder hard enough to make him yelp. His hands dug into her backside, shoving her up as he thrust down. She wrapped her legs around him and did her best to squeeze him breathless.

She squeezed him inside her, too. He groaned and gasped and spent himself at the same instant as she cried out, wordlessly this time. "My God," he said, like a man waking from the delirium of the Spanish influenza. And he had been in a delirium, though one far more pleasant than the influenza brought.

Laura Secord's face was still slack with pleasure; a pink flush mottled her breasts. She shook her head, as if she too were returning to herself. "Which of us is going to the opium den?" she murmured. Before Moss could answer—if, indeed, he'd been able to find anything to say—she got out of bed and squatted over the chamber pot. A doctor friend of Moss' had once told him getting rid of the stuff like that did only a little good, because a woman couldn't get rid of all of it, but he supposed—he hoped—it was better than nothing.

Once that was done, she turned modest again, and dressed quickly and with her back to him. He got into his own clothes. "I'd better head back down to Berlin," he said.

"Empire, you mean," Laura Secord told him.

Moss laughed. They disagreed on so many things . . . but when their bodies joined, it wasn't sparks flying, it was thunder and lightning. He'd never known nor imagined anything like it. "I still say it's Berlin, and so does everybody else," he answered, "and if you don't like that, you can let me know about it, and maybe I'll come up here and argue about it."

"Would you like to come up here and argue about it next Sunday?" she asked. "You never can tell when the weather in these parts will change, but it should still be good then."

"Next Sunday?" Moss said. "I can do that." His pulse quickened at the thought of it. "As a matter of fact, I can hardly wait."

As the clock in Jeremiah Harmon's drugstore chimed six, Reggie Bartlett put on his coat and hat. "Where's the fire?" the druggist asked him. "Are you going to leave before you get paid?"

"Not likely, boss," Reggie answered. "My wallet's been whimpering at me for the last couple of days. Thank heaven it's finally Friday."

"Well, I've got the prescription a whimpering wallet needs," Harmon said. "Here you are, Reggie." He counted out banknotes, then added a coin. "One week's pay: seventeen dollars and fifty cents."

"Thank you." Bartlett put the notes in his wallet and the coin— he saw it was dated 1909—in his pocket. "And do you know what, boss? I'm happier, I'm a hell of a lot happier, to get this than I was when you paid me millions and millions every week a couple of months ago."

"Of course you are—you're a sensible fellow," Harmon said. "When I paid you millions and millions, three days after you got them they'd be worth even less than they were when I gave them to you. Seventeen-fifty's not a whole lot of money, Lord knows, but it'll still be worth seventeen-fifty next Friday."

"I hope it will, anyhow," Reggie said. "I don't think I'm ready to put any of it in the bank just yet, though. A lot of people who put money in the banks got wiped out after the war."

"And isn't that the sad and sorry truth?" his boss said. "I was lucky, as these things go: I got mine out while it was still worth something, anyhow, and I spent it on whatever I needed then, and ever since I've been living week to week and hand to mouth like everyone else."

"I never had enough in the bank to worry too much about what I lost," Reggie said. "If I can keep my head above water for a little while now . . ." The new money had been in circulation for six weeks, and was still holding its value against the U.S. dollar and the German mark. Maybe it would go on doing that.

"What do you think of President Burton Mitchel these days?"

Harmon asked slyly. "Don't you wish you'd voted Whig in the election last fall?"

"Long as I didn't vote for Jake Featherston, who I did vote for doesn't matter a hell of a lot," Bartlett answered. "And Mitchel's had nothing but good luck since he got the job."

"I wouldn't say the way he got it was good luck," Harmon observed, his voice dry.

"Not for Wade Hampton V, that's for sure," Reggie agreed. "But good luck for the country? I reckon it is. Those wild men in the Freedom Party even got the damnyankees to feel sorry for us when they shot Hampton. Now that we aren't sending every dime in the country up to the USA, all the real money that's been hiding can come out again." He reached into his pocket. He hadn't had a half dollar in there for years. "And besides, Mitchel's got Congress eating out of the palm of his hand. Whatever he wants, they give him. Even the Freedom Party Congressmen have quit arguing with him."

"Maybe it's the sign of a guilty conscience, though I wouldn't have bet they were possessed of any such equipment," Harmon said. "I don't know how long the honeymoon will last, but Mitchel's making the most of it."

"Anything that makes the Freedom Party shut up is good in my book." Reggie touched a finger to the brim of his hat. With September heading into October, he'd traded in his flat-crowned straw for a fedora. "I'll see you tomorrow morning for my half-day."

"Good night, Reggie," Harmon told him.

Bartlett left the drugstore. Light was draining out of the sky. At this season of the year, nightfall came earlier, perceptibly earlier, every day. Street lamps threw little puddles of light down at the feet of the poles they surmounted. With dusk, people hurried wherever they were going, wanting to get there before full darkness if they could.

A man Reggie recognized passed him under one of those street lamps. The fellow came into Harmon's drugstore every so often, and was an outspoken Freedom Party backer. Reggie didn't know whether he was a Freedom Party goon, but he looked as if he might have been.

To stay on the safe side, Reggie stuck his hand in the pocket in which he still carried a pistol. The Freedom Party man knew he didn't have any use for Jake Featherston. If the fellow also knew he'd been the one who helped aim Tom Brearley at Roger Kimball, all sorts of fireworks might go off.

Whatever the Freedom Party man knew, he kept walking. His head was down, his face somber and, Reggie thought, a little confused. Was he looking for the certainty he'd known before Grady Calkins shot the president of the Confederate States, the certainty that Jake Featherston was on the way up and he himself would rise with his leader from whatever miserable job he held now? If he was, he wouldn't find it on the dark, dirty sidewalks of Richmond.

Posters on a board fence shouted HANG FEATHERSTON HIGHER THAN HAMAN! in big letters. Underneath, in much smaller type, they added, *Radical Liberal Party of the Confederate States*. They'd gone up less than a week after Wade Hampton V got shot, and no one, not even the men of the Freedom Party, had had the nerve to deface them or tear them down. Even the goons in white and butternut might have known some shame at being goons.

Back at his flat, Reggie took a chunk of leftover fried chicken out of the icebox and ate it cold with a couple of slices of bread and a bottle of beer to wash everything down. It was, he knew, a lazy man's supper, but he figured he had the right to be lazy once in a while if he felt like it.

After washing the dishes, he took out the new banknotes he'd got and looked at them. The one-dollar notes bore the image of Jefferson Davis, the five-dollar notes that of Stonewall Jackson: no doubt to remind people of the Stonewall, the five-dollar goldpiece hardly seen since the end of the war. Maybe, now that specie wasn't flowing out of the CSA as reparations, the government would start minting Stonewalls again.

Reggie walked into the bedroom and got out a banknote he'd kept from the last days before the currency reform: a $1,000,000,000 banknote. It might have been the equivalent of twenty-five or thirty cents of real money. It showed Jeb Stuart licking the Yankees during the Second Mexican War, and was every bit as well printed as the new banknotes, even if all the zeros necessarily made the design look crowded.

"A billion dollars," Reggie said softly. If only it had been worth more than a supper at a greasy spoon or a couple of shots of whiskey at a saloon with sawdust on the floor. But it hadn't; it was nothing more than a symbol of a whole country busy going down the drain. Reggie set it on the table by the sofa. "If I ever have kids," he said, "I'll show this to them. Maybe it will help them understand how hard times were after the war."

He shook his head. They wouldn't understand no matter what,

any more than they would understand what life in the trenches was like. Experience brought understanding. Nothing else came close.

When he got to work the next morning, he glanced affectionately at the cash register. All of a sudden, its keys corresponded to prices once more. He didn't mentally have to multiply by thousands or millions or billions any more.

A customer came in and bought some aspirins. "That'll be fifteen cents," Bartlett said. The man pulled from his pocket a $1,000,000,000 banknote like the one Reggie had contemplated the night before. Reggie shook his head. "I'm sorry, sir, but I can't take this."

"Why not?" the man said. "It's still worth more'n fifteen cents, I reckon."

"Yes, sir," Bartlett said, "but all these old banknotes have been—what's the word?—demonetized, that's it. You can't spend 'em for anything. Suppose you took one to a bank and tried to get a billion real dollars for it?"

"I wouldn't do that," the fellow said. He no doubt meant it: he was just a petty chiseler, not a big one. There couldn't be anybody in the Confederate States who didn't know you couldn't use the old money any more, not even for small purchases. Grumbling, the customer put the preposterously inflated banknote back in his pocket and handed Reggie a real dollar instead.

Reggie rang up the sale and then anxiously checked the till; coins were coming back into circulation more slowly than notes. But he was able to make change, even if he had to use ten pennies to do it. "Here you are, sir."

"Thanks." The man put the little flat tin of tablets in his pocket along with the change. Jingling, he turned away. "See you again sometime. Freedom!"

No one had said that to Reggie for quite a while. He would happily have gone another fifty or a hundred years without hearing it again, too. He had to make himself hold still and not go after the customer to beat hell out of him. "Freedom to butcher anybody you don't like, you mean," he ground out, "even if it's the president of the CSA."

He waited for the man to come back hotly at him, whether with words or with fists. That was the Freedom Party's style, and had been since its beginnings in the black days after the war. But the man only tucked his chin down against his chest, as if he were walking into a cold, rainy wind, and hurried out of the drugstore.

At the back of the store, Jeremiah Harmon coughed. "Yeah, I know, boss: I'm not supposed to do things like that," Bartlett said. "I know it's bad for business. But when those white-and-butternut boys come in, I see red. I can't help it. And this one had his nerve, going 'Freedom!' after what that Grady Calkins son of a bitch went and did."

"I didn't say anything, Reggie," Harmon answered. "As a matter of fact, I think I'm coming down with a cold." He coughed again. "I don't like to lose business, mind you, but I don't seek business from imbeciles, either. And any man who will call out 'Freedom!' with President Hampton still new in his grave is either an imbecile or whatever's one step down from there."

"A half-witted cur dog—a son of a bitch, like I said," Reggie suggested.

"It could be so," his boss said.

"When I was in the hospital after the damnyankees shot me and caught me, one of the other people in there was one of our nigger soldiers who'd lost a foot," Reggie said. "You ask me, he had more brains in that missing foot than the whole Freedom Party does in all its heads." He wondered how Rehoboam was doing down in Mississippi. Even if the black man had been a Red, he'd been a pretty good fellow, too.

Harmon chuckled. "Something to that, I shouldn't wonder. But now, if God is kind to us, the Freedom Party dealt itself a blow no one else could have given it, and one it won't get over."

"Amen," Reggie said with all his heart.

Cincinnatus Driver worked like a man possessed, unloading a truckload of filing cabinets he'd brought from the Des Moines railroad yards to the State Capitol on the other side of the river. It was, he admitted to himself, easier to work hard in Iowa in November than it had been in Kentucky in, say, July. But he would have put extra effort into things today even if it had been hotter and muggier than Kentucky ever got.

He finished faster than anyone would have imagined he could. Instead of racing back to the yard to see what other hauling work he could pick up—which was what he usually did when he finished a job—he used the time he'd saved to hurry back to the near northwest, to an Odd Fellows hall not far from his flat. He parked the truck on the street and hurried inside.

Four white men sat behind a long table in the middle of the hall.

"Let me have your name, please, and your street address," the one at the end nearest Cincinnatus said to him.

He gave the fellow his particulars. The second man behind the table checked a list. Cincinnatus had a moment's fear his name would not appear there. But the gray-haired white man ticked it off and pointed to a register in front of him. "If you'll just sign here, Mr. Driver," he said.

"I surely will, suh." Cincinnatus grinned from ear to ear. White men didn't call Negroes *mister* down in Kentucky. They didn't always do it here, either, but he liked it better every time he heard it. He wrote his name in a fine round hand.

The third man at the table handed him a folded sheet of paper. "Choose any voting booth you please, Mr. Driver," he said.

"Yes, suh. Thank you kindly, suh," Cincinnatus said, and then, because he couldn't hold it in any more, "You know somethin', suh? This here is the first time in my whole life I ever got to vote. Used to live in Kentucky, and I never reckoned I'd get me the chance."

"Well, you've got it," the polling official said. "I'm glad it means something to you, and I hope you use it wisely."

"Thank you," Cincinnatus said. He went to a voting booth—it was before the dinner hour, and he had plenty from which to choose—and pulled the curtain shut after himself. Then he unfolded the ballot, inked the little X-stamper in the booth with great care, and began to vote.

He voted for Democrats for Congress, for the State House of Representatives, and for the State Senate. That would, no doubt, have startled Luther Bliss; the boss of the Kentucky State Police had been convinced he was a Red. Apicius—Apicius Wood, now— had known better. A Red himself, Apicius could tell Cincinnatus wasn't . . . quite.

Cincinnatus finished marking the ballot, folded it again, and left the voting booth. He handed the folded sheet of paper to the fourth white man at the table. That worthy pushed it through the slot of the locked ballot box beside him. "Mr. Driver has voted," he said in a loud voice.

Mr. Driver has voted. As far as Cincinnatus was concerned, the words might have been accompanied by music from a marching band: they sounded in horns and drums in his ears. He felt ten feet tall as he strode out to the old Duryea truck, and marveled that he still fit inside the cab. But he did, and, having voted, he went off to eat a quick dinner and hunt up more work.

He was still eating on a bench down by the train tracks when

Joe Sims sat beside him. "Why are you grinnin' like a fool?" the older black man asked. "You look like you just tore off a piece your wife doesn't know about."

"I'm happy," Cincinnatus said, "but I ain't happy like that. I went down and voted—first time ever—is what I did."

Sims scratched his head. "I was happy when I voted the first time, too. It meant I was twenty-one. It meant I could buy whiskey, too, back when whiskey was still legal here. But I can't recollect looking like I just tripped over a steamer trunk full of double eagles because I made some X's."

Cincinnatus studied the other Negro, who hadn't the faintest idea how much he took for granted. "You was born here," Cincinnatus said at last. Sims nodded. Cincinnatus went on, "You knew from the time you was a little fellow you'd be able to vote when you got big."

"Well, sure I did," Joe Sims said, and then, belatedly, got the point. "Wasn't like that for you, was it?"

"Not hardly." Cincinnatus' voice was dry. "My ma and pa was slaves up till a few years before I was born. Before the USA took Kentucky away from the CSA, wasn't a legal school for niggers in the whole state. I learned my letters anyways, but I was lucky. I wasn't a citizen of the CSA; I was just somebody who lived there, and all the white folks told me what to do. Now, when I vote, I get to tell white folks what to do, and it ain't even against the law. Anybody reckons I ain't wild about that, he's crazy."

Sims took a big bite out of his sandwich. It wasn't ham, but a pungent sausage Cincinnatus hadn't seen much in Covington. Salami, people called it; it was pretty good. After chewing and swallowing, Sims said, "The stories you tell remind me of the ones I heard from my grandpa when I was growing up. I always thought he was making things out to be worse than they really were."

"Only reason you reckoned that is on account of you was born here," Cincinnatus said. "Nobody could make it out to be worse than it was—and it wasn't even so bad in Covington, because we was right across the river from Ohio. But it was bad there, and it got worse the further south you went."

"It ain't so good here, either," Sims said.

Negroes in Des Moines—Negroes in the USA generally—were fond of saying that. They weren't even wrong; Cincinnatus had seen as much. Nevertheless . . . "You don't know what you're talkin' about," Cincinnatus said. "Get down on your knees and praise the

Lord on account of you don't, too. I seen both sides now. This here may not be heaven, but it ain't hell, neither."

"Yeah, you say that every chance you get." Sims breathed pepper and garlic into Cincinnatus' face. "I can't argue with you. I never set foot inside the Confederate States. I do admit, I never heard of any colored fellow leaving the USA to go there."

"It would happen," Cincinnatus said. "About every other year, it would happen. The papers in the CSA would always bang the drum about it, too, to make the niggers there—and the white folks, heaven knows—happy about how things was."

"Happy." Joe Sims chewed on the word as he'd chewed on his salami. "How could you be happy, when you knew you were lying to each other down there?"

That was a better question than most of the ones about the Confederate States Cincinnatus heard up here. He had to think before he answered, "Well, the white folks were happy 'cause they were on top. And us niggers? We *were* happy some of the time. I don't reckon you can get through life without bein' happy some of the time." Cincinnatus crammed the rest of his own sandwich into his mouth. Indistinctly, he said, "Let's see what they got for us to do. With a new young-un in the house any day now, I got to keep busy."

"Got to stay out of there to get some rest once the baby comes," Sims said with a reminiscent chuckle. "I know all about that, damned if I don't. What are you and your missus going to call the kid?"

"Seneca if it's a boy—that's my pa's name," Cincinnatus said. "And Elizabeth's ma was called Amanda, so we'll name the baby that if it's a girl."

"Those are good names." Sims shut his dinner pail and got to his feet. "Like you say, we have to keep busy. We don't, everybody goes hungry."

Cincinnatus found enough work to put money in his pocket all through the afternoon. He went back to his apartment well pleased with himself. Elizabeth greeted him at the door with a kiss. "Did you vote?" she demanded. "Did you really and truly vote?" She wouldn't get her chance till the 1924 election, for Iowa women had only presidential suffrage.

"I really and truly voted," Cincinnatus said, and his wife's eyes shone. Joe Sims might not understand what the franchise meant to him, but Elizabeth did. She waddled back toward the kitchen, her legs so wide apart, the baby she carried might almost have fallen out between them.

Achilles was doing homework at the kitchen table. He had a sheet of paper turned upside down in front of him: his spelling words, which he was supposed to be committing to memory. "Orange," he said. "O-R-A-N-G-E. Orange."

"That's good, son." Cincinnatus made as if to clap his hands together. "The better you spell, the smarter folks'll reckon you are. I don't spell near as good as I wish I did, but I know you got that one right."

"It ain't . . . It's not"—Achilles carefully corrected himself— "that hard once you get the hang of it."

"You won't get any wrong on your test, then, will you?" Cincinnatus said.

"Hardly ever do," his son replied. Had that not been the truth, Cincinnatus would have clouted him for his uppity mouth. But Achilles was doing very well in school, which made Cincinnatus proud. The boy's eyes went far away. "Month. M-O-N-T-H. Month."

"Supper," Elizabeth announced. "I ain't gwine try an' spell it, but I done cooked it an' it's ready."

"Smells good," Cincinnatus said. It tasted good, too: roast beef with buttery mashed potatoes and greens on the side. "Turnip greens, ain't they?" Cincinnatus asked, lifting another forkful to his mouth.

"That's right," Elizabeth said. "Can't hardly get no other kind round these parts. Even black folks don't hardly seem to know about collard greens, an' they're better'n turnip greens any day of the week." She paused, looked down at her swollen belly, and laughed. "Baby just kick me."

"Pretty soon, the baby will be kicking Achilles," Cincinnatus said. He and Elizabeth both laughed then, at their son's expression. Having a new brother or sister still didn't seem real to Achilles. It would before long.

Elizabeth returned to the earlier subject: "Wish I had me a mess o' collard greens. You'd reckon everybody in the whole world'd know about collard greens, but it ain't so."

"Turnip greens are fine," Cincinnatus said. Elizabeth shook her head, stubbornly unconvinced. He reached out and patted her hand. "Life ain't perfect, sweetheart, but it's pretty good right now."

Where simple praise hadn't, that reached her. Slowly, she nodded. The baby must have chosen that moment to kick again, because she smiled and put both hands on her belly. "Reckon you may be right."

"Reckon I am," Cincinnatus said. "Buy me a newspaper tomorrow, find out who won the elections. Anybody win by one vote or lose by one vote, *I* made the difference. Never would have gotten to vote down in Kentucky. Didn't make no never mind whether the Stars and Bars or the Stars and Stripes was flyin' over the Covington city hall, neither—white folks was on top, and aimin' to stay there. Ain't like that here. Ain't quite like that here, anyway."

"This here's a better place," Elizabeth said quietly. Cincinnatus nodded. It wasn't a perfect place, but he didn't imagine there was any such thing. And, since he'd come from a worse place, a better one would do just fine.

When Anne Colleton opened the door to her hotel room for him, Roger Kimball took her in his arms. She let him, but only for a moment, and then pushed him away. She was strong, and she'd caught him by surprise to boot. He had to take a quick step back, and knocked the door closed before catching himself. "What's going on?" he asked in no small annoyance.

"I didn't invite you up here for that," Anne answered, her own voice sharp. He'd seen that grimly determined look in her eye before, but rarely with it aimed at him.

"Well, why did you ask me up, then?" he said: a serious question, seriously meant. Whatever else hadn't always been smooth with them, their lovemaking was something special. It always had been, ever since he'd seduced her the first night they'd met, on a train rolling down to New Orleans when the war was young.

"Why?" she echoed. "To say good-bye, that's why. I owe you that much, I think."

"Good-bye?" He stared at her, hardly believing he'd heard the word. "Jesus! What did I do to deserve that?"

Now her eyes softened to sadness. "You still belong to the Freedom Party. You still believe in the Freedom Party," she said, her voice sad, too, sad but firm, like that of a judge passing sentence on a likable rogue.

"Of course I do," Kimball answered. "When I join something, I don't quit when the going gets rough. The damnyankees found out about that." He'd never thought he would be grateful to Tom Brearley for breaking the news of the *Ericsson*, but he was. Now he could talk about it. "And I still say Jake Featherston's the only man who can get this country going again."

"We are going again." Anne walked over to the bed and picked up her handbag. Kimball was glad to watch her; her gray skirt, one of the new short ones, displayed most of the lower half of her calf—and her legs were worth displaying.

As she reached inside the handbag, he asked, "What are you doing?"

"I'll show you." She pulled out a banknote and held it up. "Do you see that?" After Kimball nodded, she drove the point home: "Take a good look at it. It's a one-dollar banknote. You haven't seen anything just like it since just after the war ended, not till this past fall you haven't. And it's still worth a real dollar, too."

"That's not all we need, dammit, not even close," Kimball said furiously. "We're naked to whatever the United States want to do to us." He wished Anne were naked to whatever he wanted to do to her, but a different urgency filled him fuller. "We've got no submarines, we've got no battleships, we've got no barrels—Christ, they don't even want us to have machine guns in case the niggers rise up again. You see the Whigs fixing any of that? I sure as hell don't."

Anne put the banknote back in her bag. "We will have all those things again," she said. "It may take longer than I'd hoped, but we'll have them. As long as the money stays good, we'll have them. And"—she took a deep breath—"we'll have them without murdering any more presidents to get them."

"You can't make an omelet without breaking eggs," Kimball said. "I've broken plenty of eggs myself—and you've set up plenty to be broken." That got home. Anne bit her lip and looked down at the floor. Kimball laughed. "You know what you remind me of? Somebody who likes bacon but won't butcher a hog."

"You *are* a bastard," Anne said. "I've known it for a long time, but—"

Roger Kimball loosed another loud, jeering laugh. "Takes one to know one, I reckon. That's likely the only reason we've put up with each other as long as we have—well, that and the screwing, anyway."

He'd hoped to anger her, but found he'd failed. She also laughed, and seemed to gain strength from it. "Yes, that and the screwing," she said. "I'll miss you. I'll be damned if I won't. But I won't miss the Freedom Party. Since you're staying in, I have to cut you loose. Grady Calkins showed me once and for all there's no controlling those people."

"I got into it thinking Jake Featherston needed controlling, too," Kimball said. "He doesn't. But the Yankees want to control him, and that's a fact."

"Featherston's clever," Anne admitted. "But he can't do everything himself. And if he can't control his people, he can't do anything at all." By the way she talked, controlling was the be-all and end-all.

Kimball supposed it was natural she thought that way. She'd spent her whole life till the Red uprising controlling a plantation, controlling money, controlling everyone around her. Her ancestors had done the same thing for a hundred years before her time. She was, in fact, one of the aristocrats against whom Jake Featherston had campaigned.

With a shrug, Kimball said, "Well, yeah, a bigger egg than Jake wanted got busted, but you can't blame the whole Freedom Party for Calkins."

"Why can't I? Everyone else does," Anne said. "And there's a lot of truth in it. With all the brawling, with the stalwarts with the clubs, with the riots during the campaign in '21, where else was the Freedom Party going but towards shooting a president?"

Uneasily, Kimball remembered keeping a stalwart in white and butternut from taking a shot at Ainsworth Layne when the Radical Liberal candidate spoke in Hampton Park. Even so, he said, "You're making—the whole country's making—it out to be bigger than it is. Sure, we've lost some folks for now on account of what happened down in Birmingham, but they'll be back."

Anne Colleton shook her head. "I don't think so. And that's the other reason I've gotten out of the Freedom Party—I never back a loser. Never. I think the Party's name will stink all across the CSA for years to come, and I don't want any of that stink sticking to me."

"You're wrong," Kimball told her. "You're dead wrong."

Now she shrugged. "I'll take the chance."

"Nothing fazes you, does it?" he said, and she shook her head again. He stepped toward her. "Last kiss before I go?"

He watched her consider it. Mischief filled her eyes. "Why not?" she said, and held out her arms.

When their lips met, he wondered if she'd bite him instead of kissing. But her malice was subtler than that. She put everything she had into the kiss, reminding him of what he wouldn't be getting any more. She held him tight as if no clothes separated them, grinding her crotch into his.

"Jesus!" he said, his voice hoarse, when he had to take his

mouth away from Anne's to breathe. She laughed, delighted with the effect she'd created. His hand cupped her breast. "Last lay before I go, too?"

"No," Anne said deliberately, and knocked the hand away. "Good-bye, Roger."

Rage ripped through him. "Why, you goddamn little tease," he rasped, and shoved her against the bed. She let out a startled squeak as she landed on her back. "I'll give you something to remember me by—see if I don't." He sprang on her.

Years before, he'd realized trying to take her by force wasn't a good idea. Since then, he never had tried. He'd never needed or wanted to try. Now . . . If she thought he'd just walk away after that kiss, she could damn well think again. Whatever he'd realized years before was dead as the *Ericsson*, dead as Tom Brearley.

It shouldn't have been, for his fury overpowered not only good sense but also caution. Anne might have been startled when he pushed her onto the bed, but she didn't stay that way longer than a heartbeat. With exquisite timing, her knee came up between his legs and caught him exactly where it did her the most good.

He howled and doubled up and clutched at himself, as any wounded animal might have done. Anne twisted away from him. He couldn't possibly have stopped her, not for the first few seconds there. "Now I think you'd better go," she said coolly.

He didn't want to take her any more. He wanted to kill her. But when he looked up, he discovered she'd had more in her handbag than a one-dollar banknote. She aimed a revolver straight at his head. He hadn't the least doubt she would pull the trigger if he moved in any way that did not suit her.

"Get off the bed," she said. He had to obey, though he still walked doubled over. The pistol tracked him. She'd killed before, helping to put down the Negro rebellion. No, she wouldn't hesitate now. Iron in her voice, she went on, "Go to the door, get out, and never come back."

At the door, he paused. "Can I wait till I can straighten up?" he asked, not wanting to publish his humiliation to the world.

He thought she'd send him out in anguish, but she nodded and let him have a couple of minutes. Then she gave a peremptory gesture with the pistol. Out he went. He still wasn't moving well—he felt like bloody hell—but, if he walked like an old man, he didn't walk like a wounded old man.

He made his slow, painful way back to his flat without meeting anyone he knew, for which he thanked God. "That would be just what I need," he muttered as he walked spraddle-legged up the stairs, "to run into Potter and Delamotte again." He grunted. Anne had hurt him worse than they had when he brawled with them—not in so many places, but worse.

He poured himself a tall whiskey, and then ran the bath half full of cold water. He shivered when he sat down in it, but the steam radiator made the apartment tolerably warm and the whiskey made him tolerably warm, so he didn't think he'd come down with pneumonia or the Spanish influenza. And the cold water helped numb his poor, abused balls—or maybe that was the whiskey, too.

At last, he let the water run down the drain. After cautiously drying, he put on the loosest drawers and baggiest trousers he owned. Then he went back to the kitchen and poured out some more whiskey. He didn't want food. The knee Anne had given him still left him faintly nauseated.

He drank from the second glass of whiskey. "Stupid bitch," he said, as if someone in the room might disagree. "Miserable stupid bitch." He took another big sip from the glass. He wished he'd wrung her neck, back there at the hotel. But he hadn't got the chance. Say what you would about her, Anne Colleton took a back seat to nobody when it came to nerve.

The glass was empty again. He refilled it. *Might as well get drunk,* he thought. *What else have I got to do?* Even if he never saw Anne again, he'd have no trouble getting laid. He knew that. He'd never had any trouble getting laid. Why, then, did he feel like a man whose tongue kept exploring the empty spot where a wisdom tooth had been before the dentist got his forceps on it?

"Dammit, we were two of a kind," he muttered. "We *are* two of a kind. She's just being stupid about the Party, that's all. She'll come around." He nodded. "She gives me half a chance—hell, she gives me even a quarter of a chance—I'll horn her into coming around." With better than two glasses of whiskey in him, it not only sounded simple, it sounded inevitable.

Someone knocked on the door. Kimball hurried to open it. "There she is already, by God!" he said happily. Of course she wouldn't stay away.

But the woman who stood in the hallway was darker and plainer and tireder than Anne Colleton. "You are Mr. Roger Kimball, the naval officer?" she asked.

"That's right," he answered. Only after the words were out of his mouth did he realize she had a Yankee accent—she sounded a little like Clarence Potter.

"Oh, good," she said. "I'm so glad I found you." As Anne had before, she reached into her purse. And, as Anne had before, she pulled out a pistol. Two bullets had slammed into Roger Kimball's chest before she said, "My husband was on the *Ericsson*." She kept firing till the revolver was empty, but Kimball never heard the last few shots.

XIX

Sylvia Enos sat in a Charleston, South Carolina, jail cell, wondering what would happen to her next. Looking back on it, she decided she shouldn't have shot Roger Kimball. Now she would have to pay for what she'd done. Try as she would, though, she couldn't make herself sorry she'd done it.

She shared the small women's wing of the Charleston city jail with a couple of drunks and a couple of streetwalkers. They all kept sending her awestruck looks because she was locked up on a murder charge. She hadn't imagined anything like that. It was funny, if you looked at it the right way.

A matron with a face like a clenched fist came down the hall and stopped in front of Sylvia's cell. "Your lawyer is here," she said, and unlocked the door. Then she quickly stepped back, as if afraid Sylvia might overpower her and escape. Sylvia found that pretty funny, too.

Her lawyer was a chubby, white-mustached, very pink man named Bishop Polk Magrath. He insisted that she call him Bish. She'd never called anyone Bish in her life, but didn't argue. He sat on one side of a table in a tiny visiting room, she on the other. The matron stood close by to make sure they didn't pass anything back and forth.

"I still don't understand why you're helping me," she said. She'd said that before, and hadn't got any kind of answer that made sense to her.

Now she did, after a fashion. Magrath's blue, blue eyes sparkled. "You don't seem to have realized what a *cause célèbre* your case has become, ma'am," he said. "I'll draw more notice for defending you than I would in ten years of ordinary cases."

"I don't see how you'll draw notice for defending me and los-ing," Sylvia said. "I did it." She hadn't tried to run after shooting Kimball. She'd given her revolver to the first man who stuck his head out the door of another apartment and waited for the police to come arrest her.

"Let's just put it like this, Mrs. Enos," the lawyer said: "There are a good many people in this town who think Mr. Kimball deserved what you gave him, a good many people who aren't the least bit sorry he's dead. If we can get enough of them on a jury, you might just see Rhode Island again."

"Massachusetts," Sylvia said automatically. She scratched her head. "I don't follow you at all. Isn't—wasn't—Roger Kimball a hero down here for sinking the *Ericsson?*"

"Oh, he is, ma'am. To some people, he is," Magrath said. By the expression on the matron's face, she might well have been one of those people. The lawyer went on, "But he's not a hero to every-body in the Confederate States, not after what happened last June he's not."

"Oh," Sylvia said softly. At last, a light went on in her head. "Because he was a Freedom Party bigshot, you mean."

"What a clever lady you are, Mrs. Enos." Magrath beamed at her. "That's right. That's just exactly right. There are people in this country—there are people in this town—who would be happy if the same thing that happened to Roger Kimball would happen to the whole Freedom Party."

One of those people, whoever they might be, was without a doubt paying Bishop Polk Magrath's fees. Sylvia certainly wasn't. She'd spent more than she could afford getting a passport and a one-way ticket down to Charleston. She hadn't expected she'd be going back to Boston. Maybe she'd been wrong.

"Time's up for this visit," the tough-looking matron said. Sylvia obediently got to her feet. The lawyer started to reach across the table to shake hands with her. A glance from the matron stopped him. He contented himself with tipping his derby instead. "Come along," the matron told Sylvia, and Sylvia came.

Halfway back to her cell, she asked, "Will supper be more of that cornmeal mush?" It didn't taste like much of anything, but it filled her stomach.

As if she hadn't spoken, the matron said, "You damnyankees killed my husband and my son, and my brother's got a hook where his hand used to be."

"I'm sorry," Sylvia said. "I haven't got a brother, and my son's too young to be a soldier. But the man I shot snuck up on my husband and more than a hundred other sailors after the war was over, and he didn't just kill them—he murdered them like he'd shot them in the back."

The matron said nothing more till they got back to Sylvia's cell. As she locked Sylvia inside once more, she remarked, "Grits for supper again, yes," and went on her way.

"What's your lawyer got to say?" one of the streetwalkers called to Sylvia. "A lawyer—God almighty." She sounded as if she never expected to enjoy a lawyer's professional services, though a lawyer might enjoy hers.

Two days later, the hard-faced matron marched up to Sylvia's cell and announced, "You've got another visitor." Disapproval congealed on her like fat in a pan cooling on the stove.

"Is it—Bish?" Sylvia still had to work to say that. The matron shook her head. Sylvia frowned in confusion. Now that Kimball was dead, her lawyer was the only person she knew or even knew of in Charleston. "Who is it, then?"

Through tight lips, the matron said, "Just come on." Sylvia came. Sitting in an iron cage staled very quickly.

Waiting for her in the visitors' room was a blond woman about her own age whose sleek good looks, coiffure, and clothes all shouted *Money!* "Mrs. Enos, my name is Anne Colleton."

That meant nothing to Sylvia—and then, to her dismay, it did. She'd seen the name in a couple of the newspaper stories that talked about Kimball. "You're one of the people who helped the Freedom Party," she said. Maybe Bishop Polk Magrath had been talking through that derby of his.

Anne nodded. "I was one of those people, yes, Mrs. Enos. And I was a friend of Roger Kimball's, too—I was, up till his last day on earth."

Sylvia heard, or thought—hoped—she heard, a slight stress on the past tense. "Were you?" she asked, with her own slight stress.

Maybe that was approval in Anne Colleton's eyes. "You listen, don't you?" the woman from the Confederate States said. "In fact, I'm not telling you any great secret when I say that Roger Kimball and I were more than friends, up till his last day on earth."

Whatever hope Sylvia had went up in smoke. It hadn't been approval after all. It must have been well-bred, well-contained fury. "Have you come here to gloat at me in jail, then?" she asked with gloomy near-certainty.

"What?" Anne Colleton stared, then started to laugh. "You

don't understand, then, do you, my dear?" Sylvia shook her head. She only understood that she didn't understand. Anne's voice went cold and harsh. "I'll spell it out for you, in that case. Not too long before you shot him, Roger Kimball tried to take me by force when I told him I didn't care to be more than his friend any more. He did not succeed, I might add." She spoke proudly. "I might also add that I came very close to shooting him myself before you got the chance."

"Oh," Sylvia whispered. Something more seemed to be called for. She went on, "I'm glad you didn't. It would have meant I'd spent all that money on my passport and train fare for nothing."

"We wouldn't want that, would we?" Anne Colleton said, and sounded as if she meant it. "With any luck at all, Mrs. Enos, the Confederate government or the government of South Carolina will pay your train fare north. Bish Magrath and I will do everything we can to see that that's what happens."

"Oh," Sylvia repeated in a different tone of voice. She'd put her children on the train, too, to distant cousins in Connecticut—distant, but closer than any other relatives she had close by. George, Jr., and Mary Jane had thought it would be a short get-acquainted visit. So had her cousins. Maybe, just maybe, if God and Anne Colleton turned out kind, they'd be right.

"Time's up," the matron announced, and even Anne Colleton, who seemed able to outstare the lightning, did not argue with her. Sylvia got to her feet and headed back toward her cell. When she was about halfway there, the matron said, "Some rich folks reckon they can buy their way out of anything."

I hope this one's right, Sylvia thought. Saying that out loud didn't seem to be the best idea she'd ever had.

Anne Colleton did not visit her again. Bishop Polk Magrath did, a couple of times. He didn't ask many questions; he seemed to come more to cheer her up than for any other reason. She didn't know how cheerful she should be. She'd gathered Anne Colleton was a power in the land, but how big a power? Sylvia couldn't find out till she went to court.

She came before a judge two weeks after Anne Colleton visited her. Bish Magrath kept beaming like a grandfather with plenty of candy canes in his pockets for his grandchildren to find. The lawyer at the other table in front of the judge—the district attorney, Sylvia supposed he was—seemed anything but happy. But was that because of the case or because he'd had a fight with his wife before coming here? Sylvia couldn't tell.

"I understand you have a request before we proceed, Mr. Chesterfield?" the judge asked the district attorney.

"Yes, your Honor, I do," the lawyer—Chesterfield—said. When he glanced over to Sylvia, he looked as if he'd bitten down hard on a lemon. "May it please the court, your Honor, the state must recognize the extraordinary circumstances that prompted the defendant to act as she has admitted acting. In light of the fact that the decedent did cause the death of the defendant's husband not during wartime but after he knew combat had ended, the state is willing"— he looked none too willing himself—"to further the cause of international understanding and amity by not pressing charges in this case, provided that the defendant leave the Confederate States on the first available transportation north and solemnly swear never to return to our nation again, on pain of rearrest and the charges' being reinstituted."

"How say you, Mr. Magrath?" the judge inquired.

"I am in complete accord with my learned colleague, your Honor," Magrath said placidly. "I should also like to note for the record that the government of the United States has formally requested clemency for my client from both the government of the Confederate States and the government of the sovereign state of South Carolina. It now rests in your hands, your Honor."

Things were happening too fast for Sylvia. They weren't just arranged—they were nailed down tight. "How say you, Mrs. Enos?" the judge asked her. "If set at liberty, will you quit the Confederate States of America, never to return?"

Bish Magrath had to nod before she could stammer, "Y-Yes, sir."

Bang! Down came the gavel. "So ordered," the judge declared. "Mrs. Enos, you will be on a northbound train before the sun sets this evening." Numbly, Sylvia nodded. She had her life back. Now she would have to figure out what to do with it.

Lieutenant Lije Jenkins sorted through the mail that had come into the barrel unit at Fort Leavenworth. He held out an envelope to Irving Morrell. "Letter from Philadelphia for you, Colonel."

"War Department?" Morrell asked, not that he had much doubt. Jenkins nodded. Morrell took the envelope. "Well, let's see what kind of birthday present they have for me today." His birthday still lay a month away, but he thought about it more than he had before he got married, because Agnes' came only a week afterwards.

Have to get into Leavenworth and do some shopping for her, he thought, and laughed under his breath. Amazing, the small domestic things in which he took pleasure these days because he was doing them for the woman he loved.

He opened the envelope and unfolded the letter it held. As his eyes went back and forth across the typewritten page, he stiffened. *Colonel Morrell,* the letter read, *Having completed work on the test vehicle for a new-model barrel and having also completed evaluation of optimum strategic utilization of barrels irregardless of model, you are ordered to terminate the program you now head at Fort Leavenworth and to report to the War Department Personnel Office here in Philadelphia no later than 1 March 1923 for reassignment. Each day earlier than the aforesaid date for the closure of the project will be greatly appreciated due to reduced expenditures as a result thereof.*

Only after he'd gone through the letter twice did he notice who had signed it: Lieutenant Colonel John Abell, the adjutant to General Hunter Liggett, who'd replaced Leonard Wood as U.S. Army Chief of Staff a few months into President Sinclair's administration.

"Well, well," Morrell said softly. A pigeon had come home to roost. He'd spent some time as a General Staff officer during the Great War, and had not got on well with John Abell. Abell was a brilliant man, everything a military administrator should be and then some. Morrell had always made it plain he would sooner have been out in the field fighting. When he'd got out in the field, he'd smashed the enemy. And now he was going to pay for it.

"Something wrong, sir?" Lieutenant Jenkins asked.

"No good deed goes unpunished," Morrell answered.

"Sir?" Jenkins said. Morrell handed him the letter. He read it, then stared at his superior. "Close down the Barrel Works? They can't do that!"

"They can. They are. Whether they ought to or not is a different question, but not one that's mine to answer," Morrell said. "You see why they're doing it—they need to save money." He saw no point to saying anything about John Abell. If personal animosity had dictated where the savings would come from . . . If that had happened, it wouldn't be the first time.

"But you *haven't* finished your work with the test model, sir," Jenkins protested.

"In a way, I have," Morrell told him. "I've done about everything I can do with one machine. If they'd coughed up the money for more than one, I could have done a lot more than I did. I just wish they were passing the Barrel Works on to someone else instead of closing it down."

"Yes, sir!" Jenkins' face was red with anger. "They might as well be telling us we've wasted all the time and work we put in here." He didn't think about what he would do next himself. In Morrell's book, that made him a good soldier.

"That's probably what they think," Morrell told him. He remembered how Abell had looked at him during the war when he'd agreed with Custer that the barrel doctrine the General Staff had developed needed changing. He might have been an atheist ripping into Holy Writ.

That he'd been right hadn't made things better. It might have made things worse.

"What are you going to do?" Jenkins asked.

"Obey the order," Morrell said with a sigh. "What else can I do? They have the test model. They have my reports. They can go on from there. Things won't disappear. They'll just stop for a while." That might prove as bad, but he didn't care to dwell on such gloomy possibilities.

He left the office to break the news to the men who had worked so hard for so long with the test model. The first one he ran into was Sergeant Michael Pound. "What's the matter, sir?" the barrel gunner asked. "You look ready to chew bolts and spit rivets."

"We're out of business, that's what," Morrell said, and went on to explain how and why—or what he understood of why—they were out of business.

Pound frowned. With his thick body, wide shoulders, and broad face, he could easily have looked like a lout. He didn't; his features were clever and expressive. "That's—very shortsighted, isn't it, sir?" he said when Morrell had finished. "The point is to stay ahead of everybody else, after all. How are we going to do that if we drop out of the race?"

"I don't know the answer to that question, Sergeant," Morrell replied. "I do know I've received a legal order to shut down the Barrel Works and report to Philadelphia once I've done it. I have to obey that order."

"Yes, sir, I understand," Pound said. "I hope you raise some hell when you get to Philadelphia, though."

"I intend to try, anyhow," Morrell said. "How much good that will do, God only knows. Now—what about you, Sergeant? Do you have any new assignment in mind? I'll do what I can to help you get it."

"That's very kind of you, sir." Pound scratched his brown mustache as he thought. "I suppose I'd better go back to the regular artillery, sir. Whether we have barrels or not, we'll always need guns."

"That's true. It's a sensible choice," Morrell said. He got the idea that most of Pound's choices were sensible. "I'll see what I can arrange. I hate to say it, but it's liable to be a better choice than staying in barrels, the way things are."

"If we do get in trouble again, we'll wish we'd done more now," Pound said with a massive shrug. "We'll all be running around trying to do what we should have done in years in a few weeks."

That was also likely to be true. Trying not to dwell on how likely it was, Morrell slapped Sergeant Pound on the shoulder and went on to find the rest of the test model's crew. They took the news hard, too. Then he had to break it to the crews of the other barrels, the Great War machines that also tested tactics, and to the mechanics who kept all the big, complex machines running. Little by little, he realized what a mountain of paperwork he'd have to climb by the first of March.

After he'd spread the word to the soldiers it affected, he went to tell the other person who needed to know: his wife. He found Agnes ironing clothes. "What are you doing here at this hour of the morning?" she said in surprise. Something in her smile as he kissed her told him what she hoped he was there for.

But he hadn't come home for that, however much he would have enjoyed it. He told her why he had come home. The explanation came out smooth as if he'd rehearsed it. As a matter of fact, he had rehearsed it, going over it again and again with his men.

Agnes pursed her lips. She was an Army wife, and had taken on many of the attitudes of her officer husband (she'd probably had some of those attitudes already, her first husband also being a soldier). She said, "They should be giving you all the tools you need to do the job right, not taking away the ones they did let you have."

"You know I feel the same way about it, honey, but I can't do anything about it except close down the Barrel Works, pack my bags, and hop on the train for Philadelphia. That means you get to hop on the train for Philadelphia, too."

Her eyes widened. "I hadn't thought of that," she said. "I've never been to Philadelphia, even to visit. Now we'll be living there, won't we?"

"Unless they ever really get around to moving the War Department back to Washington," Morrell answered. "They've been talking about it ever since the end of the war, but I'll believe it when I see it."

"Philadelphia," Agnes said, her eyes far away. "What's it like, living in Philadelphia?"

"Crowded," he said. "Expensive. The air is full of soot and smoke all the time. It's a big city. I don't much like big cities."

Agnes smiled. "I've noticed."

"I figured you had." Morrell smiled, too, but the smile slid into a grimace. "Just have to make the best of it, I suppose."

"Philadelphia," Agnes repeated. He wondered if she'd even heard him. "What will it be like in Philadelphia?"

As she'd come to know him, he'd also come to know her. At least half of what that question meant was, *Will I measure up to the competition?* Morrell smiled again. He was certain of the answer, and gave it: "Sweetheart, you'll knock 'em dead."

One of his wife's hands flew to her hair, patting it into place or maybe the outward expression of an imagined new style. "You say sweet things," she told him.

"Only when I mean them," he said. "Of course, when I'm talking about you, I mean them all the time."

She stepped up, hugged him, and kissed him. His arms tightened around her. One thing might have led to another—except that, with regret, he broke off the embrace. Agnes looked disappointed; yes, she'd been ready for more. But she didn't frown for long. "You're going to have a lot of work to do," she said, proving she was indeed an Army wife.

Morrell nodded. "I sure am. I haven't even told the base commandant about my orders yet—though I suppose a copy will have gone to him, too." He hugged Agnes again, briefly now. "You're really being a brick about this, honey."

"I think they're making a big mistake," she answered. "But you've got your orders, and you've got to follow them."

You've got your orders, and you've got to follow them. That was the way the Army worked, all right. Morrell had trouble imagining it working any other way. "Couldn't have put it better myself," he said. He gave Agnes one more kiss, then turned to go. "The work won't do itself, however much I wish it would."

"All right," his wife said. "I'll see you tonight, then."

He smiled at the promise in her voice. He started looking ahead toward Philadelphia, too. Whatever they set him to doing, he'd do it as well as he knew how. He'd do it well, period; he had a good notion of his own ability. And performing well with important people watching did have certain advantages. With a little luck, he'd be wearing stars on his shoulders instead of eagles before too long.

He wouldn't be so easy to move around like a pawn on a chess board then, not with general's rank he wouldn't. As a matter of fact, he'd be able to do some maneuvering of his own once he had general's rank. Maybe John Abell thought he'd done Morrell's career a bad turn. Morrell's smile was predatory. Anyone who thought that about him had another think coming.

Jefferson Pinkard walked toward the livery stable. "Freedom!" he called to other men heading the same way.

"Freedom!" The greeting came back loud and clear as it had before the stalwarts went out to the Alabama State Fairgrounds when President Hampton came to Birmingham. The Freedom Party had raised a lot more hell than anybody—anybody except Grady Calkins, anyhow—expected.

And now the price of that hell was showing. Jeff called "Freedom!" a couple more times before he went into the stable, but only a couple more times. The building had no trouble holding meetings these days. A lot of people who had been in the Party—people who'd put on white and butternut and banged heads, too—weren't any more. A lot of people who had been in the Party weren't admitting it any more, either.

Fair-weather friends, Pinkard thought scornfully. He still thought most of the same things were wrong with the Confederate States now as had been wrong with the country before Wade Hampton V got shot. He had trouble understanding why more people didn't feel the same way.

Up at the front of the stable, Caleb Briggs paced back and forth, pausing every so often to cough. Even by lamplight, the tough little dentist's color wasn't good. Pinkard wondered how long he could last, especially burning himself at both ends as he did. The damnyankees hadn't killed him all at once when they gassed him. They were doing it an inch at a time, giving him years full of hell before they put him in his grave. To Jeff's way of thinking, that was worse.

After a while, Briggs didn't seem able to stand waiting any longer. "Come on, y'all, move up to the front," he rasped. "Talking's hard enough for me; I'll be goddamned if I'm gonna shout when I don't have to. And there's room. Wish to Christ there wasn't, but there is."

A year before, the livery stable would have been packed. Men would have been milling around outside. Now there were more folding chairs and hay bales set out than people to sit on them. Jeff plopped his bottom down onto a chair in the second row. He could have sat in the first row—plenty of chairs to take—but memories of getting called on in school made him stay less conspicuous.

Caleb Briggs looked over the house. He pursed his lips, coughed again, and began: "Well, we're still here, boys." Maybe he gave a dry chuckle then, or maybe it was just another cough.

"Freedom!" Jefferson Pinkard called, along with his comrades.

"Freedom!" Briggs echoed. It sounded like a dying echo, too, enough so to send a chill through Jeff. But the dentist picked up spirit as he went on, "We *are* still here, dammit, and we aren't going to go away, either, no matter how much the niggers and the folks in striped trousers and top hats and the generals in the War Department wish we would. We're here for the long haul, and we're going to win."

"Freedom!" The shout was louder this time, stronger. Pinkard felt a little of the jolt of energy he always got from hearing Jake Featherston speak. He wondered if Caleb Briggs would last long enough to see the Freedom Party win. He had his doubts, even if victory came soon—and it wouldn't, dammit.

But Briggs was undeterred. He'd been a soldier, and pulled his weight like a soldier. "What we have to do now is make it through the hard times," he said. "They aren't over yet. They won't be over for a while. It'll be God's own miracle if we don't lose seats in Congress this fall. What we've got to do is try and hold on to as many as we can, so we don't look like we're going down the toilet in front of the whole damn country. And what we've got to do right here in Birmingham is make sure we send Barney Stevens back to Richmond in November."

Jeff clapped his hands. He wanted to see Stevens sent back to Richmond to keep the Freedom Party's seat there. He also wanted Stevens in Richmond because the Congressman was a rough customer whom he didn't particularly want coming home to Birmingham.

"We hang tough," Briggs was saying. "We try not to lose too much here in 1923, and we try to build up toward 1925 and especially 1927, when we vote for president again. Rome wasn't built in a day. The Confederate States won't be rebuilt in a day, either. But we will build our country back up, we will shove our niggers back down where they belong, and we—the Freedom Party—will be the ones who do that. So help me God, we will."

"Freedom!" Jeff yelled, along with his friends. The cry echoed from the roof, almost as it had in the days when the Party was swelling.

"One more thing, and then I'm through," Briggs said. "We got as far as we did by standing up and fighting for what we know is right. We're going to go right on fighting. Don't you have any doubts about that. We may pick our spots a little tighter than we did before, but we'll put on the white and butternut whenever we see the need."

Pinkard whooped. The chance to get out there and smash a few heads was one of the reasons he'd joined the Freedom Party. A good many other men cheered Caleb Briggs, too. But Jeff couldn't help noticing how many others sat silent.

Then he thought, *Grady Calkins would have cheered.* He shook his head, rejecting the comparison and all it implied. Calkins had been a madman. Every party had some. But Jeff wasn't crazy. Caleb Briggs wasn't crazy. And Jake Featherston sure as hell wasn't crazy.

Still, the idea left him uneasy. He didn't sit around and yarn and drink homemade whiskey, as he usually did after the business part of a meeting wound down. Instead, glum and oddly dissatisfied, he headed for the door. One of the guards there caught his eye. He reached into his pocket, pulled out a dollar, and tossed the banknote into the bucket at the guard's feet. "Thank you kindly, Jeff," the bruiser said. "Party needs every penny it can get its hands on these days."

"I know, Tim," Pinkard answered. He laughed. "And think— just last year, we had more millions than you can shake a stick at." It wasn't really funny, not for the Freedom Party. A sound currency had done as much to squeeze folks out of the Party as had Wade Hampton's assassination. Real money gave people one less thing to be angry about, and anger was the gasoline that fueled the Party's engine.

It had started to drizzle. Jeff jammed his cap down low on his head and tugged up his coat collar. He was angry, by God—angry about having to wait for the trolley in the rain. The trolley got there late, too, which did nothing to improve his mood. He threw five pennies in the fare box (bronze coins were returning faster than silver) and rode out to the Sloss Works company housing.

A woman was waiting at the trolley stop. Pinkard thought she would get on after he got off. When she didn't, he gave a mental shrug and started off toward his cottage. The trolleyman clanged his bell. The car rattled down the tracks.

"Jeff?" the woman called.

Pinkard stopped—froze, in fact. "Emily," he whispered, and slowly turned. In the darkness and drizzle, he hadn't recognized her, but he would have known her voice anywhere. His own roughened as he went on, "What the devil are you doing here?"

"Waiting for you," she answered. Her own tone was sharp: "I sure enough knew what you'd be doing this night of the week, didn't I? I just got here myself, though—didn't expect you back quite so soon. Things ain't so lively at the Party nowadays?"

"None of your business—you made sure of *that*, by God," Jeff said. "What do you want with me, anyway, you . . . tramp?" He could have used a stronger word, and nearly had.

"Wanted to see how you were," Emily answered. "Wanted to see what you were up to." She sighed and shook her head. "Not like you cared enough about me to find out any of that."

"After what you done, why should I care?" he said. "You're lucky I don't kick you down the street." Had he had some whiskey in him, he thought he would have done it.

"I got lonesome," she said. "I got lonesome when you was in the Army, and I got lonesome when you started caring more about the Freedom Party than you did about me. I don't like being lonesome, so I went and did something about it."

She didn't mean *lonesome*. She meant *horny*. Pinkard knew that. She'd been fine as long as he gave her everything she needed. When he stopped, she'd gone out and taken what she needed, as a man with a frigid wife might have done. It would have been all right in a man. In a woman . . . Pinkard shook his head. No man could put up with what she'd done, not if he wanted to stay a man.

Emily said, "I was almost hoping I wouldn't find you here, on account of that'd mean you were back at the house, not at that stinking livery stable. It'd mean you'd wised up and gotten out of the Freedom Party. But if what happened to President Hampton didn't open your eyes, I reckon nothin' ever will."

She'd hoped he'd given up the Party? Did that mean she wanted him back, or would have wanted him back? Did he want her back? She was explosive between the sheets. He knew that. But how would he keep from thinking he wasn't the only man she'd taken to bed? How would he keep from thinking she wasn't taking some other man to bed along with him? He shook his head again. He wouldn't. He couldn't.

To keep from thinking about that now, he asked, "What are you doing these days?"

"Working in a textile mill," she answered with a shrug. "It ain't a lot of money, but I don't need a lot, so I get by. I get lonesome sometimes, though."

She meant *horny* again. "Bet you can find plenty of fellows if you do." Jeff didn't try to keep the scorn from his voice.

"Of course I can. A woman always can." Emily sounded scornful, too, and weary, so weary. "Harder to find anybody who cares about more than that, though."

"Too bad," Jeff said harshly. "Too damn bad."

Emily sighed. "I don't know why I bothered doing this. Just wasted my time. Reckon I was hoping you'd changed—changed back into the fellow I knew before the war."

"He's dead," Pinkard said. "The damnyankees killed him, and the niggers killed him, and you helped kill him, too. The country he lived in is dead along with him. He ain't ever coming back. Maybe the country we had back then will. That's what the Freedom Party is all about."

"To hell with the Freedom Party!" Emily said furiously. A distant street lamp showed tears running down her cheeks. "And to hell with you, too, Jefferson Davis Pinkard."

"Go on, get out of here. Go peddle your tail somewhere else, or I'll give you what I gave you before, only more of it." Jeff made a fist and raised his arm. "I sure as hell don't need you. I don't need anybody, by God. As long as I've got the Party, that's everything I need in the whole wide world."

Emily turned away, her shoulders slumping. She was crying harder now, crying like a little lost child. Jeff headed home, a smile on his face now in spite of the chilly drizzle. Why not? He'd won. He knew damn well he'd won.

Chester Martin liked playing football. He liked it in the snow, and he liked it here in springtime, too. In that, he was very little different from anybody else in the United States. In New England and New York, a few people still enjoyed baseball, a game that had briefly flourished in the couple of decades before the War of Secession. Even there, though, football was king.

He pulled on his leather helmet. Being a burly steelworker, he played in the line on offense and defense. *In the trenches,* people called that these days. The comparison wasn't far-fetched. Plenty of times, he'd wished for a bayoneted rifle to hold off whatever charging rhinoceros the other team aimed at him. And not a game went by when he didn't wish he were wearing a green-gray steel pot on his head instead of mere leather.

Albert Bauer played beside him in the line. Bauer pointed to their opponents, a team of bruisers in dark blue wool shirts. "Here we go, Chester," he said. "Legal revenge for everything the police have given us since the end of the war—and before that, too."

"You don't need to fire me up, Al. I'm ready now." Martin looked down at his own shirt, which was bright red. "We licked 'em in the presidential election, and we licked 'em again in the Congressional election last year, and we've licked 'em a few times on the gridiron, too. I figure we can do it again."

"That's the proletarian spirit," Bauer said. "Don't take them lightly, though. The enemies of progress fight hard, even if their cause is doomed. They will lose the war. They can win the battles."

On one sideline, steelworkers' friends and families gathered to cheer their gladiators. Sue Martin waved to Chester. He waved back. On the other sideline stood friends and relatives of the cops. A stranger couldn't have guessed which side was which. Seeing how ordinary policemen's families were never ceased to surprise Martin.

The two referees were newspapermen; they'd covered both sides, and both sides trusted, or rather distrusted, them about evenly. They waved the team captains over to them and flipped a silver dollar. The cop let out a happy little grunt; he'd guessed right. "Give us the ball," he said.

"Yeah, give it to 'em in the balls," a steelworker said. He grinned, but it was a sharp-toothed sort of grin.

Martin held the ball upright with his finger as the kicker booted it down the field—the park, actually—toward the cops. Then he was on his feet and running as hard as he could. A policeman ran toward him, yelling in a language that didn't sound like English. Martin lowered a shoulder and knocked him sprawling. The first hit always felt good. He banged into a couple of other policemen before two of his teammates brought down the fellow with the ball.

When he lined up at right tackle, the cop playing opposite him looked familiar. "Have I seen you someplace before?" Martin asked.

Before the cop could answer, the center snapped the ball back to the quarterback, who stood waiting for it. The cop gave Martin a body block that took him out of the play, though the run gained only a yard or two. Then he helped him up. "I dunno. I been playing football for a while, same as most guys."

"I don't think that's it," Martin said. "Where'd you fight in the war?"

Another play intervened. This time, Martin spun past the blocker in dark blue and flattened the fullback behind the line of scrimmage. The fullback accused him of unsavory practices. He laughed.

"I was in Kentucky with the First Army—Custer's men," the cop answered with no small pride as they took their places once more. "Then I got sent to Utah, to put down the Mormon uprising. After that, I fought in Arkansas. How about you, bud?"

Before Martin could answer, the ball was snapped again. The quarterback booted it away in a quick kick. It rolled dead deep in the steelworkers' territory. Now it would be Martin's turn to try to hold the cop away from the ball carrier.

"Me?" he said as he took his stance. "I was in Virginia the whole time—on the Roanoke front till I got wounded, then up in the north."

The cop charged at him. Martin managed to hold his own. Even while he held the policeman at bay, he was puzzled. He was almost sure he'd seen the broken-nosed face in front of him twisted with fury while the policeman aimed a gun at . . . at . . .

He laughed. "What's funny?" the cop asked.

"I'll tell you what's funny," Martin answered. "You tried to shoot me a couple-three years ago, I think."

"Oh." The policeman frowned. Then he also started to laugh. "You should have been wearing a goddamn red shirt then, too. I would have hit what I was aiming at."

The ball flew back to the steelworkers' quarterback. He retreated till he stood more than five yards behind the line, then let fly with a forward pass. An end caught it and ran another ten yards before being dragged down from behind.

One more pass a couple of plays later moved the ball deep into the cops' territory. From there, the steelworkers pounded it into the end zone, running straight at their opponents and defying them to bring down the ball carrier. They were, Martin realized as he took the measure of the opposition, a little heavier and bigger and a little younger than their opponents. He smiled, thinking they would have an easy game and punish the policemen who had given them so much trouble on the picket line.

On the try for the point after the touchdown, he knocked the cop across from him over on his back. The steelworkers' kicker drop-kicked the ball through the uprights for the extra point.

"Smash 'em!" Sue yelled as the steelworkers trudged back to their side of the field for the kickoff.

"Of course we'll smash 'em!" Chester Martin yelled back. One of the referees tossed him the ball. He knelt down and held it for the kicker to send it down the field to the policemen. He didn't think he was bragging or doing anything but telling the truth. How could the cops compete against bigger, younger men?

Before long, he found out. One of the halfbacks on the policemen's team was nothing special to look at: a skinny little fellow with a blond Kaiser Bill mustache. But when he got the ball, that scrawny halfback was quick as a lizard and twisty as a snake. He did most of the work on the cops' drive, and capped it by sprinting into the end zone on a pretty fifteen-yard run.

Martin's tongue was hanging out from chasing him. "Jesus," he panted as both sides lined up for the cops' try for the point after touchdown. "If I had a gun right now, I wouldn't shoot you." He nodded to the policeman who'd fired during the labor unrest. "I'd shoot that miserable son of a bitch instead. He's trying to give me a heart attack."

"Yeah, Matt's dangerous," the cop agreed. "You try taking a shot at him, I figure it's about even money he dodges the bullet."

"Maybe," Martin said. "Have to bring along a machine gun, then, and see if he can dodge that." The cop chuckled and nodded. They both understood the weapons of war, even if they'd stood on opposite sides of the barricade. The policemen's drop-kick was also good, and knotted the game.

It swayed back and forth all afternoon. The steelworkers had size and youth and a quarterback who threw enough to keep the policemen from doing nothing but storming forward to stop the run. The cops had nothing but Matt. All by himself, he kept them in the game, tackling pass receivers on defense and running like the wind whenever the policemen had the ball. He never wore down. Martin started to wonder whether he was human or mechanical. However many times he got smashed to the dirt, he rose again as if nothing had happened. Even his mustache stayed unruffled, which made Chester all the more suspicious.

In the end, the steelworkers won, 27–23. Martin made himself a minor hero, falling on a fumble in the closing moments to ensure that the cops couldn't come back. After shaking hands with the policemen, he limped off the field, covered in glory and sweat and mud and bruises. He still had all his front teeth, which made him unusual on the team.

He took off his helmet and ran a hand through his damp, matted hair. "Whew!" he said. "This is supposed to be fun, they tell me. I feel like I've been slammed by a triphammer a couple dozen times."

His sister gave him a hug. "You were wonderful, Chester." She wrinkled her nose. "You don't smell so wonderful, though."

"If you were out there, you wouldn't smell so wonderful, either," Martin retorted. He stretched. It hurt.

His father said, "It's a different game nowadays, with all this throwing. Might as well be baseball, if you ask me. When I was playing, back around the time you were born, we just ran. That was a real man's game, if you ask me."

"Sure it was, Pa," Chester said. "Nobody had helmets then, and—"

"Nobody did," Stephen Douglas Martin broke in.

"Nobody had helmets," Martin repeated, "and the ball was solid steel, and the field was a mile and a half long and half a mile wide and uphill both ways, too, and everybody on the other side was always ten feet tall and weighed seven hundred pounds, and even dead men had to stay in the game—and run the ball, too. That's how they played it in the old days."

"And you are a heartless whippersnapper, and I ought to turn you over my knee and whip you black and blue," his father said, rolling his eyes. "But you're already black and blue, I expect. And you're wrong—dead men didn't have to stay in. They changed that rule in *my* father's day."

Laughing, they helped Sue and Louisa Martin spread out the picnic feast that had come along in a wicker basket. Steelworkers and policemen wandered back and forth, talking about the game and sharing food and beer and other potables. It was as if the two groups had never clashed anywhere save in a friendly game of football.

Chester gnawed a drumstick. When Matt, the fast halfback on the policemen's team, walked by, Martin held up a bottle of beer to get him to stop. The lure worked as well as a worm would have with a trout. "Thanks," Matt said, and sat down beside him. "I'd sure as the devil sooner drink with you than have you jump on my kidneys like you were doing all day long."

"Like heck I was." Martin had finally got used to watching his language again when his mother and sister were around. "Most of the time, I was flat on my fanny watching you run by."

They bantered back and forth, each making the other out to be a better football player than he really was. Then Matt got up and headed off to chin with somebody else, just as if he'd never clubbed a striking steelworker in all his born days. And Martin waved when he went, just as if he'd never kicked a cop. Everything in the park was peaceful and friendly. Chester Martin liked that fine.

It couldn't be plainer that no Negro ever born has got what it takes to be a true citizen of the Confederate States of America. Jake Featherston's pen raced across the page. One of those days, *Over Open Sights* would be done, and everyone in the country would realize he'd been telling the truth all along.

Anyone with half an eye to see can understand the reasons for this. They are— Before Jake could set down what they were, his secretary came back into his inner office. "What do you want, Lulu?" he growled; like any writer, he hated interruptions.

"Someone to see you, Mr. Featherston," she said.

"Who is it?" he asked. "I don't want to see any reporters right now." Fewer reporters wanted to see him these days, too. That worried him, but not enough to make him feel friendly right this second.

"It's not a reporter, sir," Lulu answered. "It's General Jeb Stuart, Jr."

"What?" Jake had trouble believing his ears. As far as he was concerned, Jeb Stuart, Jr., was the author of all his troubles. Who else had made sure he would stay a sergeant as long as he stayed in the Army? Jeb Stuart, Jr., blamed him for the death of Jeb Stuart III. Jake blamed Jeb Stuart, Jr., for suppressing an investigation that might have given warning of the great Red uprising. And now the general wanted to see him? Slowly, Jake said, "Well, I reckon you can bring him on in."

Jeb Stuart, Jr., was in his late fifties. He looked very much like an older version of his handsome son, save that he wore a neat gray chin beard rather than the little strip of hair under the lower lip Jeb Stuart III had affected. After cautious greetings, Stuart said, "You're probably wondering why I've called on you now, after pretending for so long that you and the Freedom Party and all the insults you've thrown at me don't exist."

Jake did his best to sound dry: "I'd be a liar if I said it hadn't crossed my mind—and I'm no liar."

"You say that. I wonder if even you believe it." Stuart looked at him. No—Stuart looked through him. He'd had upper-crust Confederate officers give him that look a great many times. It showed without words that they relegated him to the outer darkness: he wasn't quite a nigger in their eyes, but he might as well have been.

It also made Featherston want to punch those upper-crust Confederates right in the face. "You've got anything to say, say it and then get the hell out," he snapped. "Otherwise, just get the hell out."

"I intend to say it. You needn't worry about that," Jeb Stuart, Jr., replied. "I came to say good-bye."

"Good-bye?" Jake echoed. "Why? Are you leaving? If you are, it's about ten years too late, but good riddance anyway. I'm sure as the devil not going anywhere."

To his surprise, Stuart smiled. "I know you're not. You're not going anywhere at all in the Confederate States of America, not in politics, not any more you're not. And so, Sergeant Featherston"— he laced the title with contempt—"good-bye." He waved, a delicate fluttering of the fingers.

Jake laughed in his face. "Go ahead and dream, General." He showed what he thought of Stuart's title, too. "You fancy-pants boys won't be rid of me that easy." He couldn't help a nasty stab of fear, though. Nothing had gone right for him or the Freedom Party since Grady Calkins took a Tredegar out to the Alabama State Fairgrounds and shot down Wade Hampton V.

Stuart might have picked his pocket for that very thought. "People know what the Freedom Party is now, Featherston: a pack of murdering ruffians. They'll run your henchmen out of Congress in a few months, and you'll never, ever be president of the Confederate States. And for that, believe me, I get down on my knees and thank God."

"Go ahead and laugh," Featherston said. "The fellow who laughs last laughs best, or that's what they say. I fought the damnyankees till I couldn't fight any more, and I reckon I'll keep on fighting the traitors here the same way." Not for the life of him would he let Jeb Stuart, Jr., see how closely his words reflected Jake's own nightmares.

"There are no traitors, damn you," Stuart said.

"Hell there aren't," Featherston returned. "I'm sitting across the desk from one. God damn you, that nigger Pompey, your son's body servant, was as Red as he was black. They were going to take him away and grill him, but your precious brat didn't want 'em to, and they didn't. Who stopped 'em? You stopped 'em, that's who. If that doesn't make you a traitor, what the hell are you?"

"A man who made a mistake," Stuart answered. "I don't suppose you've ever made a mistake, Featherston?"

"Not one that big, by Jesus," Jake said.

Stuart startled him again, this time by nodding. "It couldn't have been much bigger, could it? It ended up costing me the life of my only son."

"It cost a lot more than that," Featherston said. "It cost thousands dead, by God. If any one thing cost us the war, that was it. And all you do is think about yourself. I reckon I ought to be surprised, but I ain't."

"You don't know what I think, so don't put words in my mouth," Jeb Stuart, Jr., said. Slowly, sadly, he shook his head. "I blamed you for my son's death, you know."

"I never would have guessed," Jake said with a fine sardonic sneer. "That's why I spent the next year and however long commanding a battery and staying a sergeant. I could have been in the Army for the next five wars—hell, the next ten wars—and I never would've had more than three stripes. Thank you very kindly, General goddamn Stuart, sir."

He wanted to fight with Stuart. He would have loved to spring out of his chair, smash the general to the floor, and stomp him. Every muscle quivered. *Give me an excuse,* he said silently. *Come on, you son of a bitch. Give me even a piece of an excuse.*

But Stuart only looked sad. "And that was the other half of my mistake. Yes, I blocked your promotion. It seemed the right thing to do at the time, but it turned out wrong, so wrong. If you'd ended the war a lieutenant or a captain, would you ever have done what you did with—and to—the Freedom Party?"

Featherston stared at him. That question had never crossed his mind. He tried to imagine himself without the smoldering resentment he'd carried since 1916. For the life of him, he couldn't. That endless burning inside was as much a part of him as his fingers.

He said, "It's a little fucking late to worry about that now, don't you reckon?"

"I do. I certainly do." Stuart got to his feet. "And it's a little fucking late to worry about you, Featherston. You're yesterday's news, and you won't be tomorrow's. You don't need to get up for me." Jake hadn't been about to get up for him, as he must have known. "I can find my own way out."

"Don't come back, either," Jake snarled.

Leaving the inner office, Jeb Stuart, Jr., got the last word: "I wish you the same." He closed the door behind him.

With another snarl, this one wordless, Jake snatched up his pen and began to write furiously. He filled two pages in *Over Open*

Sights in something less than half an hour. But even venting his anger through the growing book was not enough to satisfy him. He slammed his pad shut, threw it into his desk, and locked the drawer that held it. Until he was ready for it to see the light of day, it wouldn't.

He sprang up and paced the inner office like a caged wolf. The Party *would* lose ground when elections came, and they were only four months away. He saw no way around it. The trick was going to be holding as much as he could—and making people think the Freedom Party would be a force to reckon with in elections after 1923. He'd known it wouldn't be easy long before General Stuart stopped by to gloat.

He wished he could talk with Roger Kimball. But Kimball was dead, and the damnyankee woman who'd murdered him had got off scot-free. That was one more on the list he'd already started compiling against President Mitchel. "Go ahead, kiss the USA's ass," he muttered.

He wished he could talk with Anne Colleton, too. He valued her money, he valued her sense of theatrics, and he valued her brains. But she didn't value him or the Freedom Party any more. Of all the defections he'd had to endure over the past year, hers might have hurt most.

Since he couldn't talk with either of them, he telephoned Ferdinand Koenig. "Jeb Stuart, Jr.?" his former running mate exclaimed. "Well, isn't that a kick in the head? Stopped by to gloat, you say?"

"That's just what he did," Jake answered. "Said the Party was as good as dead and buried, God damn him to hell."

"Don't take it too much to heart," Koenig said. "If he's as right about that as he was during the war, we're in fine shape."

"Yeah!" Featherston said gratefully; he hadn't thought of it like that. "You've got a good way of looking at things, Ferd."

"Don't reckon you'll let us down, Sarge," Koenig answered. "I remember where we were back in 1917, and I can see where we are now. Maybe we haven't climbed all the way to the top of the mountain, but we'll get there."

Thousands of Party stalwarts might—would—have said the same thing. But Jake set no special stock in what stalwarts said. They weren't stalwarts because they were long on brains. They were stalwarts because they were long on muscle and short on temper. Ferdinand Koenig was different. He not only had good sense, he wasn't embarrassed about showing it.

"Of course we'll get there," Jake said, sounding more confident than he felt. "Just have to come through this November without getting skinned."

"Figure we will?" Koenig asked.

"That's the question, all right," Jake allowed. He let out a long, slow sigh. "We'll get hurt some. We'll have to put the best face on it we can, and then we'll have to start building toward 1925. We can't afford to waste a minute there. I only hope to God we don't lose so much, people won't take us serious any more." With Kimball dead and Anne Colleton gone, Ferdinand Koenig was the only one to whom he would have said even so much.

Koenig answered, "You never can tell, Sarge. Folks don't think we matter so much now that money doesn't burn a hole in their pockets if they leave it in there more than a minute and a half, but who knows how long that'll last? Who knows what all's liable to go wrong between now and 1925?"

"That's right," Jake said, smiling for the first time since Jeb Stuart, Jr., had left. "That's just right. With the Whigs running things, they *will* go wrong, sure as the sun comes up tomorrow." He hung up feeling better, but only for a little while. Would anything be left of the Freedom Party when a chance to rule came round at last?

"**M**ama!" Clara Jacobs screeched from what had been the storeroom. "Little Armstrong just tore up the picture I was drawing!"

She was almost four, more than twice the age of her little nephew. But Armstrong Grimes, even as a toddler, gave every sign of being hell on wheels. *He takes after Edna,* Nellie thought. *I bet Merle Grimes was a nice man even when he was a little boy.* She had such a good opinion of almost no one else in the male half of the human race; the more she got to know her son-in-law, the more he impressed her.

Fortunately, the coffeehouse was almost empty. She could hurry back to the old storeroom and mete out punishment. Armstrong hadn't just torn up Clara's picture; he'd made a snowstorm of pieces out of it. He was happily sticking one of those pieces in his mouth when Nellie yanked it away from him, upended him over her knee, and walloped his backside. "No, no!" she shouted. "Mustn't tear up things that don't belong to you!"

Her grandson howled. Since he was wearing a diaper that shielded his bottom, Nellie knew she wasn't hurting him much. The spanking made an impressive amount of noise, though, as did her yelling.

"Now," she said, "are you going to do that any more?"

"No," little Armstrong answered. Nellie wiped his nose, which was dripping yellowish snot. She didn't believe him. For one thing, he was heading toward the age where he said *no* every other time he opened his mouth. For another, a toddler's promise lasted only till he forgot he'd made it, which meant anywhere from two minutes to, in extraordinary circumstances, an hour or so.

"You be good, you hear me?" Nellie said.

"No," Armstrong Grimes answered. That was neither defiance nor ignorance, only the first thing that came out of his mouth.

"*I'm* good, Mama," Clara said, so virtuously that Nellie expected to be blinded by the halo about to spring into being above her head.

"Of course you are—when you feel like it," Nellie told her own daughter. "Pick up those scraps, and don't let him eat any more of them. Don't let him eat your crayons, either."

"I won't, Mama." Clara turned to her nephew. "You see? You can't have *anything*." Thus made forcibly aware that he was being deprived, Armstrong started crying again. Nellie had to spend more time soothing him before she could go out front again.

Edna was supposed to come get her son at half past three; she'd left him with Nellie so she could do some unencumbered shopping. She didn't show up till a quarter after four. "Hello, Ma—I'm sorry," she said in a perfunctory way. "How crazy did he drive you?"

"Crazy enough," Nellie replied. "I was thinking he reminds me of you." Edna laughed, but Nellie wasn't joking. She went on, "Please come get him when you say you will. I've got enough to do keeping up with Clara and the coffeehouse. Put Armstrong in there, too, and I start climbing the walls."

Edna sniffed. "I take care of Clara for you sometimes, and you don't hear me complaining about it."

"Oh, I do sometimes," Nellie said. "And besides, when you take care of the children, that's all you do. You have Merle to make a living for you. I've got to make my own living, and this place won't run by itself."

Before Edna could answer, Armstrong picked up something from the floor and started chewing on it. He bit Edna when she stuck her finger in his mouth to get it out. She finally did—it was a nasty little clump of hair and dust—and then whacked him a lot harder than Nellie had done. He wasn't crying now because he was angry or frightened; he was crying because his bottom hurt.

"You've never been fair with me," Edna said.

And here we go again, Nellie thought. *One more round in the fight that never stops for good.* She said, "You think being fair means doing whatever you want. I've got news for you, dearie—it doesn't work that way."

"I've got news for you, Ma—you never do what I want." Edna glared. "You do as you please, and what pleases you most is doing whatever you think will make me maddest."

"Why, you little liar!" Nellie snapped, as she might have at Clara. But Edna's charge held just enough truth to sting more than it would have had it been made up from whole cloth. "And you were the one who was always sneaking around behind my back. You ought to be ashamed of yourself."

"I had to sneak around behind your back. You wouldn't let me live any kind of life in front of your face," Edna said.

"I don't call living fast and loose any kind of a life." To forestall her daughter, Nellie added, "And I ought to know, too. I found out the hard way."

"Yeah, and you've been frozen up ever since on account of it," Edna said, another shot with all too much truth in it. "I got what I was looking for in spite of you, and do you know what else? I like it just fine." She carried her son out of the coffeehouse, slamming the door behind her hard enough to rattle the windows.

"Why is my big sister angry?" Clara asked from the door to her playroom. "If I slammed a door like that, I'd get a whipping."

"Edna's too big to get a whipping." Under her breath, Nellie mumbled, "No matter how much she needs one."

That slammed door also drew Hal from across the street. "You had another quarrel with Edna," he said. It was not a question.

"Well, what if I did?" Nellie said. "I don't suppose I would have, if she'd come and gotten her brat when she was supposed to."

Exercising her temper proved a mistake. Clara started chanting, "Armstrong is a brat! Armstrong is a brat!"

"Stop that!" Hal Jacobs said sharply, and, for a wonder, Clara stopped it. She listened to her father more often than to her mother, perhaps because Hal gave her fewer orders than Nellie did.

Nellie sighed. "I wish Edna would pay as much attention to you as Clara does." She sighed again. "I wish anyone would pay attention to me."

"I always pay attention to you, my dear," Hal said.

That was true. It was so true, Nellie had come to take it for granted in the years since she and Hal got married. Because she took it for granted, it no longer satisfied her. She said, "I wish Edna would pay attention to me."

"She is a grown woman," Hal said. "With a little luck, she is paying attention to her own husband now."

"It's not the same," Nellie replied in a sulky voice.

"No, I suppose it is not," Hal admitted. "But it is good that she should pay attention to someone, I think. And Merle Grimes is a young man worth paying attention to."

"I know he is. I was thinking the same thing myself earlier today," Nellie said. "But he's not her mother, and I am." She shook her head, discontented with the world and with Edna. "That's probably why she doesn't pay attention to me."

"Yes, it probably is," Hal said. "When I was becoming a man, I paid as little attention to my mother and my father as I could get away with."

Nellie had hardly known her own father. When she'd got away from her mother at an early age, it was to go into the demimonde. Hal didn't need to know any more about that than whatever he'd already found out. Nellie said, "But Edna isn't becoming a woman. By now, she is one, like you said. Shouldn't she have figured out that I know what I'm doing by now?"

"Maybe," Hal said. "But maybe not, too." He looked at Nellie with amused affection. "She has a stubborn streak as wide as yours. I wonder where she could have gotten it."

"Not from me," Nellie said automatically. She needed a moment to recognize the expression on her husband's face. Hal Jacobs was doing his best not to laugh out loud. Again, Nellie spoke automatically: "I'm not stubborn!" Hal let the words hang, the most devastating thing he could have done. Nellie's face went hot. She said, "I'm not that stubborn, anyway."

"Well, maybe not," Hal said; he should have been a diplomat in striped trousers, not a cobbler and sometimes spy. He went on, "You are my dear wife, and I love you exactly the way you are."

"You're sweet." That was usually another automatic reply. This time, Nellie listened to what she'd just said. "You really are sweet, Hal. I'm glad I married you. I was scared to death when you asked me, but it's worked out pretty well, hasn't it?" If she sounded a little surprised, she could hope her husband didn't notice.

If he did, he was too much a gentleman to show it. "The best five years of my life," he said. "Being here with you, and being here to watch Clara grow up . . ." His face softened. "Yes, the best years of my life."

With more than a little surprise, Nellie realized the years since the war had been the best of her life, too. She'd made more money when the Confederates occupied Washington, but she'd been worried and afraid all the time: worried about what Edna would do, afraid Bill Reach would tell the whole world what he knew, worried and afraid the U.S. bombardment would blow her and Edna and the coffeehouse to hell and gone.

Now Edna was married, Bill Reach was dead, and the country was at peace. And living with Hal Jacobs hadn't proved nearly so hard as she'd feared. "I love you, Hal," she exclaimed.

Saying it surprised her: it seemed an afternoon for surprises. And discovering she meant it surprised her even more. Hearing it made her husband's face light up. "I love it when you tell me that," Hal said. "I did not know I could be more happy than I already was, but now I am."

"I'm happy, too," Nellie said. By the way all the stories were written, she should have been in love with her husband before she married him, instead of finding out she was five years later. *Well,* she thought, *it's not like I've lived a storybook life.* She tried to remember if she'd ever told Hal she loved him before. Once or twice, maybe, in a dutiful fashion, as she occasionally gave him her body. But the words hadn't come from her heart, not till today.

Perhaps Hal sensed something of the same thing. He walked up to her and gave her a kiss a good deal warmer than the pecks that usually passed between them. She returned it with more warmth than usual, too. For once, she didn't mind the gleam that came into Hal's eye. The idea of making love while kindled suddenly struck her as delicious, not disgusting.

But Clara was still playing not far from one of the tables, and a customer chose that moment to come in. *Can't have everything,* Nellie thought as she walked over to ask the man what he wanted. She looked around. No, she couldn't have everything—she wouldn't be rich as long as she lived, for instance. What she had, though, was pretty good.

XX

As Hosea Blackford did whenever he came up to the Lower East Side of New York City, he looked around in astonishment. Turning to his wife, he said, "I can't imagine what growing up here would have been like, with the buildings blocking out the sky and with swarms of people everywhere."

Flora Blackford—after being married for a year, she hardly ever signed her name *Flora Hamburger* any more—shrugged. "It's all what you're used to," she answered. "I couldn't imagine there was so much open space in the whole world, let alone the USA, till I took that train trip out to Dakota with you this past summer. I felt like a little tiny bug on a great big plate."

Up till 1917, New York City was all she'd ever known. Up till the train trip to Dakota, all she'd known were New York City, Philadelphia, and the ninety-odd built-up miles between them. Endless expanses of grass waving gently in the breeze all the way out to the horizon had not been part of her mental landscape. They were now, and she felt richer for it.

A boy in short pants ran by carrying a stack of the *Daily Forward*. "Buy my paper!" he yelled in Yiddish. "Buy my paper!"

"I understood that." Blackford looked pleased with himself. "The German I took in college isn't quite fossilized after all—and being around your family is an education in any number of ways."

"I'll tell my father you said so," Flora said. She walked up the stairs of the apartment house that seemed so familiar and so strange at the same time.

Following her, Blackford said, "Go ahead. He'll take it the right way. He has better sense than half the people in the Cabinet, believe you me he does."

"Considering what goes on in the Cabinet, that's not saying so much," Flora answered. Her husband rewarded her with a gust of laughter. She laughed, too, but a little ruefully: the scent of cooking cabbage was very strong. "I don't think this building is ready for the vice president of the United States."

"Don't worry about it," he said, laughing again. "Compared to the farm I grew up on, it's paradise—a crowded paradise, but paradise. It's got running water and flush toilets and electricity. The farm I grew up on sure didn't, not that anybody had electricity back then."

"This building had gas lamps up until a few years ago," Flora said. It did not have an elevator; she and Blackford walked upstairs hand in hand.

Knocking at the door to the flat where she'd lived so long seemed strange, too, but it also seemed right: she didn't live here any more, and never would again. When the door swung open, David Hamburger was the one with his hand on the latch. His other hand held the cane that helped him get around.

Flora embraced her brother carefully, not wanting to make him topple over. David shook hands with Hosea Blackford, then shuffled through a turn and walked back to the kitchen table. Each slow, rolling step on his artificial leg was a separate effort, each a silent reproach against the war that, though more than six years over, would echo through shattered lives for most of the rest of the century.

Blackford shed his coat; the October evening might have had a nip to it, but the inside of the flat was warm enough and to spare. "Here, I'll take that," Flora's younger sister Esther said, and she did.

"Chess?" David asked. He pulled out the board and pieces even before Blackford could nod.

"I'll take on the winner," Isaac said. The younger of Flora's brothers wore in his lapel a silver Soldiers' Circle pin inscribed *1918*—the year of his conscription class. She thanked heaven that he, unlike David, hadn't had to go to war . . . and wished to heaven he wouldn't wear that pin. Soldiers' Circle men could be almost as goonish as the Freedom Party's ruffians down in the Confederate States. But he did as he pleased in such things. He was a man now, and let everyone know it on any excuse or none.

"Hello, Aunt Flora!" Yossel Reisen said. Coming home so seldom, Flora was amazed at how much her older sister's son grew in between times. He'd been a baby when she went off to Congress, but he was in school now. He added, "Hello, Uncle Hosea!"

"Hello, Yossel," Hosea Blackford answered absently, most of his attention on the board in front of him. He played well enough to beat David some of the time, but not too often. He'd already gone down a pawn, which meant he probably wouldn't win this game.

Abraham Hamburger came in from the bedroom, puffing on his pipe. He hugged Flora, then glanced at the chess board. Setting a hand on Blackford's shoulder, he said, "You're in trouble. But you knew that when you decided to marry my daughter, eh? If you didn't, you should have."

"Papa!" Flora said, indignation mostly but not altogether feigned.

"He's not kidding, dear," Blackford said. "You know he's not." Since Flora did, she subsided. Her husband started a series of trades that wiped the board clear like machine-gun fire smashing a frontal assault. By the time the dust settled, though, he was down two pawns, not one. Stopping David from promoting one of them cost him his bishop, his last piece other than pawns. He tipped over his king and stood up. "You got me again."

David only grunted. He grunted again when Isaac took Blackford's place. Before he and his brother could start playing, Sophie stuck her head out of the kitchen and announced, "Supper in a couple of minutes."

"We'd better wait," David said then.

"Ha!" Isaac said. "You're just afraid I'd beat you." But he scooped his pieces off the board and put them in the box. He and David had been giving each other a hard time as long as they'd been alive.

Sophie came out with plates and silverware. Behind her came Sarah Hamburger with a platter on which rested two big boiled beef tongues. While Sophie and Esther and Flora set the table, their mother went back into the kitchen, returning with another platter piled high with boiled potatoes and onions and carrots.

"Looks wonderful," Hosea Blackford said enthusiastically. "Smells wonderful, too."

Isaac gave him a quizzical look. "When I was in the Army, a lot of . . . fellows who weren't Jews"—he'd caught himself before saying *goyim* to his brother-in-law—"turned up their noses at the idea of eating tongue."

"All what you're used to, I suppose," Blackford said. "When I was growing up on a farm, we'd have it whenever we butchered a cow—or a lamb, for that matter, though a lamb's tongue has a skin that's tough to peel and so little meat, it's almost more trouble than it's worth. I hadn't eaten tongue for years before I first came here."

"I knew then you liked," Sarah Hamburger said, "so I make." Her English was the least certain of anyone's there, but she made a special effort for Blackford.

Over supper, Esther said, "What is it like, being vice president?" She laughed at herself. "I've been asking Flora what it's like being in Congress ever since she got elected, and I still don't really understand it, so I don't know why I should ask you now."

"Being in Congress is complicated, or it can be," Blackford answered. "Being vice president is simple. Imagine you're in a factory, and you have a machine with one very expensive part. If that part breaks, the whole machine shuts down till you can replace it."

"And you're that part?" Esther asked, her eyes wide.

Blackford laughed and shook his head. "I'm the spare for that part. I sit in the warehouse and gather dust. President Sinclair is the part that's hooked up to the machine, and I hope to heaven that he doesn't break."

"You're joking," David said. He studied Blackford's face. "No, I take it back. You're not."

"No, I'm not," Blackford said. "Flora has heard me complain about this for as long as I've had the job. I have the potential to be a very important man—but the only way the potential turns real is if something horrible happens, the way something horrible happened to the Confederate president last year. Otherwise, I haven't got much to do."

Abraham Hamburger said, "This Mitchel, down in the Confederate States, seems to be doing a good job."

"He does indeed," Blackford said. "I'm not telling any secrets when I say President Sinclair is glad, too. If the regular politicians in the Confederate States do a good job, the reactionaries don't get the chance to grab the reins."

"A *kholeriyeh* on everybody in the Confederate States," David muttered in Yiddish. Blackford glanced at Flora, but she didn't translate. She didn't blame her brother for feeling that way. Because of what the Confederates had done to him, she could hardly keep from feeling that way herself.

Her father nodded at what Blackford had said. "These Freedom Party *mamzrim* remind me of the Black Hundreds in Russia, except they go after Negroes instead of Jews."

"Not enough Jews in the Confederate States for them to go after," Isaac said. "If there were more, they would."

"That's probably true," Flora said, and Blackford nodded. Flora's laugh sounded a little shaky. "Funny to think of anybody going after anyone instead of Jews."

"It is, isn't it?" Isaac said. "People do it here, too, even though there are more Jews than Negroes in the USA. It makes life easier for us than it would be otherwise."

Hosea Blackford looked around the crowded apartment. Flora knew what was in his mind: with so many people in so small a space, Jews still didn't have it easy. She hadn't been able to see how crowded the flat was, how crowded the whole Lower East Side was, till she moved away. Before, they'd been like water to a fish. Only going to Philadelphia had given her a standard for comparison.

But that standard for comparison didn't mean her brother was wrong. *Easier* and *easy* weren't the same thing. She said, "Wherever we end up, no matter how hard things are for us, we manage to get by."

"That spirit is what made this country what it is today, no matter who has it," Hosea Blackford said. He stopped with a bite of tongue halfway to his mouth and an astonished look on his face. "Will you listen to me. Will you *listen* to me? If you didn't know better, wouldn't you swear that was Teddy Roosevelt talking?"

"He's set his mark on the country for a long time to come," David said. He rapped his own artificial leg, which sounded of wood and metal. "He's set his mark on me for the rest of my life. Having the Socialists running the country has turned out better for the country and better for us"—he grinned at Flora and at Hosea Blackford—"than I thought it would. I admit it. But I still think TR deserved a third term in 1920."

Flora knew her brother's opinion. She had never understood it, and still didn't. But she refused to let him get her goat. "Now we'll see how many terms President Sinclair deserves," she said, which seemed to satisfy everyone. As her husband had, she heard what she'd said with some surprise. *Will you listen to me? Will you listen to me? If you didn't know better, wouldn't you swear that was a politician talking?*

Someone had plastered two-word posters—VOTE FREEDOM!—on every telegraph pole and blank wall in the Terry. As Scipio walked from his roominghouse to Erasmus' fish store and restaurant, he wondered if all the Freedom Party men had gone round the bend. Only a handful of Negroes in Augusta, Georgia, were eligible to vote. Even if they'd all been eligible, the Freedom Party wouldn't have picked up more than a handful of their votes.

When Scipio came up to the fish store, Erasmus was scrubbing a Freedom Party poster off his door. "Mornin', Xerxes," he said. "I don't need me no extra work so early in the mornin'."

"Crazy damnfool buckra," Scipio said. "Ain't nobody here got no use for no Freedom Party."

"Freedom Party?" Erasmus exclaimed. "That whose poster this here is?" He was a clever man, and sharp with figures, but could hardly read or write. At Scipio's nod, he scrubbed and scraped harder than ever. "Mus' be tryin' to make us afraid of 'em."

"Mebbe so," Scipio said; that hadn't occurred to him. "I was feared o' they befo', but I ain't now. They shoots theyselves when they shoots de president."

Erasmus didn't answer for a moment; he was busy getting rid of the last bits of the offending poster. "There—that's better." He kicked shreds of wadded-up paper across the sidewalk and into the gutter, then glanced over at Scipio. "Them bastards ain't even collectin' 'taxes' no more. You reckon they's goin' anywheres now?"

"Pray to Jesus they ain't," Scipio answered with all his heart. He still didn't believe prayer helped, but the phrase came automatically to his lips.

"Amen," Erasmus said. Then he reached into a pocket of his dungarees and pulled out a one-dollar banknote. "And I reckon this here hammers some nails in the coffin lid, too. Give 'em one big thing less to bellyache about."

"Yeah." Again, Scipio spoke enthusiastically. The Freedom Party hadn't been alone in bellyaching about the inflation that had squeezed the CSA since the end of the Great War. He'd done plenty of that himself. "Been a year now, near enough, an' the money still worth what it say. Almost done got to where I starts to trust it."

"Wasn't all bad." Erasmus chuckled. "Still recollect the look on the white-folks banker's face when I paid off what I owed. Thought he was gonna piss his pants. Money was still worth a little somethin' then, so they couldn't pretend it weren't, like they done later. An' now I got my house free an' clear. Wish more niggers woulda did the same."

Scipio shared that wish. Most of the Negroes in Augusta hadn't been alert enough to the opportunity that had briefly glittered for them. "Reckon mos' of the buckra don' think of it till too late, neither," he said.

"You right about that," Erasmus answered. "Some folks is jus' stupid, an' it don't matter none whether they's black or white." Before Scipio could say anything about that, his boss went on, "We done spent enough time chinnin'. Got work to do, an' it don't never go away."

Once inside the fish store and restaurant, Scipio fell to with a will. Erasmus had told a couple of important secrets there. Fools weren't the only ones who came in all colors. So did people who worked hard. One way or another, they got ahead. The ones with black skins didn't get so far ahead and didn't get ahead so fast, but they did better than their brethren who were content to take it easy.

After the lunch crowd thinned out, Scipio said, "You let me go downtown for a little bit, boss? Bathsheba want some fancy buttons for a shirtwaist she makin', an' she can't find they nowhere in the Terry. Don't reckon no buckra too proud to take my money."

Erasmus waved him away. "Yeah, go on, go on. Be back quick, though, you hear?" Scipio nodded and left. He could take advantage of his boss' good nature every once in a while because he did work hard—and because he didn't try taking advantage very often.

Fewer Negroes were on the streets of downtown Augusta nowadays than had been there right after the war, when Scipio first came to town. The factory jobs that had brought blacks into town from the fields were gone now, gone or back in white hands. Two cops in the space of a couple of blocks demanded to see Scipio's passbook. He passed both inspections.

"Don't want no trouble from nobody, boy, you hear?" the second policeman said, handing the book back to him.

"Yes, suh," Scipio answered. He might have pointed out that the policeman wasn't stopping any whites to see if they meant trouble. He might have, but he didn't. Had he, it would have meant trouble for him. The cop wouldn't have needed to belong to the Freedom Party to come down hard on an uppity nigger.

The Freedom Party itself wasn't lying down and playing dead. Posters shouting VOTE FREEDOM! covered walls and poles and fences here, as they did over in the Terry. Here, though, they competed with others touting the Whigs and the Radical Liberals. The more of those Scipio saw, the happier he was.

He also grew happier when he saw exactly the kind of buttons Bathsheba wanted on a white cardboard card in the front window of a store that called itself Susanna's Notions. When he went inside, the salesgirl—or possibly it was Susanna herself—ignored him till he asked about the buttons. Even then, she made no move to get them, but snapped, "Show me your money."

He displayed a dollar banknote. That got her moving from behind the counter. She took the buttons back there, rang up twenty cents on the cash register, and gave him a quarter, a tiny silver half-dime, and a roll of pennies. By the look on her face, he suspected it would prove two or three cents short of the full fifty it should have held. A black man risked his life if he presumed to complain about anything a white woman did. The charges she could level in return . . . Reckoning his own life worth more than two or three cents, he nodded brusquely and left Susanna's Notions. He wouldn't be back. The woman might have profited from this sale, but she'd never get another one from him.

No sooner had he got out onto the sidewalk than he heard a cacophony of motorcar horns and a cry that still made his blood run cold: "Freedom!" Down the street, blocking traffic, came a column of Freedom Party marchers in white shirts and butternut trousers, men in the front ranks carrying flags, as arrogant as if it were 1921 all over again.

Scipio wanted to duck back into Susanna's Notions once more; he felt as if every Freedom Party ruffian were shouting right at him, and glaring right at him, too. But the woman in there had been as unfriendly in her own way as were the ruffians. He stayed where he was, doing his best to blend into the brickwork like a chameleon on a green leaf.

"Freedom! Freedom! Freedom!" The shout was as loud and, in Scipio's ears, as hateful as it had been during the presidential campaign two years before.

But more white men shouted back from the sidewalks and from their automobiles: "Murderers!" "Shut up, you bastards!" "Get out of the road before I run you over!" "Liars!" "Sons of bitches!" Scipio had never heard shouts like that during Jake Featherston's run for the Confederate presidency.

And, as if from nowhere, a phalanx of policemen, some with pistols, some carrying rifles, came off a side street to block the marchers' path. "Disperse or face the consequences," one of them growled. Nobody had ever spoken like that to a Freedom Party column during the 1921 campaign, either.

"We have the right to—" one of the men in white and butternut began.

"You haven't got the right to block traffic, and if you don't get the hell out of the way, you can see how you like the city jail," the cop said. He and his men looked ready—more than ready—to arrest any Freedom Party stalwart who started to give them a hard time, and to shoot him if he kept it up.

The Freedom Party men saw that, too. By ones and twos, they began melting out of the column and heading back to whatever they'd been doing before they started marching. A couple of the men up front kept arguing with the police. They didn't seem to notice they had fewer and fewer followers. Then one of them looked around. He did a double take that would have drawn applause on the vaudeville stage. The argument stopped. So did the march.

Scipio's feet hardly seemed to touch the ground as he walked back to the Terry. When he told Erasmus what he'd seen, his boss said, " 'Bout time them bastards gits what's coming to 'em. Way past time, anybody wants to know. But better late than never, like they say."

"Didn't never reckon I live to see the day when the police clamps down on the buckra marchin' 'long the street," Scipio said.

"You never lose your shirt bettin' on white folks to hate niggers," Erasmus said. "You bet on white folks to be stupid all the time, you one broke nigger. They knows they needs us—the smart ones knows, anyways. An' the Freedom Party done come close enough to winnin' to scare the smart ones. Don't reckon they gets free rein no more."

"Here's hopin' you is right," Scipio said. "Do Jesus, here's hopin' you is right."

When he got home, Bathsheba examined the buttons with a critical eye, then nodded. "Them's right nice," she said.

"You's right nice," Scipio said, which made his wife smile. He went on, "I gots somethin' else right nice to tell you," and again described the ignominious end to the Freedom Party march.

That made Bathsheba jump out of her chair and kiss him. "Them white-and-butternut fellers used to scare me to death," she said. "Tell the truth, them white-and-butternut fellers still scare me. But maybe, if you is right, maybe one fine day even us niggers can spit in their eye."

"Mebbe so," Scipio said dreamily. He'd already spit in the white man's eye as a not altogether willing member of the ruling council of the Congaree Socialist Republic. This would be different. Echoing

Erasmus, he said, "Even some o' the buckra like to see we spit in the Freedom Party's eye."

"I got somethin' else we can do about the Freedom Party," Bathsheba said. Scipio raised a questioning eyebrow. His wife condescended to explain: "Forget there ever was such a thing as that there party."

Now Scipio kissed her. "Amen!" he said. "Best thing is they disappears like a stretch o' bad weather. After the bad weather gone, you comes out in the sunshine an' you forgets about the rain. We done have more rain than we needs. Mebbe now, though, the sun come out to stay." And, in the hope the good weather would last, he kissed Bathsheba again.

Tom Colleton dumped afternoon papers from Charleston and Columbia down on the kitchen table in front of Anne, who was eating a slice of bread spread with orange marmalade and drinking coffee fortified with brandy. Headlines on all the newspapers proclaimed thumping Whig victories in the election the day before.

"Got to give you credit, Sis," Tom said. "Looks like you got out of the Freedom Party just in time."

"If you think the bottom is going to fall out of a stock, you sell it right then," Anne answered. "You don't wait for it to go any lower, not unless you want to lose even more."

Her brother had been content to look at the headlines. She studied the stories line by line, knowing headline writers often turned news in the direction their editors said they should. That hadn't happened here; the Whigs would own a larger majority in both the House and Senate of the Thirtysecond Confederate Congress than they had in the Thirty-first.

And the Freedom Party had lost enough seats to make Anne's lips skin back from her teeth in a savage smile. They hadn't lost quite so many as she'd hoped, but they'd been hurt. Nine Congressmen . . . how did Jake Featherston propose doing anything with nine Congressmen? He couldn't possibly do anything but bellow and paw the air. People weren't so inclined to pay attention to bellowing and pawing the air as they had been before Grady Calkins killed Wade Hampton V.

"Yes, I think he is finished," Anne murmured.

"By God, I hope so," Tom said. "Do you know what he reminded me of?" He waited for Anne to shake her head before continuing, "A wizard, that's what. One of the wicked ones straight out of a fairy tale, I mean. When he started talking, you had to listen: that was part of the spell. He's still talking, but the spell is broken now, so it doesn't matter."

Anne stared at her brother in astonishment, then got up and set the palm of her hand on his forehead. His oath should have left the smell of lightning in the air. "Oh, hush," Anne said absently. "I was wondering if you had a fever—fancies like that aren't like you. But you don't, and it was a very good figure indeed, even if you won't come up with another one like it any time soon."

"Thanks a heap, Sis." Tom's grin made him look for a moment like the irresponsible young man who'd gone gaily off to war in 1914 rather than the quenched and tempered veteran who'd returned. "He wasn't a wizard, of course, only a man too damn good at making everyone else angry when he was."

"He was angry all the time. He still is. He always will be, I think," Anne said. She'd just spoken of Featherston as finished. Even so, hearing Tom use the past tense in talking about him brought a small jolt with it.

Her brother said, "He sure had you going for a while."

Past tense again, and another jolt with it. But Anne could hardly disagree. "Yes, I reckon he did," she said, her accent less refined than usual. "Looking back on it, maybe he was a wizard. For a while there, I would have done anything he wanted."

Had President Hampton not been assassinated, Anne knew she would have gone on doing whatever Featherston wanted, too. She was honest enough to admit it to herself, if to no one else, not even her brother. Perhaps especially not to Tom, who'd always shown more resistance to Featherston's spell than she had.

Would I have gone to bed with him, if he'd wanted that? Anne wondered. Slowly, reluctantly, she nodded to herself. *I think I would have.* She hadn't been in control of things, not with Jake she hadn't. With every other man she'd ever known—even Roger Kimball after their first encounter—yes. With Featherston? No, and again she was honest enough to admit it to herself.

But he hadn't wanted her. So far as she knew, he hadn't wanted any woman. She didn't think that made him a sodomite. It was more as if he poured all his energy into rage, and had none left for desire.

All that flashed through her mind in a couple of heartbeats: before her brother said, "If I don't see him or hear him again, I won't be sorry."

"As long as the money stays good, you probably won't," Anne

said, and Tom nodded. She went on, "And as long as the niggers know their place and stick to it."

Tom nodded again. "Featherston's closest to sound on the niggers, no doubt about that. It's still worth a white man's life, sometimes, to get any decent work out of field hands. They'd sooner loll around and sleep in the sun and collect white men's wages for doing it."

"It won't ever be the way it was before the war," Anne said sadly, speaking in part for Marshlands, in part for the entire Confederacy. The desire to make things again as they had been before the war had won the Freedom Party votes by the thousands, and had helped win her backing, too. But the war was almost six and a half years over, and life did go on, even if in a different way.

"I want another chance at the United States one day," Tom said. "Featherston was sound about that, too, but he wanted it too soon."

"Yes," Anne said, "but we will have another chance at the United States sooner or later, no matter who's in charge of the CSA. And we'll have a good chance at them, too, as long as the Socialists hold the White House."

"They don't," her brother remarked with no small pride. "We wrecked it during the fight for Washington."

"It's almost rebuilt," Anne said. "I saw that in one of the papers the other day. We'll have a harder time knocking it down again, too, with the Yankees holding northern Virginia."

"We'll manage," Tom said. "Even if our soldiers don't get that far—and I think they will—we'll have plenty of bombing aeroplanes to flatten it—and Philadelphia, and New York City, too, I hope."

"Yes," was all Anne said to that. She would never be ready to live at peace with the United States, not even when she turned old and gray. Turning old and gray was on her mind a good deal these days. Nearer forty than thirty, she knew the time when her looks added to the persuasiveness of her logic would not last much longer.

As Tom was doing more and more often since coming home from the war, he thought along with her. "You really ought to get married one of these days before too long, Sis," he said. "You don't want to end up an old maid, do you?"

"That depends," Anne Colleton answered. "Compared to what? Compared to ending up with a husband who tells me what to do when he doesn't know what he's talking about? Compared to that, being an old maid looks mighty good, believe me."

"Men aren't like that," her brother protested. "We've got a way of knowing good sense when we hear it."

Anne laughed loud and long. What Tom had said struck her as so ridiculous, she didn't even bother getting angry. "When you finally get married yourself, I'll tell your wife you said that," she remarked. "She won't believe me—I promise she won't believe me—but I'll tell her."

"Why wouldn't she believe that about me?" Tom asked with such a tone of aggrieved innocence, Anne laughed harder than ever.

"Because it'd be lying?" she suggested, but that only made her brother angry. Changing the subject seemed like a good idea. She did: "When are you going to get married, anyhow? You were bothering me about it, but turnabout's fair play."

Tom shrugged. "When I find a girl who suits me," he replied. "I'm not in any big hurry. It's different for a man, you know."

"I suppose so," Anne said in a voice that supposed nothing of the sort. "People would talk if I married a twenty-year-old when I was fifty. If you do that, all your friends will be jealous."

"How you do go on, Sis!" Tom said, turning red. Anne had indeed managed to get him to stop thinking about marrying her off. But the dismal truth was, he had a point. It *was* different for men. They often got more handsome as they aged; women, almost never. And men could go right on siring children even after they went bald and wrinkled and toothless. Anne knew she had only a few childbearing years left. Once they were gone, suitors would want her only for her money, not mostly for it as they did now.

"God must be a man," she said. "If God were a woman, things would work a lot different, and you can take it to the bank."

"I don't know anything about that," Tom said. "If you really reckon it's fun and jolly to go up out of a trench when the machine guns are hammering, or to hope you've got your gas helmet good and snug when the chlorine shells start falling, or to sit in a dugout wondering whether the next eight-inch shell is going to cave it in, then you can go on about what a tough row women have to hoe."

"I've fought," Anne said. Her brother only looked at her. She knew what she'd been through. So did he. He'd been through some of it with her, cleaning Red remnants out of the swamps by the Congaree after the war against the USA was lost. She had some notion of what Tom had experienced on the Roanoke front, but only some. She hadn't done that. By everything she knew, she wouldn't have wanted to do it.

"Never mind," Tom said. "For now, it's over. We don't need to quarrel about it today. Might as well leave that for the generals—all of 'em'll spend the next twenty, thirty years writing books about how they could have won the war single-handed if only the fellows on their flanks and over 'em hadn't been a pack of fools."

He walked over to a cupboard and took out a couple of glasses. Then he yanked the cork from a bottle of whiskey on the counter under the cupboard and poured out two hefty belts. He carried one of them back to Anne and set it on the table by the newspapers. She picked it up. "What shall we drink to?" she asked.

"Drinking to being here and able to drink isn't the worst toast in the world," Tom said. He raised his glass. Anne thought about that, nodded, and raised hers in turn. The whiskey was smoke in her mouth, flame in her throat, and a nice warm fire in her belly. Before long, the glass was empty.

Anne went over to the counter and refilled it. While she was pouring, Tom came over with his glass, from which the whiskey had also vanished. She gave him another drink, too. "My turn now," she said, as if expecting him to deny it.

He didn't. He bowed instead, as a gentleman would have done before the war. Not so many gentlemen were left these days; machine guns and gas and artillery had put them under the ground by the thousands, along with their ruder countrymen by the tens of thousands.

She raised her glass. "Here's to freedom from the Freedom Party!"

"Well, you know I'll drink to that one." Her brother suited action to word.

Again, the glasses emptied fast. The whiskey hit—Anne understood why the simile was on her mind—like a bursting shell. Everything seemed simple and clear, even things she knew perfectly well weren't. She weighed Jake Featherston in the balances, as God had weighed Belshazzar in the Bible. And, as God had found Belshazzar wanting, so she found Featherston and the Freedom Party.

"No, I don't reckon he'll be back. I don't reckon he'll be back at all," she said, and that called for another drink.

Sam Carsten was using his off-duty time the way he usually did now: he sprawled in his bunk aboard the *Remembrance*, studying hard. His head felt filled to the bursting point. He had the notion that he could have built and outfitted any ship in the Navy and ordered its crew about. He didn't think the secretary of the navy knew as much as he did. God might have; he supposed he was willing to give God the benefit of the doubt.

George Moerlein, his bunkmate, came by to pull something out of his duffel bag. "Christ, Sam, don't you ever take a break?" he said. He had to repeat himself before Carsten knew he was there.

At last reminded of Moerlein's existence, Sam sheepishly shook his head. "Can't afford to take a break," he said. "Examinations are only a week away. They don't make things easy on petty officers who want to kick their way up into real officer country."

Moerlein had been a petty officer a long time, a lot longer than Carsten. He had no desire to become anything else, and saw no reason anyone else should have such a desire, either. "I've known a few mustangs, or more than a few, but I'll be damned if I ever knew a happy one. Real officers treat 'em like you'd treat a nigger in a fancy suit: the clothes may be right, but the guy inside 'em ain't."

"If I don't pass this examination, it won't matter one way or the other," Sam said pointedly. "And besides, officers can't be any rougher on mustangs than they are on ordinary sailors."

"Only shows how much you know," Moerlein answered. "Well, don't mind me, not that you was." He went on about his business. Sam returned to his book. He came across a section on engine maintenance he didn't remember quite so well as he should have. From feeling he knew about as much as God, he fearfully sank to thinking he knew less than a retarded ordinary seaman on his first day at sea.

Mess call was something of a relief. Sam stopped worrying about keeping a warship fueled and running and started thinking about stoking his own boiler. With the *Remembrance* still tied up in the Boston Navy Yard, meals remained tasty and varied—none of the beans and sausage and sauerkraut that would have marked a long cruise at sea.

Somebody sitting not far from Sam said, "I'd sooner spend my days belching and my nights farting, long as that meant I was doing something worthwhile."

Heads bobbed up and down in agreement, all along the mess table. "We ought to be thankful they ain't breaking us up for scrap," another optimist said.

Somebody else added, "God damn Upton Sinclair to hell and gone."

That brought more nods, Carsten among them, but a sailor snapped, "God damn you to hell and gone, Tad, you big dumb Polack."

Socialists everywhere, Carsten thought as Tad surged to his feet. A couple of people caught him and slammed him back down. Sam nodded again, this time in approval. "Knock it off," he said. "We don't want any brawls here, not now we don't. Anything that makes the *Remembrance* look bad is liable to get her taken out of commission and land the lot of us on the beach. Congress isn't throwing money around like they did during the war."

"Hell, Congress isn't throwing money around like they did before the war, neither," Tad said. "We busted a gut building a Navy that could go out and win, and now we're flushing it right down the head."

"Rebs ain't got a Navy worth anything any more," said the Socialist sailor who'd called him a Polack. "Limeys ain't, either. No such thing as the Canadian Navy these days. So who the hell we got to worry about?"

"Goddamn Japs, for one." Three men said the same thing at the same time, differing only in the adjective with which they modified *Japs*.

"Kaiser Bill's High Seas Fleet, for two," Sam added. "Yeah, us and the Germans are pals for now, but how long is that going to last? Best way I can think of to keep the Kaiser friendly is to stay too tough to jump on."

That produced a thoughtful silence. At last, somebody down at the far end of the mess table said, "You know, Carsten, when I heard you was studying for officer, I figured you was crazy. Maybe you knew what you was doing after all."

Sam looked around to see who was in earshot. Deciding the coast was clear, he answered, "Maybe you don't have to be crazy to be an officer, but I never heard tell that it hurts."

Amidst laughter, people started telling stories about officers they'd known. Sam pitched in with some of his own. Inside, he was smiling. A book about leadership he'd read had suggested that changing the subject was often the best way to defuse a nasty situation. Unlike some of the things he'd read, that really worked.

After supper, he went back to studying, and kept at it till lights-out. George Moerlein shook his head. "Never reckoned you was one of those fellows with spectacles and a high forehead," he said.

"You want to get anywhere, you got to work for it," Sam answered, more than a little nettled. "Anybody wants to stay in a rut, that's his business. But anybody who doesn't, that's his business, too, or it damn well ought to be."

"All right. All right. I'll shut up," Moerlein said. "Swear to Jesus, though, I think you're doing this whole thing 'cause you want I should have to salute you."

"Oh, no," Carsten said in a hoarse whisper. "My secret's out."

For a moment, his bunkmate believed him. Then Moerlein snorted and cursed and rolled over in his bunk and, a couple of minutes later, started to snore.

Sam ran on coffee and cigarettes and very little sleep till the day of the examinations, which were held in a hall not far from the Rope Walk, the long stone building in which the Navy's great hemp cables were made. Commander Grady slapped Sam on the back as he left the *Remembrance*. "Just remember, you *can* do it," the gunnery officer said.

"Thank you, sir," Sam said, "and, if you please, sir, just remember, this was your idea in the first place." Grady laughed. Sam hurried past him and down the gangplank.

Sitting at a table in the examination hall waiting for the lieutenant commander at the front of the room to pass out the pile of test booklets on his desk, Sam looked around, studying the competition. He saw a roomful of petty officers not a whole lot different from himself. Only a few were younger than he; several grizzled veterans had to be well past fifty. He admired their persistence and hoped he would outscore them in spite of it.

Then he stopped worrying about anything inessential, for the officer started giving out the booklets. "Men, you will have four hours," he said. "I wish you all the best of luck, and I remind you that, should you not pass, the examination will be offered again in a year's time. Ready? . . . Begin."

How many times had some of those grizzled veterans walked into this hall or others like it? That thought gave Sam a different perspective on persistence. He wondered if he'd keep coming back after failing the examination half a dozen or a dozen times. Hoping he wouldn't have to find out, he opened the booklet and plunged in.

The examination was as bad as he'd feared it would be, as bad as he'd heard it would be. As he worked, he felt as if his brain were being sucked out of his head and down onto the paper by way of his pencil. He couldn't imagine a human mind containing all the knowledge the Navy Department evidently expected its officers to have at their fingertips. Panic threatened to overwhelm him when he came upon the first question he couldn't even begin to answer.

Well, maybe these other bastards can't answer it, either, he thought. That steadied him. He couldn't do anything more than his best.

Sweat soaked his dark uniform long before the examination ended. It had nothing to do with the hall, which was very little warmer than the Boston December outside. But he noticed he was far from the only man wiping his brow.

After what seemed like forever—and, at the same time, like only a few minutes—the lieutenant commander rapped out, "Pencils down! Pass booklets to the left." Sam had been in the middle of a word. That didn't matter. Nothing mattered any more. He joined the weary, shambling throng of sailors filing out of the hall.

"There's always next year," someone said in doleful tones. Carsten didn't argue with him. Nobody argued with him. Sam couldn't imagine anyone being confident he'd passed that brutal examination. He also couldn't imagine anyone showing confidence without getting lynched.

He didn't have any leave coming, so he couldn't even get drunk after the miserable thing was over. He had to return to the *Remembrance* and return to duty. When Commander Grady asked him how he'd done, he rolled his eyes. Grady laughed. Sam didn't see one thing funny about it.

Day followed day; 1923 gave way to 1924. *Coming up on ten years since the war started,* Sam thought. That seemed unbelievable, but he knew it was true. He wished ten years had gone by since the examination. When results were slow in coming, he did his best to forget he'd ever taken the miserable thing. *There's always next year,* he thought—except, by now, this was next year.

Then, one day, the yeoman in charge of mail called out "Carsten!" and thrust an envelope at him. He took it with some surprise; he seldom got mail. But, sure enough, the envelope had his name typed on it, and DEPARTMENT OF THE NAVY in the upper left-hand corner. He stuck his thumb over that return address, not wanting his buddies to know he'd got news he expected to be bad.

He marched off down a corridor and opened the envelope where no one could watch him do it. The letter inside bore his name and pay number on Navy Department stationery. It read, *You are ordered to report to Commissioning Board 17 at 0800 hours on Wednesday, 6 February 1924, for the purpose of determining your fitness to hold a commission in the United States Navy and . . .*

Sam had to read it twice before he realized what it meant. "Jesus!" he whispered. "Sweet suffering Jesus! I passed!"

He had to remind himself that he wasn't home free yet. Everybody said commissioning boards did strange things. In this particular case, what everybody said was likely to be true. Standing there in the cramped corridor, he refused to let what everybody said worry him in the least. The worst had to be over, for the simple reason that nothing could have been worse than that examination. The worst was over, and he'd come through it. He was on his way.

These days, Lucien Galtier thought of himself as an accomplished driver. He didn't say he was an accomplished driver, though. The one time he'd done that, Georges had responded, "And what have you accomplished? Not killing anyone? Bravo, *mon père!*"

No matter how accomplished he reckoned himself (Georges to the contrary notwithstanding), he wasn't planning on going anywhere today. That he had a fine Chevrolet mattered not at all. He wouldn't have gone out on the fine paved road up to Rivière-du-Loup even in one of the U.S. Army's traveling forts—why the Americans called the infernal machines *barrels* he'd never figured out. The snowstorm howling down from the northwest made the trip from the farmhouse to the barn cold and hard, let alone any longer journey.

When he got inside, the livestock set up the usual infernal racket that meant, *Where have you been? We're starving to death.* He ignored all the animals but the horse. To it, he said, "This is ingratitude. Would you sooner be out on the highway in such weather?"

Only another indignant snort answered him as he gave the beast oats for the day. When it came to food, the horse could be—was—eloquent. On any other subject, Galtier might as well have been talking to himself whenever he went traveling in the wagon. He knew that. He'd known it all along. It hadn't stopped him from having innumerable conversations with the horse over the years.

"I cannot talk with the automobile," he said. "Truly, I saw this from the moment I began to drive it. It is only a machine—although this, I have seen, does not keep Marie from talking with her sewing machine from time to time."

The horse let drop a pile of green-brown dung. It was warmer in the barn than outside, but the dung still steamed. Lucien wondered whether the horse was offering its opinion of driving a motorcar or of conversing with a sewing machine.

"Do you want to work, old fool?" he asked the horse. The only reply it gave was to gobble the oats. He laughed. "No, all you want to do is eat. I cannot even get you a mare for your amusement. Oh, I could, but you would not be amused. A gelding is not to be amused in that way, *n'est-ce pas?*"

He'd had the vet geld the horse when it was a yearling. It had never known the joys not being gelded could bring. It never would. Still, he fancied it flicked its ear at him in a resentful way. He nodded to himself. Had anyone done such a thing to him, he would have been more than merely resentful.

"Life is hard," he said. "Even for an animal like yourself, one that does little work these days, life is hard. Believe me, it is no easier for men and women. Most of them, most of the time, have very little, and no hope for more than very little. I get down on my knees and thank the Lord for the bounty He has given me."

Another ear flick might have said, *Careful how you speak, there—I am a part of your bounty, after all.* Maybe the horse was exceptionally expressive today. Maybe Galtier's imagination was working harder than usual.

"Truly, I could have been unfortunate as easily as I have been fortunate," Galtier said. The horse did not deny it. Galtier went on, "Had I been unfortunate, you would not be eating so well as you are now. Believe me, you would not."

Maybe the horse believed him. Maybe it didn't. Whether it did or not, it knew it was eating well now. That was what mattered. How could a man reasonably expect a horse to care about might-have-beens?

But Lucien Galtier cared. "Consider," he said. "I might have been driven to try to blow up an American general, as was that anglophone farmer who blew himself up instead, poor fool. For I will not lie: I had no love for the Americans. Yes, that could have been me, had chance driven me in the other direction. But I am here, and I am as I am, and so you have the chance to stand in your stall and get fat and lazy. I wonder if that other farmer had a horse, and how the unlucky animal is doing."

His own horse ate all he had given it and looked around for more, which was not forthcoming. It sent him a hopeful look, rather like that of a beggar who sat in the street with a tin cup beside him. Galtier rarely gave beggars money; as far as he was concerned, men who could work should. He did not insist that the horse work, not any more, but he knew better than to overfeed it.

After finishing in the barn, he walked through the snow to the farmhouse. The heat of the stove in the kitchen seemed a greater blessing than any Bishop Pascal could give. As Galtier stood close by it, Marie poured him a cup of steaming hot coffee. She added a hefty dollop of cream and, for good measure, a slug of applejack, too.

"Drink it before it gets cold," she said in a tone that brooked no argument. "You should be warmed inside and out." And, before he could answer, almost—but not quite—before he could even think, she added, "And do not say what is in your mind, you dreadful brute of a man."

"I?" After sipping the coffee, which was delicious, Galtier said, "I declare to the world that you have wronged me."

"So you do," his wife replied. "You should remember, though, that declaring a thing does not make it true."

She was laughing at him. He could hear it in her voice. She was also laughing because of him, a very different business. He waggled a forefinger at her. "You are a very troublesome woman," he said severely.

"No doubt you have reason," Marie said. "And no doubt I have my reasons for being troublesome. One of those reasons that comes straight to my mind is that I have a very troublesome husband."

"Me?" Lucien shook his head. "By no means. Not at all." He took another sip of fortified coffee. "How could I possibly be troublesome when I am holding here a cup of the elixir of life?" He put down the elixir of life so he could shrug out of his wool plaid coat. It was not quite warm enough in the bitter cold outside, but much too warm for standing by the stove for very long. As Lucien picked up the coffee cup again, Georges came into the kitchen. Lucien nodded to himself. "If I am troublesome, it could be that I understand why."

"How strange," Marie said. "I just now had this same thought at the same time. Men and women who have been married a long while do this, they say."

"How strange," Georges said, "I just now had the thought that I have been insulted, and for once I do not even know why."

"Never fear, son," Galtier said. "There are always reasons, and they are usually good ones."

"Here, then—I will give you a reason," Georges said. He left the kitchen, and flicked the light switch on the way out. The electric bulb in the lamp hanging from the ceiling went dark, plunging the room into gloom.

"Scamp!" Galtier called after him. Georges laughed—he was being troublesome, all right. Muttering, Galtier went over and turned on the lamp again. The kitchen shone as if he'd brought the sun indoors. "Truly electricity is a great marvel," he said. "I wonder how we ever got along without it."

"I cannot imagine," Marie said. "It makes everything so much easier—and you were clever enough to squeeze it out of the government."

"And the Americans," Galtier said. "You must not forget the Americans."

"I am not likely to forget the Americans." His wife's voice was tart. "Without the Americans, we would not have the son-in-law we now have, nor the grandson, either. Believe me, I remember all this very well."

"Without the Americans, we would not be living in the Republic of Quebec," Galtier said, looking at the large picture as well as the small one. "We would still be paying our taxes to Ottawa and getting nothing for them, instead of paying them to the city of Quebec . . . and getting nothing for them." Neither independence nor wealth reconciled him to paying taxes. Wealth, indeed, left him even less enthusiastic than he had been before, for it meant he had to pay more than he had when he was not doing so well.

"When the Americans came, we thought it was the end of the world," Marie said.

"And we were right," Lucien answered. "It was the end of the world we had always known. We have changed." From a Quebecois farmer, that was blasphemy to rank alongside *tabernac* and *calisse*. "We have changed, and we are better for it." From a Quebecois farmer, that was blasphemy viler than any for which the local French dialect had words.

His wife started to contradict him. He could tell by the way she opened her mouth, by the angle at which her head turned, by any number of other small things he could not have named but did see. Before she could speak, he wagged a finger at her—only that and nothing more. She hesitated. At last, she said, "*Peut-être*—it could be."

That was a greater concession than he'd thought he could get from her. He'd been ready to argue. Instead, all he had to say was, "We are lucky. The whole family is lucky. Things could so easily be worse." He thought again of the farmer out in Manitoba who'd tried to kill General Custer.

"God has been kind to us," Marie said.

"Yes, God has been kind to us," Galtier agreed. "And we have been lucky. And"—he knew just how to forestall an argument, almost as if he'd read a book on the subject—"this is excellent, truly excellent, coffee. Could you fix me another cup, exactly like this one?" His wife turned to take care of it. Galtier smiled behind her back. He'd had good luck and, wherever he could, he'd made good luck. And here he was, in his middle years and happy. He wondered how many of his neighbors could say that. Not many, unless he missed his guess. With an open smile and a word of thanks, he took the cup from Marie.

Jake Featherston tore open the fat package from the William Byrd Press. *Dear Mr. Featherston,* the letter inside read, *Thank you for showing us the manuscript enclosed herewith. We regret that we must doubt its commercial possibilities at the present time, and must therefore regretfully decline to undertake its publication. We hope you will have success in placing it elsewhere.*

He cursed. He couldn't place *Over Open Sights* anywhere, and a lot of the letters he got back from Richmond publishers—and even from one down in Mobile—were a lot less polite than this one. "Nobody wants to hear the truth," he growled.

"Nothing you can do about it now, Jake," Ferdinand Koenig said, slapping him on the back in consolation. "Come on. Let's get out of here."

"Stupid bastards," Featherston snarled. "And they're proud of it, damn them. They want to stay stupid." But he was glad to escape the Freedom Party offices. Even to him, they stank of defeat.

When he went out onto the streets of Richmond, he could have pulled the brim of his hat down low on his forehead or tugged up his collar so it hid part of his face. He could have grown a chin beard or bushy side whiskers to change his looks. He didn't. He hadn't. He wouldn't. As always, he met the world head-on.

The world was less fond of him than it had been before Grady Calkins murdered Wade Hampton V. About every other person on the street recognized him, and about every third person who did recognize him showered him with abuse. He gave as good as he got, very often better.

Koenig shook his head while Jake and a passerby exchanged unpleasantries. After the man finally went on his way, Koenig said, "Christ, sometimes I think you look for trouble."

"No such thing." Featherston shook his head. "But I'll be goddamned if I'll run from it, either. After the damnyankee artillery, fools with big mouths aren't enough to put me off my feed."

"I still think you ought to lay low till it gets closer to the next election, let people forget about things," Koenig said.

He was one of the very few people these days who spoke frankly to Jake instead of telling him what they thought he wanted to hear. That made him a valuable man. All the same, Jake shook his head again. "No, dammit. I didn't do anything I'm ashamed of. The Party didn't do anything I'm ashamed of. One crazy man went and fouled things up for us, that's all. People need to forget about Calkins, not about me."

"They didn't forget last November," Koenig pointed out.

"We knew that was going to happen," Featherston said. "All right, it happened. It could have been a lot worse. A lot of people reckoned it would be a lot worse."

"You know what you sound like?" Koenig said. "You sound like the War Department in the last part of 1916, the first part of 1917, when the damnyankees had started hammering us hard. 'We hurt the enemy very badly and contained him more quickly than expected,' they'd say, and all that meant was, we'd lost some more ground."

Featherston grunted. Comparing him to the department he hated hit home. Stubbornly, he said, "The Freedom Party's going to get the ground back, though. The War Department never did figure out how to manage that one."

"If you say so, Sarge," Ferdinand Koenig replied. He didn't sound like a man who believed it. He sounded like a man humoring a rich lunatic—and he made sure Featherston knew he sounded that way.

"We can come back," Jake insisted. As long as he believed it, he could make other people believe it. If enough other people believed it, it would come true.

He and Koenig turned right from Seventh onto Franklin and walked on toward Capitol Square. Jake's hands folded into fists. After the war was lost—*thrown away,* he thought—discharged soldiers had almost taken the Capitol; only more soldiers with machine guns had held them at bay. A good bloodbath then would have been just what the CSA needed.

And in 1921 he'd come so close to storming his way into power in spite of everything the Whigs and all their Thirds and Fourths and Fifths could do to stop him. Sure as hell, he would have been elected in 1927. He knew he would have been—if not for Grady Calkins.

If even he was thinking about what might have been instead of what would be now—if that was so, the Freedom Party was in deep trouble. A man with a limp—*wounded veteran,* Jake judged—came toward him along Franklin. Jake nodded to him—he still had plenty of backers left, especially among men who'd fought like him.

"Freedom!" the fellow said by way of reply, but he loaded the word with loathing and made an obscene gesture at Jake.

"You go to hell!" Featherston cried.

"If I do, I'll see you there before me," the man with the limp answered, and went on his way.

"Bastard," Jake muttered on his breath. "Fucking bastard. They're all fucking bastards." Then he saw a crowd on the sidewalk ahead and forgot about the heckler. "What the hell's going on here, Ferd?"

"Damned if I know," Koenig answered. "Shall we find out?"

"Yeah." Jake elbowed his way to the front of the crowd, ably assisted by his former running mate. He'd expected a saloon giving away free beer or something of that sort. Instead, men and women were trying to shove their way into . . . a furniture store? He couldn't believe it till Ferdinand Koenig pointed to the sign taped in the window: NEWEST MAKES OF WIRELESS RECEIVERS, FROM $399.

"They're all the go nowadays," Koenig said. "Even at those prices, everybody wants one."

"I've heard people talking about them," Featherston admitted. "Haven't heard one myself, I don't think. I'll be damned if I can see what the fuss is about."

"I've listened to 'em," Koenig said. "It's—interesting. Not like anything else you'll ever run across, I'll tell you that."

"Huh." But, having got so close to the store's doorway, Featherston decided not to leave without listening to a wireless receiver. More judicious elbowing got him and Koenig inside.

The receivers were all big and boxy. Some cabinets were made of fancier wood than others; that seemed to account for the difference in price. Only one machine was actually operating. From it came tinny noises that, after a bit, Jake recognized as a Negro band playing "In the Good Old Summertime."

"Huh," he said again, and turned to the fellow who was touting the receivers. "Why would anybody want to listen to this crap, for God's sake?"

"Soon, sir, there will be offerings for every taste," the salesman answered smoothly. "Even now, people all over Richmond are listening to this and other broadcasts. As more people buy receivers, the number of broadcasts and the number of listeners will naturally increase."

"Not if they keep playing that garbage," Ferdinand Koenig said. He nodded to Featherston. "You were right—this is lousy."

"Yeah." But Jake had listened to the salesman, too. "All over Richmond, you say?"

"Yes, sir." The rabbity-looking fellow nodded enthusiastically.

"And the price of receivers has fallen dramatically in the past few months. It will probably keep right on falling, too, as they become more popular."

"People all over Richmond," Jake repeated thoughtfully. "Could you have people all over the CSA listening to the same thing at the same time?"

To his disappointment, the salesman replied, "Not from the same broadcasting facility." But the fellow went on, "I suppose you could send the same signal from several facilities at once. Why, if I might ask?"

Plainly, he didn't recognize Featherston. "Just curious," Jake answered—and, indeed, it was hardly more than that. Behind his hand, he whispered to Koenig: "Might be cheaper to make a speech on the wireless than hold a bunch of rallies in a bunch of different towns. If we could be sure we were reaching enough people that way—"

One of the other customers in the shop was whispering behind *his* hand to the salesman. "Oh?" the salesman said. "He *is?*" By the tone of voice, Jake knew exactly what the customer had whispered. The salesman said, "Sir, I am going to have to ask you to leave. This is a high-class establishment, and I don't want any trouble here."

"We weren't giving you any trouble." Featherston and Koenig spoke together.

"You're from the Freedom Party," said the customer who'd recognized Jake. "You don't have to give trouble. You *are* trouble."

Several other men from among those crowding the shop drifted toward the fellow. A couple of others ranged themselves behind Featherston. "Freedom!" one of them said.

"I am going to call for a policeman if you don't leave," the salesman told Jake. "I do not want this place broken apart."

If breaking the place apart would have brought the Party good publicity, Featherston would have started a fight on the spot. But he knew it wouldn't—just the opposite, in fact. The papers would scream he was only a ruffian leading a pack of ruffians. They hadn't talked about him and the Party like that when he was a rising power in the land, or not so much, anyhow. Now they thought they scented blood. He wouldn't give them any blood to sniff.

"Come on, Ferd," he said. "If anybody starts trouble, it won't be us."

"Look at the cowards cut and run," jeered the man who'd recognized him. "They talk big, but they don't back it up."

He never knew how close he came to getting his head broken and his nuts kneed. Jake's instinct was always to hit back at whoever and whatever struck at him, and to hit harder if he could. Only a harsh understanding that that would bring no advantage held him back.

"One day," he growled once he and Ferdinand Koenig were out on Franklin again, "one fine day I'm going to pay back every son of a bitch who ever did me wrong, and that loud-mouthed bastard will get his. So help me God, he will."

"Sure, Sarge," Koenig said. But he didn't sound sure. He sounded like a man buttering up his boss after said boss had come out with something really stupid. Featherston knew flattery when he heard it, because he heard it too damn often. He hadn't heard it much from Koenig, though.

Sourly, he studied the man who'd run for vice president with him. He and Koenig went back to the old days together, to the days when the Freedom Party operated out of a cigar box. If Koenig hadn't backed him, odds were the Party would still be a cigar-box outfit. Koenig was as close to a friend as he had on the face of the earth. And yet . . .

"If you don't fancy the way things are going, Ferd, you can always move on," Jake said. "Don't want you to feel like you're wearing a ball and chain."

Koenig turned red. "I don't want to leave, Jake. I've come too far to back out now, same as you. Only . . ."

"Only what?" Featherston snapped.

"Only Moses got to the top of the mountain, but God never let him into the Promised Land," Koenig said, going redder still. "Way things are these days, I don't know how we can win an election any time soon."

"We sure as hell won't if people lie down and give up," Jake said. "Long as we don't quit, long as we keep fighting, things will turn our way, sooner or later. It'll take longer now than I reckoned it would in 1921; I'd be a liar if I said anything different. But the time is coming. By God, it *is.*"

Koenig grunted. Again, the sound failed to fill Featherston with confidence. If even the man closest to him had doubts, who was he to be sure triumph did lie ahead? He shrugged. He'd kept firing against the damnyankees up to the very last minute. He would struggle against fate the same way.

There ahead lay Capitol Square, with its great statues of George Washington and Albert Sidney Johnston. Pointing, Jake said, "Look at 'em, Ferd. If Washington had given up, we'd still belong to England. And Johnston died so the Confederate States could be free.

How can we do anything else and still look at ourselves in the mirror afterwards?"

"I don't know," Koenig said. "But you don't see people building statues to what's-his-name—Cornwallis—or to General Grant, the Yankee who licked Johnston. Damned if I know what happened to Cornwallis. Grant died a drunk. They were both big wheels in their day, Sarge."

"And we'll be big wheels in ours." Jake understood what Koenig was saying, but wouldn't admit it even to himself. Admitting it would mean he might also have to admit he wasn't sure whether he'd end up among the winners or the losers when the history books got written. He couldn't bear that thought.

"Hope you're right," Koenig said.

"Hell, yes, I'm right." Jake spoke with great assurance, to convince not only his follower but also himself. Ferdinand Koenig nodded. If he wasn't convinced, Featherston couldn't prove it, not from a nod.

And what about you? Jake asked himself. He'd been—the Freedom Party had been—*that* close to seizing power with both hands. Now, with Wade Hampton dead, with the Confederate currency sound again . . . He kicked at the sidewalk. The Party should have gone forward again in 1923. Instead, he counted himself lucky, damn lucky, it hadn't gone further back.

Could things turn around? Of course they *could*—that was the wrong question. How likely were they to turn around? Coldly, as if in a poker game, he reckoned up the odds. Had he been in a poker game, he would have thrown in his cards. But the stakes here were too high for him to quit.

"It'll work out," he said. "Goddammit, it *will* work out." He did his best to sound as if he meant it.

About the Author

HARRY TURTLEDOVE was born in Los Angeles in 1949. After flunking out of Caltech, he earned a Ph.D. in Byzantine history from UCLA. He has taught ancient and medieval history at UCLA, Cal State Fullerton, and Cal State L.A., and has published a translation of a ninth-century Byzantine chronicle, as well as several scholarly articles. His alternate history works have included many short stories and the Civil War classic *The Guns of the South*, the World War I epic *Great War* series, and the Worldwar tetralogy that began with *Worldwar: In the Balance*. He is a Hugo winner, a Nebula finalist, and the winner of the Sidewise Award for best Alternate History for his novel *How Few Remain*.